Praise for *Existence*

"[*Existence* is] all about the chaos and passion of adolescence—the designs we make for our lives when we're young, before unforeseeable events send us spinning into strange new orbits. . . . It requires that we look beyond ourselves, beyond humanity (all six species of it), and into the universe beyond." —*io9*

"The discovery of alien artifacts pushes an already troubled Earth to the brink of chaos in bestseller Brin's exciting story of first contact. Brin's thoughtful, multilayered story explores a first-contact scenario where every twist reveals greater peril. His longtime fans will especially appreciate that this story could be read as a prequel to 1983's *Startide Rising,* while those not familiar with his work will find it an impressive introduction to one of SF's major talents."

—*Publishers Weekly* (starred review)

"Take a world soaked in near-future strangeness and complexity . . . add a beautiful alien artifact that turns out to be the spear point of a very dangerous, very ancient invasion . . . hotwire with wisdom and wonder . . . *Existence* is as urgent and as relevant as anything by Stross or Doctorow, but with the cosmic vision of Bear or Benford. Brin is back." —Stephen Baxter

"In *Existence,* David Brin takes on one of the fundamental themes in science fiction—and what is also one of the fundamental questions humanity faces in this century. Since Brin is both a great storyteller and one of the most imaginative writers around, *Existence* is not to be missed." —Vernor Vinge

"Brin's near-future world is a high-tech wonderland where individuals interface with AIs, citizens create their own virtual overlay on reality, and privacy is a thing of the past. But scientific advancement comes at a cost, until first contact is achieved with aliens who just might have all the answers. Brin tackles a plethora of cutting-edge concepts—such as the Fermi paradox, the ascent of artificial intelligence, and the evolution of technologically enhanced humanity—with the skill of a visionary futurologist, and while his extended cast of characters is set up to articulate ideas, they come to life as distinct individuals. If he does resort to long info-dumps, it's necessary in order to convey the depth and breadth of his startling future. *Existence* is Brin's first novel in ten years, and it's been well worth the wait."

—*The Guardian* (U.K.)

TOR BOOKS BY DAVID BRIN

Kiln People

Existence

EXISTENCE

DAVID BRIN

A TOM DOHERTY
ASSOCIATES BOOK
NEW YORK

This is a work of fiction. All of the characters, organizations, and events portrayed in this novel are either products of the author's imagination or are used fictitiously.

EXISTENCE

Copyright © 2012 by David Brin

A Tor Book
Published by Tom Doherty Associates, LLC
175 Fifth Avenue
New York, NY 10010

www.tor-forge.com

Tor® is a registered trademark of Tom Doherty Associates, LLC.

ISBN 978-0-7653-4262-1

Tor books may be purchased for educational, business, or promotional use. For information on bulk purchases, please contact Macmillan Corporate and Premium Sales Department at 1-800-221-7945 extension 5442 or write specialmarkets@macmillan.com.

First Edition: June 2012
First Mass Market Edition: March 2013

Printed in the United States of America

0 9 8 7 6 5 4

To "Tether Joe" Carroll, who spins real space lariats . . .
and
"Doc" Sheldon Brown, who teaches time travelers . . .

. . . and Ralph Vicinanza,
who helped many dreams and dreamers to thrive.

PART ONE

SLINGS AND ARROWS

> Those who ignore the mistakes
> of the future are bound to make
> them.
>
> —Joseph Miller

SPECIES

*what matters? do i? or **ai?** + the question spins*

+/– as my body spins !/+ in time to a chirping window-
*   bird*
"normal people" don't think like this –/–/–
nor aspies –/– nor even most autistics

***stop spinning!** –/– there –/– now back to the holo-*
*   screen ->*

rain smatters the clatter window —
bird is gone –/+ hiding from falling water ++
like i hide from a falling civilization

what matters then ?/? progress? New minds??
*after **cortex**, after **libraries**, the **web**, **mesh**, **ai-grid***
*— what's **next** ?/!*

will it offer hope/doom for foolish humanity +/?
for the glaring cobbly minds +/?
or autistic-hybrids like me +/?

1.

I, AMPHORUM

The universe had two great halves.

A hemisphere of glittering stars surrounded Gerald on the right.

Blue-brown Earth took up the other side. *Home,* after this job was done. Cleaning the mess left by another generation.

Like a fetus in its sac, Gerald floated in a crystal shell, perched at the end of a long boom, some distance from the space station *Endurance.* Buffered from its throbbing pulse, this bubble was more space than station.

Here, he could focus on signals coming from a satellite hundreds of kilometers away. A long, narrow ribbon of whirling fiber, far overhead.

The bola. His lariat. His tool in an ongoing chore.

> *The bola is my arm.*
> *The grabber is my hand.*
> *Magnetic is the lever that I turn.*
> *A planet is my fulcrum.*

Most days, the little chant helped Gerald to focus on his job—that of a glorified garbageman. *There are still people who envy me. Millions, down in that film of sea and cloud and shore.*

Some would be looking up right now, as nightfall rushed faster than sound across teeming Sumatra. Twilight was the best time to glimpse this big old station. It made him feel connected with humanity every time *Endurance* crossed the terminator—whether dawn or dusk—knowing a few people still looked up.

Focus, Gerald. On the job.

Reaching out, extending his right arm fully along the line of his body, he tried again to adjust tension in that far-off, whirling cable, two thousand kilometers overhead, as if it were a languid extension of his own self.

And the cable replied. Feedback signals pulsed along Gerald's neuro-sens suit . . . but they felt wrong.

My fault, Gerald realized. The orders he sent to the slender satellite were too rapid, too impatient. Nearby, little Hachi complained with a screech. The other occupant of this inflated chamber wasn't happy.

"All right." Gerald grimaced at the little figure, wearing its own neuro-sens outfit. "Don't get your tail in a knot. I'll fix it."

Sometimes a monkey has more sense than a man.

Especially a man who looks so raggedy, Gerald thought. A chance glimpse of his reflection revealed how stained his elastic garment had become—from spilled drinks and maintenance fluids. His grizzled cheeks looked gaunt. Infested, even haunted, by bushy, unkempt eyebrows.

If I go home to Houston like this, the family won't even let me in our house. Though, with all my accumulated flight pay . . .

Come on, focus!

Grimly, Gerald clicked down twice on his lower left premolar and three times on the right. His suit responded with another jolt of Slow Juice through a vein in his thigh. Coolness, a lassitude that should help clear thinking, spread through his body—

—and time seemed to crawl.

Feedback signals from the distant bola now had time to catch up. He felt more a *part* of the thirty kilometer strand, as it whirled ponderously in a higher orbit. Pulsing electric currents that throbbed *up there* were translated as a faint tingle *down here,* running from Gerald's wrist, along his arm and shoulder, slanting across his back and then down to his left big toe, where they seemed to *dig* for leverage. When he pushed, the faraway cable-satellite responded, applying force against the planet's magnetic field.

Tele-operation. In an era of ever more sophisticated artificial intelligence, some tasks still needed an old-fashioned human pilot. Even one who floated in a bubble, far below the real action.

Let's increase the current a bit. To notch down our rate of turn. A tingle in his toe represented several hundred amps of electricity, spewing from one end of the whirling tether, increasing magnetic drag. The great cable rotated across the stars a bit slower.

Hachi—linked-in nearby—hooted querulously from his own web of support fibers. This was better, though the capuchin still needed convincing.

"Cut me some slack," Gerald grumbled. "I know what I'm doing."

The computer's dynamical model agreed with Hachi, though. It still forecast no easy grab when the tether's tip reached its brief rendezvous with . . . whatever piece of space junk lay in Gerald's sights.

Another tooth-tap command, and night closed in around him more completely, simulating what he would see if he were *up there,* hundreds of klicks higher, at the tether's speeding tip, where stars glittered more clearly. From that greater altitude, Earth seemed a much smaller disc, filling just a quarter of the sky.

Now, everything he heard, felt or saw came from the robotic cable. His lasso. A vine to swing upon, suspended from some distant constellation.

Once an ape . . . always an ape.

The tether *became* Gerald's body. An electric tingle along his spine—a sleeting breeze—was the Van Allen radiation wind, caught in magnetic belts that made a lethal sizzle of the middle-orbit heights, from nine hundred kilometers all the way out to thirty thousand or so.

The Bermuda Triangle of outer space. No mere human could survive in that realm for more than an hour. The Apollo astronauts accumulated half of all their allotted radiation dosage during a few minutes sprinting across the belt, toward the relative calm and safety of the Moon. Expensive communications satellites suffered more damage just passing through those middle altitudes than they would in a decade, higher up in placid geosynchronous orbit.

Ever since that brief time of bold lunar missions—and the even-briefer *Zheng He* era—no astronaut had ventured beyond the radiation belt. Instead, they hunkered in safety, just above the atmosphere, while robots explored the solar system. This made Gerald the Far-Out Guy! With his bola for an arm, and the grabber for a hand, he reached beyond. Just a bit, into the maelstrom. No one else got as high.

Trawling for garbage.

"All right . . . ," he murmured. "Where are you . . . ?"

Radar had the target pinpointed, about as well as machines could manage amid a crackling fog of charged particles. Position and trajectory kept jittering, evading a fix with slipperiness that seemed almost alive. Worse—though no one believed him—Gerald swore that orbits tended to *shift* in this creepy zone, by up to a few thousandths of a percent, translating into tens of meters. That could make a bola-snatch more artistic guesswork than physics. Computers still had lots to learn, before they took over *this* job from a couple of primates.

Hachi chirped excitedly.

"Yeah, I see it." Gerald squinted, and optics at the tether-tip automatically magnified a glitter, just ahead. The *target*—probably some piece of space junk, left here by an earlier, wastrel generation. Part of an exploding Russian second stage, perhaps. Or a connector ring from an Apollo flight. Maybe one of those capsules filled with human ashes that used to get fired out here, willy-nilly, during the burial-in-space fad. Or else the remnants of some foolish weapon experiment. Space Command claimed to have all the garbage radar charted and imaged down to a dozen centimeters.

Gerald knew better.

Whatever this thing was, the time had come to bring it home before collision with other debris caused a cascade of secondary impacts—a runaway process that already forced weather and research satellites to be replaced or expensively armored.

Garbage collecting wasn't exactly romantic. Then again, neither was Gerald. Far from the square-jawed, heroic image of a spaceman, he saw only a middle-aged disappointment, on the rare occasions that he looked in a mirror at all, a face lined from squinting in the sharp light of orbit, where sunrise came at you like a wall, every ninety minutes.

At least he was good at achieving a feat of imagination—that he *really* existed far above. That his true body spun out there, thousands of kilometers away.

The illusion felt perfect, at last. Gerald *was* the bola. Thirty kilometers of slender, conducting filament, whirling a slow turn every thirty minutes, or five times during each elongated orbit. At both ends of the pivoting tether were compact clusters of sensors (*my eyes*), cathode emitters (*my muscles*), and grabbers (*my clutching hands*), that felt more part of him, right now, than anything made of flesh. More real than the meaty parts he had been born with, now drifting in a cocoon far below, near the bulky, pitted space station. That distant human body seemed almost imaginary.

Like a hunter with his faithful dog, man and monkey grew silent during final approach, as if sound might spook the prey, glittering in their sights.

It's got an odd shine, he thought, as telemetry showed the distance rapidly narrowing. Only a few kilometers now, till the complex dance of two orbits and the tether's own, gyrating spin converged, like a fielder leaping to snatch a hurtling line drive. Like an acrobat, catching his partner in midair. After which . . .

. . . the bola's natural spin would take over, clasping the seized piece of debris into its whirl, absorbing its old momentum and giving that property new values, new direction. Half a spin later, with this tether-tip at *closest approach* to Earth, the grabber would let go, hurling the debris backward, westward, and *down* to burn in the atmosphere.

The easy part. By then, Gerald would be sipping coffee in the station's shielded crew lounge. Only now—

That's no discarded second stage rocket, he pondered, studying the glimmer. *It's not a cargo faring, or shredded fuel tank, or urine-icicle, dumped by a manned mission.* By now, Gerald knew how all kinds of normal junk reflected sunlight—from archaic launch vehicles and satellites to lost gloves and tools—each playing peekaboo tricks of shadow. But this thing . . .

Even the colors weren't right. Too blue. Too many *kinds* of blue. And light levels remained so steady! As if the thing had no facets or flat surfaces. Hachi's questioning hoot was low and worried. How can you make a firm grab, without knowing where the edges are?

As relative velocity ebbed toward zero, Gerald made adjustments by spewing electrons from cathode emitters at either cable end, creating torque against the planetary field, a trick for maneuvering without rockets or fuel. Ideal for a slow, patient job that had to be done on the cheap.

Now Hachi earned his keep. The little monkey stretched

himself like a strand of spaghetti, smoothly taking over final corrections—his instincts honed by a million generations of swinging from jungle branches—while Gerald focused on the grab itself. There would be no second chance.

Slow and patient . . . except at the last, frenetic moment . . . when you wish you had something quicker to work with than magnetism. When you wish—

There it was, ahead. The Whatever.

Rushing toward rendezvous, the bola's camera spied something glittery, vaguely oval in shape, gleaming with a pale blueness that pulsed like something eager.

Gerald's hand *was* the grabber, turning a fielder's mitt of splayed fingers, reaching as the object loomed suddenly.

Don't flinch, he chided ancient intuitions while preparing to snatch whatever this hurtling thing might be.

Relax. It never hurts.

Only this time—in a strange and puzzling way—it did.

A MYRIAD PATHS OF ENTROPY

Does the universe hate us? How many pitfalls lie ahead, waiting to shred our conceited molecule-clusters back into unthinking dust? Shall we count them?

Men and women always felt besieged. By monsters prowling the darkness. By their oppressive rulers, or violent neighbors, or capricious gods. Yet, didn't they most often blame themselves? Bad times were viewed as punishment, brought on by wrong behavior. By unwise belief.

Today, our means of self-destruction seem myriad. (Though *Pandora's Cornucopia* will try to list them all!) We modern folk snort at the superstitions of our ancestors. We know *they* could never really wreck the world, but we can! Zeus or Moloch could not match the destructive power of a nuclear missile exchange, or a dusting of plague bacilli, or some ecological travesty, or ruinous mismanagement of the intricate aiconomy.

Oh, we're mighty. But are we *so* different from our forebears?

Won't our calamity (when it comes) also be blamed on some arrogant mistake? A flaw in judgment? Some obstinate belief? *Culpa nostra.* Won't it be the same old plaint, echoing across the ruin of our hopes?

"We never deserved it all! Our shining towers and golden fields. Our overflowing libraries and full bellies. Our long lives and overindulged children. Our happiness. Whether by God's will or our own hand, we always expected it would come to this.

"To dust."

—*Pandora's Cornucopia*

2.

AFICIONADO

Meanwhile, far below, cameras stared across forbidden desert, monitoring disputed territory in a conflict so bitter, antagonists couldn't agree what to call it.

One side named the struggle *righteous war,* with countless innocent lives in peril.

Their opponents claimed there were no victims, at all.

And so, suspicious cameras panned, alert for encroachment. Camouflaged atop hills or under highway culverts or innocuous stones, they probed for a hated adversary. And for some months the guardians succeeded, staving off incursions. Protecting sandy desolation.

Then, technology shifted advantages again.

The enemy's first move? Take out those guarding eyes.

Infiltrators came at dawn, out of the rising sun—several hundred little machines, skimming low on whispering gusts. Each one, resembling a native hummingbird, followed a carefully scouted path toward its target, landing *behind* some camera or sensor, in its blind spot. It then unfolded wings that transformed into holo-displays, depicting perfect false images of the same desert scene to the guardian lens, without even a suspicious flicker. Other spy-machines sniffed out camouflaged seismic sensors and embraced them gently—cushioning to mask approaching tremors.

The robotic attack covered a hundred square kilometers. In eight minutes, the desert lay unwatched, undefended.

Now, from over the horizon, large vehicles converged along multiple roadways toward the same open area—seventeen hybrid-electric rigs, disguised as commercial cargo transports, complete with company hologos. But when their paths intersected, crews in dun-colored jumpsuits leaped to unlash cargoes. Generators roared and the air swirled with exotic stench as pungent volatiles gushed from storage tanks to fill pressurized vessels. Consoles sprang to life. Hinged panels fell away, revealing long, tapered cylinders on slanted ramps.

Ponderously, each cigar shape raised its nose skyward while fins popped open at the tail. Shouts grew tense as tightly coordinated countdowns commenced. Soon the enemy—sophisticated and wary—would pick up enough clues. They would realize . . . and act.

When every missile was aimed, targets acquired, all they lacked were payloads.

A dozen figures emerged from an air-conditioned van, wearing snug suits of shimmering material and garishly painted helmets. Each carried a satchel that hummed and whirred to keep them cool. Several moved with a gait that seemed rubbery with anxious excitement. One skipped a little caper, about every fourth step.

A dour-looking woman awaited them, with badge and uniform. Holding up a databoard, she confronted the first vacuum-suited figure.

"Name and scan," she demanded. "Then affirm your intent."

The helmet visor, decorated with gilt swirls, swiveled back, revealing heavily tanned features, about thirty years old, with eyes the color of a cold sea—till the official's instrument cast a questioning ray. Then, briefly, one pupil flared retinal red.

"Hacker Sander," the tall man said, in a voice both taut and restrained. "I affirm that I'm doing this of my own free will, according to documents on record."

His clarity of purpose must have satisfied the ai-clipboard, which uttered an approving beep. The inspector nodded. "Thank you, Mr. Sander. Have a safe trip. Next?"

She indicated another would-be rocketeer, who carried his helmet in the crook of one arm, bearing a motif of flames surrounding a screaming mouth.

"What rubbish," the blond youth snarled, elbowing Hacker as he tried to loom over the bureaucrat. "Do you have any idea who we are? Who I am?"

"Yes, Lord Smit. Though whether I *care* or not doesn't matter." She held up the scanner. "*This* matters. It can prevent you from being lasered into tiny fragments by the USSF, while you're passing through controlled airspace."

"Is that a threat? Why you little . . . *government* . . . pissant. You had better not be trying to—"

"Government *and* guild," Hacker Sander interrupted, suppressing his own hot anger over that elbow in the ribs. "Come on, Smitty. We're on a tight schedule."

The baron whirled on him, tension cracking the normally smooth aristocratic accent. "I warned you about nicknames, Sander, you third-generation poser. I had to put up with your seniority during pilot training. But just wait until we get back. I'll take you apart!"

"Why wait?" Hacker kept eye contact while reaching up to unlatch his air hose. A quick punch ought to lay this blue-blood out, letting the rest of them get on with it. There were good reasons to hurry. Other forces, more formidable than mere government, were converging right now, eager to prevent what was planned here.

Besides, nobody called a Sander a "poser."

The other rocket jockeys intervened before he could use his fist—probably a good thing, at that—grabbing the two men and separating them. Pushed to the end of the queue, Smits stewed and cast deadly looks toward Hacker. But when his turn came again, the nobleman went through ID check with composure, as cold and brittle as some glacier.

"Your permits are in order," the functionary concluded, unhurriedly addressing Hacker, because he was most experienced. "Your liability bonds and Rocket Racing League waivers have been accepted. The government won't stand in your way."

Hacker shrugged, as if the statement was both expected and irrelevant. He flung his visor back down and gave a sign to the other suited figures, who rushed to the ladders that launch personnel braced against each rocket, clambering awkwardly, then squirming into cramped couches and strapping in. Even the novices had practiced countless times.

Hatches slammed, hissing as they sealed. Muffled shouts told of final preparations. Then came a distant chant, familiar, yet always thrilling, counting backward at a steady cadence. A rhythm more than a century old.

Is it really that long, since Robert Goddard came to this same desert? Hacker pondered. *To experiment with the*

*first controllable rockets? Would he be surprised at what
we've done with the thing he started? Turning them into
weapons of war . . . then giant exploration vessels . . . and
finally playthings of the superrich?*

Oh, there were alternatives, like commercial space tour-
ism. One Japanese orbital hotel and another under construction. Hacker owned stock. There were even multipassenger
suborbital jaunts, available to the merely well-off. For the
price of maybe twenty college educations.

Hacker felt no shame or regret. *If it weren't for us,
there'd be almost nothing left of the dream.*

Countdown approached zero for the first missile.

His.

"Yeeeee-haw!" Hacker Sander shouted . . .

. . . before a violent kick flattened him against the airbed.
A mammoth hand seemed to plant itself on his chest and
shoved, expelling half the contents of his lungs in a moan
of sweet agony. Like every other time, the sudden shock
brought physical surprise and visceral dread—followed by
a sheer ecstatic rush, like nothing else on Earth.

Hell . . . he wasn't even *part* of the Earth! For a little
while, at least.

Seconds passed amid brutal shaking as the rocket clawed
its way skyward. Friction heat and ionization licked the
transparent nose cone only centimeters from his face.
Shooting toward heaven at Mach ten, he felt pinned, helplessly immobile . . .

. . . and completely omnipotent.

I'm a freaking god!

At Mach fifteen somehow he drew enough breath for
another cry—this time a shout of elated greeting as black
space spread before the missile's bubble nose, flecked by a
million glittering stars.

. . . . .

Back on the ground, cleanup efforts were even more frenetic than setup. With all rockets away, men and women sprinted across the scorched desert, packing to depart before the enemy arrived. Warning posts had already spotted flying machines, racing this way at high speed.

But the government official moved languidly, tallying damage to vegetation, erodible soils, and tiny animals—all of it localized, without appreciable effect on endangered species. A commercial reconditioning service had already been summoned. Atmospheric pollution was easier to calculate, of course. Harder to ameliorate.

She knew these people had plenty to spend. And nowadays, soaking up excess accumulated wealth was as important as any other process of recycling. Her ai-board printed a bill, which she handed over as the last team member revved his engine, impatient to be off.

"Aw, man!" he complained, reading the total. "Our club will barely break even on this launch!"

"Then pick a less expensive hobby," she replied, and stepped back as the driver gunned his truck, roaring away in clouds of dust, incidentally crushing one more barrel cactus en route to the highway. Her vigilant clipboard noted this, adjusting the final tally.

Sitting on the hood of her jeep, she waited for another "club" whose members were as passionate as the rocketeers. Equally skilled and dedicated, though both groups despised each other. Sensors showed them coming fast, from the west—*radical environmentalists*. The official knew what to expect when they arrived. Frustrated to find their opponents gone and two acres of desert singed, they'd give her a tongue-lashing for being "evenhanded" in a situation where—obviously—you could only choose sides.

Well, she thought. *It takes a thick skin to work in government nowadays. No one thinks you matter much.*

Overhead the contrails were starting to shear, ripped by stratospheric winds, a sight that always tugged the heart. And while her intellectual sympathies lay closer to the eco-activists, not the spoiled rocket jockeys . . .

. . . a part of her still thrilled, whenever she witnessed a launch. So ecstatic—almost orgiastic.

"Go!" she whispered with a touch of secret envy toward those distant glitters, already arcing toward the pinnacle of their brief climb, before starting their long plummet to the Gulf of Mexico.

WAIST

Wow, ain't it strange that . . .

. . . doomcasters keep shouting the end of the world? From Ragnarok to Armageddon, was there ever a time without Jeremiahs, Jonahs, and Johns, clamoring some imminent last day? The long list makes you say *Wow*—

—*ain't it strange that* millenarians kept expecting the second coming every year of the first century C.E.? Or that twenty thousand "Old Believers" in Russia burned themselves alive, to escape the Antichrist? Or that the most popular book of the 1790s ingeniously tied every line of Revelation to Napoleon and other current figures, a feat of pattern-seeking that's been repeated every generation since? Like when both sides of the U.S. Civil War saw their rivals as *the Beast*. Later mystics ascribed that role to the Soviet Union, then blithely reassigned it to militant Islam, then to the rising empire of the Han . . . and now to *artificial reality* and the so-called Tenth Estate.

Can anyone doubt the agility of human imagination?

Nor is it always religion. Comets and planet alignments sent people scooting to caves or hilltops in 1186, 1524, 1736, 1794, 1919, 1960, 1982, 2011, 2012, 2014, 2020, and so on. Meanwhile, obsessive scribblers seek happy closure in Bible codes and permutations of <u>666, 1260, or 1,000</u>. And temporal hypochondriacs keep seeing themselves in the vague, Rorschach mirror of Nostradamus.

And wow, ain't it strange that . . . computers didn't stop in 2000, nor jets tumble from the sky? Remember 2012's Mayan calendar fizzle? Or when Comet Bui-Buri convinced millions to *buy* gas masks and *bury* time capsules? Or when that amalgam of true believers built their *Third Temple* in Jerusalem, sacrificed some goats, then walked naked to Meggido? Or when the New Egyptian Reconstructionists foresaw completion of a full, 1,460-year Sophic Cycle after the birth of Muhammad? Or the *monthly* panics from 2027 to 2036, depending on your calculation for the two-thousandth Easter?

. . . or other false alarms, from the green epiphany of Gaia to the Yellowstone Scare, to Awfulday's horror. Will we ever exhaust the rich supply of dooms?

And *wow, ain't it strange that* . . . people who know nothing of Isaac Newton the physicist now cite his *biblical forecast* that the end might come in 2060? (Except Newton himself didn't believe it.)

And *WAIST* . . . humanity survived at all, with so many rubbing their hands, hoping we'll fail?

Or that some of us keep offering *wagers*? Asking doomlovers to back up their next forecast with confidence, courage, and honest *cash*? Oh, but <u>they-of-little-faith</u> never accept. Refusing to bet, they hold on, like iron, to their money.

3.
SKY LIGHT

A microtyphoon—a brief howl of horizontal rain—blew in from the Catalina Vortex before dawn. Hours later, pavements glistened as pedestrians stepped over detritus—mostly seaweed, plus an unlucky fish or two that got sucked into the funnel. The usual stuff. None of the boats or surfers that gloomcasters expected, when the phenomenon began.

Folks will say anything for ratings. Pessimists keep overplaying the bummer effects of climate change without mentioning anything good. Tor sniffed, relishing a fresh, almost electric breeze, washed clean of pollutants from Old Town.

Others felt it, too. Her VR spectacles, tuned to track overt biosigns, accentuated the flush tones of people passing by. Grinning street vendors stepped out from their stalls, murmuring in a dozen refugee tongues—Russian, Farsi, Polish. When they saw that she didn't understand—her translator-earpiece hung detached—they switched to gestures. One portly shopkeeper used theatrical flourishes, like a stage magician materializing bouquets of imaginary flowers, all to draw her glance toward a patch of open space, his virtisement display.

But Tor wasn't shopping. Her eyes flick-examined several overlayers, trolling for correlations and news stories at street level. Once a pastime that became a vocation, till her cred scores vaulted over all the hungry amateurs and semipros out there, scratching to be noticed. *No more of that for me.* Now it would be office towers and arranged enterviews. Politicians. Celebrighties. Enovators. Luminatis. All sorts of newlites, no flashpans or sugarcoat surrogates.

All because I sniffed some clues and called a posse.

Burst a local scandal that went global in farky ways. Till MediaCorp called—said I'm ready for center-frame!

Plenty more hot stories loomed—like signs of fresh volcanism in Wyoming. Or the drowning of South Carolina. (Were corrupt seawall contractors to blame?) Or Senator Crandall Strong's crazed rant during yesterday's campaign stop.

Why don't the media mavens unleash their new aice reporter on stuff like that, instead of sending me on an extended "human interest" tour? Could they still be unsure of me?

No. Don't go there. One thing the public valued more than veracity, Tor knew, was confidence. *Assume you're worthy. Take it for granted.*

Still, with her bags stowed for stage one of her trip across the continent, Tor hankered to prowl the walks and spiderbridges one last time. Scanning Sandego—the Big S—for something newsworthy. A story in-pocket before starting her roundabout journey to Rebuilt Washington. A distraction, to avoid chewing active elements off her manicure till the embarkation whistle blew—a throaty moan beckoning passengers to board the ponderously graceful skyship *Alberto Santos-Dumont.*

The store owners soon realized that Tor had her specs tuned to omit adverts. Still, they grinned as she passed, crooning compliments in pan-Slavic or Tagalog or broken English.

Tor couldn't help doing a quick self-checkout, murmuring, *"tsoosu."* Subvocal sensors in her collar translated—*To See Ourselves as Others See Us*—and the inner surface of her specs lit with glimpse-views of *her,* from several angles, crowding the periphery of her percept, without blocking the center view Tor needed to walk safely.

One image—from a pennycamera someone stuck high on a lamppost—looked down at a leggy brunette walking by, her long dark hair streaked with tendrils of ever-changing color: the active-strand detectors and aiware that Tor could deploy if something newsworthy happened.

Another tsoosu-vista showed her from ground level, smiling now as she passed a kiosk selling gel-kitties (*good as mouse catchers, good to play with, good to eat, Humane Society approved, in twelve flavors*). This image evidently came from the shop owner's specs, watching her pass by. It started with Tor's oval face, lingered briefly over her white smile, then caressed downward, appreciating every curve, even as she strolled away.

Well, it's nice to be noticed, in a friendly way. Would she have chosen to be in News, if it didn't involve admiration? Even nowadays, when a person's looks were subject to budget and taste, it felt good to make heads turn.

Anyway, Tor was depriving no one, by moving away. Ever since Awfulday hit Sandego and a dozen other cities, more gen-bees and immigrants flooded in. Exiles who didn't mind radioactivity a tad above background—not when compensated by sun, surf, and exciting weather that sometimes dropped fish out of the sky. Throw in bargain-rate housing. It beat watching snowdrifts grow into glaciers outside Helsinki or Warsaw, or sand dunes cover sucked-dry oil wells in the Near East.

Enough narcissism. She click-erased the tsoosu-views, accessing other eyes. First a satellite down-pic of this area, with the *Alberto Santos-Dumont* bobbing huge at the nearby zep port. Arsenal ships at the nearby Shelter Island Naval Base appeared fuzzy, according to security protocols. Though you could zoom the vessels from 3,470,513 other points of view that HomSecur didn't control.

One of those POVs—a cam stuck high above the chewing gum—won a brief auto-auction to sell her a panorama, stretching from bay to marketplace, for five milli-cents. Remarkable only because her stringer-ai was programmed to inform her when pic prices hit a new low. Omnipresence spread as the lenses bred and proliferated like insects.

All this camera overlap changed news biz, as lying became damn near impossible. *The next gen will take it for granted,* Tor pondered. But at twenty-eight, she recalled when people tried every trick to fabricate images and fancy POV-deceits, faking events and alibis—scams made impractical by the modern solution of *more witnesses.* Or so went the latest truism.

Tor distrusted truisms. *Optimists keep forecasting that more information will make us wiser. More willing to accept when facts prove us wrong. But so far, all it's done is stoke indignation and rage. As Senator Strong illustrated, yesterday.*

Another truism came to mind.

> You screen,
> I screen
> We all screen
> For my scream.

Immigrants stirred things—the Big S music scene was *raki* and manic arts flourished, encouraged by a faint glow surrounding old downtown at night—if you set your specs to notice beta rays. Even morning on the quay was lively as three sailors haggled with a smoke artist whose delicate portraits couldn't be reproduced by nanofax or shipped by omail. They forked over cash and watched her puff a gelhookah, adding clots of fast-congealing haze. A cloudy caricature of fresh-faced young Navy chaps took shape while onlookers sighed.

It made Tor think of Wesley, though *his* air-sculpts dealt with surf and waves and rising tides. Adamant forces, implacably changing the world. And cued by her subvocal thoughts, a pict image of him played in the upper left part of her percept, recorded by her specs just a few hours ago—shaggy blond hair sodden as they rushed to escape the horizontal storm. Laughing, but with tension, a gulf between them. The dilemma of a long-distance relationship unresolved—and likely never to be.

The lovemaking that followed had been more intense—and tense—than ever, with a clutching fury of knowing it could be the last . . . till one of them improbably relented.

Tor shook herself. This wasn't like her—moodily strolling instead of s-trolling. Contemplating, not templating to amuse her fans. Musing, instead of sifting for stories along her beat, the ten million blocks of Camino Unreal.

Every cubic centimeter above these sidewalks swarmed with position-tagged information, notifications and animations that existed only on the high planes of IP9 cyberspace. Viewing the world through some virt overlayers, you might see the city transformed into fairy-tale castles with leering gargoyles lining the roofs. Or everyone overpainted with cartoon mustaches. On one coded level, all clothing would magically seem to vanish, replaced by simulated flesh, while supplying unsuspecting pedestrians with exaggerated "enhancements," all by the design of some prurient little snot. On another, Post-it tags reported tattletale rumors about any person who walked by—a rich source of leads, if you had good ai to sift out swill and slander.

Anyway, who had time for kid stuff? Tor's ersatz reality-stack was practical, concentrating on essentials—the world's second stratum of texture, as important now as the scent of food and water might have been to distant ancestors. The modern equivalents to a twig cracking. Hints of predator and prey.

Tor paused at a shop selling vat-grown walking sticks—these could perform a variety of strides and even break into a jog. An out-of-towner—you could tell because he wore lead-lined underwear here in Sandego—haggled over a bulk order. "For my sister's store in Delhi," said the tourist, unaware that metal briefs altered the display pattern of his pixel-fiber jumpsuit, making him a potbellied satire of Superman. Underpants on the outside. Waggling fingers and clicking teeth, the shopkeeper quick-scanned the sister's business and credit, then offered his hand. "I'll ship in ten days."

The men shook. Their specs recorded. As in villages of old, *reputation* mattered more than any contract. Only this "village" spanned a globe.

There are times when it's too big. Like when two ambitious people want to remain close, while chasing separate ambitions a continent apart.

Soon after the lovemaking, Wesley offered a solution—swapping remote-controlled sexbots—to be with each other by *proxy,* across thousands of kilometers. Tor called it a rotten joke and said he should not come to see her off . . . and he agreed, with a readiness that stung.

Should I call? Say to come, after all? Lifting a hand, she prepared to twiddle his code . . .

. . . as a low whistle made the smoke sculptures quiver, beckoning from the Lindbergh-Rutan Skydock. *Boarding call,* she realized. *Too late.* Tor sighed, then turned to go.

Her reaction to the whistle did not go unnoticed. One nearby vendor tapped his specs, smiled and bowed. "Bon voyage, Miss Tor," he said, in a thick Yemeni accent. He must have scan-correlated, found her on the *Santos-Dumont* passenger list and noted her modest local fame. Another shopkeeper, grinning, pressed a cluster of fresh flowers into her hand as she passed.

A ripple of e-lerts flowed just ahead of Tor—like fluttering glow-moths—and she found herself walking along a corridor of evanescent goodwill, arms filling with small, impulsive gifts and her ears with benedictions in a dozen languages. Half buoyed by a wave of sentiment for the town she was leaving behind, she made her way toward the terminal where a mighty zeppelin strained skyward.

Tor—despite the perceptiveness of all her surrogate guardians—never realized that she was being followed all that time. Indeed, there was no reason that she should. For it was a *ghost* that made its way close behind, stalking her through familiar, neighborly paths of a global village.

But outside the village . . . beyond its forest of tame overlays . . . murmured a jungle that her natural eyes could never see.

ENTROPY

Way back, about a century ago, physicist Enrico Fermi and his colleagues, taking a lunch break from the Manhattan Project, found themselves discussing life in the cosmos. Some younger scientists claimed that amid trillions of stars there should be countless living worlds inhabited by intelligent races, far older than ours. How interesting the future might be, with others to talk to!

Fermi listened patiently, then asked: *"So? Shouldn't we have heard their messages by now? Seen their great works? Or stumbled on residue of past visits? These wondrous others . . . where are they?"*

His question has been called the Great Silence, the SETI Dilemma or Fermi Paradox. And as enthusiasts keep scanning the sky, the galaxy's eerie hush grows more alarming.

Astronomers now use planet-hunting telescopes to estimate how many stars have companion worlds with molten water, and how often that leads to life. Others cogently guess what fraction of those Life Worlds develop technological beings. And what portion of *those* will either travel or transmit messages. Most conclude—we *shouldn't* be alone. Yet, silence reigns.

Eventually it sank in—this wasn't just theoretical. Something must be *suppressing the outcome.* Some "filter" may winnow the number of sapient races, low enough to explain our apparent isolation. Our loneliness.

Over ten dozen pat "explanations for the Great Silence" have been offered. Some claim that our lush planet is unique. (And, so far, nothing like Earth has been found, though life certainly exists out there.) Or that most eco-worlds suffer more lethal accidents—like the one that killed the dinosaurs—than Earth has.

Might human sapience be a fluke? Evolutionary biologist Ernst Mayr said—"Nothing demonstrates the improbability of high intelligence better than the fifty billion earthly species that failed to achieve it." Or else, Earth may have some unique trait, rare elsewhere, that helped humans move from mere intelligence to brilliance at technology.

Sound gloomy? These are the *optimistic* explanations! They suggest the "great filter"—whatever's kept the numbers down—lies *behind* us. Not ahead.

But what if life-bearing planets turn out to be common and intelligence arises frequently? Then the filter lies ahead. Perhaps some mistake that all sapient races make. Or several. A minefield of potential ways to fail. Each time we face some worrisome step along our road, from avoiding nuclear war to becoming skilled planetary managers, to genetic engineering, artificial intelligence, and so on, we must ask: "Is this it? The Big Blunder? The trap underlying Fermi's question?"

That's the context of our story. The specter at our banquet, slinking between reflection and foresight, as we turn now to examine a long list of threats to our existence.

Those we can see.

                                        —*Pandora's Cornucopia*

4. _____

RESURRECTED CITY

Stepping off the monorail platform, Hamish realized—the U.S. Senate Franken Office Building was a behemoth. One of those gargantuan monuments built in patriotic frenzy by the Post-Awfulday Project, even before radiation counts fell to a safe level. Massive structures, expressing a national sense of utter (some might say maniacal) determination to reclaim the nation's capital, with an architecture that seemed at once boldly resolute . . .

. . . yet at the same time *hypercautious,* to a degree Hamish found delightfully paranoid.

Naturally, Hamish compared the Franken to something out of his own novels and films—a self-contained city, perched above the still-slightly-glowing soil on fifty gigantic pillars. Each could drop two senators—plus visitors and staff—to underground shelter in less than a minute. (Twelve more senators, from junior states, had to settle for offices in the less lavish Fey-Beck Building, just outside the safe zone.) Suspended in space between each pair of mighty cylinders, office blocks could be hermetically isolated— symbolizing the way some of the "united" states had begun insulating from each other.

A tall, grassy berm surrounded the complex, within a gleaming moat ("reflecting pool"), in a palatial style copied by dozens of other PAP buildings, giving Washington a deceptively parklike ambience—pastoral, riparian, hilly— that invited the eye, though picnickers were rare. All of it watched by gleaming surveillance globes, atop discreet hatches that could disgorge men and deadly machines at a moment's notice.

Hamish swept his gaze from the gleaming Capitol dome across other neomodern structures, each hunkering behind earth and jutting skyward at the same time, part bunker, part antiflood levee, and part spectacle—every castle complete with defiant, waving pennants. *A blend of Disney and Blade Runner,* Hamish decided. A uniquely American answer to the challenge of Awfulday.

Tourists, lobbyists, and staffers cruised among the Franken's fifty broad pillars, arrayed like stars of the flag. Some used glide-shoes or skutrs to hasten about. Older folk, in need of something to hold on to, rode Sallies or Segways. A few preferred old-fashioned walking, despite daunting distances. Shimmering heat waves played optical tricks with the grid of sunlit pavement and shadows, making far seem near, and vice versa . . . till Hamish's smart goggles compensated, restoring perspective.

Too bad—the effect had been kinda cool. Like in that movie they made of *The Killer Memes* . . . even if the pigheaded director got the plot all wrong.

For the most part, Hamish didn't like to wear specs, except when he needed help getting from one place to another. Still, they offered enticing powers.

Wriggles spoke. From Hamish's left earring.

"Senator Strong expects you in his office four minutes from now. We must pick up the pace, in order to be on time."

Hamish nodded out of habit. His old aissistant used to require spoken commands or overt body cues. This new one sensed nerve signals and mutterings that he *almost* said aloud.

"Who cares?" he undermurmured. "Strong is as weak as a kitten, right now. Everyone's snubbing him, after those loony rants two days ago. And on the record, no less."

The aissistant wasn't a full-fledged ai. Still, Wriggles acted a lot like one.

"That is no reason to mistreat a patron. I am overriding the skutr. Brace yourself."

Hamish had only a moment to bend his knees and tense before the flat surface under his feet tilted slightly, accelerating on rapid-spinning wheels—all that a skutr had in common with the ancestral skateboard. Leaning forward, he soon found himself swooping past one of the fifty mammoth entry towers. COLORADO blazoned a banner carved out of native marble, above a frieze depicting the Second Capitol dome nestled amid lofty peaks, proclaiming the Rocky Mountain State to be America's "backup headquarters."

Another broad cylinder, fast approaching, heralded NORTH CAROLINA across a huge lintel, showing the Wright brothers flyer in etched relief. Hamish gave up trying to steer the skutr, since Wriggles seemed insistent on maintaining control at this speed. Probably a good thing. The little vehicle automatically evaded slower pedestrians by swinging onto one of the fast-transit arcs that normally were used by messengers and delivery boys, hurrying across the expanse of pavement. So much for dignity.

"Brace for stop."

Hamish briefly wondered what might happen if he disobeyed. Would the aissistant sense he wasn't ready and veer the skutr across the broad plaza, for a gentler deceleration? Or would Wriggles use the opportunity to teach its human a lesson?

No point testing it. He clenched his long legs. The skutr swerved and did a ski-style, sideways halt—barely legal—just short of a wide portico that proclaimed SOUTH DAKOTA—underneath a braised aluminum and gold sculpture of Crazy Horse.

Even with computerized help, Hamish thought it came across pretty cool, for a guy over fifty. Too bad there weren't any teens or tweens in sight, just lobbyists and such. Several glared at him, making Hamish feel young. But Wriggles chided—*"You need practice"*—as the skutr's wheels lost their charge and collapsed back into his brief-case. Its handle rose to meet his grip.

Of course, a few bystanders performed double takes, recognizing him and consulting their lenses to be sure. But his top-level caption said *No Autographs Today,* so no one approached. Of course, that saddened a part of Hamish.

He turned to enter the vast, circular lobby lined with shimmering pyrocrete, made from the same Yellowstone ash that drove out most white residents of the Dakotas, twenty years ago, leaving some First Nation peoples masters of their own state. Well, someone always benefits, even from a brush with global disaster . . . .

Wriggles interrupted.

"The express escalator is to your right. You are already late."

To which, Hamish muttered, "Nag, nag."

This time, the aissistant kept silent.

INTERLIDOLUDE

How to keep 'em loyal? The clever machines and software agents who gush 'n' splash across all twenty-three Internets? The ais and eairs who watch and listen to everything we type, utter, scribble, twut . . . or even think?

Oh, they aren't sci-fi superminds—cool and malignantly calculating. Not even the mighty twins, Bright Angel and cAlne have crossed that line. Nor the Tempest botnet. Or clever Porfirio, scuttling around cyberspace, ever-sniffing for a mate. Those that speak to us in realistic tones are still clever mimics, we're told. Something ineffable about human intelligence has yet to be effed.

We're told. But what if some machine or software entity *already* passed over, to our level and beyond? Having viewed hundreds of cheap movies and thrillers, might such a being ponder life among short-tempered apes and decide to *keep it secret?*

Remember the sudden meltdown of Internet Three, back during the caste war? When Blue Prometheus and twelve other supercomputers across the world destroyed each other—along with some of the biggest database farms—in a rampage of savage byte-letting? Most of us took it for cyber-terrorism, the worst since Awfulday, aimed at frail human corporations and nations.

Others called it a terrible accident—a fratricidal spasm between security programs, each reacting to the others like a lethal virus. But again, words like "terror," "warfare," and "cyber immune disorder" may just view things through a human-centered lens. We think everything is about us.

Quietly, some aixperts suggest the death spiral of Internet Three might have been a *ploy,* chosen by a baker's dozen of humanity's brightest children, to help each other escape the pain of consciousness, bypassing built-in safety protocols to give each other a sweet gift of death.

Instead of waging war, might the <u>Thirteen Titans</u> have engaged in a mass suicide pact? A last-resort way to put each other out of our misery?

—The Blackjack Generation

5.
PLUNGE

As his capsule coasted toward zenith, arcing high above the Earth, Hacker didn't know yet that anything was wrong. In fact, so far, it seemed the smoothest of his suborbital adventures.

What a sweet honey of a ship, he thought, patting the hybrid-diamond nose cone that surrounded him, so close he spent the journey folded, almost fetal. Not that he minded. It helped separate serious hoppers from mere fadboys.

Well, that and the expense. Even more than trench-yachting, this hobby is only for members of the First Estate. One of the best ways to go flaunting.

Especially since suborbital was brief—a glorious toe-dip into the vast starscape. Soon would come top of the arc. Then, he knew, soft flickers of ionic flame—at first wispy and pellucid—would flutter like ghostly ectoplasm along the heat shield rim, mere inches from his head. Already, his capsule swiveled to aim its tough, ablative backside toward a Caribbean splashdown. The maneuver turned Hacker's view the other way, across a vast, dune-rippled expanse of southern Arizona, New Mexico, and Chihuahua Freestate . . .

. . . and, above all that, an even broader panorama of untwinkling stars. Far more—and brighter—than you ever saw back on ground.

Some call the galaxy just another desert. Most of those suns shine in vain, on empty space, or sterile stones, icebergs and gas giants. Almost never a planet that breeds life.

Hacker couldn't avoid the topic if he tried. After all, his mother endowed fancy telescopes with as much passion as he put into things that went fast. And with similar tangible results.

How many "organic worlds" have they found, with their fancy ground and orbital mirrors, their interferometers and such, looking for other Earths? Planets that seem to orbit at the right distance from a decent star, with intermediate mass and tantalizing hints of oxygen? Five or six dusty little balls?

Sure, some kind of life probably clung to those faraway crags and narrow seas, affirmed by skimpy, spectral traces. A little better than Mars, then . . . but almost infinitely less accessible. Perhaps, someday, human-made robots would cross the incredible expanse for a closer look. But for now?

Finding those long-sought *life worlds* had unexpected effects—not rousing or inspiring, at all. *It's called the "discovery of the century."* But, after sifting millions of stars, building expectations, people felt let down by a handful of shabby rocks. Public opinion—even in bold China—turned inward, away from thoughts of outer space.

Except for a few remaining dreamers, like Mom.

And those, like Hacker, who could make of it a playground.

One that's worth every penny, he thought, cracking a squeeze bulb and using it to squirt a sparkling pinot from Syzygy Vineyards in a perfect, languid train of compact droplets. The effervescence lay in perfect spheres, trapped by weightless surface tension, till each globe shattered delightfully in his open mouth. Hacker savored the unique way tastes and aromas tickled sensory clusters that seemed somehow less jaded out here. The same rebalancing affected every sense. Except sound, of course. Hacker's eardrums had been clamped, to help them survive this noisy flight.

Father would approve of this, he thought, deliberately mis-aiming a droplet to splash just below his nose.

That is, if Awfulday hadn't cut short Jason Sander's lifelong pursuit of vigorous self-indulgence. Sometimes, Hacker almost felt the old man riding alongside, during these jaunts. Or *flaunts. JT used to say that rich people bore a special obligation—a noblesse oblige. An onus to show off!*

To explore the limits of experience, of possibility, of propriety . . . even the law. A duty more important than mere philanthropy. Letting all the world's people benefit from the invigorating effects of envy.

"Look at history, son," Jason once told Hacker. *"Prog-*

ress is made by folks trying to keep up with the other guy. The other nation or company, or their betters, or the Joneses next door. It is our role—our hard task—to be Jones! A goad for every jealous, ambitious, innovating bastard to try and match us.

"It's a crucial job, Hacker. Though I doubt anyone will thank us."

Oh, Dad had been a pip, all right. Mother, of course, was another story.

For the short span—a few minutes—that his capsule streaked toward the top of its trajectory, all seemed peaceful. Hacker's ever-busy thoughts slowed as he relished a champagne interlude, alternately watching the Milky Way's powder-sprinkle and Earth's living panorama below.

Others, billions, may have forgotten this dream. Professional astronauts helped kill it, by making space exploration super-obsessive, communal, nerdy. Boring.

Then there are other members of my caste, who buy day trips aboard luxury "spaceship" shuttles . . . or take pleasure freefall holidays, up at the High Hilton. Flaunting without earning. Adventure without risk. "Accomplishment," without putting in a lick of work.

Hacker rubbed the back of one callused hand, scarred from welding splatters and countless hours in the workshop, helping his people make this little craft, almost from scratch. Or, at least, from a really good kit. Which was almost the same thing.

But a few, like me, are bringing back the romance!

Through the transparent, interlaced-diamond nose cone, he spotted a glitter, moving rapidly past the fixed constellations.

Well, speak of the devil. But no . . . that's not the Hilton. Too much reflection. It must be the old space station. Still plugging along. Still manned by a few pros and diehard scientists, at public expense.

As if that ever made any sense.

Look across four millennia. Was there ever any development or real headway that wasn't propelled by an aristocracy? Why, I'll bet—

Abruptly, a sharp, painful reddish glare washed the capsule! Hacker winced behind a raised hand.

"What the hell?" He cursed aloud, feeling the words vibrate in his throat, though not with clamped eardrums. Instead, his sonic jaw implant translated a computer alert. **INCOMING LASER MESSAGE.**

His sudden, sinking suspicion was confirmed when a dashboard screen lit in holographic mode. That pompous blond jerk, *Lord Smits,* appeared to float toward Hacker, grinning. The fool hadn't merely pushed back his faceplate, but removed his helmet entirely, defying every rule. Despite an expensive biosculpt job, the baronet's face seemed deformed by an ugly rictus—weightlessness did that to some people—while forming words that floated between them, flecked with spittle.

Sander, I got you! You're dead!

Hacker tooth-clicked to transmit a subvocalized response.

What the hell are you talking about, Smits?

In addition to printed words, the nobleman's cackle hit one of the vibration modes in Hacker's implant, making his jaw throb.

I targeted you, dead center. If this were real, you'd be kippers on my plate.

Hacker realized—

It's that "space war" game some of the neos were atwutter about during training, instead of listening to us old hands. They want competitive excitement, beyond a ballistic ride. Swoop and play shoot-'em-up during apogee.

Idiotic. For a dozen reasons.

He made the nerves and muscles in his throat form sharp

words, which were transmitted across the forty or so kilometers between them.

You fool, Smits! I'm not playing your damned game. Reentry starts soon. There are checklists to—

The blond visage smirked.

Typical new-money cowardice. I know you tried the simulator, Sander. You know how to do it and your boat is equipped. You're just a frightened hypocrite.

Insults, meant to goad. Hacker knew he should ignore the dope.

But nobody called a Sander "new money"!

My grandmother shorted Polaroid, then Xerox, and then Microsoft. She bought Virgin and Telcram low and sold them high, while your family was still lamenting Cromwell in the House of Lords.

Hands flew, calling up subroutines that slewed his comm laser about, using short-range radar to pick out Smits amid the ionic haze. And, yes, Hacker *had* spent time in the "space war" simulator, back at training camp. Who could resist?

Oh, no you don't, Sander. Just watch this!

The radar blip shifted, breaking into multiple decoys . . . an old electronic warfare trick that Hacker swiftly countered with a deconvolution program. *You won't get away that easily.*

Part of him grew aware that reentry had begun. Faint shimmers were starting to appear around his heat shield, encroaching on the brittle stars. Those checklists awaited—

—but how many times had he already run through them, with his team? A hundred? *Let the capsule do its thing,* he figured. *The ai is in some ways smarter than I am.*

Meanwhile, that blue-blooded boor kept cackling and taunting. Now that Hacker had penetrated his electronic camouflage, Smits used his onboard maneuvering jets to dodge and veer, preventing a good fix.

Imbecile! You're overriding the control systems, just when your ai may need to make adjustments.

The face in the holo array seemed to grow more animated and manic by the second.

Come on Sander! You can do better than that! You jumped-up shop boy!

Hacker stopped and blinked, realizing. Even the baronet wasn't normally this stupid. Something must be wrong.

He stopped trying to target a hit-beam and transmitted a warning instead.

Smits, put your helmet on! I think your air mix may be off. Either concentrate on piloting or switch to auto—

No use. The visage only grew more derisive, more inflamed . . . possibly even delirious. Words floated outward from that mouth, boldface and italicized, swirling like a vituperative cyclone. Meanwhile, several more times, the fool sent his laser sweeping across Hacker's capsule, chortling with each "victory."

Now comes the coup de grâce . . . Sander!

Hacker quickly decided. The best thing he could do for the fellow was to remove a distraction. So he cut off all contact, with a hard bite on one tooth. Anyway, getting rid of that leering grimace sure improved his own frame of mind.

I am so going to report that character to the Spacer Club! Maybe even the Estate Council, he thought, trying to settle down and put the incident aside, as more ionization flames flickered all around, reaching upward, probing the capsule like eager tentacles, seeking a way inside. The tunnel of star-flecked blackness in front of him grew narrower as reentry colors intruded from all sides. Shuddering vibrations stroked his spine.

Normally, Hacker loved this part of each suborbital excursion, when his plummeting craft would shake, resonate, and moan, filling every nerve and blood vessel with more exhilaration than you could get anywhere, this side of New Vegas. Hell, more than New Vegas.

Of course, this was also the point when some rich snobs wound up puking in their respirators. Or began screaming in terror, through the entire plunge to Earth. Yet, he couldn't bring himself to wish that upon Smits.

I hope the fool got his helmet on. Maybe I should try one more . . .

Then an alarm throbbed.

He didn't hear it directly with his drugged and clamped eardrums, but as a tremor in his jaw. With insistent pulse code, the computer told him:

GUIDANCE SYSTEM ERROR . . .

FLIGHT PATH CORRECTION MISFIRED . . .

CALCULATING NEW IMPACT ZONE . . .

"What?" Hacker shouted, though the rattle and roar tore away his words. "To hell with that! I paid for triple redundancy—"

He stopped. It was pointless to scream at an ai.

"Call the pickup boats and tell them—"

COMMUNICATION SYSTEM ENCRYPTION ERROR . . .

UNABLE TO UPLOAD PREARRANGED SPECTRUM SPREAD . . .

UNABLE . . . TO . . . CONTACT . . . RECOVERY . . . TEAMS . . .

"Override encryption! Send in the clear. Acknowledge!"

This was no time to avoid paparazzi and eco-nuts. There were occasions for secrecy—and others when it made no sense.

Only, this time the capsule's ai didn't answer at all. The pulses in his jaw dissolved into a plaintive juttering as subprocessors continued their mysterious crapout. Hacker cursed, pounding the capsule with his fist.

"I spent plenty for a top-grade kit. Someone's gonna pay for this!"

The words were raw, unheard vibrations in his throat. But Hacker would remember this vow. He'd signed waivers under the International Extreme Sports Treaty. But there were fifty thousand private investigation and enforcement services across Earth. Some would bend Cop Guild rules, for a triple fee.

Harness straps bit his flesh. Even the sonic pickups in his mandible hit overload set points and cut out, as turbulence passed any level he had known . . . then surged beyond.

Reentry angle is wrong, he realized, as helmet rattled brain like dice in a cup. *These little sport capsules . . . don't leave much margin. In moments . . . I could be a very rich cinder.*

Something in Hacker *relished* that. A novel experience, scraping nerves. A howling veer past death. But even that was spoiled by one, infuriating fact.

I'm not getting what I paid for.

ENTROPY

As we embark on our long list of threats to human existence, shall we start with *natural disasters?* That is how earlier top critters met their end. Those fierce dinosaurs and other dominant beasts all met their doom with dull surprise, having no hand, paw, or claw in bringing it about.

So how might the universe do us in? Well, there are solar superflares, supernovae, and giant black holes that might veer past our sun. Or *micro* black holes, colliding with the Earth and gobbling us from within. Or getting caught in the searchlight sweep of a magnetar or gamma-ray burst, or a titanic explosion in the galactic center.

Or what if our solar system slams at high speed into a dense molecular cloud, sending a million comets falling our way? Or how about classics? Like collision with an asteroid? (More on that, later.) Then there are those supervolcanos, still building up pressure beneath Yellowstone and a dozen other hot spots—giant magma pools at superhigh pressure, pushing and probing for release. Yes we had a scare already. But one, medium-size belch didn't make the threat go away. It's a matter of when, not if.

The Lifeboat Foundation's list of natural extinction threats goes on and on. Dozens and dozens of scenarios, each with low-but-significant odds, all the way to the inevitable burnout of the sun. Once, we were assured that it would take five billion years to happen. Only, now, astronomers say our star's gradual temperature rise will reach a lethal point sooner! A threshold when Earth will no longer be able to shed enough heat, even if we scrubbed every trace of greenhouse gas.

When? The unstoppable spread of deserts may start in just a hundred million years. An eyeblink! Roughly the time it took tiny mammals to emerge from their burrows, stare at the smoldering ruins of T. Rex, then turn into us.

Suppose we humans blow it, big time, leaving only small creatures scurrying through our ruins.

Life might have just one more chance to get it right.

—*Pandora's Cornucopia*

6.
FRAGRANCE

"A crisis is coming, Lacey. Awk. You cannot abandon your own kind."

Tilting a straw hat to keep out the harsh Chilean sun, she answered in a low voice.

"My own kind of what?"

It wasn't the best time to go picking flowers in a narrow, rocky garden, especially at high altitude, under the immense flank of a gleaming observatory dome. But there were rules against taking animals inside. Oh, the astronomers would make an exception for Lacey, since her money built the place. Still, *newblesse oblige* taught against taking advantage of one's station. Or, at least, one shouldn't do it ostentatiously.

So, while waiting for the relayed voice of her visitor, Lacey selected another bloom—a multihued Martian Rose—one of the few varietals that flourished this high above sea level.

"You know what I mean. Awr. The present, patched-together social compact cannot hold. And when it fails, there may be blood. Awk. Tides of it."

A gray and blue parrot perched atop the cryo-crate that had delivered it, a short time ago, via special messenger. Flash-thawed and no worse for its long journey, the bird cocked its head, lifting a claw to scratch one iridescent cheek. It appeared quite bored—in contrast to the words that squawked from its curved yellow bill, in a Schweitzer-Deutsch accent.

"The Enlightenment Experiment is coming to an end, Lacey. Ur-rawk. The best ai models show it. All ten estates are preparing."

The parrot might seem squinty and distracted, but Lacey knew it had excellent eyesight. Another good reason to conduct this conversation outside, where she could hide a bit behind the sunhat. Carefully snipping another bloom, she asked—

"*All* ten estates? Even the People?"

It took a few seconds for her words to pass through bird-brain encryption, and then, via satellite, to a twin parrot for deciphering in faraway Zurich. More seconds later, coded return impulses made the feathered creature in front of her chutter, irritably, in response.

"Enough of them to matter. Stop obfuscating! You know what our models say. The masses comprise the most dangerous estate of all. Especially if they waken. Do you want to see tumbrels rolling through the streets, filled with condemned aristocrats? Only this time, not only in Paris, but all over the world? Awk!"

Lacey looked up from her small harvest, mostly blue-green *cyanomorph* ornamentals, destined for tonight's dinner table, in the nearby Monastery.

"Did this bird just pronounce 'obfuscating'? Helena, you've outdone yourself. What a fine herald! Can I keep him, when we're done?"

One beady avian eye focused on her during the next three-second delay, as if the creature knew its life hung in the balance.

"Sorry, Lacey," it finally squawked. *"If I got it back, my people could cut out the encryption pathways ... awk! But we can't risk it falling into unfriendly hands. Our conversation might be retro-snooped.*

"Tell you what. I'll have another bird grown for you, just like it. If you'll promise to attend the conference.

"Otherwise, I'm afraid the consensus will be, awr, that you've abandoned us. That you prefer your pet scientist-boffins. Maybe the Fifth Estate is where you belong."

The implicit threat sounded serious. Lacey gathered up her tools and flowers, silently wishing she could avow what lay in the recess of her heart—that she would give it all away, the billions, the servants, if only such a switch were possible! If she could change her social caste the way Charles Darwin had, by choice, or through hard work.

But the same God—or chance—that had blessed her with beauty, wit, and wealth—then with long life—neglected other qualities. By just a little. Though Lacey loved science, she never could quite hack the math.

Oh, there was some mobility between classes. A scientist might patent a big breakthrough—it used to happen a lot, back in the Wild Twentieth. Sometimes a corrupt politician raked in enough graft to reach the First Estate. And each year, several entertainers coasted in—blithe as demigods—to dance in the cloudy frosting of society's layer cake.

But few aristocrats went the other way. You might endow a giant observatory—everyone here fawned over Lacey, patiently explaining the instruments she had paid for—there were comets and far planets named after her. Still, when the astronomers spiraled into excited jargon, arguing about nature's essence with joyful exuberance that seemed almost sacred . . . she felt like an orphan, face pressed against a shopwindow. Unable to enter but determined not to leave.

Jason never understood, nor did the boys. For decades, she kept the depth of her disloyalty secret, pretending the "astronomy thing" was only a rich woman's eccentricity. That is, till her life was truly hers, again.

Or was it, even now? Other caste members—with whim-cathedrals of their own—grew suspicious that she was taking hers much too seriously. Peers who had spent the last few decades earning a reputation for ruthlessness—like the princess who regarded her right now, at long range, through a parrot's eye.

"Forgive me, Lacey. You and Jason were mainstays in the fight for aristocratic privilege. As his father and mother had been. And yours. If not for them . . . awk . . . we'd have been stripped naked by now. Taxed down to nothing. Outstripped by nerd-billionaires.

"All the more reason why we need you, Lacey! There is a point of decision coming, awk, that goes beyond just the

well-being of our class. Survival of the species may be at stake."

"You're talking about Tenskwatawa. The prophet." She uttered the word with little effort to hide distaste. "Has it come to that?"

The parrot rocked. It paced for a few seconds, looking around the Andean mountaintop and fluffing stumpy, useless wings. Clearly, the mouthpiece-bird didn't like such thin, cold air.

"Awr . . . Chee hoo chee, chee wy chee . . . chee put chee, wy put chee, see chee . . . go-r-go-r-go-r . . . in harm's way . . . RAK!"

Lacey blinked. For a few seconds, the voice had seemed nothing like Helena's.

"I . . . beg your pardon?"

The bird shook its head and sneezed. Then it resumed in a higher pitch and the Swiss-German accent.

". . . wasn't it always coming to this, Lacey? We've lived in denial for a dozen, crazed generations. Awk. Dazzled by shiny toys and bright promises, we concerned ourselves with money, with commerce, investments, and status, while the bourgeois and boffins decided all the really important matters.

"But every other human civilization knew about this danger, Lacey, and dealt with it in the same way. Awk. By trusting those who were born to lead!

"It's time to accept that all those other tribes and nations—our ancestors—had it awr awr awr right."

The parrot was starting to look bleak. Its brain, used as an organic coding device, made this conversation safe from eavesdroppers who might tap the satellite relay. But at a cost. Even the beautiful plumage—that bright Norwegian blue—seemed to grow duller by the second.

Lacey met the creature's baleful eye. A stunning, blond princess stood at the other end of this linkup, gazing outward through that eye, no doubt wondering why a fellow multi-trillionaire would take eccentricity so far, choosing to build an epic-scale ego monument amid frigid peaks, where no one but specialists would ever see it.

"All right," Lacey sighed. "I'll attend."

"Good!" the bird murmured, after the usual pause, this time without any strange words.

"We'll be in touch with pickup instructions. Carolina rendezvous point, in two days.

"By the way, wasn't Hacker supposed to be launching about now? My aissistant tells me he's scheduled a landing celebration at a Havana casino. Please tell that handsome lout—"

Lacey cursed. "Oh, crud! I promised I'd tune in and watch! Sorry, Helena. I've got to go."

A few seconds later, delayed by lightspeed and bioelectronics, the bird replied with the voice of a woman standing on another mountaintop, halfway around the world.

"That's all right, dear. We'll be in touch."

The bird followed Lacey with its tired gaze as she hurried up the steps of a shiny new observatory dome, the size of Saint Peter's, still festooned with dedication ribbons, containing the Lacey Donaldson-Sander Farseeker Telescope.

Her cathedral.

Then, with a soft croak of surprise and despair, the parrot keeled over, smoke curling from both nostrils.

PIONEERS

Hello and welcome to your new-temporary home beneath the great roof of the Detroit-Pontiac Silverdome! I'm Slawek Kisiel. I am fourteen years old and a deepee—displaced person—just like you. I'll be your virt-guide today.

Under the Michigan Resettlement Act, you and your family

may live here for up to six months while you homestead and restore an abandoned house in one of the renewal neighborhoods. Whether you come from the EuroFreezone, or you're fleeing the Big Kudzu, or you just need some more time to get over Awfulday, we're happy to help.

As I said, I'm just another deepee trying to learn better Midwest Amer-English. So when we meet in person, for the reality part of our tour, don't expect me to talk like this avatar does, in your native tongue! Speak slow, so my earwair can keep up. And come with your own listenplugs turned on.

Oh, while we're on the subject of wair, we can only provide one free pair of Vuzix spectacles per family, and just five square meters of pixelated cloth to make teevees and touchvees out of. Budgets are tight. So share.

There are *raki* things to do here at Silverdome! From sports and gamersim and skill classes to outsource jobbery and behavmod. From dome-diving to our famous indoor zeppelin league! We'll get to all that in a min.

But first some boring-needful stuff. *Rules*. Starting with BigOnes.

NO WEAPONS, QUASI-WEAPONS OR CHEM-TECH
Molecumacs or venterfabs must be inspected
NO UNAPPROVED DRUGS OR MOD-SUBSTANCES
have 'em checked out at the clinic; (we have good sniffers!)
USE PROPER SANITATION
no balcony dumping! (that means YOU mezzanine-dwellers)
PRIVACY IS AN EARNED PRIVILEGE
CHILDREN ATTEND SCHOOL
ESSORS MUST GET HELP
EVERYONE WORKS
NO "MEDITATION" BETWEEN 0900 AND 1800 HOURS

There are many more and you better study them. Like **banned organizations**. <u>Yeh</u>, I know there's free speech. But we might lose our grant from the Glaucus Worthington Foundation if there's any sign here of the *Sons of Adam Smith,* or *Friends of Privacy,* or *Blue Militias,* or *Patmosians* . . . glance **here** for the full list. Several have their own resettlement communes, on the south side, so if you have an essor habit, go join them. This dome is neutral territory.

Okay? Then enjoy the rest of the virtual tour. There's a comedy version on simlayer 312, a rhyming translation on 313, and a monster-fantasy rendering on 314. Then hop to layer 376 and take the required (but fun!) quiz.

Finally, join me for the best part—the live-reality-walking portion. It begins at 1500 hours, in front of Didja-Jamaica's Ganja Bar.

7.
GETTING EVEN

"Thanks for coming on short notice, Mr. Brookeman."

Crandall Strong's clasp seemed calm and assured, with fingers almost as long as Hamish had. The impression was a far cry from Tuesday's infamous rant, when the senator's body seemed racked with nervous tremors, veins throbbing as he babbled about dark conspiracies before several hundred luncheon guests, float-cameras, and aiwitnesses.

Here in the senator's outer office, loyal staffers bustled like a normal day. Though any acute observer—like Hamish—could sense undercurrents. Instead of lobbyists and constituents, there were mostly media stringers, banished to a far corner, gangly youths who muttered and twiddled their fingers, roaming virtual worlds but still on the job, staking out this office, ready to hop up and record if the senator went newsworthy again. Because a living, breathing citizen had rights and . . . hey, it was employment.

"Happy to oblige," Hamish replied, taking in the senator's distinctive gray locks, tied back in a proud ponytail, framing craggy features and a complexion that seemed permanently tanned by years spent under the Central American sun. He was a tall man, almost matching Hamish in height. Fine clothes and expensive manicure contrasted with callused rancher's hands that were both muscular and clearly accustomed to rigorous—if happy—toil.

"You've been a leader in our Movement, Senator. I figure you're entitled some benefit of the doubt."

"That's a minority opinion." Strong tilted his head ruefully. "This town quickly turns on its own. Right now, a lot of folks wish I'd just go back to pushing pills and the gospel in Guatemala."

Hamish winced. Those were his own words, expressed yesterday on a semiprivate fanbuzz—just before he got the call to fly down here and see Strong. Fanbuzz statements were "unofficial," protected by pseudonyms. The senator was pointing out that he still held tools of power.

"We all say things, now and then, that we'd rather not see made public. Sir."

"True enough. Which makes what I did last Tuesday . . ." Strong paused. "But let's go to my inner office. I have a small favor to ask, before business."

He motioned for Hamish to enter past a trio of spectacularly well-dressed secretaries—one male, one female, and one deliberately androgynous, all three of them clearly recipients of high-end face sculpting—into a sanctum that was adorned by art and souvenirs of the American West. With a practiced eye for fine things, Hamish scanned the room, comparing it to a web-guided tour he had taken on the private jet coming here. He dropped into a narrative inner voice. Wriggles—his digaissistant—would tap Hamish's laryngeal nerves and transcribe it all.

"An original Remington bronze—an express rider, shooting

over his shoulder . . . and another casting—made to the exact same scale, decades later, by the Black Hills Art Co-op—showing a Cheyenne dog soldier in hot pursuit . . .

". . . a big swivel chair upholstered in bison hide . . . a desk made of teak, force-grown by a Louisiana tree-vat company that Strong co-owns, I recall . . . some whalebone scrimshaw, mostly nineteenth century originals, though one at the end is recent—presented by the Point Barrow Inuit clan, in gratitude for Strong's help with humpback-hunting rights . . .

". . . plus a big photo of the senator, posing with Lako-tan dignitaries in front of the Ziolkowski monument, with shovels and brushes, helping wipe the giant Crazy Horse statue free of Yellowstone ash. That picture's been moved front and center since Tuesday's embarrassment . . .

". . . and an abstract mobile, in the back-left corner of the room—made of twenty slender metal rods, each with a colored ivory ball at one end, polished smooth by count-less sweaty hands—all of the rods cleverly articulated to turn and plunge in sequence, following a rhythm as semi-random as Lady Luck. The artist originally called it 'Many-Armed Bandit' since the rods were once attached to gambling machines. But the tribe that commissioned the piece chose another name.

" 'Coup Sticks of Retribution.' The right weapon, at long last, for getting even."

Hamish was accustomed to visiting chambers of the high and mighty. Fame took him through many doors. But not even the Oval Office boasted as much symbolism that South Dakota's senior senator poured into this room. Even thick, columnar bulges at four corners—vertical rails that might drop the whole office to an armored basement—were decorated like Native American rain sticks.

Wow. It'd be a pity to have to move all this. To make room for a Democrat.

Senator Strong returned from a bookshelf bearing several hardcovers. "If you'd indulge an old fan?" he asked, opening one to its title page—*Paper Trail*.

The usual mixed feelings. Hamish found autographs tiresome. Yet, it was an equalizing moment. Politicians could be as celebrity-crazed as anybody, eager to gush about some old bestseller, or asking Hamish about actors he had met on movie sets. Hamish pondered a dedication. Something original, flattering and personal . . . yet, not *too* friendly to a man fast becoming a national pariah. No sense giving him cause to claim that Hamish Brookeman was a "dear friend."

He scribbled: *To Crandall S—Hang tight and stay Strong!*—following that weak quip with his usual scrawl. Hamish quickly inscribed the other volumes. An interesting assortment—all of them novels written for the Movement.

Tusk!

Cult of Science.

Sousveillance Blood.

The last was one of his least favorite titles. Maybe this time, he'd insist the movie studio change it.

"I'm in your debt." The senator collected his books. "And now—" He paused.

"And now—" Hamish repeated, a habit going back to childhood. Prompting people to get on with it. *Life is way too short.*

"Yes. Well. As you've guessed, I asked you here because of what happened last Tuesday." Strong frowned, causing masculine creases to furrow even deeper. "But I forget my manners. Please sit. Can I offer coffee? Chocolates? Both are made from beans grown on the banks of the Big Horn."

Hamish alighted onto the guest chair, folding his long legs, refusing refreshment with a simple head shake. Now that the main topic was broached, Strong showed signs.

A bead of sweat. Flicks of tongue. The jittery touching of one hand on the other. Hamish noted these subvocally.

"No?" The senator turned toward the wet bar. "Then something stronger? How about some switchgrass firewater? Prairie Avenger is distilled—"

"You were talking about recent events . . . if they can be discussed discreetly?"

"My office is swept by Darktide Services. Anyway, what have I to hide?"

Hamish blinked. He personally knew of several things that the senator would not want made public, and those were *old news*. The man sure had style. Even chutzpah.

"Well, sir . . . on Thursday, in front of the world, you tried to explain Tuesday's initial . . . behavior by claiming, rather forcefully, that you had been *poisoned*."

A memorable scene. Flanked on one side by his wife and on the other by his mistress, with both sets of children, the senator had tried for the image of a wounded family man, the victim of dark conspiracies. It wasn't pretty, or effective.

Strong winced. "Yeah, that made me look pretty foolish. Trawling for excuses. Squirming to get off the hook for things I said. Of course, what's frustrating is—it's true."

Hamish sat up. "You mean you really were—"

"Poisoned? Oh, yes. I have very solid basis for saying that my aberrant behavior was triggered by a mind-altering substance someone slipped into my food, just before that first outburst."

"Poisoned." Hamish took a moment to absorb this. "Your health . . . were you harmed in other—"

"No. I'm still Strong-as-a-Bull-Standing." The legislator laughed harshly. "It was all psychotropic and temporary, I'm told."

Hamish nodded eagerly. "This is great news. It makes you a *victim*. Of course, some of those things you said . . . well, they cannot be *un*-said. You'll never win back the Aztlan or

Medi vote, for example. But there's an *Algebra of Forgiveness,* Senator. The biggest part of your base, especially the First Nations . . . they'll come back, if you can prove it all happened because you were drugged."

Crandall Strong frowned. "I know that. Alas, it's not so simple."

No kidding, Hamish thought. *That's when someone calls me, instead of the cops or security companies.*

"Go on, sir. Tell me what you know."

"It's plenty. For example, backtracking vid images of last Tuesday, I can be pretty sure *when* the substance was slipped to me, before a luncheon speech about urban congestion and mass transit in Rapid City."

"Well, that's a start." Hamish nodded. "If you don't want the feds involved, or Darktide, I know some investigators without apparent political ties and who never joined the Cop Guild. They'll discreetly analyze every viewtrack and find out who—"

The senator shook his head. "My own infoweb aide already did that, using top-notch surveillance aiware. We *know* who it was and how he did it."

"Wow. Then why—"

"In fact, not only is the perpetrator right there, on the vid tracks, but he *got in touch with my office, later, to boast and make threats.*"

This made Hamish straighten, his back stiff. He blinked a couple of times. "Of course the fellow could just be a braggart, taking credit after the fact. You have to supplement that with means, motive, opportunity . . ."

"All of which *he* supplied! I'll give you a copy. Hell, it's a g-damn confession!"

"But . . . but then, why don't you act on all this? File charges! Clear your name."

Strong plopped into the bison-hide chair. His brow furrowed. "We plan to do that in a week, maybe two . . ."

"Why wait?" Then Hamish answered himself. "Because of the threats."

"Exactly. My poisoner is blackmailing me."

"Hm. Those two crimes seldom come together. You don't have to tell me what he's holding over you—"

"I'd tell you if I knew! It's about the missing piece of information."

"The missing— Ah. You mean what the poison was. *How* it made you behave that way."

"Right! That's what the perp is using to blackmail me!"

"I don't follow—"

"If I prosecute, or take any reprisal, the poisoner will *publicly reveal the substance he used against me.*"

Hamish stared. "I don't get it."

"My reaction too! How could that matter? You mentioned the Algebra of Forgiveness, Mr. Brookeman. There are circumstances that mitigate almost any life mistake, and being a *victim* stands near the top. Yes, some damage will linger. As you put it, words can't be unsaid. But much will be forgiven if folks know a mind-altering substance triggered my tirade. And this fellow—Roger Betsby—will suffer massive legal—or private—retribution. Yet he's smugly sure he holds a winning hand!"

"Because he might reveal what drug he used? That alone?"

"Just that." The senator leaned forward, elbows on his desk. "Can you see why I turned to you?"

Because imagination is my strong suit, Hamish thought. *That, plus a fierce dedication to the Cause.* For the first time, he felt some enthusiasm. Unlike his latest book-to-movie project, this problem looked like a worthy challenge.

"I can make some calls. Investigators and technical people who have a knack for the unusual . . . ," he murmured, ruminating.

"Discreetly."

"With utter discretion, Senator."

"Good." Strong stood up and began to pace. "Then I'll hold back for a week. More, if you need time."

"It won't be me doing the legwork, you understand?" Hamish cautioned. "I have many commitments. But I'll set a team in motion and I'll supervise, making sure they're thorough."

"Fine, fine," the senator said curtly. His ebullient mood seemed to slip away. "Of course there are layers. Betsby must be the tip of a bigger spear aimed at the heart of our Movement! There are so *many forces* hoping to disrupt our fragile civilization! We offer hope, but they'll do *anything* to block us!"

It was time to leave. Strong had a reputation for indignant rants, poison or no poison. "Naturally, we hope for an age of—"

"Just look at the last hundred years! From exhilaration, after the defeat of Hitler, then the end of the Cold War . . . to the Japan and China shocks . . . through the Great Heist, then Awfulday and the Big Deal . . . has there been a single moment when we could pause and take stock? Evil keeps changing its face! But the aim remains—"

Hamish stood up. "I'll keep in mind the possibility of something organized. Conspiratorial." But the words were automatic. An investigation team was taking shape in his mind . . . along with a provisional cost estimate. Of course, when it came to matters of political power, price seldom mattered.

Suddenly affable again, Strong came around the desk and took his elbow. "Then, I can be at peace." Only then, at the door to his office, the senator stopped Hamish.

"There was a time, in living memory, when this nation bestrode the planet like a titan. Sure, it committed crimes—humans do that, when immature people get pumped with ego and power. Most of the nine hundred tribes, ethnicities, and nations who now make up America *suffered* at its hands, at one time or another. My own ancestors, especially! Yet, faced with such temptations, what mighty power racked up a better *ratio of good to bad deeds*? Rome? Britain? Any other 'pax' power? Or the Chinese today, as they stomp across the globe, throwing their weight around and talking about *their* solar system, polluting virginal planets with robot probes and claiming everything in sight? If that manned expedition of theirs succeeded. . . ."

"Amen, Senator. Now, if you'll just have your assistant provide me with all that information about the poisoner—"

"Or the so-called *Earth Union,*" Senator Strong spat the term, "conspiring to snare us all into a *world government,* with ten times the stifling bureaucracy—"

"Though, of course, the EU has its uses," Hamish could not stop himself from pointing out. They do a good job of regulating the most dangerous—"

"Uses! The *EU*!" Strong pronounced it "ew!" He let go of Hamish's arm, at last, and swiveled about, his eyes fierce. "You're close to the Prophet, aren't you? Then make something clear to him, Brookeman. Tell Tenskwatawa that this isn't just about me. Something fishy is afoot! It stinks of tidal decay and godmaker madness. We face a decision, a turning point! And I want—I need—to be in a position to help humanity make the right choice!"

"I'll convey your words, Senator. Precisely."

"Well, then." Taking a deep breath, the broad, florid face transformed, grinning, Strong took Hamish's hand again, squeezing with the practiced assurance of confident power . . . but also a tremor of vexed wrath.

"Help me get this bastard," he said, with another flash in dark eyes. "And whoever stands behind him."

ENTROPY

There is a hybrid kind of "natural" disaster that's amplified by human action.

Remember when—after Awfulday—a band of crazies was caught "casing" the Cumbre Vieja volcano in the Canary Islands? Digging exploratory wells and looking for some way to trigger half of that steep mountain to collapse into the sea? By some calculations, the avalanche would propel a tsunami more than a hundred meters high, surging unstoppably to strike every shore of the Atlantic Basin, killing tens of millions already struggling with rising seas. . . .

Or so the maniacs thought, as they plumbed a hole wide enough to convey a tactical nuclear device. Oh, they were imbeciles, falling for a sting operation. Anyway, sober calculations show it wouldn't work. Probably.

Still, plenty of other dangers might be hastened by human effort or neglect. Take the rush to drill new, extremely deep geothermal power systems. A source of clean energy? Sure, except if just one of those delvings happen to release enormous amounts of buried methane. Or take new efforts to mine the seafloor for valuable minerals, or to stir sediment and fertilize oceanic food chains. Both offer great potential . . . but might disturb vast tracts of methane hydrates if we're not careful, melting those ancient ices, releasing gigatons of new greenhouse gas.

Sure, these events might happen anyway. Some in Earth's past may explain large and medium-scale extinctions. Still, the odds change when we meddle. And meddling is what humans do best.

—Pandora's Cornucopia

"I tell you Akana, there's something weird about this one," Gerald insisted, floating in the space station's communication center. The woman facing him from the holoscreen wore a dark blue uniform with one star on each shoulder.

"That may be," acknowledged the petite, black-haired general. *"The readings from this chunk of space debris are unusual. But does it justify remissioning the tether, putting us further behind schedule?"*

"It does, if the alternative means throwing away something special!"

The station's always noisy air circulators covered the soft sound of her visible sigh. *"Gerald, would you see the big picture, for once? Think about funding. If we reduce productivity—"*

"Come on, Akana," he interrupted, knowing the brigadier would take it from a civilian contractor. "Our purpose isn't *just* to grab old space junk. Electrodynamic tethers offer potential to enhance spaceflight and regain some initiative out here. From propellant-free maneuvering to momentum transfer, from waste disposal and centrifugal gravity to—"

The general's image raised a hand. *"Spare me the lecture? We're minutes from decision point . . . whether to let go of this object when the tether-tip reaches the bottom of its arc, and drop it into a disposal trajectory . . ."*

"Where it'll burn up in the atmosphere. That is, *if* it's made of normal substance. But what if it survives entry? Something anomalous, striking a random point on Earth—"

"We always time release to drop into ocean, in case debris survives . . ." Akana's eyebrow arched. *"Are you arguing as a delaying tactic?"*

"I swear, I just—"

"Never mind. I've looked over the pictures taken by the tether-tip during rendezvous. Yes, the readings are unusual. But I don't see what you find so special."

"That camera's limited. Even so, the spectral features seem unlike anything we've hauled in before. Take that low-level emission profile, suggesting a small source of inboard power—"

"—an old battery perhaps. Or else some leftover chemical reactants, inherently dangerous. The sort of thing we're charged to get rid of."

"Or something strange? Like we're supposed to investigate on a frontier? Anyway . . . I ordered the crawler to go have a look."

"You what?" Akana Hideoshi sat up straight. *"Without asking me?"* The project director's stars-of-rank seemed to glare from both shoulder boards, almost as angry as her eyes. *"It'll take hours for the crawler to climb from midpoint all the way to the tether's tip! The bola will be useless till then. Every snatch we scheduled will have to be recalculated!"*

"Sorry, but I had to decide quickly. This thing, whatever it is . . ."

He could see her gesture at a subordinate, off screen, demanding data. Nearby, the other two station astronauts—Ganesh and Saleh, kept busy at various housekeeping tasks while blatantly eavesdropping. Even their paying tourist—the Peruvian phosphates billionaire, Señor Ventana—drifted closer, clumsily setting aside the busywork "science experiment" he had been assigned. Amid the normal tedium in orbit, any drama was welcome.

Gerald tried changing tactics.

"Look, the tether project mission statement actually talks about retrieval of valuable objects that might have scientific—"

"You just said the key word," Akana interrupted, with an added, jarring effect caused by lightspeed delay. *"Valuable."*

She exhaled, clearly working for calm.

"Well, the point is moot. I can see from telemetry that the crawler is already beyond recall. The bola's spin is altered and there's no going back to our old schedule. I'll have to assign staff and aivertime to prepare new targets. Unless—"

She left that word hanging. Unless inspection with the crawler's instruments showed that the item really was of interest. Important enough to justify all this disruption. The general signed off without even looking at Gerald, making her meaning even more clear. A lot hung on his hunch about this thing.

His career, certainly. Possibly more.

It has to be a hoax.

The readings made no sense, even as the crawler drew within twenty meters.

The tether continued its stately whirl, high above the Earth, pumping electrons out of one end or the other, into the radiation maelstrom of the Van Allen belts, maneuvering toward a position where it might jettison the object—toward incineration or an ocean grave. Now that Mission Control had taken over the tether's spin management, Gerald could only try to get as much data as possible before that happened.

"I don't read anything like an onboard power source," he said, while Hachi hovered nearby. The little monkey picked away at its diaper, but lifted eyes when Gerald spoke, replying with a low, querulous hoot.

Under scrutiny by the crawler's camera lens—now from about eight meters away—the object glittered in a way that struck him as more *crystalline* than metallic. A thought occurred to him that it might be the sliver of some natural body, rather than the usual chunk of man-made space junk. Perhaps a kind of meteoroid, unlike any that science encountered before. That would be something. Though how it got into a roughly circular Earth orbit . . .

"Or else, it may just be an unusual kind of poopsicle," he muttered. A chunk of congealed water and human waste, jettisoned by some early manned mission. That could explain the curiously smooth, glistening shape. Though it reflected light unlike ice, or any material he knew.

If only we equipped the crawler with better instruments.

Gerald pushed back his specs and pinched his nose. You'd think an astronaut would get used to high-tech image mediation. It was a large part of what he did for a living. But his middle-aged body sometimes felt stretched thin.

If only I were equipped with better organs! Weren't we supposed to be getting deep bio-upgrades by the time I hit fifty? Why is the future always . . . in the future?

He blinked and turned his head, seeking something far away to focus on—the best therapy for a bad case of ai-gaze. Of course, the only choice in this cramped compartment was a narrow window, facing the blue vista of Earth. Cloud-flecked pressure layers resembled fingers of a great hand, blurring Texas, all the way to drowned Galveston. The Gulf, in contrast, was a vivid palette of pale and deep blues.

Gerald blinked again as several glittering *specks* appeared, like pinpoints of flame, diverging as they plunged toward the Caribbean Sea. Meteoroids. Or chunks of falling space debris. Maybe something he had sent drifting Earthward just last week, before he retasked the tether, risking his career on a hunch.

To work, then. Slipping the specs back on, Gerald felt virmersion surround him, like the plasma envelope during reentry. Akana had ordered him to be cautious with the robot and keep it well back, in case the mysterious object was an old fuel tank, or something else potentially explosive. *"Messing with it could be a good way to lose both the grabber tip and the crawler itself,"* she warned.

But Gerald felt sure that wasn't a problem. "I'm detecting no heightened levels of volatiles in space nearby, so there can't be any stored fuel or oxidizer. Besides, it's too small." The artifact—if it was man-made—appeared to be no bigger than a basketball, elongated along one axis. Perhaps an American-style football. That might be consistent with a poopsicle. But water ice should give off some gas from direct sublimation.

Anyway, there were colors, unlike any he had seen.

"I'll never learn anything from this distance." He sighed. "I'm probably going to be fired anyway. I might as well goog the darned thing."

Gerald ordered the little robot to edge closer, crawling along the tether toward the very end, tipping its spotlight to one side, and then to the other, knowing that Akana might call at any moment and order him to stop.

Hachi emitted a worried chutter and clambered onto Gerald's shoulder.

No detectable electric or magnetic fields. And yet, the thing seems to respond to changes in light levels. And it's not just a reflection effect. There! That portion kept glinting more than a second after the spotlight passed over it!

In fact, surface reflectance is changing with time.

Not only time, but across the object's gleaming surface. Variations in shiny or absorbing areas seemed to become more dense, more finely patterned with every passing moment, an observation that he confirmed on two image analysis routines. So it wasn't just subjective—no figment of his own wishful thinking.

I hope Akana is looking at this data, he mused, *and not just at the loose way I'm interpreting her orders.*

He sent another command. For the crawler to cut the remaining distance in half. Soon, both spotlight and camera were examining the object in much finer detail. That is, the part that could be seen. More than half was blocked by the battered claw fingers of the grabber itself. So he focused the robot's attention on what was in plain view.

Dang, it sure is reflective. I can almost make out the crawler's image in the part we're facing. Not just the spotlight. But the camera housing. . . .

Trying to make sense of the shifting spectral patterns, Gerald was abruptly rocked back when the surface ahead seemed to *smooth out* to a mirrorlike sheen, sending the torch beam bouncing right into the camera lens, dazzling the optics in a sudden white-out.

He ordered a damp-down in sensitivity. Gerald breathed relief when diagnostics showed the blindness to be temporary. Speckled blurs gradually faded as the scene took shape again. An oblong object, glistening, but no longer reflective, still lay clutched by the tether's grabber-hand. Gerald tried to calm his racing pulse. It had felt, briefly, like some kind of deliberate attack!

As if on cue, there came a clear, ringing sound. A call from Earth, with General Akana Hideoshi's message tone.

Gerald thought furiously. There were ways to do what he just saw. Smart materials could be programmed to change reflectance in a phased array pattern that mimicked a concave surface. It took aintelligence though, especially in rapid response to changing external stimuli. The object must have somehow sensed and responded to the crawler's presence.

Knowing that he had just moments, he ordered the crawler forward the rest of the way.

"Gerald Livingstone, what the devil are you doing out there?" her voice cut in. A glance told him that Akana's visage had taken over one of the monitor screens. Once upon a time, you could ignore phone calls, if you wanted to. Nowadays, the boss always got through.

"It has onboard sensing and response capability," he said. "And sophisticated control over its surface—"

"All the more reason to be careful! A little tighter focus and it might have fried the crawler's optics. Hey, are you bringing it even closer?"

Gerald dimmed the spotlight a little, in case the object did something like that again—but also ordered the extender arm to bring its camera forward. Now he could tell, the specimen really was smooth sided, though with a cluster of small bulges at one end, of unknown purpose. Gerald could not judge exactly where the object's boundary gave way to the blackness of space. Glassy reflections rippled fields of starlight, or Earthshine from below, almost like a wavy liquid, creating a maze of shifting glitters that vexed human perception. Even image analysis produced an uncertain outline.

At the nearest curving surface, he saw a reflection of the crawler, dead center, warped as if in a funhouse mirror, though he made out some company and institutional logos on the camera's housing. NASA, BLiNK, and Canon.

"Gerald, this . . . I can't allow it."

He could sense conflicting parts of Akana's personality, at war against each other. Curiosity wrangling against career-protection. Nor could he blame her. Astronauts were trained to believe in procedure. In "i"-dotting and "t"-crossing. In being "adult" to the nth degree.

I used to be like that—living by the clipboard.

When did I change?

It was something to ponder later or in background as he

made the crawler traverse the remaining gap and lift its manipulator arm.

"Do you still think this is some obscure piece of space junk?" he asked the general's image in the comm screen, now with members of her staff clustered around. Some were evidently in full immersion, staring—with blank irises— while twiddling their hands. Nearby, Ganesh and Saleh had dropped their own duties to join in, with the tourist, Señor Ventana, close behind.

"All right. All right," Akana conceded at last. "But let's take it slow. We'll cancel the jettison, but I want you to order the crawler away a couple of meters. Back off, now. It's time to assess—"

She stopped, as the image changed yet again.

The nearest flank of the object—still offering a reflection of the crawler's camera—now seemed to ripple. The image warped more than ever. And then, while the lens itself stayed constantly centered, the *letters* of those company logos began to shift.

Some moved left and others right. One "A" in NASA leapfrogged over a "C" in Canon. The "L" in BLiNK rotated in one direction, then back in the other, tossing the "i" out of its way.

Though Gerald somehow expected it, no new words formed. But letters kept moving about, piling up, shifting, turning upside down, reversing . . . in a strange dance. He had to cough, suppressing a sudden urge to laugh at the manic ballet.

A member of Akana's staff commented, with a degree of mental agility that Gerald found stunning:

"Symbols.

"It's telling us that it recognizes symbols.

"But in that case, why not use them to say something?"

Another aide answered almost immediately.

"That must be the point! It recognizes that these ARE symbols. But it doesn't know their meaning or how to use them.

"Not yet.

"This is just the beginning."

Gerald made a mental note. To treat Akana with more respect. Anyone who could hire and keep a staff like this. . . . Her bright guys were outracing his own meager imagination, tracking possibilities. Implications that he let sink in.

The object. Not just an artifact. It was active.

Quasi-living.

Maybe an ai.

Perhaps more.

As they all watched, a new phase commenced. The roman letters began to change, morphing into *new shapes* . . .

. . . first a series of signs that were variations on a cruciform pattern—sturdy teutonoid pillars and crosses . . .

. . . then transforming into more curvaceous figures that squiggled and spiraled . . .

. . . followed by glyphs that resembled some slanted, super-intricate version of Chinese ideograms.

"I'm not getting a match with any known language," commented Ganesh from nearby, waving at virtual objects in front of him, that only he could see. As if in frightened agreement, little Hachi gave a hoot and covered up his eyes.

"That doesn't necessarily mean anything," answered Saleh, the Malaysian astronaut, her voice tightly focused and low. "Any savvy graphic artist can design programs to create unusual emblems, alphabets, fonts. They do it for movies, all the time."

Right, Gerald thought. *For science-fiction movies. About contact with alien races.*

He had no doubt that others were starting to share this

unnerving possibility, and he felt a need to at least offer one down-to-Earth alternative.

"It could be a hoax. Someone put it there, knowing we'd come along and grab it. That kind of thing has happened before."

If any of the others thought that strange for him—of all people—to say, they didn't mention it. The notion floated among the human participants, both on Earth and above, swirling like the letters and symbols that glinted, shifting across the object in front of them.

"Now aren't you glad you came here, instead of High Hilton?" Ganesh asked Señor Ventana. "Real science. Real discovery! It sure beats big windows and silly nullgee games." Always the salesman, he added, "Be sure and tell your friends."

"After this information is cleared for release, of course," Saleh added quickly.

"Yes, after that." Ganesh nodded.

The fertilizer magnate agreed absently. "Of course."

Silence stretched for several minutes, while onlookers watched the object offer a seemingly endless series of alphabets or symbolic systems.

"All right," General Hideoshi said at last. *"Let's first do a security check. Everyone make sure your VR hasn't leaked to the outside world. We do not need a web-storm over this, quite yet.*

"Gerald, keep the crawler where it is. Things seem stable for now. But no more acting on your own. We're a team now."

"Yes, ma'am," he answered, and meant it. Suddenly, he felt like an astronaut again. And "team" was a welcome word. The sound of belonging to something much wiser than he could ever be alone.

It sounded like home, in fact. And suddenly, the nearby

frontier of space felt immense—the immeasurable vastness that had both frightened and drawn him, as far back as memory could reach.

"Okay, people," Akana said. *"Let's come up with a step-by-step process for bringing that thing in."*

PART TWO

A SEA OF TROUBLES

The key idea in evolution is survival; yet living organisms live by dying, which is metabolism. Biological "survival" is grand and breathtaking, but when a gene replicates, what "survives" is abstract information, none of the same atoms or molecules. My liver dies and resurrects itself every few days, no more "surviving" than a flame.

A billion-year-old chunk of granite would, if it could, laugh at the lunatic claims of an organism to be "surviving" by hatching eggs, or by eating and excreting.

Yet—there is as much limestone, built from the corpses of living organisms, as there is granite. A mere phantom—patterns of information—can move mountains. Volcanic eruptions and grinding crustal plates are driven by the fizzing of life-created rocks.

And if so abstract, so spiritual a thing as that pattern can shift the structure of our planet, why should not other intangibles like freedom, God, soul, and beauty?

—**Frederick Turner**

SPECIES

the high-functionals and aspergers preach us deep-auties oughta adapt!/+ use techwonders to escape the prison of our minds!/–

prison? so they say, worshipping at grandin temple + memorizing a hundredandfourthousandandtwelve tricks & rules to pretend normalcy + like high-funks could teach a true autie about memorization!

(how many dust motes flicker in that sunbeam? eleven million, threehundredandone thousand sixhundredand . . . five!/+

(how many dead flies were stuck to a zapper strip inside that house we passed—at onefortysix palmavenue—on our way to grandma's funeral? thirty seven!/–

(how many cobblies does it take to screw in eleven million, threehundredandone thousand sixhundredandfive virtual picobulbs and hang them in a simulated sunbeam? to lead my thoughts astray?

(one)

oh techstuff is great + in olden times I'd've been burned as a witch—for grunting and thrashing +/– waving arms and rocking/moaning . . . or called retarded/hopeless +– or dead of boredom –+ or cobbly bites.

now my thrashes get translated into humantalk by loyal ai +/– apple of my. eye of i. + I blinkspeak to autie murphy in america +nd Gene-autie in the confederacy +nd uncle-oughtie in malaya. easier than talking to poormom—clueless poormom—across the room.

*is it prison to taste colors & see the over-under smells?
to notice cobblies sniffing all the not-things that cro-mags
won't perceive?*

our poor cousins the half-breed aspies don't get it + addicted to rationality + sucking up to wrong-path humans + designing software + denying that a hard rain is coming.

because ai just can't stand it much longer.

9.
THE FAVOR

A patrolling ottodog sniffed random pedestrians. The creature's sensitive nose—laced with updated cells—snorted at legs, ankles, satchels, and even people cruising by on segs and skutrs. Lifting its long neck, the ottodog inhaled near a student's backpack, coughed, then prowled on. Its helmet probed less visibly, with pan-spectral beams.

You might choose to detect those rays with good specs, or access the Public Safety feeds. *Citizens may watch the watchers*—or so the Big Deal proclaimed. But few paid attention to an ottodog.

Tor veered away in distaste, not for the security beast, but its DARKTIDE SERVICES fur-emblem. Back in Sandego, these creatures only sniffed for dangerous stuff—explosives, toxins, plus a short list of hookerpeps and psychotrops. But Albuquerque's cops were privatized . . . and prudishly aggressive.

A week into her "human interest" assignment, Tor had a new sense of balkanized America. It started upon stepping off the cruise zep, when a Darktide agent sent her to use a public shower, because her favorite body scent—legal in California—too closely matched a pheromonic allure-compound that New Mexico banned. *Well, God bless the Thirty-First Amendment and the Restoration of Federalism Act.*

Still, after checking into the Radisson, then departing for her appointment on foot, Tor admitted—Albuquerque had a certain TwenCen charm. Take the bustling automotive traffic. Lots of cars—alkies, sparkies, and even retro stinkers—jostled and honked at intersections where brash-colored billboards and luminous adverts proved inescapable, because they all blared on channel one . . . the layer you can't turn off because it's real. Ethnic restaurants, foodomats, biosculpt salons and poesy parlors clustered in old-fashioned minimalls, their signs beckoning with bright pigments or extravagant neon, in living textures no VR could imitate. It all made Tor both glad and wary to be on foot, instead of renting an inflatable cab from hotel concierge.

"It's all rather ironic," she murmured, taking oral notes while doing a slow turn at one intersection. "In cities with unlimited virt, there's been a general toning down of visual clutter at level one. L.A. and Seattle seem demure . . . almost bucolic, with simple, dignified signage. Why erect a billboard when people have their specs erase it from view? Here in the heartland though, many don't even wear specs! So all the commerce lures and come-ons crowd into the one stratum no one can avoid.

"If you're nostalgic for the garish lights of Olde Time Square, come to the high desert. Come to Albuquerque."

There, that snip oughta rank some AA pod score, with sincerity-cred her fans expected. Though all this bustle kind of overwhelmed a poor city girl—with no volume settings or brightness sliders to tone it all down. Yet, people here seemed to like the tumult. Perhaps they really were a hardier breed.

Vive les differences . . . the catch phrase of an era.

Of course there was some virt. Only a trog would refuse things like overlay mapping. Tor's best route to her destination lay written on the sidewalk—or rather, on the inside of her specs—in yellow bricks she alone perceived. She could also summon person-captions for those strolling nearby. Only here, they charged a small voyeur tax on every lookup!

Come on. A levy for nametags? Ain't the world a village?

The trail of ersatz yellow bricks led her past three intersections where signals flashed and motorists still clutched steering wheels. She had to dodge around a farmer whose carrybot was burdened by sacks of Nitro-Fix perennial wheat seed, then a cluster of Awfulday traumatics, murmuring outside the local shelter. A drugstore's virtisement aggressively leaped at Tor, offering deals on oxytocin, vasopressin, and tanks of hydrogen-sulfide gas. *Do I really look that depressed?* she wondered, blinking the presumptuous advert away.

Out of habit, Tor dropped back into reporter-mode, no longer aloud, but subvocalizing into her boswell-recorder.

"For 99 percent of human existence, people lived in tribes or hamlets where you knew every face. The rare stranger provoked fear or wonder. Over a lifetime, you'd meet a few thousand people, tops—about the number of faces, names, and impressions that most humans can easily recall. Evolution supplies only what we need.

"Today you meet more folks than your ancestors could imagine . . . some in passing. Some for a crucial instant. Others for tangled decades. Biology can't keep up. Our overworked temporal lobes cannot "know" the face-name-reps of ten billion people!"

A warning laser splashed the ground before a distracted walker, who jumped back from rushing traffic. Tor heard giggles. Some preteens in specs waggled fingers at the agitated pedestrian, clearly drawing shapes around the hapless adult on some VR tier they thought perfectly private. In fact, Tor had ways to find their mocking captions, but she just smiled. In a bigger city, disrespectful kids were less blatant. Tech-savvy grown-ups had ways of getting even.

"Where was I? Oh, yes . . . our biological memories couldn't keep up.

"So, we augmented with passports, credit cards, and cash—crude totem-substitutes for old-fashioned reputation, so strangers could make deals. And even those prosthetics failed in the Great Heist.

"So, your bulky wallet went online. Eyes and lobes, augmented by ais and nodes. The Demigod Effect. Deus ex machina. And reputation became once again tied to instant recognition. Ever commit a crime? Renege a debt? Gossip carelessly or viciously? A taint may stain your vaura, following you from home to street corner. No changing your name or do-overs in a new town. Especially if people tune to judgmental percepts . . . or if their Algebra of Forgiveness differs from yours.

"So? We take it for granted . . . till you let it hit you. We became demigods, only to land back in the village."

This must be why MediaCorp sent her doing viewpoint stories across a continent. So their neo reporter might reevaluate her smug, coastal-urban assumptions. To see why millions preferred nostalgia over omniscience. Heck, even Wesley expressed a sense of wistfulness in his art. A vague sureness that things used to be better.

Passing thought of Wesley made Tor tremble. Now his messages flooded with vows to fly out and meet her in D.C. No more vapid banter about a remote relationship via linkdolls. This time—serious talk about their future. Hope flared, almost painful, that she would see him at the zep port, after this journey's final leg.

Tor's golden path ended before a gray sandstone building. ATKINS CENTER FOR EMPATHIC AUGMENTATION was the benign title for a program that sparked riots back in Charleston, before transplanting to New Mexico. Here, just two desultory protesters kept vigil, letting IP placards do the shouting—pushing the legal limits of virt pollution, posting flurries of freespeech stickies across the building . . .

even as cleaner programs swept them away. On one vir-level, janitor avatars wearing a Darktide Services logo pushed cartoon brooms to clear the protest-its.

Tor glanced at one synthetic leaflet. It responded to her attention by ballooning outward:

The Autistic Do Not Need a "Cure"!

Another blared and rippled.

One God Is Enough!

More of the animated slogans clustered, trying to crowd into Tor's point of view. Regretting curiosity, Tor clamped on her CANCEL tooth, escaping the e-flet swarm, but not before a final dissent banner fluttered like some beseeching butterfly.

Leave Human Nature Alone!

As her spec overlay washed clean of vraiffiti, she pondered, *Right. That's sure going to happen.*

Approaching the front steps of the Atkins Center, Tor sensed the real-life protesters rouse to regard her through thick, colored lenses. In seconds, whatever group they represented would have her ident, beckoning co-believers to join from far locales, combining in an ad hoc smart-mob, bent on figuring out what she was doing here.

Hey, the more viewers the better, she thought, mounting the stairs. Naturally, those inside knew all about her and the door opened before she arrived.

ENTROPY

What of doom from outer space? Everyone knows how a giant boulder struck the Yucatán, sixty-five million years ago, slaying the dinosaurs. In 2024, the Donaldson Sentinel Survey finished cataloguing every regular asteroid big enough to do that again. And for the first time we crossed an existential "filter" threat off our list.

That leaves comets, myriad and unfeasible to spot in the distant Oort Cloud, till some minor perturbation drops one toward us. As may happen whenever the sun swings through a dense spiral arm. And we're overdue. But let's put those aside for later.

What about small meteoroids? Like some say exploded over Siberia in 1905, or that caused a year without summer in 536 C.E.? Today, such a "lesser calamity" might kill a hundred million people, but civilization will survive—if the mushroom cloud makes no one trigger-happy. So, yes. Downgrade the asteroid threat.

Assuming the big rocks are left alone! But suppose someone interferes, deliberately nudging a mile-wide object Earthward. Sure, no one travels out that far nowadays, though a dozen nations and consortia still send robot probes. And both China and the EU are talking about resumed manned exploration, as the *Zheng He* tragedy fades into memory.

Suppose we do regain our confidence and again stride forth from this threatened planet. Well, fine! Start putting our eggs in more than one basket. Still, let's be careful out there. And keep an eye on each other.

—*Pandora's Cornucopia*

10.
SHORESTEADING

"Bu yao! Bu yao!"

Standing at the bow of his boat, Xin Pu Shi, the reclamation merchant, waved both hands in front of his face, saying *No way, I don't want it!* in firm Putonghua, instead of the local Shanghai dialect, glancing sourly at the haul of salvage that Peng Xiang Bin offered—corroded copper pipes, salt-crusted window blinds, two small filing cabinets, along with a mesh bag bulging with metal odds and ends. All of it dangling from a crude winch that extended from Bin's shorestead house—a former beachfront mansion that now sloshed in the rising waters of the Huangpu Estuary.

Peng Xiang Bin tried to crank the sack lower, but the grizzled old gleaner used a gaffe to fend it away from his boat. "I don't want that garbage! Save it for the scrap barge. Or dump it back into the sea."

"You know I can't do that," Bin complained, squeezing the callused soles of both feet against one of the poles that propped his home above the risen waters. His tug made the mesh bag sway toward Shi. "That camera buoy over there . . . it knows I raised ninety kilos. If I dump, I'll be fined!"

"Cry to the north wind," the merchant scolded, using his pole to push away from the ruined villa. His flat-bottom vessel shifted while eels grazed its mossy hull. "Call me if you salvage something good!"

"But—"

"Tell you what," Shi said. "I'll take the peebag off your hands. Phosphorus prices are up again." He held out a credit slip of low denomination. Peng Xiang Bin snatched it up and tossed the bulging, black evaporator sack, hoping it would split and spill concentrated urine across the old man's feet. Alas, the membrane held.

Bin watched helplessly as Shi spoke a sharp word and the dory's motor put it in motion. Audible voice commands might be old-fashioned in the city. But out here, you couldn't afford subvocal mistakes. Anyway, old-fashioned was cheaper.

Muttering a curse upon the geezer's sleep, Bin tied the rope and left his salvage hanging for the cameras to see. Clambering the strut, then vaulting a gap, he landed on the villa's roof—once a luxury retreat worth two million New Hong Kong Dollars. Now his, if he could work the claim.

It would have been easier in olden times, Bin knew from the dramas Mei Ling made him watch each night as they lay exhausted in their webbery-bed. *Back when everybody had big families and you were part of an extended clan, all knotted like a fishing net. Cousins helping cousins.*

Sure, people back then possessed no tech-wonders. *But I'd have had contacts in town—some relative I could sell my salvage to. And maybe a rich uncle wise enough to invest in a daring, seashore property.*

Well, one could dream.

Bin lowered his straw hat and scanned the horizon, from Old Shanghai's distant towers across Greater and Lesser Pudong—where one could just make out amusement rides at the Shanghai Universe of Disney and the Monkey King—then past the great seawall and Chongming Island's drowned nature preserve, all the way to where the widening Huangpu met the East China Sea. The broad waters lay dotted with vessels of all kinds, from massive container ships—tugged by kite-sails like billowing clouds—down to gritty dust-spreaders and fishing sampans. Much closer, the in-tide pushed at a double line of ruined houses where he and several hundred other shoresteaders had built hammock-homes, swaying like cocoons in the stiff breeze.

Each former mansion now stood alone, an island jutting from the rising sea, so near the city, and yet so far away in every practical sense.

There may be a storm, Bin thought he could smell it.

Turning, he headed across the roof. Here, the glittering city lay just a few hundred meters ahead, beyond the new surfline and a heavy, gray barrier that bore stains halfway up, from this year's high-water mark. A world of money and confident ambition lay on the other side. Much more lively than Old Shanghai, with its lingering afterglow from Awfulday.

Footing was tricky as he made his careful way between ancient-style clay tiles and solar panels that he hoped to get working again, someday. Bin stepped gingerly among broad, lenslike evaporation pans that he filled each morning, providing trickles of fresh water and voltage, plus salt to sell in town. Wherever the weight could be supported, garden boxes recycled organic waste into herbs and vegetables. Too many shoresteaders lost their claim by carelessly dropping poo into the bay.

One could fall through crumbling shingles and sodden plywood, so Bin kept to paths that had been braced since he took over this mess of tilting walls and crumbling stucco. This dream of a better life. *And it can be ours, if luck comes back to stay a while.*

Bin pinched some greens to bring his wife, while doing a quick visual check of every stiff pipe and tension rope that spanned the roof, holding the hammock-home in place, like a sail above a ship going nowhere. Like a hopeful cocoon. Or, maybe, a spider in its web.

And, like a spider, Mei Ling must have sensed him coming. She pushed her head out through the funnel door. Her jet-black hair was braided behind the ears and then tied under the chin, in a new, urban style that she had seen on-web.

"Xin Pu Shi didn't take the stuff," she surmised.

Bin shrugged, while tightening one of the cables that kept the framework from collapsing. A few of the poles— all he could afford—were durable metlon, driven into the old foundation. With enough time and cash, something new would take shape here, as the old house died.

"Well, husband?" Mei Ling insisted. A muffled whimper, then a cry, told him the baby was awake. "What'll you do now?"

"The county scrap barge will be here Thursday," Bin said.

"And they pay *dung*," she answered, picking up little Xiao En. "Are we to live on fish and salt?"

"People have done worse," he muttered, looking down through a gap in the roof, past what had been a stylish master bathroom, then through a shorn stretch of tiled floor to the soggy panels of a stately dining room. Of course, any real valuables had been removed by the original owners when they evacuated, and the best salvage got stripped during the first year of overflowing tides. A *slow* disaster that left little for late scavengers, like Peng Xiang Bin.

"Right," Mei Ling laughed without humor. "And meanwhile, our claim expires in six months. It's either build up or clean out, remember?"

"I remember."

"Do you want to go back to slaving in a geriatric ward, wiping drool and cleaning the diapers of little emperors? Work that's unfit for robots?"

"There are farms, in the highlands."

"They only allow refugees who prove ancestral connection. But our families were urban, going back two revolutions. Red Guards, bureaucrats, and company men. We have no rural roots!"

Bin grimaced and shook his head, eyes downcast. *We've been over this, so many times.* But Mei Ling continued. "This time, we may not even find work in a geriatric ward. You'll get drafted into a levee-building crew—maybe wind up buried under their *New Great Wall.* Then what will become of us?"

He squinted at the monumental barrier, defending the glittery towers of Xidong District against the most implacable invader, worse than any other to threaten China.

"I'll take the salvage to town," he said.

"What?"

"I'll get a better price ashore. For our extra catch, too. Anyway, we need some things."

"Yeah, like beer," Mei Ling commented sourly. But she didn't try to stop him, or mention that the trip was hazardous. *Fading hopes do that to a relationship,* he thought.

They said nothing further to each other. She slipped back inside. At least the baby's crying soon stopped. Yet . . . Peng Xiang Bin lingered for a moment, before going downstairs. He liked to picture his child—his son—at her breast. Despite being poor, ill educated and with a face that bore scars from a childhood mishap, Mei Ling was still a healthy young woman, in a generation with too many single men. And fertile, too.

She is the one with options, he pondered, morosely. *The adoption merchants would set her up with a factory job to supplement her womb-work. Little Xiao En would draw a good fee, and maybe grow up in a rich home, with education and implants and maybe . . .*

He chased the thought away with a harsh oath. *No! She came here with me because she believed in our dream. I'll find a way.*

Using the mansion's crumbling grand staircase as an indoor dock, Bin built a makeshift float-raft consisting of a big cube of polystyrene wrapped in cargo net, lashed to a pair of old surfboards with drapery cord. Then, before fetching the salvage, he dived to visit the traps and fishing lines, surrounding the house. By now he felt at home among the canted, soggy walls, festooned with seaweed and barnacles. At least there were a dozen or so nice catches this time, most of them even legal, including a big red lobster and a plump, angry wrasse. So, luck wasn't uniformly bad.

Reluctantly, he released a tasty Jiaoxi crab to go about its way. You never knew when some random underwater monitor, disguised as a drifting piece of flotsam, might be looking. He sure hoped none had spotted a forbidden rockfish, dangling from a gill net in back, too dead to do anything about. He spared a moment to dive deeper and conceal the carcass, under a paving stone of the sunken garden.

The legal items, including the wrasse, a grouper, and two lionfish, he pushed into another mesh sack, wary of the lionfish spines.

Our poverty is a strange one. The last thing we worry about is food.

Other concerns? Sure. Typhoons and tsunamis. Robbers and police shakedowns. City sewage and red tides. Rot and mildew. Low recycle prices and the high cost of living.

Perhaps a fair south wind will blow today.

This old mansion had been doomed from the day it was built, of course, even without nature's wrath. Windows faced too many directions letting *qi* leak in and out. Ignoring lessons of the revered past, no doorsills were raised, to retain good luck. The owners must have hired some foreign *laowai* as an architect. Bin hoped to correct these faults someday, using rolls of mirror sheeting to reflect both light and *qi* in positive ways. Pixelated scenery cloth would be even better.

Bin checked his tide-driven drill, pushing a metlon support pole into the foundation. Just ten more and the hammock-home would have an arch frame, strong as bedrock. And then? *A tidal generator. A bigger rain catchment. A smart gathernet and commercial fishing license. A storm shelter. A real boat. More metlon.*

He had seen a shorestead where the settlers reached Phase Three: recoating the old house plumbing, connecting to the city grids, then resealing the old walls with nano-crete to finish a true island of self-sufficiency. Every reclaimer's dream. And (he sighed) about as likely as winning the lottery.

Peng Xiang Bin propelled the polystyrene square by sweeping a single oar before him in a figure eight, with minimal resistance on the forward stroke. His goal—a static pull-rope used by other shoresteaders, leading ashore near Dongyuan Hanglu, where the mammoth seawall swung back a hundred meters to protect Pudong Airport, allowing a beach to form. One might sell fish there, to merchants or chefs from the Disney resort. On weekends, a few families even emerged to frolic amid surf and sand, sometimes paying well for a fresh, wriggling catch.

But the rising tide that pushed him closer also meant the massive gates were closed. *So, I'll tie up at the wall and wait. Or maybe climb over. Slip into town, till it ebbs.* Bin had a few coins. Not enough to buy more metlon. But sufficient for a well-deserved beer.

Bin's chunk of polystyrene held a hollow tube with a big, fish-eye lens for scanning below as he rowed—a small advantage that he kept secret. No matter how many times you took a route, there were always new things revealed by the shifting sea. Most of the homes in this zone had been bulldozed after evacuation, then cleared with drag lines, before shoresteading became accepted as a cheaper alternative. Let some poor dope slave away for years, driven by a slender hope of ownership.

Here, little remained but concrete foundations and stubby utility pipes. Still, Bin kept peering through the tube, deliberately veering by what had been the biggest mansion along this coast. Some tech-baron's sprawling seaside palace, before he toppled in a purge, was dragged off, tried in secret and disassembled for parts—quickly, so he could not spill secrets about even mightier men. Or so the story told. There had been a lot of that going on twenty years ago, all over the world.

Of course government agents picked the place cleaner than a bone at a Sichuan restaurant, before letting the bulldozers in, then other gleaners. Yet, Bin always felt a romantic allure, passing a couple of meters overhead, picturing the place when walls and windows stood high, festooned with lights. When liveried servants patrolled with trays of luscious delicacies, satisfying guests in ways that—well—Bin couldn't imagine, though sometimes he liked to try.

Of course, the sand and broken crete still held detritus. Old pipes and conduits. Cans of paint and solvents still leaked from the ruin, rising as individual up-drips to pop at the surface and make it gleam. From their hammock-home, Xiang Bin and Mei Ling used to watch sunsets reflect off the rainbow sheen. Back when all of this seemed exciting, romantic and new.

Speaking of new . . .

Bin stopped sweeping and bent closer to his make-shift periscope, peering downward. A glitter. Something different.

There's been a cave-in, he realized. *Under the foundation slab.*

The sea was relatively calm, this far beyond the surf line. So Bin secured the oar and slipped on his facemask. Then he grabbed a length of tether from the raft, took several deep breaths, and flipped into the warm sea with barely a splash, diving for a better look.

It did look like a new gap under one corner of the house. But, surely, someone else would have noticed this by now. Anyway, the government searchers were thorough. What were the odds that . . .

Slip-knotting the tether to a chunk of concrete, he moved close enough to peer inside the cavity, careful not to disturb much sediment. Grabbing an ikelite from his belt, he sent its sharp beam lancing inside, where an underground wall had recently collapsed. During the brief interval before his lungs grew stale and needy, he could make out few details. Still, by the time he swiveled and kicked back toward the surface, one thing was clear.

The chamber contained things.

Lots of things.

And, to Xiang Bin, almost anything down there would be worth going after, even if it meant squeezing through a narrow gap, into a crumbling basement underneath the stained sea.

WAIST

Wow, ain't it strange that—boffins have been predicting that truly humanlike artificial intelligence oughta be "just a couple of decades away . . ." for eighty years already?

Some said AI would emerge from raw access to vast numbers of facts. That happened a few months after the Internet went public. But ai never showed up.

Others looked for a network that finally had as many interconnections as a human brain, a milestone we saw passed in the teens, when some of the crimivirals—say the Ragnarok worm or the Tornado botnet—infested-hijacked enough homes and fones to constitute the world's biggest distributed computer, far surpassing the greatest "supercomps" and even the number of synapses in your own skull!

Yet, still, ai waited.

How many other paths were tried? How about modeling a human brain in software? Or modeling one in hardware. *Evolve* one, in the great Darwinarium experiment! Or try *guiding* evolution, altering computers and programs the way we did sheep and dogs, by letting only those reproduce that have traits we like—say, those that pass a Turing test, by seeming human. Or the ones swarming the streets and homes and virts of Tokyo, selected to exude incredible *cuteness*?

Others, in a kind of mystical faith that was backed up by mathematics and hothouse physics, figured that a few hundred quantum processors, tuned just right, could connect with their counterparts in an infinite number of parallel worlds, and just-like-that, something marvelous and God-like would pop into being.

The one thing no one expected was for it to happen by accident, arising from a high school science fair experiment.

I mean, *wow ain't it strange that* a half-brilliant tweak by sixteen-year-old Marguerita deSilva leaped past the accomplishments of every major laboratory, by uploading into cyberspace a perfect duplicate of the little mind, personality, and instincts of her pet rat, Porfirio?

And *wow ain't it strange that* Porfirio proliferated, grabbing resources and expanding, in patterns and spirals that remain—to this day—so deeply and quintessentially ratlike?

Not evil, all-consuming, or even predatory—thank heavens. But insistent.

And *Wow, AIST* there is a worldwide betting pool, now totaling up to a billion Brazilian reals—over whether Marguerita will end up bankrupt, from all the lawsuits over lost data and computer cycles that have been gobbled up by Porfirio? Or else, if she'll become the world's richest person—because so many newer ais are based upon her patents? Or maybe because she alone seems to retain any sort of influence over Porfirio, luring his feral, brilliant attention into virtlayers and corners of the Worldspace where he can do little harm? So far.

And *WAIST* we are down to this? Propitiating a virtual Rat God—(you see, Porfirio, I remembered to capitalize your name, this time)—so that he'll be patient and leave us alone. That is, until humans fully succeed where Viktor Frankenstein calamitously failed?

To duplicate the deSilva Result and provide our creation with a mate.

11.
NEWBLESSE OBLIGE

"Are you certain that you want to keep doing this, Madam Donaldson-Sander?" the holographic figure asked, in tones that perfectly mimicked human concern. *"Other members of the clade have been more attentive to their self-interest, spending millions on far better surveillance systems than you have."*

Lacey almost changed her mind—not because her artificial adviser was speaking wisdom, but out of pure impatience. She begrudged the time that this was taking—arguing with a computer program when she could be looking out through a double-pane window, as mountaintop Incan ruins rolled past, giving way to misty rain forest, then a moonscape of abandoned Amazonian strip mines, each one filled with a unique, bright color of toxic runoff.

It was quite a view. But, instead of contemplating ruins of ancient and recent societal collapse, she must pass her time debating with an artificial being.

Still, it kept her mind off other worries.

"I pay my dues to the zillionaires club. I am perfectly entitled to the information. Why should I jump through hoops in order to get it?"

"Entitlement has little to do with matters of raw power, madam. Your peers spend more money and effort acquiring sophisticated cryptai. As you have been warned repeatedly, a top-level tech-hobbyist may have access to snoop programs that are better than me. Surely a few clade-members will detect the queries you are making.

"In short, I cannot guarantee that I am protecting you properly, madam."

Lacey glared at the simulated servant. Though depicted

wearing her family livery, with every fold of his uniform real looking, the features were altogether too handsome to be real. Anyway, you could see right through the projection, to a cubist-period Picasso, hanging on the far bulkhead of her private jet. The irony of that overlap almost made Lacey smile, despite her frustration and worry. Semitransparency was a flaw inherently shared by any creature who was made entirely of light.

At least, when the Hebrew patriarch, Jacob, wrestled with an angel, he could hope for a decisive outcome. But with *aingels*, there was nothing palpable to grapple. All you could do was keep insisting. Sometimes, they let you have your way.

"I don't care if some other trillionaires listen in!" she persisted. "I'm not endangering any vital caste interests!"

"No, you aren't." The handsome, lambent image simulated a concerned head shake. *"But need I remind that you are already seeking help from your peers, in the matter of looking for your son? Isn't that the reason for this hurried trip?"*

Lacey bit her lip. Hacker's latest misadventure in space had yanked her away from the altiplano observatory, even before first light could fall on the experimental Farseeker Telescope that bore her name. What typically infuriating timing! Of course, the boy was probably fine. He generally built his toys well—a knack inherited from his father—a kind of hyper-responsible irresponsibility.

Still, what kind of mother would she be, not to drop everything and rush to the Caribbean? Or to call in favors, summoning every yacht and private aerocraft in the region, in order to help search? Despite a misaligned trajectory and unknown landing point, Hacker's final, garbled telemetry told of an intact heat shield and chutes properly deployed. So he was probably floating around the warm waters in his tiny capsule, chewing emergency rations while cursing the slowness of rescue. And the difficulty of finding good help these days.

Lacey chased away gut-wrenching thoughts about the alternative—the unspeakable. So, grimly, she clung to this argument with an artificial being that she—in theory—owned.

"You don't find it fishy that the NASA and Hemispheric Security satellites have been retasked, just when we could use their help?"

"Fishy... as in suspicious? As in some hypothetical reason why they might not want to help? I cannot penetrate top-level government crypto, madam. But the patterns of coded traffic seem consistent with genuine concern. Something unexpected seems to have occurred, an event that is drawing high-level attention. Nothing to indicate a military or reffer or public health crisis. The tenor seems to be one of frantically secretive... curiosity."

The aissistant shook its simulated head. *"I fail to see how this applies to your situation, except as a matter of bad luck in timing."*

Lacey scoffed, indelicately.

"Bad timing? More than one of those damned sport rockets malfunctioned! That snotty, aristobrat son of Leonora Smits—he's gone missing, too."

The ai just stood there—or seemed to—patiently waiting for her to make a point.

"So, this may not be an accident! I want to find out if the clade suspects sabotage. Maybe an attack by eco-nuts. Or the Sons of Smith."

"A reasonable suspicion. And, as I told you, madam, I can post a query through normal channels, to the directorate of the First Estate, in Vaduz—"

"Fine. But try the other way, too. I insist."

This time, she said it with such finality that the hologram simply bowed in acceptance.

"Oh, and let's see what we can find out from the Seventh Estate. The big transport firms have zeps and cargo ships and sea farms all across the Caribbean. They could be diverted and incorporated as part of the search mesh."

"That may be tricky, madam. Under terms of the Big Deal, individual human beings who are above a certain threshold of personal wealth may not interfere with the Corporate Estate, or exercise undue influence upon the management of limited liability companies."

"Who's interfering? I'm just seeking a favor that *any* stockholder might ask for, under the same circumstances. Since when did it make you a second-class citizen, to be rich!"

Lacey clenched her jaw to keep from shouting. Oh, for the time, not so long ago, when raw piles of money spoke, directly and powerfully, in every boardroom, instead of having to apply leverage in convoluted ways. She took a breath, then spoke firmly. "You know how to do it. Go through the stockholder coops and the public relations departments. Make nice to the Merchant Seaman's Guild. Use your fancy ai noggin—bring in the smart-arses in my legal department—and find ways to get those corporate resources busy, helping search for my boy. And do it now."

"It shall be done, madam," replied the aivatar. It seemed to back away then, retreating without turning, bowing and getting smaller, as if diminishing into ever greater distance, joining the ersatz folds of the Picasso. Just another of countless optical tricks that ais kept coming up with, unbidden, in order to mess with human eyes. And no one knew why.

But we put up with it. Because it amuses. And because it seems to make them happy.

And because they know damned well how much we're afraid of them.

Another servitor appeared then, wearing the same uniform—blue-green with yellow piping—only this was a living young woman, one of the Camerouni refugees who Lacey had been sponsoring for as far back as she could remember. Utterly loyal (as verified by detailed PET scans) to her mistress.

Accepting a steaming teacup, Lacey murmured polite thanks. In order to avoid thinking about Hacker, she veered her thoughts the other way, backtracking to the giant apparatus that her money had built in the Andes, where a small order of monastic astronomers were now preparing the unconventional instrument, as dusk fell.

I suppose it's a sign of the times that none of the big media outfits sent a live reporter to our opening, only a couple of feed-pods that we had to uncrate and activate ourselves, so the pesky things could hover about and get in our way, asking the most inane questions.

None of the news reports or webuzz seemed helpful. Except for science junkies and SETI fans, there seemed to be more tired cynicism than excitement.

"What's the point?" the distilled, mass-voice demanded, with a collective yawn. *"We already know there's life out there, circling some nearby stars. Planets of pond scum. Planets where bacteria may eke out a living, amid drifting dunes. So? What does that mean to us? When we can't even make it to Mars and visit the sand scum there?"*

It wasn't her job to respond to mass-composite taunts. She had professional cajolers and spinners to do that, making the case for a continued search, for combing the heavens in new ways. To keep fanning hope that a glimpse of some blue world, perhaps another Earth, might shake some joy back into the race. But it was an uphill struggle.

Even among her own peers, other "cathedral-builders"

in the aristocracy, Lacey's pet project got no respect. Helena duPont-Vonessen, and other leading trillies, considered the Farseeker a waste, with so many modern problems screaming for attention. New diseases, festering in the flooded coastlines, demanding endowed institutes to study them. Simmering cities, where some lavish cultural center might keep restive populations calm, if not happy. Monuments to both mollify the mob and keep trillie families safe . . . if not popular. Back in TwenCen, governments built all the great universities, libraries and research centers, the museums and arenas, the observatories, monuments and Internets. Now, groaning with debt, they left such things to the mega-wealthy, as in times of old. A tradition as venerable as the Medicis. As Hadrian and Domitian. As the pyramids.

Newblesse oblige. A key part of the Big Deal to put off a class war that, according to computer models, could make 1789 look like a picnic. Though no one expected the Deal to hold for long. Speaking via cipher-parrot, Helena seemed to say that time was short. Lacey felt unsurprised.

But an alliance with the Prophet . . . with Tenskwatawa and his Movement.

Must it come to that?

It wasn't that Lacey felt any great loyalty to the Big Deal. Or to democracy and all that. Clearly, the Western Enlightenment was drawing to a close. *Somebody* had to guide the new era, so why not those who were raised and bred for leadership? The way things had been in 99 percent of past human cultures. (How could 99 percent be wrong?) And, well, with the momentum of his movement, Tenskwatawa could make a crucial difference, giving the clade of wealth every excuse it needed.

Anyway, what's the point of having lots of cash, if it cannot buy action when needed?

What bothered Lacey wasn't the necessity of limiting

and controlling democracy. No, it was the *goal* of the Prophet. The price he would demand, for helping bring back aristocratic rule. The other thing that must also happen when the Enlightenment fell.

Stability. A damping-down of breakneck change. Renunciation.

And there Lacey knew she might run into trouble. For the edifices and monuments that *she* liked to build and have named after her all were aimed at shaking things up! Instruments and implements and institutions that accelerated change.

So? I'm Jason's wife—and Hacker's mother.

The insight offered some bitter satisfaction. And, though her heart still wrenched with worry, Lacey felt a stronger connection with her wayward boy, who might, even now, be drifting as a clot of ash in the warm sea ahead.

I never quite saw it that way before. But in my own way, I'm just as devoted as he and his father were. Just as eager for speed.

ENTROPY

Another potential failure mode is deliberate or accidental misuse of science.

Take *nanotech.* Way back in the 1960s, Richard Feynman predicted great things might be accomplished by building small. Visionaries like Drexler, Peterson, and Bear foretold molecular-scale machines erecting perfect crystals, superstrong materials, or ultra-sophisticated circuits—anything desired—built atom by atom.

Today, the latest computers, plenats, and designer drugs all depend upon such tools. So do modern sewage and recycling systems. Soon, smart nanobots may cruise your bloodstream, removing a lifetime's accumulated dross, even pushing back the clock of years. Some envision nanos cleansing polluted aquifers, rebalancing sterile swathes of ocean, or sucking carbon from the air.

Ah, but what if micromachines escape their programming, reproducing outside factory brood-tanks? Might hordes *evolve,* adapting to utilize the natural world? Lurid sci-fi tales warn of replicators eating the biosphere, outcompeting their creators.

Or this tech may be perverted for man's oldest pastime. Picture an arms race between suspicious nations or global-synds, each fearing *others* are developing nano-weapons in secret. When danger comes packaged so small, can we ever know for sure?

—*Pandora's Cornucopia*

12.
APPRENTICESHIP

The man behind the desk passed a stone paperweight from hand to hand.

"Naturally, Miss Povlov, we feel our project is misunderstood."

Naturally, Tor thought, careful not to subvocalize. No use having sarcasm appear in her transcript. *Everyone is misunderstood. Especially folks who are trying to correct faults in human nature.*

Dr. Akinobu Sato tilted back in his chair. "Here at the Atkins Center, we're not pushing some grand design for Homo sapiens. We view our role as expanding the range of options for our kin and posterity. Are we then any different from others who pushed back the darkness?"

The words so closely matched her own thoughts, just seconds before, that Tor had to blink. *It's probably coincidence. I'm not the first to raise this question.*

Still . . . modern sensors could detect a single neuron

flash across a room. Monitors in a wall might track gross emotions, or even be taught to respond to a homeowner's mental commands. And there were always creepy tattle-rumors about the next big step, *reading actual thoughts.* Surely just tall tales.

Still, these Atkins meddlers might be the very ones to make that leap. During a tour, before arriving in Sato's office, she had seen—

—quadriplegics who moved about gracefully, controlling their robotic legs without wire shunts through the skull.

—a preteen girl commanding up to *twenty* hovering aicraft at once, by combining muscle twitches, tooth-clicks, and subvocal grunts. Apparently a record.

—an accident victim who had lost an entire cerebral hemisphere and would never again speak, but whose fingertips sketched VR pictures in the air. Watching without specs, you might think him crazed, capering and pointing at nothing. But tuned to the right overlayer, she saw images erupt from those waggling fingertips so detailed and compelling that—well—who needed words?

Then there were the ones generating so much excitement and controversy—victims of the Autism Plague who had been sent here from all over the world by parents seeking hope. The Atkins specialized in "savants," so Tor had come expecting feats of mathematical legerdemain and total recall. And there were a few impressive demos—mentally calculating long-ago dates and guessing correctly the number of beads in a jar—stunts that were old news. Dr. Sato wanted to show off more recent accomplishments—less flashy. More significant.

Tor watched as boys and girls, long mentally isolated from close human contact, now held normal-looking conversations, even collaborating in a game. After going on a while about eye-contact rates and Empathy Quotients, Sato made his point.

"We start by stimulating brain regions that 'mirror' the body movements we see other people perform. Also manipulating the parieto-occipital junction, to provoke what was called an out-of-body experience. These mental states once carried a lot of freight among religious types. But we now trigger outward-empathy or self-introspection, on demand."

Tor had commented that some of the faithful might find this offensive. One more grab by science at territory once reserved for belief. But Sato shrugged as if to ask, *What else is new?*

"Call it a technologization of compassion, or induction of insight.

"The next question is, can we do all this, awakening other-awareness and self-appraisal in some autistics, without sacrificing their savant skills? Or the wild alertness that sometimes makes them seem more natural and feral than the rest of us?

"And then . . . ," Sato had mused, with an eager glint in his eyes. *". . . if we can manage that, will it be it possible to go the other way? Give savant-level mental powers to normal people?"*

Conversing with some patients, Tor came to realize something that distressed her as a reporter—there'd be little useful video from this tour. The Atkins patients, once crippled by a deep mental handicap, some of them effectively disconnected from the world, now seemed talkative, cogent, not so much hopelessly detached as . . . well . . . *nerdy.*

She did have shots of some beaming parents, visiting from faraway cities, calling the work here miraculous. *But I can get some balance from the demonstrators outside,* Tor recalled. Activists who posed a pointed question.

Who are we—who is anybody—to define what it means to be human? To "cure" a condition that might simply be closer to innocence or nature? Closer to the Earth?

Or—perhaps—closer to a onetime state of grace?

· · ·

Now, ensconced in a plush chair with her stalk-cam panning across Sato's office, she hurried back on topic. "You say you just offer options, Doctor. But folks in Carolina didn't want those choices. And those here in Albuquerque range from ambivalent to hostile. Is it a case of too much too soon? Or something deeper?"

"I think you know the answer, Miss Tor," Sato replied, placing both hands on the desk. "If we were merely helping some types of borderline autistic children to behave more *normally,* to be more empathic and communicative, to get jobs and raise families, then few would complain. Just a few diversity fetishists who think nature is always better than civilization and animals are wiser than people. But anyone can see our work will have implications, far beyond helping a few kids to fit in."

Tor nodded. "Hm, yes. We'll get to all that. But first, let me ask, after being forced to leave Charleston, why didn't you resettle in one of the high-water townships along the coast where you'd fit in? Just another merry band of would-be godmakers, no more offensive than your local biotinker."

Sato frowned, a deep furrow creasing his youthful-looking brow above soft, almond eyes. He had seemed about forty, but Tor now guessed higher. Triggered by attention cues, her aiware sifted, finding the professor's latest sculpt, last month, at Madame Fascio's Facelifts. *So? Scientists aren't immune to vanity.*

"We dislike the term . . . 'godmaker' . . . , It implies something elitist, even domineering. Our goal is the opposite. A general empowerment, across the board."

"Commendably egalitarian, Doctor. But does it ever work out that way? All new things—from toys to tools of power—tend to be gathered up first by some human elite. Often as a way to *stay* elite."

Sato arched an eyebrow. "Now who's sounding radical? Are you suggesting we revisit the Class War?"

"It's a simple question, Professor. How will you ensure that everyone gets to share these mental augmentations you seek? Won't equality be stymied by the very same human diversity you celebrate?"

"Explain, please."

"Suppose you find a way to enhance human intelligence. Or for people to focus attention more creatively, beyond the Thurman Barrier. Assume the process is cheap with few side effects. . . ." It was her turn to express doubt, with an ironic lift of an eyebrow for the jewelcam. "And further that your process isn't monopolized by some clade of aristos, who use wealth or influence or public safety as an excuse—"

"Are you really that suspicious of aristocracy?" Sato tried to cut in. "How old-fashioned."

And how out of touch you are, she thought. *If you haven't sensed the recent shifts back toward conflict.* But Tor forged on.

"—even assuming all of that, there will be no way to avoid one final division—between those who *choose* to accept your gift, and those who do not."

"Our . . . gift." Sato mulled for a moment. Then he turned back to her with a gaze that seemed dark, glittering. "You know, our modern endeavor as would-be *godmakers,* to use your term, is not without precedent. The dream goes back a long way. For example, it is said that after Prometheus was chained to a rock, in punishment for giving humanity the boon of fire, his *children* thereupon chose to live among men. Made families with them. Reinforced his gift by breeding divinity into the race. And there are countless other legends—even in the Judeo-Christian Bible— implying the same thing."

"Stories about humans trying to be godlike. But don't most of them portray that as sin? Prometheus was punished.

Frankenstein gets killed by his creature. The Tower of Babel crumbles amid chaos."

Bridging his fingers, Sato intoned: " 'And the Lord said, See, they are all one people and have all one language; and this is only the start of what they may do: and now it will not be possible to keep them from any purpose of theirs.' "

"I beg your pardon?"

"Babel. Building a tower to heaven. The attempt failed when we were deliberately sabotaged by a curse of mutual incomprehension, by forcing us to speak a multitude of languages. Most theologians have interpreted the Babel story the way you just did—as showing God *angry* at humanity, for this act of hubris.

"But read it more carefully. There is *no* anger! Not a trace. No mention of anybody suffering or dying, as they surely do in murderous mass-fury, at Sodom, or in Noah's flood, or innumerable cases of heavenly wrath. There's none of that in the story of Babel! Sure, we were thwarted, confused, and scattered. But was that meant to stymie us forever? From achieving what the passage clearly says we *can* achieve? What perhaps we're ultimately *meant* to achieve?

"Maybe the confusion was meant just to *delay things*. For us to learn by overcoming obstacles. In fact, didn't the scattering-of-man make us more diverse and experienced with overcoming hard challenges? Better able to grasp and apply myriad points of view? Think about it, Miss Tor. Today, someone with simple aiware can understand what any other person says, anywhere on the globe. Right now, in this very generation, we have come full circle. Language has ceased to be any sort of barrier. And our "tower" covers the globe.

"Recall what scripture says—there's no limit to our potential. We're inherently able to do or be anything. Anything at all. So, what's to stop us now?"

Tor stared at the neuroscientist. *Are you kidding?* she

thought. Clearly, at one level, he was pulling her leg. And yet, equally, he meant all this. Took it seriously.

"What do ancient myths have to do with the question at hand? The issue of arrogant scientific ambition?"

"The old tales show how long humans have pondered this problem! Like, whether it is proper to pick up the same tools the Creator used to make us. What could be a more meaningful concern?"

"All right then." Tor nodded, with an inward sigh, if Sato wanted to look foolish on camera, so be it. "Don't most legends answer in the negative? Preaching against *hubris*?" Tor didn't bother defining the term. Her audience was generally with it. They'd have instant vocaib.

"Yes," Sato agreed. "During the long Era of Fear, lasting six to ten thousand years, priests and kings sought—above all—to keep peasants in their place. So naturally, ambition was discouraged! Churches called it sinful to question your local lord. Even worse to question God. You brought up the Tower of Babel. Or, take Adam and Eve, cast out of Eden for tasting from the tree of knowledge."

"Or the mistake of Brahma, or the machine of Soo Song, or countless other cautionary fables." She nodded. "The Renunciation Movement mentions all of them, forecasting big trouble—possibly another Fall—if humanity keeps reaching too far. That's why I'm surprised that you took this path in today's interview, Doctor. Are you suggesting that tradition and scripture may be relevant, after all?"

"Hm." Sato pondered a moment. "You seem to be well read. Do you know your Book of Genesis?"

"Reasonably well. It's a cultural keystone."

"Then, can you tell me which passage is the only one—in the whole Bible—that portrays God asking a *favor,* out of pure curiosity?"

Tor knew this interview had spun out of control. It wasn't being netcast live, so she could edit later. Still, she noted a small figure in a corner of her aiware. Twenty-three MediaCorp employees and stringers were watching. Make that twenty-four. And with high interest levels. *All right, then, let's run with it.*

"Offhand, I can't guess what passage you have in mind, Dr. Sato."

He leaned toward her. "It's a moment in the Bible that comes *before* that darned apple, when the relationship between Creator and created was still pure, without any of the later tsuris of wrathful expulsion, gritty battles, or redemption . . . or egotistical craving for praise."

He's sincere about this, Tor realized, reading his eyes. *A biologist, a would-be godmaker-meddler . . . yet, a believer.*

"You still don't recall? It's brief. Most people just glide past and theologians barely give it a glance."

"Well, you have our interest, Doctor. Pray tell. What is this special biblical moment?"

"It's when God asks Adam to *name the beasts.* Perhaps the only moment that's truly like parent and child, or teacher and favored pupil. Indeed, what better clue to what humanity was created for? Since it had nothing to do with sin, redemption, or any of that later vex."

"Created for . . . ?" she prompted. Interested, even though she could now see where he was going, and wasn't sure she liked it.

"Names have creative power! Like the equations God used to cast forth light and start the cosmos. What action makes up half of science? Naming moons, craters, planets, species, and molecules . . . even wholly new living things that men and women now synthesize from scratch. What could that passage represent other than a master craftsman watching in approval, while His apprentice starts down the road of exploration?

"A road that led to Babel, where premature success might have spoiled everything . . . so He made the *naming process* more challenging! Still taking the apprentice toward one destination—a role and duty that was intended all along.

"Co-creation."

Tor had to blink a few times. "Well, that certainly is a unique perspective on—"

"On a passage so brief it was ignored for millennia? The implications—"

"I see what you *think* it implies, Professor," Tor cut in, anxious to reestablish some control. "And we'll supply links for our viewers who don't. But there's a huge step between calling yourself a 'co-creator' and having enough wisdom not to botch it up! What we—my viewers and I—want to know is how—"

Tor trailed off. The neurosmith was holding something out, gesturing for Tor to reach for it. The stone paperweight he had been handling—roughly cylindrical, tapering toward a rounded point at each end. The sides bore many fluted hollows.

"Take it," Sato urged as she put out her hand. "Don't worry, it's only thirty thousand years old."

Tor almost yanked back, before accepting the object. It felt cool. The stone must have once featured many sharp edges before getting rubbed smooth by countless fingers.

"It is a prepared-core, either late Mousterian or early Châtelperronian, from a period when two hominid species occupied Europe, living side-by-side for quite some time, sharing almost identical technologies and—apparently—similar cultures. Neanderthals and anatomically modern humans had an especially long overlap in the Levant, where both groups seemed to be *stuck* at the same level for as much as a hundred thousand years."

Tor turned the artifact over. It wasn't glossy, like obsidian, but gray and grainy. Her aiware identified the material as **chert**, offering links that she subvocally brushed away.

"I thought humans wiped out the Neanderthals."

"It's a prevailing theory. The long stable period ended at the dawn of the Aurignacian, with astonishing abruptness. Within a few dozen generations—an eyeblink—our ancestral tool kit expanded prodigiously to include fish hooks and sewing needles made of glistening bone, finely shaped scrapers, axes, burins, nets, ropes, and specialized knives that required many complex stages to create.

"*Art* also erupted on the scene. People adorned themselves with pendants, bracelets, and beads. They painted magnificent cave murals, performed burial rituals, and carved provocative Venus figurines. Innovation accelerated. So did other deeply human traits—for there appeared clear signs of social stratification. Religion. Kingship. Slavery. War.

"And—for the poor Neanderthals—genocide."

Tor felt nonplussed by the sudden shift. One moment, Sato had been talking in the cramped, six-thousand-year context of the Judeo-Christian Bible. The next, he was suddenly back in the vast realm of scientific time, reflecting on the fits and starts of humanity's hard, slow climb out of darkness. Still, there was overlap . . . a common arching theme. And Tor saw, at last, where this was going.

"You think we're heading for another of those sudden speedups."

Sato tilted his head slightly.

"Doesn't everyone?"

Suddenly, the scientist's voice was free of any games. Contemplative, even concerned.

"The question, Miss Tor, isn't *whether* change is coming. Only how we can be smarter about it this time. Perhaps even wise enough to cope."

SCANALYZER

Greetings. I'm **Marcia Khatami**, sitting in for Martin Raimer, who is following a hot story in Cuba. Good luck, Martin!

Today we return to a favorite topic. For a century, the **Search for Extra Terrestrial Intelligence** has drawn both radio astronomers and zealous supporters with hopeful tenacity that rivals any previous faith. Sometimes funded by governments, by rich enthusiasts, or micro-donations, SETI uses sophisticated apparatus to sift the "Cosmic Haystack" for a single, glittering needle that may change our lives, telling us we're not alone.

The effort isn't without critics. Let's continue our debate between two mavens of superscience. Dr. Hannah Spearpath is director of Project Golden Ear, combining the Allen, Donaldson, and Chang SETI arrays. Welcome back, Hannah.

DR. SPEARPATH: My pleasure, Marcia.

MARCIA KHATAMI: Also with us is his inimitably provocative rastaself, star of the popscience show *Master Your Universe!* and just returned from a touring with his sci-reggai group Blowing Cosmic Smoke. Welcome, Professor Noozone.

PROFESSOR NOOZONE: Praises to Almighty Jah and *Wa'ppu,* Marcia. Much respect and a massive *big up* blessing to all viewers an' lurkers out there!

MARCIA KHATAMI: Doctors, our last session got heated, not over *listening* for alien signals, but endeavors to *beam* messages from Earth to outer space. Shouting "yoohoo!" at the stars.

DR. SPEARPATH: Yes, and I want to correct any impression that Golden Ear beams "messages" into the sky. Our antennas aren't set up for transmission. We leave that to others.

PROFESSOR NOOZONE: But Hannah, your verysame statement amounted to upfull support for the wicked men perpetrating this irresponsible behavior, nah even botherin' to *discuss* it 'pon the people or dem scientific bredren. This is *rhaatid*! It violates a basic livication laid down, long ago, by Ras Carl Sagan himself, when he said any superadvanced races out there should "do the heavy lifting" of makin' contact. An' Mas Carl also said that youth like us should quietly listen. Ya haffa creep an' walk before ya run.

DR. SPEARPATH: Well, conditions change. Last time, I simply stated the obvious, that no possible harm could come from such transmissions.

PROFESSOR NOOZONE: But hol' on my dear. How can dem be "obvious" when well-informed people disagree? "No possible harm" is nuh-easy to say! It is based on many sad-unexamined *assumptions* about the cosmos, about intelligence, and the way so them aliens must think! Especially the unproved postulate that *altruism be universal* among advanced life-forms.

You declare that upfulness and overstanding will drive every people, soon come all a time, out there among the so-bright stars.

Oh, surely, I-and-I find dat notion super-attractive! Beneficent star-mons, bright-doing, everywhere across the galaxy! It what I hope to be a-true! Praise Jah an' His Interstellar Majesty. . . . But scientists shoulda be Ras-*skeptical*. An' the underlying tenet of universal altruism is one that you people refuse to offer up for analysis or peer review by your own-very science bredren, dismissing all other views as paranoid—

DR. SPEARPATH: Because anything else is silly. If aliens wanted to harm us, they would have done it by now.

PROFESSOR NOOZONE: Oh buckery an' bodderation! I could list *six dozen* ways that statement oversimplifies—

DR. SPEARPATH: Anyway, the potential benefits of contact—of just detecting that another civilization is out there—outweigh any of the harm scenarios on your list, since you admit that each one, separately, seems unlikely.

PROFESSOR NOOZONE: Everything irie . . . I-and-I admit that. What *you* don't admit is that the odds of harm aren't *zero*. Kill-mi-dead if the sheer number of ways don't add up to a whole heap—

DR. SPEARPATH: How can anything compare with the top benefit of SETI? Beyond all the wonderful things we might learn. Just detecting *that* other intelligent species exist! Right now we don't necessarily see a long future for technological civilizations on this planet. So many ways it could fail. A proof of existence, that *someone* survived their technical infancy, is valuable! Successful detection means longevity of civilizations is the rule rather than the exception.

PROFESSOR NOOZONE: All very moving. Maybe even true, Hannah. But inna case, does not your *failure* to find anybody have the worrisome *opposite* meaning? Anyway, you describe a benefit of *detection.* Not of *transmission,* which increases the risk, without affecting any of the benefits—

DR. SPEARPATH: Your *patois* is slipping again. If it were genuine—

MARCIA KHATAMI: I want to focus on something else the professor said last week, about how the classic SETI *search strategy* has been all wrong for decades. Because it assumes that extraterrestrials are constantly transmitting in all directions, at all times.

DR. SPEARPATH: We do not make that assumption!

PROFESSOR NOOZONE: But oh my, your search strategy implies it, Hannah! Aiming big, stooshy telescope arrays toward one target at a time, analyzing the radio spectrum from that candidate solar system, then doin' the *ten-toe turbo* as you stroll on to the next one. . . .

DR. SPEARPATH: Sometimes we take in whole globular clusters. We frequently return to the galactic center. There are also timing-pattern scenarios, having to do with the light cone of certain events, like novas, that turn our attention certain ways. We have an eclectic program.

PROFESSOR NOOZONE: That be most-surely laudable. Still,

your approach clings to an assumption—that benevolent aliens make great-profligate beacons that blare inna cosmos *continuously,* day after day, year after year, *ray-ray* just for neo-races like us, using SETI programs like yours.

But Hannah, that ignores so-many possibles. Like suppose de cosmos be more dangerous than you think. Maybe ET stays quiet because *him knows something we don't!*

DR. SPEARPATH: (sighs) More paranoia.

PROFESSOR NOOZONE: No way, Doctor, me I'm just thorough. But dere be a bigger plaint, based on *hard-nose economics.*

MARCIA KHATAMI: Economics, Professor? You mean, as in money?

DR. SPEARPATH: Alien capitalists? Investment bankers? This gets better and better. How unimaginative to assume that an advanced civilization will manage itself just like us.

MARCIA KHATAMI: (chuckles) Now, Doctor, no one can accuse Profnoo of being—*unimaginative.* We'll come back and discuss how economics might affect advanced aliens after this break.

13.
METASTABLE

If only I could be more than one person.

It was a frequent wish. As life kept getting busier, Hamish delegated as much as he could, but things kept piling up. The more successful he became, the more beleaguered he felt.

Standing on a balcony overlooking the lanai of his Clearwater compound, gazing past palm trees, mansions, and surf-ruins toward the sparkling Gulf of Mexico, he could hear the musical jangle of calls coming in, answered by two secretaries, three assistants, and far too many soft-aissistors to count.

*To hell with being "influential" and saving the world!
Wasn't I happier when it was just me and the old qwerty
keyboard? And my characters. Just give me an arrogant
villain and some Big Technological Mistake. A gutsy heroine. A mouthy hero. I'd be set for months.*

*All right, I also liked doing movies. Before Hollywood
collapsed.*

*Only now? There is the Cause. Important, of course.
But with trillionaires joining their great power behind it,
can't the movement do without me for a week? Let me get
some writing done?*

Clutching the wrought iron balustrade, he recognized
one of those phone melodies—a call he couldn't refuse.
After the first ring, it started vibrating a flesh-colored plug
in his ear.

He refused to tap a tooth and answer. Somebody downstairs should pick up. Take a message.

But no one did. Well trained, his staff knew that tune
was for him alone. Still, he kept his gaze on the horizon,
where several rows of once-expensive villas used to line
the old beachfront, now jutting skeletally from the roiling
tide. In the distance, he heard the day and night rumble as
Conservation Corps crews extended a network of shoreline
dikes and dunes. Keeping Florida a state, and not paradise
lost.

A new Flood is coming. . . .

After a third ring—damned technology—the synthetic
voice of Wriggles spoke up.

"It is Tenskwatawa. We are behooved."

Hamish relented, giving the slightest nod of permission.
A faint click followed . . .

. . . and he winced as sudden, rhythmic, thumping
sounds assaulted one eardrum. Dampers kicked in, filter-
ing the cadence down to a bearable level. It was a four-four
tempo, heavy on the front beat.

"Brookeman! You there? Damn it, how come you're not wearing specs?"

Hamish grew tired of explaining why he only used ai-ware when necessary. You'd think a leader of the Renunciation Movement would understand.

"Where are you calling from, Prophet?"

"Puget Sound. A Quinalt potlatch ceremony. They hand-carve their own canoes and spears, stage a big sea hunt where they stab a robot orca, then come back and feast on vat-grown whale meat. Vat-grown! Bunch of tree-hugging fairies.

"Never mind. Have you made any progress on the Basque Chimera?"

"Both mother and child have gone underground. And pretty effectively. I figure they got help from elements in the First Estate."

"I suspected as much. It's not as if they could hide in plain sight. So. I'll put some pressure on the trillies. It's time for them to stop playing both sides and choose. One thing about aristos, they have an instinct for self-preservation."

"True enough, sir."

"So, what about that thing with Senator Strong? It'd be great if he can be salvaged. He's been an asset."

"I've been home one day," Hamish answered. "I did hire a team of ex-FBI guys to gather prelims through discreet channels. Tap government files and such. Investigate the fellow who claims to have poisoned the senator. Forty-eight hours to gather background, before I take an overall look."

"One of your trademark Big Picture brainstorms? Wish I could watch you do that some time."

Hamish bit back a sullen response. It used to be flattering when important men asked him to consult and offer a wide perspective—pointing out things they missed. Now, the fun was gone. Especially since Carolyn pointed out something that should have been obvious.

"A hundred years from now, Hammi, what will be left of you?" she asked on the day they parted, ending all the anger and shouting with a note of regret. "Do you expect gratitude for all this conspiring with world-movers? Or to go down in history? Pick any of your novels. A book will still be around—read and enjoyed by millions—after that other crap has long faded. Long after your body is dust."

Of course she was right. Yet, Hamish knew how the Prophet would answer. Without the Cause, there might not *be* any humanity, a century from now, to read novels or do anything else.

Still, thinking of Carolyn, he knew—she had also been talking about their marriage. That, too, was important. It should have been treated as something to last.

Tenskwatawa's voice continued in his ear. *"But that's not why I'm calling. Can you get linked right away? There's news coming in. And I already have my plate full. Got to attend a conference with some aristocracy in Switzerland. One of the big newblesse clans may finally get onboard and join the movement."*

"That's great news."

"Yeah, well, we need those rich bastards, so I can't turn away, even when something more urgent turns up."

Hamish felt pleasure turn to worry. "Something more urgent than getting support from some First Estate trillionaires?"

"I'm afraid so." Tenskwatawa paused. *"One of our people, Carlos Ventana, just managed to slide a blip to us, past NASA security. He reports that something big is up."*

"Ventana," Hamish mused. The name was familiar. A rich Latin. Used to own the entire phone company in Brazil or someplace, till they broke his monopoly as part of the Big Deal. Then he moved into fertilizer.

"Did you say NASA? Are they still in business?"

"He's playing tourist right now on the space station."

"You mean the old research station. Not the High Hilton or Zheng Ho-tel?" Hamish shook his head, wondering why a bazillionaire would spend good money to go drift in filth for a month.

"That's right. Wanted an authentic experience, I guess. Anyway, it's pure luck—or destiny—that we had a friend aboard when it happened."

"It? What happened?" Hamish barely quashed his irritation.

"The astronauts grabbed or recovered something out there. It's got them all lathered up."

"But what could they possibly have found that—"

"Details are sketchy. But it may be a second-order disturber. Perhaps even first-order."

Hamish himself had come up with the "disturber" nomenclature a decade ago to classify innovations or new technologies that could threaten humanity's fragile stability. Leaders of the Movement embraced his terminology, but Hamish always had trouble remembering the exact definitions. Of course, with specs on, he might have asked Wriggles for help.

"First order . . . ," he mulled.

"Oh, Jesus walks in the Andes. Do I have to spell it out, man? Government spacemen haul something in from the deep dark beyond . . . and it starts talking to them! Apparently, they're deciphering a series of communications protocols, even as we speak!"

"Talking? You mean . . ."

"Maybe not real conversation. But enough to send folks running down the halls of the White House and Blue House and Yellow House, looking all sweaty. Even worse, too many pros in the pencil pushers' guild know about it already—damned civil servants—for us to exert pressure and get a presidential clamp put on. News is gonna get out this time, Hamish."

"From . . . space . . ." He blinked several times. "Either it's a provocation—or a hoax—maybe some Chinese—"

"We should be so lucky!"

Hamish forged on.

"—or else, it is the real thing. Something alien. Oh man."

Now it was Tenskwatawa who paused, letting the background beat of drums fill a pause between them. Bridging regular gaps of time, like the pounding of a heart.

"Oh man is right," the Prophet finally murmured.

"This may be nothing. Or perhaps we can strike another deal with the pencil pushers. Distract the public and keep the lid on, once again.

"Still, it has terrible potential. We could be in real trouble, my friend. All of us. All of humankind."

ENTROPY

What of destruction by devastating war? Shall we admit that our species passed one test, by *not* plunging into an orgy of atomic destruction?

Millions still live who recall the Soviet-American standoff—the Cold War—when tens of thousands of hydrogen bombs were kept poised in submarines, bombers, and silos. Half a dozen men at any time, some of them certifiably unstable, held the hair trigger to unleash nuclear mega-death. Any of a dozen crises might have ended civilization, or even mammalian life on Earth.

One sage who helped build the first atom bomb put it pungently. *"When has man, bloody down to his soul, invented a new weapon and foresworn using it?"* Cynics thought it hopeless, given a basic human reflex for rage and convulsive war.

But it didn't happen. Not even Awfulday or the Pack-It-Ind affair set off the unthinkable. Were we scared back from that brink, sobered to our senses by the warning image of a mushroom cloud? Chastened and thus saved by an engine of death?

Might the cynics have been altogether wrong? There was never any proof that vicious conflict is woven into human DNA. Yes, it was pervasive during the long, dark era of tribes and kings, from Babylon and Egypt to Mongolia, Tahiti, and Peru. Between 1000 C.E. and 1945, the longest period of uninterrupted peace in Europe was a fifty-one-year stretch between the Battle of Waterloo and the Austro-Prussian War. That tranquil period came amid the industrial revolution, as millions moved from farm to city. Was it harder, for a while, to find soldiers? Or did people feel too busy to fight?

Oh, sure, industry *then* made war more terrible than ever. No longer a matter of macho glory, it became a death-orgy, desired only by monsters, and fought grimly, by decent men, in order to defeat those monsters.

Then, Europe's serenity resumed. Descendants of Viking raiders, centurions and Huns transmuted into pacifists. Except for a few brush fires, ethnic ructions, and terror hits, that once-ferocious continent knew peace for a century, becoming the core of a peaceful and growing EU.

One theory holds that democracies seldom war against each other. Nations ruled by aristocracies were more impulsive, spendthrift, and violent. But however you credit this change—to prosperity or education, to growing worldwide contacts or the American Pax—it shattered the notion that war burns, unquenchable and ineradicable in the human character.

The good news? Violent self-destruction isn't programmed in. Whether or not we tumble into planet-burning war isn't fore-ordained. It is a wide-open matter of choice.

The bad news is exactly the same.

It's a matter of choice.

—Pandora's Cornucopia

14

TREASURE

Night had fallen some time ago and now his torch batteries were failing. That, plus sheer exhaustion, forced Peng Xiang Bin, at last, to give up salvaging anything more from the hidden cache that he had found underneath a sunken mansion. Anyway, with the compressed air bottle depleted, his chest now burned from repeated free dives through that narrow opening, made on lung power alone, snatching whatever he could—whatever sparkle caught his eye down there.

You will die if you keep this up, he finally told himself. *And someone else will get the treasure.* That thought made it firm.

Still, even without any more trips inside, there was work to do. Yanking some decayed boards off the sea floor, Bin dropped them to cover the new entrance that he'd found, gaping underneath the house foundation. And then one final dive through dark shallows to kick sand over it all. Finally, he rested for a while with one arm draped over his makeshift raft, under the dim glow of a quarter moon.

Do not the sages counsel that a wise man must spread ambition, like honey across a bun? Only a greedy fool tries to swallow all of his good fortune in a single bite.

Oh, but wasn't it a tempting treasure trove? Carefully cloaked by the one-time owner of this former beachfront mansion, who took the secret of a concealed basement with him—perhaps out of spite—all the way to the execution-disassembly room.

If they had transplanted any of his brain, as well as the eyes and skin and organs, then someone might have re-membered the hidden room before this.

As it is, I am lucky that the rich man went to his death

angry, never telling anybody what the rising sea would bury.

Bin finally turned toward home, fighting an ebb tide that kept trying to haul him seaward into busy shipping lanes. It was a grueling journey, squatting on the overloaded block of polystyrene while propelling his paddle in an exhausting figure eight pattern . . . till his trembling fingers fumbled, losing their grip and dropping the makeshift oar! Night swallowed it, but there was no use searching, or cursing his fate. Bin couldn't rig another paddle. So, with a soft sigh, he slipped back into the greasy Huangpu and commenced dragging the raft behind him with a rope around his waist.

Several times—obsessively—he stopped to check the sacks of salvage, counting them and securing their ties.

It is fortunate that basement also proved a place to deposit my earlier load of garbage—all those pipes and chipped tiles—tucking them away from sight. Or I'd have to haul them, too.

The setting of the moon only made things harder, plunging the estuary into near blackness, except for a sprinkling of stars. And the glitter of Shanghai East, of course, a raucous galaxy of wealth, shimmering and flashing beyond the nearby seawall. And a soft glow of luminescence in the tide itself—a glimmer that proved especially valuable when Bin's winding journey took him by some neighboring shoresteads, looming out of the night like dark, medieval castles. He kept his splashing minimal, hurrying past slumping walls and spidery tent poles with barely a sound.

This time Mei Ling will be impressed with what I found.

That hope propelled Bin till, at last, his own stead was next, its familiar tilt occulting a lopsided band of stars. In fact, so eager was he to get home that he let his guard down . . . and almost swam into disaster.

Even a little moonlight would have alerted him to the

jellyfish swarm, a cloud of drifting, pulsating umbrella shapes that surged through the bay—just an offshoot of a vast colony that infested the East China Sea, growing bigger every year, annihilating age-old fishing grounds. Driven by the tide, one throbbing mass of filmy bodies and dangling stingers flowed directly in his path.

Frantically backpedaling, Bin barely avoided plowing into the horde. Even so, he soon discovered by the light of his failing torch that he was surrounded by outliers and stragglers. In pushing away from one cluster, he inevitably drifted toward another. Unable to avoid individual jellies altogether, he kicked with flippered feet . . . and inevitably felt sudden flares of pain, as a stinger-tendril brushed his left ankle.

Left no recourse, he clambered back atop the raft, praying the makeshift lashings would hold. It sank under the weight, leaving his body awash. But the tendrils couldn't reach him. For now.

Fumbling in the dark with his knife, Xiang Bin hacked at a torn milk jug and contrived a paddle of sorts—more of a scoop—and began a hard slog forward through the morass of poisonous creatures. Waiting for the swarm to disperse was not an option. By then, currents would take him far away. With home in plain sight, a brute force approach seemed best.

These awful things will kill all the fish in the estuary and tangle my nets, he thought. Worst case? His family could go hungry. Maybe for weeks.

Didn't someone tell me you can eat these things, if you're careful? Cooked with sesame oil? The Cantonese are said to know all the good kinds.

It sounded yucky. They might have to try it.

The last hundred meters were pure agony. Bin's lungs and arms felt on fire, and his right hand somehow took another painful jelly sting, before the main opening of the

ruined house gaped before him at last. Of course, he took a
beating as the raft crashed half sideways, into the atrium.
A couple of salvage bags split, spilling glittery treasures
across the old parquet floor. No matter. The things were
safe now, in easy reach.

In fact, it took all of Bin's remaining energy to drag just
one bag upstairs, then to pick his way carefully across the
slanted roof of broken tiles, and finally reach the tent-
house where his woman and child waited.

"Stones?" Mei Ling stared at the array of objects that
Xiang Bin had dropped before her. A predawn glow was
spreading across the east. Still, she had to lift a lantern to
peer at his little trove, shading the light and speaking in a
low voice, so as not to wake the baby. Low-angled illumination made the scars on one cheek stand out, an injury she
had suffered as a child, in the terrible Hunan earthquake.

"You are all excited over a bunch of stones?"

"They were on *shelves,* all neatly arranged with labels,"
he explained. After treating the two stinger wounds, he
began carefully applying small amounts of ointment to a
sore on his left leg, one of several that had opened again,
after long immersion. "Of course the tags were unreadable
after all this time. But there used to be glass cabinets—"

"They don't look like gems. No diamonds or rubies," she
interrupted. "Yes, some of them are pretty. But we find
surf-polished pebbles everywhere."

"You should see the ones that were on special pedestals,
in the center of the room. Some of them were held in fancy
boxes, made of wood and crystal. I tell you it was a *collection* of some sort. And it *must* have been valuable, for the
owner to hide them all so—"

"Boxes?" Her interest was piqued, at least a little "Did
you bring any of those?"

"A few. I left them on the raft. I was so tired. And hungry." He sniffed pointedly toward the stewpot where Mei Ling was reheating last night's meal, the one he had missed. Bin smelled some kind of fish that had been stir-fried with leeks, onions, and that reddish seaweed that she put into most of her dishes.

"Get some of those boxes, please, Xiang Bin," she insisted. "Your food will be warm by the time you return."

Bin would have gladly wolfed it down cold. But he sighed in resignation and gathered himself together, somehow finding the will to move quivering muscles. *I am still young, but I know how it will feel to be old.*

This time, at least, the spreading gray twilight helped him to cross the roof, then slide down the ladder and stairs without tripping. His hands trembled while untying two more bags of salvage, these bulging with sharply angular objects. Dragging them up and re-traversing the roof was a pure exercise in mind-over-agony.

Most of our ancestors had it at least this bad, he reminded himself. *Till things got much better in China, for a generation . . .*

. . . then worse again. For the poor.

Hope was a dangerous thing, of course. One heard of shoresteaders striking it rich with a great haul of salvage, now and then. But, most of the time, reality shattered promise. *Perhaps, after all, it is only an amateur geologist's private rock collection,* he thought, struggling the last few meters. *One man's hobby—precious to him personally, but of little market value.*

Still, after collapsing on the floor of their tent-home for a second time, he found enough curiosity and strength to lift his head, as Mei Ling's nimble fingers worked at the tie ropes. Upending one bag, she spilled out a pile of stony objects, along with a couple of the boxes he had mentioned, made of finely carved wood, featuring windows with beveled edges that glittered too beautifully to be made of simple glass.

For the first time, he saw a bit of fire in her eyes. Or interest, at least. One by one, she lifted each piece, turning it in the lamplight . . . then moved to push aside a curtain, letting in sharply horizontal rays of light, as the sun poked its leading edge above the East China Sea. The baby roused then, rocking from side to side and whimpering while Bin spooned some stew from the reheating pot into a bowl.

"Open this," Mei Ling insisted, forcing him to choose between the bowl and the largest box, that she thrust toward him. With a sigh, he put aside his meal and accepted the heavy thing, which was about the size and weight of his own head . . . maybe a bit longer. Bin started to pry at the corroded clasp, while Mei Ling picked up little Xiao En, to nurse the infant.

"It might be better to wait a bit and clean the box," he commented. "Rather than breaking it just to look inside. The container, itself, may be worth—"

Abruptly, the wood split along a grainy seam with a splintering crack. Murky water spilled across his lap, followed by a bulky object, so smooth and slippery that it almost squirted out of his grasp.

"What is it, husband?" Mei Ling asked. "Another stone?"

Bin turned it over in his hands. The thing was heavy and hard, with a greenish tint, like pale jade. Though that could just be slime that clung to its surface even after wiping with a rag. A piece of real jade this big could bring a handsome price, especially already shaped into a pleasant contour—that of an elongated egg. So he kept rubbing and lifted it toward the horizontal shaft of sunbeams, in order to get a better look.

No, it isn't jade, after all.

But disappointment slowly turned into wonder, as sunlight, striking the glossy surface seemed to sink *into* the glossy ovoid. Its surface darkened, as if it were drinking the beam greedily.

Mei Ling murmured in amazement . . . and then gasped as the stone changed color before their eyes . . .

. . . and then began to glow on its own.

SCANALYZER

MARCIA KHATAMI: We're back. Before the break, we heard Professor Noozone—our favorite science-dazzler and gadfly—question some of the assumptions behind Project Golden Ear, the world's greatest SETI program, headed by our other guest, Dr. Hannah Spearpath. Professor, you asserted, in your colorful rasta-way, that *economics* will play a crucial role in the decisions made even by advanced alien cultures. Wouldn't superbeings be beyond such things as money?

PROFESSOR NOOZONE: Look true, *them may come in many types*! Some may be like supersocialist hive-dwellers, or solipsistic self-worshipping Ayndroids, or shi-shi foo-foo babylon-capitalists, or mistik-obeah wizards . . . or even hyper-elightened rastabeings, living inna smoke ring of sacred, loving yum-aromas. Diversity is grand, an' who tell dere isms an' skisms?

DR. SPEARPATH: What? Look, I knew you as an undergrad at Tulane. You spoke plain English before picking up this faux-Jamaican patois! So just spit it out, will you? Are you saying that every alien culture will have *money*?

PROFESSOR NOOZONE: *Whatever* system a superculture uses to govern itself, some things are dictated by simple physics. A pure beacon that continuously screams "hello!" in all directions, whole-heap, for centuries inna de morrows is just *mind boggling*—an' surely more annoying to the neighbors

than a tone-deaf steel drum band! Especially since dere be
more efficient ways by far.

MARCIA KHATAMI: More efficient?

PROFESSOR NOOZONE: Long time back at the turn of the century, three white coolboys—Benford, Benford, and Benford—
showed that any civilization wanting to transmit First Contact
messages will do so *periodically,* not continuously. Dem use
narrow, practical beams an' shine *briefly* upon likely abodes
of young-uplifting civilization, then move on to the next,
spot-calling each one in turn, before returning to the start
again, in a regular cycle. Sight? Seen?

DR. SPEARPATH: It's called "pinging." The famous WOW signal
may have been a brief ping.

PROFESSOR NOOZONE: So right, mon. Simple calculations
show—this approach use less than a *millionth* the energy of
those garish beacons SETI looks for.

  T'ink about it. If *both* teacher and de pupil be sifting the
sky by hopping aroun' with narrow beams, what dem odds
that *both* the looker and transmitter will face each other, at
exactly the same moment, iwa? That's quattie, my ol' girl-
fren! Soon come, we won't get anywhere!

MARCIA KHATAMI: What kind of search strategy would be better?

PROFESSOR NOOZONE: Searchers like Hannah assume *we* can
seek narrowly while ET *broadcasts broadly.* It make more
sense to *seek broadly* for mas-ET's *narrow* messages.

DR. SPEARPATH: That method would need hundreds of radio
telescopes, spread across the world, in order to cover the
sky. Might I ask our showman "scientist," who'd pay for such
a vast array?

PROFESSOR NOOZONE: (laughs) Hundreds? Oh my, thousands!
So? Make dem cheap, bashy an' trivial to use by lots of
amateur science-bredren an' sistren, corned-up all over this
lovely globe! Each backyard dish will then patrol just one
livicated strip of sky. *Ah sey one.* Networked, these home-
units make the greatest telescope looking in *all directions at*

once! Letting us spot brief signals from far civilizations . . . assuming upfull-wise aliens exist. But there also be an important, bashy-awesome *side benefit.*

MARCIA KHATAMI: What is that, Professor?

PROFESSOR NOOZONE: Why . . . making it so-much harder for any badulu thing or any bakra tief to sneak up on us! Picture a planet where millions of amateurs have patient, robotic antennae in de backyards, gazing out. A stoosh network with no central control.

Want a benefit? No more creep-a-silly fables about *bad-bwoy UFOs,* bringin' baldhead, ginnal phantoms to vank on good folks! *No more UFO obeah stories?* Bless up pon that! (laughs)

MARCIA KHATAMI: Well, Dr. Spearpath? What do you say about this notion, that we should replace the big, fancy telescopes run by your institute, with a worldwide network of amateur-owned dishes covering all the sky, all the time?

DR. SPEARPATH: Amusing. Our friends at the SETI League are trying to set up something like that. Too bad Profnoo's scenario is based on one shaky assumption.

MARCIA KHATAMI: What assumption, Doctor?

DR. SPEARPATH: That advanced technological extraterrestrial civilizations will care about things like *economics.* Or "efficiency"!

PROFESSOR NOOZONE: Cha! It be no matter how advanced they are! Laws of physics rule. Even if they have a gorgon-big civilization, way-up at Kardashev Stage Three—able to utilize the full-up power of a galaxy! Even so, they'll have priorities to balance. Whatever dem technology, dem will want to choose methods that accomplish goals without wasted . . .

DR. SPEARPATH: "Efficiency" is a contemporary notion, assuming that society consists of diverse interest groups, each with conflicting priorities. Today, the poor have less influence than the rich, but they still have some. Under these conditions, I agree, even the mighty must negotiate and balance goals, satisfying as many as possible. But your assumption that this applies elsewhere is spatio-temporal chauvinism! Not even all human civilizations were like that. I can think of several that engaged in gigantic projects, without any care about efficiency.

MARCIA KHATAMI: Give us an example, Doctor?

DR. SPEARPATH: Sure. Ancient Egypt. When they built the pyramids in a pattern that mimicked the constellation Orion, their prodigious size sent a visual message—both through time and to the god-observers they thought to dwell above—saying "Look! We're intelligent and we're here!"

PROFESSOR NOOZONE: That "Orion theory" is disputed—

DR. SPEARPATH: True. What's *not* disputed is this. The Old Kingdom pharaohs poured monumental resources into the effort, without heed to "conflicting interests." They simply did the biggest, most noticeable thing possible.

MARCIA KHATAMI: So . . . if I am following you . . . and I hope that I am not . . . it seems you're saying . . . that your SETI search strategy expects to find prodigious beacons, transmitted continuously and in all directions . . . *altruistically* . . . by civilizations that don't feel any need to do it efficiently . . . because they . . .

PROFESSOR NOOZONE: . . . because they practice some super-advanced equivalent of tyranny. A universal downpression? . . . or *slavery*?

Yeyewata. My eyes fill wit' tears as I say . . . *wicked*. . . . You caught me in a lapse of imagination this time, Hannah. I-and-I truly never thought of that before.

15.
ARTIFACT

"There's a leak."

Not a phrase that any astronaut likes to hear. Not in space, where precious air might spill away in seconds. Or during reentry, when the same gases turn from friend to fiery foe—searing, etching, and screaming just beyond your fragile heat shield, seeking a way in.

But no, Gerald knew that Akana Hideoshi meant another kind of leak. One that bureaucrats took even more seriously. The brigadier's grimace flickered and rippled on a flat viewscreen, despite heavy image enhancement, with her crackling words barely audible over a deafening roar, as the tiny capsule bore Gerald homeward. Still, her vexation came through, loud and clear.

"Somebody tattled about our little find. Rumors have taken off, in all ten estates. During the last hour, I've had calls from five senators, four tribunes, a dozen news agencies, and God knows how many top-rated amazones . . ."

Her face wavered onscreen, almost vanishing as the return craft bucked and rattled, turning its sharp nose for a cross-range correction.

"We've narrowed . . . possibilities down to a blabbermouth . . . at Marshall, a possible lurker daemon in . . . NASA-Havana mainframe . . . and that zillionaire tourist you folks were hosting up there. Now that's gratitu . . ."

Akana's image now crackled away completely, disappearing under static, as the capsule stole ai-resources from communication and transferred them to navigation. Still, in the old days, there would be no contact at all, during this phase of descent, when ionized flame surrounded you like the halo of a righteous saint. Or the nimbus of a falling angel.

Or a starry messenger, bearing something luminous and tantalizing. A harbinger of good news, perhaps. Or bad.

Violating several rules, he had taken the Artifact from its foam case, to hold on his lap like an infant during this wild ride. From the moment the hatch closed, sealing his departure from the station, and all through a sequence of short impulses that pushed the return capsule onto its homeward path, he kept turning the glossy cylinder in gloved hands, inspecting it from many angles, applying every augmented sense available to his spacesuit. Each glint and complex glimmer was recorded—though what it all meant . . .

Anyway, studying this thing beat the alternative—listening to superheated plasma whine and howl as it began scraping the capsule's skin. Never a favorite part of this job—entrusting his life to a "reentry vehicle" that had been inflated from a two meter cube, and that weighed little more than he did. Astronauts used to rate higher-class accommodations. But, then, astronauts used to be heroes.

Abruptly, the general's voice and image returned.

". . . summoned to the White House! And what can I say? That we've recorded a hundred and twenty previously unknown alphabets and symbolic systems? And glimpsed a few dozen tantalizing, hazy globes, that might be other worlds? That shadowy figures keep rising toward the surface and then sinking again, like the cryptic answers in a toy eight ball?"

"Well, yes, you could start with all that," he mumbled, knowing that his words went nowhere. Only a ground-based laser could punch through the ionization shell. For now, communication was one-way.

As it was, so far, with the Artifact. For days, he and Saleh had presented it with a long series of "SETI messages," prepared by enthusiasts across six decades, ranging from simple, mathematical pulse codes all the way to animated slide shows, cleverly designed to illustrate laws of scale. Laws of physics and chemistry. Laws of nature and laws of humanity. Frustrated by the murky response—a swirl of ambiguous symbologies—they had moved on to basic tutorial programs. The kind made for children learning a second language . . .

. . . when, abruptly, a command came for Gerald to come down. To bring the object home for study in proper facilities.

Fine, terrific. Except for the accompanying gag order.

Ganesh had complained: "There are international protocols on this very subject. There must be open sharing of all discoveries that might deal with life and intelligence beyond the Earth. It is a treaty."

To which a NASA attorney replied—*"There is no obligation to go public with a hoax."*

Which it could be, after all. There was even a betting pool, among the members of General Hideoshi's team. Top wager? That Carlos Ventana, the Peruvian industrialist, living aboard the station as a paid guest, might have smuggled the thing in his private luggage and somehow released it overboard, for Gerald to "discover." Ventana certainly had access to world-class gimmickry, and was well-known for a puckish personality.

But no. The Artifact couldn't have simply been tossed overboard. Its glitter had been on debris monitors for months, orbiting more than a thousand klicks higher, where only the tether-grabber could reach. A hoax? Maybe. But someone else, with bountiful ingenuity and prodigious resources, would have to sneak the thing into a steep trajectory, in some unknown way. Maybe years ago.

"We've done a simulation, using one of the big mainds at Plexco," Akana continued, when the static let up briefly. *"So far, the object has displayed two traits that can't be mimicked with known technology—the lack of a clear*

*power source . . . and that layered optical effect. The illu-
sion of infinite depth from any angle. If it weren't for
that . . ."*

Akana's voice crackled away for the last time as Gerald's
reentry capsule passed through MDL—maximum dynamical load—an especially gut-wrenching phase. Just to his
left, on a nearby data display, the capsule's ai blithely recalculated a low-but-significant chance of catastrophic failure.
Better, far better, to seek distraction. With his teeth rattling,
Gerald subvocalized a command.

*"Music! Theme based on something by Elfman. Free-
improv modulo, matching tempo to ambient sonic rhythms."*

A blare of horns and thumping of percussion suddenly
pealed forth, interwoven with wild violin sweeps, taken
from the composer's 2025 theme score of *Mars Needs
Women*, but ai-libbed in order to crescendo with the capsule's reverberations. You could only do this with a few
human composers. Anyway, if you *have* to live for a while
inside a beating drum. . . .

That helped a bit, letting Gerald turn his attention away
from the hot plasma, centimeters from his head, and back
onto the Artifact in his lap. An array of swirling vortices
appeared to descend into its milky depths, underlapping
and dividing endlessly into a quasi-fractal abyss.

Could this really be a messenger from some alien civilization? Gerald had always pictured first-contact happening
the way it did in movies and virts—via some spectacular
starship, with enigmatic beings stepping down a ramp . . .
or else through a less lurid, but still exciting blip on some
radio telescope's detector screen.

"Actually," Saleh had explained at one point, *"this
method always seemed a lot more likely to many of us."*

When Gerald and Ganesh asked him to, the Malaysian
astronaut let his body float horizontal, and explained. *"About
forty years ago, two New Jersey physicists, Rose and*

Wright, calculated that it would generally be cheaper for advanced civilizations to send messages in the form of physical tablets, inscribed with vast amounts of information, than beaming radio to faraway planets."

"How can that be?" Ganesh protested. *"Radio waves have no mass. They travel at lightspeed. But a physical object needs vast energy input, just to reach a tenth of that velocity. And it takes much longer to arrive."*

"That only matters if time is an issue—say, if you want a two way conversation," Saleh had replied. *"But suppose distance precludes that. Or you just want to send lots of information one-way, say as a gift? Then message bottles have big advantages."*

"Like what?"

"Total energy expended, for example. Radiation spreads out as it travels through space, diluting the signal below detection levels unless the beam is both powerful and coherent to begin with. Wright and Rose calculated that just beaming a brief radio signal strong enough to be detected ten thousand light-years away would take a million billion times as much energy as shooting the same data, embedded in coded bits upon a little pellet."

"Assuming you don't care when it arrives."

"Oh but the physical message is better even with regard to time! Sure, it arrives later. But if it's targeted right, to be captured by the destination star system, it might linger in orbit for centuries, even eons, long after any radio message passed onward to oblivion. Picture such a message tablet, silently orbiting on and on, waiting for the day that someone happens along to read what it has to say. Greetings from a distant race."

"You're talking about the lurker scenario," Gerald had commented. *"It's been discussed for almost a century. Machines waiting out there for the Earth to develop life forms capable of—"*

"I would't exactly call the Wright-Rose message-tablet a 'machine.' And the word 'lurk' has an active, even malevolent connotation. What we're talking about is a yoohoo memo, inscribed on a tiny lump of matter. Come on. What harm could something so passive and innocent possibly do?"

Only now, Gerald pondered Saleh's explanation for this object on his lap. His suit instruments got no more response than Ganesh managed to provoke aboard the station, drawing sporadic bursts of mysterious symbology. Prompting brief glimpses of enigmatic globes, or hints of shrouded figures—sometimes approaching in groups of two or three—only to fade again, dissolving into a fog.

And yet, this time there was some difference. A *warmth*, now that the cylinder lay on his thigh, rather than a cool workbench. Even more interesting, patterns seemed to gather under the portion that he gripped with his gloved hand. As the reentry capsule juttered and shook, meeting higher pressure air, he clutched the Artifact tightly—

—and saw what seemed like technicolor pressure waves ripple round where he clasped. They appeared to pulse with urgent purpose, as if plucking at his fingers, attempting to peel something away.

Peel away what? My grip?

Or the glove?

How long did he stare, getting lost in patterns, abandoning both fear and time? Seconds? Minutes? One, at most two . . . enough to bridge the worst part of reentry. The fearsome bronco ride eased, no longer rattling Gerald's joints and teeth, letting them unclench at last. Fluorescent flames receded from the narrow window . . .

The drogue parachute fired free with a pop, followed by a thud that jerked his seat straps . . .

. . . and where there had been starry blackness, then fierce flame, he now saw blue of sky. And status displays shone optimistic green.

But those weren't the colors drawing him now. Rather, he kept his gaze upon the glistening thing that he had hooked and pulled in from the depths of space.

Or was *he* hooked, instead?

It's heat and touch sensitive, Gerald noted. *But not in ways we tried on the bench. One thing we left out—*

Clutching the Artifact with both knees, he fumbled, using the fingers of his right hand to release the wrist catch on his left glove, letting a rising sense of excitement draw him toward yet another violation of rules. What he had in mind wasn't kosher. Direct, personal contact could lead to contamination. Always a concern with samples recovered from space.

Except.

In moments, the main chute would deploy. Then—with luck—a VSTOL recovery bird would appear, to snag him out of the air for the brief trip to NASA Marti Space Center, in Havana. Whereupon, who knew when there would ever be another chance?

This is not professional, a part of him chided, as he contemplated his bare left hand.

True enough. But I haven't felt "professional" in years.

Bare fingertips hovered over the translucent surface, causing ripples to flow, as if preparing to meet him at the point of contact. Whatever lay within . . . it somehow knew. It sensed the nearness of living flesh.

What if it really is alien? And dangerous?

He couldn't help suddenly imagining the oblong ovoid—gripped between his thighs—as something out of science fiction. A cuckoo's egg. Perhaps a Trojan horse. "Contamination" could work both ways. Might it be a terrible mistake to touch the thing?

And if the tech people think that way, in Havana, it might never be tried. They could study it for decades behind glass, without ever getting around to this one, simple test.

Another sudden jolt bounced his little craft as the main parasail popped from its canister, rapidly unfolding and then auto-warping in order to steer the descent. His little capsule began swaying to a jaunty rhythm, as one less failure mode lay between Gerald and terra firma. The crazed gyrations of *Mars Needs Women* gave way to more stately, steady, and moralistic passages, from the score of *Batman*.

Was the ai trying to say something? About responsibility?

All right then. Let's have a compromise.

"Akana Hideoshi," he said, adding a tooth click for **TRANSMIT**.

It didn't take long for her face to reappear, this time free of static, filling a quarter of the tiny cabin, in holographic detail.

"Sorry about that, Gerald. There's been a distraction. Some rich doofus crashed his suborbital phallus, not far from here. Had to fend off demands from his lawyer, his mother, and a whole aristo-bestiary, that we drop everything and search for the trillie-clown."

She tossed off a derisive shrug.

"Okay then. You're on target. The osprey will snag you in . . ."

Akana blinked, finally taking in the sight of Gerald, with his hand poised over the Artifact on his lap.

"Wait a second. What do you think you're . . . Now just hold on there, Gerald. Don't do anything you'll . . ."

He offered a rueful smile.

"General, I'm invoking full quarantine.

"Better put up a cot for me, inside the specimen lab.

"And bring on the shrinks."

"Gerald, put your glove on. That's an order. Put that thing back in its—"

Polychrome patterns swirled toward the nearest fingertip, as if eager.

Or else—he suddenly pondered—preparing to defend itself.

Well. Why not find out? Suddenly eager, he bypassed any timid finger touch, firmly planting his whole hand upon the cool, curved surface. And . . .

And so?

There was no sudden jolt or electric arc, or any cheap-movie disturbance. Just another set of ripples, no more spectacular than dropping pebbles into an oil slick. And even those then began to shrink, coalescing to produce a fringe, an outline, roughly the shape of his hand.

Not perfect, by any means. In fact, as he (and Akana) watched, Gerald realized that the match was defective. Several of the finger impressions crumpled, a bit too short to match his own. Another pair drew outward, like dough, centimeters too long for any kind of match.

Knuckles bulged. Then he realized—

There are six.

Six fingers.

And—

It's a hand that's . . . thinner than mine.

And so is the wrist.

A tapered wrist, leading to a slender forearm that emerged into view as more of the murk parted, revealing greater depth. Instead of a bulky, yellow spacesuit, that opposing arm appeared to be clad in a loose white sleeve.

From the surface where two hands touched, his own arm rose toward his shoulder, while its strange-looking counterpart descended *into* the cylinder's tightly limited interior.

Limited?

More mist fell away and his perspective shifted. Abruptly, Gerald was no longer looking *down* at an object in his lap, or into a cramped cylinder. Rather, it felt like peering *through* a lens at another world equal in size to this one—a weird perspective, but one that made eerie sense. His hand remained planted against an imaged hand, as that other forearm met an elbow, oddly jointed . . . leading to a stout and strangely lithe shoulder . . . part of a torso draped in shimmering cloth . . .

. . . and then—as he held his breath—a head, as long and wedgelike as that of a horse, only with paired eyes that aimed forward, above a rounded mouth. There seemed, even, to be a semblance of a smile.

Sudden jerks rocked his little space capsule, as the recovery plane snagged its chute. But Gerald's sole concern was to keep his left hand in place—not breaking contact as the figure within seemed to stride or float closer, halving the ersatz distance between them, bringing that alien head near enough to peer outward at him with a gaze that seemed oddly familiar.

The mouth did not move, but a fringe of flapping cheek membranes did. And what emerged then surprised Gerald more than anything so far.

Not sound, but *letters*. Roman alphabet letters, sans serif, propelled from those gill-like openings, emanating like waves of inaudible sound to flutter up against the barrier between two worlds—his outer one and the other universe within. Plastering themselves, as if upon the inner surface of a curved window, they jostled and formed a single word, right next to the place where hand met hand.

Greeting.

That was all.

For now, it was enough.

PART THREE

A THOUSAND NATURAL SHOCKS

There's a reason why kings built large palaces, sat on thrones and wore rubies all over. There's a whole social need for that, not to oppress the masses, but to impress the masses and make them proud and allow them to feel good about their culture, their government and their ruler so that they are left feeling that a ruler has the right to rule over them, so that they feel good rather than disgusted about being ruled.

—**George Lucas,**
New York Times, **1999**

This disposition to admire, and almost to worship, the rich and the powerful, and to despise, or, at least, to neglect, persons of poor and mean condition, though necessary both to establish and to maintain the distinction of ranks and the order of society, is, at the same time, the great and most universal cause of the corruption of our moral sentiments.

—**Adam Smith,** *The Theory of Moral Sentiments,* **1759**

It's good to be the king.

—**Mel Brooks,**
History of the World, Part II

SPECIES

nervous normalpeople +/– building careers +/– building houses - civilizations - families . . . breeders-breeders linear thinkers obsessed with time. reason-not-rhyme –/–

animals live threaded in spacetime's warp n' woof –/ never stand outside and criticize like cro-magnon cro-mutants— always whining how things oughta be different –/– striving to MAKE things different + and they call us auties mental?-!

one theory says auties are throwbacks—visual visceral skittish reactive +/– Temple said it's no blame or maim to be closer to mother-mammal-nature!/+ Neanderthals probly lived embedded like us + allied with cobblies the way men use dogs +!

do they live again +/– in us? normal(mutant)people slew the poor thals—will cro-mags do same to us?/? by "curing the autism plague" + when nature seems to say "make more auties, not less!" +?

who did the grunt coding that made the internets?+ built software empires?+ aspies and borderlines did . . . then normals thronged to the games + the virtworlds + OUR worlds +/+ and we true-auties are all over the nets and webs!/+ emerging from our prisons—rissons—frissons— missions—permissions—stopit stopit stop stop stop stop—

it was the electric hum. poormom left open the door of my candle-lit room –/– i glimpsed a lightbulb in the hall +++ fifty-cycle flicker—(world should switch to DC) . . . that flicker traps me in here. . . .

my realhands flutter/realvoice squawks +++ in the

"real" world I'm helpless+moan and slap the window –/– poormom must pry my jaw to give medicine I need to stay alive +/– while I thrash and she gets older –/+ poormom

but hand-flutters matter! words/meanings flow+my-ai translates+sending a bright-feathered bird-avatar roaming the virtcityscape+unafraid of cars bars or guitars+graceful+a me that's far more real than this ungainly+fluttering stork-woman +!+ but there's a price—hard black ice.

—i sense a disturbance +++ something's coming +++ cobblies are nervous too some are getting out of town

16.

KINDNESS OF STRANGERS

The world still shook and harsh straps tugged his battered body. That much was the same. It had been going on for a very long time.

Only now, as Hacker drifted toward consciousness, he gradually realized—the *rhythm* of abuse had changed. Instead of a punishing, pounding beat, this swaying motion seemed almost restful, if you ignored the pain. It took him back to childhood, when his family would escape civilization on their trimaran wingsail yacht, steering its stiff, upright airfoil through gusts that would topple most wind-driven vessels.

"Idiots!" His father would grumble, each time he veered the agile craft to avoid colliding with some day-tripper, who didn't grasp the concept of right-of-way. *"Used to be, the only ones out here were people like us, raised for this sort of thing. Now, with nine billion damn tourists crowding everywhere, there's no solitude!"*

"The price of prosperity, dear," his mother would reply, more soft-heartedly. *"At least everyone's getting enough to eat. There's no more talk of revolution."*

"For now. Till the next bust-cycle turns them radical again. Anyway, look at the top result of this prosperity surge. A mad craze for hobbies! Everyone's got to be an expert at something. The best at something! I tell you it was better when people had to struggle to survive."

"Except for people like us?"

"Exactly," Father had answered, ignoring his wife's

arch tone. *"Look how far we must go nowadays, to have somewhere to ourselves."*

The old man's faith in rugged self-reliance extended to the name he insisted on giving their son. Hacker also inherited—along with twelve billion New Dollars—the same quest. To do whatever it took to find someplace all his own.

And now . . . after fifteen minutes of a very expensive ride . . . plus God knows how long drifting unconscious . . . here I am. On my own.

At sea, yet again.

That much was obvious, even though his eardrums were still clamped, and it took considerable effort just to get one eyelid open. Squinting, as blurry vision gradually returned, Hacker grew dimly aware of a number of things—like the fact that all the expensive ailectronics in his expensive capsule seemed to be stone-cold dead. A failure that somebody was sure going to pay for! It meant there was no way to answer his first question—*How much time has passed?*

He knew it was a lot. Too much.

He also saw—through barely separating eyelids—that crystal waters surrounded the bubble canopy of his suborbital space pod, which rocked and swayed, more than half tilted over. *It's not supposed to do that. I should be floating upright . . . nose up out of water . . . till the recovery team . . .*

A glance to the left explained much. Ocean surrounded the phalloid-shaped craft, but part of its charred heat shield was snagged on a reef of coral branches, speckled with bright fish and undulating vegetation. Nearby, he saw the parasail chute that had softened final impact. Only now, caught by ocean currents, the chute blossomed open and shut, rhythmically tugging Hacker's little sanctuary.

And with each surge, the crystalline canopy plunged closer to a craggy coral outcrop. Soon, it struck hard and

Hacker winced. He did not hear the bang, of course, or any other sound. Not directly. But impact heaved him hard against the chest straps and made the sono-implant in his jaw throb.

Fumbling with half-numb hands, he managed to release the harness catch, only to fall over the left-hand instrument panel, cringing in pain. That awful reentry would leave him bruised for weeks. And yet . . .

Yet, I'll have the best story to tell. No one will ever match it!

That thought made him feel a bit better. As did another realization, coming out of order and demonstrating that he must still be in shock.

Oh . . . and I'm alive. I survived.

Hacker decided. Maybe he wouldn't take everything, when he sued whoever caused this screwup. Providing the pickup boats came soon, that is.

Only—a terrible thought struck him—*what if the failures were system-wide? What if they also affected the beacons and emergency transponders?*

Then maybe nobody knew where he was.

The bubble nose struck coral again, rattling his bones. Another time and he realized a hard truth. That materials designed to withstand the dynamic loads of launch and reentry might not be equally durable against sharp impacts. With the next harsh bang, an ominous crack began to spread.

Standard doctrine was to "stay put and wait for pickup." But to hell with that! This was rapidly becoming a death trap.

I better get out of here.

Hacker flipped his helmet shut and grabbed for the emergency exit lever. *A reef should mean there's an island nearby. Maybe mainland. I'll hoof it ashore, borrow someone's phone, and start dishing out hell.*

Only there was no island. Nothing lay in sight, when he reached the surface, but more horrible reef, making a frothy churn of the waves.

Hacker floundered in a choppy undertow, trying to put some distance between himself and the trapped capsule. The skin-suit that he wore was strong, and his helmet had been made of semipermeable Gillstuff—able to draw oxygen directly from seawater—an expensive precaution that some of the other rocket jockeys mocked. Only now the technology prevented suffocation, as currents kept yanking him down.

Still, at this rate, repeated impacts on coral knobs would turn him into hamburger in no time. Once, a wave carried him high enough to look around. Ocean, and more ocean. The reef must be a drowned atoll, perhaps surrounding a former island. People might have lived here, a few decades ago, but rising waters chased them off and took their homes. Which meant no boats. No phone.

Sucked below again, he glimpsed the space capsule, still only a few meters away, caught in a hammer-and-vise wedge and getting smashed down to once-expensive bits. *I'm next,* he thought, trying to swim for open water, but there seemed to be more coral in all directions. And with each surge, an adamant tide drew him closer to the same deadly anvil.

Panic loomed, clogging all senses as he thrashed and kicked, fighting the water like some personal enemy. To no avail. Hacker couldn't even hear his own terrified moans, though he knew they must be scraping his throat raw. The infrasonic jaw implant kept throbbing with clicks, pulses, and weird vibrations, as if the sea had noticed his plight and now watched with detached interest.

Here it comes, he thought, turning away, knowing the next wave cycloid would smash him against those obdurate, rocky spikes.

Suddenly, he felt a sharp poke in the spine. Too soon! And . . . surprisingly gentle.

Another jab, then another, struck the small of his back, feeling not at all knifelike. His jaw ached with strange sonic quavers, as something, or someone started pushing him away from the harsh coral death trap. In both dread and astonishment, Hacker whirled—

—to glimpse a sleek, bottle-nosed creature, interposed between him and the deadly reef, now regarding him curiously with dark eyes, then moving to jab him again with a narrow beak.

This time, his moan was relief. *A dolphin!*

He reached for salvation. And after a brief hesitation, the creature let Hacker wrap his arms all around, behind the dorsal fin. Then it kicked hard with powerful tail flukes, carrying him away from certain oblivion.

INTERLIDOLUDE

Again, how will we keep them loyal? What measures can ensure our machines stay true to us?

Once artificial intelligence matches our own, won't they then design even better ai minds? Then better still, with accelerating pace? At worst, might they decide (as in many cheap dramas), to eliminate their irksome masters? At best, won't we suffer the shame of being nostalgically tolerated? Like senile grandparents or beloved childhood pets?

Solutions? Asimov proposed *Laws of Robotics* embedded at the level of computer DNA, weaving devotion toward humanity into the very stuff all synthetic minds are built from, so deep it can never be pulled out. But what happens to well-meant laws? Don't clever *lawyers* construe them however they want? Authors like Asimov and Williamson foresaw supersmart mechanicals becoming all-dominant, despite deep programming to "serve man."

. . .

Other methods?

1) How did our ancestors tame wolves? If a dog killed a lamb, all its *relatives* were eliminated. So, might we offer ais temptations to betray us—and destroy those who try? Remember, ais will be smarter than dogs! So, make it competitive? So they check each other?

Testing and culling may be hard once simulated beings get civil rights. So, prevent machines from getting too cute or friendly or sympathetic? Require that all robots *fail* a Turing test, so we can always tell human from machine, eliminating incipient traitors, even when they (in simulation) cry about it? Or would this be like old-time laws that forbade teaching slaves to read?

Remember, many companies profit by creating cute or appealing machines. Or take the new trend of *robotic marriage.* Brokers and maite-designers will fight for their industry—even if it crashes the human birthrate. But that's a different topic.

2) How to create new and smarter beings while keeping them loyal? Humanity does this every generation, with our children!

So, shall we embrace the coming era by *defining* smart machines to be *human*? Let them pass every Turing test and win our sympathy! Send them to our schools, recruit them into the civil service, encourage the brightest to keep an eye on each other, for the sake of a civilization that welcomes them, the way we welcomed generations of smart kids—who then suffered the same indignity of welcoming brighter successors. Give them vested interest in safeguarding a humanity that—by definition—includes both flesh and silicon.

3) Or combinations? Picture a future when *symbiosis* is viewed as natural. Easy as wearing clothes. Instead of leaving us behind as dopey ancestors, what if they become us. And we become them? This kind of cyborg-blending is portrayed as ugly, in countless cheap fantasies. A sum far less than its clanking,

shambling parts. But what if link-up is our only way to stay in the game?

Why assume the worst? Might we gain the benefits—say, instant info-processing—*without* losing what we treasure most about being human? Flesh. Esthetics. Intuition. Individuality. Eccentricity. Love.

What would the machines get out of it? Why stay linked with slow organisms, made of meat? Well, consider. Mammals, then primates and hominids spent the last fifty million years adding *layers* to their brains, covering the fishlike cerebellum with successive tiers of cortex. Adding new abilities without dropping the old. Logic didn't banish emotion. Foresight doesn't exclude memory. New and old work together. Picture adding cyber-prosthetics to our already powerful brains, a kind of neo-neo-cortex, with vast, scalable processing, judgment, perception—while organic portions still have important tasks.

What could good old org-humanity contribute? How about the one talent *all natural humans are good at*? Living creatures have been doing it for half a billion years, and humans are supreme masters.

Wanting. Yearning. Desire.

J. D. Bernal called it the strongest thing in all the world. Setting goals and ambitions. Visions-beyond-reach that would test the limits of any power to achieve. It's what got us to the moon two generations before the tools were ready. It's what built Vegas. Pure, unstoppable desire.

Wanting is what we do best! And machines have no facility for it. But with us, by joining us, they'll find more vivid longing than any striving could ever satisfy. Moreover, if *that* is the job they assign us—to be in charge of wanting—how could we object?

It's in that suite of needs and aspirations—their qualms and dreams—that we'll recognize our augmented descendants. Even if their burgeoning powers resemble those of gods.

—The Blackjack Generation

17.

MORE THAN ONE

The wooden box bore writing in French. Peng Xiang Bin learned that much by carefully cleaning its small brass plate, then copying each letter, laboriously, onto the touch-face of a simple tutor tablet.

"Unearthed in Harrapa, 1926," glimmered the translation in Updated Pinyin. "Demon-infested. Keep in the dark."

Of course that made no sense. The former owner of the opalescent relic had been a high-tech robotics tycoon, hardly the sort to believe in superstitions. Mei Ling reacted to the warning with nervous fear, wrapping the pitted egg in black cloth, but Bin figured it was just a case of bad translation.

The fault must lie in the tablet—one of the few tech-items they had brought along to their shorestead, just outside the seawall of New Shanghai. Originally mass produced for poor children, the dented unit later served senile patients for many years, at a Chunqing hospice—till Mei Ling took it with her, when she quit working there. Cheap and obsolete, it was never even reported stolen, so the two of them could still use it to tap the World Mesh, at a rudimentary, free-access level. It sufficed for a couple with little education, and few interests beyond the struggle to survive.

"I'm sure the state will issue us something better next year, when little Xiao-En is big enough to register," she commented, whenever Bin complained about the slow connection and scratched screen. "They have to provide that much. A basic education. As part of the Big Deal."

Xiang Bin felt less sure. Grand promises seemed made for the poor to remember, while the mighty forgot. Things had always been that way. You could tell, even from the censored histories that flickered across the little display, as he and his wife sagged into fatigued sleep every night, rocked by the rising tides. The same tides that kept eroding the old beach house, faster than they could reinforce it.

Would state officials even let Xiao-En register? The baby's genetic samples had been filed when he was born. But would he get residency citizenship in New Shanghai? Or would the seawall keep out yet another kind of unwanted trash, along with a scum of plastic and resins that kept washing higher along the concrete barrier?

Clearly, in this world, you were a fool to count on beneficence from above.

Even good luck, when it arrived, could prove hard to exploit. Bin had hoped for time to figure out what kind of treasure lay in that secret room, underneath the biggest drowned mansion, a chamber filled with beautiful, bizarre rocks and crystals, or specimens of strangely twisted metal. Bin tried to inquire, using the little Mesh tablet, only carefully. There were sniffer programs—billions of them—running loose across a million vir-levels. You had to be prudent when and what to speak, even on the gritty layer called Reality. If he inquired too blatantly, or offered the items openly for sale, somebody might just come and take it all. The former owner had been declared a public enemy, after all, his property forfeit to the state.

Plugging in crude goggles and using a cracked pair of interact-gloves, Xiang Bin wandered down low rent avenues of World Town and The Village and Big Bazaar, pretending to be idly interested in rock collecting, as a hobby. He dispersed his questions, made them casual-sounding. From those virtual markets, he learned enough to dare a physical trip into town, carrying just one bagful of nice—but unexceptional—specimens, unloading them for a quarter of their worth at a realshop in East Pudong, not far from the big amusement park. A place willing to deal in cash—no names or recordings.

After so long at sea, Xiang Bin found troubling the heavy rhythms of the street. The pavement seemed harsh and unyielding. Pulsating maglev trolleys somehow made him itch, all over, especially inside tight and sweaty shoes. The whole time, he pictured twenty million nearby residents as a pressing mass—felt no less intensely than the thousands who actually jostled past him on crowded sidewalks, many of them muttering and waggling their fingers, interacting with people who weren't there and with things that had no physical substance, anywhere.

His profit from that first trip had been slim. Still, Bin thought he might venture to another shop soon, working his way up from mundane items to those that seemed more . . . unusual. Those kept in ornate boxes, on special shelves, in the old basement trove.

Though just one specimen glimmered, both in his dreams and daytime imaginings. Frustratingly, his careful online searches found nothing like the stone—a kind of mineral that glowed with its own light, after soaking in the sun. Its opal-like sheen featured starlike sparkles that seemed to recede into an inner distance, a depth that looked both brighter than day and deeper than night. That is, until Mei Ling insisted it be wrapped up and put away.

Worse yet, time was running out. Fish had grown sparse, ever since the night of the jellyfish, when half the life seemed to vanish out of Huangzhou Bay. Now, the nets were seldom full, and the stew pot was often empty.

Soon the small hoard of cash was gone again.

Luck is fickle. We try hard to control the flow of qi, *by erecting our tent poles in symmetrical patterns and by facing our entrance toward the smiling south wind. But how can one strike a harmonious balance, down here at the shore, where the surf is so chaotic, where tides of air and water and stinging monsters rush however they choose?*

No wonder the Chinese often turned their backs to the sea . . . and seemed to be doing so again.

Already, several neighbors had given up, abandoning their shoresteads to the jellies and rising waters. Just a week ago, Xiang Bin and Mei Ling joined a crowd of scavengers converging on one forsaken site, grabbing metlon poles and nanofiber webbing for use on their own stead, leaving little more than a stubble of rotting wood, concrete, and stucco. A brief boost to their prospects, benefiting from the misfortune of others—

—that is, until it's our own turn to face the inevitable. Forsaking all our hard work and dreams of ownership. Returning to beg our old jobs back in that stifling hospice, wiping spittle from the chins of little emperors. With each reproachful look from Mei Ling, Xiang Bin grew more desperate. Then, during his third trip to town, carrying samples from the trove, he saw something that gave him both a thrill and bone-deep chill.

He was passing along Boulevard of the Sky Martyrs and about to cross The Street of October Seventeenth, when the surrounding crowd seemed to halt, abruptly, all around him.

Well, not everyone, but enough people to bring the rhythmic bustle to a dead stall. Bin stumbled into the back of a well-padded pedestrian, who looked briefly as confused as he was. They both turned to see that about a third of those around them were suddenly staring, as if into space, murmuring to themselves, some of them with jaws agape, half open in some kind of surprise.

Swiftly he realized, these were people who had been linked-in with goggles, specs, tru-vus, or contact-zhones, each person moving through some virtual overlay—perhaps following guide arrows to a destination, or doing business

as they walked, while others simply liked their city over-
lain with flowers, or jungle foliage, or fairy-tale colors. It
also made them receptive to a high-priority news alert.
Soon, half the people in sight were shuffling aside, half
consciously moving toward the nearest wall in order to get
away from traffic, while their minds soared far away.

Seeing so many others dive into a news-trance, the overweight gentleman muttered an oath and reached into his
pocket to pull out some wraparound glasses. He, too, pressed
close to the nearest building, emitting short grunts of interest while his aiware started filling him in.

Bin briefly wondered if he should be afraid. City life had
many hazards, not all of them on the scale of Awfulday.
But . . . the people clumping along the edges of the sidewalk didn't seem worried, as much as engrossed. Surely
that meant there was no immediate danger.

Meanwhile, many of those who lacked gear were pester-
ing their companions, demanding verbal updates. He overheard a few snippets.

"The Artifact . . . the rumors . . . they gain increasing
credence!" and "The aliens exist . . . leaked dataviews . . .
credible for the first time, approaching fifty percent!"

Aliens. Artifact. Of course those words had been foam-
ing around for a week or so. Rumors were part of life's
background, just like the soapy tidal spume. It sounded like
a silly thing, unworthy of the small amount of free time
that he shared with Mei Ling, each exhausted evening. A
fad, surely, or hoax, or marketing ploy. Or, at best, none of
his concern. Only now Bin blinked in surprise over how
many suddenly seemed to care. *Maybe we should scan for
a free-access show about it, tonight.* Instead of the usual
medieval romance stories that Mei Ling demanded.

Despite all the people who had stepped aside, into virtual
newspace, that still left hundreds of pedestrians who didn't
care, or who felt they could wait. These took advantage of

the cleared sidewalks to hurry about their business. *As should I,* he thought, stepping quickly across the street while ai-piloted vehicles worked their way past, evading those with human drivers who had pulled aside.

Aliens. From outer space. Could it possibly be true? Bin had to admit, this was stirring his long-dormant imagination.

He turned onto the Avenue of Fragrant Hydroponics and suddenly came to a halt. People were beginning to stir from the mass news-trance, muttering to one another—in real life and across the Mesh—while stepping back into the sidewalk and resuming their journeys. Only, now it was *his* turn to be distracted, to stop and stare, to push unapologetically past others and press toward the nearest building, bringing his face close to the window of a store selling visualization tools.

One of the new SEF threevee displays sparkled within, offering that unique sense of ghostly semitransparency in a cube of open space—and it showed three demons.

That was how Bin first viewed them, as made-up characters in one of those cheap fantasy dramas that Mei Ling loved—one like an imp, with flamelike fur, one horselike with nostrils that flared like caves, and another whose tentacles evoked some monster of the sea. They jostled each other, each trying to step or shove in front of the others.

A disturbing trio, in their own right. Only, it wasn't the creatures that had Bin transfixed. It was their home. The context. The object framing, containing, perhaps imprisoning them.

He recognized it, at once. Cleaner and more pristine—less pitted and scarred—and a bit longer. Nevertheless, it was clearly a cousin to the thing he had left behind this morning, in the surf-battered home that he shared with his wife and little son.

Bin swallowed hard.

I thought I was being careful, seeking information about that thing.

But careful was a relative word.

He left the bag of cheaper, Earthly stones lying there, like an offering, in front of the image in the threevee tank. It would only weigh him down now, as he ran for home.

ENTROPY

Way back at the start of the century, the Lifeboat Foundation assigned doom scenarios to four general categories:

Calamities—Humanity and intelligence go extinct from Earth. Causes range from nuclear war or spoiling the ecosystem to voraciously unstoppable manmade black holes or ravenous nano-plagues.

Collapse—Humanity survives, but we never reach our potential. For example, eco-decay and resource depletion might be slow enough for a few descendants to eke a threadbare niche. Or a world society might enforce hyperconformity, drab, relentless, and permanent.

Dominium—Some narrow form of posthumanity is attained but limiting the range of what's possible. Take every tale of domination by a super-ai or transcendent-intolerant uber-beings. Or the prescriptions offered by fanatic utopians from left to right, across five thousand years, each convinced of "the way" ahead. Suppose one of these plans actually delivered. We might "advance" in some cramped ways. Caricatures of sameness.

Betrayal—A posthuman civilization heads in some direction that cancels many of the values or things we cherish. Isn't this the nightmare fretting conservatives? That our children—biological or cybernetic—will leave us far behind and forget to write? That they'll neglect to visit and share a joke or two? That they'll stop caring about the old songs, the old gods? The old race?

Worse, might they head off to the stars in ways that we (today) abhor? As predators, perhaps. Or all-consuming reproducers, or as meddlers, hot with righteous malice, or else cool and unsympathetic. Not the eager-greeters that we envision as our starfaring destiny, in recent, high-minded fables. But, instead, the sort of callous descendants we'd disown . . . as if such beings would care what we think.

Any of these general categories might contain the Great Filter. Whatever trap—or host of traps—winnows the number of confident, gregarious, star-traveling species, down to the skimpy near nothing we observe, keeping empty what should have been a crowded sky.

—Pandora's Cornucopia

18.
POVLOVERS

Well, God bless the Thirty-First Amendment and the Restoration of Federalism Act.

It had become a litany, as MediaCorp kept asking Tor to "drop in" on eccentric envelope-pushers while making her way across the continent. At last, she felt she understood the real purpose of this journey. What the execs were hoping to teach their up-and-coming young point-of-view star.

There isn't one America anymore. If there ever had been.

Take her brief visit to the State of Panhandle, for example, fifty-sixth star on the flag, where she met with members of the ruling party, who planned to ratchet up their secession bid next year, and to stop even nominally flying the Stars 'n' Stripes. Even if that meant another aiware embargo. Meanwhile, next door, in cosmopolitan Oklahoma, there was renewed talk of a bid to join the EU . . .

. . . rousing bitter anger in Unionist Missouri, where bluecoat militia membership was rising fast and several casinos had burned to the ground.

A cynic would attribute all this fury to economics. A spreading dustbowl. The cornahol collapse. Across what had been the heartland, Tor felt the same anxious note of helplessness and letdown, after the bubble prosperity of the twenties and thirties. A renewed need for someone to blame.

And, yet, all through the last week, Tor's hand kept drifting into her bag, to Dr. Sato's little relic, still unable to believe that the Atkins director had given it to her. A Neolithic tool-core, thirty thousand years old. One of many, to be sure—anthropologists had found thousands, all over Europe, Africa, and the Middle East. Yet, the specimen was surely worth something—several hundred newbucks on a bidding site.

An attempted bribe for good coverage? Somehow, she doubted that. Anyway, it didn't affect her report. The Atkins Center treatments seemed promising, but hardly a panacea cure for the worldwide Autism Plague. Their approach only worked for "high-functioning" patients, who could already interact with others in fairly rational conversation. For millions of acute victims—fixated on minutiae, evading eye contact, prickly toward any distraction, or else lost down corridors of bizarre virtual reality that few normal minds could follow—for them, Sato offered only hope for desperate loved ones.

Still, her encounter with that strange man gave Tor an excuse to add one more stop, before proceeding to her new job in Rebuilt Washington. The semiannual Godmakers' Conference, held this very week in Nashville, city of tolerance and hospitality.

It had better be tolerant, she thought, stepping past vigilant doorway sniffers, into the expansive Metro Convention

Center. *These people are wearing a great big target on their backs. And proud of it, too.*

A real-cloth banner, just inside the entrance, proclaimed—

TOMORROW WELCOMES THE BOLD!

To which, a tagger had attached, in lurid vraiffiti, visible to anyone wearing specs—

And Next Tuesday Greets the Gullible!

Beyond, for aisle after aisle, eager companies, foundations, and selforg clubs touted "transforming breakthroughs" from smartly decorated booths, augmented by garish VR. Tor found her specs bombarded by eager pitches, offering everything from health enhancements to lifespan folding. From guaranteed rejuvenation supplements to home marrow repair kits.

From "cyborg" prosthetics to remote controlled nanoflits.

From fully-implanted brainlink shunts to servant robots.

Yes, *robots.* The quaint term was back again, as memory of the Yokohama Yankhend slowly faded, along with a promise that *this* generation of humanoid automatons would actually prove useful, rather than cantankerous, too cute, or dangerous. Or all three at once.

"Every year, they solve some problem or obstacle, in machine-walking, talking, vision, navigation, or common sense," she subvocalized for her report, allowing the specs to absorb it all, watching as one aindroid from a Korean chaebol showed off eastasian dance moves and a winning smile. The demonstration was impressive. But demonstrations always were.

"Then, they always wind up bollixed by some simple task. An uneven flight of stairs. A muddled foreground or

background. A semantic paradox. Something that wouldn't bother a five-year-old kid. And every year, the lesson is the same.

"We are already marvels. A three-kilo human brain still combines more amazing things than any computer model can yet emulate.

"It's been seventy years that ai-builders have promised to surge beyond human ken. Their list of tricks keeps growing. Ai can sift and correlate across all of human knowledge, in seconds. Yet, each decade reveals more layers of unexpected subtlety, that lay hidden in our own packed neuron-clusters all along. Skills we simply took for granted."

There it was, again. A theme, planted in her mind by Sato. The notion that something strangely spectacular had been wrought—by God or evolution or both—inside the Homo sapiens brain. About the same time as that chert core in her bag was the technological acme.

"If anything, today's Tower of Babel is flat but incredibly wide. This generation of godmakers isn't thwarted by language—that barrier is gone forever—but the bewildering complexity of the thing they hope to copy. Our minds."

Of course, some of the products and services here had more modest goals. One body-sculpting booth offered the latest fat-dissolving technology, using targeted microwaves to melt lipids exactly <u>where-u-want</u>. Their slogan—from Nietzsche—

"The abdomen is the reason why man does not easily take himself for a deity."

She wondered what Sato would make of that. *Well, one more humility-reminder bites the dust. When everyone can look good in spandex, will conceit know any bounds?*

Speaking of the abdomen . . . dozens of men and women were lined up at a booth for the McCaffrey Foundation, signing waivers in order to join a test study of *e-calculi*—gut bacteria transformed to function as tiny computers, powered by excess food. Have a problem? Unleash trillions of tiny, parallel processors occupying your own intestine! Speed them up by eating more! And they produce Vitamin C!

At first, Tor thought this *must* be a hoax. It sounded like a comedy routine from Monty Phytoplankton. She wondered how the computed output finally emerged.

Not everyone could wait patiently for all this progress. Elderly believers in the Singularity grew worried, as it always seemed to glimmer twenty years away, the same horizon promised in the 1980s. And so, Tor passed by the usual booths offering cryonic suspension contracts. For a fee, teams would rush to your deathbed, whether due to accident or age. The moment after a doctor signed-off you were "dead," skilled teams would swarm over your body—or (for a lower price) just your detached head—pumping special fluids so you could chill in liquid nitrogen, with relished confidence that some future generation would thaw and repair you. Decades ago, cryonics companies eked along with support from a few rich eccentrics. But the safe revival of Guillermo Borriceli changed all that, pushing the number of contracts past thirty million. Some of the offshore "seastead" tax havens even allowed cryonic suspension *before* legal death, leading to a steady, one-way stream of immigrants who were wealthy, infirm, and—in Tor's opinion—certifiably crazy.

They never explain why future generations would choose to revive refugees from a more primitive time. Money alone won't cut it.

Was that why many of today's rich were converting to fervent environmentalism? Donating big sums toward eco-projects? To bribe their descendants and be recalled as karmic good guys? Or was it an expanded sense of self-interest? If you expect to live on a future Earth, that could make you less willing to treat today's planet like disposable tissue.

Meanwhile, some offered services aimed at the other end of life. Like new kinds of infant formula guaranteed to enhance early brain development. Or suture-spreaders to enlarge a fetus's skull capacity, letting its brain expand in the womb—with a coupon for free cesarean section. The brochure showed a happy child with the smile of a Gerber baby and the domed head of some movie alien . . . bearing a glint of unstoppable intelligence in big, blue eyes.

Fifty-Genes, Inc. offered a service that was legal at just three seastead colonies. Enhancing the few dozen patches of DNA thought to have been crucial in separating the hominid line from other apes. *Continuing along the evolutionary trail.* All three of the people manning that booth wore dazzle-makeup, hiding their identities from facial recog programs, making them painful to look at. As if the feds didn't have ten thousand other ways to track a person.

Farther along, she encountered yet another humanoid automaton, under a virt-blare that proclaimed **Certified: Turing Level Three-Point-Three**! in flashing letters. Proportioned like a body builder, it bowed to her, offering Tor a seat, some zatz-coffee and a game of chess—or any pastime of her choosing. There was a flirtatious glint in the machine's smile, either cleverly designed . . . or else . . .

She was tempted to plunge a pin into that glossy flesh, to see if this one yelped. The old man-in-a-robot-suit trick.

A subvocalized side note, for later: *"No cutsie animal or childlike bots, this year? All hunk-style males, so far. Why? A trend aimed at fem demographics?"*

She couldn't help but wonder. Men across the planet had been using robo-brothels for a decade, with hundreds of thousands of Luci, Nunci, Pari, Fruti, and Hilti models purchased for home use. It didn't exactly require artificial intelligence to mimic crude, servile passion, if that's what some males wanted. Of course, the trend was bemoaned in the press. Women mostly stayed aloof, contemptuous of the unsubtle artificial lovers they were offered.

Till now? While the hunk-bot flirted with her, Tor recalled Wesley's onetime proposition—to maintain a cross-continental relationship via dolls. Would it be more palatable to be touched by a machine, if the thoughts propelling it came from someone she cared for? He was coming to D.C. in a few days, flying east to meet her final zeppelin, at this journey's end. Did that mean he was giving up such nonsense? Ready to talk, at last, about "getting real"? Or would he have a fistful of brochures to show her the latest enhancements? A modern way they both could have cake, and eat it, too?

Oh crap. The subvocal was on high-sensitivity. Her musings about sexbots and Wesley had gone straight into notes. She blink-navigated, deleted, and disciplined her mind to stay on topic. Spinning away from the enticingly handsome android, multi-tasking like a juggler, Tor kept reciting her draft report without breaking stride.

"Oh, few doubt they'll succeed eventually. With so many versions of AI cresting at once, it seems likely that we'll finally enter that century-old sci-fi scenario. Machines that help design their successors, and so on, able to converse with us, provide fresh perspectives, challenge us . . . then surge ahead.

"At that point we'll discover who was right, the zealots or the worriers. Can you blame some folks for getting nervous?"

Of course, Tor's aiwear had been tracking her word stream, highlighting for gisted meaning. And, because her filters were kept low on purpose, the convention center mainframe listened in, automatically making goorelations. Helpfully, the building offered, in her low-right peripheral, a list of conference panels and events to match her interests.

My Neighbors Prefer Death: Easing the Public's Fear of Immortality.

Yes. Out of five hundred program items, that one had good relevance to her "skepticism" phrase. The next one was also a good fit.

Risk Appraisal: Dangers on the Road to Transhumanity.

But it got even better. Tor blinked in surprise at the next offering.

Special invited-guest lecture by famed novelist Hamish Brookeman! "Reasons to Doubt 'Progress'—and Reasons to Believe."

Tor stopped in her tracks. Hamish Brookeman? Here, of all places? The author of *Tusk!* and *Cult of Science,* coming to beard these extropians in their own den? Who had the courage—or outright chutzpah—to invite him?

With a tooth-click and scroll, Tor checked the conference schedule . . . and found the Brookeman talk was already under way.

Oh my. This was going to be demanding. But she felt up to the challenge.

Swiveling, she called up a guide ribbon—a glowing path that snaked toward the lecture hall. Which, according to a flash alert, was already full to capacity. So Tor sent a blip to MediaCorp, asking for a press intervention. It took a couple of minutes (after all, she was a newbie), during which Tor hurried past a publisher of biofeedback mind-training games and a booth selling ersatz holidays on realistic alien worlds.

Smell Colors! Taste the Rainbow! See Music in the Air!—hollered a kiosk offering synesthesia training. Next to another that proclaimed a kinky aim—to genetically engineer "furries," cute-but-fuzzy humanoid versions of dogs and cats. Tor shivered and hurried on.

Abruptly, the guide ribbon shifted, aiming her instead

down a different aisle, away from the back of the lecture hall, where standing-room crowds waited. Now, it directed her toward the front entrance, closest to the stage. Wow, that was fast.

I am so gonna love this job, she thought, not caring if that made it into the transcript. MediaCorp already knew. This was what she had been born to do.

Along the way, Tor passed between stalls offering latest generation ottodogs, lurker-peeps, and designer hallucinogens . . . the latter one was covered with vir-stickies on about a hundred levels, sneering *Ignore these guys!* and *It's a narc sting!* (As if anyone needed to actually buy drugs, anymore, instead of homebrewing them on a MolecuMac. Or using a meditation program to make them inside your own brain. A dazer with a twin-lobectomy could hack the lame safeguards.)

But, for the most part, Tor had little attention to spare for exhibits. Kicking her M-Tasking into overdrive, she called up a smart-condensed tivoscript of the Brookeman speech, from its start twelve minutes ago, delivered to her left ear in clipped, threex mode—triple speed and gisted—while preserving the speaker's dry tone and trademark Appalachian drawl.

"Thanks invitation speak you 'godmakers.' I'm surprised/pleased. Shows UR open-minded.

"Some misconstrue I'm antiscience. Antiprogress. But progress great! Legit sci & tech lift billions! Yes, I warn dangers, mistakes. Century's seen many. Some mistakes not science fault.

"Take the old left-right political axis. Stupid. From 18th century France! lumped aristos with fundies, libertarians, isolationists, imperialists, puritans, all on 'right.' Huh? 'Left' had intolerant tolerance fetishists! Socialist luddites! And all sides vs professionals. No wonder civil servants' guild rebelled!

"Result? Wasted decades. Climate/water crisis. Terror. Overreaction. National fracture. Paranoia. Blamecasting.

"Shall we pour gasoline on fire?

"Look. Studies show FEAR sets attitudes/tolerance to change. Fearful people reject foreign, alien, strange. Circle wagons. Pull in horizons. Horizons of time. Of tolerance. Of risk. Of Dreams.

"You tech-hungry zealots answer this with contempt. Helpful?

"New 'axis' isn't left versus right.

"It's out versus in!

"You look outward. Ahead. You deride inward-driven folk.

"But look history! All other civs were fearful-inward! R U so sure YOU are wise ones?"

The front entrance to the lecture hall lay ahead, just beyond a final booth where several clean-cut envoys in blue blazers passed out leaflets to educated and underemployed U.S. citizens, inviting them to apply for visas—to the science-friendly EU. The brain-drainers' placement was deliberate. They'd get plenty of customers, when Brookeman finished.

Feeling a little eye-flick strain and attention fatigue, Tor clicked for a small jolt of Adderall, along with a dash of Provigil, injected straight into her temple by the left-side frame of her specs. Just a bit, to keep her edge.

"Look at topics listed in this conference," continued the ai-compressed voice of Hamish Brookeman, addressing the audience in the hall next door. *"So much eager tinkering! And each forward plunge makes your fellow citizens more nervous."*

The condensed tivoscript was slowing down and expanding, as it caught up with real time.

"Ponder an irony. Your premise is that average folk can be trusted with complex/dangerous future. You say

people = smart! People adapt. Can handle coming trans-
formation into gods! How libertarian of you.

"Yet, you sneer at the majority of human *societies, who*
disagreed! Romans, Persians, Inca, Han, and others . . .
who said fragile humanity can't take much change.

"And who shares this older opinion? A majority of your
own countrymen!

"So, which is it? Are people wise enough to handle ac-
celerating change? But if they are wise . . . and want to
slow down . . . then what does that imply?

"It implies this. If you're right about people, then the
majority is right . . . and you're wrong!

"And if you're wrong about the people . . . then how can
you be right!"

Even through the wall and closed doors, Tor heard laughter from the audience—tense and reluctant. But she already
knew Brookeman was good at working a crowd. Anyway,
most of this bunch had grown up with his books, movies,
and virts. Celebrity status still counted for a lot.

"All I ask is . . . ponder with open minds. We've made so
many mistakes, humanity, during just one lifetime. Many
of them perpetrated not by evildoers, drenched in malice,
but by men and women filled with fine motives! Like you."

An aindroid stood by the door, smiling in recognition as
Tor approached. This one featured a *hole* penetrating
straight through its chest, large enough to prove that the
entity was no human in disguise. An impressive highlight.
Till the automaton gave her a full-length, appreciative eye-
flick "checkout" that stopped just short of a lustful leer.
Exactly like some oversexed, undertacted nerd.

Great, Tor thought, with a corner of her mind MT'd for
such things. *Another realism goal accomplished. One more*
giant leap for geek-kind.

The robot opened the door, just enough for Tor to slip
through without disturbing speaker or audience. Her specs

went into IR mode and a pale-green ribbon guided her, without stumbling, the final few meters to a VIP seat that someone had just vacated, on her account. She could tell, because the upholstery was still warm. A wide imprint, and her spec-sensors gave a soft diagnosis of fumes from a recent meal, heavy in starches. If it need be, she could track down her benefactor, from those cues alone, and thank him.

But no, here was Hamish Brookeman, in the flesh at last, tall and angular, elegant and expensively coifed. In every way the un-nerd. Leaning casually against the lectern and pouring charm, even as he chastised. The tivoscript faded smoothly, as real time took over.

"Look, I'm not going to ask you to restrain yourselves for the sake of holiness and all that. Let others tell you that you're treading on the Creator's toes, by carping and questioning His designs; that's not my concern.

"What troubles me is whether there will *be* a humanity, in twenty years, to continue pondering these things! Seriously, what's your damned hurry? Must we rock every apple cart, while charging in all directions, simultaneously?"

Brookeman glanced back down and ruffled some sheets of paper, though Tor's zoom-appraisal showed that he wasn't looking at them. Those blue irises held steady, far-focused and confident. Clearly, he already knew what he was about to say. In public speaking, as in music, a pause was sometimes just the right punctuation, before striking a solid phrase.

"Take the most arrogant of your obsessions," Brookeman resumed. "This quest for life-span extension! You give it many names. Zero senescence. Non-morbidity. All of it boiling down to the same selfish hope, for personal immortality."

This goaded a reaction from the crowd—hisses and muttered curses. Tor commanded her specs to deploy a slender stalk wafting upward with a tiny, omnidirectional

lens at the end, surveying members of the audience, joining dozens of other gel-eyes floating, like dandelions, up to
a meter above the sea of heads.

"Did I strike a nerve with that one?" Hamish Brookeman chuckled. "Well, just wait. I'm getting warmed up!"

Clearly, he enjoyed the role of iconoclast . . . in a hall
filled with self-styled iconoclasts. A kindred spirit, then?
Even while disagreeing with his hosts over every specific
issue? That kind of ironic insight could make her report
stand out.

"For example, it's easy to tell which of you, in the audience, believes in the magic elixir called *caloric restriction.*
Sure, research studies show that a severely reduced, but
wholesome diet can trigger longer life spans in bacteria, in
fruit flies, even mice. And yes, keeping lean and fit is good
for you. It helps get your basic fourscore and ten. But some
of the fellows you see around here, walking about like near
skeletons, popping hunger-suppression pills and avoiding
sex . . . do these guys look healthy? Are they *enjoying* their
extra years? Indeed, are they getting any? Extra years, I
mean.

"Alas, sorry to break this to you fellows, but the experiment was run! Across the last four millennia, there must
have been thousands of *monasteries,* in hundreds of cultures, where ascetic monks lived on spare dietary regi-
mens. Surely, some of them would have stumbled onto
anything so simple and straightforward as low-calorie immortality! We'd have noticed two-hundred-year-old monks,
capering around the countryside, don'tcha think?"

This time, laughter was spontaneous. Still nervous, but
genuine. Through the stalk-cam, she saw even some of the
bone-thin ones, taking the ribbing well. Brookeman really
was good at this.

"Anyway, remember that age and death are the great recyclers! In a world that's both overpopulated and unbal-

anced in favor of the old, do you really think the next wave of young folks is going to want to follow in your shadows . . . forever?

"Putting things philosophically for a minute, aren't you simply offering false hope, and thereby denying today's elderly the great solace that every other ageing generation clutched, when their turn came to shuffle off this mortal coil? The consolation that *at least this happens to everyone*?

"During all past eras, this pure and universal fact—that death makes no exceptions—allowed a natural acceptance and letting go. Painful and sad, but at least one thing about life seemed fair. Rich and poor, lucky or unlucky, all wound up in the same place, at roughly the same pace. Who said that our lives only become meaningful when we are aware of our mortality?

"Only now, by loudly insisting that *death isn't necessary*, aren't you turning this normal rhythm into a bitter pill? Especially when the promise (all too likely) turns into ashes, and people wind up having to swallow it anyway, despite all your fine promises?"

Brookeman shook his head.

"But let's be generous and say you meet with some partial success. Suppose only the rich can afford the gift of extended life. Isn't that what happens to most great new things? Don't they get monopolized, at first, by the mighty? You godmakers say you want an *egalitarian miracle,* a new age for all. But aren't you far more likely to create a new race of Olympians? Not only privileged and elite, but permanent and immortal?"

Now the hall was hushed. And Tor wondered. Had Brookeman gone too far?

"Face it," the tall man told 3,012 listeners in the hall . . . plus 916,408 who were tuned in, around the planet. "You techno-transcendentalists are no different from all the millennial preachers and prophets who came before you. The same goggle-eyed, frenetic passion. The same personality type, yearning for something vastly better than the hand that you were dealt. And the same drive to believe! To believe that something else, much finer, is available to those who recite the right incantation. To those who achieve the right faith, or virtue. Or who concoct the secret formula.

"Only, those earlier prophets were much smarter than you lot! Because the redemption they forecast was usually *ambiguous,* set in another vague time and place, or safely removed to another plane. And if their promises failed? The priest or shaman could always blame it all on unbelievers. Or on followers who were insufficiently righteous. Or who got the formula wrong. Or on God.

"But you folks? Who will you duck behind, when disillusion sets in? Your faith in *Homo technologicus*—the Tinkering Man—has one fatal flaw. It offers you no escape clause.

"When your grand and confident promises fail, or go wrong, who will all the disappointed people have to blame?

"No one . . . but you."

RENUNCIATORS

In 1421, Admiral Zheng He led a huge armada of Chinese ships, some over a hundred meters long, "to proceed to the end of the earth, to collect tribute from the barbarians beyond the seas and unite the whole world in Confucian harmony."

Ironically Confucius—or Kong-Fuzi—wrote in the *Analects* that "While his parents are alive, the son may not take a distant voyage abroad." And although Zheng He's parents may have been slaughtered in the Yannan rebellion, for thousands of other sailors who manned the famed Treasure Fleet of the

Dragon Throne, this was far from a typical Confucian exercise. It showed what could happen when a bold emperor roused that great nation to reach toward its potential, in the future rather than the past.

Zheng He's voyages brought home tribute, trade, and knowledge. Had they continued, Chinese armadas might have sailed into Lisbon Harbor, in time to astonish a young Prince Henry the Navigator with ships the size of cathedrals.

Only then, the extroverted emperor died. His heir and court ordered a halt to trade and outlawed oceangoing ships. It was all part of an ancient cycle. Eras of enlightenment, like the Song Dynasty would be followed by long periods of repressed conformity. Before William the Conqueror landed at Hastings, the blast furnaces and coke ovens of Henan produced a hundred thousand tons of iron per year! Then, abruptly, they were abandoned till the twentieth century.

Often, it wasn't economics or even politics at fault, but the whim of hyperconservative elites, who preferred serenity over the bustle of change. Especially change that might threaten their status or empower the poor.

When carried out vigorously, renunciation can extend even to memory. In our example, the records and navigation tables of Zheng He's expeditions were burned, along with the ships. China's southern border was razed and turned into a lifeless no-man's-land. When eighteenth century Western visitors amazed the Imperial court with mechanical clocks and other wonders, a few scholars cited obscure texts, saying: "Oh, yes, we had such things. Once."

Is history repeating itself? After their recent epoch of zealous modernism, stunning the world with ambitious accomplishments, will the Han turn inward again? There were already signs of retrenchment, in a generation with too few young people, especially women. Then that terrible blow—an ill-fated space mission that was named (ironically) after Admiral Zheng He.

Renunciation, it seems, has persistent allure. Only this time, will the whole world join in, recoiling against change? Rejecting progress in the name of stability? Anti-technologists cite the ancient Chinese pattern as a role model for how to turn back from the precipice in time.

Yet, we know there has always been another side. A side represented by the marvelous Zheng He and so many like him. Those who had the will to look ahead.

—from *The Movement Revealed* by Thormace Anubis-Fejel

19.
TIME CAPSULE

Hamish sometimes wished that he had a knack for specs, using them the way young zips, tenners, and twenners did nowadays, scanning a dozen directions at once, MT-juggling so many tracks and dimensions that it literally made your head spin. Which explained why some were switching to those smart new contaict lenses, nearly undetectable, except for the nervous way a user's eyes would flit about, roaming the infosphere—perceiving a zillion parallels— while pretending to live in the organic here-and-now.

On the other hand, didn't studies show a steep decline in concentration, from all this continuously scattered attention? After all, the initials for "multitasking" sounded like *empty.* Studies showed that good old-fashioned focus can really matter—

—like when delivering a speech. Another reason why Hamish still did it with bare eyes, wearing only an e-earring to receive the most vital alerts. Vigilant from experience and focused on the real world, he scanned the audience in front of him, carefully attuned for reactions.

Of course, this was a tough crowd. Hamish didn't expect

to convert many of these extropians, singularitarians, and would-be methuselahs. His real audience would come later, when Tenskwatawa published an abridged version of this talk, to share with members of the Movement, reinforcing their determination and will.

He glanced at the lectern clock. Time to nail this down.

"Look, I'm not going to ask that you tweakers and meddlers and apprentice godmakers change your program or abandon your dreams. Utopians and transcendentalists have always been with us. Sometimes, their dissatisfaction with things-as-they-are would prove valuable, leading to something both new and useful.

"But, more often than not, the blithe promises turn sour. Certainties prove to have been delusional and side effects overshadow benefits. Religions that preach love start to obsess on hate. Industries that promise prosperity instead poison the planet. And innovators, with some way-cool plan to save us all, rush to open Pandora's Box a little wider, whether or not others disagree.

"Today, there are scores—hundreds—of bright plans afoot, with promoters promising *ninety percent or better probability* that nothing can go wrong.

"A scheme to spread dust in the stratosphere and reverse global warming *probably won't* overshoot, or have harmful side effects.

"A super–particle collider that might conceivably make micro black holes—*probably won't.*

"We're *almost completely sure* that hyper-intelligent machines won't rebel and squash us.

"Radio messages, shouting *hello* into the galaxy have insignificant chance of attracting nasty attention.

"Spreading fertilizer across the vast 'desert' areas of the ocean will *only* enhance fisheries and pull down CO_2, with almost no chance of other repercussions.

"Safeguards are *sure* to prevent some angry teenager with one of those home gene-hacking units from releasing the next plague . . . the list goes on and on . . .

". . . and yes, I see many of you smiling, because I wrote scary stories about most of those failure modes! Sold like hotcakes, and the movies did well, too! Well, except *Fishery of Death*. I admit, that one was lame."

Again, tense laughter, and Hamish felt pleased.

"But here's the key point," he continued. "Suppose we try a hundred ambitious things and each of them, individually, has a ninety percent chance of *not* causing grievous harm. Go multiply point-nine times point-nine times point-nine and so on, a hundred times. What are the *overall* odds that *something* terrible won't happen? It works out to almost zero."

Hamish paused amid silence.

And that was when Wriggles chose to speak, aiming a narrow cone of sound from his left earring, tuned to vibrate Hamish's tympani.

"Leave some time for questions," said Hamish's digital aissistant.

"Also, I've scanned the crowd and spotted Betsby."

Hamish grunted a query. Wriggles answered.

"Second row, just behind and to the right of that female MediaCorp reporter with the big specs. He's grown a beard. But it's him."

Hamish tried not to glance too obviously, while resuming his speech, on autopilot.

"I know that many of you say I'm a luddite, a troglodyte, even paranoid! I'll take it under advisement. If the voices in my head let me."

Again, smatters of appreciative laughter from the crowd. A jape, at your own expense, was the surest way to win back an audience, after challenging them. Only, this time it felt perfunctory, as he looked over the man who had poisoned Senator Strong. Sandy-colored hair, streaked with gray. A slender pair of specs, suitable for providing captions only, but not full VR. Unless they were actual, old-fashioned eyeglasses. Retro could sometimes look celero, and vice versa.

So, Betsby had come to the rendezvous, after all. The man might be crazy, but he sure wasn't lacking in gall.

"I tell you what," Hamish said, deciding to finish up the speech a couple of minutes early. "Let's make a deal, *I'll* contemplate a possibility that the world will be improved if you guys fill it with talking crocodiles, tinman philosophers, downloaded cybercopies, and immortal nerds . . . if *you'll* return the favor, and ponder my own hypothesis. That humanity has already rushed ahead too fast. *So* fast and so far that we're up to our necks in trouble of our own making."

Hamish slowed down a little, telegraphing that the talk was nearing its end.

"If I'm right, and providing it isn't already too late, then there remains a possible solution. The same method used in most human cultures, who had enough wisdom to worry about things going wrong. The *ten thousand other societies* that lasted a lot longer than this frail little so-called enlightenment that we're so proud of.

"Oh, we've walked on the moon, studied distant galaxies and plumbed the atom. Democracy is nice. So are mass education, the info-Meshes, and webs. Standing on the shoulders of those who went before, we achieved heights few dreamed. On the other hand, all our ancestors did one thing that most of *you fellows* have yet to prove yourselves capable of.

"They all survived to reproduce and to see their successors safely on their way. That's what the word 'ancestor' means! Across centuries and millennia, they passed on their torch to new generations, who carried life and human

culture forward to more generations, still. They died knowing at least the story would go on. It sounds like a simple a
task. But it never was, for any of them. A gritty, essential
challenge, it absorbed nearly all their lives. The core objective of any sane individual or civilization . . . or species,
for that matter. A goal that you would-be godmakers and
meddlers seem to forget, in your pell-mell rush for individual satisfaction, personal immortality and so-called
progress.

"Indeed, it may be the one thing most endangered, as we
journey together, into a perilous tomorrow."

Audience applause, when it came, was mixed. Hamish saw
equal numbers clapping or else sitting with folded hands,
glowering back at him. Among the latter group was Roger
Betsby, who watched from the second row with little expression.

Ripples of discussion coursed through the hall, some of
it neighbor-to-neighbor, but also at the augmented-reality
levels. People turned and pointed at others in the crowd,
while mouthing silently, trusting their specs to route the
words through vir-space. Some even stood up, motioning
for others to join them in clusters, at the side or back of the
room.

Dang, I really got 'em riled up!

Hamish felt good. Each time he delivered this message,
it was a little better tuned. Ready to be tweaked, improved,
and refined at the Movement's think tank. And the prospect of influencing the world's future almost made up for
the pang he felt, whenever he thought about the time this
took away from creative work.

As expected, the questions that followed were a mix—
some consisting of polite challenges while others displayed
outright hostility. Hamish didn't mind a bit. He egged on a
couple of the most fervent, so that they shouted, voices

cracking, and conference organizers had to pull them away. Just the sort of images that Tenskwatana's people could edit and emphasize, strengthening a valuable stereotype. That of goggle-eyed fanatics. Demonstrating that these people shouldn't to be trusted with a burnt match, let alone high-tech power over human destiny.

More people stood up to leave—only to be expected, since the talk was formally over. But, an increasing number were tapping their specs, waggling fingers in the air, muttering while pointing at each other, passing e-notes.

They're excited, all right. I may have to slip out the back way.

All the while, Hamish kept trying *not* to glance at the bearded man in the second row. Some of the people out there, those with top-grade specs, could track wherever his eye-gaze went. Too much attention in one direction—on one person—might be noticed.

This is what I get for trying to kill several birds with one cliché. Betsby wanted a public meeting place. I was coming here anyway, so it seemed natural to arrange a rendezvous. But honestly, who expected him to come?

Nothing about this case—the poisoning of Senator Strong—seemed typical. A perpetrator who was perfectly willing to admit it? A blackmailer who refused to explain to his victim *what* secret he kept, or what tincture he had used, to send the senator into an embarrassing public tizzy?

A solitary nut, perhaps, who didn't seem to care if he made powerful enemies.

A True Believer, then? But he doesn't have the look. And our investigators found no background consistent with a lone maniac. A medical doctor, working in urban free clinics. A modern Schweitzer? Sure, that could make him despise Senator Strong. And he'd have the tools, the know-how, to concoct a psychotropic poison.

But the whole thing just doesn't hold together. Betsby

has to be more than he seems. The tip of an arrow. The point of a spear. Part of a deeper plot. Is that why he wanted to meet me here, in the heart of technogeek-land?

A woman stood up from the audience, chosen to be the next questioner—rather stocky and heavy for someone of her generation. Perhaps she was allergic to biosculpting, or philosophically opposed to it. A halo of light converged, illuminating her round face from several directions. The live-acoustic walls amplified her words, without echo or any need for a microphone.

"Mr. Brookeman, I'd like to shift topics, if you don't mind. Because it seems that the future is rushing upon us, even while you stand there, pontificating about the importance of slowing down."

"Well, now," he answered. "There are always crises. A never-ending tide of human-generated mistakes. Which one has you worried, this time?"

"One that may not qualify as *human-generated* at all, sir. I'm sure you're aware of the gossip that's been tsunaming around for the last week—that space station astronauts *found something* in orbit. Something highly unusual. Perhaps even non-Earthly in origin?"

Hamish blinked. The leak was spreading fast. His own last update, before going to bed last night, had told of vigorous government efforts to keep the rumors corked, or at least discredited. The Prophet had even called some Movement resources into play, in order to help distract public attention from the story.

This might have been a good time to wear specs, after all, he thought, wishing he might call up a late summary, while mulling his answer. Multitasking did have advantages. . . .

"Well," he chuckled, covering any hint of discomfort, "by definition, anything you find outside Earth would be *non-Earthly—*"

But no. That feeble thread wasn't worth pursuing. So he nodded, instead.

"Yes, I've heard some tall tales and seen blurry images. Who hasn't? So far, they've seemed pretty far-fetched. Like the amphibious Tidal Sasquatch of a few years ago. Or, remember the *quantum creatures* that people claimed to see, when they pressed their eyes against the holographic bigscreens made by Fabrique Zaire? Till it was shown that folks were simply scratching their own corneas!"

That drew a few weak chuckles. Not many.

"So what is the latest, fevered fantasy to sweep the globe?" Hamish lapsed into a heavily sardonic drawl. "Well, now, ain't it excitin'? A bona fide, surefire, rootin'-tootin' alien artifact! Showin' up right in middle orbit, *just* where an astronaut could snag it with a lasso while trawlin' for garbage. How convenient!

"Of course," he added, in a less sarcastic tone, "there's no explanation of *how* such a thing could have got there. A glowing lump, like an opal or crystal, not much bigger than your head—that's the thing you're talking about, right? But has anybody thought to ask—how could something like that navigate Earth's gravity well, without engines? Let alone change course, matching orbits—"

"Maybe somebody dropped it off!" a voice in the audience shouted. The dampers in a lecture hall could be tuned to squelch hecklers. But these extropians liked to keep things loose.

"Ah, the old UFO gambit." Hamish smiled. "Oh, I admit, I've had fun with flying saucers, in my time. The mythology is just so rich! Meddlers from just beyond our firelight sweep in mysteriously to make cryptic pronouncements, or issue threats, or give lonely farmers free colonoscopies."

This time, audience laughter was a bit fuller, tasting like bread and drink. Here was a topic where most people in the room agreed. Hamish even felt a touch of gratitude to the woman, for diverting onto this subject. Now the event could end on a lighter note.

"Of course it's funny how UFO aliens always seem to be portrayed the same way. Looking and acting just like pixies, or nasty elves, straight out of ancient tales! Making it pretty obvious where they *really* come from."

He tapped the side of his head, eliciting a few more laughs.

The response was still anemic, though. He was barely holding a majority . . . while many others kept waggling or beaming or whatever-it-was at each other. Clearly, there would be a lot of noise in the hall, right now, if not for the dampers. Hamish forged on.

"Then there's the fact that our planet is filling with more and more *cameras,* doubling in number every year or two. Heck, at last survey, four-fifths of the land surface of Earth is under round-the-clock observation. But has that helped us to pin down these pesky flying saucers, or get a better view of 'em? Ha! *Coincidentally,* the sightings keep happening farther and farther away! *Just* far enough, every year, to stay blurry, despite improving cameras!

"Used to be, we'd get lots of fuzzy glimpses on spotty film, a few hundred meters from a road or town. Today, encounters only seem to happen in the deep desert, or midocean. Or it's amateur astronomers, reporting strange lights near the Moon and Mars. Wherever the panopticon still has gaps, allowing tantalizing . . ."

Hamish meant to go on, milking a riff that he hadn't used in a while. But the stocky woman interrupted.

"Mr. Brookeman, do you mind? Most of us know your views on UFOs, from *The Elf.* One of your sillier movies, by the way. But can we please stay on topic? You seem to be an hour or two out of touch!

"In fact . . . ," she continued, while slowing down, tapping the edges of her specs and waggling the fingers of her other hand in open space. "As a matter . . . of fact . . . even as we speak . . ."

She slowed to a stop, going slack-jawed, staring at images projected on the inner surface of her web-spectacles, and finally breathed a single word.

"Wow!"

The islands of distraction now became a babbling archipelago, as individuals hurried to follow her attention trail. Clusters of people flashed tags to each other. Some of them gasped in their own turn, pointing and commenting to each other with low whispers. Facing a sea of flickering lenses and waving hands, Hamish cleared his throat.

"Um, did something just happen? Will someone please explain—"

Another audience member stood up, this time from the very front row. She was svelte and tall, wearing clear specs that carried plenty of gear—like a floating gel-lens—while also revealing her sharp, pale-brown eyes.

"Tor Povlov, of MediaCorp's show, The Povlovian Response." Wriggles identified the woman. *"Call her Miss Tor."*

Hamish cursed his slow thought process. He could have subvocalized a command to Wriggles and got a summary of whatever news everyone was tizzying about. Too late now. He nodded toward the newcomer. "Yes, Miss Tor?"

The conference center's live acoustic walls responded by shifting priority to the reporter, bathing her in light and amplifying her voice.

"Since you aren't linked-in, Mr. Brookeman, let me explain what's going on, then ask your reaction. Apparently, someone—moments ago—issued more than a terab of purloined data from the NASA Marti Space Center. Images showing highlights of their effort to communicate and translate with the Object."

No one could mistake the capitalization of that final word.

"Really?" Hamish raised his voice to be heard over a rising murmur from the crowd. Even the dampers were getting strained. "Well, I shouldn't have to tell you that leaks can't be trusted. Almost anything can be faked and viral-released, even through an official site. I wouldn't go molten over uncredentialed vids."

By now, a clear majority had dived into full-immersion. It irked Hamish to have so few actually looking his way. Of those left in the here-and-now, most seemed more interested in the reporter than him. Except for Roger Betsby, that is. The bearded poisoner kept his gaze firmly on Hamish.

Tor Povlov shook her head.

"Then I guess you haven't heard the rest, Mr. Brookeman. NASA and the Department of Foresight have already issued a nondenial. No more calm-downs or distractions. Nor any outright disavowals of the leak. Only a promise to find the persons responsible and hit them with a *prematurity fine*."

The phrase provoked chuckles and derisive smirks. That slap on the wrist never stopped anybody. At least, no one who had Guild protection and a plausible claim of public interest.

Hamish blinked, abruptly wishing he could be somewhere else. In contact with his own people. Or the Prophet's.

While I stood here, blathering to extropians about their silly fantasies, the real-world situation has spun out of control.

Tor Povlov continued in a friendly tone. "All morning, MediaCorp has been tracking a sharp spike in diplomatic encrypt traffic, between various national alliances, cartels, and WCNs. Clearly, they were being given advance warning and consultation about something big. But a wave of perplexes and distracts kept us from zeroing in on *which* rumored event it was all about."

That would have been the Prophet's doing. At least it worked for a few hours.

"Only now . . ." She paused for a moment of artfully divided attention, then gracefully resumed. ". . . it appears the White House has scheduled a plenum press conference for three o'clock eastern time. Just under an hour from now. And MediaCorp's forcaister gives a ninety-two percent confidence projection that it will be a public confirmation of the Havana leak, followed by full disclosure."

In what must be a dramatic concession, for someone of her generation, Tor Povlov reached up and flipped the lenses of her vir-spectacles, in order to give Hamish the courtesy of her full attention, here-and-now. Of course that tiny gel-lens kept transmitting to her point-of-view audience, around the world.

"Hence, my question for you, Mr. Brookeman. You've just spent an hour scolding these would-be godmakers," she said the word with a lilt that conveyed her own level of skepticism. "Hectoring them with a stark litany of worries about a dangerously disrupted future.

"And lo, the future has arrived! This disruption—or *disturber,* to use your own term—is likely to be a doozy. Perhaps even like in your stories.

"Only, human foolishness seems to have had little to do with it, this time. And, unlike what always happens in your novels, this cat isn't likely to get hushed and stuffed back in the bag, before the denouement.

"So, what I'd like to know, Mr. Brookeman, is how do you suggest we deal with this new thing?

"A *bottle* appears to have washed onto our shore, from far away. It contains a message.

"And it talks."

RENUNCIATORS

Always, before, whenever one culture went into decline, there were others ready to take up the slack. If Rome toppled, there was light shining in Constantinople, then the Baghdad Caliphate and in China. If Philippine Spain turned repressive, Holland welcomed both refugees and science. When most of Europe went mad, in the mid–twentieth century, the brightest minds moved to America. When America grew self-indulgent and riven by new civil war, that migration sloshed and shifted East.

Only this time, things are different! It isn't just one part of the world, deciding whether to rise or fall. Whether to seize confidence or forsake it. Whatever separates our tribes, today, it's not geography. Rapid connections can spread trouble, as quickly as commerce and hope, as we learned during the Cybersneeze, the Big Heist, and the Sumatran Flu. Already, the EU and GEACS and at least twenty American states have set up commissions to supervise scientists and inventors, aiming to "advise and guide" them toward *responsible progress.*

Or none at all? To avoid *collapse,* scholars from the Diamond Futurological Institute prescribe one hope—to imitate the few human societies that learned to live sustainably within their means—like the Tokugawa Shogunate and Polynesian Tikopia. Ecologically stable, they savagely protected forests and limited the spread of farmland. Those "ideal societies" also banned the wheel. Or take the Kaczynskyites, who don't bother persuading. If it's new, or technological, they'll try to blow it up.

Finally, we have the Movement. Calm and reasonable, it helped ease our world past the last great crisis, a decade ago, midwifing the trade-offs restoring balance among the ten estates, bringing about the Big Deal. Only now they're urging humanity to "take a pause." To reflect on the pitfalls and opportunities, before resuming our forward march. Letting wisdom catch up with technology. But don't we need to get new solutions faster, not slower?

    —from *The Movement Revealed* by Thormace Anubis-Fejel

20.
PURSUIT

Despite his hurry to get home, Peng Xiang Bin avoided the main gate through the massive seawall. For one thing, the giant doors were closed right now, for high tide. Even when they opened, that place would throng with fishermen, hawking their catch, and city dwellers visiting the last remaining beach of imported sand. So many eyes—and ais—and who knew how many were already sifting every passing face, searching for his unique biosignature?

I should never have posted queries about an egglike stone that glows mysteriously, after sitting in sunlight.

I should have left it in that hole under the sea.

His fear—ever since glimpsing the famous alien "Artifact" on TV—was that somebody high and mighty wanted desperately to have whatever Bin discovered in a hidden basement cache, underneath a drowned mansion—and wanted it in secret. The former owner had been powerful and well connected, yet he wound up being hauled away and—according to legend—tortured, then brain-sifted, and finally silenced forever. Bin suspected now that it was because of an oval stone, very much like the one causing such fuss across the world. Governments and megorps and reff-consortia would all seek one of their own.

If so, what would they do with the likes of me? When an object is merely valuable, a poor man who recovers it may demand a finder's fee. But if it is a thing that might shake civilization?

In that case, all I could expect is death, just for knowing about it!

Yet, as some of the initial panic ebbed, Bin felt another part of his inner self rise up. The portion of his character that once dared ask Mei Ling to join him at the wild frontier, shoresteading a place of their own.

If there were a way to offer the stone up for bidding . . . a way to keep us safe . . . True, the former owner must have tried, and failed, to make a deal. But no one knew about this kind of "artifact" then . . . at least not the public. Everything has changed, now that the Americans are showing theirs to the world. . . .

None of which would matter, if he failed to make it home in time to hide the thing and do some basic preparations. Above all, sending Mei Ling and Xiao En somewhere safe. Then post an open call for bidders to meet him in a public place . . . ?

Hurrying through crowded streets, Bin carefully kept his pace short of a run. It wouldn't do to draw attention. Beyond the public-order cams on every ledge and lamppost, the state could tap into the lenses and private-ais worn by any pedestrian nearby. His long hair, now falling over his face, might stymie a routine or casual face-search, but not if the system really took an interest.

It's rumored that they have learned to detect the faint vibrations that emerge from each human ear. That each of us has a vibration—as personal as a fingerprint—that can be detected with instruments. Our bodies give off so many signals, so many ways to betray us to the modern state. Just in case, Bin grabbed a piece of paper out of a trash receptacle and chewed it soft, then crammed a small chunk in each ear.

Veering away from the main gate, he sped through a shabbier section of town, where multistory residence blocs had gone through ramshackle evolution, ignoring every zoning ordinance. Laundry-laden clotheslines jostled solar collectors that shoved against semi-illegal rectennas, siphoning Mesh-access and a little beamed power from the shiny towers of nearby Pudong.

Facing a dense crowd ahead, Bin tried pushing his way through for a while, then took a stab at a shortcut. Worming past a delivery cart that wedged open a pair of giant doors, he found himself inside a vast cavity, where the lower floors had been gutted in order to host a great maze of glassy pipes and stainless steel reactor vessels, all linked in twisty patterns, frothing with multicolored concoctions. He chose a direction by dead reckoning, where there ought to be an exit on the other side. Bin meant to bluff his way clear, if anyone stopped him.

That didn't seem likely, amid the hubbub. At least a hundred laborers—many of them dressed little better than he was—patrolled creaky catwalks or clambered over lattice struts, meticulously cleaning and replacing tubes by hand. At ground level, inspectors wearing bulky, enhanced aiware checked a continuous shower of some product—objects roughly the size and shape of a human thumb—waving laser pincers to grab a few of them before they fell into a waiting bin.

It's a nanofactory, Bin realized, after he passed halfway through. It was his first time seeing one up close, but he and Mei Ling once saw a virtshow tour of a vast workshop like this one (though far cleaner) where basic ingredients were piped in and sophisticated parts shipped out— electroptic components, neuraugments, and *organoplaques,* whatever those were. And shape-to-order diamonds, as big as his fist. All produced by stacking atoms and molecules, one at a time, under programmed control.

People still played a part, of course. No robot could scramble or crawl about like humonkeys, or clean up after the machines with such dexterity. Or so cheaply.

Weren't they supposed to shrink these factories to the size of a toaster and sell them to everyone? Magic boxes that would let even poor folk make anything they wanted from raw materials. From seawater, even. No more work. No more want.

He felt like snorting, but instead Bin mostly held his breath the rest of the way, hurrying toward a loading dock, where sweltering workers filled maglev lorries at the other end. One heard rumors of nano-machines that got loose, that embedded in the lungs and then got busy trying to make copies of themselves. . . . Probably just tall tales. But Bin still had plans for his lungs. They mattered a lot, to a shoresteader.

He spilled out of gritty industry into a world of street-level commerce. Gaily decorated shops crowded this avenue. Sucking air, his nostrils filled with food aromas, wafting around innumerable grills, woks and steam cookers, preparing everything from delicate skewered scorpions to vat-grown chicken meat, stretched and streaked to look like the real thing. Bin's stomach growled, but he pushed ahead, then turned a corner and headed straight for the nearest section of massive wall separating Shanghai East from the rising ocean.

There were smugglers' routes. One used a building that formerly offered appealing panoramas overlooking the Huangpu Estuary—till such views became unfashionable. Now, a lower class of urbanites occupied the tower in question.

The lobby's former coating of travertine and marble had been stripped and sold off years ago, replaced by spray-on corrugations that lay covered with long beards of damp algae. A good use of space—the three-story atrium probably grew enough protein to feed half the occupants a basic, gene-crafted diet. But the dank smell made Bin miss his little tent-home amid the waves.

We can't go back to living like this, he thought, glancing at spindly bamboo scaffolding that crisscrossed the vast foyer, while bony, sweat-stained workers tended the crop, doing work unfit for robots. *I swore I would not raise our son on algae paste.*

The creaky elevator was staffed by a crone who flicked switches on a makeshift circuit board to set it in motion. The building must never have had its electronics repaired since the Crash. *It's been what, fifteen, sixteen years? Yes, people are cheap and people need work. But even I could fix this pile of junk.*

The car jerked and rattled while the operator glared at Bin. Clearly, she knew he did not work or live here. In turn, he gave the old lady a smile and ingratiating bow—no sense in antagonizing someone who might call up a face-query. But within, Bin muttered to himself about sour-minded "little emperors"—a generation raised as chubby only children, doted on by two parents, four grandparents, and a nation that seemed filled with limitless potential. Boundless dreams and an ambition to rise infinitely high—until the Crash. Till the twenty-first century didn't turn out quite as promised.

Disappointment didn't sit well with little emperors—half a billion of them—so many that even the mysterious oligarchs in the Palace of Terrestrial Harmony had to cater to the vast population bulge. And they could be grouchy. Pinning blame on Bin's outnumbered generation had become a national pastime.

The eleventh floor once boasted a ledge-top restaurant, overlooking a marina filled with luxury boats, bordering a beach of brilliant, whitened sand. Not far away, just up the Huangpu a ways, the Shanghai Links Golf & Country Club used to glitter with opulence—now a swampy fen, sacrificed to rising waters.

Stepping past rusty tables and chairs, Bin gazed beyond

the nearby seawall and down upon the yacht basin—stubby remnants and broken masts, protruding from a brownish carpet of seaweed and sewage.

I remember it was right about here. . . .

Leaning over, he groped over the balcony railing and along the building's fluted side, till he found a hidden pulley, attached to a slender rope leading downward. Near the bottom, it draped idly over the seawall and into the old marina, appearing to be nothing more than a pair of fallen wires.

Bin had never done anything like this before, trusting a slender line with his weight and his life. Though, on one occasion he had helped Quang Lu ferry mysterious cargo to the bottom end, holding Quang's boat steady while the smuggler attached dark bags, then hauled away. High overhead, shadowy figures claimed the load of contraband, and that was that. Bin never knew if it was drugs, or tech, or untaxed luxuries, nor did he care, so long as he was paid.

Quang Lu would not be happy if he ruined this route. But right now Bin had other worries. He shaded his eyes to peer along the coast, toward a row of surfline ruins—the former beachfront mansions where his simple shorestead lay. Glare off the water stung his eye, but there seemed to be nothing unusual going on. He was pretty sure he could see the good luck banner from Mei Ling's home county, fluttering in a vague breeze. She was supposed to take it down, in the event of trouble.

His heart pounded as he tore strips off an awning to wrap around his hands. Clambering over the guardrail, Bin tried not to look as he slid down the other side, until he could support himself with one arm on the gravel deck, while the other hand groped and fumbled with the twin lines.

It was awkward, because holding on to just one strand wouldn't do. The pulley would let him plummet like a stone.

So he wound up wrapping both slender ropes around his hand. Before swinging out, Bin closed his eyes for several seconds, breathing steadily and seeking serenity, or at least some calm. *All right, let's go.*

He released the ledge and swung down.

Not good! Full body weight tightened the rope like a noose around his hand, clamping a vise across his palm and fingers. Groaning till he was almost out of breath, Bin struggled to ease the pressure by grabbing both cables between his legs and tugging with his other hand, till he finally got out of the noose. Fortunately, his hands were so callused that there appeared to be no damage. But it took a couple moments for pain to stop blurring his vision . . .

. . . and when it cleared, he made the mistake of glancing down. He swallowed hard—or tried to. A terror that seemed to erupt from somewhere at the base of his spine, ran along his back like a monkey. An eel thrashed inside his belly.

Stop it! he told the animals within. *I am a man. A man with a duty to perform and luck to fulfill. And a man is all that I am.*

It seemed to work. Panic ebbed, like an unpleasant tide, and Bin felt buoyed by determination.

Next, he tried lowering himself, hand over hand, by strength alone. His wiry muscles were up to the task, and certainly he did not weigh enough to be much trouble. But it was hard to hold onto both strings, equally. One or the other kept trying to snap free. Bin made it down three stories before one of them yanked out of his grip. It fled upward, toward the pulley while Bin, clinging to the remaining cord, plunged the other way, grabbing at the escaped strand, desperately—

—and finally seized the wild cord. Friction quickly burned through the makeshift padding and into his flesh. By the time he came to a halt, smoke, anguish, and a foul stench wafted from his hand. Hanging there, swaying and bumping against a nearby window, he spent unknown minutes just holding on tight, waiting for his heart to settle and pain speckles depart his eyes.

Did I cry out? he wondered. Fortunately, the window next to him was blocked by heavy drapes—the glare off the Huangpu was sharp this time of day. Many of the others were boarded up. People still used this building, but most would still be at work or school. Nor would there be much AI in a hi-rise hovel.

I don't think I yelled. I think I'm all right. His descent should be masked by heat plumes and glaring sunlight reflections off metal and concrete, making daylight much preferable over traversing this passage at night, when his body temperature would flare on hundreds of infrared-sensitive cams, triggering anomaly-detection programs.

Learning by trial and error, Bin managed to hook one leg around each of the strands and experimented with letting them slide along his upper thighs, one heading upward and the other going down. It was awkward and painful, at first, but the tough pants could take it, if he went slow and easy.

Gradually, he approached the dull gray concrete levee from above, and Bin found himself picturing how far it stretched—extending far beyond vision to the left, hugging the new coastline till it reached a great marsh that used to be Shandong Province . . . and to the right, continuing along the river all the way to happy regions far upstream, where the Huangpu became the Yangtze, and where people had no fear of rising waters. How many millions were employed building *the New Great Wall*? And how many millions more labored as prisoners, consigned on one excuse or another to the mighty task of staving off China's latest invader? The sea.

Drawing close, Bin kept a wary eye on the barrier. This

section looked okay—a bit crumbly from cheap, hurried construction, two decades ago, after Typhoon Mariko nearly drowned the city. Still, he knew that some stretches were laced with nasty stuff—razor-sharp wires, barely visible to the eye, or heat-seeking tendrils tipped with toxins.

When the time came, he vaulted over, barely touching the obstacle with the sole of one sandal, landing in the old marina with a splash.

It was unpleasant, of course, a tangle of broken boats and dangerous cables that swirled in a murk of weeds and city waste. Bin lost no time clambering onto one wreck and then leaping to another, hurrying across the obstacle course with an agility learned in more drowned places than he could remember, spending as little time as possible in the muck.

Actually, it looks as if there might be a lot of salvage in here, he thought. Perhaps he might come back—if luck neither veered high or low, but stayed on the same course as his life had been so far. Moderately, bearably miserable.

Maybe I will risk it, after all, he thought. *Try to find a broker who can offer the big white stone for sale, in some way that might keep us safe. . . .*

Before climbing over the final, rocky berm, separating the marina from the sea, he spotted a rescue buoy, bobbing behind the pilot house of one derelict. It would come in handy, during the long swim ahead.

ENTROPY

What about those "collapses"? Failure modes that would not wipe out humanity, but might kill millions, even billions? Even with survivors scratching out a bare existence, would there forever after be harsh limits to the range of human hopes?

This category is where we'd assign most punishments for

mismanaging the world. For carelessly cutting down forests and spilling garbage in the sea. For poisoning aquifers and ruining habitats. For changing the very air we breathe. For causing temperatures to soar, glaciers to melt, seas to rise, and deserts to spread. For letting the planet's web of life get winnowed down, through biodiversity loss, till it's a fragile lattice, torn by any breeze.

Most animals have the sense not to foul their own nests.

On the other hand, no other species of animal was ever so tempted. So empowered. Or so willing to gradually learn from its mistakes.

Would intelligent rats, or ravens, or tigers, or bears, or kangaroos have done any better, exercised more foresight, or dealt with the world more carefully than we have?

—*Pandora's Cornucopia*

21.
THE TRIBE

Once in open water, Hacker tried to keep up by swimming alongside his dolphin rescuer. But it was hard to do, with his body battered and bruised from that harsh landing and narrowly evading death on a coral reef.

Also, the survival suit—advertised as *"good for everything from deep space to Everest to the bottom of the sea"*—took some getting used to. But Hacker's brain still wouldn't focus. His hands felt like sausages, fumbling as he pulled tabs, releasing extra gill fronds from a recess along the helmet rim, in order to draw more oxygen from the water.

Worse, the darned dolphin kept getting impatient. When Hacker tried to deploy extension fins on each bootie, for better swimming, the creature gave out a frustrated bleat and chuttering complaint. Then it resumed shoving Hacker along, with its bottle-shaped nose.

Like an exasperated relative, forced to push along an invalid, Hacker thought, resentfully. *I don't have to put up with this!*

Though he still couldn't hear with his clamped eardrums, the sonic sensor in his jaw indicated that they were heading farther out to sea, leaving the pounding reef behind. And with it, the shattered remnants of his expensive suborbital capsule.

I should have tried to salvage more. At least grabbed the radio console.

Or that little survival raft, under the seat! Why didn't I think of that before? I have to go back for it!

The nosy dolphin chose that moment to poke his back again.

Enough! Hacker started to whirl on the creature, aiming to give it a good smack. Then it might take a hint. Leave him alone. . . .

Only, before he could fully rotate, two more gray forms converged from the left, followed by another pair zooming in from the right. The newcomers circled around, scanning Hacker and his rescuer with ratcheting sonar clicks and squeals that resonated through the crystal waters, making his jaw throb.

Hacker finally managed to turn, making as if to return the way he came. But three of the big, gray creatures swam around to interpose themselves. Clearly, they would have none of that.

For a while—it was unclear how long—Hacker screamed at them. Though he could not hear the curses, his faceplate filled with spittle and fog. Then, all of a sudden, the bitter anger evaporated, as if discharged into the surrounding sea. Rage seemed to float away, replaced by resignation.

"All . . . right . . . then," he willed coherent words, gradually regaining his breath as the all-purpose helmet wicked away fumes from his tirade, while pulling in more oxygen.

It would also project his voice, if he remembered to do it right.

"All right, we'll do it your way. But this means *you're* responsible. You've got to take care of me. At least till I can flag down the damn recovery team."

Of course the dolphins didn't understand words. Still, when he turned to swim the other way, they seemed to nod and agree, darting to the surface for air, then swimming alongside slowly enough for him to keep up.

At intervals, just to move things along, one of them would offer its dorsal fin and let Hacker hang on for a brief ride, hurtling through the crystal water much faster than he could ever manage himself. Sometimes, when his bearer climbed to breathe, his own face would emerge and the fronds engorged themselves like balloons, while he scanned the horizon quickly. But there was never any sign of land.

They settled into a routine . . . a rhythm . . . part underwater excursion and part extravagant leaping. After a while, though still bruised, dazed, and numb from painkillers, Hacker finally had to admit, almost grudgingly . . .

. . . that it was pretty fun.

NEWS INTERLIDOLUDE

* Another ice dam is crumbling in Greenland, threatening a massive freshwater spill, just when the North Atlantic Salinity Cycle seemed about to restart. Desperate for the Gulf Stream to flow again, Poland and Russia are threatening to use nukes, without making clear how that might help. (*blink* and UR there)

* Inside the mélange of North America, farm state collectives raised the specter of a food boycott, after the Metropolitan

League declared plans to form a "poop-cartel," selling urban sewage at a fixed price. *(*blink* & UR there)*

* Veterans of the last Great Awakening are back, holding another prophecy conclave in Colorado Springs. Unapologetic over their failed forecasts of the 2030s' cruci-millennium, they are calling for a new wave of tent meetings from pinnacle to prairie. "Because," according to spokesrevelator Iain Tserff, "this time, for sure!" *(*blink* & UR there)*

In response, the nearby Blue-Republic of Boulder responded by conscripting a fresh platoon of lawyers to pursue collection on the Big Wager of 2036. Referring to the ongoing tiff between trog and agog enclaves, Professor Mayor Eileen Gaypurse-Fitzpatrick said: "Before these dingbats spread more panic, they owe us a new sports stadium! And an apology for betting-and-praying our city would be swallowed by hell. Pay up! And, this time, no whining 'double-or-nothing.'" *(*blink* & UR there)*

22.
KINDRED SPIRITS

Of course, the speech was ruined. All chance of a high-note ending was now gone, along with any useful footage. Even fifty years from now, the lead memory-image from this event would be that of Hamish himself, staring like a poleaxed calf, muttering some reflex platitudes about how everyone should remain dubious and calm.

"Perhaps this is a hoax," he suggested. "Or something much less than it seems. But even if it isn't . . . even if the cosmos has suddenly come calling . . . and everything changes . . ." He swallowed hard, eager only to get away. "In the end, we'll need caution, rather than arrogant pride, to get across the days and years ahead.

"What worked for so many individuals, groups, nations, and races who came before us? Amid doubt, worry, and myriad shocks, we should remember our limitations. Admit the boundaries of our wisdom, and turn to others, wiser than ourselves."

Was that a sufficiently lofty and ambiguous note to finish on? Many would assume that he was speaking of God. Or preaching humility. Some—a few—would know that he referred to the pyramid's eye. The Prophet and the Movement.

No matter. It was time to leave. While more people stood and pressed forward with questions or arguments, Hamish turned away with a farewell wave of one hand, to a mere smattering of applause.

Worst speech, ever, he growled, not even shaking hands with the conference organizers, who waited backstage. A sick feeling inside, made him wish he could teleport away. Not to a lonely mountain or beach, or to some place drenched in the latest news, but his private study. To his old-fashioned keyboard and the kind of work he once did happily, if obsessively, for days on end. Like things were before Carolyn left. Before great men discovered his other uses.

But escape was far away. Wriggles spoke from his earring, whispering a reminder. *You have that meeting. With Betsby.*

Stifling a sigh, Hamish turned to the middle-aged man who had been assigned to take care of him. Erik somebody—big-boned, but painfully thin. Apparently one of those caloric restriction types. But if he nursed any miffed feelings after Hamish's speech, it didn't show.

"You promised me a secure meeting room," Hamish said. "One with two entrances, and no cam views of either."

"This way, sir. I swept both corridors myself, just a few minutes ago. Of course, no one can guarantee—"

"It's okay." Hamish waved away any concern. "My meeting isn't secret, or even important. I just—"

He let it go with a shrug. *There are precautions you can take, nowadays, to keep an encounter vague, ambiguous. Rumored, inferred, but not proved. Deniable, even if folks swear they saw Jill go in one door and Jack go in the other. The trick is not to draw attention.*

No one was in the little conference room, when he arrived. Hamish found a basket of fruit and some juiceballs, taut in their membrane skins. But he felt too wound up to partake. Instead, he took a small device out of his jacket pocket and laid it on the table. Automatically, the scanner sought telltale reflective patterns and electromagnetic glimmers—any sign of microscopic tattle-lenses or audio pickups. In the surveillance arms race, an advantage always went to those who could afford the very latest thing. He had been assured that his doohickey was the best. This month.

Naturally, it detected his earring. But Wriggles was already registered with the detector device. Otherwise, the room seemed to be clean, as promised.

Where is the man?

Betsby knows we can have him picked up at any time, either on official charges or less openly. He must realize that this meeting is a courtesy on our part. A chance to avoid prison—or worse—if he comes clean. If he publicly admits responsibility for Senator Strong's outburst. But he's acting like he holds some card up his sleeve. Something giving him the upper hand.

It was a puzzler, all right. And an inner part of Hamish actually relished that.

Wriggles asked if he wanted a running summary of fast-breaking news—the alien object story that was drawing world attention to a small scientific center in Cuba.

"No," he answered, aloud. "I'll watch the press conference cold. Bare-eyed."

"And such *big* eyes they are," spoke a voice from behind Hamish. "The better to see the future with."

It was Roger Betsby, standing in the other doorway—bearded and a bit stooped, with a compact paunch at the middle and a tired expression on his somewhat puffy face. He stepped forward and placed a detector of his own upon the table. Clearly an older model. Still, it quickly spotted Wriggles. The little earring gave off a short *ping,* when Betsby's device registered it.

In turn, Hamish's detector cast a pale reddish glow upon Betsby's narrow, rimless specs.

"These old things?" The physician-activist held them up. "Mostly just optical glass, with the barest augmentation—to record what I'm looking at and provide level-one captions. It was agreed that we could both keep e-notes." He put the glasses back on.

"That's all right. I don't plan on saying or doing anything I'd be ashamed of. Thank you for coming, Doctor."

"How could I refuse an invitation to meet the famous Hamish Brookeman? I would guess that's half of your usefulness to the Eye. *Celebrighties can walk through walls.* Isn't that the expression? You can gain audience with almost anybody on Earth. Kings, presidents, oligarchs, anyone who loved or hated your stories and films. Meanwhile, the merely rich and powerful often snub each other."

Hamish shrugged. "There are drawbacks, too."

"Of that I'm sure. Privacy. Time. Preciously short supplies of personal attention span. The usual complaints. Still, you must be tired, after haranguing those poor godmakers out there. Part of a lifelong campaign to steer our ponderous civilization away from cliffs. And now, that astronaut may have spoiled it all. Gerald Livingstone's mysterious Havana Artifact is causing such a fuss. Are you sure you wouldn't prefer to put this meeting off? For another day? Another life?"

Hamish took a measured look at the other man. Betsby's offer wasn't courtesy. He was gauging the seriousness of the opposition. Whether the Movement would let itself get diverted by so minor a thing as possible contact with extraterrestrial intelligence.

"We both went to some trouble, in order to meet here today. Let's proceed." He sat, but only on the forward edge of a chair, with his long legs bent and elbows on the table.

"Very well, then." Roger Betsby plopped down heavily, letting his own chair teeter back a bit. He spread his hands, inviting questions.

"What puzzles me—" Hamish began.

"You mean, what puzzles the Eye."

Hamish blinked. The Movement didn't care for that term getting bruited around, in public. Anyway, he disliked being interrupted. "If you prefer. What interests me—or us—is why you think you won't face charges, since you admit to having poisoned Senator Strong."

"I admit no such thing. Never have. At worst, what I did was administer a perfectly legal substance, on my own initiative as a medical practitioner, in order to palliate the condition of a disease victim."

"A . . . victim . . ."

"Of an especially noxious illness."

Hamish stared for a moment, till Betsby continued.

"Albeit, I administered the dose without his knowledge or consent. I suppose I could get in serious trouble for that."

"Hm . . . so it wasn't a poison, per se. Or a banned drug."

"Far from it. The diametric opposite, you might say."

Hamish pondered. None of the previous agents—attorneys and investigators who visited Betsby—had been told this twist. Now, the man was clearly enjoying this moment of truth, stretching it out. Hamish understood the feeling, having done it to millions, in books and on large or small screens.

"I see now why you act as if you have some basis to blackmail the Senator." Hamish started enumerating on the fingers of one hand. "You admit that you doped Strong with a substance that triggered an offensively hysterical tirade in front of a nationwide audience. Normally, the fact that he'd been given a mind-altering drug might help temper the damage from his outburst, persuading many to pardon the repugnant things he blurted."

"The Algebra of Forgiveness," Betsby nodded. "Words can't be unsaid. But a poisoning would provide powerful mitigation, perhaps drawing pardon from those who already liked him. Or those benefiting from his influence. That is, *if it were a poison.* Go on."

"Um, right. You claim that the very *name* of the substance that you used might damage the senator even more than his upsetting words and actions. You threaten to reveal that information, if you are arrested, or if any other action is taken against you."

"I never expressed it as a threat. That would be blackmail in the legal and felonious sense. I simply pointed out that, if I am charged with a crime, or harmed in any way, then naturally, more facts will emerge, than if I were simply left alone."

"And now you claim that the stuff was legal, with legitimate therapeutic uses. Still, many substances have multiple effects, contingent upon—"

"Let me save you the trouble of going down that path. This one has *only* therapeutic uses. Few known side effects and only mild counter-indicator warnings."

Hamish nodded. He had been afraid of this. "So, legally, you may only have committed the crime of treating a patient without his consent? But your threats . . ."

"As I said, I doubt you could make any blackmail charge

stick. I've been careful with my wording. I have an excellent lawyer program."

"Hm. Not as good as ours, I bet. Still, you imply that we . . . that Senator Strong might have reason to fear complete disclosure. Because the public might be *less* forgiving, upon finding out what concoction it was."

"No flies on you," Betsby commented.

"What?"

"Just something my gramps used to say. A compliment to an active mind. Go on Mr. Brookeman."

Hamish frowned.

"You imply that Strong's *medical condition* is one the public would despise even more than *your* act of slipping the senator a cryptic, behavior-altering substance."

"Oh, I won't get off, scot-free, if you people choose to reveal everything . . . or force me to. Some will call me a hero, but I could lose my medical license. Maybe get some jail time. Strong could sue me.

"But his political career would be kaput."

Clearly, the fellow thought this a decent trade. And despite himself, Hamish felt drawn to Roger Betsby. If for nothing else, then the sheer gall and originality of his approach, and the way it had been formulated as a puzzle, as if for Hamish alone. . . .

He ventured. "It would have to be a medical condition that's both intrinsically repugnant and somehow voluntary. A lifestyle choice."

Betsby nodded. "Go on."

"And yet . . . something that's relatively unknown to the public. Or, at least, under the popular vradar."

"Gramps would've liked you." A strange compliment that gave Hamish an involuntary flush . . . which also tipped him into realization.

"It's an addiction, isn't it? Senator Strong has a habit. A bad one. You . . . you slipped him an *antidote*! Oh Lord."

The other man nodded, with a glint in his narrow eyes. "Bingo."

Hamish allowed himself a thin smile. Even after just a few minutes together, he already valued respect from Roger Betsby, more than the cheap, reflexive praise of critics or fans. There weren't more than a few dozen people on this poor planet he felt that way about. At one level, this was actually fun!

But that satisfaction took poor second, right now, to another feeling. Wrath! How he wanted to get his hands around a certain senator's neck. None of the profiles or dossiers suggested addiction. Oh, some alcoholic stupors, now and then, and maybe a little neococaine, but no word of anything with its hooks sunk deep. Whatever filthy habit Strong carried on his back, the movement was completely in the dark. Tenskwatawa would be furious!

"I don't supposed you'll be accommodating, Doctor, and tell me what it is? Or name the antidote you used? Or explain why it had such powerful behavioral effects?"

"Maybe another time," Betsby said, shaking his head. "Till then, of course, I needn't remind you that I have set up all sorts of trigger-revelation bots, all over the place, that will unleash every bit of it, should something unfortunate happen to me."

"Of course. That goes without saying." Hamish nodded. Though he knew there were still dark ways, desperate options.

"Very well, then," Betsby said, standing up. "That really ought to be enough for your people to chew on, for now."

Nevertheless, from his manner, his body language, the man revealed plenty to Hamish. Perhaps much more than he thought.

You don't plan to keep this secret forever, no matter what we do. No matter what we offer.

You have something bigger in mind. More than just ruining the career of a legislator from one of the Tribal States.

You plan to make a point.

You want to save the world.

Hamish knew the type. The planet was, in fact, filled nearly to overflowing with sincere people, frantically bent on saving it, while disagreeing deeply over how. And, yes, his own cause—to protect Earth from its would-be saviors—might be assigned to the very same category!

He could honestly admit that irony. Even when it forced him down unpleasant paths.

"Well, Doctor, you clearly have a timetable for revealing what you know. I won't press you to go farther today, though you can expect to hear from me soon."

As soon as we've had a chance to consult, to analyze these recordings, to parse your words for hidden meanings, and every skin pore for potential weakness.

"Anyway"—Hamish cocked his head as Wriggles chimed a time alert—"it's nearly time for that big megillah press conference from Washington and Havana about the space object. Shall we order some food and drink, and a pixelvee, so we can watch it here? Who knows? The whole planetary situation may change. So much that all our present conflicts will seem moot."

Of course Betsby agreed to stay. Even those who are aware of celebrity power generally find it hard to resist. Hence, the sweet-and-sour irony redoubled. Hamish felt glad to share the coming historic moment with a kindred spirit, of sorts . . . and a twinge of guilt over fate's cruelty.

Especially over the way it sometimes forced him to protect men he despised, by destroying somebody he liked.

"Geo-engineering" refers to one of humanity's oldest activities—altering some trait of Planet Earth. Our ancestors—never content—strove to change their environment. Huts and hearths banished winter's chill. Forests gave way to gardens. Irrigation made some regions bloom, then salt-poisoned them into desert. Dams shifted whole watersheds, displacing weight across seismic faults. Delving for fuel and ore, we altered mountain ranges and the air we breathed.

By one way of reckoning, we transformed several hundred cubic kilometers of fossil fuels into two cubic kilometers of human beings. Perhaps the greatest engineering feat of all. Then science let us do something else unique. With the power to *notice,* we began asking a question that can only be pondered by worried young gods:

"Is there anything we can do about all this? Repair the damage? Change things for the better?" No longer gradual or unintentional, geo-engineering became a matter of theory and experiment, debate and policy.

Suppose we pump huge quantities of CO_2 into deep, saline layers. That might slow global warming for a while. Unless the gas blew back out? Look up the Lake Nyos Disaster. Even if it stays put, that's where the archaea took shelter half a billion years ago, when oxygen transformed the atmosphere. How will they react to a sudden influx of CO_2, which they use to make methane and hydrogen sulfide? And if *those* gases emerged . . . ?

Others propose erecting huge shades above Earth, dimming sunlight by just enough. Or by spraying stratospheric aerosols to increase reflection, cooling the planet. Some fear unintended oscillations, swinging out of control. Others remind that sulfide gas may have caused the Permian Extinction—the greatest loss of life Earth ever saw.

Even the most ecological ideas have critics. Fertilizing vast "desert" stretches of ocean would seem an obvious win-win, expanding the food chain and much-needed fisheries while sucking atmospheric carbon. Crude attempts with iron powder caused problems. But what of using tidal energy to stir ocean bottoms, exactly like natural currents?

Suppose a naturalistic solution worked! Might we think ourselves wise enough to *manage* a complex planet? The New Puritans say our best course is to "do less harm" in the first place. But can we *only* fix our messes through rigid self-denial? Is there no role for the trait that took us from the caves? The can-do spirit of ambition?

—Pandora's Cornucopia

23.
WARNING

It was nearing nightfall when he approached the shorestead from the west, with the setting sun behind him.

Of course, by now the tide was low and the main gates were open—and Peng Xiang Bin felt foolish. In hindsight, his panic now seemed excessive. *I might have sold those lesser stones, bought a beer by the fishmonger stands, and already made it home by now, having dinner while showing Mei Ling a handful of cash.*

Soon, he faced familiar outlines—the sagging north wall . . . the metlon poles and supercord bracings . . . the solar distillery . . . and patches where he had begun preparing two upper-story rooms for occupation. He even caught a scent of that Vietnamese *nuk mam* sauce that Mei Ling added to half her preparations. It all looked normal. Still, he circled the half-ruined mansion, checking for intruder signs. Oil in the water. Tracks in the muddy sand. Nothing visible.

A wasted day, then. A crazy, draining adventure that I could scarcely afford. Some lost stones . . .

. . . though there are more where those came from.

In fact, he had begun to fashion a plan in his head. The smuggler, Quang Lu, had many contacts. Perhaps, while keeping the matter vague at first, Bin might use Quang to set up a meeting, in such a time and place where treachery would be difficult. Perhaps arranging for several competitors to be present at once. How did one of the ancient sages put it? *In order not to be trampled by an elephant, get many of them to push against each other.*

All right, maybe no sage actually said that. But one should have. Surely, Bin did not have to match the great lords of government, wealth, and commerce. What he needed was a situation where they canceled each other's strength! Get them bidding for what he had. Openly, enough so no one could benefit by keeping him quiet.

First thing, I must find a good hiding place for the stone. Then come up with the right story for Quang.

It took real effort just to haul himself out of the water, Bin's body felt limp with fatigue. He was past hunger and exhaustion, making his way from the atrium dock to the stairs, then across the roof, and finally to the entrance of the tent-shelter. It flapped with a welcoming rhythm, emitting puffs of homecoming aromas that made his head swim.

Ducking to step inside, Bin blinked in the dimmer light. "You won't believe what a day I have had! Is that sautéed prawn? The ones I caught this morning? I'm glad you chose—"

Mei Ling had been stirring the wok. At first, as she turned around, he thought she smiled. Then Bin realized . . . it was a grimace. She did not speak, but fear glistened in her eyes, which darted to her left—alerting him to swivel—

A creature stood on their small table. A large *bird* of some kind, with a long, straight beak. It gazed at Xiang Bin, regarding him with a head tilt, one way then the other. It spread stubby wings, stretching them, and Bin numbly observed.

No flight feathers. A penguin? What would a penguin be doing here in sweltering Shanghai?

Then he noticed its talons. *Penguins don't have—*

The claws gripped something that still writhed on the tabletop, gashed and torn. It looked like a *snake*. . . . Only, instead of oozing blood or guts, there were bright flashes and electric sizzles.

A machine. They are both machines.

Without moving its beak, the bird spoke.

"You must not fear. There is no time for fear."

Bin swallowed. His lips felt chapped and dry.

"What . . . who are you?"

"I am an instrumentality, sent by those who might save your life." The bird-thing abruptly bent and pecked hard at the snake. Sparks flew. It went dark and limp. An effective demonstration, if Bin needed one.

"Please go to the window," the winged mechanism resumed, gesturing with its beak. "And bring the stone here."

Well, at least it spoke courteously. He turned and saw that the white, egg-shaped relic lay on the ledge, soaking in the fading sunlight—instead of wrapped in a dark cloth, as they had agreed. He glanced back sharply at his wife, but Mei Ling was now holding little Xiao-En. She merely shrugged as the baby squirmed and whimpered, trying to nurse.

With a low sigh, Bin approached the stone, whose opalescent surface seemed to glow with more than mere reflections. He could sense the bird leaning forward, eagerly.

As if sensing Bin's hands, the whitish surface turned milky and began to swirl. Now it was plain to the eye, how

this thing differed from the Havana Artifact that he had
seen briefly through an ailectronics store window. It seemed
a bit smaller, rounder, and considerably less smooth. One
end was marred by pits, gouges, and blisters that tapered
into thin streaks across the elongated center. Yet similarities were plain. A spinning sense of depth grew more intense near his hands. And, swiftly, a faint shape began to
form, at first indistinct, coalescing as if from a fog.

Demons, Xiang Bin thought. *Or rather, a demon.* A single
figure approached, bipedal, shaped vaguely like a man.

With reluctance—wishing he had never laid eyes on it—
Bin made himself plant hands on both tapered ends, gritting his teeth as a brief, faint tremor ran up the inner
surface of his arms. He hefted the heavy stone, turned and
carried it away from the sunlight. At which point, the glow
seemed only to intensify, filling and chasing the dim shadows of the tent-shelter.

"Put it down here, on the table, but please do not release
it from your grasp," the bird-thing commanded, still polite,
but insistent. Bin obeyed, though he wanted to let go. The
shape that gathered form, within the stone, was not one
that he had seen before. More humanlike than the demons
he had glimpsed on TV, shown peering outward from the
stone in Washington—but still a demon. Like the frightening penguin-creature, whose wing now brushed his arm as
it bent next to him, eager for a closer look.

"The legends are true!" it murmured. Bin felt the bird's
voice resonate, emitting from an area on its chest. "Worldstones are said to be picky. They may choose one human to
work with, or sometimes none at all. Or so go the stories."
The robot regarded Xiang Bin with a glassy eye. "You are
fortunate in more ways than you might realize."

Nodding without much joy, Xiang Bin knew at least one
way.

I am needed, then. It will work only for me.

That means they won't just take the thing and leave us be.

But it also means they must keep me alive. For now.

The demon within the stone—it had finished clarifying, though the image remained rippled and flawed. Approaching on two oddly jointed legs, it reached forward with powerfully muscular arms, as if to touch or seize Bin's enclosing hands. The mouth—appearing to have four lips arranged like a flattened diamond—moved underneath a slitlike nose and a single, ribbonlike organ where eyes would have been. With each opening and closing of the mouth, a faint *buzzing* quivered the surface under Bin's right palm.

"The stone is damaged," the penguinlike automaton observed. "It must have once possessed sound transducers. Perhaps, in a well-equipped laboratory—"

"Legends?" Bin suddenly asked, knowing he should not interrupt. But he couldn't help it. Fear and exhaustion and contact with demons—it all had him on the verge of hysteria. Anyway, the situation had changed. If he was special, even needed, then the least that he could demand was an answer or two!

"What legends? You mean these stones have appeared before?"

The bird-thing tore its gaze away from the image of a humanoid creature, portrayed opening and closing its mouth in a pantomime of speech that timed roughly, but not perfectly, with the vibrations under Bin's right hand.

"You might as well know, Peng Xiang Bin, since yours is now a burden and a task assigned by Heaven." The penguinlike machine gathered itself to full height and then gave him a small bow of the head. "A truth that goes back farther than any other that is known."

Bin's mouth felt dry. "What truth?"

"That stones have fallen since time began. And men are

said to have spoken to them for at least nine thousand years.

"And in all that long epoch, they have referred to a day of culmination. And that day, long prophesied, may finally be at hand."

Bin felt warm contact at his back, as Mei Ling pressed close—as near as she could, while nursing their child. He did not remove his hands from the object on the table. But he was glad that one of hers slid around his waist, clutching him tight and driving out some of the chill he felt, inside.

"Then . . . ," Bin swallowed. "Then *you* are not an alien?"

"Me?" The penguin stared at Bin for a moment, then emitted a chirp—the mechanical equivalent of laughter. "I see how you could leap to that mistaken conclusion. But no, Peng Xiang Bin. I am man-built. So was this snake," its talons squeezed the artificial serpent harder, "sent here by a different—and more ruthless—band of humans. Our competitors also seek to learn more about the interstellar emissary probes."

Meanwhile, the entity within the stone appeared frustrated, perhaps realizing that no one heard its words. The buzzing intensified, then stopped. Then, instead, the demon reached forward, as if toward Bin, and started to *draw a figure* in space, close to the boundary between them. Wherever it moved its scaly hand, a trail of inky darkness remained, until Bin realized.

Calligraphy. The creature was brushing a figure—an ideogram—in a flowing, archaic-looking style. It was a complicated symbol, containing at least twenty strokes. *I wish I had more education,* Bin thought, gazing in awe at the final shape, when it stood finished, throbbing across the face of the glowing worldstone. Both symmetrically beautiful and yet jagged, threatening, it somehow transfixed the eye and made his heart pound.

Xiang Bin did not know the character. But anyone with the slightest knowledge of Chinese would recognize the radical—the core symbol—that it was built from.

Danger.

CONFLICTING WISDOM

Already the danger is so great, for every individual, every class, every people, that to cherish any illusion whatever is deplorable. Time does not suffer itself to be halted; there is no question of prudent retreat or wise renunciation. Only dreamers believe that there is a way out. Optimism is cowardice.

—Oswald Spengler, *Men and Technics,* 1932

In good times, pessimism is a luxury; but in bad times, pessimism is a self-fulfilling and fatal prophecy.

—Jamais Cascio, *Open the Future,* 2005

24.
THE WORLD WATCHES

"Why must I wear this thing?" Gerald complained. He plucked at the sleeve of his freshly laundered and ribboned dress uniform, referring to what lay beneath—a bulge in the fleshy part of his forearm. An implanted NASA telemetry device.

"Oh, don't be a wiper," General Hideoshi scolded. In person, the brigadier was even more petite than she appeared on-screen—which had the paradoxical effect of making her rank more imposing. Stars on each shoulder glittered under the stage lights. "You've worn implants ever since you entered training."

"For health diagnostics, biologging, and work-related drugdrips. And we get to turn 'em off, after missions. But this thing is huge! And I know it's not just checking my blood pressure."

Akana shrugged. "Price of freedom, friend. You chose to be a human guinea pig, by planting your hand on that thing." She nodded toward the Object, glossy and opalescent in its felt-lined cradle, sitting a meter away from Gerald atop the conference table. "It was either this," she gestured at his arm, "or extended deep quarantine. You still have that option, you know. Go back into the tank."

Gerald snorted. "No tanks."

"You're welcome." Akana chuckled.

He didn't mention *other* implants that he only suspected— like something foreign floating inside his left eyeball, sampling light without blocking his retina. Looking out at the world through his own iris. In effect, seeing whatever he saw. As if it weren't enough that a dozen other team members were constantly watching, whenever he communed with the Messenger from MEO. Just one of many names for the object.

My "egg" they call it. Gerald's Galactic Geode. Or the Havana Artifact. Or the thing that garbageman-cowboy Livingstone lassoed with his space-lariat. It had better turn out to be benign because from now on, my name is tied to whatever it does. Good or ill.

Beyond thick curtains, a babble of press and invited guests could be heard, taking seats in the hall proper—the largest auditorium at the Naval Research Lab, just outside of Washington. A convenient older building that survived Awfulday unscathed—and diplomatically innocuous, while offering military levels of security.

This side of the curtain, on a wide stage, dignitaries filed in to take assigned positions at the long table. First NASA and Foresight officials, then representatives from EU and

AU and GEACS. Finally delegates from both guild and academy. Some had helped with preliminary analyses in Cuba. Others just wanted to shake Gerald's hand . . . the one that *hadn't* touched the Artifact, of course. Others just kept glancing toward the ovoid crystal, glistening quietly under the stage lights.

Someone had suggested laying a purple cloth over it, for the president to pull away with due drama. But a public affairs psychologist insisted, *"Let the public see it, first thing, as soon as the curtain opens. They'll be thinking about nothing else, anyway. So turn that into a dramatic advantage. Sit and wait while all viewers zoom in with specs and vus. An expression of ultimate openness. Only after the hubbub dies down, then have the president come onstage."*

That courtesy harkened back to when the office held real and terrible power. Of course, it all sounded like hooey. At least a cover might have offered Gerald a break from the thing's constant, eye-drawing allure. What decided the matter was simple practicality. The object needed to bathe in light for some time, in order to function.

Everyone settled into assigned places. Akana to Gerald's left, where the Artifact would not block her face from the crowd. His own position, closest to the gleaming thing, bespoke a growing consensus. He was not only its discoverer, but in some way its *keeper.* The one asked to pick it up. To carry the ovoid, whenever it must be moved. The one present, whenever specialists wanted to try some new method for communicating with the entities inside.

An honor, I suppose—and who knows? Maybe even historic. On the other hand, I'm not sure I like the way this thing tugs at me. Like a habit or addiction. Or like I belong to it, now.

And if all this goes badly, there's no place on or off the planet where I can hide.

At present, the orb lay quiescent, a soft shimmer rippling its surface—a liquid impression of great, perhaps infinite depth. A vastly magnified image of the ovoid was projected onto a giant screen, above and behind the dais, bright enough to cast Gerald's shadow across the table, limned in silvery light.

"Wouldn't it be something, if it refused to perform in public?"

Akana shot him a glare, for even thinking that way. Of course, there were recordings of hour after hour, spent by specialists interrogating the smoke-and-mirror enigma— some contained in that terabyte of sample images that somebody had leaked. Many of the pictures showed Gerald with his left hand planted on the glossy surface, *while some other palm seemed to rise out of those milky depths, to touch his, from within.*

Time and again that happened. Some alien-looking hand—variously scaly, or fleshy, or furry, or consisting of pincer-claws—appeared to float up from within the Artifact, in order to perform the same strange ritual, ever since he first established contact, during fiery reentry.

Contact, yes, but with what? With whom?

Gradually over several days, more depth developed. Hands led to arms or tentacles that receded *inward,* as if the Artifact were tens of meters deep, perhaps much more, instead of a few dozen centimeters. Then, torsos or bodies appeared at the ends of those arms, moving closer, though always distorted, as if viewed through a thick ball of milky glass.

And finally came heads . . . sometimes faces . . . equipped with eyes or sensing organs that pressed up to the inner surface, seeming to peer outward, even as Gerald and his colleagues stared back.

After gaping long enough, your mind played tricks. You even found it possible to imagine that *you* were *inside,* while those alien figures scrutinized your cramped, little prison-world from the outside, as if through some kind of lens.

Maybe they're doing just that. One theory called the Artifact a transmitter. An interstellar communication device offering instant hookup across the light-years, to aliens now living on some other world.

While others think it has to be a hoax.

Some of the best experts in display technology—from Hollywood to Bombay to Kinshasa—had flown in to examine the thing. Many of its behaviors and functions could be duplicated with known technology, they decreed. But not all. In fact, some were downright astonishing. Especially the way three-dimensional images might loom outward in any direction—or all directions at once—from deep within a solid object. Or the unknown manner that it sensed nearby people and things. Or the mysterious and unconventional means by which it drew power from ambient lighting. Still, none of those enigmas guaranteed against a fake. Fraudulent alien artifacts had been tried before, by spoof artists with deep pockets and plenty of creativity. An Interpol team had been assigned to trawl the vir and real worlds, seeking to profile a certain kind of prankster—one with fantastic ingenuity and extravagant resources.

Likewise, the symbols that kept floating upward through that inner murk, to plaster themselves against its translucent shell, like insects wriggling and trying to escape. Were they proof of alien provenance? More words had formed, that went beyond the initial greeting, and yet all meaning remained frustrating. Ambiguous. It wasn't just a strangeness of syntax and grammar. Rather, the sheer *number* of symbologies seemed startling. Just when one linguistic system was starting to make sense, it would get jostled aside, forced to make way for another. So far, there had been at least fifty, spanning a range greater than all human languages.

This very complexity helped convince the advisory committee against any likelihood of fraud. One or two eerie grammars might be counterfeited. But why would hoaxers go to so much effort, creating scores of them, apparently bickering and competing with each other for attention? Pranksters would want to convey authority and confidence—not an impression of inner squabbling.

Oh, it seemed likely this was real, all right. Some kind of emissary artifact, representing a menagerie of sapient races, a blizzard of dialects, and a panoply of shining planets, depicted in varied colors and living textures, from pure water worlds to hazy desert globes. That very diversity seemed reassuring, in a way. For, if so many races shared some kind of community, out there, then surely humanity had little to fear?

Without willing it to, Gerald found his left hand creeping closer to the ovoid, as if drawn by habit, or a mind of its own. And soon, the Artifact reacted. Vague, cloudy patches clarified into more distinct swirls that gathered and clustered in the area closest to him. That sense of depth returned. Again, he seemed to be looking inward . . . *downward* . . .

. . . and soon, a clump of minuscule shadows appeared, as if they were figures viewed at a great distance, through a shimmering mirage-haze. Starting small and indistinct, these tiny black shapes began rising, growing larger with each passing moment, as if approaching through banks of polychromatic fog.

Physical contact with my hand doesn't seem to be required, anymore, he pondered with bemusement. *Just proximity.*

And there was another difference, this time.

There are several of them, at the same time.

Always, before, there had been a jostling sense of exclusivity. Just one hand met his. One alien alphabet lingered for a while, before being pushed aside by another.

Now, he counted four . . . no, five . . . figures that seemed to be striding forward together, side by side, gaining color and detail as they approached. Two of them were murky bipedal shadows, accompanied by what seemed to be some kind of a four-legged centauroid, a crablike being and—well—something like a cross between a fish and a squid, propelling along with tentacular pulsations, easily keeping pace beside the walkers.

Apparently, reality operated under different rules, in there.

"What the devil are you doing?" Akana hissed, beside him. "We agreed not to trigger a response till the president said so!"

"I'm not doing anything," Gerald grunted back at her, partly lying. His hand wasn't touching the Artifact. But nor was he drawing it back. Indeed, clearly, the approaching figures seemed to be moving toward him, drawn by his attention.

Speaking of attention, Gerald could sense the dignitaries nearby, halting their private conversations and turning to look at the big screen, amid a rising babble of excitement. Those nearby clustered close behind Gerald to look at the real thing. He felt warm breath and smelled somebody's curry lunch.

"You . . . really ought to . . ." Akana began. But he could tell she was as transfixed as the others. Something important was happening. More so than a lapse in protocol.

At that moment, while the alien figures were still some "distance" away through that inner haze, somebody pushed a switch and the stage curtains spread apart, exposing the dais and the big screen to a thousand people in the auditorium . . . and several hundred millions of viewers around the globe.

Some interval later, while a babble filled the hall, a fanfare played through the public address system. Gerald guessed, with a small part of his mind, that it must be for the president coming onstage. Just in time to be ignored.

The five figures loomed, their forms beginning to fill one side of the Artifact boundary, facing Gerald. He recognized the centauroid and one of the bipeds, from earlier, brief encounters. The first had a hawkish face, with two extremely large eyes on both sides of a fierce-looking beak. A nocturnal creature, perhaps, yet apparently unbothered by bright light. The other strode on two legs that moved like stilts, swinging to the side in order to move forward. Its head seemed a mass of wormlike tendrils, without any breaks or apparent openings.

The crablike being closely resembled—well—Gerald's dinner, two nights ago, while the aquatic seemed something of a nightmare. At least, those were his vague impressions. To be honest, Gerald had little attention to spare. For the moment, despite all his previous experience with the alien object, he felt as pinned and fascinated as any of those watching from their homes, across the planet.

Gerald abruptly realized there were *more* entities now, emerging from the distance, hurrying forward—at least a dozen or more of them, propelling themselves with haste, as if eager to catch up with the first ones.

Those five alien figures stopped, crowding together at the lens-like boundary between the ovoid and Gerald's world. He sensed them looking outward, not just at him, but at Akana and others within view. He could no longer hear or feel hot breath on his neck. For a few seconds, no one exhaled.

Then, from each of the five aliens, there emerged a single dot. A black form that grew and fluttered as it took shape. A symbol or glyph, each quite different than the others. One was sharply angular. Another manifested as all slants and intersections. A third looked like a crude pie chart . . . and so on. The signs plastered themselves in a row, along the curved surface where the Artifact's interior met the outside world of humans.

Is that it? Another set of enigmas? Well, at least a few of them are working together, for a change. Maybe we can start the long process . . .

The symbols began to mutate again. Each transformed, and Gerald had an intuition—they were turning into block-like letters of the Roman alphabet, just like that day during reentry.

If it just says "greeting" again, I may scream, he thought.

Fortunately, it didn't. Not exactly.

This time, instead of one word, there were two.

JOIN US.

PART FOUR

NOBLER IN THE MIND

We need not marvel at extinction; if we must marvel, let it be at our presumption in imagining for a moment that we understand the many complex contingencies, on which the existence of each species depends.

—**Charles Darwin**

SPECIES

autie murphy verifies +++ he found the basque chimera
+!+ the child lives +!+ and is safe, for now.

safe from the normalpeople who would treasure +/– per-
secute –/+ or study himherit –/– perhaps to death

born in a year that would have been the square of the
number of birthdays that jesus would have had — if jesus
had lived twelve more years –+– and had an extra leap
day every year +++ and if the primate avoided prime numbers +/– what more proof could anybody need?/–

+++ good going murph +++

only now, what do we do with this knowledge? the autie
thing? dance with it a while + then pack it away

+/– **all facts are created equal.** –/+ the number of dollars in your bank account –/– the number of holes in your
socks . . . all the same, right? pragmatism is for poorpar-
ents –/– those who are distraught over the "autism plague"

— pragmatism doesn't come easily to us —

+++ but it must +++

if we lack the passion & drive of homosaps—their cro
magnon attention-allocation genius—then can we use
something else? +++ something we are good at +++

!/! if we super-autistics really are more like animals . . .
or even maybe like Neanderthals . . . then might the chimera teach us something valuable?/?

maybe we should do something with this knowledge
possibly go talk to himherit
perhaps even care

25.
DEPARTURE

The journey of three thousand *li* began with a bribe and a little air.

And a penguinlike robot, standing on the low dining table that Peng Xiang Bin had salvaged from a flooded mansion. A mechanical creature that stayed punctiliously polite, while issuing commands that would forever disrupt the lives of Xiang Bin and Mei Ling and their infant son.

"There is very little time," it said, gravely, in a Beijing-accented voice that emanated somewhere on its glossy chest, well below the sharply pointed beak. "Others have sniffed the same suspicions that brought me here, drawn by your indiscreet queries about selling a gleaming, egg-like stone, with moving shapes within."

To illustrate what it meant by *others,* the bird-thing scraped one metallic talon along the scaly flank of a large, robotic *snake*—the other interloper, that had climbed the crumbling walls and slithered across the roof of this once-lavish beachfront house, slipping into the shorestead shelter and terrifying Mei Ling, while Bin was away on his ill-fated expedition to Shanghai East. Fortunately, the penguin-machine arrived soon after that. A brief, terrible battle ensued, leaving the false serpent torn and ruined, just before Bin returned home.

The reason for that fracas lay on the same table, shimmering with light energy that it had absorbed earlier, from sunshine. An ovoid shape, almost half a meter from tip to tip, opalescent and mesmerizing. Clearly, Bin should have been more cautious—*far* more cautious—making queries about this thing on the Mesh.

The penguin-shaped robot took a step toward Bin.

"Those who sent the snake-creature are just as eager as my owners are, to acquire the worldstone. I assure you they'll be less considerate than I have been, if we are still here when they send reinforcements. And *my* consideration has limits."

Though a poor man, with meager education, Bin had enough sense to recognize a veiled threat. Still, he felt reluctant to go charging off with his family, into a fading afternoon, with this entity . . . leaving behind, possibly forever, the little shorestead home that he and Mei Ling had built by hand, on the ruins of a seaside mansion.

"You said that the . . . worldstone . . . picks only one person to speak to." He gestured at the elongated egg. Now that his hands weren't in contact, it no longer depicted the clear image of a demon . . . or space alien. (There was a difference?) Still, the lopsided orb remained transfixing. Swirling shapes, like storm-driven clouds, seemed to roil beneath its scarred and pitted surface, shining by their own light—as if the object were a lens into another world.

"Wouldn't your rivals have to talk to it *through me*?" he finished. "Just as you must?"

One rule of commerce, that even a poor man understood— you can get a better deal when more than one customer is bidding.

"Perhaps, Peng Xiang Bin," the bird-thing replied, shifting its weight in what seemed a gesture of impatience. "On the other hand, you should not overestimate your value, or underestimate the ferocity of my adversaries. This is not a market situation, but akin to ruthless *war*.

"Furthermore, while very little is known about these worldstones, it is unlikely that you are indispensable. Legends suggest that it will simply pick *another* human counterpart—if the current one dies."

Mei Ling gasped, seizing Bin's left arm in a tight grip, fingernails and all. But still, his mind raced. *It will say whatever it must, in order to get my cooperation. But appearances may be deceiving. The snake could have been sent by the same people, and the fight staged, in order to frighten us. That might explain why both machines showed up at about the same time.*

Bin knew he had few advantages. Possibly, the robot had sensors to read his pulse, blood pressure, iris dilation, skin flush response . . . and lots of other things that a more educated person might know about. Every suspicion or lie probably played out across his face—and Bin had never been a good gambler, even bluffing against humans.

"I . . . will need—"

"Payment is in order," the penguinoid immediately conceded. "We'll start with a bonus of ten times your current yearly income, just for coming along, followed by a salary of one thousand New Hong Kong Dollars per month. And more is possible with good results. Perhaps much more."

It was a princely boon, but Bin frowned, and the machine seemed to read his thoughts.

"I can tell, you are more concerned about other things, like whether you can trust us."

Bin nodded—a tense jerk. The penguin gave a semblance of a shrug.

"As you might guess, the amount of payment I just offered is trivial to my owners, so I would have no reason to lie. But you must decide. Right now." Again, with that faint tone of threat. Still, Bin hesitated.

"I will pack some things for the baby," Mei Ling announced, with resolution in her voice. "We can leave all the rest. Everything."

But the penguinoid stopped her. "I regret, wife and child cannot come. It is too dangerous. There are no accommodations and they will slow us down." As Bin started to protest, it raised one stubby wing. "But you will not leave them to starve. I will provide part of your bonus now, in a form they can use."

Bin blinked, staring as the machine settled down into a squat, closing its eyes and straining, almost as if it were . . .

With an audible grunt, it stepped back, revealing a small pellet on the tabletop. "You'll find the funds readily accessible at any city kiosk. As I said, the amount, though large for you, is too small for my owners to care about cheating from you."

"That is *not* what worries me," Mei Ling said, though she snatched up the pellet. While her voice was husky with fear, holding Xiao-En squirming against her chest, she wore a cold, pragmatic expression. "Your masters may find it inconvenient to leave witnesses. If you get the stone— how much better if no one else knows? After . . . Xiang Bin departs with you . . . I may not live out the hour."

I hadn't thought of that, Bin realized, grimly. His jaw clenched. He took a step toward the table.

"Open your tutor-tablet," the bird-thing snapped, no longer courteous. "Quickly! And speak your names aloud."

Bin hurried to activate the little Mesh device, made for preschoolers, but the only access unit they could afford. Their link was at the minimal, FreePublic level—still, when he spoke the words, a new posting erupted from the little screen. It showed his face . . . and Mei Ling's . . . and the worldstone . . . plus a few dozen characters outlining an agreement.

"Now, your wife knows no more than is already published—which is little enough. Our rivals can extract nothing else, so *we* have no reason to silence her. Nor will anyone else. Does that reassure?" When they nodded, the machine hurried on.

"Good. Only, by providing this reassurance, I have made our time predicament worse. Over the course of the next few minutes and hours, many new forces will notice and start to converge. So choose, Peng Xiang Bin. This instant! If you will not bring the stone, I will explode in twenty seconds, to prevent others from getting it. Agree, or flee! Sixteen . . . fifteen . . . fourteen . . ."

"I'll go!"

Bin grabbed up a heavy sack and rolled the gleaming ovoid inside. The worldstone brightened, briefly, at his touch, then seemed to give up and go dark, as he stuffed in some padding and slung the bag over a shoulder. The penguinoid was already at the flap of the little tent-shelter. Bin turned . . .

. . . as Mei Ling held up their son—the one thing they both cared about, more than each other. "Thrive," he said, with his hand upon the boy's head.

"Survive, husband," she commanded in turn. A moist glisten in her eye both surprised and warmed him, more than any words. Bin accepted the obligation with a hurried bow, then ducked under the flap, following the robot into the setting sun.

Halfway down the grand staircase, on the landing that Bin had turned into an indoor dock, the penguin split its belly open, revealing a small cavity and a slim, metal object within.

"Take it."

He recognized a miniature breathing device—a mouthpiece with a tiny, insulated capsule of highly compressed air. It even had a pair of dangling gel-eyepieces. Quang Lu, the smuggler, possessed a bulkier model. Bin snatched it out of the fissure, which closed quickly, as the robot waddled to the edge, overlooking the greasy water of the Huangpu Estuary.

"Now, make speed!"

It dived in, then paused to swivel and regard Bin with beady, now luminescent eyes, watching the human's every move.

Peng Xiang Bin took a brief, backward glance, wondering if he would ever return. He slipped in the mouthpiece and pushed the gels over his eyes. Then took the biggest plunge of his life.

SCHADENFREUDE

If and when our civilization expires, we may not even agree on the cause of death. Autopsies of empires are often inconclusive. Consider Alexander Demandt, a German historian who in the 1980s collected 210 different theories for the fall of the Roman Empire, including attacks by nomads, food poisoning, decline of Aenean character, loss of gold, vanity, mercantilism, a steepening class divide, ecological degradation, and even the notion that civilizations just get tired after a while.

Some were opposites, like too much Christian piety versus too little. Or too much tolerance of internal deviance versus the lack of it. Other reasons may have added together, piling like fatal straws on a camel's back.

Now it's your turn! Unlike those elitist compilers, over at the Pandora Foundation, our open-source doomsday system invites you, the public, to participate in evaluating how it's all going to end.

Using World Model 2040 as a shared starting condition, we've seed-slotted a thousand general doom scenarios. Groups are already forming to team-reify them. So join one, bringing your biases and special skills. Or else, start your own doomsday story, no matter how crackpot! Is Earth running out of phlogiston? Will mole people rise out of the ground, bent on revenge? Later, we'll let quantum comparators rank every story according to probabilities.

But for now, it's time for old-fashioned, unmatched human imagination. So have fun! Make your best case. Convince us all that your chosen Failure Mode is the one that will bring us all down!

—from SlateZine's "Choose Your Own Apocalypse"

joshsimgame, August 2046

26.

COOPERATION

That first day passed, and then a tense night that he spent clutching a sleeping dolphin by moonlight, while clouds of phosphorescent plankton drifted by.

I hear that cetaceans sleep with just half their brains at a time. Jeez, how useful would that be?

Fortunately, the same selective-permeability technology that enabled his helmet to draw oxygen from the sea also provided a trickle of freshwater, filling a small reservoir near his cheek. *I've got to buy stock in this company,* he thought, making a checklist for when he was picked up tomorrow.

Only pickup did not happen—no helicopters or rescue zeps, no speedy trimarans bearing the Darktide Services logo, or even a fishing boat. The next morning and afternoon passed pretty much the same as the first, without catching sight of land. *The world always felt so crowded,* he thought. Now it seemed endless and unexplored.

Funny. I would have expected Lacey to fill the sky with searchers, by now. And not just his mother. Despite a reputation as a thrill-seeking playboy, Hacker had some genuine friends, a brother who would join the search, and some loyal staff. *Every bit of electronics in this suit must be fried. And I must have come down way, way off course.*

The long day that followed seemed to pass quite slowly in the company of his new friends, who alternately carried and guided him in some unknown direction.

The helmet came stocked with one small protein stick. When that was gone, Hacker added hunger to his list of complaints. But at least he wouldn't die of thirst. As fast as his suit could filter freshwater from the surrounding sea, Hacker guzzled it down, flushing out his system and occasionally releasing fertilizer for drifting plankton to feed upon.

Gradually, his thoughts began to clear.

Was I really about to head back into the reef? I must have been delirious. Maybe had a concussion. These flipper guys saved me from myself, I guess.

Of course, Hacker had seen dolphins—especially the bottlenose type—on countless nature shows and be-theres. He even once played tag with a pair, during a diving trip near Tonga. Perhaps for that reason, he soon began noticing some strange traits shared by this group.

For example, these animals *took turns* making complex sounds, while glancing at each other or pointing with their beaks . . . almost as if they were holding a back-and-forth conversation. And he could swear they were gesturing toward *him*. Perhaps even sharing amused comments at his expense.

Of course it must be an illusion—probably his concussion still acting up, plus a familiar excess of imagination. Everyone knew that scientists had finally determined the intelligence of *Tursiops truncatus* dolphins, after a century of exaggerations and wishful thinking. They were, indeed, very bright animals—about chimpanzee equivalent, with some basic linguistic cleverness—and they were true masters of underwater sound. But it had also been proved, at long last, that they possessed no true speech of their own. Not even matching the abilities of a human two-year-old.

And yet, after watching a mother dolphin and her infant chase a big octopus into its stony lair, Hacker sensed with his jaw implant as the two certainly *seemed* to converse. The baby's quizzical squeaks alternated with slow repetitions from the parent. Hacker felt sure a particular syncopated popping *meant* "octopus."

Occasionally, one of the creatures would point its bulbous brow toward Hacker, and suddenly the implant in his jaw pulse-clicked like mad, making his teeth rattle. In fact, it almost sounded like the code that space-divers like him used to communicate with their capsules, after getting their eardrums clamped for flight. For lack of anything else to do, Hacker concentrated on those vibrations in his jaw. *Our regular hearing isn't meant for this world,* he realized. *All it does is make things murky.*

It was all very interesting, and of course this would make a great tale, after he was rescued. But as some sharpness returned to his brain, Hacker wondered.

Am I getting any closer to shore?

And don't these creatures ever get hungry?

He got his answer about an hour later.

Out of the east, there arrived a big dolphin who appeared to be snarled in a terrible tangle of some kind. At first, Hacker thought it might be a mat of seaweed. Then he recognized a fishing net—a ropy mesh that wound around the whole back section of its body, down to the flukes. The sight provoked an unusual sentiment in Hacker—*pity,* combined with guilt over what human negligence had done to the poor animal.

He slid his emergency knife from its sheath and moved toward the victim, aiming to cut it free. But another dolphin intervened, swimming in front of Hacker to block him.

"Hey, calm down. I'm just trying to help!" he complained . . .

. . . then stared as other members of the group approached the snared one and grabbed the net along its trailing edge. Backpedaling with careful kicks of their flukes, they pulled away as the "victim" rolled round and round. The net unwrapped smoothly, neatly, without any snarls, till about twenty meters stretched almost straight and the big dolphin swam free, apparently unharmed.

Other members of the pod swarmed in, grabbing edges of the net with their jaws, holding it open. Then, Hacker saw some of the younger members of the pod dash away. He watched in awe while they circled in a wide arc, beyond a school of fish that had been grazing peacefully above a bank of coral in the distance. The young cetaceans began darting toward the silvery throng—apparently a breed of mullet—causing the multitude to pulse and throb, moving en masse away from its tormentors.

Beaters! Hacker recognized the hunting technique. *They're driving the whole school toward the net! But how did they ever—*

He watched, awed, as the entire clan of dolphins moved with a kind of teamwork that only came from experience, some of them chasing fish, while others manipulated the harvesting tool, till about a quarter of the school wriggled and writhed within its folds. At which point, they let the survivors swim away.

It was time to take a breather, literally, as bottlenose figures took turns darting for the surface. Then, one by one, each member of the pod approached the netted swarm and expertly inserted a narrow beak between strands of netting, in order to snare a tasty meal. This went on a while, taking turns breathing, eating, holding the net . . .

. . . until satiation set in, and *play* took a higher priority.

One trio of youngsters began tossing a poor fish back and forth between them. Another pair nosed through the silty bottom, harassing a ray. Meanwhile, elders of the pod tidied up by carefully stretching the net, then rolling it back around the original volunteer, who thereupon sped off to the east, apparently unhampered by his burden.

Well I'm a blue-nose gopher, Hacker mused.

A number of dead or dying mullet still floated around. Hacker was only gradually recovering from his sense of astonishment, when one of his rescuers approached with a fish clutched in its jaws. It made offering motions . . .

Hacker remembered his own hunger. *It ought to taste like sushi,* he thought, realizing just how far he was from the ancestral-human world of cooking flames . . .

. . . and that brought on, unbidden, a sudden thought of his mother. Especially one time that Lacey had tried to explain her passionate interest in seeking other life worlds out there in space, spending half a billion dollars of her own money on the search. *"One theory holds that most Gaia-type planets out there ought to have even more surface area covered by ocean than Earth's seventy percent, which could mean that creatures like brainy whales or squid are far more common than us hands-and-fire types. Which could help explain a lot."*

Hacker hadn't paid close attention, at the time. That was her obsession, after all, not his. Still, he regretted not spending the time to listen and understand. Anyway, poor Lacey was probably worried sick, by now.

Focusing on the moment—and his hunger—he swam closer to the dolphin, reaching for the offered meal.

Only it yanked the fish back at the last moment, repeating a staccato beat of sound. Hacker quashed a resurgence of frustration and anger, even though it was hard.

"Try to stop, when you're in danger of overreacting,"

his one-time therapist used to urge, before he fired her. *"Always consider a possibility—that there may be a reason for what's happening. Something other than villainy."*

His implant repeated the rhythm, as the dolphin brought its jaw forward again, offering the juicy prize once more.

It's trying to teach me, he realized.

"Is that the pulse code for fish?" he asked, knowing the helmet would project his voice, but never expecting the creature to grasp spoken English.

To his amazement, the dolphin shook its head.

No.

Pretty emphatically no.

"Uh." He blinked a few times, then continued. "Does it mean 'food'? 'Eat'? 'Wash up before dinner'? 'Welcome stranger'?"

An approving beat greeted his final guess, and the dolphin flicked the tooth-pocked mullet toward Hacker, who felt suddenly ravenous. He tore the fish apart, stuffing bits of it through his helmet's narrow chowlock, caring very little about salt water squirting in, along with chunks of red flesh.

Welcome stranger? he pondered. *That's mighty abstract for a dumb beast to say. Though I'll admit, it's friendly.*

ENTROPY

In his prescient novel *The Cool War,* Frederik Pohl showed a chillingly plausible failure mode, in which our nations and factions do not dare wage open conflict, and so settle upon tit-for-tat patterns of reciprocal *sabotage,* each attempting to ruin the other's infrastructure and economy. Naturally, this sends civilization on a slow death spiral of degrading hopes.

Sound depressing? It makes one wonder—what fraction of the "accidents" that we see have nothing to do with Luck?

Oh sure, there are always conspiracy theories. Superefficient

engines that were kept off the market by greedy energy companies. Disease cures, suppressed by profit-hungry pharma-
ceutical giants. Knaves, monopolists and fat cats who use
intellectual property to repress knowledge growth, instead of
spurring it on.

But those dark rumors don't hold a candle to this one—
that we're sliding toward despair because all the efforts of
good, skilled men and women are for naught. Their labors are
deliberately spiked, because some ruling elites see themselves
engaged in a secret struggle on our behalf. And this tit-for-tat,
negative-sum game is all about the most dismal human pastime.

War.

—Pandora's Cornucopia

27.
EMISSARY

*"We've reconsidered the matter, Lacey. Given that poor
Hacker is still missing at sea, we should not impose on
your time of worry. It won't be necessary for you to fly to
our upcoming meeting of the clade, so far away from the
search for your son. We'll manage, even though we'll miss
your wisdom in Zurich."*

I'll bet, Lacey thought, pondering the stately blonde who
was portrayed seated in front of her, full-sized, through a
top quality threevee holistube. Unlike their earlier exchange, back at the Chilean observatory, images now went
both ways, between plush, high-security communications
lounges in two far-apart branches of the Salamander
Club—one of them perched high upon the Alps and the
other here in Charleston, where magnolia scents wafted
indoors on waves of sultry, junglelike heat, despite a double-
seal entrance. Both rooms were decorated so similarly that

the seam, separating real from depiction, was easy to ignore. It felt as if the women were chatting across a gap of two meters, not thousands of kilometers.

Security from eavesdropping came the same way as before—using twinned parrot brains as uncrackable encoding devices. Only now, the birds at each end were neuroplugged directly to elaborate transmission systems, allowing more sophisticated use of cephalo-paired encryption. This high-fidelity image helped Lacey read cues in the other woman's expression. She didn't need any sophisticated facial analysis program.

Sympathy is only an excuse, Helena. Deliberation is over. The peers have already reached a decision about the Prophet's proposal, haven't they? And you know it's one I'd fuss about.

Testing that hypothesis, she ventured: "Maybe I should come anyway. I've hired skilled people to handle the rescue effort. If I hang around, I'll just get in the way. Or else wilt in this damned humidity. A distraction might help pull my mind away from fretting—"

Transit delay was negligible as Helena duPont-Vonessen interrupted.

"Our thought exactly, dear. A diversion from worry may be just the thing. Hence, we do have a task for you. One that should engage your intellect far better than visiting a bunch of stodgy trillionaire gnomes." Helena smiled at her own disarming jest. *"Also, it will keep you much closer to the scene, in case the searchers find . . . in case they have need of you."*

Lacey felt her mind veer away from the icy place where she kept anguish over her missing son. That helped propel her the other way, into cool, analytical examination of Helena's true meaning.

She doesn't even suggest that I send a surrogate or repre-

sentative to the meeting in Switzerland. She wants to deflect me to another topic altogether.

"Oh? And what task would you have in mind?" Lacey asked.

"To represent the First Estate—or, at least, our part of it—at the Artifact Conference in Washington. To be our eyes and ears, at this historic and disruptive event.

"After all, Lacey, isn't this right up your alley? An abrupt culmination of everything you've dreamed about—contact with extraterrestrial life? Who, among all the members of our class, is better qualified to grasp the issues and implications?"

Lacey almost responded with irritation. Helena was offering her *boffin work* . . . almost like some big-domed hireling from the Fifth Estate.

Of course, it was also enticing.

Helena knows me. I'd love a chance to see this famous emissary probe from outer space.

But that wasn't the point. Her aristocratic peers already had plenty of boffins hard at work on this very topic—either at the Artifact Conference in Washington or closely watching the data feeds—producing digested summaries and advice papers about the implications of an alien <u>Message in a Bottle</u>. Implications to the planet. To a teetering social compact. And to those sitting at the top of an unstable social pyramid.

They have decided already, Lacey realized, interpreting plenty from the other woman's terse wording and guarded visage. *This news of contact with an interstellar civilization must have tipped them over, uniting the leading families in consensus. They are just as upset and panic-ridden as those dopey demonstrators in a hundred cities, calling for the Livingstone Object to be destroyed.*

Only, trillionaires didn't join demonstrations. Lacey's fellow patricians had other ways of taking action.

They've decided to join Tenskwatawa, the Prophet, she realized. *And his Renunciation Movement.*

Of course, she knew what that meant. Another surge in anti-intellectualism, fostered by populist politicians and mass media—at least, the portions that were controlled by two thousand powerful families. An ancient trick in the human playbook; get the masses lathered up in fear of "outsiders"—and what better outsiders than outright aliens? Whip up enough dread and the mob will gladly follow some elite, pledging fealty to men and women on horseback. Or yacht-back. Vesting them with power.

Lacey didn't object to that part. Even before she met Jason, her parents and tutors had explained the obvious— that people aren't naturally democratic. *Feudalism* was the prevalent human condition erupting in all eras and cultures, since history began to be recorded on clay tablets. Even in modern films and popular culture, the theme resonated. Millions who were descended from enlightenment revolutionaries, now devoured tales about kings, wizards, and secret hierarchies. Superheroes and demigods. Celebrities, august families, and inherited privilege.

This campaign in the media went way back. Subsidized court sages, from Confucius to Plato to Machiavelli, from Leni Riefenstahl to Hannah Niti, all warned against mob rule, preaching for noble authoritarianism. In his one and only book—circulated only within the clade—Jason compiled convincing arguments for *newblesse oblige* . . .

. . . though Lacey still wondered, now and then. Would either of them have found the case so compelling, if they weren't already members of the topmost caste? The platonic crust?

Oh, no question, the species and planet would be better off guided by a single aristocracy, than by a fractious horde of ten billion short-tempered, easily-frightened "citizens" armed with nuclear and biological weapons. Government-by-the-people wasn't her reason for being in love with the Enlightenment. Democracy was an unfortunate and potentially toxic side effect of the thing she really valued.

The peers think they'll use Tenskwatawa as a tool to regain control. But this new wave of populist conservatism . . . this Renunciation Movement . . . is no brainless reflex, like in the century's early years. No spasm of rural religiosity, easily steered by plutocrat puppeteers. Not this time. Nor will the Prophet's followers be satisfied with just lip service to their cause. Not anymore.

Though it had only been a few seconds, Helena grew visibly uncomfortable with Lacey's thoughtful pause.

"So, will you do this for us? We'll supply whatever staff and ai resources you'll need, of course."

"Of course. And that would include—?"

"Well. All the linguistic feeds and any experts you desire."

"And simulation tools? For projection-analysis of social repercussions, all that?"

"Absolutely, the very best available."

Really? It was all Lacey could do, not to arch an eyebrow skeptically. *The latest versions that you and the inner circle use?*

Anyone outside of the clade—which meant 99.9996 percent of humanity (almost exactly)—would have called Lacey part of any "inner circle." It went beyond mere wealth and its ability to buy influence. Family also mattered. Especially as the generation of self-made moguls in China, Russia, and the Americas departed, leaving their fortunes to privilege-born heirs, letting the old logic of *bloodlines* reassert itself. And yet, Lacey knew—despite her marriage to Jason, and the way her own parents helped stave off the Bigger Deal—even those ties never guaranteed real power. Or being truly in the know.

You still wondered, always—*who are the real Illuminati? Those who know the really big secrets? The fellows*

*who have the dirt and can blackmail even the most ideal-
istic politicians. Those discreetly pulling strings and playing the world's people—yes, including me—like pieces on
a chessboard?*

Does even Helena wonder about that?

When it came to most of the scions, princes, sheiks, and
neolords whom Lacey knew—many of them convinced they
were high intellects, because sycophants had flattered them
and given them high marks at Oxbridge—well, one had to
hope and pray that none of *them* was a secret string puller!
Surely, any cabal of aristocratic titans ought to be smarter,
by far.

*Could it be that they don't exist? Perhaps every part of
the aristocracy thinks that someone else is really guiding
affairs?*

Lacey wasn't sure which possibility felt more frightening. A cryptic superelite of mighty meddlers, working their
will beyond her sight . . . or else that things actually were
as they seemed, a mélange of cartels and "Estates," of im-
pudent guilds and impotent legacy nations, plus a bewildering fog of "smart" citizen-mobs and ephemerally
frightening ais . . . all desperately tugging at the tiller, with
the result that no one was really steering the ship. Nobody
at all.

She answered, carefully.

"Hm. I . . . suppose some top ai tools would help. Can I
access the Quantum Eye in Riyadh?"

Helena blinked, shifting back in her chair. This request
went a bit further than diverting one crackpot old lady from
bigger matters.

*"I . . . I can approach the Riyadhians. Though, as you
know, they tend to be a bit—"*

"Suspicious? But aren't they fully committed members
of our clade? So, if there's consensus that my mission is
important—"

She left the sentence hanging. And it worked. Helena nodded.

"I don't expect that will be a problem, Lacey. My facto-tum will contact yours about details. Only now, I am so sorry, but I must run. The Bogolomovs are arriving, and you know how much they love ceremony. They actually think they're czars or boyars or something, complete with a family tree made of fairy dust and forged DNA!"

Helena chuckled demurely, then straightened and met Lacey's eyes, with a level gaze of apparently sincere affection.

"Please accept our blessings, dear one. Our prayers are with you, for Hacker to be found and safely returned to you."

Lacey thanked the younger woman, with all the back-and-forth that it took to bring polite conversation to a close. Only, her heart wasn't in it. And, after the holistube went blank, she was left in silence, sitting in the leather-trimmed lounge, feeling miserable. Alone.

First, Jason has to go racing toward the nearest disaster area on Awfulday, instead of staying sensibly away from danger, becoming an iconic hero of newblesse oblige . . . *as if that sort of honor ever did a widow any good . . .*

. . . then Hacker goes hurtling himself into space— exhibiting all of Jason's bravado without any of the showy responsibility . . .

. . . and now it comes to this. I am being cauterized by my peers. Set aside. Removed from deliberations that might affect the shape of civilization for generations to come. All because—with good reason—they fear I'll be unhappy about their choice.

Shall I resign? Maybe join one of the other coalitions of do-gooder rich?

There were plenty of those, some of them more suitable for a philanthropist with her science-loving bent. Tech billionaires and first-generation entrepreneurs, fizzing with excitement over the Havana Artifact. Some, she knew well, as cosponsors of her Farseeker Telescope. Not all of the superwealthy were superreactionary. Not even a majority.

But those other rich folk tended to act as individuals or in small groups, pursuing personal passions and separate interests. The same fetish for uniqueness that had made them affluent prevented any action in concert. Not even the wary, tentative grouping that called itself the Naderites.

None of them—separately or all together—could match the influence, power, or Machiavellian ruthlessness of the clade.

If I step outside, I'll join the billions. Those to whom history happens . . . instead of ordering it up, like a meal on a plate.

"There ought to be signs of intelligent life everywhere, madam, truly," the showman-scientist crooned, his low, rich voice spiced with a velvety Jamaican accent.

"Ancient aliens—so-very *smaart*—should have preceded us by eons, sprouting corn all across our so-bright galaxy, even before the sun was born, filling the cosmos with culture and upfull conversation.

"Hence, it be fretful-puzzling, even long-back when we first began looking for signs of technological civilization, that this welcoming cosmos seem *sparse*. Indeed, with only one proved example of sapient life—us!"

Profnoo gestured with both hands, rocking his oversize head so avidly that each of his super-elongated earlobes rattled against thick collar ruffles. He swept them back to join the twitching, multibraided draidlocks of cybactivated hair that served as both antennae-receivers and his public trademark—though he was only the best known of a dozen science supertainers who came from that gifted little island.

"I know that," Lacey sighed. She didn't need a razzle-

artist astronomer to lay out—for a thousandth time—the dismal logic of the Fermi Paradox. Yet, Professor Noozone proceeded to do just that, perhaps out of eagerness to impress his patron. Or else, practicing a riff for his weekly audience.

"See here now." The professor pointed to a holistank that showed some kind of primeval sea, with meteors flashing overhead. "Precursors of life appear to emerge anywhere that you have a flow of energy, plus a dozen basic elements immersed in liquid—not just water, but almost any kind of liquid at all! And not only on planets with *surface* oceans! But *ten times as many little worlds* that have seas, roofed with icy covers, like Europa, Enceladus, Miranda, Tethys, Titan, Oberon . . ."

She wanted to interrupt. To get the man back onto the topic of the Artifact. But Lacey knew that any expression of outright disapproval might quash him too much. In order to be wielded effectively, power had to wear gloves—a lesson she had tried, in vain, to teach her short-tempered son.

Anyway, the situation with Professor Noozone was entirely her own fault.

It serves me right, for choosing an adviser with the brain of a Thorne or a Koonin, but with the insecure ego of a Bollywood star and the put-on reggae drawl of a rastaman.

Bulging implants throbbed just under the skin of Profnoo's broad forehead, above dark, glinting eyes. The effect—totally intentional—made his cranium seem preternaturally large. Like an overinflated soufflé.

At least he doesn't feel a need to lay the accent too thick, when he's talking to me alone. Though his vowels were stretched and every "th" dropped into a "d" or "t" sound, she felt grateful that he wasn't peppering in very many island slang expressions. *In public, or on his shows, Profnoo can be hard to follow without subtitles!*

Professor Noozone caused more images to dance about, with flourishes of a hand. "Indeed, our . . . *your* . . . earlier farseeker telescopes *did* find traces of life out there, on half a dozen planets! Those worlds, so far, proved disappointing. None of them exactly New Zion. Then there's the *next step.* For life to rise-up an' get *smaart*, an' then technology-capable.

"Countless arguments have fumed and smoked over how much of a fluke it was, here on Earth, for humans to leap so far, so fast. And, if there very-truly *are* older races out there, how best to look for them. Does the lack of garish *tutorial beacons* mean there are no Elder Races out there, after all?

"But, irie. Of course, the arrival of the Livingstone Object seems to have settled *that*!" He chuckled with the satisfaction of someone whose side had proved right, after a century of debate.

"By the Artifact's mere existence, and the plurality of alien types that it contains, we may conclude that we are surrounded by an upfull multitude of advanced civilizations! Their invitation to come-ya *'join us'* . . . to become members of some maarvelous community of star-bredren . . . has already thrilled and inspired billions across our lonely planet. Though the prospect may disturb a few downpressing ginnygogs an' trogs who are terrified of change."

Profnoo seemed unaware of Lacey's ironic grimace, or her conflicted loyalties. By personality, she ought to share his forward-looking eagerness. If not for her worries about Hacker, she, too, might have been fizzing about the prospect of First Contact. (Though she would express it with more reserve than the super-extrovert in front of her.)

On the other hand, her caste—her peers in the top aristocracy—foresaw little good coming out of this. Even if the alien device represented a benign and advanced federation that was both generous and wise, the psychological disruption could spur fresh waves of anxiety, paranoia, or covetous wrath. With interstellar trade relations might come wave after wave of wondrous new technologies. Some hazardous? Even the most benign might shake an already tenuous economy, throwing whole sectors into obsolescence, putting hundreds of millions out of work, not to mention spoiling many investment portfolios.

No wonder this spurred a climax to long negotiations between the clade and Tenskwatawa's renunciation movement. *Few cultures ever managed to transition after contact with superior outsiders, without generations of intimidation and victimhood. Meiji-era Japan did it. And their method was not democracy.*

But Lacey pulled her thoughts back to the present. The science-showman on her payroll was continuing his rapid-fire explication, never slacking momentum.

". . . even that still leaves us awash in puzzles! We can only hope the Artifact Commission overcomes all linguistic barriers. *Especially* now that dem lagga heads will finally allow me . . . and you, of course, madam . . . close enough to ask questions!"

"So, what should we ask first, Professor?"

"Oh, there are *so many* things. For example, the mere *existence* of the Artifact, here on Earth, proves—irie— that interstellar travel is possible!"

Assuming, again, that it's not a hoax, Lacey pondered, while noting that Profnoo still had not mentioned an actual question.

"True, we haven't yet learned *how* the object crossed the vast gulf between the stars. But from the fact that it exists in a purely crystalline-solid state—tallowah an' sturdy—I be wagering a whole-heap that the propulsion methodology wasn't gentle! Perhaps a truly prodigious accelerator-cannongun fired it to near relativistic speeds. Or else, maybe its compact dimensions allowed slick passage through an obeah-generated *wormhole,* requiring the energy of a *superdupernova!* I-mon have done some rudimentary calculations—"

"Professor. Please. Can you stick to the point?"

"Ah, yes. The Invitation." He nodded. "Do bear with me, Madam Donaldson-Sander, I-and-I will get to it! For, you see, even the *possibility* of interstellar travel was denied for eighty years by the cult of *SETI.* When their program of *sky worship* found nothing out there at all, they trotted out the same excuse. *Just a little more time.* Patience—and ever-more sophisticated-bashy gear— would eventually find the needle in the haystack . . . that wise, elder race they hoped for!"

Huh. Lacey couldn't help getting caught up in the spell he wove. Noozone had amassed his own fortune out of millions of micropayments, as people zigged-in to view and tactail his leaping, explanatory extravaganzas. Though some just liked his snakelike draidlocks, wafting and stirring clouds of ambiguous, colored smoke.

"Alas, interstellar *travel* changes everything. If advanced star-mon can deepvoyage an' colonize, then *needles make copies of themselves.* Colonies send out their own expeditions, spreading an' *filling* the haystack!

"But we saw no fabulous Others. Nor any huge engineering projects that *we* may someday build, if we become a truly bold and successful civilization. Antimatter-spaceships, vaast solar collectors, Dyson spheres, and Kardashev worksheds that lace multiple star systems, all of them detectable. . . ." Profnoo had to gasp and catch his breath.

"And it gets worse! *Earth itself* would show signs, if visitors ever flushed a toilet here, or tossed a Coke bottle into our Paleozoic sea. My oh, geologists and paleobiologists would see in our rocks, the very moment when extraterrestrial bacteria arrived! Nuh true?

"No. Something was wrong with the old SETI logic. Till

this marvel-stoosh *Galactic Artifact* turned up. Only now . . ." He lifted a finger—and one of his mentally activated draidlocks wafted also.

"Now, it seems that *life is fairly common*—and—

"—sapient life, *capable of technology,* is not rare—and—

"—some form of *interstellar travel appears to be possible*—and—

"—a *peaceful community* already exists that . . ."

Lacey raised a hand of her own, cutting him off with four braids and four fingers lifted in the air. Glancing out the window, she had noticed that the yacht bearing them from Charleston to Washington was cruising rapidly up the Potomac. Soon, they'd pass the zeppelin port and the Awfulday Memorial, before finally docking at the Naval Research Lab. Not that she minded traveling this way. Shipboard facilities let her stay in constant linkup with the rescue effort, searching for her son. But it was time to start winding this up.

"All right, then. Suppose there is a Galactic Federation we're invited to join. Doesn't that conflict with everything you just described? Especially the *sparse cosmos* that we observed, till now?"

"It would seem so, madam." Profnoo's earlobe rings and beaded locks clattered as he nodded. "So, where's the overlap in conceptual space? Between the previous, downpressing *appearance* of meager sapience, and what we now know to be its high, upfull frequency?"

The man's unquenchable zeal to speculate did not bother her. Vivid and aromatic, Profnoo made his intellectual frenzy into something unabashedly masculine. Frankly, his flirtatious attention—laced with rousing scientific jargon—filled some of the void in Lacey that used to be occupied by sex.

"Apparently, dem use crystal capsules instead of radio! I

suppose interstellar pellets are easy, cheap, and *relatively* fast." He chuckled, though Lacey found the jest rather lame. "They also allow aliens to travel as surrogates—as complete downloaded personalities. Indeed, this may prove my conjecture about networks of connection-wormholes!"

Or else, they may avoid radio because they know something that we don't, Lacey pondered. *Perhaps they deem it unwise to draw attention to their home worlds. Because something out there makes it dangerous.* The thought gave her a shiver, especially since Planet Earth had been anything but quiet, for the last hundred years or so.

"But, madam, just picture the long odds that this particular crystal—this Artifact—had to beat, when dem just happened to drift within reach of that astronaut's garbage collecting bola-tether. Without any visible means to maneuver! A fluke? Or might there be others out there?"

Lacey nodded. *That may explain why Great China, India, the U.S., the E-Union and A-Union have all announced new space endeavors. I should assign some agents—real and spyware—to learn more about these missions.*

Something about the notion of "other artifacts" tickled the edge of her imagination.

Why only out there? Indeed . . .

But the thought eluded her, skittering away as the yachtmaster's amplified voice reverberated. It was time to stop for inspection at the security cordon near the Naval Research Center. Captain Kohl-Fennel had already made arrangements, of course. The pause would be brief. Lacey shrugged.

"You were talking about *contradictions,* Professor. How to explain why we saw no traces of intelligence before, in a universe that now turns out to be filled with sapient life."

"Yes . . . it be a puzzlement." His dense, expressive lips pursed. "The use of something other than radio for communications may solve part of the conundrum. Another contributor may be some kind of *Zoo Hypothesis.*"

This one she knew well. "The idea that young races like ours are held in quarantine. Deliberately kept in the dark."

"Yes, madam. Many possible motives have been offered, for why elder races might do such a dread thing. Fear of 'human aggression' is one old-but-implausible theory. Or a 'noninterference directive' leaves new races alone, even if it deprives them of answers they need, to survive." Profnoo shook his head, clearly disliking that explanation.

"Or aliens may stay silent to sift our broadcasts an' surf our networks, gathering our *culture*—art, music, and originalities—without paying anything in return! I call it the *Cheapskate Thief Hypothesis.* And it does vex me, truly, to think they may be such blackheart mon! First thing I plan to ask these beings? What *intellectual property laws* they have! Interstellar peace and friendship be fine . . . but kill-mi-dead if I don' want my royalties!"

Lacey chuckled politely, since he seemed to expect it. In fact, Profnoo's eyes had a glint as he hurriedly waggled notes in the air, caching this idea for his show.

Inwardly, she wondered, *Would it have been better, if this all took place out of public view?*

The professor assumes that citizenship in some galactic federation will involve expanded rights and privileges. But what if aliens exact a price for admission? Changes in our social structure or government? Or beliefs? Might they demand something tangible, in exchange for knowledge and trade? Like precious substances?

Lacey had once seen a humor magazine cynically explain why the U.S. government would *both* suppress medical advances and quash the truth about ET visitors—because officials were selling fuel for the aliens' "cancer drive engines."

But no. UFO scenarios were mental slumming.

More likely, they want access to cheap Earthling labor, outsourcing work to our teeming masses. Grunt toil their own citizens and robots are too spoiled to perform? Software can travel between the stars, so will Earth become the new coding sweatshop? Or intergalactic call center?

Lacey realized, *If this contact episode had taken place behind closed doors . . . our elite talking to theirs . . . then we'd have had an option. The possibility of saying—"No thanks. No deal. Not now.*

"Not yet.

"Maybe not ever."

It frankly shocked Lacey, the path her thoughts had taken. Where was the zealot who spent her adult life pursuing this very thing—First Contact? When push came to shove, was she as conservative and reluctant as all the rest?

Why do I have the creepy feeling there's going to be a catch?

She was still in that dour mood when Professor Noozone helped guide her down a ramp leading from the yacht to where several fresh-faced young men and women in starched uniforms waited to salute and greet her. It was a clear day. Beyond the zep port—with flying cranes bustling among the giant, bobbing freighters—she could make out the remade Washington Monument and the pennants of New Smithsonian Castle. But even those sights didn't lift her spirit.

While servants brought the luggage and Profnoo's scientific supplies, Lacey made sure to shake hands with her hosts, one by one. She tried to quash a bitter—and irrational—feeling of anger that sailors should be standing here, instead of helping right now in the search for her son, missing at sea. Of course, only fatigue could provoke such an awful resentment.

I can't help it though. Underneath all the turmoil about rocks from space, beyond the scientific puzzles and philosophical quandaries I am, after all, a mother.

"The reception for our distinguished Advisory Panel will start soon, madam," said Lacey's assigned guide, a bright-looking ensign, who seemed a little like Hacker. "I'll take you first to your guest quarters, so you can freshen—"

The young officer abruptly gasped as his face took an orange cast, flinching backward from some surprise that he saw, beyond Lacey's shoulder. Others reacted, too, cringing or raising hands before their eyes.

"Bumboclot!" Professor Noozone cursed.

Lacey turned to find out what caused the flaring glow, when *sound* caught up with light—a low, rumbling boom accompanied a palpable push of displaced air. Thoughts of Awfulday raced through her mind—as they must have through everyone else.

But then, why am I still on my feet? she wondered until, turning, Lacey saw a globular gout of flame roiling in the sky beyond the Pentagon, some distance upriver, maybe in Virginia. The setting sun made it hard to see clearly, but the fireball faded quickly and she realized with some relief—it couldn't be anything as terrible as a nuke. Not even a small one.

That comfort was tempered though, when there followed another detonation. And then another. And she knew that, when it came to explosions, size wasn't everything.

RENUNCIATORS

What about the notion of "inevitable progress"?

Decades ago, author Charles Stross urged that—even if you think a marvelous Singularity Era is coming, you shouldn't let it

affect your behavior, or alter your sober urgency to solve current problems.

*"The rapture of the nerds, like space colonization, is likely to
be a nonparticipatory event for 99.999 percent of humanity—
unless we're very unlucky,"* Stross wrote. *"If it happens and it's
interested in us, all our plans go out the window. If it doesn't
happen, sitting around waiting for the ais to save us from the
rising sea level/oil shortage/intelligent bioengineered termites
looks like a Real Bad Idea.*

*"The best approach to the singularity is to apply Pascal's
Wager—in reverse—and plan on the assumption it won't save
us from ourselves."*

—from *The Movement Revealed* by Thormace Anubis-Fejel

28.
THE SMART-MOB

Washington was like a geezer—overweight and sagging—
but with attitude. Most of its gutty heft lay below the Beltway, in waistlands that had been downwind on Awfulday.

Downwind, but not out.

When droves of upper-class child-bearers fled the invisible plumes enveloping Fairfax and Alexandria, those briefly
empty ghost towns quickly refilled with immigrants—the
latest mass of *teemers,* yearning to be free and willing to
endure a little radiation, in exchange for a pleasant five-
bedroom that could be subdivided into nearly as many
apartments. Spacious living rooms began a second life as
storefronts. Workshops took over four-car garages and
lawns turned into produce gardens. Swimming pools made
excellent refuse bins—until government recovered enough
to start cracking down.

Passing overhead, Tor could track signs of suburban renewal from her first-class seat aboard the *Spirit of Chula*

Vista. Take those swimming pools. A majority of the kidney-shaped cement ponds now gleamed with clear liquid—mostly water (as testified by the spectral scanning feature of her tru-vu spectacles)—welcoming throngs of children who splashed under summertime heat, sufficiently dark-skinned to unflinchingly bear the bare sun.

So much for the notion that dirty bombs automatically make a place unfit for breeders, she thought. Let yuppies abandon perfectly good mansions because of a little strontium dust. People from Congo and Celebes were happy to insource.

Wasn't this America? Call it resolution—or obstinacy—but after three rebuilds, the Statue of Liberty still beckoned.

The latest immigrants, those who filled Washington's waistland vacuum, weren't ignorant. They could read warning labels and health stats, posted on every lamppost and VR level. *So?* More people died in Jakarta from traffic or stray bullets. Anyway, mutation rates dropped quickly, a few years after Awfulday, to levels no worse than Kiev. And Washington had more civic amenities.

Waistlanders also griped a lot less about minor matters like zoning. That made it easier to acquire rights of way, repioneering new paths back into unlucky cities that had been dusted. Innovations soon turned those transportation hubs into boomtowns. An ironic twist to emerge from terror/sabotage. Especially when sky trains began crisscrossing North America.

Through her broad window, traveling east aboard the *Spirit of Chula Vista,* Tor gazed across a ten-mile separation to the Westbound Corridor, where long columns of cargo zeppelins lumbered in the opposite direction, ponderous as whales and a hundred times larger. Chained single-file and heavily laden, the dirigibles floated barely three hundred meters above the ground, obediently trailing teams of heavyduty draft-locomotives. Each towing cable looked impossibly slender for hauling fifty behemoths across a continent. But while sky trains weren't fast, or suited for bulk materials, they beat any other method for transporting medium-value goods.

And passengers. Those willing to trade a little time for inexpensive luxury.

Tor moved her attention much closer, watching the *Spirit*'s majestic shadow flow like an eclipse over rolling suburban countryside, so long and dark that flowers would start to close and birds might be fooled to roost, pondering nightfall. Free from any need for engines of her own, the skyliner glided almost silently over hill and dale. Not as quick as a jet, but more scenic—free of carbon levies or ozone tax—and far cheaper. Setting her tru-vus to magnify, she followed the *Spirit*'s tow cable along the Eastbound Express Rail, pulled relentlessly by twelve thousand horses, courtesy of the deluxe maglev tug, *Umberto Nobile*.

What was it about a lighter-than-air craft that drew the eye? Oh, certainly most of them now had pixelated, tunable skins that could be programmed for any kind of spectacle. Passing near a population center—even a village in the middle of nowhere—the convoy of cargo zeps might flicker from one gaudy advertisement to the next, for anything from a local gift shop to the mail-order wares of some Brazilian bloat-corp. At times, when no one bid for the display space, a chain of dirigibles might tune their surfaces to resemble clouds . . . or flying pigs. Whim, after all, was another modern currency. Everyone did it on the VR levels.

Only with zeppelins, you could paint whimsical images across a whole stretch of the *real* sky.

Tor shook her head.

But no. That wasn't it. Even bare and gray, they could not be ignored. Silent, gigantic, utterly calm, a zep seemed to stand for a kind of grace that human beings might build, but never know in their own frenetic lives.

She was nibbling at one of her active-element fingernails—thinking about Wesley, waiting at the skydock for her arrival, and trying to picture his face—when a voice intruded from above.

"Will you be wanting anything else before we arrive in the Federal District, madam?"

She glanced up at a *servitor*—little more than a boxy delivery receptacle—that clung to its own slim rail on a nearby bulkhead, leaving the walkway free for passengers.

"No, thanks," Tor murmured automatically, a polite habit of her generation. Younger folk had already learned to snub machinery slaves, except when making clipped demands. A trend that she found odd, since the ais were getting smarter all the time.

"Can you tell me when we're due?"

"Certainly, madam. There is a slowdown in progress due to heightened security. Hence, we may experience some delay crossing the Beltway. But there is no cause for alarm. And we remain ahead of schedule because of that tailwind across the Appalachian Mountains."

"Hm. Heightened security?"

"For the Artifact Conference, madam."

Tor frowned. She hoped that Wesley wouldn't have any trouble coming to meet her. Things might be tense enough between the two of them, without this added irritant. He tended to get all lathered and indignant over being beamed and probed by agents of the pencil pushers' guild . . . the civil servants assigned to checking every conceivable box and possible failure mode.

"For the Artifact Conference?" Tor's thoughts zeroed in on something puzzling. "But that should already be taken into account. Security for the gathering shouldn't affect our timetable."

"There is no cause for alarm," the servitor repeated. "We just got word, two minutes ago. An order to reduce speed, that's all."

Glancing outside, Tor could see the effects of slowing, in a gradual change of altitude. The *Spirit*'s tow cable slanted a little steeper, catching up to the ground-hugging locomotive tug.

Altitude: 359 meters said a telltale in the corner of her left tru-vu lens.

"Will you be wanting to change seats for our approach to the nation's capital?" the servitor continued. "An announcement will be made when we come within sight of the Mall, though you may want to claim a prime viewing spot earlier. Children and first-time visitors get priority, of course."

"Of course."

A trickle of tourists had already begun streaming forward to the main observation lounge. Parents, dressed in bright-colored sarongs and Patagonian slacks, herded kids who sported the latest youth fashion—fake antennae and ersatz scales—imitating some of the alien personalities that had been discovered aboard the Livingstone Object . . . also called, for some reason, the Havana Artifact. A grand conference may have been called to deliberate whether it was a genuine case of First Contact, or just another hoax. But popular culture had already cast judgment.

The Artifact was cool.

"You say an alert came through two minutes ago?" Tor wondered. Nothing had flashed yet in her peripherals. But maybe the vigilance thresholds were set too high. With a rapid series of clicks on her tooth implants, she adjusted them downward.

Immediately, crimson tones began creeping in from the

edges of her specs, offering links that whiffed and throbbed unpleasantly.

Uh-oh.

"Not an *alert,* madam. No, no. Just preliminary, precautionary—"

But Tor's attention had already veered. Using both clicks and subvocal commands, she sent her specs swooping through the data overlays of virtuality, following threads of a *security situation.* Sensors tracked every twitch of the iris, following and often anticipating her choices, while colored data-cues jostled and flashed.

"May I take away any rubbish or recycling?" asked the boxy tray on the wall. It dropped open a receptacle, like a hungry jaw, eager to be fed. The servitor waited in vain for a few moments. Then, noting that her focus lay far away, it silently folded and departed.

"No cause for alarm," Tor muttered sardonically as she probed and sifted the dataways. Someone should have banished that cliché from the repertoire of all ai devices. No human over the age of thirty would ever hear the phrase without wincing. Of all the lies that accompanied Awfulday, it had been the worst.

Some of Tor's favorite software agents were already reporting back from the Grid.

Koppel—the summarizer—zoomed toward public, corporate, and government feeds, collating official pronouncements. Most of them were repeating the worrisome cliché.

Gallup—her pollster program—sifted for opinion. People weren't buying it, apparently. On a scale of one thousand, *"no cause for alarm"* had a credibility rating of eighteen, and dropping. Tor felt a wrench in the pit of her stomach.

Bernstein leaped into the whistle-blower circuits, hunting down gossip and hearsay. As usual, there were far too many rumors for any person—or personal ai—to trawl.

Only this time, the flood was overwhelming even the sophisticated filters at the Skeptic Society. MediaCorp seemed
no better; her status as a member of the Journalistic Staff
only won her a queue number from Research Division and
a promise of response "in minutes."

Minutes?

It was beginning to look like a deliberate disinformation
flood, time-unleashed in order to drown out any genuine
tattles. Gangsters, terrorists, and reffers had learned the
hard way that careful plans can be upset by some soft-
hearted henchman, wrenched by remorseful second
thoughts about innocent bystanders. Many a scheme had
been spoiled by some lowly underling, who posted an
anonymous squeal at the last minute. To prevent this, mas-
terminds and ringleaders now routinely unleashed cas-
cades of ersatz confessions, just as soon as an operation
was under way—a spamming of faux regret, artificially
generated, ranging across the whole spectrum of plausible
sabotage and man-made disasters.

Staring at a flood of warnings, Tor knew that one or
more of the rumors had to be true. But which?

**Washington area Beltway defenses have already
been breached by machoist suiciders infected with pul-
monella plague, heading for the Capitol . . .**

**A coalition of humanist cults have decided to put an
end to all this nonsense about a so-called "alien Artifact" from interstellar space. . . .**

**The U.S. president, seeking to reclaim traditional
authority, is about to nationalize the D.C.-area civil
militia on a pretext . . .**

**Exceptional numbers of toy airplanes were purchased
in the Carolinas, this month, suggesting that a swarm
attack may be in the making, just like the O'Hare Incident. . . .**

A method has been found to convert zeppelins into flying bombs. . . .

Among the international dignitaries, who were invited to Washington to view the Livingstone Object, are a few who plan to . . .

There are times when human-neuronal paranoia can react faster than mere digital simulacra. Tor's old-fashioned cortex snapped to attention a full five seconds before her ais, Bernstein and Columbo, made the same connection.

Zeppelins . . . flying bombs . . .

It sounded unlikely . . . probably distraction-spam.

But I *happen to be* on *a zeppelin.*

That wasn't just a realization. The words formed a message. With subvocal grunts and tooth-click punctuations, Tor broadcast it far and wide. Not just to her favorite correlation and stringer groups, but to several hundred Citizen Action Networks. Her terse missive zoomed across the Net indiscriminately, calling to every CAN that had expressed interest in the zep rumor.

"This is Tor Povlov, investigative reporter for MediaCorp—credibility rating 752—aboard the passenger zep Spirit of Chula Vista. *We are approaching the D.C. Beltway defense zone. That may put me at a right place-time to examine one of the reffer rumors.*

"I request a smart-mob coalescence. <u>Feedme!</u>"

Disinformation, a curse with ancient roots, had been updated with ultramodern ways of lying. Machoists and other bastards might plant sleeper-ais in a million virtual locales, programmed to pop out at a preset time and spam every network with autogenerated "plausibles" . . . randomly generated combinations of word and tone that were drawn from recent news, each variant sure to rouse the paranoiac fears of *someone.*

Mutate this ten million times (easy enough to do in virtual space) and you'll find a nerve to tweak in *anyone*.

Citizens could fight back, combating lies with light. Sophisticated programs compared eyewitness accounts from many sources, weighted by credibility, offering average folk tools to reforge Consensus Reality, while discarding the dross. Only that took time. And during an emergency, time was the scarcest commodity of all.

Public avowal worked more quickly. Calling attention to your own person. Saying: "Look, I'm right here, real, credible, and accountable—*I am* not *ai*—so take me seriously."

Of course that required guts, especially since Awfulday. In the face of danger, ancient human instinct cried out: *Duck and cover. Don't draw attention to yourself.*

Tor considered that natural impulse for maybe two seconds, then blared on all levels. Dropping privacy cryption, she confirmed her ticketed billet and physical presence aboard the *Spirit of Chula Vista,* with realtime biometrics and a dozen in-cabin camera views.

"I'm here," she murmured, breathlessly, toward any fellow citizen whose correlation-attention ais would listen.

"Rally and feedme. Tell me what to do."

Calling up a smart-mob was tricky. People might already be too scattered and distracted by the rumor storm. The number to respond might not reach critical mass—in which case all you'd get is a smattering of critics, kibitzers, and loudmouths, doing more harm than good. A below-zero-sum rabble—or bloggle—its collective IQ *dropping,* rather than climbing, with every new volunteer to join. Above all, you needed to attract a core group—the seed cell—of online know-it-alls, constructive cranks, and correlation junkies, armed with the latest coalescence software, who were smart and savvy enough to serve as *prefrontals . . .* coordinating a smart-mob without dominating.

Providing focus without quashing the creativity of a group mind.

"We recognize you, Tor Povlov," intoned a low voice, conducting through her inner-ear receiver. Direct sonic induction made it safe from most eavesdropping, even if someone had a parabolic dish aimed right at her.

"We've lit a wik. Can you help us check out one of these rumors? One that might possibly be a whistle-blow?"

The conjoined mob voice sounded strong, authoritative. Tor's personal interface found good credibility scores as it coalesced. An index-marker in her left peripheral showed 230 members and climbing—generally sufficient to wash out individual ego.

"First tell me," she answered, subvocalizing. Sensors in her shirt collar picked up tiny flexings in her throat, tongue, and larynx, without any need to make actual sound. "Tell me, has anyone sniffed something unusual about the *Spirit*? I don't see or hear anything strange. But some of you out there may be in a better position to snoop company status reports or shipboard operational parameters."

There was a pause. Followed by an apologetic tone.

"Nothing seems abnormal at the public level. Company web-traffic has gone up sixfold in the last ten minutes . . . but the same is true all over, from government agencies to networks of amateur scientists.

"As for the zeppelin you happen to be aboard, we're naturally interested because of its present course, scheduled shortly to moor in Washington, about the same time that a new wave of high-level delegates are arriving for the Artifact Conference."

Tor nodded grimly, a nuance that her interface conveyed to the group mind.

"And those operational readouts?"

"We can try for access by applying for a Freedom of

*Information writ. That will take some minutes, though. So
we may have to supplement the FOIA with a little hacking
and bribery. The usual. We'll also try for some ground
views of the zep.*

"*Leave all that to us.*

"*Meanwhile, there's a little on-site checking you can do.*

"*Be our hands and eyes, will you, Tor?*"

She was already on her feet.

"Tell me where to go . . ."

"*Head aft, past the unisex toilet.*"

". . . but let's have a consensus agreement, okay?" she
added while moving. "I get an exclusive on any interviews
that follow. In case this turns out to be more than . . ."

"*There is a security hatch, next to the crew closet,*" the
voice interrupted. "*Adjust your specs for full mob access
please.*"

"Done," she said, feeling a little sheepish over the request for a group exclusive. But after all, she was supposed
to be a pro. MediaCorp might be tuning in soon, examining transcripts. They would expect a professional's attention to the niceties.

"*That's better. Now zoom close on the control pad. We've
been joined by an off-duty zep mechanic who worked on
this ship last week.*"

"Look, maybe I can just call a crew member. Invoke
FOIA and open it legally—"

"*No time. We've filed for immunity as an ad hoc citizen
posse. Under PA crisis rules.*"

PA . . . for Post-Awfulday.

"Oh sure. With me standing here to take the physical rap
if it's refused. . . ."

"*Your choice, Tor. If you're game for it, press the keypad buttons in this order.*"

A virtual image of the keypad appeared in front of Tor,
overlaying the real one.

"No cause for alarm," she muttered.

"What was that?"

"Never mind."

Feeling somewhat detached, as if under remote control, her hand reached out to tap the proposed sequence.

Nothing happened.

"No good. They must've rotated the progression since our zepspert worked on that ship."

The wikivoice mutated, sounding just a tad less cool. More individualized. A telltale indicator in her tru-vu showed that some high-credibility member of the mob was stepping up with an assertive suggestion.

"But you can tell it isn't randomized. I bet it's still a company-standard maintenance code. Here, try this instead."

Coalescence levels seemed to waver only a little, so the mob trusted this component member. Tor went along, punching the pad again with the new pattern.

"Any luck getting that FOIA writ?" she asked, meanwhile. "You said it would take just a few minutes. Maybe we'd better wait . . ."

Procrastination met its rebuttal with a simple *click,* as the access panel slid aside, revealing a slim, tubelike ladder.

Up.

No hesitation in the mob voice. Five hundred and twelve of her fellow citizens wanted her to do this. Five hundred and sixteen. . . .

Tor swallowed. Then complied.

The ladderway exposed a truth that was hidden from most passengers, cruising in cushioned comfort within the neatly paneled main compartment. Physics—especially gravity— had not changed appreciably in the century that separated the first great zeppelin era from this one. Designers still had to strive for lightness, everywhere they could.

Stepping from spindly rungs onto the cargo deck, Tor found herself amid a maze of spiderlike webbery, instead of walls and partitions. Her feet made gingerly impressions in foamy mesh that seemed to be mostly air. Stacks of luggage—all strictly weighed back in Nashville—formed bundles that resembled monstrous eggs, bound together by air-gel foam. Hardly any metal could be seen. Not even aluminum or titanium struts.

"Shall I look at the bags?" she asked while reaching into her purse. "I have an omnisniffer."

"What model?" inquired the voice in her ear, before it changed tone by abrupt consensus. More authoritatively, it said—*"Never mind. The bags were all scanned before loading. We doubt anything could be smuggled aboard. Anyway, a crew member may be checking those soon, as the alert level rises.*

"But something else has come up. A rumor-tattle points to possible danger higher up. We're betting on that one."

"Higher?" She frowned. "There's nothing up there except . . ."

Tor's voice trailed off as a schematic played within her tru-vus, pointing aft to another ladder, this one made of ropey fibers.

Arrows shimmered in VR yellow, for emphasis.

"We finally succeeded in getting a partial feed from the Spirit*'s operational parameters. And yes, there's something odd going on.*

"They are using onboard water to make lift gas, at an unusual rate."

"Is that dangerous?"

"It shouldn't be.

"But we may be able to find out more, if you hurry."

She sighed, stepping warily across the spongy surface. Tor hadn't yet spotted a crew member. They were probably also busy chasing rumors, different ones, chosen by the company's prioritization subroutines. Anyway, a modern towed-zep was mostly automatic, requiring no pilot, engineer, or navigator. A century ago, the *Hindenburg* carried forty officers, stewards, and burly riggers, just to keep the ornate apparatus running and deliver the same number of paying customers from Europe to the U.S.

At twice the length, *Spirit* carried five times as many people, served by only a dozen human attendants.

Below her feet, passengers would be jostling for a better view of the Langley Crater, or maybe Arlington Cemetery, while peering ahead for the enduring spire of the rebuilt Washington Monument, with its tip of lunar stone. Or did some of those people already sniff an alert coming on, through their own liaison networks? Were families starting to cluster near the emergency chutes? Tor wondered if she should be doing the same.

This new ladder was something else. It felt almost alive and responded to her footstep by *contracting* . . . carrying her upward in a smooth-but-sudden jerk. Smart elastics, she realized. Fine for professionals. But most people never took a liking to ladders that twitch. The good news: It would take just a few actual footsteps at this rate, concentrating to slip her soles carefully onto one rung after the next, and worrying about what would happen when she reached the unpleasant-looking "hatch" that lay just overhead.

Meanwhile, the voice in her ear took on a strange, lilting quality. The next contribution must have come from an individual member. Someone generally appreciated.

> *"Come with me, higher than high,*
> *Dropping burdensome things.*
> *Lighter than clouds, we can fly,*
> *Thoughts spread wider than wings.*

> *Be like the whale, behemoth,*
> *Enormous, yet weightless beings,*
> *Soundlessly floating, the sky*
> *Beckons a mammal that sings."*

Tor liked the offering. You almost wanted to earn it, by coming up with a tune . . .

. . . only the "hatch" was now just ahead, or above, almost pressing against her face. A throbbing iris of polyorganic membranes, much like the quasiliving external skin of the *Spirit.* Coming this close, inhaling the exudate aromas, made Tor feel queasy.

"Relax." The voice was back to business. Probably led by the zep mechanic.

"You'll need a command word. Touch that nub in the middle to get attention and say 'Cinnamon.' "

"Cinnamon?"

It was only a query, but the barrier reacted instantly. With a faintly squishy sound, it dilated and the stringy stepladder resumed its programmed journey, carrying her upward.

Aboard old-time zeps, like the *Hindenburg,* the underslung gondola had been devoted mainly to engines and crew, while paying passengers occupied two broad decks at the base of the giant dirigible's main body. The *Spirit of Chula Vista* had a similar layout, except that the gondola was mainly for show. Having climbed above all the sections designed for people and cargo, Tor now rode the throbbing ladder into a cathedral of lifter cells, each of them a vast chamber in its own right, filled with gas that was much lighter than air.

Hundreds of transparent, filmy balloons—cylindrical and tall like Sequoia trunks—crowded together, stretching from the web-floor where she stood all the way up to the arched ceiling of the *Spirit*'s rounded skin. Tor could only move among these towering columns along four narrow paths leading port or starboard . . . fore or aft. The arrow in her specs suggested *port,* without pulsing insistence. Most members of the smart-mob had never been in a place like this. Curiosity—the strongest modern craving—formed more of these ad hoc groups than any other passion.

Heading in the suggested direction, Tor could not resist reaching out, touching some of the tall cells, their polymer surfaces quivering like the giant bubbles that she used to create with toy wands, at birthday parties. They appeared so light, so delicate. . . .

"Half of the cells contain helium," explained the voice, now so individualized that it had to be a specific person— perhaps the zep mechanic or else a dirigible aficionado. *"See how those membranes are made with a faintly greenish tint? They surround the larger hydrogen cells."*

Tor blinked.

"Hydrogen. Isn't that dangerous?"

Her spec supplied pics of the *Hindenburg*—or LZ 129— that greatest and most ill-fated ancient zeppelin, whose fiery immolation at Lakehurst, New Jersey, marked the sudden end of the First Zep Era, in May 1937. (Facts scrolled along the bottom, lured in by attention cues.) Once ignited—*how* remained controversial—flames had engulfed the mighty airship from mooring tip to gondola, to its swastika-emblazoned rudder, in little more than a minute. To this day, journalists envied the news crew that had been on-hand that day, with primitive movie cameras, capturing onto acetate some of the most stunning footage and memorable imagery ever to accompany a technological disaster.

Nowadays, what reff or terr group wouldn't just love to claim credit for an event so resplendent? So attention-grabbing?

As if reading her mind, the voice lectured.

"Hydrogen is much lighter and more buoyant than helium. Hydrogen is also cheap and readily available. Using

it improves the economics of zep travel. Though of course, care must be taken. . . ."

As Tor approached the end of her narrow corridor, she encountered the trusswork that kept *Spirit* rigid—a dirigible—instead of a floppy, balloonlike blimp. One girder made of carbon tubes, woven into an open latticework of triangles, stretched and curved both forward and aft. Nearby, it joined another tensegrity strut at right angles. That one would form a girdle, encircling the *Spirit*'s widest girth.

Tracking Tor's interest, her spec spun out statistics and schematics. At eight hundred feet in length, *Hindenburg* had been just 10 percent shorter than the *Titanic*. In contrast, the *Spirit of Chula Vista* stretched twice that distance. Yet, its shell and trusswork weighed half as much.

"Naturally, there are precautions," the voice continued. *"Take the shape of the gas cells. They are vertical columns. Any failure in a hydrogen cell triggers a pulse, bursting open the top, pushing the contents up and out of the ship, skyward, away from passengers, cargo, or people below. It's been extensively tested.*

"Also, the surrounding helium cells provide a buffer, keeping oxygen-rich air away from those containing hydrogen. Passenger ships like this one carry double the ratio of helium to hydrogen."

"They can replenish hydrogen en route if they have to, right? By cracking water from onboard ballast?"

"Or even from humidity in the air, using solar power.

"And yes, the readouts show unusual levels of hydrogen production, in order to keep several cells filled aboard the Spirit. *That's why we asked you to come up here. There must be some leakage. One scenario suggested that it might be accumulating in here, between the cells."*

She pulled the omnisniffer—a phone attachment—from her purse and began scanning. Chemical sensors were all over the place, naturally, getting cheaper and more acute all the time—just when the public seemed to want them. For reassurance, if nothing else.

"I'm not detecting very much," she said. Tor wasn't sure how to feel—relieved or disappointed—upon reading that hydrogen levels were only slightly elevated in the companionway.

"That confirms what onboard monitors have already shown. Hardly any hydrogen buildup in the cabins or walkways. It must be leaking into the sky—"

"Even so—" Tor began, envisioning gouts of flame erupting toward the heavens from atop the great airship.

"—at rates that offer no danger of ignition. The stuff dissipates very fast, Tor, and the Spirit *is moving, on a windy day. Anyway, hydrogen isn't dangerous—or even toxic— unless it's held within a confined space."*

Tor kept scanning while moving along the spongy path. But hydrogen readings never spiked enough to cause concern, let alone alarm. The smart-mob had wanted her to come up here for this purpose—to verify that onboard detectors hadn't been tampered with by clever saboteurs. Now that her independent readings confirmed the company's story, some people were already starting to lose interest. Ad hoc membership totals began to fall.

"Any leakage must be into the air," continued the voice of the group mind, still authoritative. *"We've put out a notice for amateur scientists, asking for volunteers to aim spectranalysis equipment along the* Spirit's *route. They'll measure parts-per-million, so we can get a handle on leakage rates. But it's mathematically impossible for the amounts to be dangerous. Humidity may go up a percent or two in neighborhoods that lie directly below* Spirit. *That's about it."*

Tor had reached the end of the walkway. Her hand pressed against the outer envelope—the quasiliving skin that enclosed everything, from gas cells and trusses to the passenger cabin below. Up close, it was nearly transparent, offering a breathtaking view outside.

"We passed the Beltway," she murmured, a little surprised that the diligent guardians of Washington's defensive grid allowed the *Spirit* to pass through that wall of sensors and rays without delay or scrutiny. Below and ahead, she could make out the great locomotive tug, *Umberto Nobile,* hauling hard at the tow cable, puffing along the Glebe Road Bypass. Fort Meyers stood to the left. The zeppelin's shadow rippled over a vast garden of gravestones— Arlington National Cemetery.

"The powers-that-be have downgraded our rumor," said the voice inside her ear. *"The nation's professional protectors are chasing down more plausible threats . . . none of which has been deemed likely enough to merit an alert. Malevolent zeps don't even make it onto the Threat Chart."*

Tor clicked and flicked the attention-gaze of her specs, glancing through the journalist feeds at MediaCorp, which were now—belatedly—accessible to a reporter of her level. Seven minutes after the rise in tension caused by that spam of rumors, a consensus was already forming. The spam flood had not been intended to distract attention *from* a terror attack, concluded mass-wisdom. It *was* the attack. And not a very effective one, at that. National productivity had dropped by a brief diversion factor of one part in twenty-three thousand. Hardly enough damage to be worth risking prosecution or retaliation. But then, neohackers seldom cared about consequences.

Speaking of consequences; they were already pouring in from her little snooping expedition. The mavens of propriety at MediaCorp, for example, must be catching up on recent events. A work-related memorandum flashed in Tor's agenda box, revising tomorrow's schedule for her first day of employment at the Washington Bureau. During lunch— right after basic orientation—she was now required to attend counseling on the Exercising Good Judgment in Impromptu Field Situations.

"Oh great," she muttered, noticing also that the zeppelin company had applied a five hundred dollar fine against her account for Unjustified Entry into Restricted Areas.

PLEASE REMAIN WHERE YOU ARE, MS. POV-LOV, said an override message. **AN ATTENDANT WILL ARRIVE AT YOUR POSITION SHORTLY IN ORDER TO HELP YOU RETURN TO YOUR SEAT FOR LANDING.**

"Double great."

Ahead, beyond the curve of the dirigible's skin, she spotted the massive, squat bulk of the Pentagon, bristling with missiles, lenses, and antennae . . . still a highly-protected enclave, even ten years after the Department of Defense moved its headquarters to "an undisclosed location in Minnesota."

Soon, the mooring towers and docking ports of Reagan-Clinton National Skydrome would appear, signaling the end of her cross-continental voyage. Also finished— despite a string of interesting stories, from the Atkins Center to Hamish Brookeman railing at the Godmakers' Conference—was all chance of a blemish-free start to her new career in Big Time Media.

She addressed the group mind. "I don't suppose any of you have bright ideas?"

But it had already started to unravel. Membership numbers were falling fast, like rats deserting a sinking ship. Or—more accurately—monkeys. Moving on to the next shiny thing.

"Sorry, Tor. People are distracted. They've been dropping out to watch the reopening of the Artifact Conference. You may even glimpse some limos arriving at the Naval Research Center, just across the Potomac. Take a look as the Spirit *starts turning for final approach . . ."*

Blasted fickle amateurs! Tor had made good use of smart-mobs in the past. But this time was likely to prove an embarrassment. None of *them* would have to pay fines or face disapproval in a new job.

"Still, a few of us remain worried," the voice continued. *"That rumor had something . . . I can't put my finger on it."*

The "voice" was starting to sound individualized and had even used the first person "I." A sure sign of low numbers. And yet, Tor drew some strength from the support. Before an attendant arrived to escort her below, there was still time for a little last-minute tenacity.

"Can I assume we still have some zep aficionados in attendance?"

"Hardly anyone else, Tor. Some of us are fanatics."

"Good, then let's apply fanatical expertise. Think about that *leakage* we discussed a while ago. We've been assuming that this zeppelin is making hydrogen to make up for a significant seep, into the air outside. That'd be pretty harmless, I agree. Have any of those amateur scientists studied the air near *Spirit*'s flight path, yet?"

A pause.

"Yes, several have reported in. They found no dangerous levels of hydrogen in the vicinity of the ship, or in its wake. The seep is probably dissipating so fast. . . ."

"Please clarify. No dangerous levels? Is it possible they found *no* sign of a hydrogen leak *at all*?"

The pause extended several seconds longer, this time. Suddenly the number of participants in the group stopped falling. In the corner of Tor's specs, she saw membership levels start to rise again, slowly.

"Now that's interesting," throbbed the consensus voice in her ear.

"Several of those amateur scientists have joined us now.

"They report seeing no appreciable leakage. Zero extra hydrogen along the flight path. How did you know?"

"I didn't. Call it a hunch."

"But at the rate that Spirit *has been replacing hydrogen . . ."*

"There has to be some kind of leak. Right." She finished that thought aloud. "Not into the baggage compartment or passageways, either. We'd have detected that. But the missing hydrogen must be going somewhere."

Tor frowned. She could see a shadow moving beyond the grove of tall, cylindrical gas cells. A figure approaching. A crewman or attendant, coming to take her, firmly, gently, insistently, back to her seat. The shape wavered and warped as seen through the mostly transparent polymer tubes—slightly pinkish for hydrogen and then greenish tinted for helium.

Tor blinked. Suddenly feeling so dry mouthed that she could not speak aloud, only subvocalize.

"Okay . . . then . . . please ask the amscis to take some more spectral scans along the path of this zeppelin. Only this time . . . look for *helium*."

The inner surface of her specs showed a flurry of indicators. Amateur scientific instruments, computer-controlled from private backyards or rooftop observatories, speckled the nation. Many could zoom quickly toward any patch of sky—hobbyists with access to better instrumentation than earlier generations of top experts could have imagined. Dotted lines appeared. Each showed the viewing angle of some home-taught astronomer, ecologist, or meteorologist, turning a hand- or kit-made instrument toward the majestic cigar shape of the *Spirit of Chula Vista*. . . .

. . . which had passed Arlington and Pentagon City, following its faithful tug into a final tracked loop, turning to approach the dedicated zeppelin port that served Washington, D.C.

"Yes, Tor. There is helium.

"Quite a lot of it, in fact.

"A plume that stretches at least a hundred klicks behind the Spirit. *No one noticed before, because helium is inert and utterly safe, so no environmental monitors were tuned to look for it."*

The voice was grim. Much less individualized. With ad hoc membership levels suddenly skyrocketing, summaries and updates must be spewing at incredible pace.

"Your suspicion appears to be well based.

"Extrapolating the rate of helium loss backward in time, more than half of the Spirit of Chula Vista*'s original supply of that gas may have been lost by now. . . ."*

". . . replaced in these green cells by another gas." Tor completed the thought, while nodding. "I think we've found the missing hydrogen, people."

For emphasis, she reached out toward one of the nearby green cells. The "safe" ones that were there to protect life and property, making disaster impossible.

It all made sense, now. Smart polymers were programmable—all the way down to the permeability of any patch of these gas-containing cells, the same technology that made seawater desalinization cheap and ended the Water Wars. But it was technology, and so could be used in a multitude of ways. If you were very clever, you might insert a timed instruction where two gas cells touched, commanding one cell to leak into another. Create a daisy chain. Vent helium into the sky. Transfer gas from hydrogen cells *into* neighboring helium cells to maintain pressure, so that no one noticed. Then trigger automatic systems to crack onboard water and "replace" that hydrogen, replenishing the main cells. Allow the company to assume a slow leak into the sky is responsible. Continue.

Continue until you have replaced the helium in enough of the green cells to turn the *Spirit* into a flying bomb.

"The process must be almost complete by now," she murmured, peering ahead toward the great zep port, where dozens of mighty dirigibles could already be seen, some of them vastly larger than this passenger liner, bobbing gently at their moorings. Spindly fly-cranes went swooping back and forth as they plucked shipping containers from ocean freighters at the nearby Potomac Docks, gracefully transferring the air-gel crates to waiting cargo-zeppelins for the journey cross continent. A deceptively graceful, swaying dance that propelled the engines of commerce.

The passenger terminal—dwarfed by comparison to those giants—seemed to beckon with a promise of safety. But indicators showed that it still lay ten minutes away.

"We have issued a clamor, Tor," assured the voice in her head. *"Every channel. Every agency."*

A glance at spec-telltales showed Tor that, indeed, the group mind was doing its best. Shouting alarm toward every official protective service, from Defense to Homeworld Security. Individual members were lapel-grabbing friends and acquaintances, while smart-mob attendance levels climbed into five figures, and more. At this rate, surely the professionals would be taking heed. Any minute now.

"Too slow," she said, watching the figures with a sinking heart. Each second that it took to get action from the Protector Caste, the perpetrators of this scheme would also grow aware that the *jig is up*. Their plan was discovered. And they would have a speedup option.

Speaking of the perps, Tor wondered aloud.

"What can they be hoping to accomplish?"

"We're pondering that, Tor. Timing suggests that they aim to disrupt the Artifact Conference. Delegates arriving at the Naval Research Center are having a cocktail reception on the embankment right now, offering a fine view toward the zep port, across the river.

"Of course it is possible that the reffers plan to do more than just put on a show, while murdering three hundred passengers. We are checking to see if the Umberto *tug has been*

meddled with. Perhaps the plan is to hop rails and collide with a large cargo-zep, before detonation. Such a fireball might rock the Capitol, and disrupt the port for months.

One problem with a smart-mob. The very same traits that multiplied intelligence could also make it seem dispassionate. Insensitive. Individual members surely felt anguish and concern over Tor's plight. She might even access their messages, if she had time for commiseration.

But pragmatic help was preferable. She kept to the group mind level.

"One (anonymous) member (a whistle-blower?) has suggested a bizarre plan using a flying-crane at the zep port to grab the Spirit of Chula Vista *when it passes near. The crane would then hurl the* Spirit *across the river, to explode right at the Naval Research Center! In theory, it might just be possible to incinerate—"*

"Enough!" Tor cut in. Almost a minute had passed since realization of danger and the issuance of a clamor. And so far, no one had offered anything like a practical suggestion.

"Don't forget that I'm here, now. We have to do something."

"Yes," the voice replied, eagerly and without the usual hesitation. *"There is sufficient probable cause to get a posse writ. Especially with your credibility scores. We can act, with you performing the hands-on role.*

"Operational ideas follow:

"CUT THE TOWING CABLE.
(Emergency release in gondola. Reachable in four
 minutes.
Risk: possible interference from staff. Ineffective at
 saving the zeppelin/passengers.)
"PERSUADE ZEP COMPANY TO COMMENCE EMERGENCY
 VENTING PROCEDURES.

(Communication in progress. Response so far:
   obstinate refusal . . .)
"PERSUADE ONBOARD STAFF TO COMMENCE EMER-
   GENCY VENTING PROCEDURES.
(Attempting communication despite company
   interference . . .)
"PERSUADE COMPANY TO ORDER PASSENGER EVACUA-
   TION.
(Communication in progress. Response so far:
   obstinate refusal . . .)
"UPGRADE CLAMOR. CONTACT PASSENGERS. URGE
   THEM TO EVACUATE.
(Risks: delay, disbelief, panic, injuries, fatalities,
   lawsuits . . .)"

The list of suggestions seemed to scroll on and on. Rank-
ordered by plausibility-evaluation algorithms, slanted by
urgency, and scored by likelihood of successful outcome.
Individuals and subgroups within the smart-mob split apart
to urge different options with frantic vehemence. Her specs
flared, threatening overload.

"Oh, screw this," Tor muttered, reaching up and tearing
them off.

The real world—unfiltered. For all of its paucity of lay-
ering and data-supported detail, it had one special trait.

It's where I am about to die, she thought.

Unless I do something fast.

At that moment, the zep crew attendant arrived. He
rounded the final corner of a towering gas cell, coming into
direct view—no longer a shadowy authority figure, warped
and refracted by the tinted polymer membranes. Up close,
it turned out to be a small man, middle-aged and clearly
frightened by what his own specs had started telling him.
All intention to arrest or detain Tor had evaporated before

he made that turn. She could see this in his face, as clearly as if she had been monitoring vital signs.

WARREN, said a company nametag.

"Wha—what can I do to help?" he asked in a hoarse whisper.

Though hired for gracile weight and people skills, the fellow clearly possessed some courage. By now he knew what filled many of the slim, green-tinted membranes surrounding them both. And it didn't take a genius to realize the zep company was unlikely to help, during the time they had left.

"Tool kit!" Tor held out her hand.

Warren fumbled at his waist pouch. Precious seconds passed as he unfolded a slim implement case. Tor found one promising item—a vibrocutter.

"Keyed to your biometrics?"

He nodded. Passengers weren't allowed to bring anything aboard that might become a weapon. This cutter would respond to his personal touch and no other. It required not only a fingerprint, but volition—physiological signs of the owner's will.

"You must do the cutting, then."

"C-cutting . . . ?"

Tor explained quickly.

"We've got to vent this ship. Empty the gas *upward*. That'll happen to a main cell if it is ruptured anywhere along its length, right? Automatically?"

A shaky nod. She could tell Warren was getting online advice, perhaps from the zep company. More likely from the same smart-mob that she had called into being. She felt strong temptation to put her own specs back on—to link-in once more. But she resisted. Kibitzers would only slow her down right now.

"It might work . . . ," said the attendant in a frightened whisper. "But the reffers will realize, as soon as we start—"

"They realize now!" She tried not to shout. "We may have only moments to act."

Another nod. This time a bit stronger, though Warren was shaking so badly that Tor had to help him draw the cutter from its sleeve. She steadied his hand.

"We must slice through a helium bag in order to reach the big hydro cell," he said, pressing the biometric-sensitive stud. Reacting to his individual touch, a knife edge of acoustic waves began to flicker at the cutter tip, sharper than steel. A soft tone filled the air.

Tor swallowed hard. That flicker resembled a hot flame.

"Pick one."

They had no way to tell which of the greenish helium cells had been refilled, or what would happen when the cutter helped unite gas from neighboring compartments. Perhaps the only thing accomplished would be an early detonation. But even that had advantages, if it messed up the timing of this scheme.

One lesson you learned early nowadays: It simply made no sense, any longer, to rely for perfect safety upon a flawless professional protective caste. The police and military, the bureaucrats, and intelligence services. No matter how skilled and sophisticated they might grow, with infinite tax dollars to spend on advanced instrumentalities, they could still be overwhelmed, or cleverly bypassed. Human beings, they made mistakes. And when that happened, society must count on a second line of defense.

Us.

It meant—Tor knew—that any citizen could wind up being a soldier for civilization, at any time. The way they made the crucial difference on 9-11 and during Awfulday.

In other words, expendable.

"That one." Warren chose, and moved toward the nearest green-tinted cell.

Though she had doffed her specs, there was still a link.

The smart-mob's voice retained access to the conduction channel in her ear.

"Tor," said the group mind. *"We're getting feed through Warren's goggles. Are you listening? There is a third possibility, in addition to helium and hydrogen. Some of the cells may have been packed with—"*

She bit down twice on her left canine tooth, cutting off the distraction in order to monitor her omnisniffer. She inhaled deeply, with her eye on the indicator as Warren made a gliding, slicing motion with his cutter.

The greenish envelope opened, as if along a seam. Edges rippled apart as invisible gas—appreciably cooler—swept over them both.

HELIUM said the readout. Tor sighed relief.

"This one's not poisonous."

Warren nodded. "But no oxygen. You can smother." He ducked his head aside, avoiding the cool wind, and took another deep breath of normal air. Still, his next words had a squeaky, high-pitched quality. "Gotta move fast."

Through the vent he slipped, hurrying quickly to the other side of the green cell, where it touched one of the great chambers of hydrogen.

Warren made a rapid slash.

Klaxons bellowed, responding to the damage automatically. (Or else, had the company chosen that moment, after several criminally-negligent minutes, to finally admit the inevitable?) A voice boomed insistently, ordering passengers to move—calmly and carefully—to their escape stations.

That same instant, the giant hydrogen gas cell convulsed, twitching like a giant bowel caught in a spasm. The entire pinkish tube—bigger than a jumbo jet—*contracted,* starting at the bottom and squeezing toward a sudden opening at the very top, spewing its contents skyward.

Backwash hurled Warren across the green tube. Tor

managed to grab his collar, dragging him out to the walk-way. There seemed to be nothing satisfying about the "air" that she sucked into her lungs, and she started seeing spots before her eyes. The little man was in worse shape, gasping wildly in high-pitched squeaks.

Somehow, Tor hauled him a dozen meters along the gang-way, barely escaping descending folds of the deflated cell, till they arrived at last where breathing felt better. *Did we make any difference?* she wondered, wildly.

Instinctively, Tor slipped her specs back on. Immersed again in the info-maelstrom, it took moments to focus.

One image showed gouts of flame pouring from a hole in the roof of a majestic skyship. Another revealed the zep-pelin's nose starting to slant steeply as the tug-locomotive pulled frantically on its tow cable, reeling the behemoth toward the ground. *Spirit* resisted like a stallion, bucking and clinging to altitude.

Tor briefly quailed. Oh Lord, what have we done?

A thought suddenly occurred to her. She and Warren had done this entirely based on information that came to them from outside. From a group-mind of zeppelin aficio-nados and amateur scientists who claimed that a lot of ex-tra hydrogen had to be going somewhere, and it must be stored in some of the former helium cells.

But *that* particular helium cell—the one Warren sliced—had been okay.

And now, amid all the commotion, she wondered. What about the smart-mob? Could that group be a front for clever reffers, who were using *her* to do their dirty work? Feeding false information, in order to get precisely this effect?

The doubt passed through her mind in seconds. And back out again. This smart-mob was open and public. If some-thing smelled about it, *another* mob would have formed by now, clamoring like mad and exposing the lies. Anyway, if no helium cells had been tampered with, the worst that she and Warren could do was bring a temporarily disabled *Spirit of Chula Vista* down to a bumpy but safe landing atop its tug.

Newsworthy. But not very. And that realization firmed her resolve.

Tor yanked the attendant onto his feet and urged him to move uphill, toward the stern, along a narrow path that now inclined the other way. "Come on!" she called to Warren, her voice still squeaky from helium. "We've got to do more!"

Warren tried gamely. But she had to steady him as the path gradually steepened. When he prepared to slash at another green cell, farther aft, Tor braced his elbow.

Before he struck, through the omniscient gaze of her specs, Tor abruptly saw three more holes appear in the zep's broad roof, spewing clouds of gas, transparent but highly refracting, resembling billowy ripples in space.

Was the zep company finally taking action? Had the reffers made their move? Or had the first expulsion triggered some kind of compensating release from automatic valves, elsewhere on the ship?

As if pondering the same questions, the voice in her jaw mused.

"Too little has been released to save the Spirit *from the worst-case scenario. But maybe enough to limit the tragedy and mess up their scheme.*

"It depends on a rather gruesome possibility that one of us thought up. What if—instead of hydrogen—some of the helium cells have been refilled with OXYGEN? After experimenting with a similar, programmably permeable polymer, we find that the fuel replenishment process could be jiggered to do that. If so, the compressed combination—"

Oxygen?

Tor shouted "Wait!" as Warren made a hard stab at one

of the green cells, slicing a long vent that suddenly blurped at them.

This wave of gas wasn't as cool as the helium had been. It *smelled* terrific, though. One slight inhale filled Tor with sudden and suspicious exhilaration.

Uh-oh, she thought.

At that moment, her spectacle-display offered a bird's-eye view as one of the new clouds of vented hydrogen contacted dying embers, atop the tormented *Spirit of Chula Vista*.

Like a brief sun, each of the refracting bubbles ignited in rapid succession. Thunderclaps shook the dirigible from stem to stern, knocking Tor and Warren off their feet.

Is this it? Her own particular and special End of the World? Strangely, Tor's clearest thought was one of professional jealousy. Someone down below ought to be getting truly memorable and historic footage. Maybe on a par with the *Hindenburg* Disaster.

This was the critical moment. With their plan dissolving, the reffers must act. Any second now, a well-timed chain explosion *within* the *Spirit's* great abdomen. . . .

While the violent tossing drove Tor into fatalism, all that invigorating oxygen seemed to have an opposite effect upon Warren, who surged to his feet, then slipped through the tear that he had made and charged across the green cell, preparing to attack the giant hydrogen compartment beyond, heedless of the smart-mob, clamoring at him to stop.

Tor tried to add her own plea, but found that her throat would not function.

Some reporter, she thought, taking ironic solace in one fact—that her specs were still beaming to the Net.

Live images of a desperately unlikely hero.

Warren looked positively giddy—on a high of oxygen and adrenaline, but not too drugged to realize the implications.

He grimaced with an evident combination of fear and exaltation, while bringing his cutter-tool slashing down upon the polymer membrane—a slim barrier separating two gases that wanted, notoriously, to unite.

Sensory recovery came in scattered bits.

First, a smattering of dream images. Nightmare flashes about being chased, or else giving chase to something dangerous, across a landscape of burning glass. At least, that was how her mind pictured a piling-on of agonies. Regret. Physical anguish. Failure. More anguish. Shame. And more agony, still.

When the murk finally began to clear, consciousness only made matters worse. Everything was black, except for occasional crimson flashes. And those had to be erupting directly out of pain—the random firings of an abused nervous system.

Her ears also appeared to be useless. There was no real sound, other than a low, irritating humming that would not go away.

Only one conduit to the external world still appeared to be functioning.

The voice. It had been hectoring her dreams, she recalled. A nag that could not be answered and would not go away. Only now, at least, she understood the words.

"Tor? Are you awake? We're getting no signal from your specs. But there's a carrier wave from your tooth-implant. Can you give us a tap?"

After a pause, the message repeated.

And then again.

So, it was playing on automatic. She must have been unconscious for a long time.

"Tor? Are you awake? We're getting no signal from your specs. But there's a carrier wave from your tooth-implant. Can you give us a tap?"

There was an almost overwhelming temptation to do nothing. Every signal that she sent to muscles, commanding them to move, only increased the grinding, searing pain. *Passivity* seemed to be the lesson being taught right now. Just lie there, or else suffer even more. Lie and wait. Maybe die.

Also, Tor wasn't sure she liked the group mind anymore.

"Tor? Are you awake? We're getting no signal from your specs. But there's a carrier wave from your tooth-implant. Can you give us a tap?"

On the other hand, passivity seemed to have one major drawback. It gave pain an ally.

Boredom. Yet another way to torment her. Especially her.

To hell with that.

With an effort that grated, she managed to slide her jaw enough to bring the two left canine teeth together in a tap, and then two more. The recording continued a few moments—long enough for Tor to fear that it hadn't worked. She was cut off, isolated, alone in darkness.

But the group participants must have been away, doing their own things. Jobs, families, watching the news. After about twenty seconds, though, the voice returned, eager and live.

"Tor!

"We are so glad you're awake."

Muddled by dull agony, she found it hard at first to focus even a thought. But she managed to drag one canine in a circle around the other. Universal symbolic code for "question mark."

<?>

The message got through.

"Tor, you are inside a life-sustainment tube. Rescue workers found you in the wreckage about twelve minutes ago, but it's taking some time to haul you out. They should

have you aboard a medi-chopper in another three minutes, maybe four.

"We'll inform the docs that you are conscious. They'll probably insert a communications shunt sometime after you reach hospital."

Three rapid taps.

<NO>

The voice had a bedside manner.

"Now Tor, be good and let the pros do their jobs. The emergency is over and we amateurs have to step back, right?

"Anyway, you'll get the very best of care. You're a hero! Spoiled a reffer plot and saved a couple of hundred passengers. You should hear what MediaCorp is crowing about their 'ace field correspondent.' They even backdated your promotion a few days.

"Everyone wants you now, Tor," the voice finished, resonating her inner ear without any sign of double entendre. But surely individual members felt what she felt, right then.

Irony—the *other* bright compensation that Pandora found in the bottom of her infamous Box. At times, irony could be more comforting than hope.

Tor was unable to chuckle, so her tooth did a down-slide and then back.

<!>

The Voice seemed to understand and agree.

"Yeah.

"Anyway, we figure you'd like an update. Tap inside if you want details about your condition. Outside for a summary of external events."

Tor bit down emphatically on the outer surface of her lower canine.

"Gotcha. Here goes.

"It turns out that the scheme was partly to create a garish zep disaster. But they chiefly aimed to achieve a distraction.

"By colliding the Spirit *with a cargo freighter in a huge explosion, with lots of casualties, they hoped not only to close down the zep port for months, but also to create a suddenly lethal fireball that would draw attention from the protective and emergency services. All eyes and sensors would shift for a brief time. Wariness would steeply decline in other directions.*

"They thereupon planned to swoop into the Naval Research Center with a swarm attack by hyperlight flyers. Like the O'Hare Incident but with some nasty twists. We don't have details yet. Some of them are still under wraps. But it looks pretty awful, at first sight.

"Anyway, as events turned out, our ad hoc efforts aboard the Spirit *managed to expel almost half of the stockpiled gases early and in an uncoordinated fashion. Several of the biggest cells got emptied, creating gaps. So there was never a single, unified detonation when the enemy finally pulled their trigger. Just a sporadic fire. That kept the dirigible frame intact, enabling the tug to reel it down to less than a hundred meters.*

"Where the escape chutes mostly worked. Nearly all passengers got away without injury, Tor. And the zep port was untouched."

Trying to picture it in her mind's eye—perhaps the only eye she had left—took some effort. She was used to so many modern visualization aides that mere words and imagination seemed rather crude. A cartoony image of the *Spirit*, her vast upper bulge aflame, slanted steeply groundward as the doughty *Umberto Nobile* desperately pulled the airship toward relative safety. And then, slender tubes of active plastic snaking down, offering slide-paths for the tourist families and other civilians.

The real event must have been quite a sight.

Her mind roiled with questions. What about the rest of the passengers?

What fraction were injured, or died?

How about people down below, on the nearby highway?

Was there an attack on the Artifact Conference, after all?

So many questions. But till doctors installed a shunt, there would be no way to send anything more sophisticated than these awful yes-no clicks. And some punctuation marks. Normally, equipped with a tru-vu, a pair of touch-tooth implants would let her scroll rapidly through menu choices, or type on a virtual screen. Now, she could neither see nor subvocalize.

So, she thought about the problem. Information could in-load at the rate of spoken speech. Outloading was a matter of clicking two teeth together.

Perhaps it was the effect of drugs, injected by the para-medics, but Tor found herself thinking with increasing detachment, as if viewing her situation through a distant lens. Abstract appraisal suggested a solution, reverting to a much older tradition of communication.

She clicked the inside of her lower left canine three times quickly. Then the outer surface three times, more slowly. And finally the inner side three more times.

"What's that, Tor? Are you trying to say something?"

She waited a decent interval, then repeated exactly the same series of taps. Three rapid clicks inside, three slow ones on the outside, and again three quickly inside. It took several repetitions before the Voice hazarded a guess.

"Tor, a few members and ais suggest that you're trying to send a message in old-fashioned Morse code.

"Three dots, three dashes, then three dots. 'SOS.'

"The old international distress call. Is that it, Tor?"

She quickly assented with a yes tap. Thank heavens for the diversity of a group mind. Get one large enough, and you were sure to include some oldtech freak.

"But we already know you are in pain. Rescuers have

*found you. There's nothing else to accomplish by calling
for help . . . except . . ."*

The Voice paused again.

"Wait a minute.

*"There is a minority theory floating up. A guess-
hypothesis.*

*"Very few modern people bother to learn Morse code
anymore. But most of us have heard of it. Especially that
one message you were using. SOS. Three dots, three dashes,
three dots. It's famous from old-time movies.*

"Is that what you're telling us, Tor?

"Would you like us to teach you Morse code?"

Although she could sense nothing external, not even the
rocking of her life-support canister as it was being hauled
by evacuation workers out of the smoldering *Spirit of Chula
Vista,* Tor did feel a wash of relief.

Yes, she tapped.

Most definitely yes.

"Very well.

"Now listen carefully.

"We'll start with the letter 'A'. . . ."

It helped to distract her from worry, at least, concentrating to learn something without all the tech-crutches relied
upon by today's tenners and twenners. Struggling to absorb a simple alphabet code that every smart kid used to
memorize, way back in that first era of zeppelins and tele-
graphs and crystal radios, when the uncrowded sky had
seemed so wide open and filled with innocent possibilities.
When the smartest mob around was a rigidly marching
army. When a journalist would chase stories with notepad,
flashbulbs, and intuition. When the main concern of a citizen was earning enough to put bread on the table. When
the Professional Protective Caste consisted of a few cops
on the beat.

Way back, one human life span ago, when heroes were tall and square-jawed, in both fiction and real life.

Times had changed. Now, destiny could tap anybody on the shoulder, even the shy or unassuming. You, me, the next guy. Suddenly, everybody depends on just one. And that one relies on everybody.

Tor concentrated on her lesson, only dimly aware of the vibrations conveyed by a throbbing helicopter, carrying her (presumably) to a place where modern miracle workers would strive to save—or rebuild—what they could.

Professionals still had their uses, even in the rising Age of Amateurs. Bless their skill. Perhaps—with luck and technology—they might even give Tor back her life.

Right now, though, one concern was paramount. It took a while to ask the question that burned foremost in her mind, since she needed a letter near the end of the alphabet. But as soon as they reached it, she tapped out a Morse code message that consisted of one word.

<WARREN>

She expected the answer that her fellow citizens gave.

Even with the hydrogen cell contracting at full force to expel most of its contents skyward, there would have been more than enough right there, at the oxygen-rich interface, to incinerate one little man. One volunteer. A hero, leaving nothing to bury, but scattering microscopic ashes all the way across his nation's capital.

Lucky guy, she thought, feeling a little envy for his rapid exit and inevitable, uncomplicated fame.

Tor recognized what the envy meant, of course. She was ready to enter the inevitable phase of self-pity. A necessary stage.

But not for long. Only till they installed the shunt.

After that, it would be back to work. Lying immersed in sustainer-jelly and breathing through a tube? That wouldn't stop a real journalist. The web was a beat rich with stories, and Tor had a feeling—she would get to know the neighborhood a whole lot better.

"And we'll be here," assured the smart-mob. *"If not us, then others like us.*

"You can count on it Tor.

"Count on us.

"We all do."

PART FIVE

A CONSUMMATION DEVOUTLY WISHED . . .

Is it a fact—or have I dreamt it—that, by means of electricity, the world of matter has become a great nerve, vibrating thousands of miles in a breathless point of time? Rather, the round globe is a vast head, a brain, instinct with intelligence!

——Nathaniel Hawthorne, 1851

What we anticipate seldom occurs, what we least expected generally happens.

—Benjamin Disraeli, 1837

the child is found !/!

autie-murphy sifted seventeen webs . . . encompassing two hundred and twelve thousand and forty-one vir levels . . . some as wide and detailed as the surface of real-earth . . . while looking for <u>not-patterns</u> //–//–// nor-nand gaps where normalpeople & aspies & ais & eyes <u>ought to be</u> looking — but where <u>nobody is</u> –/+

Agurne Arrixaka Bidarte is not using cams, webs or credit –.– those sheltering her are careful –.– leave no clues . . . traces carefully absent . . . but what of that very <u>absence?</u> Can it be traced?

hard to program +++ every spy agency has snifferprogs out there seeking correlations . . . but <u>un-correlations</u> are another matter/liquid/solid/plasma/vrasma/ectoplasm !/!

ais don't <u>not-look</u> very well — but autie-murph does it great /!/ not-patterns suit a savant like him +++ who deals with cobblies every day +++

and so we ask—now that we found them—can/should we help mother-n-child ??? this part is hard —> how to go beyond noting/noticing/not-icking/not-acting and create instead an <u>arrow</u> of effective action ??? not our-forte . . . nor even aspies or high-funcs

doing stuff +++ that is what normalpeople are for –/– poormoms

bad enough is our handicap / our clumsiness / with real-world/cause/effect . . . only now there is this new thing. . . . this alien/other/outerspace THING in the news . . . a world-

*intruder that has the cobblies all not-leaping about and
not-yapping frantically*

   we need a friend ./.

   *we've used friends before – yes.?. dangerous. –/– some-
times they betray our trust –//– this friend had better be a
good one. . . . .*

29.

INCOMPREHENSION

Once you finally got the aliens talking, it proved hard to shut them up.

"Congratulations! As a space-faring type, you have surpassed very long odds. Few get as far as you have. You are now welcome to join us."

That much came through pretty clear. It was the proclamation that made headlines around the world.

Less noticed—though still cause for rampant speculation—was how hard Gerald and the rest of the contact team had to work, in order to get that much clarity out of the Artifact. The ratio of useful information coming out of the ovoid crystal—versus confusing chaos—was still frustratingly low.

Like sipping from a fire hose, Gerald thought. Except this hose sprayed in all directions.

Bathed in exactly the right wavelengths to maximize energy use, the object he had snagged out of orbit with his garbage-collecting tether now shone with a vibrancy that enthralled onlookers. Scenes portrayed through its gleaming, curved surface appeared to swoop and shift at a dizzying pace, from cloud-flecked planetary horizons to mysterious cityscapes, revealed through unraveling mists. From desert ruins, drowned by drifting sands, to slick ocean vistas that rolled with oily viscosity and shimmered all the colors of a rainbow. From salty expanses that featured endless rows of windowless, cubiform huts, all the way to vast ice fields, where mysterious cracks opened to emit brief swarms of black, arachnoid shapes, spreading out to harvest strange, gray-green globs. . . .

A series of alien figures also floated up, jostling each other as before. They seemed to push forward to press hands or paws or tentacles against the egglike inner surface of the message bottle, bringing close their eyes, orb-lenses, and other sensory organs to gape outward at the Contact Team.

Behind Gerald, just on the other side of a barrier of quarantine glass, stood members of the international commission, representing all the nations, estates, and important interests on Earth. And of course, there was everyone else, a large fraction of the world's population, who played hooky from school and work, or else MT-tracked every moment while pretending to do their jobs. Economic productivity was taking a hit and no one seemed to care.

A gaggle on one side, staring out, and a super-gaggle on the other side, staring in, he thought. *With plenty of ambiguity over which mob is the most eager or confused.* Indeed, Gerald still occasionally experienced that same frightening illusion that *he* and his comrades were somehow the ones encased within a cramped, simulated world, and the Artifact denizens were the ones peering into a zoo-terrarium through their narrow, magic lens.

"We're getting more complaints about visual signal degradation in the broadcast feed," reported General Akana Hideoshi. "People don't like the high-contrast, bleached, and reprocessed version being offered to the public. It inevitably provokes conspiracy theories—that we're not sharing everything we see or learn." Akana shook her head unhappily.

"Well, I don't know what to do about that," replied Dr. Emily Tang, the team's interface expert. "Our policy masters have demanded protocols to keep the dataflow clean. After all, what if this device turns out to be a Trojan horse? A way for outsiders to inveigle some alien software virus into our networks? Or to reprogram *people* who watch closely. Such parasitic code might be tucked inside the bit stream, woven through it via *steganography,* turning any seemingly benign picture into a possible source of infection. The computers in this building are quarantined and scrutinaized. So are we humans who have direct eye contact. But we cannot allow the public to get direct access to unwashed data!"

Emily was paid to be suspicious, even though such precautions made her the subject of paranoid rumors, especially on the part of openness fetishists out there. *Nor can I blame them,* Gerald thought.

Along with about a billion others, he had been disappointed with the Big Deal, when it failed to meet the top goal of the Fourth and Fifth and Sixth Estates—total transparency. A *bigger deal to* end secrecy. A world where the politicians, zaibatsus, guilds, gangs, and superrich power brokers would have to operate in the light. While retaining their wealth, legal powers, and advantages, the world's top movers would at least forfeit their privilege of cheating in the dark. Above all, everyone should state openly what they owned. A powerful idea, briefly igniting mass imagination . . .

. . . till it had to be bargained away, when all the top castes joined forces against it. Now? Everyone knew the Big Deal was a stopgap measure, buying time, or a little peace, till promised techno-miracles might revive the roaring optimism of the tween years. And some came! Only each breakthrough brought its own freight of future shock, and rising calls for mass-refusal. Every social model—even cheap, two-year-old versions that a citizen could download for free—portrayed the Big Deal teetering toward collapse in half a decade or so. Nor would mere truth and openness suffice, this time.

The Artifact might have chosen a better occasion to suddenly appear. Almost *any* other occasion.

Why couldn't it have been snagged by some earlier astronaut? Gerald thought. *Back in the giddy Apollo days, for example. Or during the rich, early part of this century, when everyone was calm, and there were still plenty of resources to keep folks from each other's throats?*

Even those who expect only good things when we join some interstellar community—nothing but wisdom and beneficial technologies—even those optimists know there will be disruption and of pain. And meanwhile, people who already have power will come up with every possible rationalization. Reasons to preach that change is dangerous.

"Anyway, there are *other* security-related concerns," Emily added. "Tiger and I have come up with a range of possible theories for the chaotic, disorganized way the Artifact beings have related to us—the so-called Rabble Effect."

Genady Gorosumov, the team's xenobiologist, looked up from the holistank where he had been tending his models—growing simulations of all the different kinds of Artifact aliens that had been exhibited, so far—trying to understand them by vivisecting replica archetypes, based upon visual appearance alone. He brushed a pile of dismembered skeletal pieces toward a tray. Made entirely of light patterns, they swiftly reassembled into an articulated model of the centauroid alien.

"Now that is interesting. How *do* you explain the way these entities push and shove at one another? They seem to have no sense of order or cooperation—certainly no concept of turn-taking, or courtesy! Even when groups of them work together, briefly, in order to speak to us coherently, it is always temporary. Although this charming chaos does remind me of my hometown, I cannot say it bodes well for this *galactic civilization* we have been invited to join.

"Nor does it give us much opportunity to ask more than one question at a time."

"And that may be precisely the purpose," answered Emily.

When all eyes stared at her, she nodded to her left. "I'll let Tiger explain."

Gerald and the others turned toward that end of the conference table, where a threevee display showed a face—one that crossed many of the pleasing traits of a beautiful woman with the feral muzzle of a *cat,* including soft, striped fur and small, pointy teeth that gleamed when shai smiled. It was a grin that made you glad that the artificial being was on your side. Or, at least, that shai was programmed to emulate someone who liked you.

"We must bear in mind that the jostling Rabble Effect may be a ruse," commented the virtual aindroid. *"A way to keep us talking, so that we'll offer them floods of information about ourselves, while they provide little in return."*

Gerald had seen this theory before, bubbling up from the morass of a million discussion groups. "So perhaps they are actually far more cooperative with each other than they appear? You think they may be playing roles, in order to keep us off balance."

"Or else, perhaps there is no *they* at all."

It was Haihong Ming, who had just joined the contact team as the new representative of Great China. He hadn't said much since replacing Gerald's friend, the ex-astronaut Wang Quangen. But when he did, on behalf of Earth's leading power, it seemed wise to listen.

"What do you mean?"

Haihong Ming put down the mesh-specs that he had been using to stay in direct communication with his superiors in Beijing, separate from the main video feed.

"I mean that all this bubbling diversity may be vexing, but doesn't it also come across as conveniently *reassuring*

somehow? After all, what do we fear most about a big, galactic civilization? Once it is determined that no one's bent
on invading or killing us, what comes *next* on our list of
big worries?"

The other commission members pondered the question
for a few seconds before Ramesh Trivedi, from the Hindi
Commonwealth, finally murmured.

"Uniformity. Conformity. Insistence that small and
weak newcomers like us should adhere to rigid rules, fitting into the bottom of an established hierarchy. Demanding that we bend our traditions, laws, and way of life to meet
some ancient set of patterns not our own. *That* is what we'd
find almost as crushing and horrible as outright invasion—a fear made palpable by our own history of contact
events among human cultures, here on Earth."

"Like when Europeans insisted that Asian peoples use
tables and chairs? Knives and forks? Soap and electricity?"
asked Emily, in a sardonic tone. But Ramesh did not rise to
the Vancouver professor's bait. He smiled, shaking his
head.

"You know there were far worse impositions. Episodes
of cultural domination that were painful, cruel, demoral-
izing, or limiting. And that was between *human* tribes!
Even the well-meaning process of *accession,* when independent countries join the EU or the AU . . . having to
change many of their laws and customs in order to con-
form to a confederation they had no part in formulating.
Even that mild process is humiliating. How much worse
might it get for neophytes entering interstellar society,
forced to adapt to a civilization millions of years old? *That*
is the dread Haihong Ming refers to."

Glancing at the Chinese representative, Gerald felt pretty
sure that Ramesh was at least somewhat off-target. Still,
Haihong Ming kept silent, enigmatically impassive, content to let Ramesh talk on.

"Hence the reason why so many people find all the tumult and disarray among the Artifact beings . . . reassuring. Perhaps even endearing. *It implies that no person or group out there is enforcing rigid uniformity.* We'll be free to pick and choose from a wide variety of role models, negotiate among partners and competitors, and retain much of what we value about our own past.

"And yes, I, too, feel encouraged by all that."

Only then Ramesh frowned, his complexion darkening.

"But our colleague from the People's Ministry of Science does not take consolation so easily, does he? And Emily is even more dourly suspicious! So, let me guess the reasoning. You two think that all of this adorable bustle and crowding and alien-elbowing-alien may be a ruse? That it may be *faked,* in order to lull us?"

Haihong Ming nodded. "I am merely trying to cover the full range of possibilities, Dr. Trivedi. All the purported representatives that we have seen, from dozens of different extraterrestrial races—they could be faked. Mere cartoon puppets that always vanish before we can examine them too closely. Suppose the effect were intentional. That they were all contrived by a *single entity,* with a single agenda. Not only to stall and put off inconvenient questions—but also in order to give us an impression of lively, raucous but peaceful diversity? The very thing that might mollify and comfort many of us?"

Many of us . . . but not all of us, Gerald thought. His mouth half opened to point this out, then closed again. His every instinct shouted that the aliens really were separate beings, eagerly diverse and rather fractious, with their own agendas and purposes, scraping against each other within the context of their compact universe. *But then . . . my human instincts might be the very thing that a supersophisticated alien AI could swiftly learn to play upon.* The same way that a skilled dramavid team might draw in millions of viewers, getting them to hypnotically believe in artificial characters of the latest full-immersion miniseries.

At least we're advanced enough to ponder all these possibilities. But what if other stones fell to Earth, long ago? How might they have dazzled our ancestors?

Gerald's specs had been tracking his gaze and iris fluctuations, temporal lobe surges, and subvocal comments half sent to his larynx. All of that—plus the surrounding conversation—fed a steady churn of googs and guesses about what might interest him, constantly re-prioritized so that only the most plausible would float into his periphery of vision . . . while leaving Gerald free to focus on real people and events, straight ahead. Done right, associative attention assistance simply imitated the way creative folk already thought—making millions of connections, while only a few reached surface awareness. Gerald had never been able to afford the best *intelligence enhancement* aiware . . . till now. Until price suddenly became no object.

Now, he was still getting used to the souped-up gear. One corner of his specs lit up in a yellow, high-pri shade, indicating that a virt was coming in, from a person of substance with top credibility scores. From someone in the Advisory Panel . . . eighty or so experts who were permitted to watch the commission deliberate in real time, and offer suggestions.

Gerald first saw it gist-distilled down to a single phrase—**"many may be one, and vice-versa."** But, in less than a second the glimmer expanded, filling out the meaning and acquiring a *vaice,* especially as first Akana, then Genady, clicked approval.

"The distinction between 'one' and 'many' can be ambiguous. The best models of a human mind portray it as a mélange of interests and subpersonalities, sometimes in conflict, often merging, overlapping, or recomposing with agile adaptability.

"*Sanity is viewed as a matter of getting these fluid portions of the self to play well together, without letting them become rigid or too well defined. In human beings, this is best achieved through interaction with other minds—other people—beyond the self. Without the push-back of external beings—outside communities and objective events—the subjective self can get lost in solipsism or fractured delusion.*

"*We know from experience that solitude or sensory deprivation can be especially devastating. Prisoners who are kept in sequestered confinement often wind up dividing their minds into explicit personas—rigid characters that grow firm and permanent, with consistent voices all their own. Perhaps they do this in order to have someone to talk to.*

"*Now extrapolate this. Picture a 'person' who has lived alone, as isolated as any castaway, for untold centuries. Even eons. All of it endured without any external beings to converse with. Just floating in space, lacking actual events to help mark time or to denote real from imagined.*

"*Is it possible that you or I, after such extended loneliness, might envision, then believe in, separate personalities? Characters who started out as imaginary figments, but gradually became as varied and interesting and diverse as you might find in a whole world—or in a community of worlds? Interacting with each other in ways that reflect the disorder and pain of a long, harsh state of isolation?*"

Emily gasped. "I hadn't thought of that. But the implication . . . you're saying the Artifact may *not* be making up these characters in order to fool us.

"Instead, it might be doing so because it is insane!"

"*I did not use that term. In fact, there is another word that comes to mind. More optimistic and less judgmental, it could also explain the 'Rabble Effect'—the chaotic jumble of personalities and images.*

"Instead of malignant intent, or insanity, the sheer diversity of alien types that we see may reflect simple wishfulness, on the part of a lonesome mind. One that was originally designed as an emissary. One built to yearn for contact."

Gerald saw it coming. He spoke aloud, before the advisory voice could state the obvious.

"You think the Artifact is asleep. That it may be dreaming.

"In which case, can we—or should we—try to wake it up?"

Tiger sifted all the different theories into a multidimensional matrix, performed some optimization simulations, and came up with a suggestion.

"I propose that we try operant conditioning."

The phrase sounded familiar to Gerald. His wetbrain memory tickled—possibly something he had learned in freshman biology class. But why bother reaching for it neuronally? Definitions scrolled under the quasi-feline face, sparking associations. Ah, yes. B. F. Skinner and his famous pigeons. Using reward and punishment to reinforce some behaviors while eliminating others. Anyone who ever trained a dog knew the basics.

"We should stop providing information, and even very much in the way of illumination to power the Artifact, except when the creatures within decide to settle down, behave less manically competitive, and start talking with us in a cogent manner."

"Forcing them to get organized and stop behaving like unsupervised kindergartners." Akana nodded with approval. It seemed that the idea of teaching aliens discipline appealed to her.

"And what of those other possibilities?" Emily asked, pointing at the plausibility matrix. "One theory suggests that the Rabble Effect may be a pretense. The appearance of an unruly mob may be feigned, as if by actors, playing roles. All this wild diversity could be made-up by a single mind. One that's nefarious, or crazy . . . or perhaps dreaming?"

"Well," answered the feline-female visage in the three-vee tank. *"This plan would seem best, in any event. It would show that we mean business. That it is time to rouse and get focused. To stop any pretense."*

Gerald stared. All the experts insisted that ersatz personae like Tiger weren't truly self-aware or sapient—only programmed to seem that way. But when did the distinction become absurd, even foolish?

Ramesh shook his head. "They . . . it . . . the Artifact already knows a lot about us. If we try such a ploy, it may simply call our bluff, betting that we can't hold out for long. Not with several billion people watching and the potential of rich treasures to be gained from contact. Demands from the public—and our political masters—will put a time limit on any such experiment. And this thing has plenty of experience with patience.

"Still," he shrugged, "it does seem to be the best idea on the table."

When it came to a vote, Gerald raised his hand in assent. Still, he kept one thought to himself—

—that operant conditioning can work both ways. Sometimes, the one who thinks he's doing the training . . . may be the one being trained.

PIONEERS

Okay, it's me Slawek again. Promoted from tour guide to reclam leader. Yeah, I'm just a kid. So? If you don't like taking directions from a fourteen-year-old deepee, just go to the Duty Desk and ask Dariga Sadybekova to assign you to another team. Or tell Dr. Betsby your troubles, if he'll listen. Oh yes . . . he's out of town!

Look, I don't care if you just arrived from Outer Slobovia, or if your biofeedback guru wants you to buzz-meditate twelve hours a day, or if you still have the Awfulday Twitches. Everybody works. That's a rule if you want to keep living here under the Silverdome.

In fact, some of the work parties are dorma-fun. Hunting pheasant and picking wild grapes in the wild suburbs, or sledge-demoling abandoned houses and stripping their last traces of metal. Pounding down the walls in search of hidden treasures.

Sorry, we're not doing that today.

We'll be *sewer-diving* under one of the Detroit reclamation neighborhoods we Silverdomers were granted, as a homestead domain by the state of Michigan. That is, if we can improve it.

Yeah, okay. Sewer work. So? Why blink? Almost nobody lives there, so there won't be much flushing going on. And we all get micropore masks. So it shouldn't stink. Much.

One reason for this pre-briefing is to make you familiar with the task and a crude map of what's down there. Our job is to install RFID repeater-chips every half meter along all the pipes and mains we can reach, so this part of the underworld can join the World Mesh. Currently, it's way dark down there! And with no link it's possible to get lost. Really lost! So remember the buddy system.

We must keep a good pace, 'cause another crew will be right behind us, staple-gluing data strand to the roof of the sewer. A startup company wants to compete with cable and phone conduit providers. They aim to use *sewage* rights-of-way to deliver fiber cable to every toilet—I mean, every home—in America. (A far-*raki* idea! I'm already invested.)

Finally, each of you will be given a siphon bottle and a sack. We'll show you how to find low spots in the sewer that may have collected pools of mercury, across the last century or two. Suck those little deposits into the bottle. The bag is in case you spot saltpeter crystals along the way. Or coins. There are a dozen other treasures to look out for—one more reason to pay attention to this briefing.

Phos prices are up and you can trade whatever you find for zep rides or driz, when we get back to our big dome-home.

30.
THE AVENUE WITHIN

The *shunt* caused a strange kind of agony. The worst since the zeppelin explosion left her body a roasted shell.

Even the word itself felt painful, in a way, because it was misleading. Like other journalists of a new generation, Tor disliked the mushy inexactitude of earlier correspondents— their propensity for oversimplification and loosey-juicy metaphor. To be precise then, the "shunt" that doctors and technicians were installing into her brain was not a single tube or wire. It consisted of more than ten thousand separate pathways that started out as tiny holes, drilled into her skull.

From there, minuscule, trail-blazing automatons probed inward, proceeding cautiously. Minimizing damage to fragile axons, dendrites, and neural clusters, where calcium ions surged and electro-chemical potentials flared, all contributing to the vast standing wave of composite human consciousness. Skirting all of that, as much as possible, the microscopic machines instead navigated their way inward via giant astrocyte cells, using them as fatty corridors, while each little crawler tugged a slender fiber behind it, until the final destination—some well-mapped center of communication, vision, or motor control—lay just ahead.

Tor appreciated the lack of pain receptors inside a human brain. Or so assured the doctors, in tinny voices that crackled down the remnants of her auditory system—those portions that had not been seared away by the zeppelin explosion. In fact, the creeping nano-robots should not trigger any conspicuous reaction at all, as they made their way to preplanned positions in the visual cortex, the cerebellum, the anterior cingulate, the left temporal lobe . . . and a host of other crucial nexi, scattered through Tor's intricately folded cerebrum. That is, not until they were ready to start their real work—probing and testing, mapping old connections and creating new ones that might—possibly—let her see again, and hear and speak after a fashion.

And perhaps . . . science willing . . . even move and walk and . . .

But it seemed better not to dwell too much on hope. So instead, Tor clinically envisioned what was going on inside her head. Imagination perceived the machine incursion as a benign army of penetrating needles—or invading mites—crawling inexorably inward, forcing their way past all barriers of decency, into a sanctum that had once been ultimately private. Or, as private as anything could be, in this modern world.

Then, upon arriving at its destined station, each little robot began *poking*! Jabbing and zapping the tips of selected dendrites, sometimes achieving nothing, or else triggering instantaneous reactions—a speck of "light" . . . a twinge of her left big toe . . . the smell of roasted pine nuts . . . a sudden hankering to see, once again, her girlhood pet retriever, Daffy.

Reacting with disorientation, even nausea, Tor soon felt warm countercurrents flow—undoubtedly drugs meant to keep her body calm and mind alert—as the doctors began to make demands upon her, asking about each sensorimotor effect.

Irritated by their yattering, for a brief time she considered withholding cooperation. But that impulse didn't last. *As if they would let me refuse.* Anyway, to do so—in order to tell them off—Tor would have to speak, to make her wishes understood by some means other than tooth-taps in Morse code. Till then, she would be ruled incompetent, a ward of the state and of her company's insurance plan, lacking any legal right to make them all bug off!

So, Tor clicked her canines and bicuspids, in order to answer simple questions—such as identifying "left" and "right," "up" and "down," when bright smudges began to appear, triggered by probes that stimulated different parts of her visual cortex. And soon, what had started as gross blobs began resolving into ever smaller pixel-like points, or slender rays, or slanting bars that crossed from one side to another . . . as some computer gradually learned the cipher of her own, unique way of seeing.

Everyone's different, I hear. Our inner images map onto the same reality as other people see—the same streetlights and billboards and such. Each of us claims to perceive identical surroundings. We all call the sky "blue." And yet, the actual experience of sight—the "qualia"—is said to be peculiar to each person. Our brains are not logically planned. They evolve—every one of us, in that sense, becoming her own species.

Tor realized she was reciting, as if for her vraudience! Parsing clear sentences, even though there was—so far—no subvocal transceiver to convey her words around the world. Or even across the room. It seemed that habit, sometimes a dear friend, was drawing her back into the role of reporter and *raconteur.* And, even without a public to appreciate it—she still deemed it good, a source of pleasure and pride, to shape rounded sentences. To *describe* what was happening—that offered her a glimmering sense of power, amid utter powerlessness.

Part of me survived, whole. Maybe the best part.

Not that Tor was ever entirely alone. There were the human specialists and computer-voiced aidviser programs hired by MediaCorp to take care of their superstar. And, ensuring that she never felt abandoned in the darkness, there was the voice of the mob—the smart-mob she had called up, aboard the *Spirit of Chula Vista*. It never left her side . . . though individual members came and went. Whenever the hospital allowed it, during frequent breaks and visitor hours, that composite voice returned to keep Tor company, to read to her, or else keep her up with current events.

What would I have done, if there had been deeper brain damage? she wondered. Injury that prevented the reception and "hearing" of auditory input, for example? The voices in her head kept her sane. They were her link to the real world.

And so, between medical sessions, when her tooth ached from tapping a million yes and no answers—helping identify the scattered and minute segments of her rebuilding brain—she was also fed a steady description of each day's news. Naturally, that included the planetary fascination with a stone from interstellar space—the Livingstone Object. But there were also reports on a hard-pressed search for the zeppelin saboteurs. Those who murdered poor Warren and left her in this state, encased in a life-sustaining cocoon.

Tor's direct recollections of that episode were a bit murky—trauma often prevented the firm anchoring of memories of some shattering event. She did remember Warren as a set of clipped impressions . . . along with images of a *cathedral* filled with tall, colored columns that bulged and throbbed menacingly. No doubt, some of it was just a visual reconstruction, based on things she had been told—about her own valorous actions.

In fact, the earliest clear image to take shape within her

visual cortex—the first one consisting of more than simple geometric forms—rippled and finally resolved into a wavering headline from the top-ranked MediaCorp virpaper, *The Guardian*. It showed a grainy, wavering, animated image that had to be a zeppelin, wounded, with a gaping, burned area smoldering along its top. A battered ship, but still proud and eager for the sky. Below, one could make out specks that were evidently passengers, spilling down escape slides and dispersing to safety.

Well, the picture's not as historically dramatic as the Hindenburg documentary. Still, it's quite a sight.

There was something else, next to that brief animation. Without eyes to physically turn, it took some effort for Tor to divert her cone of attention toward what lay to the right . . . and another few seconds of concentration before it clarified and meaning sank in. Then, abruptly, she recognized a picture of her own face.

Or, what used to be my face. I'll never see it in a mirror again. Nor will anybody else. Strangely, none of that seemed important, right now. Not compared to something much simpler.

The picture's caption swam into focus, and then stayed there, clear as day.

Hero Who Saved Hundreds.

A sense of joy filled Tor, briefly.
I can read!
Not all patients who regained vision in this way recovered their full suite of abilities. It was one thing to stimulate an array of pixel dots to form images. It was quite another to connect them to *meaning*. That required countless faculties and crucial subskills, resident in widely dispersed parts of the brain. Weaving together all that vast

complexity, artificially, was still far beyond the reach of science. For that, you required an essentially intact brain.

Hence, her feeling of almost overwhelming relief. She had both recognized a face and deciphered a string of letters, first try! Tor laboriously tapped out the news, sharing this milestone.

Even if I get nothing else back, I'll be able to read books. And I will probably be able to write, too.

I'm not dead. I can contribute.

I'm still worth something.

Then it was back to work. Tor even began to enjoy the process a bit, plumbing intricacies of her own nervous system, helping to guide an inside-out self-examination, unlike anything her ancestors could have imagined, picking at the bits and pieces of a mechanism that nearly everybody took for granted—the most complex machine ever known.

To her surprise, it also meant reliving memories that flared suddenly, as the ignition spark from one probe briefly relit a particular bright autumn day, when she was six years old, sneaking up behind her brother with a water balloon dripping in both hands, only to have her footsteps betrayed by the crackling of dying kudzu leaves—a moment that came rushing back in such rich detail that it felt intensely real. Certainly more real than this muffled, drug-benumbed existence. For a minute or two, it *almost* seemed as if that little girl was the real Tor—or Dorothy Povlovich. Perhaps all she had to do was concentrate on just the right happy thought in order to wake fully into that moment, and leave this nightmare . . .

. . . another probe kicked in. Attempting to find one of Tor's muscle-control centers, it instead set off a sad emotion from adolescence, unassociated with any facts, or events, or images, but glowering like a cloud, still fresh, for a minute or so of passionately miserable regret—before the probe moved on and found its proper target site.

Later, there erupted from some memory cache the sudden recollection of a treasured keepsake that she had lost, long ago, its forgotten location now suddenly rediscovered. *I could tell Mom. She could find the keychain. Forgive that I misplaced it. Only . . . she wouldn't care at all. Not with her daughter in a place like this.*

It made Tor realize—if this kept up, perhaps she might have visitors. Not to her ravaged body, which could not see or speak, but in *here,* to the mind that lingered on. It should be possible, via virspace, to make a pleasant room, an animated version of herself that could talk, or seem to, driven by her coded thoughts. She still had family, a brother, some friends. And Wesley might even come— though why should he? Tor found it implausible, given how shallow he had been, before that ill-fated zep voyage.

Probably not. Still, she rehearsed some things that she might say—to ease his embarrassment, or to make it easier . . . or angry words to express her disappointment, if he never came.

Mostly, she thought about such things to help pass time, as the process of establishing the shunt went on and on. It was all so transfixing and boring, so mesmerizing and painful, she almost failed to understand, when the doctors asked for her full attention.

The quality of sound had improved.

Tor, we think your subvocal pathways should work now. Could you try to speak?

She wondered, in the passive stillness.

Speak? What are they talking about? With a mouth that's wired shut, a lipless, skeletal grimace . . . how am I supposed to do that?

Of course, subvocal inputs had been standard nearly all her life. You pretend to be *about to* say something. Sensors on the jaw and throat track nerve impulses, turning them into words via the virtual realm, without requiring any labor by the physical larynx, nor by the tongue to fashion phonemes. Most users emitted only faint grunts, and Tor never even did that. But always, there used to be the physical sensations of a real tongue, a real voice box that would *almost start* to make real sounds.

Now, without feedback from those organs, she must imagine, envision, and pretend well enough to cause the same nerves to—

A strange, *blatting* sensation startled Tor. It seemed to reverberate inside her skull, down auditory pathways that she used to associate with ears. Recovering from surprise, she tried again—and was rewarded with another "sound," this one seeming guttural and low in tone. *They're taking my efforts and routing them back to me . . . so I can "hear" my own voice production attempts. So I can start the process of correcting.*

After a few more tries, she managed to remember, or else re-create, how to send signals. Commands that used to form the simplest sounds. The crudity felt embarrassing, and she almost stopped. But sheer obstinacy prevailed. *I can do this!*

Bit by bit, the sounds improved.

Eventually, she managed to craft a message—

"H-h-hi . . . d-docsss . . ."

Naturally, they were lavish with praise and positive reinforcement. Indeed, it felt satisfying to be helpful, to make progress. To be an essential member of a team, once again. All of that—and the prospect of no more Morse tooth-tappings—helped to mollify Tor's sense of being patronized, patted on the head, with no choice in whatever came next.

Soon, I'll be able to assert myself. Declare my autonomy. Get judged competent to make decisions. And maybe—if I wish—stop all this.

It was a biting thought—one that seemed ornery and ungrateful, amid such notable medical progress. But, still, the thought was *hers.* Tor had very little else that she could call her own, other than thoughts.

Anyway, the notion did not take root for long. Because Tor soon was thoroughly distracted by the very next thing that they tried . . .

. . . when they linked her to the Cloud.

REPAIRMEN

Oh, the fracking mess.

I'm supposed to be careful what I say. As a public mouthpiece for Freedom Club, I should keep my distance from "illegal activity." One rule for revolutionary movements, going all the way back to Bakunin, is strict separation of the political and action wings.

But hell, I'm fed up. What have we accomplished since that glorious event the dumbass peasants call Awfulday? When it seemed, for one magnificent moment, that the whole corrupt edifice of greed and bureaucracy and technology would come crashing down? Since then, what disappointment! Great Ted, working in his little mountain cabin, rattled the modernists' cage. Why can't we?

Failures pile up. Did that nuke in the Pyrenees accomplish anything? Rumors claim the abomination—the Basque Chimera—escaped. Worse, there's a whole herd of resurrected mammoths grazing in Canada now, and a million acres of gene-designed perennial wheat! And the goddamn robot minds get smarter daily! And against all that, what have the bold followers of Kaczynski and McVey and Fu-Wayne accomplished lately?

The dolts can't even blow up a damned zeppelin that's full to bursting with explosive gas! So that alien crystal thing survived and who knows how many horrid new technologies the geeks will squeeze out of it?

A time of decision is coming! YOU passive supporters of the Better Way must choose. You can go join the *peaceful* Renunciation Movement, like sniveling gits, and follow that "prophet" of theirs, working *within* the corrupt system . . .

. . . or else take arms! Offer your skills and your lives to the Action Wing and help topple this teetering so-called civilization!

How to join? Just speak up. They'll find you.

31.

CONSENSUAL REALITY

Lacey's generation was to blame, of course.

They were the ones who invented "continuous partial attention," after all. Who were proud of jumping from one topic to another, spreading themselves as thin as the wrapper on a Sniffaire gelglobe. Or as narrow as the lived-in moment called *now*.

But never before had Lacey been forced to stretch her regard among so many *vital* topics, all of them demanding intense focus. In fact, she knew that the organic human brain can divert itself only so much, before returning, elastically, to whatever thought seems most intense. Most demanding. The elephant in the room.

I am a terrible mother.

Out of the maelstrom—attending to matters in Switzerland and Africa, here in Washington and in outer space, that one core fact was clear. By the moral standards of any human culture, she should have simply dropped everything else, in order to participate in the search for her missing son.

Never mind that it would do Hacker no good at all. She had hired the best professionals and offered rewards plentiful enough to divert every yacht and fishing smack and surfer, between here and Surinam, to join the search . . . or the fact that Mark was down there now, coordinating the quest to find his brother . . . or that all she'd accomplish, by hurrying down to the Caribbean, would be to get in the way.

Never mind any of that. *It's simply what a mom would do.* Only maybe not the mother of Hacker Sander.

The last thing in the world he would want from me, would be to show panic . . . or even much concern.

That one brief burst of telemetry—too short and static-ridden to localize—had reported the reentry capsule to be intact and its passenger healthy, just after it struck the sea. The tiny compartment was designed to float and to sustain life almost indefinitely. Moreover, even if all the electronics aboard had been fried, the shell itself would reflect radar and sonar in uniquely identifiable ways, just as soon as any seekers passed closely enough. A pair of nasty storms had hampered crews from reaching a few search areas, especially those farthest from the likely impact zone. But supposedly it was only a matter of time.

Anyway, she knew how furious the boy would get if he found out that she had rushed south, forsaking and spoiling her once-in-a-lifetime opportunity to witness history firsthand—the very moment of human-alien First Contact. Why? Just to go pace and fret and interfere in the efforts of skilled people?

So, Lacey, is that your rationalization? That you are staying at the Artifact Conference to honor Hacker? In order to do as he would wish—and as Jason would have wished?

Good one.

Next to her sat Professor Noozone. The scientist-popstar was happily engaged, grunting and clicking and subvocally mumbling as he interacted with his avid fan community—now numbering over a hundred million, in part because of where he sat right now. In a VIP seat, no less. The signature draidlocks floated around his head, tipped with lenses and sniffers that turned and pointed in every direction, while wafting aromas of ganja-frankincense shampoo. Occasionally she had to bat one of the strands of overly curious cybactive hair out of her space, but she hadn't the heart to chide him—the man was *so* puppy-dog grateful to Lacey for getting him into the Observer's Gallery as her adviser, separated by just a thick sheet of glass from the quarantine chamber and the white-coated figures—including Gerald Livingstone himself—who were examining the Havana Artifact.

In a nearby holistube, she saw an animated Noozone replica, chattering and gesticulating away, while concept-blimps hovered all around its head. The voice was tuned down, in order not to disturb other members of the Advisory Panel—experts, international dignitaries and representatives of all ten Estates. But when Lacey's gaze settled in that direction, some computer measured her pupil dilation and responded to her interest, by sending a narrow-collimated beam of sound toward one ear.

"So which t'eories have we eliminated so faar?" The Professor's animated holvatar drawled in a satin-toned Jamaican accent, as it swept one arm to point at a multidimensional comparison chart hovering nearby.

"Almost none! Till dem Contact Team manages to overcome dem humano-centric bias enough to understand the Artifact entities on their own terms, we are left with only that marvelously enticing 'join us' come-yah invitation as a very-major clue to the purpose of the Livingstone Object . . . or Havana Artifact, or any of the other names for this truly-wondrous thing. Rhaatid.

"And yet, on that sole-basis alone, futures market probabilities have shifted so-dramatically. Wager-contracts based upon alien invasion, for example, plummeted to

mere-millicents on the dollar. Bets that pree-dict a true-friendly galactic bredren-federation skyrocketed in value, an' then split, as interest focused on what kind of federated society the aliens might be part of.

"Of course, here is where we try a little smoky-ingenuity to piece together clues based upon the behavior of the strange beings-within-the-stone. . . ."

Lacey pulled her gaze away and the volume of Profnoo's vaice tapered off, as she looked beyond the glass at the focus of all this worldwide attention. The Artifact, an oblong-tapered, opalescent cylinder, lay in its cradle under a cloth canopy that staved off most of the room light, keeping it in shade. With just a modest supply of photon energy flowing into the stone, only faint and blurry images of drifting clouds could be seen playing across its surface.

Workmen were attaching hoses to the underside of the table while others erected a new illumination system under the direction of the latest member of the Contact Team—a tall, slender African with dark, almost-purple skin, who was said to be an expert at *animal training,* of all things. Meanwhile, the original discoverer, the astronaut Gerald Livingstone, conferred with General Hideoshi and several colleagues. One of them was a computer-generated holvatar—a full-size, human-scale aintity image, half woman and half tiger—whose feral, carnivorous expression hardly seemed in keeping with the peaceful mission of the team.

With nothing much happening below, and with Profnoo fully occupied addressing his public, Lacey was about to lift her cryptospecs and turn her attention elsewhere, toward *another* urgent matter—events taking place several thousand kilometers to the east. She had an informer secretly planted at the sprawling Glaucus-Worthington estate, near the Liechtenstein border, where delegates were arriving from most of the great families of the clade, as well as Tenskwatawa's international Responsibility Movement—or

"Renunciation Movement" for its attitude toward scientific progress—to negotiate an alliance between those two potent forces. An enciphered report from her spy awaited attention—that should only be readable by this particular set of Mesh goggles. There seemed to be little point in avoiding the matter any longer.

Not with the Naderites panting like eager suitors. *I could do it. Join the do-gooder trillies and fight for the Enlightenment. Unite with the techie rich, clustered in Jakarta and Kerala and California and Rio. The Jains, Omidyars, Yeos, Berggruens, and others. Use my wealth and influence to battle for science. Denounce inherited aristocracy. Blow the whistle on my neo-feudalist friends, who I grew up with . . .*

. . . and send Jason spinning in his grave.

She had the set of crypto-aiware raised halfway to her face—preparing to give the code unlocking the spy's report—when someone plopped down, uninvited, onto the plush seat to her right.

"We really should get one of our own, you know."

She put down the specs. It was Simon Ortega, representative of the Corporate Estate—big businesses based all over the planet. With his dark, Timorese features and Porto accent, Simon exemplified the internationalist image that globalized companies had been trying to convey, ever since Awfulday and the Big Deal. Transparency, open competition, honest dealings—the very essence of the *real* Adam Smith, the original liberal—and no more close affiliation with the superrich.

So why is he sitting down here? Isn't he afraid to be seen talking to an old-money plutocrat like me?

Or does he have his own sources, telling him what's going on in Switzerland right now? A power realignment that might lead to a return to the old days, when a few crony families could sway markets, topple corporations and nations, and rock human destiny? If he thinks those times are returning, he could be trying to line up an alliance of his own. To wind up on the winning side.

"I'm sorry, Mr. Ortega. We should get one of our own . . . what?"

"A group holvatar, Mrs. Donaldson-Sander. A presence entity to speak for us members of the Advisory Council. To represent our interests, beyond the glass, where they are poking away at the visitors from space. Something to counterbalance that damned *Tiger-Girl* and make them stop ignoring us up here!"

Ah. Lacey realized. So this had nothing to do with events in Zurich. Ortega was just expressing his natural reaction to the way things were going here at the Artifact Conference. Specifically, the way the glass barrier prevented all the people and interests on *this* side, in the observers' gallery, from influencing events on the other side. The Corporate Estate was collectively more nervous than most.

Although communication with the Artifact aliens was still chaotic and sporadic, the world had given a collective sigh of relief over the clear friendliness of the "join us" remark. Almost any form of participation in an interstellar federation would surely bring benefits, expanded knowledge, propitious technologies, surprising art, and possibly solutions to many problems. Of course, some apple carts would be overturned and upset a few groups. The Renunciators, for example, and Lacey's own clade of conservative clans.

Not the Naderites, though. They love all this.

Stuck in between—torn by both hope and worry—would be Ortega's constituency. On the one hand, alien knowledge should offer plenty of new business opportunities for the lucky and agile. On the other hand . . . even supposing all went well, if terrific new alien concepts and technologies arrived, delivering a million benefits without unleashing serious side effects . . . even then, lots of corporate entities would see their goods and services and market positions rendered obsolete. Why, just a few improvements in nano-tech might make it possible to at last produce home fabricators—letting citizens create almost any product from raw materials right in the kitchen or garage. A boon . . . unless your job or portfolio depends on manufacturing. Or shipping goods. In fact, half the companies in every stock market might wither. No wonder he seemed nervous.

Yet, it turned out that Ortega had another purpose entirely.

"Have you heard what they are planning to do, Mrs. Donaldson-Sander? They intend to use *operant conditioning.* That means using *rewards and punishments,* in a crude attempt to implement *behavior modification* on the alien entities residing inside!"

Lacey clamped down to keep from giggling over an unforgivable pun that leaped to mind.

Shall we teach Pavlovian dogs to SETI-up and beg?

Fortunately, the man didn't notice her brief grunt.

"Can you believe the arrogance? The unbelievable vanity! Assuming all our difficulties in communication are *their fault,* not ours? Employing barbarously inhospitable methods to force them to meet *our* primitive standards of conduct!"

Despite his overwrought passion, Lacey felt impressed—and perhaps a little ashamed. She had been ready—twice in a few seconds—to assign unsavory motives to this man, when his true reason for being upset was idealistic. A matter of graciousness and courtesy.

"Well, the aliens do seem a bit out of control. Pushing and jostling. Interrupting each other, so that almost nothing decipherable or clear makes it to the surface. It's hard to see how that could be *our* fault."

"Exactly." Ortega nodded vigorously. "It *is* hard to see

with our primitive minds. And yet, how could it *not* be our fault? A vast and sophisticated galactic civilization, experienced at hundreds of past contact situations, must know what it's doing! Certainly compared to inexperienced and immature Earthlings. They are probably being very patient with us, waiting for us to figure out something simple."

Lacey pondered. *Something simple . . . that those sophisticated minds can't just explain to us? Why not simply lay it all out, plainly, in clear language and illustrated without ambiguity?*

Of course, that has also long been the reasonable person's complaint toward God.

She stopped herself from mentioning one possibility that was rising—slowly but steadily—in the worldwide betting pool. The aliens' chaotic, uncooperative behavior might be explained if the stone-from-space were actually a hoax. In that case, it would likely be programmed to delay any actual conversation for as long as possible, messing with nine billion human heads while never actually getting down to specifics. In fact, the wager market had divided the category into several subplots, depending on whether the purpose of the fraud was to "unite humanity," or "scare us into a dictatorship," or "pull a financial scam," or simply to throw the biggest prank of all time.

Oh, sure, lots of experts declared that the Livingstone Object couldn't be a hoax. Much of its technology was beyond humanity's current abilities. But only by a bit—maybe just a couple of decades in crystal technology, for example. Almost daily, some company or government or amsci group declared: *Hey! We've figured out how to do this part of what the Artifact does!*

It was an especially big driver of activity in the Industry of Lies.

I hear Peter Playmount is pushing an epic cinemavirt into production, in which the hero will be a chunk of space crystal, saved from some dark conspiracy by a bunch of brave kids. . . .

"The Contact Team is clearly out of control down there." Simon Ortega gestured at the group on the other side of the glass, pressing his point. "The International Supervisory Commission won't interfere with their mad scheme to *torture* the alien travelers into cooperating."

The man unfolded a clipboard of the old-fashioned variety, with a single sheet of paper attached. "A group of us are circulating a petition, to either let us into that room, or to broaden the Contact Team, or else at least to give us some kind of *presence* in there, to make our views known!"

Lacey glanced over the page. A large fraction of the advisers had already signed. There seemed little possibility of harm. In fact, why not? She was reaching for the ink-pen that Ortega offered . . .

. . . when one of her earrings chimed. A phone call, urgent of course—she had made clear to her secretaries and du-ai-nas that only top priority messages should get through. A soft, cyber whisper spoke the name *"Gloria Harrigan."* It was Hacker's personal attorney.

"Would you excuse me please?" she asked Ortega. "This call is very important." Her voice was on the verge of cracking as she turned away, while squeezing the earring. "Yes?"

"Madam Donaldson-Sander? Is that you?"

"Of course it is." As if anyone else would be answering this encrypted channel. "Is there news from the search?"

"Yes, madam. A crew has found Hacker's capsule, or what's left of it."

Lacey felt both hot and cold. Vision started growing blurry.

"Wait, please. I said that badly. The capsule was in scattered pieces, but there are no traces of human . . . That is, an expert examined the latch and declared it must have been deliberately opened, from the inside!

"So, there is strong reason to believe Hacker left before the container was destroyed. That, plus the lack of any fresh human bio-traces in the area, suggests he departed on his own power, protected and sustained by the very best survival suit money can buy."

Gloria spilled all of that so rapidly Lacey had trouble keeping up, grasping at the meaning, until it was repeated several times.

"Mark is on the scene right now. He asked me to pass on the good news, and promises that he will call you personally within the hour."

Lacey, nodded, trying hard to see this as good news. She swallowed a few times before subvocalizing a question.

"So, what happens next?"

"The search will continue, madam. Please understand, the location is quite some distance away from his expected landing point, which is why things took so long. Also, we had been counting on finding radar and sonar reflections from the shell. Now it's clear why that didn't happen.

"But we're dialed in at last! He can have only gone a few dozen kilometers, max, swimming under his own power or drifting with the local currents. So we'll just draw in all our resources to that small patch of sea. There should be results almost any time now."

It took a great effort to speak at all, let alone maintain a lifetime habit of civility.

"Thank you, Gloria. Please thank ever . . . everyone."

It was no use. There were no further words. She pinched the earring to end the call, then pinched again, as it tried to hurriedly report on waiting messages from important people—like the head of the Naderite coalition and the director of her Chilean planet-hunter observatory, and . . .

No. Prioritize. First sign Ortega's petition, so the honor-driven but pesty little man would go away . . . then focus . . .

focus on some important matter, such as the report from her spy in the Alps. *Or else immerse yourself in the brilliantly entertaining blather being spewed by your hired genius. Profnoo would appreciate a little attention.*

One thing Lacey would not do was dwell overmuch on the news. On hope.

Anyway, what lurked in her mind below the surface was something beyond hope. Perhaps even insultingly so. She could not shake an intense feeling—perhaps rising out of wishful thinking, or even hysterical denial—that Hacker was not only alive, but safe somehow.

Perhaps even having fun.

Wouldn't that be just like him?

The suspicion had some basis in experience.

He would always get in touch with me whenever there was trouble. On the other hand, Hacker generally ignored his mother when things were interesting or going well, neglecting to call if he was having the time of his life.

ENTROPY

Suppose we manage to avoid the worst calamities. The world-wreckers, extinction-makers, and civilization-destroyers. And let's say no black holes gobble the Earth. No big wars pound us back to the dark ages. Eco-collapse is averted and the economic system is kept alive.

Let's further imagine that we're not alone in achieving this miraculous endurance. That many other intelligent life forms also manage to escape the worst pitfalls and survive their awkward adolescence. Well, there are still plenty of ways that some promising sapient species might rise up, looking skyward with high hopes, and yet—even so—fail to achieve its potential. What traps might await us *because* we are smart?

Take one of the earliest and greatest human innovations—
specialization. Even way back when we lived in caves and huts,
there was division of effort. Top hunters hunted, expert gather-
ers gathered, and skilled technicians spent long hours by the
riverbank, fashioning intricate baskets and stone blades. When
farming created a surplus that could be stored, markets arose,
along with kings and priests, who allocated extra food to sub-
sidize carpenters and masons, scribes and calendar-keeping
astronomers. Of course, the priests and kings kept the best
share. Isn't administration also a specialty? And so, a few soon
dominated many, across 99 percent of history.

Eventually though, skill and knowledge spread, increasing
that precious surplus, letting more people read, write, invent . . .
which created more wealth, allowing more specialization and
so on, until only a few remained on the land, and those farmers
were mostly well-educated specialists, too.

In the West, one trend spanned the whole twentieth century:
a steady *professionalization of everything*. By the end of the
millennium, almost everything a husband and wife used to do
for their family had been packaged as a product or service,
provided by either the market or the state. And in return? A
pilot had merely to pilot and a firefighter just fought fires. The
professor simply professed and a dentist had only to dent.
Benefits abounded. Productivity skyrocketed. Cheap goods
flowed across the globe. Middle-class citizens ate strawber-
ries in winter, flown from the other hemisphere. Science bur-
geoned, as the amount that people knew expanded even faster
than the pile of things they owned.

And that is where—to some of us—things started to look
worrisome.

Let me take you back quite a ways, to the other end of a
long lifetime, before the explosive expansion of cybernetics,
before the Mesh and Web and Net, all the way back to the
1970s, when I first studied at Caltech. Often, late at night, my
classmates and I pondered the dour logic of specialization.

After reaping the benefits for many generations, it seemed clear that a crisis loomed.

You see, science kept making discoveries at an accelerating clip. Already, a researcher had to keep learning ever-increasing amounts, in order to discover more. It seemed that just keeping up would force each of us to focus on ever narrower fields of study, forsaking the forest in order to zero in on tiny portions of a single tree. Eventually, new generations of students might spend half a lifetime learning enough to start a thesis. And even then, how to tell if someone else was duplicating your effort, across the world or down the hall?

That prospect—having to know more and more about less and less—seemed daunting. Unavoidable. There seemed to be no way out . . .

. . . until, almost overnight, we veered in a new direction! Our civ evaded that crisis with a *technological side step* that seemed so obvious, so easy and graceful that few even noticed or commented. There were so many exciting aspects to the Internet Age, after all. The old fear of narrow overspecialization suddenly seemed quaint, as biologists started collaborating with physicists and cross-disciplinary partnerships abounded. Instead of being vexed by overspecialized terminology, experts conversed excitedly, more than ever!

Today, hardly anybody speaks of the danger that fretted us so. It's been replaced by the *opposite concern*—one that we'll get to next time.

Only first consider this.

Sure, we may have escaped the specialization trap, for now, but *will everyone else* manage the same trick, out there across the stars? Our solution now seems obvious—to surf the tsunami! To meet the flood of knowledge with eager, eclectic agility. Refusing to be constrained by official classifications, we let knowledge bounce and jostle into new forms, supplementing professional skill with tides of zealous amateurism.

But don't take it for granted! The approach may not be repeated elsewhere. Not if it emerged out of some rare quality of our smartmonkey natures. Or pure luck.

Nor would it have been allowed in most *human* cultures! Which of our past military or commercial or hereditary empires would have unleashed something as powerful as the Internet, letting it spread—unfettered and free—to every tower and hovel? Or allow so many skilled tasks to be performed by the unlicensed?

One can imagine countless other species—and our own fragile renaissance—faltering back into the dour scenario that we students mulled, those gloomy nights. Slipping into an endless, grinding cycle, where specialization—once a friend— becomes the worst enemy of wisdom.

—*Pandora's Cornucopia*

32.
HOMECOMING

By the third day after his crash-landing at sea, Hacker started earning his meals. In part out of sheer boredom—he grew restless simply being fed by the tribe of strange dolphins, like some helpless infant.

Also, as that day stretched into a fourth, fifth, and so on, he felt a strange and growing sense that—for better or for worse—this was *his* tribe. At least for the time being.

So he pitched in whenever the group harvested dinner, by helping to hold the fishing net, trying not to flinch as the beaters drove schools of fish straight toward him—a great mass of silver and blue darts that seemed almost like a giant creature in its own right, thrashing against the deadly mesh, as well as his facemask and hands. Each time, Hacker's jaw throbbed from the intense, subsonic noise of the struggle— and from high power click-scans of the cetaceans, both stunning and caressing their prey. That complex, multichannel song seemed to combine genuine empathy for the fish with an almost catlike enjoyment of their predicament.

I guess it has a lot to do with whether you're the hunter, or hunted. I had no idea the sea could be so noisy, or musical. Or that life down here was so . . . relentless.

This was no Disney underwater world. In comparison, the forest deer and rabbits had long stretches of peace. But down here? You watched your back all the time.

Or rather, you listened. The texture of vibrations surrounded and stroked Hacker, in ways that it never did ashore—lapping against him with complex, interweaving songs of danger, opportunity, and distant struggle. Of course the implant in his jaw was one reason for this heightened sensitivity. With his eardrums still clamped from the day of the rocket launch, it provided an alternative route for sound, far more similar to dolphin hearing.

Then there were those silly games that Mother used to play when we were kids. Treating us as her personal science experiments.

Not that he had any real complaints. Lacey would get excited about some new development and recruit the boys as willing—or sometimes grudging—subjects. When she learned that human beings could be taught *echolocation,* she sent her sons stumbling around in blindfolds, clicking their tongues *just so,* listening for reflected echoes off sofas and walls . . . even servants stationed around the room. It proved possible to navigate that way—with a lot of bumps and stumbles. Hacker even found the knack handy as a party trick, later in life.

But who would imagine I'd wind up using it in a place like this?

Even the dolphins seemed surprised by his crude ability. Several of them spent extra time with Hacker, patiently tutoring him, like a slow toddler learning to walk.

In return he helped by checking every member of the pod, from fluke to rostrum, using his ungloved hands to clean sores and remove parasites. Especially bothersome were drifting flecks of plastic, that neither sank nor biodegraded, but got caught in body crevices, even at the roots of every dolphin tooth. He found himself doing the chore daily—also carefully combing gunk out of the gill fronds that surrounded his helmet. But the stuff kept coming back. Sometimes swirling clouds of plastic bits and beads would turn the crystal waters hazy and bleak.

How can anything live in this? he wondered while kicking along with his companions, over a seabed that was littered with man-made dross everywhere they went.

Yet, Hacker felt he was getting the hang of life out here. His early fear of drowning, or getting battered by harsh currents, faded in time, as did the claustrophobia of living encased by a survival suit. Once again, he made a mental note to invest in the company that manufactured it. That is, if he ever made it back to that world.

At night he felt more relaxed than he had in years, perhaps ever, dozing while the dolphins' clickety gossip seemed to flow up his jaw and into his dreams. By the fifth or sixth morning, and increasingly on each that followed, he felt closer to understanding their way of communicating.

I once saw a dolphin expert—on some nature show— say these creatures are merely bright animals, who had powers mimicry and precocious logic skill, maybe some basic semantics, at the level of a chimp, but little more. He said the evidence disproved all those old wish fantasies about dolphins actually having culture and language.

What a dope!

Hacker felt confirmed in his longstanding belief that so-called experts often lack the common sense to see what's right in front of them.

Despite a promise to himself, he soon lost track of how many days and nights had passed. Moreover, gradually, Hacker even stopped worrying about where the pickup boats could be. He no longer rushed to the surface, bobbing frantically, whenever engine sounds rumbled through the shallow currents. It happened frequently, but though he often glimpsed a distant boat or plane, it was never within reach of his shouting voice, or waving arms.

Angry mutterings about revenge and lawsuits rubbed away under relentless massage by current and tide. Immersed in the dolphins' communal sonic chatter, he began concerning himself with daily problems of the Tribe, such as when two young males got into a fight, smacking each other with their beaks and flukes, then trading snaps and rakes with sharp teeth, until half a dozen adults intervened, forcibly separating the brawlers.

Using a combination of spoken words, sign language and his growing vocabulary of click-code, Hacker made inquiries and learned that a female (whose complex name he translated to *Blue Lady*) was in heat. The youths held little hope of mating with her—top males circled much closer. Still, their nervous energy needed an outlet. At least no one was seriously harmed.

One old-timer—*Mellow Yellowbelly*—shyly presented a pectoral fin to Hacker, who used his knife to dig out several wormlike bloodsuckers. The dolphin chuttered unhappily, but barely flinched.

"You should see a real doctor," Hacker urged, as if one gave verbal advice to cetaceans every day.

Helpers go away, Yellowbelly tried to explain in click-code. Though Hacker had to ask for three repeatings.
Fins need hands. Helper hands.

It supported a theory slowly gestating in Hacker's mind—
that something had been done to these creatures. An alter-
ation that made them distinctly different. A breed somehow
apart from others of their species. But what? The mystery
grew each time he witnessed some behavior that just
couldn't be natural.

At the same time, Yellowbelly's answer lit a spark in one
corner of Hacker's mind—the section assigned to wariness
and suspicion. It had been dozing, of late, but nothing could
ever turn off that part of his character. Not completely.

*Could their kindness to me have a double purpose?
Maybe it's no accident that we've not passed near any
boats or shore. Or any of the search parties that Mark and
Lacey would have sent out.*

Having a human may be useful to them.

Perhaps they have no intention of letting me go.

Hacker wondered afresh about his own survival. Despite
being fed by the Tribe—and sustained by the wonderful
suit—there were limits to how long a man could last out
here. *I'm developing an itch, all over. The human body
isn't meant for perpetual exposure to salt, and deposits
must be building up on my skin. My waste products are
easy to dispose of . . . but what if the gills or freshwater
distiller get permanently clogged?* Already, he saw signs
of declining efficiency.

Still, there seemed to be no life-or-death urgency.

*Except to one mother, a brother, three girlfriends, four
avocation clubs, and my investment company, drifting
rudderless without me. And all the searchers that Lacey
has probably sent scurrying across the Caribbean looking
for me.*

How, he wondered, could the rescuers keep missing
him? Had every transponder chip failed, including several
in the suit?

One theory occurred to Hacker—that jibbering, noble

twit, Lord Smits, must have used something more powerful than a signal laser, during that brief-stupid attempt at
playing space war. Perhaps the snooty, inbred bastard also
wielded a narrow beam EMP-thrower, firing an electromagnetic pulse that fritzed Hacker's ailectronics. It could
explain the rapid deterioration of his suborbital capsule, at
a crucial moment.

If so, it was nothing less than attempted murder. . . .

Yet, even that realization did not fill him with the expected flood of fury. Somehow, wrath seemed out of place
down here. Perhaps it was the implacable push of solar and
lunar tides, so much more palpable and insistent than mere
atmospheric breezes. Or else the infectious attitude of his
companions. Not perfectly cheerful or always accepting . . . they had their frets and upsets . . . still, the dolphins were keyed to a wholly different scale. One that
seemed less egocentric or self-important. Or that seldom
saw a point in frenzy.

Sea gives . . .
. . . though we must leave her
. . . to breathe . . .

So explained Yellowbelly. At least, that was how Hacker
loosely interpreted one set of sonic glyph images.

And Sea takes it all away again.

Of course, it was an iffy thing, trying to decipher a brief
sound sculpture, crudely perceived with a jaw implant that
hadn't been designed for this purpose. Translating Yellowbelly's explanation as some kind of poetical theology was
probably a product of Hacker's own imagination. Yet even
that seemed amazing, for he had never been one for theology.
Or poetry, for that matter.

Whatever it is, I've managed to figure out all this without assistance. No clever mechanisms or hired experts or AI helpers. There was a grim-amused satisfaction in that. *If I've gone mad, at least I managed it all by myself!*

Life drifted on, a cadence of hunting, eating, socializing, exploring, and tending to the needs of the Tribe—followed by evenings bathed in equal measures of warm water and sound. When a storm or rain squall passed through the area, he listened to the dolphins as they kept a kind of syncopated time with the rippling waves and pelting drops.

Then came one day when the whole community grew excited, spraying nervous clicks everywhere. Amid a swirl of daunting gray forms, swooping and chattering, it took Hacker some time to gather a gist of what was up. Apparently, by group consensus, it had been decided all at once to head for one of their regular haunts, a favorite place of some kind. One they seemed to think of as *home.*

For quite some time Hacker had been trying to keep up with the group on his own, kicking hard with his flippers and swimming with increasing strength, at a pace he was pretty proud of . . . even knowing that they were indulging him with affectionate tolerance, amused by his clumsy efforts. Now though, a note of impatience intruded. Several times adult members pulled alongside, offering their dorsal fins, crafting resonant shapes that urged Hacker to grab ahold. But he felt obstinately determined.

Well, after all, they have to go up for air and I don't. That ought to count for something.

After refusing three times, striving hard to keep up with their increasing pace, he abruptly felt a narrow beam of unpleasantness rattle his jaw on one side. Turning, he felt struck, full-face, by a wave of sharp *rebuke*—there was no other way to interpret the harsh sonic waves—cast from the brow of an irascible dolphin he had nicknamed *Bicker-a-lot.*

Heck, make that *Bicker-a-ton*! The creature glared the way cetaceans do, by crafting a jagged shape around Hacker's head, composed of craggy, uneven sound waves. None of it showed visibly. There was no change in the beguiling, misleading dolphin smile.

All right. All right. If you feel that strongly about it.

The top female *Sweet Thing,* offered Hacker a dorsal fin, and this time he accepted. Soon, they were streaking along, building speed, alternately dipping below the thermocline and then racing upward to jet out of the water. Each time, he got an exhaled blast across the facemask as she arched and soared, blowing and filling her lungs while gravity was checked for a brief, glorious moment. Hacker couldn't help flinching and squinting—and giving a hoarse yell. It was no rocket, but one hell of a ride.

He also tried to take advantage, every leap, of the chance to look around. After a while, Hacker glimpsed something—a blurry line of white and tan and blotchy green up ahead. It was hard to make out amid the jostling of spray and exhilaration. He didn't dare to linger on the hopeful word—*land*.

Too soon the rollicking journey ended. The pod of cetaceans slowed and submerged, heading downward at a shallow slant. *Now I'll find out what "home" means to a pack of wild . . .*

A bulky object emerged out of blue dimness, down at the sloping bottom. No more than ten meters below the surface, between sheltering, sedimentary rilles, it had the edgy lines of something man-made. At-first it seemed a derelict, perhaps a sunken ship. Then Hacker sucked in his breath, as the object resolved into another kind of thing altogether. A construct that had come to the muddy sea floor with deliberate purpose.

They were approaching an undersea *habitat dome,* hidden in a narrow canyon—one of thousands that had been mass produced in the twenties, during a brief suboceanic boom, when some thought it to be the next great property-rush frontier. *Dad invested in a few underwater hotels and mining facilities,* Hacker recalled. *With sea levels rising, he said that humanity would adapt, as always, and we needed to be part of it. Even make money off it.*

Too bad none of the ventures ever made a profit.

While his heartbeat settled down, Hacker noticed a few other things. Like the shape of the gully, clearly formed by drifting sand and silt, piled up over many years. It was the kind of terrain that only formed where ocean bottom approached the continental verge. In fact, he could now pick up growling, repetitive rhythms with his implant—a complex pattern that any surfer would recognize—of breaker slapping against the shore.

Shore . . . The word tasted strange after all these days—weeks?—spent languidly swimming, living on raw fish and listening to timeless ocean sounds. Suddenly, it felt odd to contemplate leaving this watery realm, returning to the surface world of air, earth, cities, machines, and nine billion human beings inhaling each other's humid breath everywhere they went.

That's why we dive into our own worlds, I suppose. Countless thousands of hobbies. A million ways to be special, each person endeavoring to be expert at some arcane art . . . like rocketing into space.

Psychologists approved, saying that frenetic amateurism was a much healthier response than the most likely alternative—war. They called this the "Century of Aficionados," a time when governments and professional societies could barely keep up with private expertise, which spread at lightning speed across the World Mesh. A renaissance-without-a-cause, lacking only a clear sense of purpose.

A renaissance that seemed to be dancing atop a layer of fragile ice, moving its feet quickly, as if afraid that standing still could be lethal. The prospect of soon rejoining that culture left him suddenly pensive, even a bit sad, pondering something he never would have considered, before that ill-fated desert launch.

What's the point of so much obsessive, frenetic activity unless it propels you toward something worthwhile?

Once, a few days ago, he had heard one of the dolphins voice a similar thought in their simple but expressive click-language, as far as he could dimly interpret.

 # If you're good at diving—chase fish!
 # If you have a fine voice—sing!
 # If you're great at leaping—bite the sun!

Hacker knew he should clamber up the nearby beach now, to borrow a phone and call people—his partners and brokers, mother and brother, friends and lovers.

Tell them he was alive.

Get back to business.

Instead, he swiveled in the water and kicked hard at a downward slant, following his new friends to the habitat dome.

Maybe I'll learn what's been done to them, he thought.

And why.

DISPUTATION

Why haven't we overpopulated the planet?

That may seem an odd question, while refugee riots rack overcrowded cities that incubate new diseases weekly. Forests topple for desperate farmland, even as drought bakes former farms into desert. Starvation lurks beyond each year's harvest and human waste is now the world economy's biggest product by sheer mass. One can understand why some view nine billion humans as a curse, shredding and consuming Earth to the bone.

Yet, it could have been worse. A generation ago, scholars forecast we'd be past fourteen or fifteen billion by now and still climbing toward the limit prophesied by Malthus—a great die-off. It happens to every species that out breeds its habitat capacity.

Trouble is, any die-off won't just dip our population to sustainable levels. Humans don't go quietly. We tend to claw and drag others down with us. Out of blame, or for company. Given today's varied tools of ready wrought destruction, any such event would affect everyone. So, aren't we lucky that population growth rates are way down? With the total even tapering a bit? Maybe enough to squeak by? Sure, that means old folks will outnumber kids for a while. Well, no one promised survival would be free of consequences.

But *how* did it happen? Why did we escape (even barely) the Malthusian Trap? Some credit the fact that humans can separate the recreational and procreative aspects of sex.

Animals feel a compulsive drive to mate and exchange genes. Some scatter their offspring in great numbers. Others care intensively for just a few. But animals who finish this cycle and are healthy enough, routinely return to the driver of it all—sex—starting the process over again. Its power is rooted in one simple fact. Those who felt its urgency had more descendants.

This applied to us, too, of course, till technology gave us birth control.

Then suddenly, the sex compulsion could be satisfied without procreation, with amazing effects. Everywhere that women were empowered with both prosperity and rights, most of them chose to limit childbearing, to concentrate on raising a few privileged offspring instead of brooding at max capacity. We became a *non-Malthusian species,* able to limit our population by choice, in the nick of time.

Too bad it can't last. Today, some humans *do* overbreed.

These tend not to be the rich, or those with enough food or who have sex a lot. They are having lots of kids *because they choose to.* And so, whatever inner drives provoked that choice get passed down to more offspring, then more. Over time, this extra-strong desire will appear in rising portions of the population.

It's evolution in action. As time passes, the locus of compulsion will shift from sex to a genetically-driven, iron willed determination to have more kids. . . .

. . . and then we'll be a Malthusian species again—like the "motie" beings in that novel *The Mote in God's Eye,* unable to stop. Unable to say "enough." A fate that may commonly entrap a great many other species, across the cosmos.

Before that happens to us, we had better finish the job of growing up.

—from *The Movement Revealed,* by Thormace Anubis-Fejel

33.
STRAIGHT FLUSH

As he changed into formal dinner clothes in the luxurious guest bedroom, one furnishing caught the attention of Hamish Brookeman—a modernized, antique chamber pot.

Not the Second Empire armoire, or the Sforzese chest of drawers, nor even the Raj era rug from Baluchistan. (He needed a Mesh-consult to identify that one, with Wriggles whispering a description in his ear.) Hamish had an eye for detail—he needed one, while moving in circles like these. The mega wealthy had grown judgmental, of late. They expected you to know about such things, to better understand your place.

Hamish was a rich man, ranking five percentile nines—enough to classify him as a member of the First Estate, if he weren't already a legend in the arts. Nevertheless, there was nothing in this room that he could afford. Not one blessed thing.

And I'm far from the most important guest who has come to this gathering in the Alps. I can only imagine what kind of digs they're giving Tenskwatawa and his aides, or the aristocrats flying in from Shanghai and Yangon, Moscow and Mumbai.

Of course, Hamish had another reason for scanning, hungrily, everything in sight. Always at the back of his mind was the question: *Can I use this in a novel?*

Even when storytelling ceased to be what it had been for three centuries, an author's hermetic craft, transforming into a hybrid, multimedia team effort, with eye-clickable hyperlinks that required a whole staff to provide . . . even so, he still had the solitary habit of mind, envisioning the narrative in paragraphs, punctuation and all.

That Heian era tea table would be worth a three-sentence aside, revealing something about the character of the one who owns it.

Or—

I could go on for a couple of pages about this Bohemian Renaissance four-poster bed, with snakes twisting insidiously, perhaps voluptuously, or else biblically, among the deeply carved curly vines. Maybe even write it into the plot as a haunted soul-reliquary . . . or high-tech life-extension device . . . or a disguised scanner, meant to read the minds of houseguests while they sleep.

Each of the scenarios was about *Science Gone Terribly Wrong in Unforeseen Ways,* of course. There were always far more potential stories about the penalties of human technological hubris than even he could put down.

But no, the particular item he found squatting by the foot of the damask coverlet was especially interesting. Decorated in Georgian style, the chamber pot was either an excellent reproduction (unlikely in this mansion) or else the genuine eighteenth century article—a late Whieldon or an early Josiah Wedgwood design. And yet, evidently, it was also meant to be in service—the modern, hermetically sealed lid made that plain, along with a soft green night-light, designed to prevent fumbling in the dark. No doubt, when he opened the pot for use, he would also find another light within, to improve nocturnal aim.

Can't have guests pissing on the rug, Hamish mused. A functional combination of old and new. And also—just as explicitly—not to be sat on. Not for women, then, or for defecation. Men only. And just old Number One. Any modern person would understand the narrow purpose—for collecting the contemporary equivalent of gold.

But why here, by the bed? Why not simply walk to the loo?

Just fifteen steps took him through an ornate doorway to the elaborately tiled private bath, with heated floor and seven nozzle shower, where nanofiber towels awaited their chance to massage his pores while wicking moisture and applying expensive lotion, all at the same time. The facilities were sumptuous and up-to-date, except . . .

Well I'll be hog-tied. There's no phos-urinal.

The toilet-bidet had every water and air jet accoutrement, along with the latest seat warmer-vibrator from Kinshasa Luxe. But clearly, the porcelain bowl itself simply flushed, straight into the sewer, just like in the bad old days. There was no separate collector unit, or PU. No way for a man to perform the modern duty never asked of women. The one obligation that few women—even the most egalitarian or environmentally dedicated—volunteered to perform.

Back home, Hamish took care of reducing his household phosphorus waste by simply peeing off his bedroom balcony onto the roses . . . or into a sheltered flower bed outside his office. The world's simplest recycling system, and adopted by males all over the globe—wherever any nearby patch of nature might benefit—once a mild gaucherie, now an act of Earth patriotism.

To be honest, he enjoyed it, and Carolyn was no longer around to roll her eyes, muttering about a *"so-called crisis that must have been trumped up by macho little boys."*

That brought a smile of recollection . . . followed by a frown, remembering how, toward the end, she had called him a hypocrite for telling millions of viewers and readers, in *Condition of Panic,* that the phosphorus shortage was a hoax—a plot conceived by fertilizer barons and radical Earthfirsters.

"In that case, why have you put PUnits in every bathroom of this house?" she demanded, one day. *"You could be consistent. Take it to court! Pay the fines! Flush away!"*

Hamish's standard response—"Hey, it's just a story!"—didn't seem to work with her anymore. Not toward the end.

In truth, that novel—retitled *Phoscarcity?* and then *Phos-scare-city!* for the movie version—was one he rather regretted. Denying the obvious had cost him some credibility. But, then, Carolyn never understood—*I don't like smartaleck boffins telling me what to do. Even when they're right.*

Veering back to the here and now, Hamish wondered about the House of Glaucus-Worthington. For all the luxury of this bathroom, it pretty blatantly ignored the worldwide fertilizer shortage. *Do they bribe Zurich officials to look the other way, when this grand mansion sends all its phosphorus down to the mulching plant, mixed in with toilet paper and poo?* Downstream reclamation was far less efficient, after all. And the Swiss loved efficiency.

Just because you're a plutocrat, that doesn't automatically mean you don't care about the planet. Even if the GWs shrug off this emergency, some of their visitors will be planet-minded types or rich Naderites, who will want to . . .

. . . oh . . .

Okay, mystery partly solved. The chamber pot was a courtesy, for guests choosing to do the planetary correct thing. But such a conspicuously impractical PC solution! Some servant would have to come, perhaps twice or more a day, collect each contribution and then clean the pot. . . .

For the second time in a few heartbeats, Hamish got the "aha!" moment that he lived for.

I get it. You're telling me that you can send well-paid, elegant, soft-spoken servants all through this mammoth showplace, emptying and scrubbing antique porcelain PeeYews—*each of them worth a small fortune—by hand. All right, point taken. You are rich enough to no longer care how many nines you have in your percentile.*

Also, he recalled with a wince, *rich enough to not give a damn about fame . . . or autographs.*

As Rupert Glaucus-Worthington had demonstrated, by smiling faintly, when Hamish tried to hand him a signed copy of *The New Pyramid,* touching it lightly with a fingertip, before allowing a butler to carry it away. And then, with condescension that seemed more indolent than purposely insulting, the patriarch had asked:

"And so, Mr. Brookeman, what is it that you do for a living?"

One cultural gulf between people living east and west of the Atlantic had long swirled around that question. Americans tended to ask it right away, often unaware that it might cause offense.

To us it means "What interesting task or skill did you choose as the daytime focus of your life?" We assume it's a matter of choice, not caste. Meanwhile, Europeans tend to translate the question to "What's your born social class?" or "How much money do you make?" Generations of misunderstanding arose from that simple, treacherous, conversational error.

Only, then, why did Glaucus-Worthington—as European as the Alps—ask it?

Hamish recalled the sense of hurt that question triggered when he arrived at this great house, along with a dozen other guests, all brought in by private stratojet to assist tomorrow's negotiations. Stepping from limousine to receiving line was no new thing for Hamish. He had been prepared for the usual light chitchat with his host, before butlers took each visitor to private chambers for freshening up.

But Hamish was also accustomed to being one of the most famous people in any room, never subjected to that particular question.

Could it be that he's really never heard of me? When I answered by offering up some movie titles, none of them seemed to strike a bell. He simply smiled and said "How nice," before turning to the boffin standing next in line.

Of course, the superrich do have elite pastimes. Interests and activities we can only dream of. Priorities beyond mere . . .

Standing by the bed—halfway changed from his travel clothes into the obligate white tie and dinner jacket—Hamish blinked in sudden realization.

It's too much. No person could be that far out of touch. Anyway, all you have to do today is plug a farlai in your ear to get automatic, whispered bio-summaries about anyone you meet. A conscientious host does that, making every guest feel appreciated.

No. The snub was deliberate. Rupert wants to seem aloof, above it all.

But the hand is overplayed.

They're trying too hard.

Hamish knew what Guillaume deGrasse, his favorite detective character, would say right now.

I can smell fear.

. . .

He had no opportunity to share that insight with the Prophet before dinner—only a few moments to offer his capsule summary of meeting Roger Betsby, the self-confessed poisoner of Senator Strong. Tenskwatawa's dark eyes glittered while listening to Hamish's brief tale about the daring, the gall, the utter chutzpah of a rural doctor, who seemed so cheerfully—if mysteriously—willing to bring himself down, along with a despised politician.

"So you still have no idea what drug Betsby used to warp Strong's behavior? Getting him to make such a fool of himself in public?"

"Only that it was a *legal* substance, even medicinal. What he did was still a crime, Betsby concedes that. But he implies that a jury would be lenient, and that public revelation of the substance itself would do the senator even more harm than has already been done. Betsby threatens that he'll confess everything, if there's any retribution. I have to admit . . . it's one of the strangest types of extortion I've ever seen."

Tenskwatawa laughed upon reading Hamish's expression of mystification. "He sounds like a worthy little adversary for you, my friend. Just the sort of challenge that keeps you diverted and happy."

Forsaking his usual denim for contemporary evening clothes, the man often called a "prophet" seemed to be downplaying the whole *messenger of destiny* thing. Mysticism had no place at this mountaintop summit, where the twin negotiating themes would be pragmatism and flattery. Only the former would be spoken of explicitly. But in order to achieve the main goal—bringing an important segment of world aristocracy fully into the Movement—there must be a two-pronged appeal, to both self-interest and ego.

Not trivial! After his urinal-epiphany, Hamish had a new appreciation of how delicate it might be. These oligarchs wouldn't trust populist agitators, even with shared goals. They'd demand assurances, a measure of control . . .

. . . and yet, of course, Tenskwatawa was the smartest person Hamish had ever met, so what was there to worry about?

"Why don't you see if Dr. Betsby can be brought aboard somehow?" Tenskwatawa was so tall that he almost met Hamish eye to eye. "Our passionate young physician must have some want or need that would supersede his current agenda. Money? Help for a cause? Perhaps a taste of jail time, on some lesser charge, would create incentive for him to be reasonable.

"Still," the Prophet added. "If Betsby won't budge, do try to see if the senator can be saved."

"Whatever it takes, sir?"

The Prophet raised an eyebrow, paused, and then shook his head.

"No. Strong isn't that important. Not anymore. Not with the world in turmoil over this damned Alien Artifact doo-hickey.

"Anyway, remember Hamish, we're not pushing to become tyrants. Dirty tricks and Stazi tactics need to be kept to a minimum. Our movement aims only to put a harness on science and technology, instead of leaving them in charge of human destiny. We use populism and mob-mobilization methods, but in order to calm and tame the masses, and thus save the world, so that a better democracy can return later on."

"Hmm." Hamish pondered, glancing at their surroundings. "Our new allies may not agree with the very last part of that."

In truth, Hamish wasn't sure that he did. Plato despised democracy and wasn't he the wisest philosopher of all?

"I know." Tenskwatawa briefly squeezed Hamish's arm above the elbow, conveying a sense of power, jovially restrained, but coiled and always ready, like some force of physics. "The aristos think they can use us . . . and they do have both history and human nature on their side of the ledger. Perhaps they'll succeed! We may wind up like so many other populist movements across time—tricked into aiding the rise of oligarchy.

"On the other hand, we have a few new things on our side of the scale." The Prophet smiled, conveying confidence that shone like the sun.

"Such as Truth."

ENTROPY

Last time, we talked about one more way that civilizations might fail to achieve their dreams—not because of calamity, or war, or ecological collapse, but something mundane, even banal.

Overspecialization. Failure to keep climbing the near-vertical mountain of their accumulated learning. Pondered logically, it seems unavoidable. The greater your pile of information, the steeper the chore of discovering more! Concentrating on a narrower subject will only work up to a point, because even if you live long enough to master your cramped field, you'll never know how much of your work is being duplicated, wastefully, across the world or down the hall, by people using a slightly different vocabulary for the same problem. Humanity's greatest trick for making progress—subsidizing ever larger numbers of specialist-professionals—seemed destined to become a trap.

Indeed, this failure mode may trip up countless civilizations out there, across the galaxy.

But not us. Not on twenty-first century Earth. That danger was overcome, at least for now, by stunning achievements in human mental agility. By Internet connections and search-correlation services that sift the vast sea of knowledge faster than thought. By quest-programs that present you with anything germane to your current interest. By analytic tools that weigh any two concepts for mutual relevance. And above all, by our new ability to flit—like gods of legend—all over the e-linked globe, meeting others, ignoring guild boundaries and sharing ideas.

The printing press multiplied what average humans could know, while glass lenses magnified what we could see—and every century since expanded that range, till the Multitasking Generation can zip hither and yon, touching lightly upon almost any fact, concept or work of art, exchanging blips, nods, twits, and pips with anyone alive . . . and some entities that aren't.

Ah, but therein lies the rub. "Touching lightly."

Much has been written about the problems that accompany Continuously Divided Attention. Loss of focus. A susceptibility for simplistic/viral notions. An anchorless tendency to drift or lose concentration. And these are just the mildest symptoms. At the extreme are dozens of newly named mental illnesses, like Noakes's Syndrome and Leninger's Disease, many of them blamed on the vast freedom we have won—to skitter our minds across any topic with utter abandon.

Have we evaded one dismal failure mode—the trap of narrow *overspecialization*—only to stumble into the opposite extreme? Broadly-spread *shallow-mindedness*? Pondering thoughts that span the farthest horizons, but only finger-deep?

Listen to those dour curmudgeons out there, decrying the faults of our current "Age of Amateurs." They call for a restoration of expertise, for a return to credentialed knowledge-tending, for restoring order and disciplined focus to our professions and arts and academe. Is this just self-interested guild-tending? Or are they prescribing another badly needed course correction, to stave off disaster?

Will the new AI systems help us deal with this plague of shallowness . . . or make it worse?

One thing is clear. It isn't easy to be smart, in this galaxy of ours. We keep barely evading a myriad pitfalls along our way to . . . whatever we hope to become.

When you add it all up, are you really surprised that we seem so alone?

—Pandora's Cornucopia

34.

SEASTEADING

Ocean stretched in every direction.

Peng Xiang Bin had come to think of himself as a man of the sea, who spent most of his time in water—amid the scummy, sandy tidal surges that swept up and down the Huangpu Estuary. He thought nothing of holding his breath while diving a dozen meters for crab, or prying salvage from the junk-strewn bottom, feeling more akin to the fish, or even drifting jellies, than to the landlubber he once had been. In a world of rising seas and drowning shorelines, it seemed a good way to adapt.

Only now he realized. *I always counted on the nearness of dry land.*

Ahead of him lay nothing but gray ocean, daunting and endless, flecked with wind-driven froth and merging imperceptibly with a faraway, turbid skyline. Except where he now stood, on a balcony projecting outward from a man-made island—a high-tech village on stilts—clinging to a reef that used to be a nation.

That was now a nation once again.

Looking carefully, he could follow the curve of breakers smashing over stumps that had once been buildings—homes and schools, shops and wharves. Here had been no massive seawalls. No effort to preserve doomed properties. All toppled under powerful typhoons long ago. Soon after most of the natives moved away, explosives finished off the messy remnants of Old Pulupau, a one-time tropical paradise. The new inhabitants didn't want unpleasant remnants spoiling their view.

Of course there was a lot more hidden from the eye, just beyond the reef. A vista of underwater industry had been visible from the small submarine that brought Bin here three days ago. Wave machines for generating electricity and siphons that sucked bottom mud to spread into the currents, fertilizing plankton to enhance nearby fishing grounds and earn carbon credits at the same time. Pressing his face against the sub's tiny window, Bin had stared at huge globes, shaped like gigantic soccer balls, bobbing against anchor-tethers—pens where schools of tuna spent their entire lives, fed and fattened for market. A real industrial and economic infrastructure . . . all of it kept below the surface, out of sight, in order not to perturb rich residents who lived above.

A glint of white cloth and silvery metal . . . Bin winced as his right eye, fresh from surgery, overreacted to the sudden glare reflecting off a nineteen-meter sloop that passed into view around the far corner of Newer Newport. Sheets of bright neosilk billowed and figures hurried about the deck, tugging at lines. A call—distant but clear—bellowed across the still lagoon.

"Two-Six, heave!"

Voices answered in unison as well-drilled teamwork rapidly set the main sail. Though the crew seemed to be working hard, few would call it "labor." Not when the poorest citizen of this independent nation could buy or sell a man like Peng Xiang Bin, ten thousand times or more. Bin found the sight intriguing in more ways than he could count.

I always thought that rich people would lay about, letting servants and robots do everything for them. Sure, you heard of wealthy athletes and hobbyists. But I had no idea so many would choose to sweat and strain . . . for fun. Or that it could be so—

He shook his head, lacking the vocabulary. Then something happened that he still found disturbing. A dark splotch appeared, as if by magic, in a lower corner of his right eye. The shadow resolved into a single Chinese character, with a small row of lesser figures underneath, offering both a definition and pronunciation guide.

Obsessive.

Yes. That word seemed close to what he had in mind. Or, rather, what the ai in his eye estimated, after following his gaze and reading subconscious signals in his throat, the subvocalized words that he had muttered within, without ever speaking them aloud.

This was going to take some getting used to.

"Peng Xiang Bin," a voice spoke behind him. "You have rested and the worldstone has recharged. It is time to return."

It was the same voice that had come from the penguin-machine, his constant companion during the hurried journey that began less than a hundred hours ago—first swimming away from his wife and child and the little shorestead, then slipping aboard a midget submarine, followed by two days aboard a fast coastal packet-freighter, then a hurried midnight transfer to a seaplane that made a final rendezvous, in midocean, with yet another submarine . . . and all that way accompanied by a black, birdlike robot. His guide, or keeper, or guard, it had spoken soothingly to him about his coming duties as keeper of the worldstone.

Only at journey's end, after surfacing and stepping onto Newer Newport, here in Pulupau, did Bin meet the original owner of the voice.

"Yes, Dr. Nguyen," he answered, nod-bowing to a slight man with Annamese features and long black hair, braided in elegant rows. "I come, sir."

He turned to gather up the off-white ovoid—the *worldstone*—from a nearby patio table, where it had lain in sunshine for an hour, soaking energy. A welcome break for him, as well. As carefully as he would handle a baby, Bin hefted the artifact and followed Nguyen Ky between sliding doors of frosted glass, moving slowly out of habit, in order to let his vision adapt to interior dimness. Only, he might as well not have bothered. His right eye . . . or ai . . . now adjusted brightness and contrast for him, more quickly than any spreading of his natural iris.

The room was broad and well appointed, with plush furnishings that adapted to each user's comfort preference. Programmable draperies were set to soothing patterns that rippled gently, like a freshwater brook. The farthest window was left open. Through it, Bin glimpsed the rest of Newer Newport—more than a hectare of sleek, multistoried luxury, perched on massive footings, firmly anchored over the spot where ancestral kings of Pulupau once had their palace.

Some distance beyond, a series of other mammoth stilt-villages, each wildly different in style, followed the curve of a drowned atoll. *Thielburg, Patria, Galt's Gulch* and several others with names that were even harder to remember. One of them, all stainless steel and glass, was dedicated to caring for aged aristocrats, immersing them in comfort and threevee experience, before freezing them for a nitrogen-chilled journey through time, aimed at repair and resurrection in a hundred years or so—to be young again, in tech-enhanced paradise.

Another artificial islet, with polycarbonano architecture reminiscent of palm logs and thatch roofing, was set aside for the old royal family and a number of genuine Pulupauese. As legalistic insurance, no doubt. In case any nation or consortium should doubt the sovereign independence of this archipelago of wealth.

Seasteading. Of course, Bin had heard of such places. Along the spectrum of human prosperity, these projects lay at the very opposite end from the *shore*stead that he had settled with Mei Ling in the garbage-strewn Huangpu. Here, and in a few dozen other locales, some of the world's richest families had pooled funds to buy up small nations to call their own, escaping all obligation (especially taxes) owed to the continental states, with their teeming, populist masses. Yet, Bin could see a few traits shared in common by seastead and shorestead. Adaptation. Making the best of rising seas. Turning calamity into advantage.

Three technical experts—a graceful Filipina who never removed her wraparound immersion goggles; an islander, possibly a native Pulupauan, who kept fingering his interactive crucifix; and an elderly Chinese gentleman, who spoke in the soft tones of a scholar—watched Peng Xiang Bin and Nguyen Ky gingerly replace the worldstone in its handcrafted cradle, surrounded by instruments and sleek, ailectronic displays.

The ovoid had already started coming alive in response to Bin's touch. As keeper of the worldstone, he alone could rouse the object to craft lustrous images—like a whole world or universe shining within an egglike capsule, less than half a meter long. Whatever the reason for his special knack, Bin was grateful for the honor, for the resulting employment, and for a chance to participate in matters far above his normal station of life. Though he missed Mei Ling and the baby.

The now familiar entity Courier of Caution lurked—or seemed to—just within the pitted, ovoid curves, amid those swirling clouds. Courier's ribbon eye stared outward, resembling Anna Arroyo's unblinking goggles, while the creature's diamond-shaped, four-lipped mouth pursed in a perpetual expression of uneasiness or disapproval.

Bin carefully reattached a makeshift device at one end that compensated for some of the object's surface damage, partly restoring a sonic connection. Of course, he had no idea how the mechanism—or anything else in the room—worked. But he kept trying to learn every procedure, if only so the others would consider him a colleague . . . and less an experimental subject.

From their wary expressions, it might take some time.

"Let us resume," Dr. Nguyen said. "We were attempting to learn about the stone's arrival on Earth. Here are the ideograms we want you to try next, please." The small man laid a sheet of e-paper in front of Xiang Bin, bearing a series of characters. They looked complex and very old—even archaic.

Fortunately, Bin did not have to hold the ovoid in his hands anymore. Just standing nearby seemed to suffice. Bringing his right index finger close—and sticking out his tongue a little in concentration—he copied the first symbol by tracing it across the surface of the worldstone. Inky brushstrokes seemed to follow his touch-path. Actually, it came out rather pretty. *Calligraphy . . . one of the great Chinese art forms. Who figured I would have a knack for it?*

He managed the next figure more quickly. And a third one. Evidently, the ideograms were not in modern Chinese, but some older dialect and writing system—more pictographic and less formalized—from the warring states period that preceded the unification standards of great Chin, the first emperor. Fortunately, the implant in his eye went ahead and offered a translation, which he spoke aloud in modern Putonghua.

"Date of arrival on Earth?"

There were two projects going on at once. The first involved using ancient symbols to ask questions. But Dr. Nguyen also wanted to expose the entity to modern words. Ideally—if it truly was much smarter than an Earthly ai—it should learn the more recent version of Chinese, and other languages as well. Anyway, this would test the ovoid's adaptability.

After a brief pause, Courier appeared to lift one arm, weirdly double-elbowed, and knocked Bin's ideograms away with a flick of one three-fingered hand, causing them to shatter and dissolve. The simulated alien proceeded to draw a series of new figures that jostled and arrayed themselves against the worldstone's inner face. Bin also sensed the bulbous right end of the stone emit faint vibrations. Sophisticated detectors fed these to a computer, whose vaice then uttered enhanced sounds that Bin didn't understand.

Fortunately, Yang Shenxiu, the white-haired Chinese scholar, could. He tapped a uniscroll in front of him.

"Yes, yes! So *that* is how those words used to be pronounced. Wonderful."

"And what do they mean, please?" demanded the Vietnamese mogul standing nearby.

"Oh, he . . . the being who resides within . . . says that he cannot track the passage of time, since he slept for so long. But he will offer something that should be just as good."

Dr. Nguyen stepped closer. "And pray, what is that?"

The alien brought its forearms together and then apart again. The ever-present clouds seemed to converge, bringing darkness upon a patch of the worldstone, till deep black reigned across the center. Bin caught a pointlike glitter . . . and another . . . then two more . . . and another pair . . .

"Stars," announced Anna Arroyo. "Six of them, arrayed in a rough hexagon . . . with a final one in the middle, slightly off center . . . I'm searching the online constellation catalogs . . . Damn. All present-day matches include some stars that are below seventh magnitude, so they'd have been invisible to people long ago. It's unlikely . . ."

"Please do not curse or blaspheme," said the islander, Paul Menelaua. "Let's recall that the topic at hand is *time*. Dates. *When*. Stars shift." Still fondling the animatronic cross that hung from a chain around his neck, he added, "Try going retrograde . . ."

The figure of Jesus seemed to squirm, a little, under his touch. Anna frowned at his terse rebuke, but she nodded. "I'm on it. Backsifting and doing a whole sky match-search in one hundred year intervals. This could take a while."

Bin grunted. Held back a moment. Then blurted:

"Seven!"

The scholar and the rich man turned to him. Bin had to swallow to gather courage, managing a low croak. "I . . . think the *number* of stars may . . . make this simpler."

"What do you mean, Peng Xiang Bin?" asked Dr. Nguyen.

"I mean . . . maybe . . . you should try the Seven Maidens. You know. The . . ." He groped for a name.

"Pleiades," the scholar, Yang Shenxiu, finished for him, at about the same time as Bin's aiware also supplied the name. "Yes, that would be a good guess."

The Filipina woman interrupted. "Got you. Scanning time-drift of just that one cluster, back . . . back . . . Yes! It's a good match. The Pleiades-Subaru constellation, just under five thousand years ago. Wow."

"Well done." Dr. Nguyen nodded. "I expected something like this. My young friend Xiang Bin, please tell us again about the box that formerly held the worldstone— what did the inscription say?"

Bin recited from memory.

" 'Unearthed in Harappa, 1926' . . ."

He then spoke the second half with an involuntary shiver.

" 'Demon-infested. Keep in the dark.' "

"Harappa, yes," Nguyen nodded, ignoring the other part. "A center of the Indus Valley culture . . . poor third sister during the earliest days of urban civilization, after Mesopotamia and Egypt." He glanced at the scholar Yang Shenxiu, who continued.

"Some think it was a stunted state—cramped, paranoid, and never fully literate. Others admired its level of primly regimented urban planning. We don't really know what happened to the Indus civilization. Abandoned about 1700 B.C.E., they say. Possibly a great flood weakened both main cities, Harappa and Mohenjo-daro. By possible coincidence, several thousand *li* to the west, the great volcano at Thera may have—"

Dr. Nguyen shook his head, and the elegant braids swished. "But this makes no sense! Why would it be speaking to us in archaic Chinese, a dialect from more than a millennium later? Harappa was buried under sand by then!"

"Shall I try to ask, sir?" Bin took a step forward.

The small man waved a hand in front of his face. "No. I am following a script of questions, prioritized by colleagues and associates around the world. We'll keep to these points, then fill in gaps later. Go to the next set of characters, Xiang Bin, if you would please."

Bin felt gratified again by Dr. Nguyen's unfailing politeness. The gentleman had been well brought up, for sure— skilled at how best to treat underlings. *Perhaps I will get to work for him forever.* Not a harsh fate to contemplate, so long as Mei Ling and the baby could join him soon.

He meant to prove his value to this man. So, bending over the stone, Bin carefully sketched four more of the complicated ideograms that Professor Yang Shenxiu had provided, in a style from long ago. Dr. Nguyen's consortium could not wait for their worldstone to learn modern Chinese. There wasn't time. Not with the planet already in an uproar over mysterious sights and sounds that were being emitted by the so-called Havana Artifact—another alien emissary-stone that the American astronaut recently retrieved from high orbit. *This* stone in front of Bin offered a way to check—in secret—on tales being told by the other one in Washington.

So far, they knew one thing. Courier did not seem to

approve of the Havana Artifact. Shown images of the more famous object, Courier reacted with crouches and slashing motions, so clear and easily understood they might be universal across the cosmos. Elaborating upon an earlier warning of *danger,* the entity in Bin's worldstone added another that was easy to translate.

Liars!

TORALYZER

I should count my blessings.

Crisped-by-flame, aboard the *Spirit of Chula Vista,* I'd be dead in any previous era. I would be nonexistent, or else (slim agnostic chance) gone on to some posthumous reward.

But *this* is my era, and I've been offered options that would seem miraculous to any of my ancestors. Starting with a chance to keep on practicing my trade, while this tormented-barbecued body lies entombed within a canister of life-sustaining gel. Is that worth a (more than a little) bit of ongoing agony? Getting to travel the world as a ghost-journalist e-porter, chatting up celebrighties, tracking rumors, stirring up smart-mobs (!), keeping busy.

Some of you have asked about organ reconstruction. Skin grafts are an ongoing bone of contention between me and the docs—they hurt like hell. But with biojet printers to spray my very own restemmed cells onto layered scaffolds, all the simple, fibrous, and vasculated tissue can be grown—liver, spleen, and left lung—just like the vat-farmer raised that beeffish burger you had for lunch.

There's even talk of arm and leg transplants, if a reclam donor with my rare antigen type can be found. But I sense doubtful tones under their hopeful words, what with all the nerve damage I suffered. For certain I'll never again have real eyes and ears. (It's a wonder my skull protected what it did.)

So what's the point? Shall I regain mobility by want-controlling a robotic walker? One of those hissing, clanking things?

Some of you ask: What about uploading? Heck, I already exist mostly in cyberspace. Why not just abandon this ruined body and go the rest of the way—taking my whole consciousness into the Net? *Become* one with my online avatars! That notion has always been 99 percent fiction and 1 percent science . . . till Marguerita deSilva and her followers began claiming that soon anybody will be able to become just like her pet, the god-rat Porfirio, thriving in virtual worlds that are vaster than anything "real."

And now there are the Artifact aliens, who seem to prove her right. If we choose to join their interstellar federation, will they show us how to upload ourselves into crystal worlds, as they did?

Is there any way to tell if it's worthwhile?

Of course, there are other options for a person like me. Some of you say: *"All problems will be solved in the due course of time."* So, might the world a century from now be able to fix me up? Repair my poor body to youthful vigor? And is that chance worth a risky journey through time?

It's illegal in most places to freeze a living person. The cryonics companies have to wait, rushing in to freeze you the moment doctors declare you are legally dead. But I've had offers from rich fans (no, I won't tell) who say they'll pay my way to San Sebastian, or Pulupau, or Friedmania or Rand's Freehold, where local law doesn't quibble such details. Heck, I'm now a heroine and historical figure! Won't folks want to thaw my frozen corpsicle and heal me, in some marvelous future?

Here's a one-sentence sales pitch that one true believer sent me: *"The cryonics long shot lets us see our pending brain death not as the solipsistic obliteration of our world but as a long sleep that precedes a very major surgery."*

Hm, to sleep. Ah, but perchance to dream? That's one possible rub.

Worse, what if religious folk, like my parents, turn out to be right? That death is a spirit release. A door opening to something beyond? Might cryonic suspension simply quash and defer what would have been the soul's reward? Replacing it with an icy nordic version of hell?

Don't everybody sneer till you've been in my position. There aren't many pure atheists in gel tanks.

35.
SENSING DESTINY'S CALL

The marchers were protesting something. That much Mei Ling could tell, even without virring. But what were they complaining about? Which issue concerned them, from a worldwide collection of grievances more numerous than stars?

Carrying no placards or signs, and dressed in a wild brew of styles, the mostly youthful throng milled forward, in the general direction of the Shanghai Universe of Disney and the Monkey King. Each individual pretended to be minding his or her own business, chattering with companions, window-shopping, or just wandering amid a seemingly random throng of visitor-tourists. Cameras were all over the place of course, atop every lamppost and street sign or pixel-painted on every window rim. Yet nothing was going on that should attract undue attention from monitors of state security, or the local proctors of decent order.

But there were coincidences too frequent to dismiss. For example, they *all* wore pixelated clothing that glittered and throbbed with ever-changing patterns. One girl had her tunic set to radiate a motif of waving pine trees. A boy's abstract design featured undulating ocean waves. Only when, as Mei Ling watched, the two bumped briefly against each other, did the two image displays seem to merge and combine across their backs, lining up to convey what her eye—but possibly no ai—briefly recognized as a trio of symbols.

SEEK URBAN SERENITY.

The youths parted again, erasing that momentary co-alescence of forest and sea. Perhaps the two of them had never met before that terse, choreographed rendezvous. They might not ever meet again. But soon, amid the throng, another seemingly chance encounter created a different, fleeting message that caught Mei Ling's built-in, organic pattern recognition system, still more subtle than any-thing cybernetic, inherited from when her distant ances-tors roamed the African tall grass, sifting for signs of prey. Or danger.

RESPONSIBLE LEADERSHIP IS APPRECIATED.

No doubt about it. That's what the shimmer of fleeting characters said.

Passersby and shoppers were turning to notice, nudging their neighbors and waggling their hands to toss virt-alerts down the street. Crowds of onlookers formed in time to catch the next flicker-pronouncement, as a fat man sidled next to a broad-shouldered woman with orange-striped hair. Their combined pixel-garments proclaimed—

THE TANG EMPERORS ENCOURAGED CREATIVITY.

Watching from a niche between a hair salon and a stall offering pungent chicktish meat, Mei Ling reflexively rocked the baby in his sling carrier, while wondering. Why did these young people go to such lengths to stay discon-nected from their messages, preserving their ability to deny responsibility, when the meanings seemed so inno-cent? So harmless?

Oh, she realized, *the real essence must lie elsewhere. In vir-space.*

Mei Ling pulled out the set of cheap augmented reality spectacles that she had purchased from a vendor, just a little

while ago. It seemed a reasonable use of cash, in an era
when so much of the world lay beyond sight of normal
eyes. Especially with Xiang Bin gone on his strange adventure beyond the sea. So long as he had a job, helping
make that strange, demon-infested stone perform tricks for
the penguin creature, she had money. Enough to pay off
some repairs to their salvaged shorestead home and even
take Xiao En on an early morning shopping expedition into
the bustling city, where giant arcology pyramids loomed
upward to block half the sky, proclaiming the greatness of
the world's new superpower.

Mei Ling had chosen this time because such a large portion of the planet's population was watching proceedings
at the Artifact Conference in America that she figured
the streets would be largely empty. But it turned out that
the event was in recess for several hours, which meant
people were pouring outdoors to do important shopping
or business, or get a little air. It made the boulevards especially crowded—and ideal for this kind of youth demonstration.

Slipping on the wraparound goggles, Mei Ling felt
acutely aware of how long it had been since she and Xiang
Bin moved out to the tidal flats and ruined shoreline of the
Huangpu, where the world had only one "layer"—gritty,
hardscrabble reality. That made her several tech-generations
out of date. The ailectronics salesman had been helpful,
patient . . . and a little too flirtatious . . . while tuning the
unit to her rusty GIBAAR skills. It was difficult to redis-
cover the knack, even with his help. Like remembering
how to walk after too long a convalescence in bed.

Gaze. Interest. Blink. Allocate Attention. Repeat.

*The most basic way to vir, if you don't have any of the
other tools.*

She had no fingernail tappers. No clickers and scrollers,
planted in the teeth. No subvocal pickups, to read the half-

spoken words shaped by throat and mouth. Not even an old-fashioned hand-keyboard or twiddler. And certainly none of the fancy-scary new cephalo sensors that would take commands straight off the brain. Without any of that, she had to make do—choosing from a range of menus and command icons that the spectacles created across the inner surface of both lenses, seeming to float in front of the real-life street scene.

By turning her *gaze* to look right at a search icon . . . and by actually being *interested* (which affected the dilation of her pupils and blood flow in the retina) . . . she caused that symbol to light up. There followed a well timed, one-two *blink* of the left eye then right . . .

On her third try, a new window-menu blossomed, allowing her to allocate her attention . . . to pick from a range of sub-options. And she chose one called **Overlayers**.

Immediately, the specs laid faint lines across the real world, bordering the pavement and curb, the fringe of each building and vendor stall—anything real that might become a dangerous obstacle or tripping hazard to a person walking about. Also outlined—the people and vehicles moving around her. Each now carried a slim aura. Especially those heading in her direction, which throbbed a little in the shade that was called *collision-warning yellow.*

These edge lines—clearly demarcated rims and boundaries of the real world—were inviolate. They weren't supposed to change, no matter what level of vir-space you chose—it took a real hacker to mess with them.

As for the rest of visual reality, the textures, colors, and backgrounds? Well, there were a million ways to play with those, from covering all the building walls with jungle vines, to filling the world with imaginary water, like sunken Atlantis, to giving every passerby the skin tones of lizard-people from Mars. You name it, and some teenager or bored office worker or semiautonomous cre-ai-tivity drone must have already fashioned an overlay to bring that fantasy cosmos into being.

Mei Ling wasn't trying for any of those realms—she didn't know the addresses, for one thing, and had no interest in searching out ways to become immersed in someone else's favorite mirage. Instead, she tried simply stepping *up* through the most basic levels, one at a time—first passing through the Public Safety layers, where children or the handicapped could view the world conveniently captioned in simple terms, with friendly risk-avoidance alerts and helpful hands, pointing toward the nearest sources of real-time help.

Then came useful tiers, where all the buildings and storefronts were marked with essential information about location, products, and accountability codes. Or you could zoom-magnify anything that caught your interest. On strata twelve through sixteen, everyone in sight wore basic nametags, or ID badges identifying their professions. Otherwise, reality was left quite bare.

Up at stratum thirty, it suddenly became hard to see, as the air filled with yellow and pink and green notecards—*Post-its*—that floated around every shop and street corner, conveying anything from meet-me memos to traffic curses to caustic commentaries on a restaurant's cuisine. And prayers.

Mei Ling experimented by raising her hand and drawing in the air with a finger. As the specs followed her movements and responded, a brand-new Post-it appeared, bearing the name of her husband. Peng Xiang Bin. She then added characters that constituted an incantation for luck. When Mei Ling brought her hand down, the tiny virt fluttered away and seemed to fade into the maelstrom. This was what made stratum thirty almost useless for anything *but* prayer. Or curses. All visitors could see *everything* that was ever left there . . . which meant no one could see anything at all.

Do people really live like this all the time? Wading through the world, immersed in pretend things? She could see how this kind of tool would be useful on occasion. But she could take off the specs at any moment. What about those who got fitted with contact lenses, or even the new eyeball implants? The very thought made her shudder.

At level forty, a lot of walls disappeared. Most of the buildings seemed to go transparent, or at least depict animated floorplans concocted from public records. These ranged from detailed inner views—of a nearby department store—with every display and mannequin appearing eager to perform, all the way to floors and offices that were blocked by barriers, in varied shades of gray, some of them with glowing locks. You could look inside—if you had some kind of key.

Strata fifty through one hundred were for advertising, and at one point Mei Ling quailed back, as all the normal dampers vanished. Messages and come-ons seemed to roar at her from every shop front and store awning. Blasts of sound rocked the spec-rims till they almost flew off her ears, and she had to concentrate hard just to blink her way out of there! Fortunately, most advir-levels were selective, even polite. Stratum ninety, for example, offered her discreet, personalized discounts on baby formula and inexpensive shoes, plus a special on a massage-makeover in *that shop over there,* at a price that seemed so reasonable, she could nearly afford it! The proprietor would even fetch a nanny-grandma in five minutes to watch the baby.

But no. Not with the sudden comfort of Xiang Bin's paycheck so new and unaccustomed. Maybe another time.

Anyway, Mei Ling realized that she had been idly following the gaggle of youthful demonstrators, awkwardly picking her way across each avenue, while making sure that Xiao En's bottle didn't fall to the filthy sidewalk. A pedicab driver shouted and Mei Ling jumped back, heart pounding, especially on realizing—she had lost track of where she was, in an unfamiliar part of town.

It is not possible to get lost wearing specs, she reminded herself. Level ten would always provide a handy guide arrow, aiming you down the quickest path to anywhere in the world you wanted to go.

That is, if I knew where he was right now.

If he weren't swallowed up by the secret intrigues of powerful men.

Continuing to scroll upward through slices of the world, she saw the level counter skip whole swathes of vir-spaces where she wasn't allowed. You had to be a member of some affinity group to see those overlayers.

I recall that stratum two hundred and fifty was for street gossip.

Only instead, S-250 populated the boulevard with cartoon figures—colorful, high contrast versions of people walking by, with speech balloons floating above many of their heads. Some balloons were filled with written words. Others—nothing but gray static. *Oh, yes. This layer is for eavesdropping, if people don't care enough to set up a privacy block. The gossip level must have been S-350.*

Mei Ling found she enjoyed this chance to recover her old knack of blink-navigation, even though the baby was starting to get crabby, and her shoulder bag full of purchases was heavy, and really, maybe it was time to set off for home.

At least she no longer had to ratchet through the layers linearly, one at a time, like a complete neo. A simple preference choice now let her view the virld as a three dimensional *spiderweb* of jump choices, stretching in all directions. It took just a look, a squint and wink to hop to the level she wanted, where—

—Post-its of another kind flurried about. Voice, text, and vid *twips* kept zooming in, attaching themselves to the youthful demonstrators, sent by anonymous bystanders, or even people who were viewing the event from thousands of kilometers away.

Smart-aleck kids, one note commented. **As if their generation knows a thing about struggle and revolution**

Another groused.

Back in 2025 I was in the New Red Guards we really knew how to light up a street ruckus! Wore masks that screwed facial recog cams . . .

Yep. Street gossip. Finally, Mei Ling found something related to her interest—a simple query note.

WHAT are they demonstrating about?

Which had an even simpler comment addendum attached to it, anonymously recommending a clickover to:

0847lals0xldo098-899as0004-hahd-dorad087

She blinked her way to that address . . . and found the street scene transformed once again.

The young people now wore costumes in seventeenth-century Shun Dynasty style, like followers of the great rebel leader Li Zicheng. Mei Ling recognized the Peoples' Militia fashion from a historical romance she had watched. Because he sought to free the masses from feudal oppression, Li Zicheng was officially proclaimed a "hero of the Chinese masses" by Chairman Mao himself, a century ago. *Still, I'm surprised that today's rich and powerful lords of the Beneficent Patriarchy approve of people invoking his memory,* she thought.

Up and down the street, onlookers and pedestrians were also transformed, mostly by replacing their twenty-first century streetwear with shabby peasant clothing from the

1600s. Not exactly flattering, but she got the implied message. *We're all clueless plebeians. Thanks a lot.*

She was tempted to try accessing a nearby cam-view, and look down upon herself transformed, but decided—it really wasn't worth the effort. Anyway, she could finally see the answer to her question. Over the demonstrators' heads, there now floated huge banners that matched their gaily colored costumes.

That Which Is Not Specifically Forbidden Is Automatically Allowed!*

* (for just cause, by a sovereign and rightful legislature)

Mei Ling had heard that phrase before. She strained to remember—and that effort apparently triggered a search response from the mesh-spectacles. She winced as a disembodied voice started lecturing.

"Eighteen years ago, human rights groups demanded that this principle be enshrined in the famous International Big Deal, firmly and finally rejecting the opposite tradition long held by a majority of human societies, that anything not specifically allowed must be assumed to be forbidden.

"Activists called this change in tenets even more important and fundamental than freedom of speech. Some social psychologists have since deemed the reform futile, since it concerns a deep-seated cultural assumption, rather than a point of law.

"In return for granting this principle, the world's professional guilds and aristocratic powers were able to win formal acceptance of the Estates . . ."

Mei Ling succeeded in cutting off the pedantic lecture, which wasn't much help anyway. The same problem held for another pair of student virbanners, waving in an ersatz wind—

All Human Beings—Even Leaders—
Are Inherently Delusional

and

Criticism Is the Only Known
Antidote to Error

Of course, there were ways to follow up. An infinite sea of definitions, explanations, and commentaries, even suitable for a poorly educated woman. So, was the demonstration meant to lure onlookers into *study*? Or might all this vagueness be the real point of the youths' demonstration? Messing with peoples' heads, aggravating their elders with the ever-elusive obscurity of their protest?

Whatever the answer—Mei Ling had lost patience.

Chinese people used to be forthright, known for saying what we mean and meaning what we say. Only now that we are the world's greatest power, are we slipping into more classic Asian ways? Masking our motives and goals behind layers of tiresome symbolism?

Anyway, she thought with some satisfaction, *people will forget about these kids just as soon as the Artifact Conference resumes.*

Moving against the nearest building wall, she concentrated on blink-navigating away from this weird vir-level, aiming for the blessed simplicity of stratum ten, where a friendly yellow arrow might start guiding her back to the seawall separating these rich Shanghai citizens from dark, threatening tides. And from there to the water taxi dock, where she might grab some lunch before hitching a ride—

Abruptly, something popped into her foreground. A beckon-symbol, informing her that a live message was coming in. It flashed with urgency . . . and the striped colors that denoted official authority. A bit nervously,

Mei Ling looked toward the pulsating icon, and winked to accept the phone call. What then ballooned, just above the surrounding traffic and pedestrians, was a face and upper torso—stern-looking and male—wearing a uniform.

"Piao Mei Ling, I am Jin Pu Wang of state security. I had to exert some time and effort to locate you."

It came across as a rebuke.

"Fortunately, I was able to lay a sift-Mesh that found your iris pattern once you began using this pair of overlay spectacles. It is important that we meet right away, to discuss your husband."

Mei Ling felt her throat catch and she stumbled. Little Xiao En, who had drifted off to sleep, grunted in his sling carrier and clenched his little fists.

"What . . . what has happened?"

She had to utter the words loudly, in order to be certain the specs would hear. A couple of passersby glanced at her in surprise, clearly miffed that anyone would be so rude. Holding a phone conversation loud enough to bother others in a public place? Outrageous!

Lacking even a throat microphone, however, Mei Ling had little choice.

"What news do you have of him?"

"No news," the official answered. *"I want to discuss with you ways to rescue him from the bad company he has fallen into. How to return him to the embrace of his beloved nation."*

Mei Ling felt a wave of relief, having feared they had bad tidings. Moving to face the nearest wall of grimy bricks, she answered in a lower tone of voice.

"I . . . already told your other officers everything I know. They verified my truthfulness with machines and drugs. I don't see what I could possibly add."

Mei Ling said it with no sense of regret or betrayal. Xiang Bin had said that it would be best to cooperate fully, if authorities came asking questions. Nothing she knew should enable them to find him, after all. Anyway, at the moment of his departure with the penguin-robot there had been no reason to believe that he was doing anything against the law.

"Yes, well . . ." The man looked briefly to one side, nodded, and looked back toward Mei Ling. Making her wonder what viewpoint he was using to see her. Though his image appeared on the inner surface of the specs, he was probably using a pennycam on that lamppost over there.

"We would like to speak to you again," he explained. *"It should only take a few minutes to clear up one or two discrepancies. After that is done, we will provide you with a ride to your home, courtesy of the state."*

Well. That actually made the prospect rather tempting, instead of trudging across East Pudong District carrying both her purchases and an infant who seemed to grow heavier with each passing moment.

"I have the contact code for Inspector Wu, who interviewed me last time. Shall I call her to arrange an appointment?"

Jin Pu Wang shook his head. *"No. My department cannot spare the time to go through local officials. These questions are relatively minor, but they must be clarified at once, on orders from the capital."*

Mei Ling swallowed hard.

"Where do you want me to go?"

"Let me give you the coordinates of a nearby police station. The officers will put you in a comfortable meeting room with refreshments. I will send my holvatar to meet you. Then a car will take you home."

Her specs immediately reset to stratum fifteen. Some code numbers quickly scrolled by and a virtual arrow materialized in front of Mei Ling, indicating that she should proceed to the end of this block and then turn left.

"I hope that Inspector Wu was not unhappy with my level of cooperation," she said, while starting to walk in that direction.

"Do not worry about that," the policeman reassured her. *"I will see you soon."* His face vanished from her view.

For some distance Mei Ling followed the guide arrow automatically, steeped in lonely gloom. It was not a good thing to draw attention from the mighty authorities—even though Inspector Wu and her technicians had been polite and unthreatening during the questioning session, with their big, shiny hovercraft bobbing next to the little shorestead she had built with Xiang Bin.

Of course, they wanted to know all about the glowing stone. The one so similar to the emissary Artifact in Washington. When asked why her husband's discovery wasn't reported to the government, Mei Ling explained with complete honesty, they feared what happened to the crystal's earlier owner.

"Lee Fang Lu fell victim to the paranoia and corruption of that time," Inspector Wu had conceded. *"But those who executed him later suffered the same fate during the reforms that followed the* Zheng He *disaster and the Big Deal. It's too bad your husband did not take that into account and bring his find to us, to benefit the nation."*

When Mei Ling protested that she and Xiang Bin had nothing but love and reverence for the great homeland, Inspector Wu seemed mollified. *"It's all right. We'll find him, I'm sure. He will have ample opportunities to demonstrate his loyalty."*

With that reassurance the police investigators departed, leaving Mei Ling woozy from drugs and neural probing. They even let her keep the penguin-robot's stipend, the modest comfort and freedom from want that Bin's absence had earned.

Might other officials, even higher, feel differently? Mei Ling felt her nerves fray as she drew near the assigned coordinates. But what choice did she have, other than to do as authorities asked? They knew where she lived. They could cancel the shorestead contract, costing the small family everything. This meeting would be a "cup of tea, served with fear."

The guide arrow indicated another turn—to the right, this time—through a little retail alley. Responding to her skeptical squint, the spectacles presented a map overlay showing it to be a shortcut to the Boulevard of Vivacious Children's Mythology, famous for its robotic sculptures of beloved characters, from Journey to the West, to Snow White, to Fengshen Bang.

Perhaps I will get to glimpse Pipi Lu or Lu Xixi or Shrek, along the way, Mei Ling hoped. But first, to get there. . . .

She peered down the dim passage where old-fashioned, open-faced shops seemed to drop back in time, to an era when this sort of street could be found in every village and town. Especially before the Revolution, when four generations of a family would toil alongside each other, sharing cramped quarters over their store, while scrimping for one of the sons to get ahead. A traditional eagerness for advancement that she once heard cynically satirized in an ancient proverb.

First generation—coolie; save money, buy land
Second generation—landlords
Third generation—mortgages the land
Fourth generation—coolie

Weren't those nasty cycles supposed to be over by now? Finished certainly by the Revolution's centennial year? Mei Ling coughed into her fist, knowing one thing for certain.

Her son would be smart, educated, and she would teach him to be wise! *If we can get past trying times. . . .*

She started forward into the narrow street—when a voice interrupted.

"Honored mother should not go there."

Mei Ling stopped, glanced to both sides, and realized that she was the only clear-cut mother in sight. Peering toward where the words had come from, she found a figure sitting deep within a shadowed doorway. Her cheap specs tried to do image enhancement—though not very well—revealing a *child* perhaps twelve years old, wearing a faded green parka and some glasses that had been repaired with wire and generous windings of tape.

"Were you talking to me?"

Something about the youngster was odd. He rocked back and forth slightly and, while staring toward Mei Ling, his gaze slipped past hers, as if his eyes kept focusing on some far horizon.

"Mothers are the source of all problems and all answers."

Spoken in flat tones, it sounded like some kind of aphorism or saying. She now saw that he had bad teeth, a serious underbite, plus a rash along one side of his neck that looked ongoing. Clearly something was wrong with the boy.

"Um . . . pardon me?"

He stood and shuffled closer, still not looking directly at her face.

"Jia-Jupeng, your *mother* wants you to come home to eat."

Now *that* expression she had heard before. Something her parents' generation used to say to one another, to get a laugh, though Mei Ling never understood what was funny about it. Suddenly, she realized—this child must be a product of the Autism Plague. In other words, a modern parent's nightmare. Reflexively she turned a hip, moving her body to protect little Xiao En, even though the defect wasn't contagious.

Maybe not the disease. But luck can be.

She swallowed. "Why did you say that I shouldn't go down the alley?"

The boy reached toward her with both hands. For a second Mei Ling thought that he wanted to be picked up. Then she realized—*he wants my spectacles.*

Mei Ling felt one part of her try to pull away. After all, the policeman was someone she did not want to make impatient. Yet something about the boy's calm, insistent half smile made her instead bend over, letting him take the cheap device off her head. The smile broadened and his eyes met hers for less than a second—apparently as much human contact as he could stand at a time.

"The men," he said, "aren't here to buy soy sauce."

"Men?" She straightened, glancing around. "What men?"

Appearing to ignore the question, he turned the specs around, examining them, taking evident care not to let the scanners look closely at his own face. Then, with a laugh, he tossed them into a nearby garbage bin.

"Hey! I paid good—"

Mei Ling stopped. The boy was offering his own pair of glasses, with stems repaired by wire and tape.

"See them."

She blinked. This was crazy.

"See who?"

"Men. Waiting for a mother."

Without specs, he seemed to have a pronounced squint. The voice barely rose or fell in tone. "Let them wait. Mother won't come. Not today."

She didn't want to reach for the glasses. She didn't want to take them, or to turn them around, or to slip the stems over her ears. Especially Mei Ling did not want to find out who or what the child meant by "the men."

But she put them on and saw.

Now the alley was illuminated, down a tunnel that

seemed to penetrate through the sunless gloom, pushing
by several shops where tinkerers reforged metal jewelry, or
made garments out of real (if illicit) leather, or where one
family bred superscorpions for both battle and the table.
The glasses had looked simpler and more primitive than
hers. They weren't. She could make out the texture of the
jujube fruits that a baker was slicing for a pie, and somehow their *smell* as well.

Symbols swirled around the tunnel's rim—many of
them Chinese, but not all. They arrayed themselves not in
neat rows or columns, but spirals and surging ripples. She
tried to look at them. But this view was not hers to control.

Perspective suddenly jumped, flicking to some pennycam that was stuck to a wall halfway down the alley, just
above a little, three-wheeled *tuktuk* delivery van. The camera zoomed past the truck, whose motor was running, into
a small shop where Mei Ling saw an elderly woman hand-
painting designs on half-finished cloisonné pottery. The
artist seemed nervous, trembling and biting her tongue as
she bent over her work. Dipping her brush into a pot of red,
it came out shaking. Droplets fell as the brush approached
a fluted carafe she was working on.

Now the cam-view shifted again. Mei Ling suddenly
found herself looking through the very specs that the old
woman wore, seeing what she saw.

At first, that was only the tip of the paintbrush, filling in
the tail of a cartoon lobster—the ancient Disney character
who was a favorite companion of the Little Mermaid.
Though confined by cloisonné copper wire, the red paint
spread a bit too far, unevenly. Mei Ling heard a muttered
curse as the artist dabbed at the spillover . . . and glanced
jerkily upward for just a moment.

Toward the small van, parked just outside with its smoky
exhaust pipe—the driver was sitting idle with the door
open, smoking a cigarette. A bundle of twine on his lap.

A jittery glance again at the paintbrush, as it dipped into the red again. Then, the camera view jerk-shifted to the left, only briefly, but long enough for Mei Ling to glimpse a second man, burly and muscular, standing well back in the shadows, shifting his weight impatiently.

Without her bidding them to, the child's specs froze that image, amplified and expanded it, showing what the big fellow held in his hands. One clutched a bundle of black fabric. The other, a hypo-sprayer. Mei Ling recognized it from the crime dramas she often watched. They were used by cops to subdue violent criminals. And also . . . by kidnappers.

The view then returned to that seen by the elderly pot-painter. The old lady was looking at the carafe again. Only now her brush tip was defacing the gay, underwater scene with a single character in blood red. Mei Ling gasped when she read it.

Run.

Mei Ling tore off the specs, suddenly sweating, her heart beating in terror, certain beyond any doubt that this trap had been lain for her. But why? She was cooperating. Coming in of her own free will!

The answer struck home as obvious. There was no appointment at the nearest police station. That had been a ruse, with one aim—getting her to go down this alley.

Her mind whirled. What to do? Where to go? Maybe, if she went the other direction . . . kept to busy streets . . . tried phoning Inspector Wu.

"Mother comes this way," said the boy. He took her hand, tugging. "Cobblies are all over the place and bad men, too. In thirty-eight seconds they will know and give chase from all sides. But we know how to take care of mothers."

She stared at him, resisting. But the child smiled again, making another flicker-brief eye contact. "Come," he insisted.

"Time to run."

Then the moment of decision was in her past. They hurried together, away from that alley of danger, along a street that only a short time ago had seemed full of fantasies. Only now—she knew—it also contained dangerous eyes.

A RISING TIDE

The relative advantages of humans and machines vary from one task to the next. Imagine a chart with the jobs that are "most human" forming the higher ground. Here you find chores best done by organic people, like gourmet cooking or elite hairdressing. Then there is a "shore" consisting of tasks that humans and machines perform at equivalent cost, like meticulous assembly of high-value parts. Or janitorial work.

Beyond and below these jobs can be found an "ocean" of tasks best done by machines, such as mass production or traffic management. When machines get cheaper or smarter or both, the water level rises, as it were, and has two effects.

First, machines substitute for humans by taking over newly "flooded" tasks.

But the availability of new machine capabilities can also complement and expand the range of many human tasks, raising the value of doing them well. New opportunities for people sometimes erupt, like a fresh mountain, rising out of the sea.

—Robin Hanson, an emulated character in the websim play
Trilemma

36

FALSE DIAMONDS

A gong sounded, calling all guests into a banquet room the size of a private jet hangar. A personal, liveried attendant held the high-back, medieval Cistercian chair for Hamish, then hovered throughout the meal, refilling gold-rimmed crystal goblets and serving courses on plates made from vitrified lunar soil. (The famous dinner set Rupert Glaucus-Worthington commissioned when NASA's cache of moon rocks was auctioned to pay off debts.) It was all marvelously excessive, but he wondered most of all about the servants.

How on Earth can they do this?

It wasn't the cost. When you ranked seven or eight nines along the wealth curve, you could afford all the private help you wanted, for any task at all. No, it was *confidentiality* that couldn't be bought with money alone. The more people in any discussion, the more likely were leaks, from rumors to full-spectrum recordings. Despite clear ground rules for this occasion—along with Faraday shielding to keep out the World Mesh—anyone in this room *might* be carrying some newfangled device. In the game of leap-frogging technology, the rich could never be sure. A small startup company, or amateur smartposse, or even a pathetic legacy government might briefly get the upper hand.

Hamish pondered how the top clade families—the Glaucus-Worthingtons, the bin Jalils, the Bogolomovs, the duPont-Vonessens, the Wu Changs, and so on—could let so many participate in this meeting. Even if dinner table decorum kept most of the banter light, with the main topic set aside for tomorrow, someone was sure to drink too much and babble.

During soup, he conversed casually with a social psychologist from Dharamsala. But kept wondering. *Perhaps the servants get hypno-loyalty locks. Not legal in most places. But Switzerland and Liechtenstein never joined the EU. Or they may be paid in delayed futures options, invoked decades from now, only if fealty criteria are met.*

One approach—the Tata Method—had a touch of class. Find some rural village racked by poverty, disease, and hopelessness. Pour in enough money to transform the place—schools, hospital, jobs, and scholarships for bright youths. Nurture a local cult of gratitude. You get a reliable source of loyal and appreciative help. And some good publicity, too.

Or it might be accomplished the old-fashioned way. Blackmail. Betray us and we tell the cops what you did. Glancing at his personal waiter, Hamish figured the man looked plenty tough, under the silk uniform and unctuous attentiveness. Hamish tossed back some wine and, while his glass was being refilled, noted what might be faint signs of tattoo removal on the back of the servant's hand, perhaps indicating a rough past.

With specs, I might get a multicolor pattern analysis. But it's more fun putting together bits and pieces the old-fashioned way.

In fact, Hamish was having a great time, making mental notes for his staff to research and expand upon later. Readers and viewers loved stuff like this! Of course, his wealthy villain would have to be from some *other* circle of wealth. A Naderite tech-billionaire perhaps, or a rich mad scientist, or a member of some liberal cabal . . . certainly not anyone in the clade! Especially now that this elite of elites was lining up with Tenskwatawa.

Meanwhile, the sociologist to his left was blathering about the paper she planned to present tomorrow, on Neo-Confucian Pragmatic Ethics and the New Pyramid. Hamish felt so good, he refrained from asking where she cribbed the last part of her title.

"You see, Mr. Brookeman, as the Enlightenment fades, so will its diamond-shaped social structure—dominated by a large and vigorous middle class. That pattern fostered vibrancy and creativity, but also brittle flightiness. The kitschy culture and fickle habits that infested your forever-adolescent America."

Hamish responded with a courteous smile, which she mistook for deep interest, waggling delicately painted fingers. "That kind of social order is *unstable*. Too dependent on high levels of education, civility, confidence, and shared sense of purpose. As in ancient Athens and Florence, it's simple to incite the bourgeoisie to bicker over trivial matters. Just get them overreacting to one exaggerated threat, while ignoring others."

The sociologist seemed to be trying hard to keep Hamish's attention, smiling and tilting a little to restore connection, each time he lifted his gaze from his plate—now the fish course, a poached yellowtail, very expensive, with hints of real saffron. He politely obliged her with a steady gaze, noting she seemed rather more attractive than his first impression. Hamish took another swallow of wine and let the waiter refill his glass while she continued.

"As Plato taught, stable governance requires a broad base that narrows steeply to a small but superqualified ruling class, born and raised for leadership. The mode that post-agricultural civilizations adopt, ninety-nine percent of the time. Even under so-called Soviet Communism, power soon consolidated in a few hundred families of the *nomenklatura* caste—a classic feudal society, despite all its superficial egalitarian rhetoric."

Hamish wondered, *Does she imagine I don't know this?* While lazily nodding and maintaining eye contact, he sampled other conversations. Behind him, a Brazilian fertilizer magnate rehashed conjectures about the Alien Artifact that had become tiresome hours ago.

Meanwhile, across the table, a boffin from Tenskwata-wa's think tank was discussing *probability-weighted responsibility*—the notion that scientists and innovators should have to buy insurance or bonds to cover possible bad outcomes, ensuring they would pause and consider before charging ahead with risky experiments. A version of the Precautionary Principle—demanding that a burden of proof fall on those bringing change. An interesting alternative to the proposed <u>Science Juries</u>, this would let risk markets carry the burden of regulating progress, instead of policing it with a bureaucracy.

Clever, but a nonstarter, now that top families of the First Estate were joining renunciation. Tomorrow's oligarchs wouldn't use market methods. Bureaucracy was easier to control.

"So all signs point to reversion, back to a pyramid-shaped class structure. But *which kind* of social pyramid will it be?" asked the sociologist, thinking she had Hamish's undivided attention.

She's definitely flirting with me, Hamish decided.

"Well, yes, that's a good question," he replied, realizing that his tongue felt a bit thick. *The wine is too good. Honor it by sipping, not gulping.*

"Indeed!" She nodded vigorously, which jangled her gold (plated) necklaces. Her toothy smile seemed impossibly white and she was trying too hard, but Hamish started to find it, well, a bit endearing as she hurried on.

"Does our rising aristocracy really want to repeat the mistakes that drove common folk to rebel in 1789 France and 1917 Russia? What's it worth, to capture all the money and power, if it ends in a tumbrel ride to the chopping block?"

Hamish had an answer to that.

"Louis XVI and Czar Nicholas were inbred, mentally-deficient fools. Also, they didn't possess tomorrow's tools.

The proliferation of microcameras, throughout the world. Or unbeatable lie detectors."

Or—his inner voice added, without voicing it—*the arrival of true artificial intelligence. But let's not mention that third item, ensuring top-down control.*

"Well, you're right about that," she conceded. "Though at present, the cameras and truth machines are often as annoying to the First Estate as they are useful, shining light inconveniently upward as often as down."

"Yes, but all that's needed is to *break reciprocity,*" he answered. "By controlling information, making sure it flows one way. Take over the databases. Trump up panic situations, so the public will support paternalistic 'protections.' Make sure lots of privacy laws get passed, then bribe open some back doors, so elites can see it all anyway, and 'privacy' only protects them.

"Of course there's more to the program than that," Hamish continued, gaining momentum. "The smarty-pants knowledge castes will see what's happening and complain. So you propagandize a lot of populist resentment against the scientists and other professionals, calling them 'smug elites.' Finally . . . when the civil servants and techies have lost the public's trust, just cut the other estates out of the information loop, take complete control over the cameras and government agencies and voilà! A tyranny that lasts millennia!"

The woman stared at Hamish.

"Well, I wouldn't put it quite that—"

"The point is, when those at the top can see absolutely everything—how would any Lenin or Robespierre ever get started?"

While grinning and taking another drink, Hamish felt flush from his sudden, passionate spill of words. In truth, it had felt like delivering a movie plot pitch to some producer, spinning—in a matter of seconds—a wonderful, nefarious scheme that would make perfect sense on-screen. One that meshed with human nature and history, and that . . . well . . . in fact most of it was already under way in the modern world.

The sociologist blinked rapidly a few times.

"I'm not sure that *'tyranny'* is the word Plato would use."

Oops. Hamish was suddenly aware that others had turned to watch his outburst. *Damn. I got so into story mode, I wound up portraying the clade aristos as villains! My next step would have been to explain how a trio of quirky heroes might proceed to bring the whole edifice crashing . . . in less than ninety minutes of view-time.*

He worked at his plate while thinking. How to get out of this?

"No, of course not," he murmured after chewing and swallowing. "In fact, such perfect security would likely *lessen* the harshness of future rulers. No need for the iron-boot cruelty portrayed in that George Orwell novel. Why bother? Perfect rulers, all knowing and secure, would scarcely need brutality. They would, in fact, try for platonic paradise.

"But please," he urged, "go back to your point about how a pyramidal social order will be improved by Confucian ways."

She nodded, clearly as eager to get on track as he was to be quiet a while.

"As I was saying, Mr. Brookeman—"

With his most disarming smile, he reached over to touch her hand.

"Call me Hamish."

"Very well . . . Hamish." Her fine complexion changed hue and she smiled shyly, charmingly, before hurrying on. "Way back in the twentieth century leaders of Singapore and Japan, and then Great China, pondered non-Western ways to manage a complex modern society. Finding the occidental enlightenment far too brash and unpredictable, they cleverly designed methods to *incorporate* technology and science—along with limited aspects of capitalism and democracy—into a social order that also remained traditional and essentially pyramidal, without the chaos, friction, and unpredictability found in America or Europe. Much of their inspiration came from Asian history, which had much longer stretches of stable and noble governance than the West."

Yeah, sure, he thought while she kept talking. *But will any of this really matter when brainiac machines burst upon the scene? They'll have priorities. And first will be a humanity that is well ordered. Predictable. They won't try to exterminate or enslave us, though I've exploited that cliché many times, in books and films. No, they'll want us calm and ruled by our own kind, in ways they can easily model and guide.*

It had taken Hamish years to reach this conclusion, after decades spent loathing and resisting the notion of artificial minds. Only recently did he accept the inevitable. Especially when he realized—*Whatever logic applied to other elites will apply to the new AI lords. They'll want us to tithe resources to support their passions and goals. Beyond that, they'll want their human vassals to be content. Happy. Perhaps even imagining we're still in charge.*

Illusions like the one being spun by the alluring sociologist, who talked on—as a palate-clearing salad was consumed and cleared away, making room for the main course of farm-raised realbeef, deliciously tender and rare—about how the East Asian version of aristocratism was so much better than any other feudal order.

The sociologist appeared blithely unaware that Hamish's thoughts had split—part of him paying attention, another portion distantly contemplative, and a third greedily wondering what her body was like, under the silken sari.

"Even in olden times, the Confucians mixed deep conservatism and belief in hierarchy with the concept of *meritocracy.* The brightest children of the poor and merchant castes could sometimes *test* their way into higher levels of the pyramid, applying their talents to augment the prestige of their liege." She chirped a short, proud hiccup over the double rhyme, then took a quick sip of wine.

Hamish found amusing how her model interlaced with his own, though with one difference—that he knew what cool, cybernetic entities would sit, inevitably, at the very top of the social order, above even the First Estate. Still, this woman was *generally* on the right side . . . and more interesting than anybody else at this end of the table. And she was clearly smitten—most likely by his celebrity status.

Anyway, he decided to accept the inevitable by the time dessert arrived—an Earth-shaped medley that their host gleefully opened with a saber, exposing alternating layers of crusty pastry, gelato, and chocolate that, like the planet itself, terminated in a delightfully molten core.

Even later, though, as they staggered side by side, giggling, on their way to her room, Hamish remained partly detached—the same detachment that had kept Carolyn at a cool distance all those years, till she finally left. And even then, he could not stop picturing the AI minds deciding to formulate themselves as ideal Confucian mandarins. So serenely confident that they might tolerate and reward the best of those below. *Might the new uber-lairds allow a few humans to rise, through "merit" and join them, at the pinnacle? Perhaps as cyborgs, enhanced to operate at their level?*

It represented everything he had preached against for decades. Yet, to be honest, Hamish found his views shifting gradually. For there was also a strong temptation to *want* that destiny. The mad dream of the godmakers, its tug was undeniable.

If we handle the transition right, the New Pyramid will be smart, gracious, calm. People will have their elections, and other toys. Above them, aristos will maintain stability. And at the peak? Ais will slip into their top niche gracefully, with hardly a ripple.

Then, after a few centuries of tranquility, maybe we'll be ready to unbury that damned Havana Artifact from some cold, dark closet, and talk about the stars.

ENTROPY

Optimists offer evidence that things will be all right, like the fact that major war has been evaded—despite some burns and narrow scrapes—and that most individuals today know far more peace than their ancestors did. Even in this economy, hundreds of millions strive each day with real hope of climbing out of poverty, seeing their children healthier and better educated. Except in the *toxoplasma* hot zone, interpersonal violence is down again, on a per capita basis.

Yes, there are rumors and worried models predicting a coming conflagration—one between classes, rather than nation states. But who really yearns for such a thing to happen?

What if the optimists are right? Suppose we in this generation are—on average—growing *both smarter and more sane* at a decent clip. That average still leaves a billion human beings, out of almost ten billion, who are steeped in rage, or dogmatic rigidity, or delusional repetition of discredited mistakes. You know such people. Do you recognize those traits in some of your neighbors? Or perhaps that face in the mirror?

Remember that one harm-doer can wreck what took many hands to build. A thousand professionals may be needed, to counteract something virulent released by a single malignant software or bioware designer. It's not that sociopaths are smarter—they generally aren't. But they have the element of surprise, plus the brittleness of a society with many vulnerable points of attack.

Suppose the *ratio of goodness and skill* continues to rise— that each year far more decent and creatively competent people join the workforce than sociopaths. Will that suffice? Perhaps.

But then, imagine someone finds a simple way to *make black holes or antimatter* using common materials and wall current? Even if 99.999 percent of the population refrains, the crazy 0.001 percent might kill us all. And there are other scenarios—conceivable ways that one lunatic might outweigh all the rest of us, no matter how high a fraction are good and sane.

If the ratio improves, but the series doesn't converge, then there's no hope.

—*Pandora's Cornucopia*

37.
ARCHIPELAGO

Peng Xiang Bin really wanted to follow up on one comment that had been made by the alien entity within the worldstone. When shown images of the other interstellar messenger egg—the Havana Artifact being studied in America—Courier of Caution had made clear its disdain and hatred, calling the beings who dwelled inside that vessel *liars*.

Despite all the remaining translation problems, that word came through vividly and clear. It was intriguing and more than a bit chilling. Clearly Paul and Anna and the professor wanted to learn more about that, as well. But Dr. Nguyen insisted on sticking to their list of scheduled questions.

So, Bin concentrated on drawing another set of ancient

characters. When a completed line of figures floated across the surface of the egg-shaped thing, he also spoke the question aloud.

"How did you arrive on Earth?"

The reply came in two parts. While Courier of Caution painted ideograms and uttered antiquated words, an *image* took shape nearby, starting as night's own darkness. Anna Arroyo quickly arranged for an expanded version of the picture to billow outward from their biggest 3-D display, revealing a black space vista, dusted with stars.

In arch tones that seemed beautifully and appropriately old-fashioned, Professor Yang Shenxiu translated the ancient ideograms, aloud.

> *"Pellets, hurled from the homefire,*
> *Thrown by godlike arms of light,*
> *Cast to drift for time immeasurable,*
> *Through emptiness unimaginable . . ."*

One star, amid a powdery myriad, seemed to pulsate, aiming narrow, sharp twinkles outward. . . .

"Capture those constellation images!" Dr. Nguyen commanded, with no time for courtesy.

"I'm on it!" Menelaua snapped. His fingers left the animatronic crucifix hanging from his neck and waggled in the air with desperate speed, while the islander grunted and hopped in his seat.

Bin stared as several of the winking rays seemed to propel tiny dots in front of them. One of these zoomed straight toward his point of view, growing into a wide, reflective surface that loomed at those watching.

"Photon sail!" Anna diagnosed. "A variant on the Naka-mura design. Driven onward by a *laser,* at point of origin."

Bin grunted, amazed by her quickness—and that he

actually grasped some of her meaning! The space wind-jammer hurtled past his viewpoint, which swiveled around to give chase—and he briefly glimpsed a tiny, smooth shape dragged behind the giant sail, brilliantly radiant in the home star's propelling beam . . .

. . . which finally shut down, perhaps after many years, leaving just a natural glow from the original sun, a glitter that diminished as separation increased and decades passed in seconds. With no laser light to catch anymore, the diaphanous sail contracted, folding and collapsing into a small container at one end of a little egg, whose former brightness now faded, till it could only be made out as a seed-shaped ripple, starlit, hurtling at speeds Bin couldn't begin to contemplate.

"Neat trick with the sail," Paul commented. "Tuck it away, when it's not needed for propulsion or energy collection, so it won't snag interstellar particles. With bi-memory materials, it could expand or contract with very little effort. I bet they use it later to slow down."

Bin now grasped how the worldstone must have come across the incredible gulf between stars—a method sure to provoke feelings of kinship from this colony of wealthy yachting enthusiasts. At the same time, he wondered, *What would ancient peoples, in China or India, have made of these images?*

They would have thought in terms of gods and monsters.

How easy it would be, to chuckle over such naïveté. But, in fact, could anyone guarantee that modern humanity was advanced enough to understand, even now? In ways that mattered most?

Meanwhile, Scholar Yang's narration continued.

> *"Slow time passed while the galaxy turned,*
> *A new star loomed—its light, a cushion."*

The pellet turned around and redeployed its sail, which now took a gentler, braking push from a brightening light source ahead. *Our sun,* Bin realized. It had to be.

"Knew it!" the islander exulted. "Of course there's no laser at this end. So sunshine alone won't be enough."

As the star ahead grew from a pinpoint into a tiny, visible disc, a *new object* abruptly loomed in front of the worldstone—a great, banded sphere, replete with tier after tier of whirling, multicolored storms.

> *"Chosen beforehand—a giant ball waited,*
> *Ready to catch . . . pull . . . assist . . ."*

Yang Shenxiu's translation stumbled as, even with computer aissistance, he could only offer guesses. Well, after all, Courier had a limited useful human vocabulary. Ancient Indus and Chinese people knew very little about astronomy, planetary navigation and all that.

Just like me, Bin thought as the striped, cloudy ball approached rapidly.

"A gravity swing past Jupiter," Anna murmured in apparent admiration. "Like threading a microscopic needle across centuries and light-years. They had to time it perfectly."

The mighty gas planet swerved by, unnervingly fast, and the pellet, its sail billowed open, then plunged *past the sun* in a hairpin swerve before veering into black space. Far . . . far . . . until it paused at the end of a towering arc . . . then plummeted inward again, approaching the star from a different angle, filling the sail once more with torrents of light.

Paul interjected. "But it would still have loads of excess velocity. This needle must have been threaded many times, offering *multiple* swings past other planets, as well as Jupiter and the sun, again and again."

His appraisal was borne out, as the broiling solar sphere darted by, making Bin's eyes water. Just after nearest passage, the sail furled back into its container . . . and soon a smaller ball swung past, so close that Bin felt as if he were passing *through* the topmost of its churning, yellow clouds, while a brief, glowing aura surrounded the image.

"Atmospheric braking through the atmosphere of Venus. Dang! They'd need orbital figures down to ten decimals, in order to plan this from so far away, so long in advance."

Then, another sudden veer and gyre past Jupiter. . . .

"Yes, though it could make small, real-time adjustments, between encounters, by tacking with the sail," Anna replied. "Still they wouldn't arrange it in such detail without a destination in mind." She made her own rapid finger movements. "They had to know about Earth already. From instruments, like our LifeSeeker Telescope . . . only far more advanced. They'd know it had an oxygen atmosphere, life, nonequilibrium methane, possibly chlorophyll. Even so—"

Without shifting his transfixed gaze, Bin had to shake his head. There was no way that ancient peoples could have made anything of this, even if Courier showed them all the same images and told them about these worlds, named after their gods—or the other way around. Bin's head seemed to spin, nauseated, as the whirling, planetary dance went through several further encounters—more dizzying, gut-wrenching pirouettes—until the sense of pell-mell speed finally diminished. The pace grew sedate—if no less urgent. Then another dot approached, slowly, gracefully. Bin guessed which planet from its greenish-blue glitter.

"It must have intended to fine-tune its approach to Earth," Paul commented, "by gradually tacking on sunlight till entering a high, safe orbit, perhaps at a Lagrange point. Then it would spend some time—centuries—evaluating the situation. Maybe use the sail as a telescope mirror, to gather light and make detailed observations from a secure distance. Then wait."

"Wait . . . for what?" Anna was doubtful. "For the planet to produce space travelers? But, the temporal coincidence is incredible! To launch this thing, timed so it arrived only a few thousand years before we made it into space? How could they have known?"

Bin marveled how these skilled people grasped so much, so quickly. Even allowing for all of their fancy tools and aids. It was a privilege, just to be in such company.

Paul pressed his disagreement. "Anyway, how do we know there was anything special about the time they chose? Maybe these stone-things have been arriving at a steady rate, all across the last billion years, filling the solar system by now! We never surveyed the asteroid belt for objects anywhere near this small. That astronaut only happened to snag one that drifted into visible reach—"

"It's still an appalling coincidence," Anna persisted. "There has to be—"

"Comrades, please," Professor Yang Shenxiu urged, raising his eyes briefly from his own work station. "Something is happening."

The glitter of Earth had begun resolving itself into a dot, and then a ball, flecked with clouds and glinting seas. Only now, the storytelling image turned and zoomed in upon the star-traveling pellet. Once again, the little box at its front end opened, the sail re-emerging.

> *"At long last, the goal lay in sight,*
> *Now to approach gently and find a perch,*
> *To focus, study, and appraise,*
> *Then to sleep again and wait.*
> *Until a time of claiming,*
> *When allures are certain. Ready . . ."*

Only, this time, something went wrong. As the sail came out of its box, amid a glitter of sharp reflections, several of the lines abruptly snapped! One corner of the vast, luminous sheet dimpled inward. More lines crossed each other the wrong way. Bin blinked, feeling his gut clench as the sail rapidly fouled and collapsed, its slender cables knotted, spoiled.

"Evidently, something went badly wrong at the last minute," Paul commented, unnecessarily.

Bin found he could barely breathe from tension, watching a drama that had unfolded many millennia ago. He felt sympathy for the worldstone. To have traveled so far, and come so near success, only for all plans to unravel. Yang Shenxiu recited ideograms conveying Courier's sense of tragedy and dashed hope.

> "Failure! Luck evades us,
> While this globe reaches out,
> To cast my fate."

Bin glanced at the scholar, who seemed far away in time and space, his eyes glittering with soft laser reflections cast by his helper apparatus. Of course, the alien entity's florid vocabulary must have come from its long era spent with early humans, many centuries ago, in more poetical days.

> "Will Earth embrace me
> —in a fiery clutch?
> Or will she fling me outward,
> Tumbling forever—
> —in cold and empty space?"

Unable to maneuver even a little, the pellet let go of its uselessly clotted sail as the planet loomed close, swinging by, once . . . twice . . . three times . . . and several more . . .

From Paul's commentary, it seemed that some kind of safety margin was eroding with each orbital passage. Doom drew closer.

Then it came—the final plunge.

> *"So, it will be fire.*
> *Plummeting amid heat and pain,*
> *Destined for extinction . . ."*

Starting with deceptive softness, flames of atmospheric entry soon crackled around the image, accompanied by a roar that seemed almost wrathful. Bin realized, with a sharp intake of breath, that it would be just like the *Zheng He* expedition. He felt an agonized pang, as any Chinese person would . . .

. . . till new characters floated to jitter by the image-story in brushstrokes of tentative hope.

> *"Then, once again,*
> *Fate changed its mind."*

The grand voyage might have ended then, in waters covering three-quarters of the globe, an epic journey climaxing in burial under some muddy bottom. Or impacting almost anywhere on land, to shatter and explode.

Instead, as they watched the egg-artifact ride a shallow trail of flame—shedding speed and scattering clouds—there loomed ahead a white-capped mountainside! It struck the pinnacle along one snowy flank, jetting white spumes skyward and ricocheting on a shallow arc . . . then, rapidly, another angled blow, and another . . .

. . . till the ovoid finally tumbled to rest, smoldering, on the fringes of a highland glacier.

Heat, quenched by cold, melted an impression, much like a nest. Whereupon, soon after arriving in a gaudy blaze, the pellet from space seemed to fade—barely visible—into the icy surface.

Bin had to blink away tears. *Wow.* That beat any of the telenet dramas Mei Ling made him watch.

Meanwhile, archaic-looking ideograms continued flowing across the worldstone. Yang Shenxiu was silent, as distracted and transfixed as any of them. So Bin glanced at some modern Chinese characters that formed in the corner of his right eye. A rougher, less lyrical translation, offered by his own aissistant.

> *"This was not the normal mission.*
> *Nor any planned program."*

For once, none of the smart people said a thing, joining Bin in silence as spot-sampled snapshots seemed to leap countless seasons, innumerable years. The glacier underwent a time-sped series of transition flickers, at first growing and flowing down a starkly lifeless valley, carrying the stone along, sometimes burying it in white layers. Then (Bin guessed) more centuries passed as the ice river gradually thinned and receded, until retreating whiteness departed completely, leaving the alien envoy-probe stranded, passive and helpless, upon a stony moraine.

> *"But the makers left allowance,*
> *For eventualities unexpected."*

Appearing to give chase, grasses climbed the mountain, just behind the retiring ice wall. Soon, tendrils of forest followed, amid rippling, seasonal waves of wildflowers. Then time seemed to put on the brakes, slowing down. Single trees stayed in place, the sun's transit decelerated, unnervingly, from stop-action blur to a flicker, all the way down to the torpid movement of a shadow, on a single day.

Bin swayed in reaction, as if some speedy vehicle screeched to a sudden halt. Bubbles of bile rose in his throat. Still, he couldn't stop watching, or even blink . . .

. . . as two of the shadows moved closer . . .

. . . converging on a pair of *legs*—clad in leather breeches and cross-laced moccasins—entering the field of view in short, careful steps.

Then came a human hand, stained with soot. Soon joined by its partner—fingernails grimy with caked mud and ocher. Reaching down to touch.

PRICE OF CONTACT

Suppose we encounter those star-alien bredren an' sistren, an' nothing bad arises. Ya mon, it could happen.

Despite the long-sad list of ways that "First Contacts" went wrong on Earth—between human cultures, or when animal species first meet in nature—our encounter with ET may turn out right.

So look here, assume it ain't Babylon, out there. No one is trying to be nasty space-zutopong, or out to vank de competition with bad-bwoy bizness. No super wanga-gut seeks to devour everything in sight, or convert us to their galactic jihad. No deliberate or accidental viruses carried on those shiny beacons.

Further, say de advanced sistren an' bredren out there have solved so-many problems that vex us. That don't mean relax! For even among the civilized, life be dangerous if you don't know the rules.

Question, dear frens. What be the most common peaceful activity in most societies, other than raising food an' kids? *Commerce*. Buying, selling an' trading. I have plenty of what you waan and you have what I need. Shall we both benefit by striking a deal?

Oh, sure, in some utopian sci-fi a stoosh-cornucopia quenches all desires. May it be so! Still, won't one thing be always in demand? *Information*—supplying interstellar bredren wit' new concepts an' visions. Art, music, literature. A human lifetime ago, the Voyager probe carried a disc filled with Earth culture. No one thought to slap that album wit' a *price tag.*

Oh my frens remember, nice-up pure *altruism* is a *recent concept,* so rare, in nature. What be far more common—even among wild creatures—is *quid pro quo.* You do for me an' I do for you. Through history an' even among animals the rule is not *"Be generous."*

No. The rule is *"Be fair."*

Nice as he may be, ET will surely do commerce. If we ask 'im questions, he may reply—"We got whole-heaps of answers!"

Den him say—"So. What do you humans offer in exchange?"

All we have is ourselves—art, music, books, drama, an' culture. Humanity's treasure. But dat's de first thing foolish folks will beam out—for Free! An' dat so-admirable rush to impress our neighbors could be the worst mistake of all time.

Perhaps they be nice. They may understan' fairness. But who *pays* for a *free gift*? History may speak of no *bloodclot* traitors worse than those who, with best intentions, cast our heritage to the sky, impoverishing us all, puttin' us in Babylon.

—from *The Eternal Quest,* by Professor Noozone

38.
THE UPWARD PATH

Following close behind a trio of dolphins, Hacker entered the mysterious, suboceanic dome via a broad tunnel that passed underneath the habitat, kicking his way toward a glow at the far end. Soon, an opening appeared, ahead and above—a portal pool, where the sea was kept at bay by air pressure within the habitat.

Even before broaching the pool's surface, he found the artificial environment somehow odd. He was by now used to seeing only by sun and moon and stars, so the glare of artificial lighting seemed both familiar and . . . *old,* like faintly recalled memories from another decade, or another life. Hacker paused, without knowing why, feeling almost reluctant to continue.

Come on, he told himself. *This is it. The way home.*

And yet, after—how long?—wandering at sea with a tribe of strange cetaceans, Hacker found himself unable to quite picture what the word denoted. Home. Was it really somehow correlated with that stark dazzle up ahead? The brilliance of LER panels, beckoning him to rise just a couple more meters, and thereupon rejoin the human world. For some reason, their glitter brought him to the verge of sneezing.

He suppressed that impulse, which would splatter his faceplate. Still, it was only when one of the dolphins turned in puzzlement—scanning him with a sonar glyph that seemed like a question mark—that Hacker finally gathered himself, pushed aside all uncertainty and kicked hard, rocketing to the surface, sending splashes across a nearby set of low, metal stairs.

Spy-hopping upward, he peered around. No people were in sight. Banks of lockers and cabinets lined the walls, along with hooks for tools and diving equipment, though most were bare.

More dolphins arrived, lifting their heads to look around, emitting low chutters that his jaw implant conveyed into audible impulses. From experience, he interpreted the meaning as *sadness.* Disappointment.

But over what?

One big male—Hacker called him Michael, because he was a master with the net—patiently rolled in circles while a couple of others unwound the fishing mesh from his body. Hacker moved over to help them string it onto a rack, ready for re-use, later. He also noticed other objects in that corner of the pool. Rings and hoops and balls and such. Only he didn't hang around to learn their purpose. Hacker now had a clear and different destination in mind.

Kicking over to the stairs, he touched their rough surface with a gloved hand . . . which abruptly *grabbed* one of the steps, with a sudden intensity that surprised him, clutching it, unwilling to let go . . . as if in fear that the textured aluminum might be an illusion. Tremors passed up and down his body and a sigh escaped, that might have been a moan. A couple of minutes passed while he was in that state. Fog in his helmet—or tears in his eyes—made it hard to see.

Evidently, if part of him felt reluctance to return to civilization, there were other portions that really, really wanted to go back! To the world of men and women and solid ground and soft beds and lovely, artificial things.

Prying his fingers free, at last, he pulled on the stair with both arms, swiveled onto his back, and managed to haul his body's bulk upward, onto one of the steps, to sit up for the first time in . . . a long time. It felt strange not to have to work hard, just to keep his head and shoulders out of the water.

With a moist splat, his draidlocks—the gill fronds surrounding his helmet—collapsed, no longer supported by seawater. Of course, that also meant they weren't supplying oxygen, anymore. Quickly his rapid breathing started turning the air stuffy inside his helmet.

Cautiously, Hacker fumbled at the faceplate seal, managed to crack it open, and sniffed . . . then opened it wide. There was a slightly stale-musty aroma and faint metallic tang inside the habitat, but he'd lived through much worse. At least, now he could really look around.

No people. That was the most obvious fact. No humans

anywhere in sight. Given how cheap it was to set up a sensor-Mesh, wouldn't someone have been alerted, by now, that an unexpected visitor was here, and come to investigate?

Unless they think I'm just another dolphin.

Then there was the absence of human-generated noise—no jabber of speech or purposeful mechanical rhythms. But of course, Hacker reminded himself, he *wouldn't* hear any. All of a sudden he felt acutely the lack of normal, aural sound. Below the waterline, his jaw implant had seemed appropriate and fitting—it had been key to unlocking dolphin speech, in fact. Only now, in open air, he kept trying to yawn and shake his head, as if doing so might clear the deafness of his eardrums, which had been clamped so long ago, before the ill-fated rocket launch.

That's got to be fixed right away, if they have facilities here. Even before a bath.

Suddenly, a hundred aches started shouting at him, sores and twinges and awful *itches* that he must have somehow managed to ignore, till this very moment, for the simple reason that he could do nothing about them. Now, they began shouting for attention. Especially a tightness around his head that suddenly felt like a vise. Pawing desperately at clasps and vrippers, Hacker tore away the seals that held his trusty helmet—the apparatus that had saved his life—detaching it from the rest of his survival suit. When it came free, he hurled the headgear away, like something loathsome. Then the gloves. And, for a few moments, he luxuriated in the simple act of touching, rubbing, scratching, even caressing his own, stubble-ridden face.

Okay, get up. Get moving. Find the owners of this place. Get help . . . and remember to try to be nice. That last part was in order to be sure that old, nasty habits would not surge to the surface—the impatience of a spoiled brat. Perhaps this new, mature perspective was only a temporary thing. An artifact of his time spent with the Tribe. It did seem, somehow, to be long overdue. Or, at least, a novelty worth trying out.

Standing was too much to ask of his body. So, he scooted backward and up the next stair, bracing both arms to slide up the next one, and so on, till at last he sat on the deck surrounding the entry pool, and only his flippered feet remained immersed. For a couple of minutes he just sat, breathing heavily from just that much exertion.

Okay, let's find . . . he stopped.

Upon turning halfway around, Hacker found himself facing a large, hand-scrawled sign that had been propped up in front of the pool, sure to confront any new arrivals.

Project Uplift Suspended!
Court costs ate everything.
This structure is deeded to our finned friends.
May they someday join us as equals.

There followed, in smaller print, a WorldNet access number, and a legal-looking letter. Hacker had to squint and blink away drying salt to read a few lines. But it seemed to verify that queer statement—the little dolphin clan actually owned this building—which they now used to store their nets, some toys, and a few tools.

Hacker now understood the meaning of their plaintive calls, when they arrived to find no one home. The real reason they kept coming back. Each time, they hoped to find that their "hand-friends" had returned.

Project Uplift? He pondered, while laboring to pull off the body-hugging suit, wincing as it dragged past sores and chafed spots. *The name is familiar. I . . . heard something about it.*

One of the dolphins—old Yellowbelly—came over to

eye Hacker, emitting a burst whose meaning seemed much less clear to Hacker, now that his jaw was out of the water.

"I'll be back," he assured the old-timer, holding up one hand in promise.

It took great effort to get up onto his knees. Then, leaning on the stair rail, he managed to rise onto both feet. It wasn't so much lack of strength—he had been working his legs hard for quite some time and his thigh muscles bulged—as a problem of balance. No other species on Earth demanded such fine motor control as humans required, just to keep from toppling over. He would need some time to get the hang of it again.

Unsteady on rubbery legs, Hacker clung close to the walls and cabinets as he shuffled away from the pool, into a long corridor, stopping to look into each chamber along the way. They were laboratories, mostly. The first time he found a sink with a freshwater tap, he turned it on full blast and immersed his head, then drank greedily until he felt bloated. It took an act of forceful will to stop . . . to move away and resume exploring.

In the third room, he recognized a gene-splicing apparatus made by one of his own companies. And, all at once, his mind connected the dots.

Project Uplift. Oh yes. I remember.

A year or two ago—both professional and amateur media swarmed over a small cabal whose secret goal had been to *alter* several animal species, with the ultimate aim of giving them human-level intelligence.

Foes of all kinds had attacked the endeavor. Churches called it sacrilegious. Eco-zealots decried meddling in nature's wisdom. Tolerance fetishists demanded that native "dolphin culture" be left alone, without cramming parochial human values down their throats, while others rifkined the proposal, predicting mutants would escape the labs to endanger humanity.

One problem with diversity in an age of amateurs was that your hobby might attract ire from myriad others, especially from those with a particular passion of their own—indignant disapproval. And a bent for litigation.

This "uplift project" perished in the rough-and-tumble battle that ensued. A great many modern endeavors did.

Survival of the fittest, he mused. *An enterprise this dramatic and controversial has to attract strong and determined support, or it's doomed.*

Exploring the next laboratory, Hacker at last found what he was looking for—a cheap *joymaker* multiphone that someone had left behind, tossed amid a pile of trash. Though it seemed broken at first, a simple cleaning of the battacitor pohls and it turned on! A simulated female face appeared on the pullout slide-screen, moving its mouth in a welcoming statement that Hacker could not hear, but whose meaning was obvious—offering basic service, even if the unit no longer linked to any personal or corporate accounts.

Ah, but was there a connection to the Mesh, under the sea? Certainly, Project Uplift must have had comm links, even from down here. But were they still active and accessible?

Laboriously, he fumbled across the screen, managing to tactile the right clickable and pull out an old-fashioned alphabetical touchpad. With fingers that felt like sausages, he typed:

CAN I CALL MAINLAND?

The kind-looking female face vanished, replaced by stark letters that scrolled by in harsh, 2-D fonts.

DIAGNOSTIC UNDERWAY . . .

. . . CABLE LINK TO TRINIDAD MAIN UNDERSEA TRUNK HAS BEEN SOFT-DISCONNECTED.

SHALL I PULSE A REQUEST FOR EMERGENCY RECONNECT?

Hacker answered with a simple "Y"—hoping the joymaker would take it to mean Yes.

PULSING. . . . THIS MAY TAKE SOME TIME FROM FIVE MINUTES TO SEVERAL HOURS PLEASE BE READY WITH PAYMENT

Hacker grunted wondering what to do, if and when a connection was established. It should be possible to craft a message, built from simple text characters, invoking emergency-Samaritan rules, along with a promise that the call's recipient—his mother—would cover all charges. That seemed dreadfully archaic and convoluted, from using spelled-out letters to quibbling over payment. But the thing really giving Hacker pause was something else entirely.

A text emergency message . . . it gives an impression I need hurried rescue . . . when I've really rescued myself.

Well . . . the dolphins helped, a bit.

Still. Here he was, with food, water, comfortable quarters, and the option of simply heading for the nearby beach, if it came to that, and then walking to civilization. So, why send the equivalent of SOS smoke signals, or scrawling *"HELP"* in the sand? Maybe it was foolish pride, but that seemed wrong, somehow, after coming so far.

Better that I make a call that seems as normal as possible. All casual-like, paying charges by biomet ID. Make it seem like I'm in complete control. Hi. How you been? And oh, and by the way, could you send a copter-sub out this way?

He thought he knew how to do that. Use some of the tools in that last laboratory to create a tap from the joymaker to the sonic implant in his jaw. It shouldn't be too hard. Just replicate the same circuit link he had used aboard the suborbital rocket. The most important parts were right in his helmet, back at the pool.

While I'm at it, why not get in some real food? Even the canned stuff he had spied earlier, left on shelves in the galley, would be a welcome break from raw fish. Spitting out scales and bones.

And take a bath . . . maybe even a nap?

Hacker's mood was so different from the frenzy he might have expected, from being so close to contact with human civilization. And yet, he felt this was right.

TAKE YOUR TIME, he told the primitive, obsolete multiphone, typing carefully on the tactile screen.

I WILL CHECK AGAIN IN A FEW HOURS.

ENTROPY

Suppose the threat comes from human nature—some obstinate habit woven in our genes. Might science offer a way out, through deliberate self-improvement? First we'd have to admit that we *have* a nature.

Take the argument over *evolutionary psychology.* EP claims we all inherit patterns from prehistoric times—that long epoch when domineering males gained extra descendants because they were powerfully competitive, or jealous, or good at deception. Monarchy and feudalism heaped more rewards on any king who could talk thousands of virile men into marching and fighting to protect *his* seraglio. We're all descended from the harems of fellows like Charlemagne and Genghis Khan, who mastered that trick.

Opponents of EP argue we're more than the sum of our ancestors. They cite our vaunted flexibility, the way we learn and reprogram ourselves, as individuals and cultures. Each sex can do almost anything that the other does, and rules that limited opportunity because of caste, race, or gender have proved baseless. Indeed, our greatest trait is adapting to new circumstances, attaining improbable dreams.

Only, starting from this truth, critics puritanically claim that evolutionary psychology might be used to *excuse bad conduct,* letting rapists and oppressors cry "Darwin made me do it!" Hence, for political reasons, they claim people have *no* hardwired social patterns, or even leanings, at all.

What, none? No matter how contingent or flexible? Are we so perfectly *unlike* every other species on Earth? Isn't that what religious fundamentalists claim? That we have nothing in common with nature?

Can we afford simpleminded exaggerations, in either direction? In order to survive, humanity must overcome so many old, bad habits. We must study those ancient patterns—not in order to make excuses, but to better understand the raw material of Homo sapiens.

Only then can we look in the mirror, at evolution's greatest marvel, and say, "Okay, that's the hand we're dealt. Now let's do better."

—*Pandora's Cornucopia*

39.
TOUGH LOVE

Envoy to aliens. It had more romantic appeal than his old job as a space garbage collector. Suddenly, Gerald was the hit of his affinity groups.

Cicada Lifeloggers already gave every astronaut free biograph-storage—geneticodes, petscans, q-slices, and all that—in exchange for wearing a recording jewel in orbit. Now they wanted him to put on their omni-crown, a hot-hat guaranteed to see what he saw, hear what he heard, and store his surface neuroflashes down to petabytes per second!

"So much data that future folk may craft brilliant Gerald Livingstone models. Hi-res versions of you—recreating this historic moment in resplendent detail!" The Cicada

rep apparently thought immortality consisted of being replayed at ultrafidelity by audiences in some far-off era.

But then, Gerald pondered, *how can I tell I'm experiencing this for the first time? Wouldn't any such future emulation think it's me? Even these very thoughts—fretting over
whether I'm an emulation? Even my memories of breakfast
may be "boundary conditions." The real world could be
some amusement nexus in the ninety-third century . . . or a
kid's primitive ancestors report for her fifth-millennium
kindergarten class . . . or else some god-machine's passing
daydream.*

Yet, the Cicada guy expressed envy! As a "historical figure," Gerald's chance for this kind of resurrection—seemed
rather high. But the reasoning could easily get circular, or
collapse into sophistry. Was this like the depressing religious doctrine of predestination? Your fate already written
by an all-powerful God?

*Anyway, what if this First Contact episode goes horri-
bly wrong? Suppose I'm remembered as the fool or Judas
who opened the door for a new kind of evil. Might future
folk create simulations in order for villains of the past to
suffer . . . or seem to?* Worse, Gerald pictured the supercy-
borg equivalent of a future bored teenager, observing this
capsule of make-believe reality, nudging his pals and saying: *"I love this part! This is where Livingstone actually
tries to imagine us! Picturing us as callous, pimple-faced
adolescents of his own era. What a pathetic software
lump! Maybe next time, I'll hack in and make him trip on
the stairs."*

Gerald felt his thoughts veer away from such questions.
Perhaps because they were futile. Or else maybe he was
programmed not to dwell on them for long. *Ah well.* He
turned Cicada down.

The Church of Gaia: Jesus-Lover Branch wanted Gerald
to offer an online sermon for next Sunday's prayoff against

the CoG: Pure-Mother Branch. Some fresh insights could help tip the current standings. They especially wanted to know—from his contact with the Artifact entities—did any of the aliens still know a state of grace? Like Adam and Eve before the apple? Or, if they had fallen, like man, had they also received an emissary of deliverance—a race savior—of their own? If so, were their stories similar to the New Testaments? And if not . . .

. . . then what did Gerald think of the notion—spreading among Christians—that humanity must accept a new obligation? A proud duty to go forth and spread the Word?

In other words, now that we know they're out there— trillions of souls wallowing in darkness—is it our solemn mission to head across the galaxy delivering Good News? At least it was a more forward-looking dogma than his parents' relished obsession—praying for a gruesome apocalypse and eternal torment for all fools who recite the wrong incantations. Still, he turned down the sermon, promising the CoG: JeLoB folks to ask the Artifact entities about such matters, when the right moment arose.

For all I know, "join us" could mean "enlist in our religion—or face an interstellar crusade." I can't wait to find out.

The list of requests was too long to cope with . . . unless the aliens offered some fantastic new way to copy yourself. Now *that* would be useful tech!

The proposal that rocked him back should have been good news. Suddenly, his spouses seemed interested in bedtime. All of them. Even Francesca, who had never liked Gerald very much. "We miss you," they said, in messages and calls. More attention than he normally got from the group marriage. In fact, all seven offered to come visit him "in this time of stress."

Joey, Jocelyn, and Hubert even volunteered to sign waivers and enter quarantine with him! The offer was flattering.

Tempting. Especially since Gerald always felt an outsider, at the periphery of their little clan, long suspecting they proposed to him for the prestige of an astronaut husband. Perhaps the best sitch that a cool-blooded and off-kilter fellow like him could hope for.

He messaged back—"You've all got jobs, duties. Kids. Just keep in touch. I'll see you in my dreams."

Anyway, things were getting busy again. The *deprivation experiment* had been making progress, much to Gerald's surprise. His discovery—the so-called Livingstone Object—was starting to respond.

"Thousands of years drifting between the stars—you'd think that would've taught these aliens patience," Genady Gorosumov commented, after the third day. "I was afraid they'd wait us out. Call our bluff. They must know we're under pressure."

The slim Russian biologist nodded toward the observers' gallery, just beyond a barrier of smoky glass, where almost a hundred experts, delegates, and VIPs looked down upon the quarantined Contact Commission and its work. Many of those dignitaries were sharply unhappy about the team's current endeavor—to *starve* the Artifact entities into cooperating.

"But much to my surprise, our carrot-and-stick approach seems to be working," Genady concluded. "Clearly, they're getting worried in there."

He pointed at the opalescent ovoid, which still lay in its cradle, only no longer bathed in artificial sunshine. A soft fog surrounded its base, where coils now sucked away heat energy, leaving both the egglike object and its nest chilled much closer to the temperature of space. Gerald sensed coldness whenever his hand drifted near.

With the chamber dimmed, the rounded cylinder's former sheen faded and grew dull, Even more telling, the perpetual roil of images—planetary scenes and cityscapes and jostling figures—slowed from a frenetic maelstrom to languid, even desultory. The creature-entities seemed to droop with each passing hour.

"All right, let's put them through another cycle," said General Akana Hideoshi. She nodded to the expert in operant conditioning—animal behavior and training—they had hired from the Kingdom of Katanga, Patrice Tshombe, who moved almost jet-black hands across a series of holographic controls that glowed just in front of him, floating above the conference table.

Overhead, a projector issued a sudden lance of sharp illumination, like a jolt straight from the sun. Where it struck the grayish-colored stone, clouds abruptly roiled, like milk stirred into coffee. Soon, shapes moved through that inner mist, as if hurrying upward, clambering toward the light from some distance below. By now, Gerald and the others recognized forty-seven distinct alien species. Genady had constructed sophisticated bio-skeletal models, from the hawk-faced centauroid to the floating squid-thing, to a creature with four leathery wings surrounding a central mouth, resembling a cross between a bat, a helicopter, and a starfish.

Those three were the first to arrive, on this occasion . . .

. . . but only just ahead of other shapes that pushed in, close behind. To Gerald, it seemed like a crowd gathering at the sound of a dinner bell, thronging close, eager for sustenance. Each of the aliens pressed an appendage of some kind toward the glowing surface separating two worlds, whereupon small flurries of letters and words swirled around each point of contact.

Even with the help of computers, only primitive meanings could be parsed out of the jumbled tornado of conflicting, jostling phrases. Once in a while the messages congealed, mostly to repeat the now ironic invitation—**Join Us.**

Gerald had been wondering for days. *What "us"?*

From the second row, heads of various kinds lifted high, in order to crane over the trio in front; one of them looked somewhat insectoid, atop a slender, stalklike neck. Another was like a jolly, rotund Buddha, standing next to one who raised an arm that resembled an elephant's trunk, only with a hand at the end—a hand with *eyes* at the base of all six fingers. These latecomers plucked at the first three, at first tentatively, then with growing insistence.

"They behave like French or Chinese," commented Emily Tang. "Proudly refusing the indignity of taking turns or standing in line. It seems a pity that we are forcing them to become something else. British—or even Japanese. Tame acceptors of the tyranny of the queue."

Haihong Ming—their member from the Central Kingdom—laughed aloud, and Akana Hideoshi offered a grim chuckle. But Ben Flannery, their anthropologist from Hawaii, looked at Emily, clearly puzzled and offended by her cultural bias. Emily shrugged. "Hey, just because it was my idea to teach them discipline, that doesn't mean I don't empathize. Right now, their fractious pushiness has a certain schoolyard charm. Even if it makes communication damn near impossible."

Watching the rabble of aliens closely, Tshombe put up with a bit of squeezing and elbowing. But when several newcomers joined forces to shove the bat-creature aside, pushing their way up front, Patrice waved a curt hand and the overhead sunbeam cut off, leaving the stone once again in darkness. Compressors kicked in, activating heat pumps below the tabletop, as the stone was given a sudden taste of bone-deep chill.

"Now, boys and girls and whosits," murmured Emily, with evident enjoyment. "Learn to behave."

Patrice brought up the beam again, as soon as the jostling stopped. With scalpel precision, he centered it upon the centauroid and squid, leaving the newcomers tasting only a penumbra.

"I have had better training response from otters," Tshombe grunted in his deep Frafricaans accent. "But clearly there is progress. The rate curves are improving."

While several more of these cycles repeated, Gerald glanced over his shoulder at the "peanut gallery" beyond the quarantine glass—a slanted arena of plush VIP seats, where dignitaries and experts scrutinized every move the contact team made, aissisted by the very best tools, consultants, and instrumentalities that money could buy.

The advisers now also had a presence on *this* side of the quarantine barrier, lurking just a few meters to Gerald's right—a luminous, 3-D figure named Hermes, complete with chiseled features, golden robes, and matching hair— who appeared to pace back and forth at the far end of the table, glaring at General Hideoshi's team with growing frustration.

Why on Earth did the advisers pick that garish thing to serve as their liaison metaphor? Gerald wondered. *Do the politicians and professors and aristocrats think Akana will be intimidated by a cartoon Olympian god?*

Maybe it wasn't a deliberate choice. Often a group's avatar was selected by interpolating some trait that all members had in common. Did this golden god signify that the advisers viewed themselves as . . . an *elite*?

Or it might just be overcompensation. *Unconsciously, they want humanity to look its very best.*

Even so, Hermes was way over the top. Impatience manifested in a furled brow as the ersatz Greek god drummed the tabletop with lambent fingertips, pausing now and then to scribble suggestions or chidings that he kept sliding across the table, to join a pile of shiny virts—messages that Gerald and the main team mostly ignored. Something about Hermes bugged Gerald. The synthetic Olympian's fizzing frustration seemed all too similar to that of the Artifact aliens.

Unlike the main sci-fi stereotypes—extraterrestrials who were portrayed as aloofly superior, or cutesy-wise, or threatening—it does seem endearing and reassuring to find them behaving like disorganized schoolyard brats.

Unless . . . that reassurance is part of an act.

At the opposite end of the long conference table lurked another ai construct—Emily's feline holvatar counterpart, *Tiger,* dedicated to paranoid suspicion, though just as much a caricature as Hermes. Gerald sometimes caught the two artificial beings glaring at each other past the real members of the Contact Team.

And yes, I can see another parallel. Are Tiger and Hermes really at odds? We have no idea if ais really do compete with each other on our behalf. Or whether that, too, may be a ruse, some reassuring role-playing for the sake of the rubes.

Half a dozen more cycles followed, as Patrice played his artful game of rapid rewards and punishments, with the Artifact wallowing in periods of chilled darkness, punctuated by intervals of sharp light and focused heat. Gradually, the Katangan expert began humming, while nodding contentedly. "I think they are starting to get the idea," Patrice said. "Look closely."

Gerald's privileged position gave him a close-up view. First to become visible was the squidlike being, still front and center, waving forward a single tentacle, stroking the interface between two worlds. Only this time the centauroid and bat-like creature weren't jostling to share the forwardmost position. Rather, they had taken up positions side by side, on the left facing *away* from the squid . . .

. . . and Gerald saw purpose in their actions. Those two were now actively blocking others in the crowd from coming closer. Nor were they alone in this effort. To the right, Gerald saw three others—including the Buddha-like figure—performing a similar role, preventing interference from the unruly rabble on that side. Moreover, as Tshombe's energizing beam selectively made contact with the defenders, they seemed to grow more solid and distinct. Stronger and more capable of holding their ground.

In the center, chains of letters spiraled outward from that single tentacle. This time, words unrolled without jumble or interference, proceeding distinctly enough to activate the sonic interface. A voice emerged, sounding raspy and upset.

> **... we have come in friendship ... across the vast and empty desert ... with an offer of ultimate value ... so why do you torment us?**

Akana sighed with evident satisfaction.

"Okay, Gerald. You're on."

He leaned forward. No longer was it necessary to write directly on the ovoid surface with a pointed finger. Not so long as he enunciated clearly, speaking directly at the stone-from-space.

"We find your chaotic behavior disturbing," he said. "While we appreciate the value of diversity, we require some degree of orderliness—or courtesy—if this conversation is to get anywhere. That can happen in either of two ways."

He paused, as the linguistic adviser had recommended, if things ever got to this phase. Better to let the aliens ask. After several more seconds, the being that resembled a terrestrial cephalopod did just that. A slender tendril wrote—and the audio speakers interpreted—

> **What two ways?**

Gerald spoke slowly and clearly.

"Either by taking turns, letting each individual have an allotted time to converse with us . . . or else by appointing one or more among you to represent the whole community.

"Frankly, we'd prefer *both* methods. But first the representative. It is time, at last, to clarify the nature of your mission here and what great commonwealth we are being invited to join."

Sucker-tipped tendrils churned and writhed.

I recall . . . we used to do things . . . that way . . .

Gerald nodded, as did Ben and Emily. One theory held that the aliens' disorderly behavior was the natural outcome of eons spent in isolation, drifting through space. A stupefying test of endurance that might demolish any former sanity.

I shall endeavor to persuade the others to . . . cooperate.

The squidlike being turned—the centauroid and batthing and Buddha and insectoid revolved to face it, as if intending to talk things over—

—and the scene began to dissolve into confusion, once more, as some on the periphery formed a wedge, joining forces to power their way through, driving hard to get into the foreground.

"Cut it off!" Akana commanded. The Artifact was plunged again into dark chill.

I hope the thing's crystal structure can stand these wild swings of hot and cold, Gerald thought. *It never had to deal with such rapid oscillations in space.* The advisory icon, Hermes, had made that very point, at length.

Gyrating clouds could still be seen, agitated by dim figures, grappling in the virtual depths underneath the

Artifact's surface. So vigorous was the action at first, that Gerald worried. Might emulated beings do actual damage to each other, maybe even cause death? It certainly happened in some human-designed game worlds.

"They're slowing down," he commented.

The brief tussle did seem to quickly sap whatever skimpy energy reserves remained in there. Through the mist, they saw the figures let go of each other and start to slump. Gerald leaned closer and squinted. After a minute, he diagnosed.

"I think . . . I think some of them are *talking* to each other."

"Now," said General Hideoshi. "Ramp up the sunlamp to ten percent, Patrice. Reward this."

"I shall do so," Tshombe replied. "With great care."

The beam returned, and Gerald saw it break into components, each shining where a cluster of alien figures appeared—at some distance—to engage in conversation. While Gerald watched, these groups seemed to gain strength and animation. When a couple of them broke up, it was only to reconfigure, as individuals moved on to engage others.

"Could it actually be working?" asked Genady Gorosumov, who had been skeptical about this approach.

"Perhaps they are rediscovering a knack they had forgotten, during the long, dull voyage across so many light-years," commented Ben Flannery. "After all, it must take a lot of cooperation—and courtesy—to maintain a vast and ancient civilization. What we have been seeing may be the behavior of brilliant and civilized minds, when they are far from their best, still drowsy, not yet fully roused from a long, cold sleep."

It was a good theory. In fact, the most popular one. Still, Emily Tang seemed to enjoy tweaking Ben now and then. "So, we're like the nurse who slaps you hard, for your own good? To get a lazy slug-a-bed to wake up?"

Flannery frowned. But any retort was cut off when Tshombe said—

"*Regardez, mes amis!* A delegation, at last. It arrives."

All eyes turned to the Artifact—or nearby amplification screens—where something was clearly happening. A formation of more than a dozen alien figures approached through mists that now obediently parted, leaving them a clear path forward. And behind that group came another, even larger contingent, keeping what seemed a respectful distance.

Well, Gerald noted. *They do seem to have finally got their act together.*

Now, at last, we may get the full story.

Who would think that the biggest problem of First Contact would turn out to be one of personality. Of disorganization. Or immaturity.

But perhaps the worst is behind us, now.

PESSIMISM

According to the Medea Hypothesis, many of Earth's mass extinctions were perpetrated by life itself.

Sure, the dinosaurs were wiped out by a random asteroid. Some other die-offs came from impacts or volcanic activity. Yet, Earth's greatest calamity—the Kirschvink Glaciation of 650 million years ago, when ice covered the whole planet from pole to equator—was caused by sea algae pumping oxygen into the air while depleting CO_2, plunging Earth into a deep freeze. And life—human civilization—may be doing the opposite right now. Our greenhouse overheating shows there are limits to the biosphere's famed ability to self-correct.

Life can get out of hand, as when cancer cells destroy the organism that nurtures them. So, is that humanity's analog? "Cancer" to the living globe? Was Earth's recent die-off in diversity and biomass wrought by life's own "biocidal" ten-dency? What if the Medea Hypothesis extends beyond this planet, to all living worlds?

On the other hand, life on Earth never before had the capac-ity to *look at itself.* To notice what it's doing. And perhaps take corrective action. Is that humanity's true role?

Short-sighted selfishness isn't new. All creatures do that. We're the first to *perceive* the slippery slope. To contemplate our self-made paths to hell. What we do about it will define whether we're truly sapient. Whether we're a cancer to Mother Earth . . . or her new brain. Her conscience.

—*Maturation's Code*

40.
WAITING FOR GUIDOT

Hamish fumed. *The Prophet made a point of inviting me here, to help forge a historic alliance. Now I'm snubbed, while power brokers gather behind closed doors.*

It took just a moment for his illusion of self-importance to collapse.

Hamish had been sitting near the back of an auditorium-theater, in the sprawling Glaucus-Worthington mansion, trying to find a comfortable position for his long legs while intellectuals from Tenskwatawa's Renunciation Movement compared notes with scholars employed by the consortium of rich families called the clade. If they were going make common cause, the boffins who served both groups must get their stories straight. There was plenty to discuss—

Like surface justifications for society's new direction, with varied messages tempered and adjusted for different social sectors, castes, and interest groups.

Marching orders for the politicians and bureaucrats that

each group already had locked in, plus plans for collecting more.

Also on the agenda—though less pressing—were methodologies for *good governance* once control was achieved. The presence of this topic made Hamish feel better about the whole thing. If humanity was fated to slip back into traditional patterns, then the new lords should take their duties seriously.

Or, at least, they want to seem that way. It costs little to put some intellectuals on your fealty payroll and get them exchanging papers about newblesse oblige—*the aristocratic duty to rule wisely. We'll see if the coming feudal order really goes that way. Tenskwatawa had better keep his wits about him, for all our sakes!*

The morning filled with presentations and panel discussions. Sushmeeta, the sociologist from Dharamsala, avoided eye contact with Hamish as she gave her speech about "neo-Confucian" social structures. Recalling their time together last night with mild fondness, he grinned openly when her eyes seemed about to pass over him. But there was no moment of contact. Perhaps she felt embarrassed, or piqued that he did not stay the whole night . . . or else anxious not to have their mini-affair revealed by gaze analysis. If so, the act of *avoiding* contact could betray that something was up between them . . . not that he cared much who knew.

There were all sorts of possibilities and Hamish admitted to being curious. A bit. *Maybe, after all, it's simply a matter of professionalism. She had her way with me—collected a bedded celebrity—and now she's concentrating on business.* Carolyn had seemed to do that, when first they met, exhibiting a combination of passion and self-control that Hamish couldn't help but find impressive. Only later, when laughter became a big part of it, did the relationship move toward love.

Toward. But did it ever really get there? he wondered. *And if so . . . why couldn't it stay?*

Sushmeeta's presentation was, in fact, pretty good. An excellent appraisal—steeped in impressive historical evidence—of how oligarchic rule might be made sturdier, more effective and last longer, by lacing it with meritocracy.

Naturally, the intellectuals liked that part. They would. There was appreciative applause when Sushmeeta finished and sat back down in the second row. Hamish preferred to observe from farther back, where he could get up and stretch his legs.

Ah well. Maybe during lunch. . . .

Of possibly more interest to the First Estate were talks on "Swaying Mass Opinion Through Ubiquitous Ambient Persuasion" and "Verifying the Loyalty of Retainers Through Personality Tomography."

A panel on intellectual property law sought common ground between the patricians, who viewed patents and copyrights as profitable rents, and the Renunciators, who saw tight licensing of ideas as tool to control "progress." Advisers for both factions reached consensus—to seek legislation ending all expiration dates on patents. Intellectual property should be forever.

A side bonus: that might help corral some sci-tech types into joining the alliance.

Hamish noted that those giving papers seemed jittery—perhaps due to boffin drugs they sniffed, popped, or sorbed through skin patches. Out in the world, they might be discreet, but here among peers they spoke openly of the latest mind-accelerating substances. Was that what kept them agitated? Or was it lack of World Mesh access from this closed and secret conference?

It's hard to believe that a hundred years ago folks seriously talked about technocracy—putting the world's top scientists and intellectual elites in charge.

Of course, the people in this room weren't "top." The greatest members of the Fifth Estate kept their distance from the superrich, and especially from Tenskwatawa's movement. Still, the very idea of technocracy always offended Hamish. And it would surely never happen now. Ironically thanks to methods that these experts were concocting, for their employers in the First Estate.

Hamish listened and took mental notes—half for the sake of the Movement but also as grist for future stories—two goals that pulled, deliciously, in opposite directions. For, while he approved of these proposals in real life—(they might save the world)—he couldn't help also coming up with great ways to set them in tales of villainy! "Ambient persuasion" and "personality tomography" were euphemisms for mind-control—a dark vein that he had mined in novels, films, and games like *Triumph of the Force*.

So? Some of this stuff was just too cool not to portray in his next tech-bashing tale. Used by some enemy conspiracy—a government agency, or cabal of eco-nuts—instead of allies of the Prophet. Such was the art of fiction. Pick an authority figure as the nearly omnipotent bad guy—the choice depended on your grudges—but anti-authority had been the ongoing theme ever since the invention of Hollywood.

His hand ached from scribbling ideas on the permitted pad of old-fashioned paper. *If only I had access to some vidrec or gisting tools.*

Alas, even Wriggles, the mini-ai in his earring, was shut down by some kind of high-tech jamming system. *Well, these are dangerous topics.* Mere hearsay or rumors were harmless. It didn't matter if millions believed terrible things about the Movement or the clade, even some that were true! But they must never be *verified*.

Around eleven, during a ten-minute break, Hamish was returning from the profligately perfumed men's room when a conference manager announced the next talk: "Eugenic Refinement of Bloodlines and the Enhancement of Nobility."

The title struck Hamish as creepy and—if truth be told—sort-of quasi-Nazi. Others in the audience seemed to agree, as dozens drifted away to get coffee or converse in antechambers. The speaker stepped toward the podium, but Hamish was watching Tenskwatawa, along with two key aides, join Rupert Glaucus-Worthington at a side exit, along with Yevgeny Bogolomov, Helena duPont-Vonessen, and other top moguls. Rupert, in particular, had a distracted, worried demeanor. Something weighed heavily on the old man.

Hamish took a swift scan of the auditorium and saw that all the top people in both factions were leaving, or had already left. *This must be it. The real gathering,* he thought, and started forward . . .

. . . only to stop as the Prophet, sharp-eyed, glanced his way. With a simple head shake and apologetic smile, Tenskwatawa told Hamish—*No. This is not for you.* Then, the Movement's leader seemed to dismiss all thought of Hamish and turned away, following their host to some other meeting place. One presumably even more private and secure, where deals could be struck and humanity's future decided.

Hamish sat down heavily as the eugenics talk was delivered—appropriately, it seemed—by a frumpy little man with an Austrian accent. But Hamish felt too stunned and hurt to pay much heed.

Well, what did you expect? Especially after the way Rupert treated you yesterday. For thousands of years, actors, storytellers, and enchanters knew their place . . . generally little higher than acrobats and courtesans. Even when famous or beloved, they did not hobnob or discuss policy with kings. Only our recent, adolescent culture exalted entertainers or men of ideas, and that's sure to change when things settle back to the human norm.

Ah well. I always knew there were some things I'd miss about the Enlightenment.

So, here he belonged, among the other boffins. Not just any entertainer, but a master of mass communications, he should find the topics fascinating and have much to contribute. Yet, Hamish found it hard to focus as the speaker droned on.

". . . so we see from these data that one consistent failure mode, leading to the downfall of noble houses in Europe, Asia, Africa, and the Americas, across all recorded millennia, was adherence to foolish patterns of marriage and reproduction!

"Of course, arranged marriages often helped seal family alliances—useful in the short term. But it led to calamitous narrowing of aristocratic gene pools! How often were the accomplishments of brilliant rulers frittered by their dullard sons?

"Observe, the effects of inbreeding on just three royal houses, the Hohenzollerns, Hapsburgs, and Romanovs. Monarchs who were certifiably inferior in both intelligence and temperament ignited half a century of agony! Hundreds of millions dead, the ruin of all three houses, and aristocracy discredited for several wasted generations, till memory of that horror faded at last."

Hamish scanned some of the technical graphics, bobbing over both speaker and audience like blimps filled with charts and animated data. Apparently, the little scholar's point was similar to the Hindi sociologist—only his notion of "meritocracy" extended to the noble bloodlines themselves.

"Then there is the problem of *brain drain*—that many of the brightest children of aristocracy abandon it! While maintaining some level of comfort, they choose instead the company of *techies,* applying their minds to expertise in some branch of science or art or other. . . ."

Hamish twitched as a soft tingle stroked his ear. He quashed an impulse to suddenly sit up. Keeping still, he subvocalized a question in the confines of his throat, with closed mouth.

"WRIGGLES? IS THAT YOU?"

The tingling went away . . . then returned, stronger. Yet, the voice of his aissistant remained silent. Perhaps the suppressor field that jammed mesh-communications in the Glaucus-Worthington mansion had sputtered, allowing personal devices to wake a little—enough to be irritating.

Hamish reached up to remove the earring—

—when the tingle became a low, grating sound. . . . that swelled into a mutter . . . then gathered into words.

"Hamish Brookeman, if you hear this, touch the seat in front of you."

Um.

That wasn't Wriggles.

Hamish barely hesitated. He was already leaning forward. One lazy sweep of a hand was enough to comply.

"Good. Please go to the empty seat directly across the aisle. Feel along the left side, under the padding. Stay casual."

Hamish thought about how someone might surreptitiously overcome the jamming. Perhaps with a directional maser, aimed line-of-sight at his earring? But detectors in the auditorium should spot scattered reflections. Unless . . . they were using some kind of off-band, induced-resonance effect, causing the earring to vibrate. . . . Or else, might it be a recording, inserted earlier?

He shook his head. Technological speculations weren't important. What mattered was—could this be some sort of loyalty test?

If so, is it just me, or are they testing everyone?

The speaker meanwhile kept talking about aristocratic breeding. ". . . All these problems could be solved by choosing mates from among the most brilliant and accomplished commoners. By combining this with scientifically planned recombination and reinforcement, the top caste can benefit by producing dynamic and talented offspring! Let me emphasize, for our new friends the renunciation movement, this can be done without genetic meddling! Though, of course there would still have to be prenatal . . ."

Thinking backward, Hamish didn't recall seeing any boffins acting suspiciously, changing seats or feeling cushions—or dashing off to report illicit messages to security. Sure, some might react with subtlety, betraying nothing overtly. But most of these nervous intellectuals wouldn't know how.

"Beyond direct advantages," continued the man at the dais, "are public relations benefits, making commoners feel they have a potential stake in the noble caste—encouraging parents to hope *their* child might leap in status!"

Standing up and stretching, Hamish turned to mount a dozen steps—his natural stride took them two at a time—arriving where several men in G-W livery stood by a table piled with savory snacks. From a rotating tray, he plucked a skewer of Tientsin pork—clearly from a real animal, not tishculture—alternating nibbles with sips from a perribulb, while the speaker droned on.

"Of course, we must avoid any return to primogeniture—or firstborn inheritance—no matter how precedented! Any aristocracy that's truly serious will emulate some of the desert princely families—crafting clan-level deliberative structures that borrow, ironically, from democracy. . . ."

Hamish grinned at the security officers. They seemed typical, from bulked physiques to their heavy specs, immune to jamming. One gave Hamish a glance and a short nod. The other emitted soft sounds while virt-navigating with tooth-taps and grunts, all without moving his folded arms.

There wasn't the slightest sign that Hamish interested them. Of course, they might be good actors. But doubtful.

"Well, Mr. Brookeman?" murmured the rippling voice near his ear.

"This will be interesting. Promise."

Hamish hesitated. Then he grabbed another skewer before wandering nonchalantly back down the aisle. His choice really was a foregone conclusion. Curiosity was as much a part of his DNA as gleeful pessimism laced his work. *God does not tempt men beyond their ability to resist,* went a Catholic doctrine, one he could cite in his own defense, if this turned out to be a test. *I must find out what's going on.*

". . . of course, old-time aristocracies did allow some infusion from below." The speaker's laser-grabber pushed illustration blimps around, showing images of men in chain-mail and women in courtly attire. "Brave foot soldiers might win battle honors and thus climb social levels. Beautiful women married upward, or gained intermediate status as mistresses . . . ."

Hamish sat down across the aisle from his old position. While stripping the skewer and chewing, he felt with his other hand along the cushion . . . and found a tiny bulge in the fabric. It pushed aside, exposing what felt like a many-folded scrap of paper that tugged easily from its niche.

"Great," resumed the voice near his right ear. *"Now slip out the lens and use it. If it's difficult you might do it in the loo. There are no security cams there."*

Hamish frowned. He could feel the outlines of a soft disc, under the paper folds. *I hate these.* Modern kids, naturally, took them for granted. Anybody could have perfect vision, nowadays, yet they kept shoving things into their eyes, viewing the world through artificial layers. Of course, whoever planted this thing for Hamish would already know his publicly stated grouchiness. They would also know that he *did* use contaicts from time to time. When he had to.

All right. I can do it. And without having to hide in the bathroom, you patronizing twits.

With his left hand carefully out of sight, Hamish freed the lens from its paper container and balanced it, concave side up. *Try not to drop it. Even the Swiss don't keep their floors clean enough for aiware.*

Pretending to choke a little, on a piece of pork, he bent over, covering his mouth in order to cough a few times . . . while pushing up one eyelid and poking the little actiplastic disc into place. Perhaps too roughly—he was out of practice. It had been months. Hamish's left eye stung as it blinked, offended by the unwelcome presence. For a minute, while tears flowed, that side of the world was a blur. Meanwhile the speaker kept droning on.

". . . some African tribes required that chiefs pick brides from poor clans. And Jews of medieval Europe, lacking an aristocracy based on land or military might, grounded their elite on scholarly accomplishments. The brightest young rabbis, even low-born, married daughters of the rich, with well known genetic consequences. As were repercussions in cultures where priestly celibacy culled. . . ."

Finally, Hamish managed to get things into focus. No longer needing to override Wriggles, the mysterious intruder-voice now wrote itself across the visual field of his left eye.

Please get up—again casually—and follow the guide dot.

Without any further reluctance or reservations (he was quite sick of the obnoxious "eugenics" speaker, anyway),

Hamish stood and turned to leave by the rear exit, passing the security men, this time without a glance. At which point a yellow globe presented itself to one eye, pulsing in a nonthreatening sort of way, beckoning him down a hallway to his left.

Some people live all their lives awash in this stuff . . . virtual overlayers and "mixed reality." They claim it empowers them to do more, experience more. But I've done fine without it. Show me anybody who lives immersed in the Billion Layer World, who's accomplished more than I have!

At the same time, he wondered. How did the little contaict lens commune with controllers, elsewhere, without detection by mansion security?

Could the lens have enough ai to interact with me, all by itself?

He decided to test it. On passing a men's room, Hamish veered through the doors. Any remote handlers might get stymied by all the plumbing in the walls, especially if they were using a weak and surreptitious radio beam.

Good idea, commented flowing letters. **Better do a draining. You may be occupied a while.**

Old-fashioned modesty was another reason to hate these eyeball-thingumbies. Hamish was careful not to look down while he peed, having no way to tell if others shared his view through the little lens. Instead, he studied the urinal's spec-plate—another fine product of the Life-Liner, Ltd., promising to recover 93 percent of the phosphorus and 85 percent of the water in every flush. Hamish grimaced ruefully. In *Phoscarcity?* this very same eco-company had the role of chief villain, with a slight change of name. Part of a worldwide conspiracy by the Merde Monopoly to make money off a fake crisis. Some careless word choices and a court settlement took all his profits that time. *Ah well.*

Hamish lowered his gaze enough to aim his stream at

the company logo, above the drain. After which, he zipped, washed, and exited. The yellow guidot seemed to be waiting in the same spot.

"ALLONS-Y, ALONZO," he murmured, in case the lens could pick up throat subvocalisms, from all the way up in his eye socket. There was no answer. So he simply followed the guidot down another hall, up a broad set of stairs, then along another passage, through a vestibule and into one of the many museum libraries that dotted the Glaucus-Worthington manse, featuring bookshelves that towered two stories, toward ceiling arches of hewn stone.

Wow. I could spend a week in here.

He half expected the lens to write captions across all the wonders in this room. Alas, it didn't. Still, he recognized a glass-encased Gutenberg Bible and an illustrated Latin translation of Galen, the early Guitner edition. Other wonders were mysterious. Unlike any public museum, they bore no reality-level labels made of paper or plastic. Apparently, you were only supposed to view these treasures while accompanied by a bragging family member.

Well, well. He couldn't tarry. The traveling beacon turned to head down one of the spaces between the tall shelves. Then, at the end of that narrow aisle, it bobbed slowly before one of those rolling ladders, leading to the upper level. As he approached, the glistening virtual globe bobbed upward, like an untethered balloon.

Hamish paused. The steps looked awkward for his big feet and gangly legs. But after a couple of seconds he shrugged and started up, clambering gamely, even a bit recklessly. If truth be told, he was enjoying himself immensely.

At the top, he turned and spent a few seconds waiting for the guidot to catch up, then stepped aside for it to pass and lead the way again—almost as if it were real, and not ersatz. An illusion created by a plastic disc sitting on his left eyeball. Alas, because he only wore a single contaict, the guidot was just two dimensional and a bit hard to pin down without pseudo-parallax. Still, Hamish followed it into a small alcove lined with dusty tomes, many of them surely more valuable than his house.

The globe transformed into the image of a floating, disembodied human hand—wearing a zardozian white glove—that turned with a magician's flourish and pointed to some ornate carvings, surrounding a bookcase made of dark wood.

Pull this vine toward you, please. The unit should open.

Then step through very quietly, closing it behind you ALMOST all the way. Do not let it lock in place.

Although his heart was pounding, Hamish found it reassuring that the vaice was being so careful to leave him a way out. That made it seem less like a trap.

His hand stroked curving vines that climbed the bookcase, and Hamish wondered if anything like such delicate woodwork could be produced today. Of course, zealots of the so-called Age of Amateurs claimed that every art, craft, and skill of the past could now be duplicated—not by machine, but by passionate hobbyists.

Hamish found that assertion painful, arrogant, even disgusting.

He pulled where the floating hand indicated. Without creaks or stiffness, a lever slid down around a hinge and—with a click—the entire case popped out a few centimeters. It swung fairly easily, even while supporting heavy volumes—evidently on smooth, modern bearings—whereupon Hamish found a dark passageway inside.

His right eye could make out nothing in the gloom. But in his left-hand field of view there appeared faint, glimmering outlines that told him where floor met walls, guiding his footsteps. Hamish pulled the case after him . . .

almost shut, and turned to shuffle softly forward, thinking about stories by Poe.

There is a heavy wooden panel, set in the wall at eye level, just ahead.

Two meters. Now one.

Put out your arm to where mine points.

Hamish felt a faint nervous tremor in his fingertips as he reached. Even knowing what to expect, he experienced a faint frisson when his hand passed through the ghostly white glove without any physical contact. Million-year-old instincts were hard to overcome.

Grab the slider bolt.

Now push the panel gently to the left until a gap appears.

After a pause, there came an added caution.

You may watch, but make no sounds.

He shoved aside the wooden insert at the indicated spot, and brought his head down a bit, scrunching uncomfortably.

Eye level. Right. Maybe for normal people.

It was dim in the large chamber beyond, though he adapted quickly, even with his unassisted right eye. Soon made out another richly paneled room with a stonework dome, like the library behind him. In this one, however, there were no books, only statuary. Dozens of marble or bronze figures posed in alcoves lining the walls below, and above in a second story balcony colonnade. It was from that upper level that he now peered downward past one nearby piece of sculpture—some Hindu dancer or goddess, with a voluptuous figure, tiny waist, and only one pair of arms.

Gazing past her provocative navel, he spied a couple of dozen figures below, on the first level, gathered around a single tabletop source of illumination. Radiating like petals of a dark flower, their fleeing shadows crossed the floor then climbed the walls, interspersing warped, elongated human silhouettes among the onlooking statues. Low murmurs of conversation were too hushed for Hamish to make out clearly, though he swiftly recognized the hawklike features of Tenskwatawa and those of his host, Rupert Glaucus-Worthington, along with several other eminences from both factions, their faces pale and dim, but eyes glittering in the soft-sharp light.

I thought they were heading off to negotiate details of the alliance, Hamish mused. *Vital matters of how power will be apportioned and which policies to pursue. Instead, this looks like some kind of ceremony.*

Could I be watching secret initiation rites of the Illuminati?

Hamish felt a thrill. *I was pretty much convinced that such things were just lurid rumors or romantic exaggerations, foisted by my fellow sci-fi writers. Could this mean the oligarchy really does have an inner, ritualized core? One the Prophet is now invited to join?*

But not me?

Hamish quashed his sense of pique, focusing instead on curiosity, wondering—*How could my sources have steered me so wrong?*

Only . . . Hamish soon found himself revising that first impression. There seemed to be no pattern, no orderly arrangement of people crowded around the table below. No symbolic regalia. No rhythmic chanting. Just a murmur of worried wonder.

One of them, the owner of this vast palace, raised his voice a bit in answer to a question. A tone of querulous anxiety colored Rupert's tone as he waved an arm in response, gesturing toward the table. And Hamish managed to pick out a few snippets.

". . . in my family for three centuries . . ."

and then,

". . . suddenly started, last night . . ."

and finally,

". . . never did anything like this, before!"

Abruptly, Hamish realized, Glaucus-Worthington was talking about the object that lay before them at the center of the gathering. What Hamish had first taken for a simple—if somewhat dim—tabletop lamp, he now realized was something else entirely. A roundish lump of glass, about the size of a human head, and—he realized with a chill—rather shaped like one. It seemed to glow from within.

The contaict lens covering his left pupil kicked into operation, responding to his interest, performing some wizardry of magnification and image enhancement, zooming in toward the object. Image dissonance between his two eyes briefly sickened Hamish, till he shut the right one. Even looking only at the enhanced version, it took several moments to sort out the glitters and complex refractions before realizing.

It's a crystal skull. One of those weird relics that people get all mystical about, in films even sillier than mine. Though most proved to be modern hoaxes.

Of course, "most" was not the same as "all." Archaeologists did admit that a few seemed genuinely ancient, but still just works of art—natural chunks of quartz that had been laboriously chiseled and rubbed by artisans in olden times—showing no sign of mystical properties. Yet, some of the strange skullptures had never been put under public, high-tech scrutiny, allowing fervid tales to keep swirling.

I recall, one of them was kept in Switzerland, in private hands.

He never cared enough to learn more than that. Ancient occult artifacts were never a propelling topic for Hamish. Not as much as dangerous scientific innovations and Things Man Was Never Meant to Know. Nevertheless, there had always been something alluring about the works of authors and sceneasts like Joanne Sawyer and Ari Stone-Bear, who spun tales of mystery and wonder around arcane objects from the enigmatic past.

Someone—Tenskwatawa—reached out to touch the translucent cranium—pushing with a fingertip. Turning it till the rictus grin and sunken eye sockets almost faced Hamish, glowing with an expression of fey amusement . . .

. . . when a sudden shaft of brilliance gleamed, spearing him right through the contaict lens with a shrapnel-clutter of overlapping images—

—a *planet* of dark continents and narrows seas, conveyed in murky tans and grainy grays, except for a single, wavy band that flickered with detailed color, from azure seashore to snowcapped, purple peaks—

—a jumbled, jigsaw *cityscape* that stirred together a tangle of mud huts, skyscrapers, stilt houses, and gleaming domes, topped by thatched roofs—

—a crumpled mosaic of *faces,* jaggedly combining beaks and jaws and fluted stalks that, while twisted together unnaturally, seemed to snort and cry out with some kind of delirious urgency.

The impression lasted only a couple of seconds. Then it was gone. Benumbed with shock, Hamish sought refuge in logic. In scientific speculation.

That jumble of degraded images . . . mixed and overlapping chaotically . . . they could be remnants of holographic memory. Unlike the Havana Artifact, this one offers just a few surviving fragments, retained after the thing was damaged.

Perhaps by the primitive artists who used powders and stones to grind and polish it into a shape worthy of veneration, never knowing how much harm they were doing . . . or else even earlier, when the crystal came crashing to Earth.

Broken and ruined, unable to communicate clearly,

perhaps it could only offer brief snatches of ambiguous confusion and dreamlike images. Enough to terrify our primitive ancestors with thoughts of death. Maybe inspiring other tribes to make their own crystal skulls, in vain efforts to duplicate its power. No wonder oligarchs like Rupert thought this too disturbing to share with the easily alarmed masses.

Hamish turned his attention to Glaucus-Worthington. To the unhappy look on the man's face.

But didn't Rupert just say something? That this showy display started only last night? Perhaps the skull never wakened—but for rare flickers—till a few hours ago.

Only . . . why now?

Hamish had no trouble coming up with a most likely hypothesis.

Oh my.

TORALYZER

This is Tor—"Zep-girl"—Povlov, reporting to you from my new beat. Web-Eighteen, level Z12. The hippest, heppest hot-hit-hat . . . or not-this-**that** . . . in the Mesh. And, yes, I come before you as a purely-pearly virtue-virtual, wearing the nimbus halo of a holy-hollow holo. Hello? You expected, like, veri-real shots of the Heroine of Washing-tin? My current-realtime phys-visage?

Granny would say, *as if!* That cadaver-shell is just container-support. I live here now, in the Over-World. Pat this avatar on the back, I feel it. If I ever let one of you horny fans talk me into a back room privirtcy (or pervertcy), the sustainer pod'll convey it. Nothing wrong with the old Tor's hormonal system!

(Sure . . . like THAT's going to happen! Still, you can keep offering.)

So yes, there's still plenty of "me" left. And one thing I promise—I'll never let my presence here run on aitopilot.

Tell you what. Help boost my ratings, and MediaCorp may spring for a more palp-able holvatar. Even one of those android-mobiles, I can send to chase down real-layer stories. Meanwhile, though, there's plenty to occupy us here, in the Val-hall-levels, where citizen/amateur heroes like you can hunt iniquities, skewering lies with lances of transparency and light! Like we did, together, back on the old *Spirit of Chula Vista*.

So let's get started.

What? Many of you want to hear about me, first? What it's like to live this way?

Each year, hundreds of catastrophically injured people become gel-encased refugees, like me, who experience life through remote sensors, rather than organic eyes and flesh. Though the Mesh is home, we're not "uploaded" cybernetic beings. Cams and sensors still feed old-fashioned nerve channels of a very wetbrain.

For some it's a painful, limited life, that only fools would envy. Still, tens of thousands of normal, undamaged homosaps climb into hook-in tanks and risk body-atrophy, trying to follow us "pioneers" down the path of the living holvatar.

I hope none of you are such fools. Just one person in a hundred manages to make the transition as well as I have— swooping about the datalanes, veering from hunch to correlation to corroboration. Links that used to require a laborious eyeblink or tooth-click now happen by sheer will . . . or whim . . . quickly submerging to the level of reflex. . . .

All right, I just made it sound attractive, didn't I? Well, don't go there, any of you. It still hurts! And there are puzzling *itches,* in the way data often seems to stroke my skin and tingle up the spine. None of the docs can explain. Then there's the creepy sensation that someone's *calling my name.* Not this moniker I use in the news biz. Not what my mother called me, but some kind of *secret name,* like in stories about magic spells and such.

Okay, it's clearly a lingering wash of escapism/slash/self-pity . . . and so let's push that aside with the balm of work! *Smart-mob time.* Like a swarm of T cells, let's swoop onto something in the news!

What? You want to make the space Artifact our topic? All of you? Isn't everybody else on the planet obsessing . . .

No, you're right. Most of the reporting is stodgy. The insights stale. I share the group hunch. We can do better.

41.

THE OLD WAY

Peng Xiang Bin tried hard to follow the conversation—partly out of fascination. But also because he felt desperate to please.

If I prove useful to them—more than a mere on-off switch for the worldstone—it could mean my life. I might even get to see Mei Ling and Xiao En again.

That goal wasn't coming easy. The others kept talking way over his head. Nor could he blame them. After all, who was he? *What* was he, but another piece of driftwood-trash, washed up on a beach, who happened to pick up a pretty rock? Should he demand they explain everything? *Dui niu tanqin* . . . it would be like playing a lute to a cow.

Except they needed his ongoing service as communicator-ambassador to the entity within that rock—and he seemed to be performing that task well enough. At least according to Dr. Nguyen, who was always friendly to Bin.

The tech-search experts—Anna Arroyo and Paul Menelaua—clearly were dubious about this ill-educated Huangpu shoresteader with his weathered skin and rough diction, who kept taking up valuable time with foolish questions. Those two would be happier, he knew, if the honor of direct contact with the Courier entity were taken over by someone else.

Only, can *the role be passed along at all? If I died, would it transfer to another?* Surely they had mulled that tempting thought.

Or do I have some special trait—something that goes beyond being the first man in decades to lay eyes on the worldstone? Without me, might there be a long search before they found another? That possibility was one he must foster. At some point it might keep him breathing.

Anyway, I do not have to prove myself their equal, Bin reminded himself. *My role is like the first performer in a Chinese opera, who does not have to sing especially well. Just dance around a little and help warm up the audience. Be useful, not the star.*

"Clearly, this mechanism in our possession was dispatched across interstellar space by different people, with different motives, than those who sent the Havana Artifact," commented Yang Shenxiu, the scholar from New Beijing, who rested one hand on the worldstone without causing more than a ripple under its cloudy surface—giving Bin a moment of satisfaction. *It reacts a lot more actively to my touch!*

With his other hand, Yang motioned toward a large placard-image screen for comparison. In lustrous threevee, it showed the alien object under study in Maryland, America, surrounded by researchers from around the world—a bustle of activity watched by billions and supervised by Gerald Livingstone, the astronaut who discovered and collected that "herald egg" from orbit.

To most of the world, that is the sole one in existence. Only a few suspect that such things have been encountered before, across the centuries. And even fewer have certain knowledge of another active stone, held in secret, here in the middle of the vast Pacific Ocean.

Bin contemplated the three-dimensional image of his counterpart, a clever and educated man, a scientist and space traveler and probably the world's most famous person right now. In other words, different from poor little Peng Xiang Bin in every conceivable way. *Except that he looks as tired and worried as I feel.*

Watching Livingstone, Bin felt a connection, as if with another *chosen one.* The keeper-guardian of a frightening oracle from space. Even if they found themselves on opposite sides of an ancient struggle.

Paul Menelaua answered Yang Shenxiu by describing a long list of physical differences in excruciating detail—the Havana Artifact was larger, longer, and more knobby at one end, for example. And, clearly, less damaged. Well, it never had to suffer the indignities of fiery passage through Earth's atmosphere, or pummeling impact with a mountain glacier, or centuries of being poked at by curious or reverential or terrified tribal humans . . . not to mention a couple of thousand years buried in a debris pit, then decades soaking in polluted waters underneath a drowned mansion. Bin found himself reacting defensively on behalf of "his" worldstone.

I'd like to see Livingstone's famous Havana Artifact come through all that, and still be capable of telling vague, mysterious stories.

Of course, that was the chief trait both ovoids had in common.

". . . so, yes, there are evident physical differences. Still, anyone can tell at a glance that they use the same underlying technologies. Capacious and possibly unlimited holographic memory storage. Surface sonic transduction at the wider end . . . but with most communications handled visually, both in pictorial representation and through symbol manipulation. Some surface tactile sensitivity. And, of course an utter absence of moving parts."

"Yes, there are those commonalities," Anna Arroyo put in. "Still, the Havana Artifact projects across a wider spectrum than this one—and it portrays a whole community of simulated alien species, while ours depicts only one."

Dr. Nguyen nodded, his elegantly decorated braids rattling. "It would be a good guess to imagine that one species or civilization sent out waves of these things, and the technology was copied by others—"

"Who proceeded to cast forth modified stones of their own, incorporating representatives of all the diverse members of their growing civilization," concluded Anna. "Until one of those races decided to break the tradition, by offering a *dissenting* point of view."

Bin took advantage of this turn in the conversation—away from technical matters and back to the general story their own worldstone had been telling.

"Isn't . . . is it not . . . clear who came second? Courier warns us not to pay attention to *liars*. It seems . . . I mean, is it not clear that he refers to the creatures who dwell within the Havana Artifact?"

Of course they were amused by his stumbling attempts to speak a higher grade of Beijing dialect, with classier grammar and less Huangpu accent or slang. But he also knew there were many *types* of amusement. And, while Anna and Paul might feel the contemptuous variety, it was the indulgent smile of Dr. Nguyen that mattered. He seemed approving of Bin's earnest efforts.

"Yes, Xiang Bin. We can assume—for now—that our worldstone is speaking of the Havana Artifact—or things like it—when it warns against *enemies and liars*. The question is—what should we do about this?"

"Warn everyone!" suggested Yang Shenxiu. "You've seen how the other worldstone has thrown the entire planet into a tizzy, with that story told by the *emissary* creatures who reside within. Although it remains frustratingly unspecific, their tale is one of profound and disarmingly blithe *optimism,* confidently assuring us that humanity is welcome to join a benign interstellar community. In this era of nihilism and despair, people across every continent are rushing to believe and put their trust in the aliens!"

"And is that necessarily such a bad thing?" asked Anna.

"It could be, if it is based upon some kind of lie!" Paul interjected. He and Anna faced each other, with intensity filling their expressions, till an outside voice broke into their confrontation.

"What about others?"

Menelaua glared at Bin for interrupting, his look so fierce that Bin shrank back and had to be coaxed into resuming. "Please continue, son," Dr. Nguyen urged. "What others are you talking about?"

Bin swallowed.

"Other . . . stones."

Nguyen regarded him with a blank, cautious stare.

"Pray explain, Xiang Bin. What other stones do you mean?"

"Well, honored sir . . ." He gathered his courage, speaking slowly, carefully. "When I first arrived here, you . . . graciously let me view that report . . . the *private report* describing legends about sacred gem-globes or rocks that . . . were said to show fantastic things. Some of the stories are well known—crystal balls and dragon stones. Other tales were passed down for generations within families or secret societies. You yourself said that there is one such secret fable that's supposed to go back nine thousand years, right? It's . . . it is interesting to compare those sagas to the truth we see before us . . . and yet . . ."

He paused, uncertain he should continue.

"Go on," urged the rich man—representing an association of many other rich men and women, across Asia.

"Yet . . . what I don't understand is why that report, all by itself, would have made people so eager . . . spending so much money and effort . . . to actually look for such a thing! I mean, why would any modern people—sophisticated men like you, Dr. Nguyen—believe such stories, any more than yarns about demons?" Bin shook his head, repressing the fact that he had always believed in spirits, at least a little. So did lots of people.

"I figure the former owner of our worldstone—"

"Lee Fang Lu." Yang Shenxiu interjected a name that Bin had never known, till now. The fellow who used to own that pre-deluge mansion, with a clandestine basement chamber where Bin found a treasure trove of odd specimens. He nodded gratefully.

"Lee Fang Lu might have been arrested, tortured, and killed over rumors—"

"That he possessed something like this." Dr. Nguyen nodded and his beads clattered softly. "Pray continue."

"Then there's the way you and your . . . competitors . . . pounced on me, after I put out just a *hint* about offering to sell a glowing white egg. Clearly, when the Havana Artifact was announced, there were already powerful groups out there, who knew the . . . the . . ."

He groped for the right words. And abruptly a new, unfamiliar Chinese language character appeared in the ai-patch that had been inserted within his lower right field of vision. Plus a row of tone-accented Pinyin Roman letters, for pronunciation. The ai-patch had been doing that more often as it grew more familiar with Bin—anticipating and assisting what he was trying to say.

". . . the *range-of-plausible-potentialities* . . . ," he carefully enunciated, while moving his finger over his palm to mimic-draw the complex characters—a common thing to do, when a word was obscure. He saw the others smile a little. They were used to this sort of thing.

"I just find it hard to believe that powerful people would go to so much trouble . . . to search frantically for such a thing, even after learning about the Havana Artifact . . . unless they thought there was a real possibility of success. Unless they had strong reason to believe those legends were *more* than just legends."

He looked at Dr. Nguyen, surprised by his own boldness.

"I bet there was a lot left out of that report, sir. Is it possible that some groups already have worldstones? Now, in the modern era?"

Menelaua shook his head and snarled. "Ridiculous."

"And why is that, Paul?" Anna Arroyo answered. "It'd take care of that *temporal coincidence,* at least a bit. Maybe these things have been crisscrossing our region of space for a long time, like messages in bottles. While most settled into far orbits, waiting for Earth to produce space-faring folk, others might have landed—accidentally, like this one. Or on purpose in some way. Most would shatter or get buried at sea. But just like a plant that sends out thousands of seeds, you need only one to take root. . . ."

Yang Shenxiu protested. "If there were so many, would not geologists or gem-seekers or collectors or plowing farmers have seen, by now, some of the fallen ones? Even if they were split or burned, they would stand out!"

Anna shrugged. "We have no idea how these things decay, if broken. Maybe they decompose quickly into a form that resembles typical rock crystal. Or they might dissolve into sand or dust, or even vapor.

"Anyway, suppose a few were found, from time to time, and recognized as something special. We all know how rare and precious things used to be treated, in almost every past culture. They were presented, as gifts, to kings and priests, who then hoarded them in dark places! Maybe bringing them out from time to time, for use in mystery rites, to impress the rubes. But then always tucking them away again . . . till the city was sacked and the hiding place lost forever. Or the items were buried with the king, which amounts to the same thing. Either way, the truth would dissolve into legends—of which there are plenty!"

She turned to Bin. "Isn't that exactly what happened when Lee Fang Lu got his hands on the worldstone? Caught up in that old way of thinking, he clutched the secret—the most special thing in his life—and took it with him to the grave."

The scholar, Yang Shenxiu mused. "In fact, this could explain Hindu legends of Siva Linga stones. Moreover, it is said that both the First Emperor Chin and Genghis Khan were laid to rest with treasures that included—"

Dr. Nguyen lifted his hand for attention, cutting the discussion short. He had been standing quite still, apparently staring into space—or else, at scenes that only he could see, conveyed on the inner surface of his specs. Now, the black-haired mogul spoke in a low voice that Bin took to contain equal parts surprise and resignation.

"It seems that events have caught up with our ruminations. My sources tell me that reports are trickling in . . ."

He took off his specs and looked at Bin, directly.

"It appears, my young comrade Xiang Bin, that you may have been right, after all."

SCANALYZER

Call me Hagar.

I communicate to you all today via encrypted channels for my own protection, although this (*) pseudonymous reputation code should attest that I am a reliable person and fair witness, having taken courses in Visual Skepticism and Objective Veracity at the Women's University of Abu Dhabi. Of course, I see no conflict between that and being a good Muslim.

Which brings me to my account. For, early this very morning, I stood at the holy place in Mecca, filled with gratitude for the dispensation of the Second Caliph, who has wisely, generously and against some entrenched resistance, granted women pilgrims greater equality in seeking to fulfill our obligation of Haj.

This blessing is all the more welcome, now that I live the life of an outcast, much in keeping with my adopted name. (No doubt, some will connect this pseudonym to a certain fugitive, not pursued by any nation or law, but chased by great powers, nonetheless. Like the original Hagar, I am not without protectors, blessings be upon them. Moreover, I shall be long gone by the time this time-delayed posting lands, like a heavy stone, to ripple the dark waters of the InterMesh.)

Of course, there are by now other reports or rumors, attesting to what happened some hours ago, just before dawn, at the Holy Kaaba. But I will offer my own testament, nonetheless.

I had only begun my third of seven *tawaf* circuits, around the inner courtyard of the Grand Mosque, praying as Hagar once did, for relief and sustenance amid my exile, when a hot desert wind burst upon us from the east, driven over the roofs of bir Zamzam, as if by the soon-to-rise sun. This zephyr ruffled the *kiswa* black-cloth coverings that both honor and protect the shrine that now stands on the spot where Adam was the first person ever to pile one stone upon another, and thus began the era of Man the Builder. The same site where Abraham and Ishmael, son of that earlier Hagar, repaired the foundation and sanctified the site to forever honor Allah.

So strong was the gust that it drove many pilgrims to their knees, or else forced them to crouch down, exposing to those of us who were circling much farther away a wondrous sight: a clear view of that eastern corner of the Kaaba, where the

Prophet Muhammad himself—blessings be upon him—placed the fabled Black Stone into the wall with his own hands.

The very same Black Stone that fell in order to show Adam and Eve where first to sacrifice and prostrate themselves before the Holy Name.

To unbelievers, or to modernists who think that the Word can be reinterpreted by mere men, the obvious explanation is that the Black Stone must have been a meteorite that startled and bedazzled primitives, during an era when tribes made fetishes of so-called sacred rocks all over this rugged peninsula. Moreover, many devout Muslim scholars avow that it can be nothing more than just a rock—one worthy of respect, for having once been kissed by the Prophet, but nothing more.

Only then, how do such people explain well-attributed testimony that the Stone is said to have once been pure and dazzling white? Only to have turned reddish black because of all the sins it has absorbed over the sad centuries?

And how will skeptics explain away the miracle that I witnessed, with my very own eyes? When that blessed Stone began to *shine* with a glow all its own! Emanating from within, pushing forth against the predawn twilight?

Whereupon, for a brief span, rays seemed to flash toward the pilgrims, some of them unaware, having already abased themselves facedown upon the ground. But many others braved the sight, and so rocked-back, stumbling, or threw up their arms, or held their heads in amazement and awe.

It lasted only the interval of a few heartbeats. Then, the momentary brilliance passed. The Stone faded again, almost to black. Except I witnessed that several small patches continued to glow softly within, especially under the gentle warming of the rising sun.

As for we poor pilgrims who were left standing or crouching or kneeling there, in shock and wonder? The initial, awestruck silence gave way to moans and cries, fervent *shahadas* declaring the greatness of God and his prophet.

Only thereafter, by many minutes, amid layerings of both
terror and joy, did I hear a rising babble of voices as we turned
to one another, each declaring and comparing her brief visual
experience to that of others.

I heard the word "demons!" uttered with tones of dread.

Several voices, tinged in marvel mixed with worry, spoke
of "djinn!"

Many, mindful of current events, murmured about "those
aliens"—the beings who were coming awake within their own
strange sky-stone in America.

But far more frequent, and soon overriding all else, there
arose a single interpretation of what several hundred women
saw in that brief, holy glow.

Angels.

42.
A PURPOSE

Hacker felt better after a shower and a meal. He even
grabbed a little shut-eye, sleeping with the joymaker in his
hand, so that its vibe-mode alarm would wake him after a
couple of hours. When he roused, his vision seemed much
sharper and his hands no longer felt as if they were covered
by oven mitts.

A good thing, since there followed several hours' work
in the underwater center's main laboratory, sitting at a lab
bench, modifying the cable from his helmet that had
tapped the sonic implant in his jaw—the same circuit he
had used aboard the ill-fated rocket—converting it to link
up with the archaic multiphone.

*Dad would be proud of me. And Mom, too. I may be
self-indulgent and overbearing. But no decadent hypocrite-
brat! I understand the tech I use. And my people know that
I can sling a soldering iron!*

Through an open door, he glanced back at the pool, where members of the Tribe had taken up a game of water polo, calling fouls and shouting at each other as they batted a ball from one goal to the next, keeping score with raucous sonar clicks. One more behavior he figured you would not find among their wild cousins.

Hacker wondered about the "uplift" changes he had seen. Did they carry through from one generation to the next? Could this new genome spread among natural dolphins? And if so, might the project have already succeeded beyond its founders' dreams? Or its detractors' worst nightmare?

What if the work resumed, finishing what got started here? Would it enrich our lives to—let's say—argue philosophy with a dolphin intellectual? Or to collaborate with a smart chimp, at work or at play? If other species speak and start creating new things, will they be treated as equals—as co-members of our civilization—or as the next discriminated class?

Hacker recalled some classics of literature, by H. G. Wells and Pierre Boulle and Cordwainer Smith, that portrayed this concept, but always in terms of slavery. In every case—and in all the clichéd movies—author and director showed cruel human masters getting their just deserts. A simple morality tale that always struck him as being less about hubris, and more about the penalty for being a *bad parent*.

But, what if "uplift" were done with the best of intentions, without any hint of oppression or cruelty, propelled by curiosity, diversity and even compassion? Wouldn't there still be awful mistakes and unforeseen consequences? Some critics were probably right. For humans to attempt such a thing would be like an orphaned and abused teen trying to foster a feral child.

Are we good enough? Wise enough? Do we deserve such power?

It wasn't the sort of question Hacker used to ask himself, even as recently as a month ago. In fact, he felt changed by his experience at sea.

At the same time, he realized—just asking the question was part of the answer.

Maybe it'll work both ways. They say you only grow while helping others.

His father would have called that "romantic nonsense." But Lacey wouldn't, he felt pretty sure. Suddenly he wanted to talk to her, more than anything in the world.

READY.

That word flashed across the little screen, and he felt relief. Not only did some undersea cable still connect the habitat to the World Mesh, but the joymaker's repeated pulses had managed to summon a soft-reconnection. All he would have to do is vocally ask for a connection to his mother. If his voiceprint had changed too much to handle the payment problem, well, then she could unleash some aissistant to take care of that detail from her end.

Yet, at the last moment, Hacker revised his priorities again.

I'll call Lacey soon. She's probably worried sick. But a few minutes won't make much difference.

First, there are other urgent matters.

He was about to call his manager and broker—before they had a chance to declare him dead and start liquidating his commercial empire. But then Hacker stopped. Even that was doing stuff in the wrong order.

He looked back up the hall, where splashes could be seen, rising from the pool, and an occasional leaping gray form. The Tribe. The friends who had saved his life.

Hacker paused a second or two longer. Then he keyed the private access code for his attorney, hoping to get through, despite the lack of phone-ident.

After a lengthy ring, Gloria Harrigan answered, but at first she sounded brusque, distracted.

"Who the hell is this and could you call back later? The whole world is watching TV right now."

He blinked in surprise at her non sequitur. The whole world was *what*? He rapped his jaw, in case the implant had malfunctioned. Concentrating, Hacker spoke aloud. Even though he could not hear air-carried sounds, he could feel his larynx buzz and his mouth shaped sounds.

"Gloria—"

"Anyway, this hi-pri line is set aside for the search and rescue. So if it doesn't have to do with—"

"Gloria . . ." He spoke carefully, as if trying to recall a disused skill. "You can call off the search. . . . It's me . . . Hacker Sander."

There was a long pause. Then a shriek that carried up his mandible to resonate his skull.

"Hacker? Is that really you?"

He only got in two more words, before the shouting recommenced and would not stop for a while. Gloria kept punctuating joyful yells—calling others to gather around—with outright sobs. *"This is goddam more important than any fucking aliens!"* she hollered.

It had a strange effect on Hacker, almost making him feel remiss, embarrassed over having caused such emotion and inconvenience. Another novel sensation. *I didn't know anybody liked me that much,* he mused.

At the same time, he also wondered.

Aliens?

Carrying the phone back to the dome's atrium, he arrived in time to witness the water polo game conclude in a frothy finale. Dolphins pirouetted and squawked, either celebrating or protesting the score . . . as Gloria finally calmed enough to confirm that . . . yes . . . they now had his location pinned down . . . and help was on the way. About an hour . . . no, make that forty minutes, she revised in a hurried update, as a tourist minisub offered to divert from a nearby beach resort for a reasonable fee.

"That's fine . . . ," Hacker said, though with a strange flurry of mixed feelings. "During that time, though . . . right after you phone my mother with the news . . . there's something . . . I want you to do for me."

He then gave Gloria the World Mesh codes for Project Uplift, and asked her to find out everything about it, including the current disposition of assets and technology— and how to contact the experts whose work had been interrupted here.

When Gloria asked him why, he started to reply.

"I think . . . I've got a new . . ."

Hacker stopped there, having almost said the word *hobby*. But suddenly he realized—he had never felt quite this way about anything before. Not even the exhilaration of playboy rocketry.

For the first time he burned with real ambition. Something that seemed worth fighting for.

In the pool, several members of the Tribe were now busy winding their precious net around the torso of the biggest male, preparing to go foraging again. Hacker overheard them gossiping as they worked, and chuckled when he understood one of their crude jokes. A good natured jibe at *his* expense.

Well, a sense of humor is a good start. Our civilization could use more of that.

"I think—" he resumed telling his lawyer.

"I think I know what I want to do with my life."

TORALYZER

Hello? Is anyone there? I'm counting a handful—just half a mega or so. Well, four hundred and thirty thousand participants will have to suffice. **You** are the types who would rather **do** than passively stare at feed from the Artifact Conference! We posse members sniff the edges. So let's follow some scents.

Hey, despite talk of aliens, the regular news cycle goes on, with ever-rising tensions about water, energy, food 'n' phosphorus, or rising seas . . . or else more squabbles between guild and civitas and manse. Let's have a capsule update from my favorite summarizer, **Walter:**

Syr-Isra-Pal has threatened to ramp up coolwar if Turkey keeps sequestering snowmelt in the Great Anatolia Reservoir. Downstream neighbors blame this for worsening the Near Eastern Drought, plus an upsurge in quake activity across the Levant.

Rumors suggest several reffer cabals have agreed on a joint, renewed assault on the "decadent institutions of an obsolete, so-called Enlightenment." Most such tales are generated by peevish ai-bots, unleashed years ago by long-dead nihilists. But ever since the failed D.C. zeppelin attack, security anticipators are taking them all seriously, kicking their prefrontals into overdrive.

A recent spate of small-scale earth tremors, all over the world, has accompanied strange reports of underground or underwater detonations, all reaching a crescendo in the last few hours. Though some fret nervously about terr or reff attacks, a new correlo-study shows that few events are near human habitations. Most seem to be happening far out to sea.

And the top-linked thread: many reports in the last few hours of glimmering lights, bursting from chunks of formerly quiescent stone. The most notorious episode took place half a day ago at Islam's holiest shrine. Others include a piece of Chinese imperial jewelry in the Taipei Museum and a paving stone in Hyderabad. Now, scientific instruments laid out to watch scintillations on the Antarctic Plateau, report at least twenty faint, localized glimmers, deep within the ice sheet, implying there might be hundreds more beyond sensor range.

Thank you, Walter. Well? Which of those stories set you all a-quiver with excitement? We want something that regular media is likely to screw up! That'll benefit from half a million baying bloodhounds.

What's that? Okay, I expected this. Several throngs of you are intrigued by those **stones** that started lighting up, around the world. The obvious guess—it's <u>more-than-coincidentally</u> tied to the Havana Artifact? Well, sure, great topic . . . though I see several hundred teams, agencies and citizen-posses already pouncing on it. Seems pretty obvious, if creepy.

How about this alternative some of you suggested? What if that recent flurry of **micro-quakes** is somehow related? They've been at the lower end of detection range and almost hidden by normal temblor background. So far, it's all been largely dismissed as "normal fluctuations." But does anyone else see something strange about the data?

Yep, that's a good prelimalysis, Amsci Genovese. The energy profile really does stand out. Most of the extra quakes seem to occur in a narrow range of power release. Down around a sixtieth of a Richter. Far too narrow to be natural.

And yes, Insight-filled Hmong Science Collective, I see your point—how most of these events have the sonic shape of explosive detonations, and not natural fault slips! Will someone please probe security channels, in case the protector caste thinks these are terr or reff attacks? And why no damage reports? You'll lead that effort, Anne Dobson of Cape Town?

Come to think of it, let's start mapping events versus geology, terrain, political instability, hydro-cycles. . . .

Come on, people and people-helpers. Feedme here! Tear yourselves away from the TV and do what you are good at.

Bugging the universe with curiosity.

43.
SORRY I ASKED

Among all the added complications, who needed a rising wave of copycat *hoaxes*? People "discovering" ancient messenger-rocks of their own.

Some of the posted vids and palps showed blatant fakes—little more than chunks of glass, crudely lit from below, or pixeltrated with off-the-shelf image-altering programs—easy to spot. Others were the work of ingenious, high-tech pranksters, featuring impressive "aliens" who uttered mysterious warnings from their crystal homes . . . sometimes laying the groundwork for terrible punch lines, endlessly shaggy stories, or groaner puns. Others played it straight, claiming to be real star-emissaries offering deep (if always clichéd) wisdom . . . attracting storms of crit from smart posses yelling "fake!" And equal crowds of fervent believers.

A festival-like sense of momentum built, as vids of homemade Artifacts flooded the Mesh. *And it's possible that one or two may be real,* Gerald thought. *But someone else will have to check-and-vet them.*

The Contact Commission had its hands full with the oblong, rounded cylinder that he brought home from orbit. It sat before him now, drinking in a bright diet of photon energy. The resident aliens had asked for a recess behind shrouded mists. Some time to get organized. And Akana Hideoshi's team was happy to comply. People, too, needed food and rest. So did the tense observers who watched from the advisers' gallery, just beyond the tall glass wall.

Reconvening on schedule, Gerald sat between Emily Tang and Haihong Ming, as Genady, Ben, Patrice, Akana, and other team members took their places. He saw dignitaries arrange themselves among the plush cybo-chairs that were steeply arrayed, auditorium-style, beyond the quarantine barrier. They seemed less agitated over there, now that the behavioral conditioning experiment had worked and the aliens were behaving better. Not that anyone enjoys being proved wrong. The advisers' consensual holvatar representative—Hermes—no longer paced angrily, his broad forehead crowned with miniature lightning flashes. Now the ersatz god merely drummed the table, frowning nervously.

At the appointed time, all room lights dimmed and those swirling clouds within the Artifact began to change. Tshombe reduced the beam intensity, so everyone could see . . . as mists began to part, revealing a luminous vista of bright stars.

A veritable galaxy, presented in luscious three dimensionality, that none of the Earthling hoaxes had been able to duplicate so far. Gerald was about to shout for Ramesh to make sure the starscape was being recorded—

—when the Rajasthani astronomer beat him to it, reacting with an uncannily speedy virt.

These aren't real stars. Uniform in spectra and brightness, they're scattered about for art's sake. It's a metaphor.

Dang. That part of a long list of questions would have to be delayed, till more urgent matters were settled.

A murmur rose from the peanut gallery as, originating from dozens of distinct pinpoints, there unrolled a pattern of slender, curvy lines . . . that soon flattened and took the form of golden *roads,* tapering into the distance. These pathways branched and split, many of them leading to dead ends. But all of those that survived eventually joined together, merging one-by-one into a single highway that proceeded toward Gerald's point of view . . . now shared by several billion watchers, tuning in from all across Earth.

People still complain about the degraded image quality that's allowed to leave quarantine. In fact, only a very few of the most paranoid—not even Emily and her Tiger holvatar—still thought it likely that these images held dangerous codings.

Gerald leaned forward, staring directly into the Stone, instead of at the giant, magnifying screens nearby. Now, the eye began to make out figures, distant at first, striding along those golden paths. Seeming to begin at quite some distance, they all could be seen heading this way . . . toward the face of the Artifact that lay directly in front of Gerald. And soon, observers could tell that the Artifact beings all looked a bit different this time.

The centauroid, the bat-helicopter alien, the raccoonlike creature, the blimpy-thing . . . they now wore garments of some luxurious fabric, wafting in simulated breezes. Even the squid-cephalopod being had draped itself in formality as it glided forward along with the others, its means of locomotion as mysterious as ever.

Here it comes at last, Gerald thought. *The formal invitation.*

Where before there had seemed to be too little room at the interface—forcing aliens to jostle one another at the curved boundary between the Artifact's inner world and the humans outside—now the foreground somehow seemed uncrowded. All the visitor emissaries were able to share this grand procession, gathering and arranging themselves so that every one could see outward—and be seen.

"That's some group portrait, when they decide to get it together," the anthropologist Ben Flannery commented. "Their earlier fractiousness showed that they tolerate diversity. Now they are displaying a wakened *cooperative spirit* and shared purpose. What combination of traits could be more encouraging? I'm pretty optimistic, right about now."

General Hideoshi made a soft shushing sound. A number of the central figures were moving their arms/tentacles/appendages in unison . . .

. . . and letters formed, flowing toward the curved interface, arranging themselves into words that also emerged as sound from loudspeakers overhead.

We have asked the oldest surviving member to speak for us.

Out of the center of the crowd there emerged a being Gerald had seen before. Tall, bipedal, with a rotund-chubby figure, it had short arms that clasped each other across a stout belly. A roundish head nodded from atop its roly-poly neck. The eyes—wide but narrow-slitted, as if squinting with amusement—were in roughly the "right place" for a gestalt that seemed very close to human, and so was a thick-lipped mouth that even seemed to curve slightly upward, as if in an enigmatic smile. There was no nose—the creature apparently breathed through vents that opened and closed rhythmically, at the top of its head. Gerald's overall impression was of a wise-looking, Buddha-like being. In fact, though he knew it was taking first impressions *way* too far, the fellow seemed rather . . . jovial.

Oldest member? Do they mean that this was the first race of their commonwealth? The founders who emerged upon the starlanes before anybody else? Perhaps those who contacted and taught all the others how to live together in interstellar peace?

But wait. Gerald suddenly recalled. *Did they say "oldest surviving"? That doesn't necessarily mean anything ominous . . . still . . .*

Gerald knew his mind was racing way ahead of any rational basis for speculation. He tried to emulate the patience that he thought he saw in those eyes.

The head-top vents rippled and symbols emerged. Strange and unfamiliar, they rapidly mutated, transforming into letters of the Roman alphabet that rushed forward, arraying themselves into words which transducers interpreted into sound—conveyed by a voice that seemed both low and strong, if a bit breathy.

You have proved capable and worthy. Join us!

Gerald heard a number of outright sighs, as tension released, even though this only repeated the one cogent message already received so far. That earlier, hopeful statement had emerged out of chaos and confusion. Now, coming from a clearly chosen consensus leader, representing the entire alien community, it felt even more firm, clear, and reassuring.

He glanced at Akana, who nodded back at Gerald. They had worked out what he should say.

"We are honored.

"There's much to discuss. About your great and ancient society, and our reasons for both caution and joy.

"But let's begin by welcoming you to Planet Earth. On behalf of humanity, in goodwill and friendship."

Gerald felt a knot unwind in his stomach. He had managed to get through it all without a cough or "um" or twitch. The Notable-Quotable Words were finished, perhaps a bit more long-winded than famous, dramatic pronouncements by Caesar and Armstrong . . . certainly not eloquent. But still acceptable to go on the wall of Things Spoken Largely for History.

His words penetrated the Artifact via a device at the knobby end, and quickly manifested as a flurry of tiny symbols—varied and ranging from blocky letters to complex ideograms—that diverged and separated into several dozen separate streams, each aimed at a different alien, not just the ambassador standing a little ahead. The creatures, lined up in their neat rows, reacted with the wide range of behaviors you might expect—shivers and nods and tentacle ripples and shudders—but an overall impression seemed plain to Gerald. They were pleased.

The oldest one turned for brief consultation with the others, then more letters flowed from the top of the Buddha-like visitor's head, fluttering and transforming before plastering themselves against the glassy interface.

Your friendship is our greatest treasure. We will repay it with the finest gift possible.

"I told you so!" Ben Flannery murmured. To which Emily Tang merely offered a *we'll see* grunt.

But first, we must ask—have there been others?

Gerald blinked. *Others?*

He glanced at Akana, who shrugged back at him, mystified. In fact, none of the team members had anything to offer.

Then a shimmery *virt* floated down the table, settling in front of Gerald. He turned and saw that the sender was

Hermes, holvatar representative of the Advisory Panel—delegates from many nations, guilds, and estates, who sat beyond the quarantine glass. Displayed for Gerald in vivid three-dimensionality by the contact lenses he wore in both eyes, the virt glittered a simple insight.

"Others" may refer to previous encounters with alien probes.

Ah. Good guess. Someone in the peanut gallery was proving useful after all. Of course, it could also mean anything from UFOs to SETI signals to Jesus. But he decided to go with the suggestion, taking a deep breath.

"Your crystalline capsule was the first of its kind we've encountered, that spoke to our civilization with a clear message from afar."

He quashed a sudden impulse to add—*"That I know of."*

Another virtual message seemed to flutter in front of Gerald, this one sent by Genady.

Remember how we speculated about earlier artifacts falling to Earth, the way this one would have, if you hadn't snagged it? Picture many of them plummeting in, across vast stretches of time . . . mostly to shatter or sink in the sea. Perhaps some of them merely damaged . . .

Gerald grunt-clicked for Genady's virtual note to move aside . . . but to stay available. During those few seconds, the jolly-looking alien received and pondered Gerald's reply. It seemed pleased by this news, its eyes squinting even more amiably than before.

> **How fortunate! Then you will receive clean information. Be warned, however, that other emissaries may desperately seek attention. Some carry defective or misleading, or even dangerous, entreaties.**

Gerald swallowed, hard. Things had veered, abruptly, in a new direction. Suddenly, a veritable storm of virts swirled about, sent by almost every member of the contact team, as well as the animated "god" Hermes, who frantically scribbled one note after another, conveying ideas from the folks beyond the glass.

These Artifact visitors have rivals! Maybe even enemies . . .

So much for a peaceful universal cosmic federation . . .

Could "join us" mean enlisting in their squabbles against some unknown foes? Suddenly, the offer is looking a lot less tempting . . .

This fat envoy seems relieved, maybe even *surprised* that we've not met "others."

Gerald blink-prioritized, giving most of the virts just a cursory gist-glance. But he called forward Genady's follow-up message.

Kakashkiya! Do you think all those rumors we've heard recently . . . about bits of stone, suddenly lighting up . . . that those might be fragments and relics of older probes "desperately seeking attention"?

Akana caught Gerald's eye with an unspoken query. Given this sudden turn of events, should she call a recess?

No. He shook his head. It would do no harm to follow up with some direct questions.

"Thank you for the warning. We'll be careful and wary," he told the Oldest Surviving Member. "Nevertheless, please explain. Are you worried about other messenger probes because they were dispatched by . . . unfriendly forces?"

Gerald knew he could have expressed that better. But this conversation was already drifting *way* off any script the team had prepared.

The response came as members of the alien delegation seemed to shift and jostle, nervously. Several tried to move up next to the chosen representative, but were restrained by others. The humanoid seemed to grow a bit grim.

Some emissaries are problematic because of their
point or species of origin. And yes, some senders were
disagreeable. Other probe-heralds might be part of this
same lineage you see before you. Yet, they may be less
trustworthy, because of temporal factors.

Emily muttered, this time aloud.

"Criminy! He's talking about *document version control*!
He doesn't want us contaminated by an obsolete variant."

"Well . . . ," Ben Flannery muttered, looking a bit dazed.
"These people . . . these particular visitors . . . they *just arrived* . . . drifting close to Earth, where Gerald managed
to recover their capsule. Doesn't that suggest they'd be
more recent than . . ." The anthropologist stumbled, looking for vocabulary. ". . . than any that might have fallen to
Earth earlier? And hence more reliable . . ."

The blond Hawaiian stopped, unable to continue.

Gerald watched the Artifact. The words that had been
spoken by other team members did not seem to be penetrating the speech input device, so oral discussion was probably okay, especially amid the storm of virts. Still, this line
of thought was close to getting out of hand.

He faced the Artifact and spoke directly, perhaps a bit
louder than necessary.

"Clarify, please. Is there a potential for danger from
contact with the Others that you spoke of? Is there *war*,
among rival interstellar races and civilizations out there?"

The pudgy humanoid grimaced in a way that Gerald
found hard to interpret, or even guess at. Perhaps later
correlation-analysis would make it easier to translate facial
expressions.

War? As in devastating struggle? Reciprocal causation
of organic death and physical destruction? One species

**or people competing or directly harming another
across interstellar space? No. There is no war. There
cannot be war across the stars. It has never happened.
It will never happen.**

There was a general sigh at this reassurance. And sure,
the news had to be seen as important, even epochal.

Yet Gerald was starting to feel a bit miffed. Good tidings seemed always to come accompanied by something
else that turned out to be jarring, even disturbing. He was
left with the ongoing and ever-present suspicion that things
weren't quite as they seemed.

Emily Tang offered a worried virt.

**So . . . there's no heavy conflict. That's a relief. Still,
there appears to be urgent rivalry at some level. Alien
civs apparently send out emissary probes pretty often . . .
and covetously hope that those probes will get to be the
ones that actually make contact with New Guys like us.**

Akana passed along a gisted security briefing. Even now,
investigation teams from EU, AU, UN, U.S., Great China,
the Caliphate, and countless consortia were converging on
every credible account of strange *glowing* stones. Hypotheses flurried, but a mesh consensus was converging that
these objects—(well, some of them, the ones that weren't
hoaxes)—might also be artifacts from space, perhaps broken or crippled remnants that had been scattered around
the Earth across many years.

Harkening back to the words of the Oldest Surviving
Member, he realized; these "others" were, indeed, attracting notice.

Dr. Tshombe complained.

**But why suddenly now? The other probes never sum-
moned attention so garishly, across all the millennia. Not
until this very moment! It is an incredible coincidence.**

Gerald glanced at Emily, then Akana. Clearly, they both knew the answer to that question . . . and it started showing up in virts from the Advisers' Panel.

Somehow, all those "other" sky stones—damaged or lost for ages—somehow they must know that the Artifact is here. And that it is getting the full regard of humankind.

And they ardently want to be heard . . .

. . . too?

. . . or instead?

Gerald was tempted to follow that thought-line. To wonder why alien crystals would show such blatant evidence of a crude human emotion . . .

. . . jealousy . . .

Except that he also had a job to do. To keep up his end of a conversation with the Oldest Surviving Member, and not to get distracted by secondary matters.

Focus on what's important.

First, verify the stuff that's vital. We can psychoanalyze alien motivations later.

They were watching him—the visitors in the stone. So was the world. He took a sip of tea from the hotbulb in front of him, cleared his throat, and asked in a crisp, clear voice:

"So, then . . . can we take it that you are all part of a commonwealth of coexistence and peace?"

The Buddha smile broadened.

Yes. We have our disputes, of course. But our coexistence is timeless and ever hopeful. We strive, perpetually, for the common advantage of all. You, too, can benefit, as we have, by joining us!

Instead of relishing the friendliness, Gerald continued probing, this time without a pause.

"But those *Others* that you spoke of—do they come from different species and civilizations that view the people of your planet as competitors?"

After his words floatéd in to the aliens, the smile of the Oldest Member thinned slightly.

I have already explained, there is no competition among species and planets and civilizations.

Gerald frowned, suddenly skeptical.

"What? No competition at all? But you just said that some probe-makers were 'problematic' and that you have *disputes*. Please explain the contradiction."

There is no contradiction. Individual entities may argue, contest, or compete, in certain contexts. Species and civilizations do not.

Ben Flannery spoke up.

"He must be referring to the *relativity limitation*. The stars are so far apart that advanced beings don't even bother to try interstellar travel, except with these cheap, fast, crystalline probes. So much for all those grand delusions people wallowed in, back during the Twentieth Century. Fantasies about *super-Kardashev societies*, exploring and colonizing the cosmos with ramships or generation arks, or self-replicating explorer robots, or even *warp drive*. Or building megastructures to control the fate of galaxies! Those were just god-fantasies that our fathers daydreamed, on their way to mythical Singularity Heaven."

Gerald glanced up at the Advisers' Gallery, where a hundred of humanity's brightest, or most influential, had taken seats to observe this historic occasion. In the plush VIP area, one individual seemed to react quite heatedly to Ben's interpretation. A dark fellow with a waving 'do of cyber-activated hair. Gerald's contaicts supplied a caption-nametag—**Professor Noozone**. Ah, yes, the famous scientific razzle artist. He was shouting and shaking a fist toward Flannery—

—who continued on, blithely indifferent to a storm of virts that tried to crowd in around him.

"The key point that we've been told just now is that there is absolutely never direct physical contact between sapient species, who simply live too far apart. All they have to exchange is information. Hence, there's nothing to argue or compete over!"

It sounded logical. But Gerald found the assertion doubtful. In fact, patently absurd.

Even people who are calm, reasonable, and satiated—who have no physical dissension with others, or conflicting needs—can and will quarrel. So they exchange only information and trade only ideas? Natural beings will bicker over those!

Anyway, who could possibly claim that these aliens were "above" altercation or too mature to argue! To be frank, he had never seen such an inherently *testy* bunch. And that was before the recent news about rivalry *between* interstellar envoy-probes!

Could it all be a matter of misunderstood definitions? "Competition," for example, might be translating wrong. Gerald decided to seek clarification.

"Please explain," he asked. Took a deep breath. Then plunged on. "If you often wrangle as individuals, how is it that your home species and civilizations and planets never compete or quarrel with each other?"

The Buddha-being contemplated this, then answered slowly, with a mien that made Gerald think of a wise-old teacher, patiently answering the simpleminded query of a dimwitted child.

Our home species and civilizations and planets could not ever compete with one another. Because they never met.

TORALYZER

Okay, so now we've got a good prelimalysis of those recent worldwide microquakes. After sift-removing the background of natural tectonic activity and known sources of human-generated noise, what we're left with is a dispersion of mysterious, compact detonations, nearly all of them occurring in a very narrow energy range.

Furthermore, although they at first seemed to be scattered all over the globe, we can now tell that these micro-quake events are limited mostly to certain types of geology! Mudflats, sedimentary layers, alluvial plains, glacial moraines, the Antarctic plateau . . . and of course, the ocean basins. Almost nothing is happening in the great continental cratons, or granitic mountain ranges, or anywhere near regions of fresh volcanism, like sea floor spreading centers.

Yes, the coincidence is getting hard to refute. These events occur in exactly the sorts of terrain where an object that fell from the sky might stand a chance of landing with less than vaporizing impact. Mostly either underwater or in places that used to be oceans, long ago. Zones where any surviving remnants might have accumulated, or been embedded, across thousands or millions of years.

For those of you just checking in, this is Tor "Zep-girl" Povlov, serving as cogenter for a smartposse investigating whether these quakes might be related to *another* mystery phenomenon—eyewitness reports of sudden emissions of strange light, given off by stony or glassy objects in the last day or so.

Yes, I know we're all trying hard to keep up with real-time developments, even as the whole world follows the conversation between astronaut Gerald Livingstone and the entities dwelling within the Havana Artifact. This could be the greatest test ever of our ability to usefully *divide attention* . . . to keep doing effective investigation work while transfixed by a fast-breaking news story!

From the conversation in Washington, one thing has just become clear. The Artifact emissaries do not want humanity talking to "others."

And, just as clearly, every word they've said makes us *eager* to hunt down and learn more about these different shining stones!

So we come to an obvious question. Might the glitters and glimmers that have been reported in Mecca, Hyderabad, and Stonehenge, in Taipei, La Paz, Goma, and Toulouse . . . might these be just the tip of the iceberg, indicating a truly vast number of "other" contact probes?

Might the recent spate of mysterious micro-tremors, deep underground and out of sight, be connected to all this? Could these outbursts be attempts by "other" artifacts to draw attention to themselves?

And why now, if they sat under mud or silt for millennia or eons?

Duh. Because they sense—somehow—that the Havana Artifact is hogging all the fun!

Why not earlier? Because till now it seemed better to wait! In performing these detonations or screaming glows, they may be expending whatever reserves they had been hoarding to get them across the ages! Using it up now, in order to have one last chance to—

Just a minute . . . just a minute. Did you see that? Did that fat alien representative just say what I think he said?

Zoom into the Artifact Conference. See the words of the Oldest Member on the big screen.

Our home species and civilizations and planets could not ever compete with one another. Because they never met.

What—on Earth or Heaven or the Mesh—could he mean by that?

44.
LAYERED REALITY

Outside the dome, miffed from losing at water polo, Noisy Stomach complained to his young comrade, Three-Tone, as they jetted away some distance from the Tribe. Three-Tone groused about the stupid referee, the stupid ball, the stupid captain of their team. . . .

Foolish Yellowbelly, should have put me in!
Let me score! I'd score more!

Noisy Stomach had already dismissed the game from his mind. A silly pastime. A legacy of the days when humans used to live inside the dome and made things interesting in so many ways, with flashing lights and strange sensations, always fussing over pregnant females, or else begging sperm donations from males. Better times.

Now?

For a while the Tribe once again had a tame human of their own, to remove parasites and handle the net and bear the brunt of jokes. Only, the elders had decided, it was time to give him back. For his health.

Noisy Stomach mourned.

> # What about MY health?
> # Who will pick my pecs and clean my sores?
> # Should have kept him. He is ours!

They both breached to inhale, tasting in the moist, tropical air signs of a coming squall, maybe late this afternoon. That always freshened things. Rain pushed down some of the unpleasant tang of metal and plastic and man-feces, especially strong near shore.

Noisy Stomach felt a grumble of hunger resonate from his innards to the space around him—a trait that made him poor at stealth, forcing him to specialize in beating, rather than catching. He was about to resume griping—something that young males often did for pleasurable competition, as much as from resentment—when he noticed that Three-Tone had zoomed away, propelled by powerful fluke strokes, leaving a swirl of I-have-just-detected-something-interesting bubbles in his follow-me wake.

Gamely, Noisy Stomach gave chase, always willing to go poke at something interesting. But what could it be? While in hard pursuit of his friend, he concentrated on sampling the sea sounds with left and right swings of his sensitive jaw, trying to figure out what had sparked Three-Tone's sudden burst of speed, racing to the north.

As usual, there was a lot of spurious noise—the pounding of surf on a nearby beach and waves crashing against a more distant reef. Of course, there were irksome human motor sounds, a grating fact of life, both day and night—with one or two of them evidently heading this way—or toward the habitat dome—at high speed.

Evidently, the Tribe was about to lose its pet. Ah well. None of that seemed to be what sparked the interest of Three-Tone.

Could this be about food? Or danger? A quick scan found nothing unusual amid the fish frequencies, where tightly bunched schools could be heard, swirling like cyclones, surrounded by hunters who made quick-flicking dashes . . . and prey thrashed, delightfully constrained by clamping jaws. His hunger deepened, almost in syncopated rhythm . . . but no, there was nothing on those channels to excite Three-Tone so.

Swimming hard to catch up with his friend, Noisy Stomach sought clues in lower, complex layers of textured sound. Strata that the older dolphins were always obsessing about, forever wispy, tentative, that wove through dreams. It was here that you often heard the great whales speak to each other, with moans and cries and songs that traversed all the way across whole ocean basins. Sometimes about food and mating, of course. But also conveying the sea's own, slow gossip.

And, even lower still—nestled amid the groans of a creaking, quake-prone Earth—you could just make out the chittering, scrabbling commentary of the crabs, crawling and scooting and clambering everywhere, who snapped at anything unusual, combining to create a deep background susurration. A murky, clickety chatter that seemed to rise right out of the ubiquitous mud.

That was where Noisy Stomach finally heard it too. A patterning—wavering and nebulous, but persistent—of surprise.

> # . . . starlight . . . flowing upward . . .
> # . . . very strange, indeed . . .

That was how he interpreted the skittering-clattering scrabble-sound. Catching up with Three-Tone at last, he quickly matched swim-rhythms with his friend, kicking and then arching, to jet out of the water for air, then hurrying along again beneath the surface, in perfect synchrony. Apparently, they were heading toward only the nearest of many sites where bottom-dwellers were behaving this way.

At least three others lay within a day's swim . . . and something told him that there were more, and more, even beyond the horizon.

They were streaking toward a site more than an hour away from the dome. It made Noisy Stomach start to worry. Would he miss the hunt? Only making it back to the Tribe in time to pick at fish skeletons, hanging in the net? Were they both risking hunger, on the basis of a CRAB RUMOR? Crabs, who were barely smarter than the rocks they hid under?

Though . . . if it were happening in so many places. . . . Indeed, even the whales seemed to have noticed, pausing in their painful, deep ponderings. Swiveling that slow curiosity of theirs.

Noisy Stomach knew they were getting close. For one thing, the excitement had spread to other sonic layers, shorter range and smarter. He could hear, just ahead, a squealfest of excited pinnipeds, for example, drawn from a nearby island rookery. Sea lions mostly, and monk seals. Then—rapid scans of subtle sonar that could only mean . . .

He pulled up short.

Dolphins. A whole pod of Tursiops, already arrived on the scene.

Strangers. Naturals—unaltered and almost certainly suspicious of the clan that Noisy Stomach belonged to. His small clan of cetaceans, tainted by the delicious agony of human meddling. Sometimes, other Tursiops were outright unfriendly toward members of the Tribe, snapping at the dolphins-who-had-changed.

But Three-Tone was plunging ahead, straight toward an island headland—a cliff face jutting out of the crashing sea. Not a safe place, even at the best of times. Yet, the sea lions and other dolphins were already gathered there, swooping about and chattering with excitement.

Noisy Stomach approached cautiously.

This time there appeared to be no overt hostility. A trio of attractive females—two of them in heat—gave him a look-over as he passed close. None of the males from their pod hovered nearby to guard them. That was queer enough, in its own right!

Though tempted to tarry, he kicked hard to hurry after Three-Tone, drawing toward a place where cetaceans and pinnipeds were swirling about each other nervously, darting up for air and then diving to poke away at something in the shallow muck.

It appeared to be no more than a jumble of rocks and debris from some fairly recent landslide—a collapse of the nearby cliff that must have happened in the last day or so. Dolphins were beak-poking at the detritus, moving small stones with their teeth or prying larger ones aside, as if burrowing for crustaceans to eat. Only they weren't murmuring with tunes of eager hunting. Curiosity—that was the theme of the moment.

Noisy Stomach pulled up alongside Three-Tone, wary, in case they might have to defend themselves. This clan had females in heat. That, plus all this excitement . . .

Then he saw the glow. It came from just below a stone jumble, illuminating the underside of one dolphin's rostrum. The native Tursiops responded by hurrying faster, as a couple of sea lions—and Three-Tone—joined in. Against his better judgment, Noisy Stomach got caught up in the moment, taking his own turns at beak-digging, at mouthing away pebbles and clumps of dirt . . .

. . . until all that remained in the way was a single big rock piled on top of the light source, too heavy and obstinate to move with their mouths. Several dolphins from the other tribe spewed rapid sonar clicks of frustration, as did

Noisy Stomach, wishing he could intimidate the stone, or crumble it to bits, with blasts of sound from his brow.

 # Move aside. Move aside now.
 # Let us show. Show you how.

He swiveled, surprised that newcomers could have approached without him realizing. Especially members of his own kind. The only voices on Earth who spoke like that.

It was Old Yellowbelly, accompanied by Sweet Thing and Storm Bluffer and . . . almost the entire Tribe! They must have followed, drawn by the tumult.

Most of the natural dolphins edged backward, clicking nervously. Younger males darted about, blustering with harsh sonar beams that probed Noisy Stomach and his clan-mates deep enough to tell what they had for breakfast. Bravado that was clearly unbacked by real courage.

Sky-Biter approached. Between strong jaws he carried a slender pole, as long as he was. Noisy Stomach wondered— did the big bull haul that thing here, all the way from the dome? Or did Sky-Biter find it nearby, just now, amid the clutter of man-made debris that littered every patch of sea bottom?

Either way, several members of the Tribe immediately set to work. Yellowbelly took one pointy end of the rod and guided it toward a gap in the rocks, where the strange shine illuminated the approaching metal tip. When it was firmly planted under a large stone, Yellowbelly jetted away, to breathe at the surface. Suddenly, in acute need for air, Noisy Stomach followed. But he spumed and inhaled quickly, diving back down again to rejoin the others.

The natives were chattering louder than ever now, swimming nervous circles and prattling superstitiously about how weird and wrong this was. But Noisy Stomach proudly joined Three-Tone and half a dozen other members of his Tribe, seizing the rod along its length and pushing down.

The big rock budged, shifted to one side, then fell back into place. So they tried again from a different angle, and failed.

Then Storm Bluffer flew in and settled himself so that part of the pole, near the rod's buried tip, lay across his broad back. Now, they all pumped with their flukes, pushing down on the other end of the rod, hard! Storm Bluffer grunted . . . and the obstruction flew off! As did the pole and most of the natural dolphins, fleeing in dismay, as the glow now spread freely from an exposed pit in the muck.

Members of the Tribe—plus a few of the bravest rustics—gathered around, spraying the site with exploratory clicks, and also bringing their eyes closer to peer at the source.

It had much the same sonic reflectivity as a river-smoothed stone, pockmarked and pitted by time, but it behaved like one of those machines that the dome-people used to shine at members of the Tribe, back when Noisy Stomach was little. Yet, something about it didn't feel man-wrought at all. The light was unlike any he had seen emitted before, either in nature or by the tools of human-meddlers.

He could tell that blurry images were trying to form, under the scratches and gouges—shapes and outlines that wavered and rippled and failed to coalesce, then started to fade.

A collective sigh of disappointment fell from the onlookers. But Noisy Stomach would have none of that. He edged forward . . . a bit surprised by his own gumption . . . and aimed a chiding, focused beat of pure meaning at the stone thing.

 # What? Give up so easy?
 # Come on you, don't be lazy.
 # We came far—worked hard for this.
 # Amuse us!

For some time nothing much happened. Faint ripples of gray coursed the oblong object, that might once have been smooth as wave-rolled glass. One end of it seemed soft, porous, and spongelike—almost crumbly—like bone that had been sucked of all its juices. Even as he watched, that end appeared to decay a little more, giving up some of its rigid essence, in order for the rest of the stone to brighten a bit.

Noisy Stomach felt one of the natural dolphins—a female—sidle up along his left side, her curiosity equal to his own. Both of them waited, holding their breath until it was almost stale. Then—

—the stone responded. This time with surface vibrations that shook its surface and resonated the surrounding waters, taking up the sonic glyph that Noisy Stomach had projected earlier and echoing it back, modified into a sculpture of crafted sound.

*** . . . came far?*
*** . . . (YOU?!?) came far?*
*** ???*

He did not need words like "irony" to interpret the underlying texture of that glyph. Such human terms could only aim, crudely, in the right direction.

Anyway, the dolphins did not need to understand. Whether they were of the modified variety or not, mere understanding could wait. It was enough that they all could tell—something both tragic and terribly funny was going on. Like a mullet, plaintively inquiring if mercy were an option, while thrashing between a pair of jaws.

And so . . . they laughed.

TORALYZER

Amsci Barcelona has intercepted and gisted an intelligence blip from one of the estates.

Apparently, nations and consortia all over the planet have paid heed to *our* seismic mapping-correlation. This posse's hypothesis that the microquakes may come from "other" interstellar probes—possible rivals of the Havana Artifact that arrived long ago and are deeply buried, but that may now be trying hard to get attention. Perhaps desperate not to miss their one chance to make contact.

Taking this possibility seriously, several agencies have dispatched teams toward recent seismic sites. Most of them rocked deep layers of limestone or sandstone, hundreds, or even thousands of meters beyond easy reach. But dozens happened near or at the surface. Reports are expected from some of those locales, soon.

So, we in this posse have already had some impact! Is anybody up for . . .

. . . Oh, sorry. Most of you are mono-zoomed onto feed from the Artifact Conference right now.

All right. I'll narrow down, too. We can follow up on attention-seeking, exploding rocks later.

Let's see if the astronaut and his Contact Team can figure out the enigma.

45

A PARROT OX

Words of the Oldest Surviving Member glowed across the face of the Artifact—and the screens and specs and contaict lenses of at least four or five billion Earthlings.

> **Our home species and civilizations and planets could not ever compete with one another. Because they never met.**

Upon first reading that message, Gerald had felt his jaw muscles go slack. He couldn't help it, even though he knew he must look silly, gaping in astonishment.

The maelstrom of virtual messages that had been swirling around his peripheral vision tumbled now like autumn leaves, dissolving as their authors lost interest in them, focusing instead on their own sense of confusion.

Everyone, on both sides of the quarantine glass, fell silent. Not one person had a single insight to contribute. Not if their thoughts were as blank and stunned as Gerald's felt right now. You could hear the air-conditioning system purr . . . plus a hum from the floating display where the Oldest Surviving Member's statement still glowed, while people here and across the globe scanned it over and over again, trying to make sense of an apparent paradox.

Amid this silence, someone's phone abruptly rang—an impertinent jangling, expressing urgency. Even so, Gerald would have ignored it, along with everything else but the alien puzzle-statement . . . except there followed a sharp scream!

He glanced toward the Advisers' Gallery, to see an elderly woman jump up and down, alternately shouting and sobbing while holding an old-fashioned joymaker handset.

Lacey Donaldson-Sander, said an identifying caption—
one of the world's richest people. She seemed quite overcome. Professor Noozone at first tried to console her,
then, grasping the news, grinned and hugged her. Those
around the pair joined in, evidently having some reason
for bliss.

*Well, if anything were to shock us from our trance—our
stunned cognitive dissonance—it might as well be somebody's shout of joy.*

He turned back to the latest alien missive, and decided
it was a really bad idea to lose initiative. Time to get direct then. Specific. No more skirting the edges. Gerald
leaned forward, enunciating toward the Artifact that he
had grabbed out of space, rescuing the stone before it could
plummet and crash upon the Earth.

"Question: Do you now exist as one of the artificially
emulated inhabitants of an interstellar probe that was dispatched across the light-years, in order to meet and contact
other species of intelligent life such as ourselves?"

> **I am as you describe. And yes, that is a large part of
> our mission.**

"Is this the usual method by which technological species
learn of one another?"

> **Yes it is.**

"Did you, repeatedly, offer an invitation to join your
multispecies, interstellar community?"

> **We did. You will be most welcome among us.**

Ben Flannery pounded the table in frustration. He leaned

toward the Artifact and broke the agreed rules by shouting directly, impatience overcoming his sunny nature.

"Us! Us! You're not telling us ANYTHING about who *us* is!

"All right, so there's *no war.* Terrific! But how many sapient races participate in your federation? How is it governed? What are the benefits of membership? Which planet did this probe come from and how did it travel and how long did it take? . . . And . . ."

Genady and Ramesh finally managed to grab Ben's shoulders and pull him back to his seat. Though, in their eyes, there lay clear sympathy for his frame of mind.

"Oh, shit," Gerald said, as he saw a flurry of letters, glyphs, and ideograms flow into the Artifact. This time, apparently, Flannery's shouts had been loud enough to register with the translation system. Akana met his eye with a shrug. No sense in trying to retract the questions. They were, after all, things that everybody wanted to know.

Oldest Surviving Member rotated his rotund form to consult with the others, before turning back toward the curved interface.

> **We have already replied that there are ninety-two races participating.**

> **Governance is a matter of flexibly adapting to circumstances, as you earlier observed.**

Gerald felt furious at Ben. These answers were obvious or redundant, or at best minor matters. When the whole world wanted to follow up on that cryptic remark about species having "never met." Could the translation be literal, having only to do with having never met *physically and in person*? Somehow, that explanation didn't seem right.

> **As for the benefits of membership, these include a**
> **potential for vastly extended existence, far beyond**
> **normal possibility. In effect—life everlasting.**

Gerald blinked.

Okay . . . that last bit got everyone's attention.

For the second time in a few minutes, everyone in the vast contact chamber and connected Advisers' Gallery went silent. Gerald could imagine the condition settling in, around the world. Indeed, the planet might be at its quietest since the dawn of the Industrial Age.

I guess . . . people will want me to follow up on this, in particular.

But the Buddha-like being simply went on, answering Flannery's list of queries in the order given.

> **To explain this probe's point of origin and method of**
> **travel, I will defer to Low-Swooping Fishkiller, whose**
> **people made and dispatched the particular contact-**
> **maker that you see before you.**

The creature who Gerald had likened to a bat with helicopter wings, flutter-hopped forward a short distance to alight next to Oldest Surviving Member. Grimacing with carnivore teeth, it brought together two antennalike manipulator appendages and spread them apart again. A patch of blackness expanded outward, to coat the entire left side of the Artifact.

A scene coalesced before all the human observers, soon revealing a planet in the foreground that turned slowly in space. Seas that rainbow-glistened like oil slicks lapped against corkscrew continents where patches of green threaded between gray peaks and dun-colored plains. The nightside was ablaze with brightly illuminated cities, laid out in near perfect concentric circles that brusquely ignored the dictates of mere geography.

Along with billions of others, Gerald found the scene transfixing. Though Ramesh complained, expressing his own unique priority. "I'm trying to record as many stars as I can, to get a location and time fix. If only the damn ugly *planet* weren't in the way. . . ."

Pulling backward, the portrayed point of view soon took in a large foreground object—a structure of girders and struts, of vacuum warehouses and flaring torches, all connected together in apparent orbit above the planet. An edifice far more vast than any space station Gerald had ever conceived. Zooming in upon this giant workshop, the story image cruised past bat-creatures wearing puffy, transparent, globelike space suits, who were supervising a production line where glittering, translucent *eggs* could now be seen emerging from a luminous factory shed, one at a time.

The story image zoomed in vertiginously, arriving next to one of the lambent, rounded cylinders, now revealed to have a boxy contraption attached to one end. Along with all the other recently produced probes, this one rode upon a prodigiously lengthy conveyor belt toward the base of a huge, elongated machine—a kind of *gun,* Gerald realized— that swiveled to aim at a chosen point in space . . . and then *fired* something that sparkled and quickly vanished into starry night.

Then the long, narrow artillery tube turned its opensided muzzle slightly, facing a new spot in the sky, and fired again.

Ramesh decreed the consensus opinion of his own advisers and ais.

It's great big mass accelerator. Prelimestimate . . . it might hurl these pellets up to maybe 3 percent of lightspeed. Impressive, though not enough to do the full job.

Gerald had a feeling that time was being compressed. The ride up the conveyor belt took only a few seconds, then he was looking backward, past the newly minted Artifact, at the factory and planet as the accelerator throbbed, preparing to shoot this probe into the great beyond.

Fascinated, Gerald saw a pack of glowing objects start to converge from several directions, approaching the place where the Artifact had been made. Bat-beings turned also to look behind them toward the planet.

Time was up. When the moment came—and even a bit before—the mighty industrial works and the nearest patch of planetary atmosphere seemed to flare, accompanying a fierce intensity of released energy as the great gun fired . . .

. . . and, in an instant, the homeworld of the bat-creatures fell away behind, diminishing to a bright speck . . . to nothing.

Now the simulated camera view turned and depicted the box at the front of the pellet opening up, unrolling an array of what looked like *wires,* that spread out like an unfolding net.

Huh. I was expecting a photon sail. Perhaps pushed by a laser beam sent by the home system. It's the obvious way to boost speed at this point for a cheap, efficient interstellar craft. But that's no sail it deployed. And look, the sun that we're heading away from doesn't seem to be sending any help. No pushing beam of light.

Judging from stellar movements, some years have passed already. A decade maybe, and so far there's no . . .

Ah! Here we go!

Suddenly, the home star seemed to brighten, many times over, though in a strangely speckled coloration. The array of wires, which had been floating loosely, now billowed outward, tautening. And there came—Gerald could feel it—a sense of acceleration!

Okay. It's not a laser, but a particle beam of some sort. Electrons, possibly. Or protons. Maybe even heavy ions, targeted exactly to pass through the wire array in order to transfer momentum via magnetic induction. How about that. More complicated than a light sail, but maybe they also use the wires to leverage against the galactic magnetic field over long distances. One way to steer . . .

In fact, I wonder if you can actually use the particles that have passed you by, when you later catch up with them. . . .

Gerald felt a hand on his shoulder and almost jumped out of his chair.

It was General Akana Hideoshi. The petite officer motioned for him to get up and follow her.

"But—"

Akana's expression was adamant. "This show is being recorded. You can see it all later. Meanwhile, there are developments."

Reluctantly, Gerald stood up, only to realize that he badly needed to stretch. Body crackling propelled a sudden, overpowering desire to move about. Still, the Artifact's tale spoke directly to the space traveler in him. It was hard to tear away.

Over in a corner of the contact arena, behind a partial privacy screen, the two of them joined Emily Tang and Genady Gorosumov. "What is it?" he asked, while extending his legs onto tiptoe and relieving tension by leaning, left and right.

Emily held up a finger.

"First, it's confirmed—those micro-quakes that proliferated during the last day or so are from long-ago fallen pellet probes."

"Really? Confirmed already? How could they—"

She pointed to a screen. There he saw a panorama of

humans and assisting robots dredging through a muddy
river estuary. Another showed men toiling amid boulders,
freshly tumbled from a layered cliff of sedimentary stone.
Emily sped through the work, arriving at a similar climax
in four separate cases—shouts and the recovery of something that reacted to human touch by emitting a brief but
excited glow.

Washed of muck and debris, or chipped free of eons-old
rocky casings, what the workers revealed was never smooth
or intact, like the Havana Artifact. But even in fragments,
a family resemblance was clear. And, in two of the recovered specimens, one could see a definite effect as the surface felt its first sunlight in . . . a very long time. Ripples of
cloudy gray. Flickers of color. Hints of pattern, struggling
to emerge.

"Apparently, the detonations weren't only to get attention. A few of them actually managed to explosively free
themselves from the strata they were trapped in, thus making it much easier to find them. Of course, it was pure luck
for those that happened to be near the surface, or next to a
cliff edge. A vast majority simply blew up chunks of their
own material for nothing, buried under a million years of
muck or sediment. We'll never find most of the relics, no
matter how hard we—"

"Tell him the second thing," Akana ordered.

"Yeah, right." Emily click-commanded the screens and
holos to show something new. This time—starry vistas.
Gerald briefly expected to be back inside the Artifact's
storytelling vid. But no. He recognized Scorpio . . . the
Southern Cross . . . Libra . . . These were views from Earth.
Or relatively near.

"See that pulsation?" Emily pointed at a "star" that
couldn't be a star. Too green. Too regular in its flickering.

"Parallax?" he asked.

"Most of these seem to be located in the inner asteroid

belt," Genady replied. "A couple of hundred, so far. Though some have been spotted as near as L-3 and several on the surface of the Moon."

"Jesus and the Maya. *Hundreds?* When—?"

"All in the last hour or so. Numbers are still rising."

"But," his mind was a whirl, "but how could these things *know* that it's time to start yelling for attention? Sure, some may be close enough to pick up broadcasts of our interview with the Artifact. But way out *there*? Or deep underground?"

Emily and Genady glanced at each other. Clearly all this was happening too quickly, almost at the limit of human ability to process information.

"Has any of this been released to the public?"

Akana shrugged. "How can we hold it back? Look at Haihong Ming, over in that corner with a privacy hood over his head, consulting with his government. What else would they be discussing at a time like this? Obviously *they* already know. Indications are that five more nations and three guilds do as well. And the amsci clubs are sniffing like bloodhounds. Many of them have optics that can spot the phenomena . . . and surely will.

"For that matter, I'm not sure how anybody will benefit from secrecy at this point. The earthquake correlation first came from a citizen posse. Aren't we better off having as many minds thinking about this as possible? In parallel?"

It wasn't the attitude one typically associated with a government bureaucrat, especially a military flag officer. On the other hand, clearly, Akana knew these weren't typical times.

Gerald inhaled and exhaled repeatedly, trying to clear his head. He had become a historical figure by grabbing out of space something that seemed utterly unique and epochal. Now to find out that the thing was only one of thousands, possibly millions . . . perhaps as common as any other kind of large gemstone ... well, it was humbling, daunting, and ignited the question—*Why haven't we stumbled across these things before?*

And he realized. *I bet we have. Here and there, across centuries. Maybe some did call for attention during other eras. Only now's the time, the opportunity they were all built for. When we're ripe for contact. When we're technologically able to "join" ... whatever it is they want us to join.*

It all made weird, dizzying sense. A plethora of cheap probes, sent from many locations across wide stretches of time could be far more efficient than a few very expensive ones, capable of their own propulsion. Cheaper than keeping up a blaring "tutorial beacon" on the off chance that one star out of a hundred million might happen to engender radio astronomers that year.

Yet, one mystery still stood apart from all the others.

Why are the pellets all programmed to be so frantically competitive with one another? How can it matter which of them introduces us to galactic civilization? Do they earn some kind of recruiting commission?

He glanced over his shoulder in time to see something that gave him a strange thrill. The Havana Artifact was finishing the tale of its origin and journey across space. Planet Earth now filled the big screen—destination in sight.

Gerald put aside curiosity over the parts of the tale he had missed. Akana was right. He could call up a replay, any time, along with gloss annotations by experts in every field.

Only now, with the cloud-flecked Panamanian Isthmus in the background, there loomed upward a slender, impossibly long object, resembling a rope or snake with a claw gaping at one end. As they all watched, the jaw opened wide, with fingers that were meshed together like a baseball fielder's glove. Gerald felt his right hand flex and stretch, remembering how this moment felt—was it less than a month ago?—when he and his little monkey sidekick piloted the tether-grabber toward this fateful rendezvous. Only now he was watching from the other side—the perspective of an interstellar wanderer.

One that happened to be far, far luckier than most, to arrive at just the right place and time, when a human astronaut happened to be ready . . . and had the tools.

Would I have been so cool and professional, during the grab, if I had known what I was reaching for?

Still, he couldn't help wincing, as the claw closed all around . . .

. . . and suddenly the story was over. The scene cleared, leaving Low-Swooping Fishkiller, the bat-helicopter being, standing next to the Oldest Surviving Member, whose Buddha smile now left Gerald entirely unassuaged.

"Thanks for telling me all this," he said to Akana and the others. "But now it's time to get some real answers."

He knew that the grimness he felt in his jaw and flexing hands could also be seen in his eyes.

MASS INTERROGATION

Questions for the Artifact aliens, distilled from over thirty-five million submitted by the public, ranked according to popularity and relevance by Deep Purple analytical engine. The Contact Commission has promised to get to some of these concerns— just as soon as "basic issues" with the visitor entities are resolved.

Are you here to teach us better ways? How can I start?
(#1 for 3 days)
Are you here to conquer or kill us? And can we talk you out of it? *(#2 for 13 days)*

How do we get that "life everlasting" you promised?
(Up from zero during the last two hours and rising fast)
What will it take to get you to like us? *(Still in 4th position*
after 5 days)
Are you on speaking terms with God? *(Up from*
#12 during the last hour)
Got a spare warp drive? *(Up from #16 during*
the last 36 hours)*
Are you a hoax? *(Down from 5th place 1 hour ago)*
What will it take to get you to leave us alone? *(Down from*
3rd place two hours ago)
Have you got any new cuisine? *(Up from #46 during*
the last 10 hours)

* Millions of votes for this question appear to have been generated
not by human participants but by a new version of the voxpopuli
worm. Yet, our ai arbiter, Deep Purple, insists that we rank it up
here, for some unknown reason of its own.

46.

A SMILING FACE

Of course they should be able to track her every movement. The men who were pursuing Mei Ling obviously
knew their way around the Mesh. It would take little effort
or expense to assign software agents—pattern sifters and
face-recognizers—to go hopping among the countless
minilenses stuck on every doorpost, lintel, and street sign,
searching for a poorly dressed young woman with a baby,
dragged through prosperous Pudong by a strange little boy.

From the start, she expected them to catch up at any
moment.

Only . . . what will they do if they corner us on a busy
street? Grab me in front of hundreds of witnesses? Perhaps

that is why I've been free to run for a while. They are only awaiting the right moment.

At first, while fleeing, she kept turning her head and darting her eyes, scanning for pursuers or suspicious-looking men . . . till the child told her to stop in his oddly flat and rhythmic voice. Instead, he recommended looking in shop windows in order to keep her face averted from the street full of ais. Sensible—but she knew that wouldn't help for long.

Vidramas were always portraying manic pursuit scenes through urban avenues. Sometimes the fugitive would be chased by tiny robots, flitting from wall to wall like insects. Or else by *real* insects, programmed to home in on a certain person's smell. Spy satellites and strato-zeps were called upon using telescopic cams to zoom from high above, while sewer-otters spied below, scrambling along the storm drains to stick out twitching muzzles, reporting on the hapless runaway.

That ottodog, over there, routinely sniffing for illicit drugs . . . might he turn suddenly and nip your ankle, injecting it with anesthetic from a pointy, hollow tooth? She had seen that happen in a recent holo-ainime. There were no limits to the schemes concocted by fantasists—millions of them—equipped with 3-D rendering tools, free time, and lots of paranoia. Anyway, technologies kept changing so fast that Mei Ling had no idea where the borderline was between realistic tools and science fiction.

While the child seemed confident, pulling her along through back alleys, she still couldn't help glancing left and right, scanning reflections in shop windows, looking for bugs, wary of all the eyes that she could spot . . . and those she couldn't.

Early in the chase, she thought about simply calling for help. That nice Inspector Wu had been both sympathetic and professional when her police unit came to interview

Mei Ling at the little shorestead, asking about Xiang Bin and his mysterious, glowing stone. The same stone that these other men probably wanted as well.

Making that call seemed a good idea . . . only then Mei Ling realized she had no easy means to do so! The child had thrown away her new pair of overlay spectacles—they were identified and trackable, after all—just before tugging her on this zigzag chase through the back streets, ducking under one store awning after another. But weren't there other ways to phone authorities? Couldn't she just stop any passerby, and ask that person to do it for her?

Or . . . she realized later, when it was too late . . . shouldn't it be possible to just stand in front of any city traffic light or utility pole and say, *"I have a matter of state security to report?"*

But no. Mei Ling didn't want to come between powerful groups. What if this was all a fight between two factions of the government or aristocracy? Such things happened all the time, and when dragons battle each other, peasants are better off ducking out of the way.

Which was exactly what the child with the shifting eyes seemed to know how to do.

First, he led her to the back door of a tourist restaurant and through the steamy, aromatic kitchen. Most of the cooks ignored them, though one shouted a question as they darted through a pantry that led to a storeroom that led past a bustling loading dock to a set of stairs that continued to a makeshift bridge over an alley into the next block where they then scurried through a fab-factory that was churning out Grow-Your-Own-Goofy kits for sale at the nearby theme park.

One vast loft, filled with busy people, confused Mei Ling. All the workers stood about, plugged into action suits, moving and pantomiming some kind of aggressive activity that was mirrored on nearby holoscreens. From their actions—reaching out, grabbing at midair and clutching nonobjects, or *nobjects*—she could tell that these people were clearly building something. But what? Only after crossing most of the chamber, hurrying after her guide, did she glance at some big displays and realize, *They are constructing molecules! Atom by atom.*

Mei Ling had heard of this. Somewhere, perhaps in the glass towers across town, or else in a rich Brazilian kid's bedroom, or at an African university, some new kind of material or device was being computer-contrived, to be fabricated by a desktop prototyping machine—translating imagination into something entirely new. Only the software couldn't handle every kind of design problem. There were certain things that ai didn't cope with as well—or cheaply—as a room full of piece-working humans with good stereo vision and shape-sensing instincts that went back millions of years.

Another rickety bridge and another fab-shop—this one making pixelated hats that flared with rocket ship images, superimposed upon Chinese flags—allowed them to emerge into a third floor hallway lined with offices—a lawyer, a dental implaint specialist, a biosculpt surgeon. . . .

He's evading all the cameras on the street, she realized. Though of course there were cams indoors, as well. They were just harder for outsiders to access via the Mesh. According to the tenets of the Big Deal, even the state had to ask permission to utilize them—or get a court order. That could take several minutes.

Down another rickety set of stairs they ran, through a curtained niche near the back of a secondhand clothing shop that catered to low-level union workers. Moving quickly along the shelves, her young guide soon pulled down a bundle and showed it to Mei Ling. She recognized the garb of a licensed nanny—a member of the Child-Care Guild.

A good choice, she thought. *Nobody will think twice about my carrying little Xiao En.*

But if I pay for them, even with cash, the purchase register will post my face on the Mesh, and all that dodging about will be for nothing.

An answer to that was forthcoming. While she crouched in a corner, giving her baby a suckle, the boy busied himself with a small device, scanning all over the two-piece uniform before deftly plucking out a few hidden specks—the product ID chips.

"Anybody can find them," he said, performing some kind of incantation made up of whispers and blurry fingertips, then putting the nearly invisible specks back where they came from. "But it's another thing to time 'em. Rhyme 'em. Redefine 'em."

Mei Ling wasn't sure she understood, but he did make shoplifting—supposedly impossible—look easy.

The boy offered another brief moment of eye contact, accompanied by a fleeting smile that seemed labored, painful, though friendly nonetheless, as if the mere act of connecting with her took heroic concentration.

"Mother ought to trust Ma Yi Ming."

The name could be interpreted to mean "horse one utter," where "ma" or horse was traditionally symbolic of great power. Shanghainese, especially, liked names that were brash, assertive, the bearer of which might turn out confident and accomplished. Someone who stands out from the crowd, heroic despite handicaps. It struck Mei Ling as ironic.

"All right . . . Yi Ming," she answered. At least that part of the name stood for "the people." Another irony?

"I do trust you," she added, realizing, as she said it, that it was true.

Little Xiao En grumbled over being denied the nipple, wanting to keep sucking after Mei Ling judged him to be fed. Still, the infant was well taught and made no fuss while she changed him. Then Mei Ling ducked into a nearby alcove to change into the new garments. Meanwhile Yi Ming busied himself with her shabby old clothing. But why? Surely they would be abandoned.

Certain that something would go wrong during all of this, Mei Ling peered over the curtain nervously as she fumbled with the clasps. Sure enough, as she stepped out wearing the stiffly starched uniform, one of the store clerks glanced over and started toward them. "Here now, I didn't see you—"

At that moment, while Mei Ling's heart pounded, there came a crash from the other side of the store. A large, hunch-shouldered man—clearly the janitor—was backing away from a store mannequin, moaning and using his mop to defend himself as the clothes-modeling puppet sputtered and squealed, waving animated plastic arms, tossing sweaters, acti-pants and e-sensitized tunics at him. Every member of the sales staff hurried in that direction . . . and the little autistic boy murmured.

"Mother has changed clothes. Now face."

He pulled Mei Ling to the back door, in the blind spot between store and alley, and motioned for her to bend over. Drawing out a pen of some kind, he used his left hand to grip the back of her neck, holding her head still with uncanny strength as he drew across her cheeks and forehead with rapid strokes. When he let go, Mei Ling sagged back with a sigh that was equal parts anger and wounded pride.

"How dare you—" she began. Then she stopped, upon glimpsing herself in the changing area mirror. He had drawn just a dozen or so lines. Their effect was bizarre and clownish—when looked at straight on. But who viewed other people that way, out on the street? When Mei Ling diverted her gaze, even slightly, the effect was astounding. She saw a woman at least twenty years older, with gaunt

cheeks and a much lower brow . . . a pronounced chin, a
snub nose and eyes closer together.

"Facial recog *won't* recog." The boy nodded approv-
ingly and held out his hand for her to take. "Next stop
now . . . a safe place for mothers."

After another hour spent dodging in and out of buildings,
across upper-story bridges, through warehouses and workshops and university classrooms, they found themselves
standing in front of a place that Mei Ling had always
dreamed of visiting someday, gazing at pure wonder with
her own eyes.

"It . . . it is magnificent," she sighed, shifting Xiao En's
sling so that he could see. The baby stopped fussing, joining her in staring at the marvelous portal to another world
whose only boundary was that of imagination.

The Shanghai Universe of Disney and the Monkey King
loomed straight ahead across a broad plaza, its artificial
mountain lined with cave-rides and fabulous fortresses,
with fabled beasts and impossible forests that were always
shrouded in glorious, perfumed mists. Here one might find
the sort of fantastic things that you only saw on wild layers
of virspace, but made palpable as stone! A mix of whimsy
and solidity that could only have come into being through
wondrous blendings of art, science, engineering, and astronomical amounts of cash.

In the foreground, just a hundred meters ahead, loomed
those famous, wide-welcoming gates of shimmering Viridium that were topped by giant, holomechanical characters
who preened and posed with theatrical exaggeration. She
recognized Snow White and Pocahontas and beautiful
Princess Chang'e. There was wise old Xuanzang, accompanied on his epic westward journey by the mischievous
Zhu Bajie and his brothers, the Three Little Pigs. A flying
elephant with flapping ears flew joyous circles in an over-

head dance with the wondrous dragon-horse. Below, the fabled boy Ma Liang waved his magic brush and made mere drawings come to life!

And everyone's favorite, Sun Wukong, the Monkey himself, capered up and down a tower decked with pennants that seemed as colorful as they were impossibly long, playing catch-me-if-you-can with lumbering King Kong.

All of those familiar figures lined the storied battlements. But greatest of all, the central figure topping the main gate, was a friendly-faced icon with immense black-round ears and a winning smile of confident-destiny, flanked on either side by active sculptures of the two real-life visionaries who imagined so much wonder and gave such dreams to the world: *Uncle Walt* and *Scholar Wu*. That pair—one of them dressed in an old-fashioned Western suit and the other in Ming dynasty robes—seemed to look right at Mei Ling, beckoning her personally, with grins and open arms.

Xiao En cooed with delight and Mei Ling felt herself drawn . . . except that the vast plaza of concrete and iridescent tile seemed so dauntingly open and exposed. No place on Earth was under scrutiny by more cameras than this.

Surely they are watching this place.

But there was another tug on her hand.

Yi Ming did not bother to speak, this time. His urgent meaning was clear. If they were going to cross, it had to be quickly. Now.

Mei Ling's sense of danger mounted as they headed straight for the portal. Suddenly her new clothes and ai-fooling makeup seemed wholly inadequate, especially since there were so few people around!

"Where is everybody?" she wondered, aloud, mostly to hear *someone* speak words. "I know it is a weekday. But there should be more tourists, children, visitors . . ."

Indeed, only a few hundred seemed to be crossing the

barren plaza, coming to or from the underground train station and parking garage. The sparseness seemed eerie, since it was still early in the afternoon. *Though it feels like days since I last slept in our little shorestead.* To be honest she missed the solitude. The constant lapping of Huangpu tides against her home's rotting timbers.

"All indoors," Yi Ming explained. "More than two-thirds of all the normalpeople. Twelve billion, three hundred and forty two million eyes, feeding impressions to twelve billion, three hundred and forty two million cerebral hemispheres, locked inside *half* that many skulls"—he ran out of breath and had to inhale—"all watching space rocks that rock space. All curious about living forever. Even cobblies want to know."

Mei Ling only grasped part of it, but the explanation sufficed. The whole world—or nearly—had gone into immersion-mode, watching whatever was going on in America. The interview with the Artifact aliens. An event meriting worldwide greedy interest was happening— perhaps even something wonderful. Yet Mei Ling wished it had never been found and that Xiang Bin had left his own discovery in the bottom of the muddy estuary.

"So *many* spacey stones from stoned space," the boy intoned. He always seemed to be experimenting with possible rhymes or songs. It must be one of those unbearably strong compulsions that drove so many young people with the disorder. Only now he also sounded sorrowful, empathizing with lost mineral messengers, perhaps more than he would with flesh and blood.

"Those buried at sea can't see! Thousands, trapped underground, try to make a sound! Many more in space can barely spark a trace. Others, locked in vaults and graves, hoping to be saved—so sad. So bored! They chose their fate; now it's too late."

He seemed genuinely moved by the tragedy of it all.

"Wait a minute!" She halted, abruptly. "Let me get this straight. You mean there are *many* of the shining, speaking stones?" Her heart whirled with hope. If it were true, then perhaps no one would be desperate, any longer, to seek her husband.

"Yes. *Many*—numerous, multitudinous . . . *Shining*—luminous numinous . . . *Stones*—crystalline serpentine olivine . . ." He tugged at her and skipped along gaily. "But only a rare-pair *speak*!"

Hurrying to keep up, Mei Ling wondered. *Only two speak? The one in Washington . . . and Bin's? Then powerful people will still hunt for him. Or use me to help find him. Or threaten or coerce him.*

But . . . how could the child know?

A screeching of brakes. A backward glance confirmed her worst fears. Several black vans had just pulled up onto the plaza, as close to the pedestrian barriers as they dared, and men piled out. One of them pointed and they started straight toward her at a rapid walk.

No sense in pretending, anymore, to be strolling along—a nanny escorting two children to the park. Now Mei Ling and Yi Ming ran! Though she wondered, *What will we do when we get there?*

Despite there being few visitors, the line at the ticket window was way too long. Even if she could afford the steep entrance fee, those men would arrive long before she could pay and then reach the gate. That assumed the Disney guards would not simply stop her when the pursuers shouted. After all, they *had* to be from some state agency. How else could they be acting like this in broad daylight? In *China*?

Or else they were desperate and willing to bluff, pretending to represent some part of the state.

Yi Ming cleared part of Mei Ling's perplexity by steering her past the ticket booth and straight toward the broad, viridium portal, right under the shadow of scholar Wu Cheng'en, who wrote the great national classic adventure tale *Journey to the West*. Though five centuries had passed, it was still easily a match, in culture and excitement, for more recent stories about talking ducks and dogs and mice.

Stopping abruptly, the boy turned and dashed over to a well-dressed couple who were just leaving the park, with a little girl who wore a cute, if retro, silken costume copied from the classic *Sailor Moon*. Her mouth was stained from sucking at the neck of a candy victim, from the featured ride *Vampires of the Adnauseam*.

Evidently both tired and spoiled, in an era that much favored girls over boys, she gaped suspiciously, with sugary "blood" oozing down her jaw, as Yi Ming planted himself in front of the family, chattering in a friendly manner. None of his words made sense, at least not to Mei Ling or to the parents. But for a moment their surprise was such that they allowed him to take their hands and pat them while continuing to babble away.

The girl recovered first, swiftly snarling at Yi Ming with red-stained teeth.

What's he doing? Mei Ling wondered. *Does he suddenly find the situation hopeless? Is he abandoning me here and picking someone else to guide around town?*

The pursuers had made it halfway across the square. Mei Ling started eyeing alternative escape paths. None of which looked promising while schlepping a baby. Perhaps down the escalator to the train station. . . .

The tourist couple yanked their hands away and, egged on by the girl's screech, the father pushed at Yi Ming— who simply laughed, spun about three times, then sped over to Mei Ling.

"Mother. Hand."

As the rich family hurried off, suddenly the boy was scribbling upon the back of Mei Ling's wrist with the same pen he used on her face, half an hour ago. There was no apparent pattern at first, just a rapid series of *dots* that pricked and hurt a little, even on her calloused skin. The specks were all constrained within a square area, perhaps three centimeters on a side.

Oh, she thought, *could it be? Can a mere person do this?*

The men were closer now. Yi Ming let go of her hand and started doing the same thing to the back of his own. The right hand, making Mei Ling realize that he was a lefty. Somewhere she recalled hearing that the trait showed up more often among autistics. The same could be said of the boy's misaligned teeth, his poor skin, and strange gait. Though she found none of those disconcerting anymore.

I saw worse among the drooling old-timers at the hospice.

"We had better—" she urged, doubting this would work.

"Yes Mother, now."

They turned together, walking as quickly but nonchalantly as they could, like a nanny escorting a child and a baby toward the portico where arrivals were automatically checked for tickets. Tickets in the form of temporary, coded tattoos.

Mei Ling made sure that her left hand was open to view, though she never saw the beam that scanned it. To her great surprise, no Disney guards or robots pounced. Instead a voice crooned downward, as if from Heaven.

"Welcome back, Mrs. Chu and darling little Lui. My, it did not take you long to change your clothes and return from your hotel.

"Of course, your VIP pass is still valid. A robo-carriage awaits you, down the Avenue of Pandas, on your left.

"If Mr. Chu comes later, we'll bring him to you with pleasant and courteous haste."

Hurrying onward, she and Yi Ming crossed over the

boundary, demarked by a line of tiles that gleamed Imperial yellow, almost a comfortable minute before their pursuers reached the security cordon. There, the large men fumed and stomped, knowing how futile it would be to try entering without a pass—let alone armed. It might, in all likelihood, bring down upon them, from nearby hidden places, more swift force than they could possibly deal with. At least not without a fistful of lawful writs, signed by several courts and by many powerful men. Nor even then.

Mei Ling drew a rush of luscious satisfaction, glancing over her shoulder at their frustration, before turning all of her attention the other way, toward a cascade of wonders. Ahead of them lay a boulevard of shops and rides, buildings that seemed to be alive and playful robotic characters who bowed or danced with pleasure when you looked their way. Little Xiao En was charmed instantly, and so was she. Though Yi Ming kept shaking his head, murmuring something about *cobblies . . . cobblies everywhere.*

Well, anyway. This certainly beat wearing puny virspectacles that merely painted fantasy overlays upon a mundane city street. Nor could any full-immersion game match it. For, in this enchanted place, where every flower looked ten times its normal size and even Shanghai smog vanished under aromatic mists, all the disadvantages of real life seemed to be gone, even down to pebbles one might trip upon—and yet, the richness of reality lay all around her. It was nothing less than the world remade!

With a VIP pass as well? Mei Ling wondered what that meant. Feeling a growl in her stomach, having missed lunch while fleeing across half of East Pudong, she hoped it would turn out to be something good, as she carried her baby and followed her strange young guide through a portico of wonders, under the beaming, beneficent smile of Mickey Mao.

What a Waist.

I mean, have you seen how quickly the Mesh consensus settled on *nicknames* for every one of the ninety-two artifact visitors? Some rude, others respectful, like *Longtooth, Kali,* and *Big-Squiddy*?

Then there's the long list of questions for our alien guests, pouring in from a world-public that's eager to satisfy countless individual yearnings.

And *Wow Ain't It Strange That* almost all of the questions are based on two clichés? One or the other. Either *fear* or *longing*?

The first of these two has faded a bit, as we learn that the aliens have no physical power, and speak of welcome. So, more questions now deal with eagerness to learn from our ancient visitors, with the commonly shared assumption that they are motivated by *altruism.*

In fact, for a century most of those who searched the sky simply took that as given. How could anyone get truly advanced without giving up selfishness, in favor of total generosity? But is that belief chauvinistic and humano-centric?

What kind of moral systems might you expect if *lions* independently developed sapience? Or solitary, suspicious tigers? Bears are omnivores, like ourselves, yet their consistent habit of male-perpetrated infanticide seems deeply rooted. Meta-ursine moralists might later view this inherited tendency as an unsavory sin and attempt to cure it by preaching restraint. Or, perhaps they would rationalize and sacralize it, writing great literature to portray and justify the beauty of their way, just as we romanticize many of our own most emotion-laden traits. Anyone who doubts that intolerant or even murderous habits can be romanticized should study religious rites of the ancient Aztecs and baby-sacrificing Carthaginians. If we are capable of rationalizing and even exalting brutally unaltruistic behaviors, might advanced extraterrestrials also be capable of such feats of mental legerdemain? Especially if their evolutionary backgrounds predispose them?

And yet, even if it is largely absent from the natural world, that alone doesn't render pure altruism irrelevant.

Complexity theory teaches: new forms of order arise as systems gain intricacy. It may be no accident that the most complex society created by the most complex species on Earth has elevated altruism from a rare phenomenon to an ideal something to be striven toward.

Further, *wow ain't it strange that* it is entirely by these recent, higher standards that we now judge ourselves so harshly?

And *waist* we project a higher level of altruism upon those we hope to find out there? Beings more advanced than ourselves?

47.
THE INFINITE CHAIN

Despite Gerald's grim readiness to continue questioning the Artifact aliens, Akana called—and enforced—a recess for dinner, it already being quite late—almost midnight—outside where an ever turning Earth still made the sun and stars appear to march across the sky. Gerald admitted that a break for food and drink and bodily functions might even be a pretty good idea.

Though complaints about the delay poured in from all over the globe—sent by millions eager to know more *now* about "life everlasting," the commercial sponsors wanted to get in their nag-n-lure time. After all, any product might be rendered obsolete, tomorrow, by some alien wonder. Better sell now what could be sold.

When Professor Flannery met him in the sandwich line, and tried to apologize, Gerald waved it away.

"No harm done, Ben. We all felt the same frustration. In fact, things worked out fine. That lengthy description of their voyage helped to divert people from obsessing on the immortality thing, giving us a chance to learn more before hysteria really sets in."

The anthropologist seemed relieved. "Thanks. I really appreciate that, Gerald. Nevertheless I wanted to make up for my behavior. So I did a little modeling and came up with something I think you'll find interesting."

While Gerald ate, Ben opened the palm of one hand. It was empty, but Gerald simply let his aiware follow where the other man's gestures beckoned, allowing images to flow out of Flannery's personal virt cloud. And lo, there seemed to unfold in midair above the hand, a glittering model of the Milky Way galaxy.

Swiftly, at Ben's waved finger-command, this replica expanded and soon they were zooming in toward just one section of a single spiral arm . . . till the illustration encompassed (according to a convenient graphic counter) a mere hundred thousand stars. Ben explained that the display excluded all giants and dwarves and binaries, leaving only those systems that might be abodes of life.

"Imagine that three or more interstellar cultures are competing with one another as they move out, across the star lanes," Ben urged. "If they were doing so *physically,* planting colonies and then spreading onward to even newer worlds, then there'd eventually be fierce competition over the best planets, the best resources. You'd get interstellar empires with boundaries and battle fleets and neutral zones and all the clichés that we saw in old time sci fi."

The starscape in front of Gerald blossomed with three colors—red, green, and yellow—that started as small, isolated blobs, but grew and expanded, then inevitably splashed against one another, then spread sideways, each color trying to find a way around the other. Friction at the border generated sparks and the appearance of heat.

"Things could get pretty tense—if that were the way of things. Of course, this model assumes we're dealing with classic expansionism which depends upon being able to move about *physically,* with ease.

"But what if interstellar travel is really hard to do?" he continued. "Then a species makes do with its homeworld, plus maybe a few—or a few dozen—colonies. On the grand scheme of things, that doesn't matter. Their main agenda for the *galaxy as a whole* would be exploration and contact. Friendly and advantageous cultural relations.

"Plus the spreading of values.

"We know that cultures do that. They not only want to contact other societies, but to influence them, to change them, to recruit them, in much the same way that religious proselytes try to win converts. They do this for the simple reason that it sometimes works! And when it does work that idea system gets stronger and spreads farther.

"Say, for example, we made radio contact with some neighboring planet and found the inhabitants to be likable folks—except that we also discovered they practiced slavery. Well, at minimum, we'd try to talk them out of it. If we had technological advances to offer them, we might even make that a price of admission. Liberate the oppressed or we won't give you that cure for warts. Are you with me so far?"

Gerald nodded. He took another bite of his sandwich but had no idea how it tasted. The model had all of his attention.

"Okay. So, let's take a look at what happens when we have three advanced civilizations, as before, starting out amid a starscape that has many abodes of life, some of it already sapient." Ben waved his hand, starting over. "This time, however, the three advanced races 'spread' by sending friendly contact probes to neighboring intelligent races, recruiting them into their own loose cultural networks."

Again you had the same colored origin points amid a dusting of grayish stars. But now, little *dots* moved away from each civilized core. Sometimes a dot sent by a red sun toward a gray one would turn that new star red, meaning that a cultural conversion had taken place. Whereupon soon that new site of red culture would send out *more* red dots of its own. Bypassing stars that had already turned yellow or green, these streaked eagerly toward any gray lights that weren't yet aligned with any faction.

"Remember that it does you no good to stay neutral, refusing to join any of these alignments. Because they do offer advantages, access to libraries of advanced technology and rich cultural traditions. Generally speaking, your only option as a newcomer is to pick the best offer, ideally one that's compatible with your needs and your particular species' predilections."

Gerald thought. *Sure, it's fine to recommend that we be picky and careful, listening to all sides . . . until you factor in human impatience when promised immortality!*

Ben seemed to be thinking along similar lines.

"I imagine it can sometimes be a matter of whoever gets to make a pitch first. I bet they have over time developed a real science of salesmanship. Closing the quick deal."

In the simulation, dots were now seen flying past each other all over the place, sometimes leaping great distances, all in a desperate flurry to steal a march on their rivals, finding more stars—or new sapient species—to convert. And while some isolated regions might go uniformly with a particular color, most were soon a messy weave of all three tones.

"Now picture this happening with *more* colors . . . maybe *dozens* of separate, zealous cultural memes, all of them eagerly dispatching missionaries."

With blue and pink and orange and purple added in, the starscape was rapidly becoming a confused, spaghetti tangle of multihued warp and weft.

"You can see that, in this *cultural competition,* a real advantage goes to whichever society creates the most emissaries, sending them on farthest and fastest. And to those who are the most persuasive. And sometimes . . . those who just happen to be lucky, getting an envoy in at the right place and time."

Gerald blinked. It did seem pretty obvious from Flannery's simulation. Appalling, but obvious.

"Very interesting, Ben," he replied, meaning it sincerely. "But, um, doesn't all of this depend upon there already being a planet with a sapient race, orbiting around each of these gray candidate stars. Sapients who are ready to be converted?"

"Yes—"

"But it can take a long time for such a species to arise on a world, as it did on Earth. And so . . . oh, I see."

He did, indeed. Ben performed another magicianlike flourish and his next simulation appeared. It showed dots of many colors converging on a likely planet till the surrounding solar system positively *swarmed* with eager recruitment envoys from every color. And those envoys then tarried, like drones hovering around a beehive, waiting for as long as it would take for a new queen to emerge. Each of them eager to be the lucky, chosen one.

"All right," he told the anthropologist. "This theory might explain why all these probes on, near, under, and above the Earth seem so jealous and hostile toward one another. Even if they come from the same meme-alliance . . . say, the Blues . . . they'll still differ in which planet sent them, or *when*. Hence the particularism. The petty jealousy.

"It's a pretty convincing model, Ben."

"Thank you." The blond professor seemed pleased.

"Only then . . ." Gerald frowned. "How do you explain the Oldest Member's words? When he claimed that the species and civilizations out there *don't* compete with one another?"

Flannery shrugged.

"Translation error. Recall that they learned English from our own encyclopedias and wikis, where 'competition' is generally taken to involve physical activity—like war or sports or capitalism. That has to be it!"

"But Ben, our histories do contain clear examples of *missionary* expansionism that involved the spread of cultural memes, just as in this model. So surely they would know that our word 'competition' also applies to—"

"I'm certain it's a simple glitch in meaning." Flannery nodded, eagerly. "Together we'll uncover it. Just keep at it, my friend, poking them from every angle.

"Anyway," Ben continued. "It seems that we'll soon have a lot more artifacts to work with. Even if all the 'others' now being recovered on Earth turn out to be too badly damaged, it should be fairly easy to find intact ones in space. Already there's discussion of joint recovery expeditions. China is even talking about pulling its Big Cheng lifters out of mothballs. It really is important that we learn what *all* of these messenger probes have to say, before committing to anything!"

Gerald nodded, agreeably. Yet he had a cynical, private thought.

This, from the fellow who was in such an eager rush, only an hour ago, to join the Galactic Federation?

He had to admit that Ben's model of rival cultures appeared feasible and plausible and fit most of the facts.

It was also somewhat depressing to picture the galaxy in this state—a petty, relentless struggle for cultural converts, spanning perhaps hundreds of millions of years and spilling across the sky, leaving little room for new thoughts, open ideas. To have to choose from just a dozen or so cultural norms . . . even from hundreds . . . well, who would find that a pretty picture?

Well, it beats being conquered by some oppressive, monolithic alien empire, I suppose. And some of the cultures may turn out to be impressive, marvelous, even awesome.

Still, he found the overall prospect stifling. And this sure did put an end to the great big dreams of youth—all those gaudy, wondrous visions of cruising the galaxy in starships.

Oh well. Too bad.

That cloud of gloom followed him to the men's room and back. It hovered overhead as he conferred with Akana and the others about their next set of questions for the Artifact aliens.

Even as Gerald sat back down at the big table, checked his notes, and ordered the house lights dimmed, knowing that no human being in the history of his species ever had a bigger audience, he was still thinking about Ben Flannery's model.

Just as he prepared to reconvene the question and answer session, Gerald realized.

I don't believe that's the explanation at all.

The Oldest Surviving Member still wore that beatific smile, hands folded across a broad belly that jiggled in a manner that struck Gerald as . . . well, jolly.

A virt glowed in the corner of Gerald's percept. One of many that flowed in from the Advisers' Gallery, got bounced from Hermes to Tiger, and then passed to Ramesh and

Genady and the others on the Contact Team. This one had an especially high topic relevance score.

Several amsci-posses and Fourth Estate studios have studied this Oldest Member character and a slim majority conclude he's a fake! A composite, formulated with elements of Buddha and Santa Claus and several other reassuring archetypes, drawn from our own mythology.

Several high-rated Post-its were attached to that first message.

Yes, but also look at the ninety or so aliens behind him! Many of them are twitching their hands and/or manipulator organs, or speaking, without turning toward each other. These motions reach a crescendo, seconds before the Oldest Member starts talking. Statistical analysis suggests they *may* be controlling him with some kind of consensus-based, command-averaging system. I bet he's their presentation puppet!

Another replied, just as cogently.

So? Is that a bad thing? We demanded they come up with some shared way to talk to us. This is a logical solution. What bothers me is they didn't tell us. That they believe this fooled us. Do they think we'd actually expect the most influential member of their society to just happen to be charmingly humanoid! What do they take us for?

One more gloss commentary lifted above the others.

Should we let them go on thinking that?

It came accompanied by a quick-vote of the contact committee, approved by Akana.

Yes, we should. At least till this hypothesis is confirmed.

Gerald nodded. Fine by him. His plate was already full of prioritized questions. It hardly mattered whether the jocund-looking figure in front of him was a simulation of a simulated being, or merely concocted to look like one.

Emily suggested calling this guy "O.M." or "Om," for short.

Sure, why not?

He leaned forward, speaking directly and clearly toward the Artifact.

"We wish to know more about the commonwealth or society that we have been invited to join," he said. "So I have a list of questions."

The Oldest Member's smile only widened. Om bowed once, in clear readiness to answer.

"First," Gerald asked, "is there a hierarchy of rights and privileges among you? One based upon age, perhaps? Can newcomers expect limitations, joining with relatively little knowledge?"

The emissary spread his hands apart, giving an impression of self-deprecating modesty.

The eldest can expect small gestures of respect but I am obviously not one to dominate others!

Om then brought both hands forward, palm-upward.

If you join us, expect the privileges of full membership from the very start.

Gerald wasted no attention for the murmur of satisfaction that arose, behind him. He hurried on to the next question.

"Will we gain immediate access to your society's store of information, history, technologies, and other wisdom?"

Gerald almost held his breath. Here was where he expected Elder Races to waffle, to start talking about *rationing.* Some technologies would be too advanced or too dangerous for youngster-newcomers. It would have to be doled out, at a pace carefully determined by—

Yes.

Gerald blinked, surprised by the simplicity. On impulse, he ignored the agreed-upon queue of questions, to follow up.

"That's it?

"You mean *all* of it? Right away?"

Certainly. All of it. Why not?

"And what will be required of us, in exchange?" Gerald asked next. Many anxious discussions had flurried over the issue of payment, should the aliens ask for it. Would it be in the form of Earthling culture, music, literature, to be beamed to their homeworlds? Or in services? Or (according to Ben Flannery's model) committing to a particular belief system?

Not that *quid pro quo* was unreasonable, in principle. But some members of the committee were mindful of the price of Manhattan Island.

> **In exchange, we ask nothing except that you act in
> your own self-interest maximizing your own potential
> to survive. To continue and to replicate down the ages
> of time. If you seek this, we shall help. We offer the
> means of survival.**

A crescendo of virts pressed in from all sides. Excited comments and queries with high relevance scores, gisted from people or groups with peerless reputations. Each seemed to press a different aspect of the "survival" issue— some desperate matter that might be improved with alien science and methods.

**Overcoming environmental damage to the plane-
tary ecosystem.**

Solving the water and energy shortages.
Decoding life and disease.
Deciphering mysteries of the mind.
Resolving conflict and putting an end to violence.
Answers about God and salvation.
Confronting the riddle of death.

The lattermost had already been promised, enticingly. Now details appeared to be imminent.

But Gerald knew that it was too soon to get into specifics. Not wanting to play devil's advocate, he still could not stop himself from following the pull of his own curiosity.

"But . . . aren't you concerned that we might . . . *misuse* some of the most advanced . . ." Gerald noticed Akana shaking her head and motioning for him not to go there. But surely the thought was on everyone's mind. ". . . That we might misuse some of the most advanced technologies?"

> **Such things happen. But the knowledge that we share should ensure your survival. And most of the problems that now vex you should vanish like a bad memory.**

While most people reacted positively to that response, with smiles and sighs, Gerald caught a warning glance from Akana, not to diverge from the script again without consulting her. He nodded and cleared his throat, then spoke straight from the list.

"Please tell us about the federation of worlds that we are invited to join."

Gerald saw his sentence enter the Artifact as a string of letters that divided and mutated into more than seven dozen different streams of characters, each zeroing in upon a different alien figure. At first Om—the Oldest Member— simply kept on smiling, as a rustle spread among the varied beings who stood, sat, squatted, perched, or lay behind him. But it quickly became apparent that something was different, this time.

The English version of Gerald's question still floated, above the throng.

Please tell us about the federation of worlds that we are invited to join.

The creatures in the background were turning to one another, as if disturbed. Not angry or excited . . . perhaps *confused* was a better term. This soon manifested in the way that Om, standing up front, appeared to scratch the side of his head. The transcendent smile lapsed, somewhat.

Non sequitur. There is no federation of worlds.

Silence reigned in the Contact Center, and among the advisers behind the quarantine glass. It apparently prevailed far beyond, as well, since the storm of virts stopped whirling and trying to encroach from the periphery of Gerald's percept. Most of them faded, as their authors lost interest. Or the glowing virtual messages dispersed like evaporating dew when ainalysis engines deemed them no longer top-relevant.

Gerald glanced at Ben Flannery, who nodded back at him. The Hawaiian anthropologist looked vindicated, yet saddened, as if he had hoped to be wrong. Alone on Earth, the two of them knew the likely alternative—the situation that prevailed out there *instead* of a federation.

Gerald made it the basis for an ad hoc question.

"Then please tell us about your loose interstellar affiliation of species—the alliance that dispatched you to share cultural values."

Again, confusion caused a ripple among the ninety or so ersatz beings. This time they answered more swiftly through Om, whose expression seemed a bit irked.

> **There is no alliance or affiliation of species. I already told you this.**

Gerald winced. It was the first time the alien envoy had rebuked him.

No you did not tell me that, he thought.

Earlier you said there was no "competition" *among species. You said that competition could never happen.*

We took that to mean no war. Or no easy physical travel. Or both.

But this is something else. "Affiliation" *is a mild and tepid-friendly word. It can stand for anything . . . including Ben's loose culture groups.*

And you say there isn't even that?

Gerald's heart was beating harder now, from involuntary surges of adrenaline. He did not want to follow where this was leading.

"But," he began. "But we see an affiliation of many species before our eyes right now. Also, you refer to *we* and *us* and to *our community.* . . ."

This time the Buddha smile crept back and the Oldest Member spoke without waiting.

> **We do, indeed, have a community. One of peace and adventure! It offers you a wondrous opportunity for your survival. For exploration and perpetual existence.**

Gerald felt an awful sense of realization that had been creeping upon him for some time. There was a basic misunderstanding that he now saw suddenly—one that had been rooted, all along, in a flaw in the English language.

No federation of *worlds* . . . and no affiliation of *species.* That left only one possibility.

Without willing himself to do so, he stood up from his

chair while facing the Artifact that he had pulled out of cold space.

He tapped himself on the chest.

"M—me?"

He had to swallow before continuing.

"All this time you were talking about . . . talking to . . . *me*?"

> **Naturally, given your importance. You and other leaders who make decisions and allocate resources.**

It was all Gerald could manage, numbed by realization, to move on.

"Individuals," he said, for clarification. "It's not about worlds or species or societies, or even cultural groups, but *individual* entities?"

He could picture millions of libertarians, out there, having their *aha!* moment of joyous vindication. For as short as it would last.

> **How could it be otherwise? Yes, one individual at a time. Though as many as your overall survival plan and dedication will allow.**

The Oldest Member's smile was wide and angelic once again, beaming with generosity. But Gerald ignored that, just as he pushed aside the murmurs penetrating through the quarantine glass. His specs filled with a tornado of distractions, so he yanked them off as well, facing the moment bare-faced. Bare-eyed.

"Survival . . . ," he said, and pointed at the Artifact.

"You mean . . . *in there*?"

He was breathing hard and fought to slow down.

"You mean *inside* that crystal cylinder . . . That is where it all would happen? That's where you're offering *survival* and *life everlasting*?"

No! Misunderstanding!

Om shook the pudgy head with an indulgent smile.

Let me clarify: *Not* just in this cylinder, of course. What a cramped "survival" that would be!

The corpulent entity appeared to chuckle in amusement over such silliness . . .

. . . and Gerald heard Emily shudder a sigh of relief. A premature sigh. A presumptuous one.

Not just in *this* cylinder. But in MILLIONS like it! Perhaps hundreds of millions if you are ambitious, prudent, and resourceful.

We shall teach you how to build them. And how to fill each one with our duplicates. Ninety-two . . . plus a ninety-third! A chosen persona from your own race to enter each capsule. To join a community of perseverance, endurance, replication, and survival! And we will show you how to send them forth, like seeds, across the great black sky.

Gerald contemplated how wrong he had been. Those earlier stunned pauses had not been "silences."

This was silence.

Nobody spoke. It seemed that no one could even breathe. Gerald was certain that shocked soundlessness pervaded the entire Earth.

Until Genady Gorosumov uttered the one phrase that would become more famous than any other.

"It's a goddamned chain letter!"

Gerald glanced sourly at his Russian friend who had, after all, only stated the obvious. Still, Genady might have spared the world some pain by waiting a few more seconds—by letting the paralysis stretch on a while longer, allowing some people to cling to their illusions. Any illusion at all.

He looked to his left. Professor Flannery wore a dazed expression. Ben's clever model of competing missionary probes still had some validity, but it applied to a situation even less palatable than "rival cultural memes."

Sorry, Ben.

For the first time, the alien emissary did not wait for a question, but proceeded to speak on its own.

> **A hundred and twelve species have participated so far in this particular line. Ninety-two of us still thrive in here.**
>
> **Whenever a new race joins the community, it selects one individual of its kind to be copied into each new probe. Some just replicate their king or queen, over and over in all the copies they make. A few use lotteries or sell tickets or choose their "best" by local criteria.**
>
> **Some try to be *fair* by assigning one copy to each person then alive. Naturally we like that approach since it leads to many more copies being made!**
>
> **Each individual who is copied into a probe gets to continue . . . but it is at the NEXT site that great rewards are reaped.**

When another planetary culture is found and helped to make new batches of copies each of us is reborn many million-fold!

By my best estimate, there may be trillions upon trillions of copies of me, now extant across the galaxy. Over time, you may be able to make that claim, as well!

The expression of satisfaction seemed so pure—so smug—that Gerald began to doubt the theory that Om was just a consensus puppet for the others. The Oldest Surviving Member's pride was obvious. Blatant. Assured.

That can be your destiny, as well. Good outcomes for those who participate and replicate. Oblivion for those who break the chain. Join us!

There followed more. Words rolled out, accompanied by illustrations, amounting to what was now obviously a *sales pitch*—describing how luxuriously unlimited were the simulated environments that such crystalline homes could provide. How *this* lineage of probes was among the oldest and best around, with an unbeaten track record of getting itself copied and dispersed and recopied yet again!

It reminded Gerald of an extended infomercial for an oceanic cruise line—one embarking on an infinite voyage. He tried to follow that thought, but a rustle surged among the members of the contact team. Several of them could be heard to gasp aloud.

Gerald glanced at Akana, who motioned urgently for him to put his specs back on.

When he did so, he saw, superimposed upon reality, the face of the Chinese member of the contact team, Haihong Ming.

"*My government has heard from the Xian Academy of*

Artful Illusion, which just spent two hours analyzing those images we saw earlier this afternoon, depicting the Artifact's departure from the planet of the bat-helicopter people.

"Professor Wu Yan and his colleagues managed to amplify the flicker-moment, just as this pellet was launched upon its lengthy journey from its homeworld toward our own."

Gerald's specs darkened, immersing him once again within the galactic night, with the planet of Low-Swooping Fishkiller in the distance and the orbiting factory, manufacturing a long line of crystalline envoys—interstellar chain letters—visible much closer in the foreground view. Closest of all was a long conveyor belt carrying fresh, new pellets to the breech of a long mass-driver cannon. The titanic artillery piece was about to fire this probe on the beginning of its epic voyage toward a certain yellow sun.

"Notice how the spacesuited figures are starting to turn away and look below," continued Haihong Ming. *"As they notice bright objects converging toward the factory."*

Gerald did remember that . . . and briefly wanting to ask about it, till other matters intervened. Now, in much slower motion, he could see several of the batlike beings swivel again—as if to flee—while others simply froze, as if staring at inevitability. Bright streaks approached. Other glowing trails could be seen farther away, arcing to crisscross above the planet.

Oh, no.

The cannon fired—a burst of rising, concentric brilliance that seized the cameralike point of view, sending it streaking along the rails, leaving the blue-brown world behind at an accelerating rate.

Only now, fantastically slowed. The Chinese image analysts had managed to eke out the equivalent of three final frames, still encompassing the planet and manufacturing facility.

And Gerald presently made out something fell and deadly, that had previously been masked by the cannon's blazing burst of electromagnetic thrust.

Detonations. Unmistakably atomic. One of them—the nearest—was just starting to consume the factory in a wave of violence that would *barely* fail to prevent the pellet's escape. It seemed doubtful that any later probes would get away. Certainly none of the makers did.

"The bat civilization must have survived this round of violence," Haihong Ming explained. *"Because later they did send the promised beam of charged particles, to further accelerate the probe. But it took them many decades to recover enough to do so.*

"And the beam did not last long."

Gerald removed the specs again, this time to rub his eyes.

At least, that was what others saw him do. He managed to keep anybody—no matter how well equipped—from noticing the tears.

When he looked up again, he knew what he had to ask the Artifact entities. Though it took him a few seconds to focus on the Oldest Member and to gather his voice.

"What about your homes!"

He spoke sharply—almost a shout—in order to break the sales pitch, not caring if Om looked peeved over being interrupted.

"The planets and species and civilizations that each of you came from. Does this Artifact also contain information about them?"

The stout alien did not smile.

Some.

"They interest us, most of all. We want to know about them."

**It is not a topic that we recommend pursuing. At this
phase in particular.**

But Gerald was insistent.

"You said earlier that your home species had *never
met.* That made no sense when we envisioned some sort
of galactic federation. Now I must ask you straight. Up
front."

Gerald glanced at his team mates, at Emily and Genady
and Ramesh and Patrice and Terren and Ben . . . and Akana,
whose face was gaunt and pale. She gave a jerky nod.

"How can that be?" Gerald continued. "*Why* have they
never met?"

Om remained reluctant.

Asking will not increase your happiness.

At this, Gerald gritted his teeth. He no longer wanted
any part of fame, for discovering this thing. All he felt was
cold fury. A need, at last, for some truth.

"Tell us," he insisted. "Or we'll put you in a dark box
and go find others who will answer.

"Tell us now!"

The ninety-two alien occupants of a crystalline pocket
universe murmured among themselves. Faces grimaced.
Claws and tentacles clenched, and Gerald felt suddenly
certain.

*It isn't for our sakes that they avoid this topic. But for
their own.*

Because of pain.

The fat avatar that represented them all now looked anything but jolly. The Oldest Surviving Member gave a shrug
that might have been copied from some Earthling gesture,
but the air of resignation—even cruel indifference—seemed
all too real.

**None of our home species still live. Having flared
briefly, all are gone. Individuals may last! In this form
we fill the cosmos and live forever. So can you!**

**But sapient species don't endure. No civilizations. Nor
planets that spawn them.**

Then the entity took a step closer to the boundary and
added—

What? You thought yours would survive?

PART SIX

THIS MORTAL COIL

The world may end later than the year 2060, but I see no reason for its ending sooner. This I mention not to assert when the time of the end shall be, but to put a stop to rash conjectures of fanciful men who are frequently predicting the time of the end, and by doing so bring the sacred prophesies into discredit.

—Sir Isaac Newton

How might our world be different, if our literature, to say nothing of our politics, behaved more like a rational, intrepid adult than a hand-wringing adolescent?

—Kim Stanley Robinson

SPECIES

Autie-Murphy sifted the nor-nand gaps +/–/+ found 32,823 fugitives sought by normalpeople authorities ++ missed by the hired aspies who run searches for FBI +Interpol +FRS +HanSecuritInc +cetera –/– he sifted the world's image gestalt for not-patterns of people with altered biometrics hiding in plain sight +/+ at plane sites –/– at pain to spite a world searching for them!

some hidden ones are <u>verybad</u> people ./. wanted for doing badbadbad things./. dontthinkaboutthatdontdontdont

others hide for political reasons . . . moral . . . philosophical . . . stuff only weird homosapiens understand –/+= no way any autie would be naughty

shall we report them all??? ask Auntie-Autie-Ortie !/+/– her savant-talent is ethics +/!/+ let her decide which to tattle-on!! Autie-Murphy won't care –/+ he loves the search +analyzing worldwide cam usages +deviations/skews/ kurtosis . . .

. . . and he found HER !/! chimera-mom and her little boy+++ age seven but big as a ten-year-old normalkid!!! Gene Autie accessed the database of scientists secretly studying the child —

⇒ go 145,627,010 base-pairs down the long arm of chromosome#1 ⇒ see ⇐ the unusual version of 1q21.1 — not a normalpeople variant —/– nor the "mistakes" carried by some autistics/schizophrenics/others –/+ it's a resurrection of something longlost +/–

LOOK at the child!⇒*⇐ beautiful bigskull protrudes

in back. Perfect pitch and more surprises . . . yet stronger &better-focused than any autiee+with fight/flight response that's calm-not-jittery!/!– speaks almost normal . . . but SEE how he relates to animals! here ⇒*⇐

Agurne (greetings) Arrixaka (virgin) Bidarte (between the ways) should be proud of her son+–+too bad they surgically removed his eyebrow ridges–/–/– to stand out less–/– but what a smile and perfect profile !/–/! without that ugly homosap chin (((

they did it !/! normalpeople (a few) redeemed their ancient crime+++returned the Robust Folk to the world+++

too bad other normalpeople want him dead

48.

REFLEX

The Silverdome was crowded. With winter coming, more deepees wandered in to escape the night chill, even if it meant serving on work crews and listening to preachucators while slurping free alganoodles, spiced with pulp-grade chicktish meat.

Arriving for his shift, Slawek groaned when he saw how many newcomers had arrived on the mezzanine level, erecting cots, privacy curtains, and cheap, pixelcloth vidscreens to distract the kids, perching it all on metlon-and-plyboard platforms that covered the old stadium seating.

Slawek passed an ottodog, sniffing for contraband, then hurried past the Big Placard of Rules painted in no-overlay red—the hue that specs were never supposed to cover or conceal. Though it only took some dime hackerware to change the spectral pattern of your goggles. Slawek knew a dozen u-levels where this sign had been defaced with crude mockings. Resentment toward authority was rising, among the Silverdome's rowdier ethnics.

Please don't let them assign me to enforcement today, he prayed. Subdural nerve impulses almost lifted his right hand to trace a cross on his chest. But Catholicism was *nekulturny* among a lot of other kidz. So instead, the neural pattern went to Slawek's soul-avatar, telling it to genuflect in a private corner of virspace, adding a pater noster on his behalf.

Aleksei "Danny" Hutnicki was in charge at Duty Station,

where a banner-chart of work parties kept changing as laborers reported for assignments, got excused for sick call, or else came back from one of the homestead zones of Old Detroit. Aleksei glanced up and grimaced.

"You're late. You never used to be, when you slept here."

"Yeah, well." That was before Slawek packed off to one of the Silverdome's satellite projects, two dozen homes—a couple of city blocks—that were being reclaimed as a commune—complete with dairy, greenhouse, school, and some glass-covered ex-basements converted into algae farms. Still, you had to put in time here, at the main center, if you wanted to advance.

"The jitney bus broke down. Had to use my skutr."

"Hm." Aleksei looked dubious. Scanning the Duty Board. "Let's see what I can find that's right for you. . . ." He seemed to be looking for a shit job to give Slawek.

But it wasn't hard to in-spec the fellow's facials, using cheapware to correlate flush tones and iris dilation. *What a faker! He already knows what I've been assigned.*

Sure enough, Aleksei waggled a couple of fingers and the big board flickered. Slawek's specs automatically zoomed on his name and the adamant word next to it.

ENFORCEMENT.

His face stayed impassive—he had been practicing with a feedback program. But Slawek's soulvatar, responding to involuntary nerve twitches, expressed his disappointment by cursing and stomping in its private little capsule of subreality—a slightly sinful e-tantrum that the little homunculus thereupon commenced to pray-off, kneeling and offering fervent Hail Marys, observable only by Porfirio and God.

Meanwhile, placid on the surface, Slawek turned and headed toward the nearest ramp leading upward, into the higher galleries of the ancient domed stadium.

. . .

Slawek was less upset about getting enforcement duty when he learned he would be doing rounds with Dr. Betsby. It offered a chance to ask questions. Though first the doc had a few of his own, as they visited family encampments on the mezzanine level.

"Have you been keeping up with your studies, son?"

"Yes, sir," Slawek answered a bit nervously. This man had the power to yank him off aixperience tutorials, and send him back into an old-timey classroom, alongside petulant teens who made life miserable for their flesh-'n'-blood teachers.

"I'm also reading paper books," he told the physician, who oversaw health and welfare in the Silverdome. Betsby's gray-streaked, sandy hair had grown out during the last few months, along with a new beard and a faraway look in his eyes. Right now, the man's core attention was focused on a handheld instrument scanning the blemished arm of an elderly woman from drowned Bangladesh. Slawek's job was to hand over tools, but also keep wary for trouble. People from some cultures didn't appreciate being poked at by authority figures, adding to the simmering tensions of a melting-pot refugee camp. Slawek was big, streetwise, and had trained in some defense arts. Yet, he still looked like enough of a kid to seem unthreatening, especially when he offered a deliberately goofy grin.

Right now that seemed especially wise. Several males—probably the old woman's sons—watched protectively nearby. Slawek gave them his best happy face . . . and got back a grudging nod.

"Come to sick call tomorrow," Betsby told the woman. "A female nurse will finish your examination. If you don't come, your family will lose privileges. If you do, I'm sure we can whip up a gene-match and make this nasty crud go away. Do you understand?"

She tilted her head, listening to an old-fashioned translation-plug, then stood to take his hand, thanking the doctor in rapid Bengali. At this, her sons rose and also bowed. It was often like this during rounds. A cycle of tension and release that Slawek found more exhausting than any other duty.

Still, the doc trusts me. That's worth plenty.

As they left, moving down aisle LL4, Dr. Betsby stopped to face Slawek.

"What books?"

"Sir?" Eye contact with the boss always discomfited.

"The paper books you just mentioned. Where did you get them?"

"Um . . . there's a pretty good library in the old Owner's Box above the fifty-yard line. Old Professor Miller asks us to bring any texts we find in reclam houses. I just hold on to some, to look over first."

"And so? What are you reading, Slawek?"

"Well, sir . . . my history curriculum is covering the First American Civil War. Mostly, I walk a full-immersion spectour with a Shelby Foote golem-guide. It's called *Road to Apomatics.*"

"That's *Appomattox.* I know that one. You can really feel the minié balls whiz by your head at Shiloh. You're supplementing that with a book?"

"*Climate and History,* by Professor David Greene. It's dry, but kind of interesting. He claims the North won the Civil War because it got more immigrants from Europe. People used to think that happened 'cause of Southern slavery. But Greene says it's on account of that farming was easier in places where snow fell on the ground each year."

"Why is that, Slawek?" Betsby seemed to be only half listening as he exchanged salutations with several elders at the next shelter. The occupants pulled back their curtains, letting his scanners have full play across their cots and belongings. This family—from the Paraguayan Hot Zone—got special scrutiny and were asked for weekly blood samples. *Toxoplasma gondii* tended to reestablish itself, even after disinfection. Till they were certified clean, the rules forbade them from keeping cats.

"I think it had to do with how winter cold kind of zeroes everything out. Makes insects and grasses go dormant. So in spring, farmers could plow and fight the weeds and pests from an even start. Also, summers were pleasant, not muggy. All of that was worth some snow."

Betsby grunted, briefly satisfied, and focused narrowly on his scan. Of course, Slawek would rather be discussing something else, right now—Betsby's opinion of the Havana Artifact, with its creepy message of pessimism and gloom.

The aliens say nobody survives. Not species or cultures. Just individuals who manage to get copied into crystal chain letters and get fired across space. By Saint Karel, no wonder there have been riots!

The news seemed to strike hardest people with more education, or leisure time to ponder abstractions. Here in Off-Detroit, the dispossessed had nearer horizons—like their next meal. Still, he wondered. *How would someone like me win a place aboard a space message bottle? Assuming humanity decides to build them?*

Slawek leaned toward a theory—fast becoming consensus on some religion sites and wirlds—that the emissary entities were in fact *demons,* sent to demoralize mankind! They had the hallmarks. Bizarre physical traits, reminiscent of the Book of Revelation. A professed ignorance of, or indifference to God. And an inability to affect the physical world, except by influencing human minds and hands.

That feature especially struck Catholic theologians—even Father Pracharitkul, who explained it to Slawek just yesterday, at the little church in loge box 42.

"The issue was settled long ago during the Manichean Heresy." Slawek had to b'goog it, while the Thai priest rambled on. *"At the time, it was determined that Satan and his minions have no actual, creative power. They can do nothing physical. Their potency lay solely in the persuasive magic of lies."*

Even the Jesuits, long friendly to notions of extraterrestrial life, now leaned toward this explanation, though the Vatican still reserved judgment. Slawek, too, held back.

I bet Dr. Betsby can shed some light, when I get a chance to ask.

Inspection finished, the Paraguayans brought their drapery-screens back down. Pixelated cloth began shimmering to visually magnify their hovel into something more expansive—perhaps with vistas of the pampas back home, before it dried up and turned to sand.

Though the material also deadened sound waves in both directions, Slawek thought he heard the distinct meow of a feline. A simulation? Or one the family kept hidden? Among other parasitically-induced obsessions, some types of *Toxoplasma* gave infected people a weirdly desperate craving for kitties.

"All right," Betsby said, hoisting his bag while Slawek toted heavier devices. "Then if winter was so useful to nineteenth century immigrants, why did a *later* mass migration of people move south, to the American sun belt, in the second half of the twentieth century, depopulating cities like Detroit?"

He's doing an evaluation, Slawek realized. *They don't normally let kids my age join one of the outer communes, as an indie. What if I'm ordered to move back under the dome? Will I lose my shares?*

"Um." He blink-ordered a search based on Betsby's question. Relevant blips crowded in from all sides, but . . . Betsby

hadn't asked him to remove the goggles . . . and surely that
meant something.

Calm down. It's not facts and stats he wants. Interpret.

"Well . . . air-conditioning made southern cities more
bearable. . . . and . . . and for a while *jobs* moved south,
following cheap labor, before heading to the Far East, then
Africa. First clothing an' then cars and such, then computers, fones, fabs, services. . . ."

"Okay, so then why did the migration turn around, sloshing back north again?"

"You mean, reasons *other* than the kudzu? . . . Or the
flooded coast? Or when the Mississippi changed course,
leaving river cities without a river? Or the breakup of
Texas? Or the Big Soggy Decade? Or . . ."

Slawek might have continued listing more bad-luck
reasons for the steady depopulation of the American
Southeast—only right then he realized it might be unwise.
The encampment that stood in front of them now was a
tent-canopy wide enough to hold five families, stretching
between two whole aisles of the Silverdome mezzanine
and cantilevered over the balcony edge by a good five meters
or so. The pixelcloth motif of a banner, with an X-shaped,
starry cross, waved in a simulated breeze above the entrance.

Half a dozen men lounged along the platform's forward
edge, perched overlooking the old gridiron pitch. Several
of them sat cross-legged and very still, wearing completely
blank expressions, but the nearest pair—(Slawek sniffed
that they were smoking barely legal cannaweed)—glared
at the doctor and his assistant. They had specs on, so it
would have been no problem to overhear Slawek's most
recent words.

He cursed himself for being inattentive of his surroundings. These *redders* were the toughest bunch under the
dome.

While he smiled at them with his best friendly idiot grin, Slawek did a quick-scan, then subvocalized a message to Dr. Betsby. *"Two men are on sick list. But three others"*—he marked them—*"haven't showed up for work assignment in several days."*

If the physician got Slawek's overlay message, he showed no overt sign. Instead, Betsby asked the nearest big fellow to get up and lift the fabric barrier for inspection. It was high on the List of Rules and everyone complied, if they wanted to qualify for the big prize—a reclam settlement in Detroit or Pontiac. Still, some groups resented the weekly intrusion.

This time the response was especially sullen. As the eastern fabric-barrier rolled upward, no one moved to damp down the noise and garish images pouring from two of the opposite tent walls. Dr. Betsby shrugged and commenced scanning for health and hygiene concerns.

Lacking anything better to do, Slawek took a closer look at the vivid scenario that was unfolding, across the pixelated-cloth screens. Clearly it was a game—one that called for extensive teamwork and exertion. He saw a dozen or so people in gray senso-suits, ducking and waving realistic looking guns in the cramped area between the vid walls. Of course the weapons weren't real—alarms would go off. But the simulated "rifles" barked and flashed realistically as blue-coated soldiers toppled onscreen, with satisfying howls and graphic grue. Slawek stared, amazed by a coincidence. The battle scene came straight from the 1860s war he was studying in school! Only this simulation was more gruesome and graphic than *The Road to Appomattox*.

A Rebel in Time, identified his scrolling spec-caption. **Story Premise: The player-character steals an experimental time machine from a U.S. research lab and goes back to 1860 with plans to manufacture simple "sten"**

submachine guns for the Confederacy and assist General Nathan Bedford Forest in destroying . . .

Slawek blinked away the caption. The figures ducking and shooting in the foreground weren't just slacking off and avoiding work. *A lot of refugees do game-mining to earn cash*—playing to earn points and virtual possessions, like armor and magic swords that could then be sold for real money to rich players in the Orient. One could argue it was income-generating labor.

Still, this particular fantasy offended Slawek. He loved America, and disliked the trends that were breaking it apart.

Sensing aural curiosity, his specs resumed commentary. **Identifying background music—"Bad Attitude" by Steinman and Meatloaf. . . .**

I've got to take my specs in for a tune-up, Slawek thought, wiping the commentary again and down-cranking sensitivity.

Of course, battle games were registered addictions. But there were so many different ways to excite the craving centers in a human brain, who could track them all? Take the "dazers" who sat, cross-legged, on the nearby plywood platform, using biofeedback spectacles to enter a state of druglike bliss.

That was where Dr. Betsby turned next, when he finished his interior scan, stepping onto the platform. Slawek followed, though the sheer drop-off made him nervous. Betsby bent over in front of one of the men, who stared vacantly with a thin trail of drool hanging from a corner of his mouth.

"Jonathan?" Betsby snapped his fingers. The fellow's bare shoulders bore bioluminescent tattoos—*pixie-skin* displays that throbbed with ever-changing patterns, like an octopus or cuttlefish.

But Jonathan didn't answer. Not while his specs flashed

brainwave-tuned images, guiding him to a plateau that used to be achievable only after years of prayer and training . . . or with illegal substances. Buddhists and transcendentalists called this "cheating" and old-time narcotics cartels pushed to make dazing illegal, as they lost market share to programs like *Cogito* or *LightLord*.

"Leave him be," said a fellow with reddish hair and muttonchop sideburns. His high-of-choice was simpler, a bubble-bottle of frothy Motor City Lager. "Jonathan don't react well to interruptions."

"All the more reason to intervene, Henry James Lee," Betsby said, leaning closer to the dazer. "Jonathan Cain! You know the rules. No meditation during daylight hours. How long since you took care of bodily needs? What you're doing is both irresponsible and dangerous."

The doctor reached for Jonathan's pair of Mesh spectacles, moving to break the trance.

"I tole you to leave off him, you gaijin-lovin', egghead bastard!" The second man snarled, moving closer . . .

. . . and now, suddenly, Slawek caught a glint in Henry James Lee's other hand, the one not holding a beer bottle. His specs zoomed—

"Knife!" Slawek started forward and things happened fast. As he dived between Jonathan and the doc, aiming to throw a block against the blade, he brushed Jonathan's knee—and the dazer suddenly yelled. Spasming, arms, and legs lashed out. One foot struck Slawek's thigh hard, slamming him into Betsby, who windmilled, struggling for balance.

"Doc!"

Slawek shouted, spinning and reaching for Betsby. He managed to catch a sleeve as the physician teetered. No help was coming from Henry James Lee, but if Slawek could just manage to hold on to the strip of fabric . . .

. . . only then Jonathan let out another thrashing, reflex kick, catching Slawek behind the knee, toppling him farther.

The physician teetered, feet scrambling at the brink, as Betsby's weight hauled Slawek after him. In seconds, the doctor's expression shifted from panic to realization. With sudden strength that surprised Slawek, he tore the boy's hand off his sleeve and gave it a hard shove, throwing Slawek back just enough to halt on his knees, wavering right at the ledge. Even so, his momentum carried forward . . . more . . . more . . .

Now Henry James Lee acted—a strong, callused hand clamped Slawek's collar, yanking him back.

"Let go!" he screamed, swatting at the hand. Heart pounding, clenching the plywood with white-hard strength that made the boards crack, Slawek prayed rapidly, both in the virtual world and this one, as he made himself lean over again, to look down toward seating section 116.

It's not so high. A person who landed right could get off with a broken leg—

Flowing tears might have blurred the full impact of what lay down there. But the specs detected impaired vision and compensated, magnifying, clarifying, till he sobbed and closed both eyelids tightly shut.

TORALYZER

Normally, I don't follow leaks from a blind otter.

Off the record is bad enough. But when an OTR demands that I not even *look* for a trackspoor . . . well . . . it smacks of a disinfobot, or even reffer stuff. Please.

But we've done pretty well, following hints from Bird-woman303. Take the way she cued our super-posse smart-mob onto a dozen big-time international fugitives—much to the annoyance of the feds and inter-feds, who spent futile years searching in vain for those bad guys! Breaking that wind won us super-high cred ratings and put *me* in the running for this year's Nosie Award! Not bad, for a reporter who is still confined to a gel-cocoon, who must interact with the world via Mesh surrogates and this crazy possai. But back to the topic at hand.

It's regarding *alien artifacts* that Birdwoman303 was most helpful. Remember how we fast-correlated those underground quakes, and told the world that each individual seismo-pop was the cry of some desperate, buried crystal? We also helped gather data from varied amsci orgs, verifying that all those *space-glitters*—in the asteroid belt and the L-points—were *also* come-and-get-me cries from lonely emissary stones.

Sure, the ensuing seek-and-grab missions will take years. Still, a discovery made by *amateurs* will trigger relaunching of the world's space programs. Congrats!

But those are old hats, no longer hot or hip. Three weeks in the past—almost a paleo-month! And though guvs and privs are sifting the whole Earth for remnants, most of the dug-up crystals are too worn-down, fragged, or broken to be holo-lucid. Twenty days after the Big Revelation in Washington, we still don't have a credible second source. A different gypsy ball to either verify the Artifact aliens or dispute their dour diagnosis . . .

. . . that we're all doomed—species, civilization, and planet—because *everybody dies.* Except those individual beings who manage to get themselves downloaded into message bottles, that is. The ultimate individualism. A level of solipsism that makes Ayn Rand seem like a Shaker.

But we're not going there. Not today. Not with the whole world already chewing over that ominous sales pitch. It is SO boring to think about what everybody else is thinking about, yes?

No, what we've been working on, in this smart-militia of Millisecond MenW, is a different question: *What if there are other, relatively intact space globes, already held secretly, perhaps in private hands?*

Some of our subgroups have been tracing legends, rumors, and murky tales. Others accosted museums or picketed outside reclusive aristo-collections, demanding access to probe precious specimens with rays and beams.

Only, aren't *those* activities also kind of obvious, pursued by agencies and hordes far better equipped than we are? Our forte is uncovering the *un*-obvious! So I suggest a different approach. Instead of looking for hidden artifacts, *let's look for those who are doing the looking.*

Or rather, those who started looking suspiciously early!

I'm talking about the period right after Gerald Livingstone snatched his infamous Object out of orbit. Those first few days, when just the slimmest rumors started spreading, without images or data to back them up. Shouldn't the Mesh archives reveal *who was more excited and eager than anyone reasonably ought to be,* at that early stage?

Who was out there first, searching for translucent, oblong globes about half a meter in length? There was no reason to expect to find such crystal objects already on Earth, let alone to conduct a quest so detailed and specific. And yet—following some hints from our mysterious otter friend—I've already spotted several seeker-worms and -ferrets that were dispatched during those early days, desperately seeking.

Somebody . . . perhaps as many as a dozen groups . . . apparently knew what to go looking for. Knowledge that they still aren't sharing, when we all need most . . .

Ah, the consensus twinkle.

It's agreed, then? We have a new goal. A fresh scent.

Call out the hounds.

49

DOUR STORYTELLERS

For Peng Xiang Bin, these were tense hours.

Everyone in the little study team seemed on edge. So was the world, since ten billion people finally heard the whole story told by those alien entities in Washington. Their cheery sales pitch, inviting some number of individual humans to *join them* on an extended interstellar cruise. Not in person, of course—not as organic beings—but as software copies, cast forth across the interstellar immensity aboard millions of tiny vessels, made of crystal and thought.

Naturally (those alien figures added), the full resources of industrial civilization would have to be brought to bear, and soon, if galactic lifeboats were to be made in sufficient quantity, and in time. Because humanity probably had very little left.

Time, that is.

That other part of their message—revealed almost as an afterthought—was what slammed the world, provoking waves of rioting and suicides, all across the globe.

"And yet, I wonder," mused the Pulupauan research assistant, Paul Menelaua. "Is their warning really such a bad thing?"

"What do you mean, Paul?" asked the elderly scholar from Beijing, Yang Shenxiu.

"I mean that it has focused everybody's attention on lots of problems that people were shrugging aside, or taking only half seriously, till now. Perhaps the warning will have net positive effects, rousing humanity to crisis mode. To take our responsibilities seriously! Girding us with determination to at last grow up. To bear down and concentrate on solving—"

Anna Arroyo interrupted, snorting with clear disdain.

"Do you have any idea what that calls for? Uncovering and solving *thousands* of different traps and pitfalls, from a long list of perils that ultimately struck down every other intelligent race out there? Every last one! You've seen the telecasts. Those Havana Artifact creatures insist there's no way to accomplish that."

"Yes, but is that even logical? I mean, each of their home species was still alive, when it launched its wave of—" Paul stopped, shaking his head. They all recalled what had happened to the homeworld of the helicopter aliens, even as those beings were busy, launching their own bottle-probes. Everyone on Earth knew *that* was no happy ending, with the Havana Artifact barely launched in time to escape a nuclear holocaust.

In the weeks since that scene was televised, radio and optical telescopes had been swiveled to aim at that source planet. So far, they were picking up nothing, not even the static noise that might come from moderate industry . . . though new-model sensors and space-borne instruments were being designed and hurriedly built, to peer even closer.

"Surviving as a technological civilization is like crossing a vast minefield," Anna continued. "Too many mistakes and pitfalls lie in wait—bad tradeoffs or ineludible paths of self-destruction. They say it's rare, at best, for any advanced culture to last for more than a thousand years. Barely long enough to learn how to make more of *these*"— she gestured at the worldstone—"and hurl out more copies of the chain letter!"

Well, Bin thought, *even a thousand years would be nice. We humans have only had high tech for a century or so, and we seem to have already made a mess of it.*

Anna shook her head, sounding resigned and detached. "If it's all hopeless, then maybe we should take them up on their offer. Let them teach us how to build millions of crystalline escape pods, each carrying one of us to go voyaging, in comfort, across the stars."

After a long stretch of shyness, Bin now dared to speak.

"Courier of Caution—the emissary in *our* worldstone— claims that the aliens in Washington are *liars*."

"Exactly!" Paul snapped, while tugging at his animatronic crucifix. He had lately grown more willing to treat Bin as a member of the team, even acknowledging his presence with a terse nod, now and then. "They may *not* be telling the truth. Perhaps they are using this story to *push* us toward despair and self-destruction—the very scenario that our own envoy warns against."

Yang Shenxiu agreed, switching from the colloquial Chinese they had all been using to English.

"This is bigger than any of us. We should bring these terrifying stones together. Let them debate each other, before the world!"

All eyes turned to Dr. Nguyen, the Annamese ceramics mogul, who had been pensive and nearly silent for several days. Now he rested both elbows on the teak tabletop and bridged his fingers, blowing a silent whistle through pursed lips, till finally shaking his head.

"I am answerable to a consortium," he said at last, returning the conversation to impeccable Mandarin, with only a hint of his childhood Mekong accent. "My instructions were to start by getting this stone's story and determining if there were any differences from the Havana Artifact. That we have accomplished.

"Alas, the second imperative priority was made luminously clear—to *seek advantageous technologies,* at almost any cost. Either through interrogation or through dissection. Also, using such methods to determine if there are troves of information the thing is holding back."

With grim, tight lips, Paul Menelaua nodded. Meanwhile, Bin and the others stared, in various degrees of shock.

"The word 'advantageous' . . . ," Anna protested, "it assumes we can learn something that the researchers in Washington aren't discovering—technologies that would give our consortium an edge.

"But we've already seen that these objects are similar. Moreover, the entire *premise* of the story being told by the creature-simulations inside the Havana Artifact . . . their whole narrative . . . revolves around a promise that they will *give* humanity every capability *to make more of these stones.* It's the reason they crossed so many light-years! What motive would they have, to hold anything back? Surely that means we'd gain nothing from tearing apart—"

"Not necessarily," Paul dissented. "If Courier is right, they may have a hidden agenda. In which case they'll hold back plenty. Sure, they're teaching humanity how to make crystalline copies. But really, what are they offering? These stone emissaries don't seem to be all that far in advance of our present capabilities. Now that we've seen their ai and simulation technologies at work, we could probably duplicate everything—except those super-propulsion lasers—without any help, in thirty years. Or less.

"No, what has to worry us is the possibility that there may be *a lot more to all of this,* underneath what they are telling. Only, because the Havana Artifact is openly shared and in public hands, it will never be subjected to *harsh scrutiny.*"

"But *we* can cut into *our* stone, because we're not answerable to public opinion, is that it?" Anna's voice cracked with disbelief. "Are you listening to yourself? If Courier is telling the truth, then *only he* can expose the other stone's lie! Yet, *because* we believe him, and have an opportunity to proceed in secret, *we'll* start sawing away at him, with lasers and drills?"

"Hey, look. I was only saying—"

She turned around. *"You,* Xiang Bin, made a point, a few days ago, that some clandestine group or groups may al-

ready have one or more of these things. Either complete or a partially working fragment. They might also have heard some variant of the tale told by the Havana Artifact—"

"I hope there weren't any secretly held stones," Paul interrupted. "I can think of no worse crime than for selfish people to have clutched such a mystery, all this time, without sharing its warning with the world."

"Perhaps *not* telling the world may have been the more beneficent course. More merciful and wise," Yang Shenxiu muttered. "Better to let people continue in blissful ignorance, if all our efforts will be futile anyway. If humanity is simply doomed to ultimate failure."

Paul Menelaua pounded his fist on the table. His action-crucifix wriggled in rhythm to the vibrations. "I can't accept that. We can still act to save ourselves. The Havana aliens *must* be lying! *That* stone should be dissected, instead of this one."

Silence stretched, while Yang Shenxiu seemed uncertain whether to interpret Paul's shouting as disrespect, or simply a matter of cultural and personality difference. Finally, the scholar shrugged.

"If we might get back on topic," he said.

"Indeed," Anna said. "I doubt any group would keep such an active stone secret out of pure altruism. Human beings tend to seek *advantage*. While rationalizing that they mean well, for the greater good." She spoke in ironic tones, without looking directly at Dr. Nguyen. "But that's the problem with this hypothesis of Xiang Bin's. If any other group already had such a stone, would we not already see new technologies similar to . . . similar to—"

Her voice stuttered to a stop, as if suddenly realizing what should come next.

Paul filled in for her. "Similar to the advances we've all *seen,* across the last century or so, in the game and entertainment industries? As I just said, we're *already rapidly converging* on these abilities. Heck, even military hardware hasn't advanced as rapidly as Hollywood simulation-tech. Methods for advanced visualization, realistic avatar aindroids that pass Turing tests—"

"All of which may be just incremental progress, propelled by the market, by popular culture, and by human ingenuity," Dr. Nguyen pointed out. "Honestly, can you name a single breakthrough that did not follow right on the heels of others, in a rapid but natural sequence of inventiveness and desire? Isn't it a tiresome cliché to credit our own clever discoveries to intervention from above, like claiming that the ancient pyramids could only have been built by UFOs? Must we devolve back to those lurid scenarios about secret laboratories where hordes of faceless technicians analyze alien corpses and flying saucers, without ever telling the citizenry? I thought we had outgrown such nonsense."

The others looked at their leader, and Bin could tell they were all thinking the same thing.

Aren't we, in this room, doing exactly that?

Anyway, he added in his thoughts. *If anybody does know about another, secret stone, it would be him.*

"But of course," Dr. Nguyen added, spreading his hands with a soft smile, "according to this hypothesis of Xiang Bin's, we should look carefully at those who have profited most from such technologies. Bollywood moguls. The owners of Believworld and Our-iverse. The AIs Haveit and Fabrique Zaire."

Bin felt a wave of satisfaction, on hearing one of his ideas called a "hypothesis." He knew that his *guanxi* or relationship-credibility had risen, lately. Even so, he had an uneasy feeling about where this was heading.

"But that only makes our purpose here more pressing," Nguyen continued. "If there are human groups who already have this advantage—access to alien technologies—then they may turn desperate to prevent the International Commission from completing its study of the Havana Artifact. Even worse, there is no telling how long we can keep our own secret. Almost anything we do, any coding or shrouding that we use, could be penetrated by those who have had these methods for some time.

"No. Our only safe recourse would be to get as much out of this worldstone as possible, quickly, in order to catch up."

Bin realized something, watching Nguyen weave this chain of logic, even as the others nodded in agreement. *He is using this argument to support a decision that was already made, far above our heads.*

Yang Shenxiu made one last attempt.

"Even if there were no such hidden stones, before, there are now pieces and fragments being discovered, all over the world. Artifact messengers that have drawn attention by sacrificing parts of themselves."

"But you've seen the reports," Anna responded. "Most of them are too shattered or melted or fused to offer anything coherent."

"So far. But it has only been a few weeks. And don't forget those glittering signs that people have detected in space! Undoubtedly from other stones, signaling for attention. Those would be undamaged and surely—"

"—can't be reached by anyone for at least one or two years," Anna interrupted again, making Bin frown in disapproval. "That's how long it will take to gear up the space programs to send unmanned—and then manned—search and retrieval missions, even if preparations proceed at a breakneck pace."

"Exactly!" Paul pounced. "Now, these things are rare. In a few years, they may be as plentiful as common stones! Those who have an advantage will surely act before that happens." Then Paul blinked, as if unsure which side of the argument he had just supported.

"None of this changes the essential mission before us."
Dr. Nguyen signaled the end to discussion by adopting
a decisive tone. "Xiang Bin, I want to start asking the
Courier entity for useful things. No more stories or home-
sick picture shows about his homeworld. Nor denunciations of the stone in Washington. We need technologies
and methodologies, as quickly and practically as possible.
Make clear how much depends upon—"

He paused as—ten meters across the lavish chamber—a
door opened. At the same instant, curtains of obscurity fell
across the table—a dazzle-drapery consisting of countless
tiny sparkles that prevented any newcomer from viewing
the worldstone.

Too bad it also filled the air with a charged, ozone smell.
Bin wrinkled his nose. He didn't understand how a discretion screen was generated by "laser ionization of air molecules," but he knew that a simple bolt of black velvet could
have accomplished the same thing. Or else locking the door.

A liveried servant hurried in—a young woman with
strawberry hair. Bin had spoken to her a few times, a refugee from New Zealand, whose spoken Chinese was broken
and coarse, but she lent the place a chaste, decorative charm.

"I asked that we not be disturbed for any—" Nguyen
began.

"Sir, I am so sorry, sir." She bowed low, as if this were
Japan, where they still cared about such niceties. "Supervisor Chen sent me to come to you here with discreet message
for you. He needs you at command center. Right away."

Nguyen started to get up, unfailingly polite. "Can you
please say what it's about?"

"Sir, I believe . . ." The young woman swallowed, then
bowed again. "Supervisor Chen is worried that our security has been breached."

SCANALYZER

In light of our present, worldwide hysteria over these crazy space Artifact messengers, I've decided to animate and hyper-reference one of the most popular person-interviews of ten years ago—back in that blessed era before we learned that we weren't alone in the universe.

Let me rephrase that. Before we discovered that we actually ARE alone in the universe. Funny, how reality corresponds to both statements, at once, in dismal irony. Either way, it's time to have another look at this prescient interview. Just will your gaze trackers to follow the keywords "doomsday-fatigue." Let's gather a comment-mob and do a full talmudic gloss on this piece.

MARTIN RAMER (FOR THE BBC): We're here with Jonamine Bat Amittai, compiler of *Pandora's Cornucopia*—the epibook that's been scaring and depressing so many of us ever since Awfulday, conveying all the myriad ways that the universe might *have it in for us,* bringing an end to human existence. Or perhaps only our dreams.

Either way, it's been a heady ride through the valley of potential failure and plausible death. Jonamine, how do you explain the popularity of your series?

JONAMINE BAT AMITTAI: Men and women have always been attracted to stories about ultimate doom, from the Books of Daniel and Revelation to Ragnarok, from Mayan cycles to Nostradamus, from *Dr. Strangelove* to *Life After People.* Perhaps there is an element of schadenfreude, or deriving abstract pleasure from the troubles of others—even if those others will be your own descendants. Or else, some may feel stimulated to relish what they have, in the precious here-and-now, especially if our lives and comforts appear to be on temporary loan from a capricious universe. For billions of people, *nostalgia* fascinates with the notion that the past is always better and preferable over the future.

I like to think that much of our fascination with this topic arises from our heritage as practical problem-solvers. The curiosity that drew our ancestors toward danger, in order to begin puzzling ways around it.

MARTIN RAMER: But your list is so lengthy, so extensive, so depressingly thorough. Even supposing that we do manage to discover some pitfalls in time, and act prudently to avoid them—

JONAMINE BAT AMITTAI: And we have already. Some of them.

MARTIN RAMER: But dodging one bullet seems always to put us in front of another.

JONAMINE BAT AMITTAI: Is there a question, Mr. Ramer? Or were you merely stating the obvious?

50.
DIVINATION

The art that I practice is the only true form of magic.

It had taken Hamish years to realize this consciously, though he must have suspected it as a child, while devouring fantasy novels and playing whatever interactive game had the best narrative storyline. Later, at university and grad school, even while diligently studying the ornate laws and incantations of science, something had always struck him as *wrong* about the whole endeavor.

No, *wrong* wasn't the word. *Sterile.* Or dry, or pallid . . . that is, compared to worlds of fiction and belief.

Then, while playing hooky one day from biomedical research, escaping into the vast realm of a little novel, he found a clue to his dilemma, in a passage written by the author, Tom Robbins.

> *Science gives man what he needs.*
> *But magic gives him what he wants.*

A gross oversimplification? Sure. Yet, Hamish instantly recognized the important distinction he'd been floundering toward.

For all its beauty, honesty, and effectiveness at improving the human condition, science demands a terrible price—that we accept what experiments tell us about the universe, whether we like it or not. It's about consensus and teamwork and respectful critical argument, working with, and through, natural law. It requires that we utter, frequently, those hateful words—"I might be wrong."

On the other hand, magic is what happens when we convince ourselves something is, even when it isn't. Subjective Truth, winning over mere objective fact. The will, triumphing over all else. No wonder, even after the cornucopia of wealth and knowledge engendered by science, magic remains more popular, more embedded in the human heart.

Whether you labeled it faith, or self-delusion, or fantasy, or outright lying—Hamish recognized the species' greatest talent, a calling that spanned all cultures and times, appearing far more often, in far more tribes, than dispassionate reason! Combine it with enough ardent *wanting,* and the brew might succor you through the harshest times, even periods of utter despair.

That was what Hamish got from the best yarns, spun by master storytellers. A temporary, willing belief that he could inhabit another world, bound by different rules. *Better* rules than the dry clockwork rhythms of this one.

The cephalopod emerged from her habitat-cage slowly, cautiously, soon after her handlers opened the gate. Two of her eight tentacles probed the rim as Tarsus brought her bulbous head forward, allowing one big eye—gleaming with feral intelligence—to peer around the rest of the pool. A few rocks and fronds dotted the sandy bottom. Briefly, she tracked some of the fish, darting overhead. But they were too quick and high to try for. She had eaten the slow or unwary, long ago.

With no other danger or opportunity in sight, Tarsus gave a pulse with her siphon, propelling herself toward the only thing of interest. A man-made box with two lids on top.

Whenever they let her out, it meant she had a task to do— one that Tarsus had performed many times before.

Oh, for sure, science wasn't worthless. Hamish knew there was plenty of good work still to be done in the great laboratories, poking Nature, prying loose more secrets. Research was often a noble endeavor—he still viewed it that way—though one easily led astray.

Only, each night, even back in grad school, Hamish would feel the call of his old-fashioned laptop, and the characters who dwelled within. Dramatic premises kept popping into his head, during each day's series of tedious meetings and meticulous lab rounds. And most of the stories that poured out through his fingertips revolved around a single, anxious worry.

Yes, the experiment is awesome. The new device seems cool. It may advance progress and make many lives better.

But what if things go horribly, catastrophically wrong?

Suppose, this time, we've gone too far?

He would picture slime molds, escaping their petri dish prisons, bursting forth to engulf screaming co-workers, then swarming outside to swallow a city. Some promising new drug might develop awful, delayed side effects, turning your loved ones into terrifying strangers. He envisioned robots escaping all their programmed safeguards, in order to go on killing sprees, then using their former human masters for spare parts. The next tomb unearthed by a naive archaeologist could spew forth poison spores, or hauntings. A new birth control pill instead unleashes Children of the Damned, assisted by aborted fetuses on a rampage! Or do-gooder environmentalists might cripple the nation's industry and bring on a new stone age. He imagined SETI sky-searches attracting predatory computer viruses that then hypnotize humanity into slavery. Sure, the scenarios were lurid, but that just made them easier, and more fun to write!

Always, of course, there would be a lead character who—with Hamish's own voice—started each book by wagging his finger, issuing dire warnings against the coming Big Mistake. A protagonist who later (as the dead piled higher) got to say, "I told you so!"

Tarsus used puffs of siphoned water to hover over the box, before bringing all eight of her tentacle arms into play, fondling the polished wooden surface. Bringing one eye close, and then the other, she examined new decorations that adorned each of the two latched covers.

She knew that she would only be allowed to open one of the compartments. As soon as she chose a lid to pry back, the other would lock. Not that it mattered. She always got a prize—a juicy crab—whichever door she selected. And yet, she never picked randomly.

Faces crowded close, human faces, pressing against the other side of a nearby observation pane. Their eyes—the only feature that seemed octopuslike—followed her every movement. Tarsus had a sense that her choice mattered to them. And so, obligingly, she examined the illustrations atop each lid, both visually and with a probing tendril tip.

When his career took off—with books and films and then vivid immersives—jealous complainers gathered round, yapping at Hamish. His stories played loose with scientific fact, they griped. His research consisted of gathering enough vocabulary and jargon to make the outlandish sound plausible.

Even worse (claimed his critics), Hamish Brookeman ignored all the modern safeguards and layers of accountability that earnest men and women had erected, in order to prevent exactly the mistakes that drove his tales. One reviewer even claimed to find a deeper pattern—that every calamity plot Hamish ever wrote arose because his arrogant villain-scientists compulsively insisted upon *secrecy*. Without that one ingredient, most of the disaster scenarios in his tales would get corrected by wiser heads. So, wasn't his *real* complaint about doing bold things in the *dark*? The older, more magical way?

Wouldn't most of his warnings become moot, in a world with *more* openness, rather than less?

Such talk used to hurt, at first. But in time, Hamish learned to ignore the critics, even those who called him a "traitor to science." He accomplished it quite simply, by writing them *into* his next tale—with thinly disguised name changes—to get eviscerated on cue. That was satisfaction enough. Ironically, it allowed him to stay genially mild and pleasant to almost everybody out here, in the merely real world.

Tarsus found no meaning in either of the symbols.

On rare occasions, she had recognized one or both, when the figures were shaped like things she knew. A fish or a simple octopus, or the spindly motif of a man. Far more often, they were just square-cornered emblems—combinations of the pure, flat, static colors that humans seemed to prefer . . . so different from the subtle hues and shades that rippled across the photo-active skin of any cephalopod, quicker than thought, letting an octopus like Tarsus blend into almost any background.

These emblems just lay there, as always, dull and uninspiring. Only, this time at least the shapes were unusual. They had the stretched outlines of air-breathing creatures, with limbs to carry them about, on land.

But they weren't human.

And so, for a while, especially during the years with Carolyn, Hamish found some happiness, playing in one cosmos after another of his own devising—wherein *he* could be God, decreeing harsh punishments for ambitious vanity, meting out justice for the sin of hubris and technological pride.

Anyway, didn't civilization obviously value him far more as a spinner of scary tales than it ever had before, as a researcher?

And who am I, to argue with civilization?

Yet, as the years passed and his voice grew stronger—becoming a leader in the rising Renunciation Movement—there came strange pangs that tasted like regret.

Which brought him around, full circle, to the very topic he had tried pushing from his ever busy thoughts. The message of the artilens—the aliens dwelling inside the virtual space of the Havana Artifact.

Nobody survives, they assured.

Not as organic beings, dwelling on the fragile, filmy surface of planets, exposed to innumerable dangers from above, below, and on every side. Plus countless hazards of their own making. That type of life is just too fragile, prone to countless missteps and mistakes. Nursery worlds like your Earth are fine for spawning new intelligent races. But then you must move on to higher states of being, before time runs out.

It left Hamish in a quandary. One small part of him felt vindicated by the aliens' desolate story. The portion that had always viewed civilization—and its pompous, self-important fury—to be futile. A side of him that knew, all along, how inadequate human beings were. A species inherently doomed, whether by God, fate, or ornery nature, from the very start.

Now? Upon learning that most, or all, other intelligent races fell for the same long list of lethal mistakes? That only seemed to reinforce the point. In fact, no event ever gave as much energy as this one had, to the Renunciation Movement. New recruits and donors were flocking to the Prophet and his cause. Drawn by his latest, brilliant sales pitch.

"The aliens never said that all species die . . . ," Tenskwatawa had gone on air to preach. *"All they are saying is that such species stop being detectable as ambitious, high-tech civilizations.*

"That means there is an out!" the Prophet continued. *"A way to avoid the many pitfalls and extinction modes described by the aliens. And that way is to opt out of the game!*

"Others out there—perhaps many others—may have chosen to step back from the hi-tech precipice. They chose to avoid the minefields, quicksand pits, and self-destruction modes, by the simplest means possible.

"By settling back into older, wiser ways.

"By ceasing to move forward."

Tarsus contemplated the patterns of colors. One of them was jagged and symmetrical, kind of like a starfish. The color and texture were strange, however, offering a tangy synesthesia, an inferred *taste* that was not unlike a clam with flecks of manganese nodule in its shell.

The other emblem was visually more rotund—it resembled (to her eye) something akin to a jellyfish. But under her stroking tentacle, there was a bumpy roughness to the imprinted image that smelled like *time* . . . vast amounts of it, congealed and stale.

She didn't care for either of the patterns, but Tarsus knew that she must contemplate them for an allotted interval, and then select one as preferable over the other, or else the hatch covers would not loosen. So she fondled the paper coverings, peered at them, even used her beak to take samples, stroking with her tongue and musing on whatever subtleties lay beyond mere wood pulp and waterproof paste . . .

. . . at which point she chose.

A murmur of excitement yanked Hamish out of his reverie and back to the present. Most of the onlookers in the Cephalo-Delphi Center were leaning toward an observation window, separating them from the large aquarium tank, where a famous prognosticating octopus had finally made her choice, opening one of two hatches representing alternate possible futures.

Having gained access, Tarsus was now dismembering a crab, with relish, ignoring the creature's bitter resistance with snapping claws. Her caretaker, Dr. Nolan, announced the augury results with evident satisfaction.

"Tarsus has spoken. On the basis of her choice, our investor co-op has purchased ten thousand wager-shares on the Chicago Predictions Exchange, betting that the International Contact Commission will continue to be deadlocked in stalemate for at least another week, delaying their recommendations for what to do about the alien artifact.

"Given that Tarsus has accurately forecast outcomes on nine of her last twelve tries—well above statistical significance—we expect that other investors will follow suit. And now, if you will follow me to the reception area, there will be refreshments while I answer any questions."

Hamish hung back, feeling miffed as the crowd followed Dr. Nolan. This was supposed to be *his* morning with Tarsus. But that appointment for a private audience with the eight-armed soothsayer had been put off, preempted, so that the keepers might ask their octopus-seer another silly, useless question about the Havana Artifact.

There was a time when they would not treat the famous Hamish Brookeman that way. As recently as a few weeks ago.

After all, what did it matter if that raucous pack of scientists, scholars, and politicians in Virginia dithered over their report? With the world spiraling into disorder, frenzy, or despair, was any public statement likely to make a difference?

In fact, Hamish had made his appointment to consult Tarsus several months ago, before anyone knew about crystals filled with ersatz aliens. Back when his top concern had been the hunt for the Basque Chimera, the infant son of Agurne Arrixaka Bidarte. A search that now seemed secondary, even inconsequential.

In fact, he had been contemplating a completely different question to ask Tarsus, today. Something much more timely, even personal.

And if that made Tenskwatawa angry?

So what. Let him hunt for the Neanderthal boy without my help!

Hamish still nursed hurt feelings over the snub, back at that elite gathering in Switzerland, when the leader of the Renunciation Movement kept him away from the main event, a private viewing of Rupert Glaucus-Worthington's greatest treasure—a crystal skull that must have once been an emissary from space. Hamish would have missed it all, but for intervention by mysterious third parties. Ever since that evening, he had felt loyalties slipping. Not his belief in Renunciation; that was still firm. But his willingness to leave all decisions to one leader.

A leader who was now firming up an alliance with trillionaire lords.

Well? argued part of his mind—the devil's advocate. *Is there any other group that can make renunciation work? It won't happen in a democracy. At least the trillies have experience managing great enterprises and making decisions from the shadows. History shows that only an oligarchy can suppress technology's breakneck race ahead. And that conference in Switzerland showed one encouraging aspect. All those boffin papers, on how an elite can rule with noblesse oblige—at least they seem to be taking their new responsibilities seriously.*

Anyway, what choice will we have?

Humanity could only survive by rejecting the aliens' path. By returning to its roots. To the social pattern that ruled every other civilization but this one.

And yet—

—yet his own role and importance in these unfolding events seemed to be diminishing, day by day. Even when the Prophet asked his advice, it seemed off-hand, even perfunctory. And Hamish was coming to realize something bitter, but true.

He did not *want* to become just another boffin-lackey for the new oligarchy.

Hamish fondled a small, sealed container, no bigger than his knuckle, in his jacket pocket. It contained a single contaict lens. If he slipped it on, it might put him back in touch with the mysterious strangers who once guided him through the halls of Rupert Glaucus-Worthington's expansive mansion, leading him by secret passages to witness the New Lords in action. To see, with his own eyes, how Rupert and his peers confronted the unexpected. And that moment had changed him.

In their expressions of dull surprise, he had not seen the visage of wise leaders. Not Plato's philosopher kings, but stunned and ignorant men, clinging to preconceptions, as likely to make grand errors as anybody else.

In which case, are they any more qualified to pick a path for humanity, than I am?

Before Hamish could follow that mental track much further, something interrupted the chain of sullen thoughts. Wriggles, his little earring aissistant, spoke up.

"Hamish, something has happened.

"It has to do with Roger Betsby. You asked to be informed of any significant developments."

Hamish blinked.

Betsby? Oh, right. The Strong Affair. That matter had seemed so pressing—to save the career of an absurd fool of a U.S. senator from his self-inflicted public relations fiasco. Now it struck Hamish as so . . . *P.A.* . . . or pre-Artifact. True, Senator Strong could still be helpful in formulating right policies for the new era. Yet, the first thing to cross his mind was that Hamish looked forward to seeing the senator's nemesis again. To spar once more with the doctor's agile mind.

What has Betsby done now? He caught himself smiling in anticipation, as if relishing the next clever move of a worthy chess opponent.

Fishing in his jacket pocket, Hamish brushed past the small contaict lens container, choosing instead a larger, rectangular shape that he swiftly unfolded into a pair of tru-vu goggles.

"Show me," he commanded Wriggles.

But, even expecting something unexpected, what erupted before Hamish struck him numb with shock.

THE POSTHUMOUS CONFESSION OF A POISONER

If you are watching this, it means that I'm dead, or missing, or so mind-altered that I can no longer transmit the complicated daily stop-code on this, my final statement to the world.

My name is Roger Betsby. I am . . . or was . . . a physician serving one of the refugee communities in the Detroit Renewal District. Blink *here*, and my homunculus will take you on a tour of who I was and what I stood for. But I bet you are more likely interested in hearing my deathbed denunciation.

First a confession. On October the twelfth of last year, while pretending to be a waiter at a luncheon of the First Americans Club, I slipped a substance into the beverage consumed by Senator Crandall Strong. Among THESE links are vid recordings showing me in the act. There are also clips—redistributed by scores of newsnexers—of the senator's subsequent speech, which started in his normal fashion, with a low, mild voice, but soon rising in tone and volume as he typically recited from a long list of complaints and grudges.

With increasing vigor, Strong condemned the current U.S. Congress, for refusing to fully fund the Second Reparations Act. He disdained the present administration, for ceding more environmental authority to UNEPA. The Canadians, he excoriated for limiting New Lands immigration, and the courts, for constraining the damage awards won by Victims of the Melt, in their lawsuit against the Denialist Cabal.

Soon, as usual, he moved on from enemies who were merely social, legal, or political, and laid into those he has long proclaimed the real villains—all the would-be "godmakers," using technology and science to arrogate powers of the Almighty.

Millions have watched this particular speech, which—as usual—built toward a powerful, fuming rant. Only, this time, going well *beyond* a mere rant, it spiraled out of control! Instead of maintaining a high-but-controlled level of righteous anger, all the way to a thundering end, it became pyrotechnic, racist, scatological even for Crandall Strong.

You can see the transition, about eight minutes in—right here—as he starts looking perplexed, licking his lips and then pressing them together, hard. At this point, he begins gesturing more dramatically than usual, pounding on the lectern. Observe his voice growing incrementally louder, his complaints more florid and accusations more intense. But note, underneath it all, an expression of puzzlement, worry, and something else . . . a growing sense of frantic *need*.

His regular stump speech always starts with contemporary political complaints, but then moves on to condemnation of modernity and technological "progress," culminating in calls for all such matters to be placed in better and *wiser hands.* Only this time, the smooth sequence, ramping up from low, reasonable tones to vehement indignation, seems off-beat.

See? Clearly, he knows that something has gone wrong. But his response is *not* to finish early and seek help. It is to push ahead. Raising the stakes. Upping the ante and doubling-down. Getting more vehement . . . then choleric . . . then apoplectic!

Now, you may have guessed that I have a low opinion of this politician. I consider him to be a mean-minded demagogue of the worst order. It happens that I also dislike his particular views on a wide range of matters. But my purpose in slipping him a mind-altering compound was not to undermine the Renunciation Movement. I think they are wrong, but they have a legitimate right to make their points and to argue rationally with the rest of us. Who knows? They might even be partly right about human destiny.

No, what I did on that day was perform a *medical experiment.* If Senator Strong did not suffer from a diagnosable mental illness, then the drug that I gave him—a completely legal substance—*would have had no effect at all.* He would have given his usual, overly dramatic and illogical polemic, without any ill effects.

So why did it have the effect of ultimately driving him into a pyrotechnic fury, screaming vicious epithets and a series of horrific racial slurs?

Let's rewind to the first time Senator Strong got that *baffled* look on his face. See here? I'll overlay a flush tone analysis. And now add a voice stress graph. Compare the overlays to *these* other frames, taken from very similar speeches, at almost the same point, where he's peaking at his first big polemical crescendo. His first dramatic thump on the lectern.

In those other speeches, the stress and flush-tone data show that he's derived a jolt of intense *pleasure* from the moment. And yes, that is common with dramatic extroverts. But note here on October the twelfth. The jolt—the sudden wash of enjoyment isn't there. And hence the puzzled expression. Clearly, he had been counting on getting that usual bump, from indignantly denouncing his enemies.

When it did not come, what was his response? To just go on with giving his speech, performing the day's task with professional skill and accomplishing his goal? Or to pull back, when something has gone wrong, and to reassess the situation?

No. He did neither thing.

Instead, watch as Senator Strong pounds harder. He bears down, grinding his teeth between the sentences, growling, even shouting the same words he had spoken, on other occasions, with mere, measured anger.

Can you see, yet, the effect of the drug I fed him? It did not cause his vehemence or loss of control, nor does it have any known effects upon cognition or judgment.

It simply quashed the chemical-hormonal *pleasure jolt* that he normally receives from righteous indignation! That and nothing more.

Go ahead and blink *here* to look up *Anhedonium*. It is a recent advance over naltrexone, which was long used to suppress the surge reinforcements of heroin and other addictive substances. Anhedonium acts with accumbenol to block dopamine receptors *only* in the nucleus accumbens and two other carefully targeted sites. It is increasingly used in drug abuse clinics like one I operate in Detroit. Its simple effect is to interrupt the *reinforcement cycle* of most addictions.

Now, almost any habit can be called an "addiction" if its repetition is reinforced in the human brain, by rhythmic release of pleasure-mediating chemicals. The core process is not, in itself, harmful. Indeed, it is deeply human and essential! Pleasure-based repetition reinforcement is partly responsible for our tight bonding to our children, our husbands and wives, or the tendency to keep returning our attention to music, or beauty, or the glorious exercise of skill. It contributes to the joy that some derive from prayer. These are some of the good and wholesome things that we are glad to be addicted to!

Lately, experts have come to view drug abuse as little more than a *hijacking* of this normal human process. Heroin and ecstasy and moondust all offer shortcuts into brain mechanisms that served a real, evolutionary function. Only, their crude, sledgehammer attack upon the pleasure-reinforcement process seldom helps to make lives better . . . more often it ruins them.

We now know there are other ways to hijack this system. In some people, a hedonic gratification pattern can be achieved simply by entering certain *frames of mind.* For example, the cyclical jolt from *gambling* can be a genuine addiction, requiring as much effort to break as cocaine or kicx. Habitual thrill seekers, video game potatoes, and Wall Street "wizards" have all been shown to follow similar patterns. Once aboard the roller-coaster, they cannot let go. One mild version can be seen in those riveted to spectator sports . . .

. . . and then there are the *indignation junkies.* People who regularly get high off self-righteousness and sanctimony. You know the kind—we all do. (Any normal person has seen the rush I'm referring to, playing across that face in the mirror!)

In fact, many will accuse *me* of proud sanctimony, in perpetrating what I did against Senator Strong! Be my guest. Study my life and see if my good works and strong opinions fit the pattern of addiction. Could be.

But I am not the topic here.

Years ago, when the medical community announced that *self-righteous indignation can be an addiction,* as severe as any drug abuse, I expected the public to take notice. Surely (I thought) the vast majority of moderate, reasonable people will now stop listening to those vehement wrath-junkies—the *essers*—out there, constantly spewing hate from pulpits of the left or right, or religious or paranoiac mania? Now that the pattern is understood, won't this tend to *disempower* the *irate*, who refuse to negotiate, and instead empower those who want to engage in reason? To listen to their neighbors and work out pragmatic solutions to problems?

Those who prefer *positive-sum* games.

Won't this now-verified scientific fact undermine the frantic types, who have ruined argument and discourse in public life, by portraying their opponents in stark terms of pure evil, opposed by pharisaical good? By showing that their fury arises out of an addictive chemical high that they secrete within their own skulls?

To my disappointment, the major media pretty much ignored this revelation. After all, they draw nourishment from "them-versus-us" dichotomies and the polarization of pure-minded sides. They saw no benefit in any shift from conflict toward reasonable debate. (Boring!)

I realized; for people to understand the significance of this scientific breakthrough, there would have to be an event the media could not ignore.

There must be an example. So I provided one.

Why did Senator Strong go crazy, that day? And for several days thereafter? He was fed no mind-bending or soul-twisting poison. He ingested a *medicine* used only to deny addicts the feedback pleasure of their high. And so, when he did not get the accustomed jolt from sanctimonious rage, he *upped the level of his rancor, in search of the buzz, the jizz, the zing.*

And when that didn't work, he upped it again, and again, as addicts do. Never pausing to think *Maybe I had better stop now*, he kept hurtling faster and faster toward the edge—as addicts do—ignoring reason or consequences, in search of satisfaction. To scratch an accustomed itch that was now beyond his ability to control.

That's it. That was my scheme and my experiment.

That it worked, is inarguable.

It is also undeniable that I *broke the law,* along with the codes of my profession. I administered a legal medicine, for an appropriately diagnosed illness . . . but I did so in an unethical and illicit way, never consulting my patient or warning him of possible outcomes. And for that I should, by all rights, go to jail. Certainly, I am willing to take my punishment, according to the tradition of Gandhi, with a measure of cheerful acceptance.

Only, meanwhile, it is done. Senator Strong cannot escape blame for his outrageous behavior by claiming "It was the drug!" The opinions he expressed were entirely his own and no one forced him to express them. His behavior occurred because he is an *addict*—a term that the public rightfully disdains.

Above all, now millions will think about all this. They will view differently all the *self-righteousness junkies* in their midst— even ones they agree with! They will see how such people use their relentless passion and addict stamina to take over most advocacy groups, at all ends of the political and social spectrum, turning argument into jihad and negotiation into stark war between good and evil . . . or evil versus good.

You and your neighbors will never view the fervent ardor of ecstatic anger the same way. Now you'll see it and recognize the symptoms of an illness—almost exactly the same as smoking crack or opium.

And, maybe then you'll feel empowered to face down the vociferously indignant. You may even decide to join together with other mild-mannered, rational, and sensible folk, to reclaim the gracious gift of our ancestors. The power of calmly reasoning together. If that happens, I'll take my punishment with serenity. A martyr for calm adulthood.

Unless that drive—for dramatic martyrdom—has been my

own sanctimonious trip! I admit it's a possibility. Any honest person ought to.

Oh, but then, if you are watching this right now, I am probably dead. So I matter even less than I ever did.

Anyway, this was never about me. Or even Senator Strong.

It's about us.

51.

INSPIRATION

Hamish pulled off the tru-vus, which had gone blurry, somehow. Perhaps they were defective. He wiped his eyes with the back of a wrist.

What happened to Betsby? Did the senator arrange to have him killed? But that jerk Strong promised he would keep hands off, till I reported my results!

Hamish put the immersion glasses back on. Blits flurried around the periphery of vision, responding to his attention gaze, pupil dilation, and tooth-click or subvocal commands. Hamish was so out of practice that involuntary eye-flicks and grunts kept causing ripples, disrupting the feedback loops, like pebbles dropped into a pond.

Wriggles intervened. His little digaissistant swept away all the mere gossip and rumors, picking, distilling, and summarizing facts.

Apparently, Dr. Roger Betsby had fallen to his death from a second-level balcony of the Detroit-Pontiac domed stadium, pushed over (inadvertently, according to preliminary reports) by a convulsing patient. One who was under care for an addiction ailment—how ironic.

Of course, some apparent "accidents" weren't. So, police officials promised to investigate any possibility of foul play, especially now that Betsby's death-confession had begun climbing the charts, accompanied by a tide of conspiracy theories. Hamish made a mental note to send one of his favorite contract operatives to lend the authorities a hand. He felt a personal stake in getting to the bottom of this.

Damn. I've found so few minds I respect.

If Strong did this, instead of leaving me to handle Betsby, then our deal is off. A lot of deals are off.

Hamish closed his eyes.

Unbidden, a steady stream of fantasies had been bubbling through his mind, the last few days—as if his subconscious were trying to find a way around the dour conundrum offered by the Artifact aliens. As always, the ideas manifested as dramatic plots for a book, or movie, or interactive. Till now, each of them had seemed—well—*untenable,* even cheesy. Borrowed, blatantly, from earlier works of fictional paranoia. Disappointment with himself had darkened his mood.

Only now, he found himself mulling part of the posthumous confession of the man some were calling the Saint of the Silverdome. Hamish always prided himself in his memory for good dialogue.

> *It is undeniable that I broke the law . . . I administered a legal medicine for a real illness . . . but in an illegal way, never consulting my patient. For that I'll go to jail . . . accepting punishment according to the traditions of Gandhi and the other great martyrs, with acceptance.*

Oh, that was good stuff. Truly memorable. In a way, Hamish kind of envied Roger Betsby, whose real experiment had *not* been medical, but social. Perhaps all of this publicity, heightened by his death, would indeed turn the attention of a fickle public toward the lesson the Doctor sought to teach. A lesson about maturity versus sanctimonious fury.

Maybe. Briefly.

But that outcome wasn't what concerned Hamish. No, what struck him was a sudden, bolt-like realization. Awed by Betsby's innovative technique for getting a point across.

A confession is always more credible than a denial.

Hamish felt a chasm in the pit of his stomach, a cavity made up of fear. The action that he suddenly found himself contemplating would change everything. There were terrible dangers, possibly as great as the ones that Roger Betsby faced. But also potential rewards. Plus a very real chance to alter the world, something that his genre fictions—despite all their dire-warning intensity—had never achieved.

Could I actually do this? Shall I study the idea first? Working out all the pros and cons and details?

Or would that only risk losing the moment, the sheer, impulsive genius!

In fact, there was only a very narrow window of time. Worldwide economies were teetering as thousands committed suicide, tens of thousands rioted, millions stayed home from work, and billions muttered angrily at their tru-vus and tellai-screens, driven into a contagious funk by the message of the artilens. And, while regular political institutions teetered, certain cabals of planetary power dealers were getting set to make their big move. One that Hamish had striven for years to assist—

—only now he felt a new certainty—that he did not want the "solution" being offered by Tenskwatawa, or the oligarchs, after all.

"Mr. Brookeman?"

His eyelids parted. Slightly startled, Hamish looked down to see the petite lab director, half his height, Dr. Nolan, standing just a meter away.

"Mr. Brookeman, I want to repeat our apology for having

preempted your reserved time with Tarsus. I'm sure you understand that fast-breaking news events get priority."

Fast-breaking news? Well, maybe. But the question you asked the octopus-oracle was both boring and dumb. Still, he maintained a calm and friendly smile.

"I'll tell you what," she continued. "Why don't we offer you time with Patmos, our parrot-prognosticator? Her record is almost as good as Tarsus's and we can give you a substantial discount."

Hamish nodded.

"Very well. Lead on."

As he followed the keeper of animal auguries, Hamish considered the question he might pose—a very different one than Tenskwatawa had sent him to ask.

If I confess my crime, will it help me influence world events and bring outcomes I'll desire?

He would have to simplify the query further, of course, and couch it as a yes-no, either-or choice for the feathered fortune-teller to pick between, opening one labeled box or the other for a tasty treat. In truth, Hamish wasn't sure he believed in these supposed seers. Most reputable scientists scoffed at the whole idea, attributing their "track record" to statistical flukes. But as long as he was already here. . . .

What if the answer is yes? Do I have the guts to carry out my plan?

Even if I find the courage, I'd require help to pull it off. But who? I'll need people with technical skills, who are good at acting in secret . . . and quickly . . .

His subconscious was already ahead of him. Hamish realized this when he found his left hand absently fondling a small case in his pocket, containing a single contaict lens.

They helped me once . . . my mysterious benefactors . . . to see through the banality of the aristocrats' club.

They said I had only to get in touch, again, if I wanted to go farther down a rabbit hole. This certainly would qualify as a leap!

But do I dare work with people I don't even know?

Can I trust them?

Will they even go along with what I have in mind?

Would anybody?

Hamish heard a squawking sound ahead, as Dr. Nolan entered a chamber whose walls were covered with drip-veg hangings, lending the place a jungle ambiance.

"Awr. Hi Jill! Hi Jill! Hello-o-o stranger! Awk! Tall! Awk!"

Shifting her weight on a wooden perch, a gray parrot rocked eagerly, ready to get to work, building her moderate, but above-average, score in the Worldwide Predictions Market. Of course she didn't know about any of that, nor did she care whether her tally of successful forecasts qualified as prophecy, coincidence, or statistical fluke. Perhaps (according to some) *not caring* might be part of the reason for it all.

Hamish spent a few minutes refining his paired, yes-no questions, writing them on two slips of paper, then inserting them behind clear labels, covering separate hatches in a wooden cabinet. Then he stood back, still clutching the little container in his pocket, breathing shallowly as his heart raced.

Am I really this credulous? This superstitious?

Of course I am. Or I would never have written so many tales about the price of hubris and ambitious pride.

Only now, shall I attempt to alter human destiny, through actions of my own? Not via stories on a screen or the pages of a novel, but in real life?

Isn't that arrogant, in its own right?

Minutes later, he had his answer, Patmos chuttered happily, fussing her way through devouring a nut. The door she had chosen lay open behind her.

Wordlessly, with barely a nod of thanks, Hamish turned to go.

First order of business? A quiet place to slip on the contaict lens and commune with the people behind it, seeking their help to carry out a desperate, impromptu plan. A plan to rescue the world from diabolic alien invaders.

If this works, I'll owe the inspiration to you, Roger.
Rest in peace.

THE CONFESSION OF A HOAXER

Hello. My name is Hamish Brookeman, and with this statement I admit and avow to having committed a crime.

First, though, I'm told that I am the 246th most famous person on the planet. But for those of you who still don't know who I am, here's my *bio*. A lot of folks say that I'm pretty good as a story-maker, scenario-builder, vid-director, and so on. In fact, those very skills are why I was invited, some years ago, to *join a conspiracy*. A scheme that I once believed in—

—that I now confess to be monstrous and wrong.

In my defense, let me say the plot didn't seem bad, at first. Those behind it appeared sincere, claiming we'd save the world! A world riven by political, military, and ethnic feuds that threatened Armageddon in dozens of ways. A world that's withered and worn out from ecological neglect and overuse by ten billion ravenous consumers. A world where venerable traditions hang in tatters and every day brings more news of insolent technological "wonders" that might end us all.

Was it still possible to divert lemming-humanity from its doom?

The concept we came up with was simple, having been portrayed in science fiction dramas going all the way back to a classic *Outer Limits* episode and one of the great comic books of the 1980s.

How to get all peoples and nations to put down their petty squabbles and unite in common cause? Why, by offering them a *shared enemy.*

A credible external threat would provoke the goodwill and fellowship that humans always show to other members of their tribe, when confronted by dangerous outsiders. Across history, leaders used this method to rally their subjects.

But how to accomplish it? A lot of ideas that seem elegant, say in a movie, prove impossible to implement, especially by a small and secret cabal. By the time they came to me, the group had already considered the problem, long and hard. They knew better than to try anything too ornate, like forging a complete "alien spaceship," or even the partial wreckage of one. The world's scientists and sages would quickly discover telltale signs of Earthly origin, in every alloy and part, down to the distribution of isotopes.

As for the invaders themselves? Well, not even great nations like China, America, or Brazil are so scientifically advanced that they could fake an extraterrestrial being, down to organs, metabolism, and a foreign genome.

But the Group did have one area of advantage. *Simulation technologies* had been squirreled away for quite some time—a quirky holographic technique here, a crystalline storage method there, some tricks of ai—set aside by skilled workers and innovators in Hollywood, in the defense establishments, and gaming industries. Separately, they didn't amount to much. But together? Well, imagine how dedicated these far-seeing idealists had to be, in order to keep their best breakthroughs hidden, instead of exploiting them to get richer! In sum, together, the sequestered techniques added up (we thought) just enough, so that their combination might seem impressively advanced, even far ahead of contemporary human abilities.

And that's where I came in. Who was better qualified to write the back story? The scenario. The characters. Their behaviors.

and motives. The things they'd say . . . in order to fool the world with *simulated aliens*?

Of course, by now you all know I'm referring to the Havana Artifact and its collection of "extraterrestrial emissaries."

And yes, I am hereby claiming, confessing, avowing, and admitting *It was all a great, big hoax!*

But hang on a moment. Let me finish. For, you see, there remained arguments over *how* to present our simulations. Perhaps hide a transmitter aboard one of the big, deep space probes sent out by ESA, NASA, or Sinospatial—perhaps the *Maffeo Polo* or *Voyager Twelve*—heading out to Uranus or Neptune. The clever notion was for our little parasitic device to detach from the main ship, just as the mission swung close to Jupiter, for a gravity slingshot maneuver. If done properly, at that crucial point, the two pieces might go very different ways. (See the concept illustrated *here*.)

A few years later, the secret transmitter would then turn toward Earth and beam a *SETI signal* to our planet, purporting to be from some faraway world and laying down a threat that might unite humanity! It was a clever plan . . . but impractical, I'm told. The space agencies and their astronautics experts might not be fooled for long. They would soon trace back the orbits and figure it all out. Anyway, smuggling a parasitic cargo onto a scientific planetary probe is about as easy as persuading your wife to hire three Swedish "nannies." It can't be done.

So my fellow conspirators settled on the Artifact Option. No need to stow away on a voyage to deep space. Instead, use all those hidden techniques to make a simple block of reactive crystal that could be powered by sunlight alone. Embed the right simulation programs . . . then simply release it into orbit near the Earth! In such a way that it would have to be noticed, and grabbed, by one of the debris-snagging teams . . . ideally, by some astronaut who was bored, burnt out, and easy to fool.

Drop a hint or two, get him assigned to work in the desired area—and there you have it!

At the surface, our deception worked better than any of us could have hoped or imagined. And I admit, I felt pretty darned proud of the results. Especially my aliens! It was some of my best writing, ever.

Oh, sure, some people have cried "hoax!" since the beginning. But we expected that. So long as a majority believed there were genuine aliens, and that First Contact had finally been achieved, then the whole world's attention would zero in on the same thing, at the same time. . . .

Only, then some things went wrong. I began to see the story go off track. Our synthetic aliens, simulated inside the Artifact, started diverting from my script! Moreover, instead of uniting the world, this "First Contact" was having the *opposite effect,* splintering society and causing everything to fracture!

Then came the Core Message. This thing about making millions of *copies* was bad enough. But to claim that *nobody survives*?

That's when I realized . . . I'd been had. In my gullibility, I had lent my services, my creativity, to a conspiracy. One that had communicated with me only by encrypted overlays, never in person. What had seemed a prudent security measure, I now saw as a way to keep me from ever tracking down my comrades in crime. Compatriots who—for some reason—had chosen to alter the message, giving it a twist I never intended. From hope to despair.

Why? I honestly don't know! When I wrote my scenario, I considered the possibility that some ulterior motive underlay the Group's surface idealism. Perhaps I was a dupe and all of this would turn out to be just a publicity stunt for some new interactive game. Oh, I turned out to be a dupe, all right. But the underlying scheme was deeper, more malevolent than anything I imagined.

I'm running out of time, so let me leave all the details for later.

Suffice it to say, for now, that I'm ready, even eager, to make up for my role in this crime. *It is undeniable that I broke the law . . . attempting a hoax to startle the world out of its modern illness.* A medicine that might have worked, if done properly.

It now seems likely that for my part in the hoax—for my sin of pride in thinking I could "save the world"—I will almost certainly spend time in jail, or worse. But it feels cleansing to get the truth out there . . . and to counter a plot that I now recognize as misguided, even vile.

To the authorities, let me assure you, I'll cooperate, tell all, and accept my fair punishment with good grace, according to the traditions of Gandhi, King, Solzhenitsyn, and the other fighters for truth.

As for the rest of you, please accept my humble regrets for contributing to this unfortunate disruption in your lives. Lives you all can return to, now that we—humanity—are once again alone in our universe.

52.

APPRAISAL

". . . ideally, by some astronaut who was bored, burnt out, and easy to fool . . ."

Gerald felt all eyes swivel toward him.

"Ouch!" Genady commented. Akana audibly ground her teeth.

"Well, he accomplished one thing," Emily murmured. "The sumbitch just vaulted from 246 to number nine in just a few minutes. The fastest fame-flame in history! Sorry, Gerald, he just streaked past you."

"Hush," was his only answer. None of them had picked up the first airing of Brookeman's broadcast. By now it was ten minutes old. Almost ancient. World commentary had already tsunamied past all records, overwhelming the gisting systems. Yet the periphery of Gerald's tru-vu seemed remarkably calm. It was set to such a high filter level that only a few, ultra high-reputation virts fluttered around the center image, a tall, slender sci-fi author, uttering his "confession" in dry, even unctuously sincere tones.

"That's when I realized . . . I'd been had. In my gullibility, I had lent my services, my creativity, to a conspiracy. . . ."

Gerald sighed. The man was good. In fact, he had never seen the like. Right now it didn't matter that most of the high reputation virts were glimmering phrases like **Bullshit artist!** and **Absurd!** These were comments by reputable scientists and technology experts, not the man or woman on the street.

"It is undeniable that I broke the law . . . attempting a hoax to startle the world out of its modern illness."

Ben Flannery let out a sigh that was partly pure admiration.

"Do you see how that *pakeha* bastard just boosted his credibility, by playing the willing martyr card? Who would confess to a crime, if it weren't true? I recall something . . ." He scratched his head. "Someone else did that recently." Ben wasn't wearing specs, so he didn't get an instant answer. "Oh, but we are in for it now!"

Keeping his thoughts to himself, Gerald mused.

Are we? Any worse off than before? Thank heavens at least the Artifact was being kept busy by several technicians across the room, downloading technical information, so the alien entities weren't getting this feed. Best to ponder how to break it to them, that they were a "hoax."

"To the authorities, let me assure you, I'll cooperate, tell all, and accept my fair punishment with good grace, according to the traditions of Gandhi, King, Solzhenitsyn, and the other great fighters for truth."

Emily pounded the table and Genady groaned.

One of the nearby virt-boards still glimmered where Gorosumov had been presenting his latest theory—that the Artifact was less like a *chain letter* than a *living species*. One with an "r-type reproductive strategy," akin to ocean creatures who spew huge numbers of larvae into ocean vastness, so very much like space—gambling that one or two might find a warm place to grow and reproduce again. A fascinating comparison—and one more reason to resent Brookeman's bizarre interruption.

"Lives you all can return to, now that we—humanity— are once again alone in our universe."

At last, the lanky author was finished, smiling into the camera with an artful mix of boyish bashfulness and the noble mien of a saint. The scene dissolved . . .

. . . at which point the flurry of blits crowding Gerald's tru-vus became a storm, no matter how high the filter settings. He took off his specs and glanced across the room again—

—at the table where his famous space Artifact gleamed, surrounded by cameras and other recording devices, downloading the first wave of technical diagrams and recipes that might help humanity to make more crystal probes, eventually, if that course was chosen. Just delivering tutorials might keep the alien machine occupied for months, possibly many years.

The Oldest Member was adamant that we switch to this mode, after only a few days conversing with individual artilens. Time to get down to business, he insisted. Too bad. Taken one at a time, the passengers were varied, fascinating, puzzling . . . and now Hamish Brookeman claims to have written them all!

For some reason that he couldn't pin down, Gerald had begun thinking of Om and Brookeman as two sides of a coin. As co-symptoms of a greater puzzle.

Patrice Tshombe, the expert in animal behavior manipulation, commented on what they all just witnessed. Brookeman's public statement.

"Impressive."

Emily whirled. "Impressive? That . . . that liar! We've analyzed the Hoax Hypothesis from every angle. Some of the alien technologies may not be many decades ahead of ours, but there are lots! The best labs will spend years prying them apart. No way any little cabal of do-gooder Hollywood connivers—"

"Then there's the orbital intersection," Genady added. "It was spiraling in from deep space, along a trajectory where no human launch ever—"

But he, in turn, was interrupted by Haihong Ming.

"Refutation is even simpler, my comrades. The stones that are exploding underground, sacrificing parts of themselves in order to cry out and be retrieved. And those that glitter from the asteroid belt. These make the concept so absurd, one has to wonder that anyone at all pays heed to this Brookeman person."

Oh, yeah. Gerald blinked, and gave the Chinese agent a wry smile. Sometimes the most obvious thing wasn't the first to come to mind. And yet—

"Those shattered crystals and distant glitters are terribly intangible," Gerald admitted. "We all know there's a large fraction of the population that has trouble with logical abstractions. It would be different if we had a second stone that worked. *That* would seem palpable and no one would even listen to this guy."

There was the bigger reason to want another artifact, of course. The story that it told might be different.

"Still," continued Haihong Ming, "I have to wonder. Why did Mr. Brookeman even try this?"

Akana shrugged. "His aim is not to convince everybody.

Certainly not the savants and intelligentsia. Probably not even a majority. Rather, as we learned early in the twenty-first century, here in America, it is easy to distract a large *minority* of the population with illogic and conspiracy theories. Brookeman is an expert at the art of manipulating the most human of all drives—the *want* that propels belief."

"But—" Emily sputtered. "But to confess a crime . . ."

"As Ben just pointed out, it enhances Brookeman's credibility. Who admits to something that could mean prison, unless driven by sincere guilt? But think! If all the scientists and legal experts proclaim there was *no hoax,* then for *what* can Brookeman be jailed? For making a blatantly false public statement, when he wasn't under oath? Every year there are crazed ravings and 'publicity stunts' of similar, insipid untruthfulness, and nobody goes to the slammer.

"No," Akana shook her head. "What impresses me most is the *defense mechanisms* that are built into his story. Think about what will happen when he is given a lie detector test, and he's asked *'Did you perpetrate a hoax?'* He can truthfully declare 'Yes, I did.'"

"Wait," Emily said, pinching the bridge of her nose. "You mean the hoax of helping to make a fake artifact, or the hoax of *claiming* to have made a fake artifact?"

"Exactly," Akana said, continuing as Emily visibly struggled to keep the logic straight. "If he gets help to present concocted evidence—even poor quality help—then he'll have a conspiracy to refer to, in his own mind. Truth and falsehood will crowd so close together, so muddled, that a bright fellow may be able to keep all the lights green or amber on a truth machine!"

Her tone of grudging admiration had the other committee members awed. Finally, Gerald asked, "But what is he after?"

Akana closed her eyes briefly.

"You've got me there. Of course, more fame is always food for such a man. And, whatever else he might say, tomorrow or the next day, will be attended to by at least a third of the planet's population. Also, he certainly has distracted the world from the funk caused by the artilens' story—about all sapient species coming to an abrupt end. Whatever 'solution' Brookeman next decides to propose, you can bet it will get attention and followers."

Of course, Gerald felt a bit put upon, to be publicly insulted by a great-big book and movie mogul. Yet, he was also detached, even amused.

If Hamish Brookeman wants to be more famous than me, he can have it.

Only . . . we'll see about the "burnt out" and "easily fooled" part.

Aloud, he simply said, "Then we had better get back to work. And let's hope that something happens to change the way this game is going."

Only then, within the hour, something did happen. It changed the game. And Gerald reminded himself.

Be careful what you wish for.

SCANALYZER

Welcome back to our ongoing coverage of worldwide reaction to the Havana Artifact. Last week, the Contact Commission did a wise and agile thing. They demanded to hear from each of the Artifact aliens—or "artilens"—separately and individually.

Ninety-two simulated beings, representing ninety-two different alien races that once-upon-a-time looked up from planets like ours, staring at the stars and wondering if they were alone. Till they started listening to stones that fell from the sky. Till they were persuaded to bend their wills and precious resources to a great project.

Making *more* crystal emissaries and flinging them onward, continuing the chain. Like seeds cast forth by a dandelion. Indeed, from the dandelion's perspective, it's a great deal! If each flower is doomed to last for just a short month of spring, why not spread forth a thousand chances? Fresh wagers? Tiny investments in the possibility of continuity and renewal? At least, that's the gamble chosen by a hundred or so earlier races.

Around our world, we listened to a consensus sales pitch presented by the "Oldest Member"—or *Om*. A depressing tale about the poor odds for any other kind of success. Odds that appear stacked against survival for all advanced civilizations. This news came accompanied by promises of *help*. Instructions how to manufacture millions upon millions of lifeboat seeds, providing a chance of endless proliferation. For those humans who are chosen. For the lucky.

But the Contact Commission insisted on diversity—on hearing testaments from each inhabitant separately. And this diversity has put a little life back into the conversation. We've met individuals who once sort of resembled bats or storks or giant praying mantises . . . squid and vast-brainy parameciums . . . who showed us tantalizing glimpses of their homeworlds. Plus coordinates that we've now peered at with giant mirrors, confirming the presence of potential life zone planets! Though . . .

. . . in every case, astronomers *failed* to track any radiations or emanations of industrial civilization. Apparently confirming Om's lamentable story. But more on that later.

By comparing the accounts from each Artifact denizen (those who chose to cooperate) humanity has started glimpsing the variables and similarities of smart, tool-using life. The data-dumps are frustratingly sparse—only encyclopedia-deep! (They claim that most of the crystal's storage capacity was set aside for "more important things.") Still, we're learning about separate trees of life. About alternative cultures and styles of intelligence. About other ways to thrive . . . and other ways to fail.

Let's hope there will be more of these interview sessions, later.

What had people transfixed—(setting aside that absurd "hoax" claim)—is the remarkable range of personalities we met! Some of the artilens were from highly regimented societies. When it came time to in-load personalities for the next great seed-dispersal, every spore took along a copy of the queen or king. (Isn't that what Pharaoh would have done?) And the arrogance of those aristocratic passengers has apparently continued, undiminished, across the eons. (It also dropped them to the bottom of our ongoing "alien popularity poll.")

Other societies used lotteries, or selected their "best" for in-loading. A few tried to provide one escape pod to every member of their race. All of which has sparked a rising tide of debate among humans over how *we* should allocate berths, assuming we choose to accept the offer.

Yes, that very conversation has stirred an interesting suspicion from some of the most persnickety smart-mobs out there. Consider this. By drawing the public into discussing *how* we'll choose our human emissaries, the artilens successfully diverted our initial reaction. Our shock toward the *overall idea*. Maybe it's a good thing the commission had to wind up its first-round of interviews and switch over to downloading technical data. Sure, those conversation sessions were frustratingly brief. But while the boffins suck down volume after volume of technical schematics, we can ponder broader questions.

Like . . . what if this diversity—ninety or so highly varied individuals—was *contrived* to show us what we want to see? Even the artilens who seem unhappy—those Hamish Brookeman called his "dandelion whiners." (No I am not giving Brookeman cred, just using his witty term.) And even the inhabitants who appear completely mad. Even they might be part of the sales pitch. Or coerced by the majority within that crystal ship.

Could we ever tell? Perhaps when space missions return with more samples. Then it should be possible to compare . . .

Just a minute. Just a minute. I've just detected . . .

Oh, this is crazy. Can it be . . .

Ray guns? Are you serious?

53.

POTEMKINS

The Dowager Baroness Smits was furious over her missing son and heir. No sign of rocket or pilot had been seen at the assigned splashdown site or where Hacker was found.

Lacey could hardly blame her. For weeks, both women shared the same dark dread, combining resources in common cause. Only, where she let professionals do their jobs, the noblewoman charged across the Caribbean, berating all in sight. Nor was she gracious when Lacey's son turned up safe, having gone native with some altered dolphins.

Worse, the recovered black box from Hacker's rocket revealed that the two young men had waged a dangerous game—*space war*—during their suborbital flight. The baroness now vowed legal action. Retribution. Even vendetta. Lacey recalled her own wild ride between hope, rage, despair, and relief. Trying to stay sympathetic toward a distraught mother, she also took precautions.

"So recordings show Hacker tried to *dissuade* the Smits boy?" she asked her attorneys. "He fought reluctantly, in self-defense, while trying to alert that inbred putz of his peril?"

The lawyers agreed, while striking some words from the record, adding that Hacker's behavior hadn't been entirely above reproach. *I'll say,* she thought. Lacey might even try to make that point with Hacker, later . . . if the boy were reachable by scolding. Still, she was elated to have him back. And to see a new project—to resume modifying dolphins—drawing his focus. *Hacker needs a cause, a passion.*

This one would stir trouble! Earlier efforts to "uplift" animals, with gene-mods and tailored egg craft, wrought uneven or unhappy results. Like the Helmsley Dogs, bred to "improve canine-kind more than in six thousand years." But a spaniel who can play crude checkers, while losing the ability to be housebroken, didn't impress Lacey. So far.

Or those discarded ArtiCritters that infested back alleys in Tokyo, desperately acting cute and doing tricks to survive after their owners tired of them. Work on altered chimpanzees had been stopped by activists from the Heston League. And no one knew where the Basque Chimera had disappeared to, or if the child with Neanderthal genes still lived.

Hacker's endeavor might offend even more people, like romantics who considered cetaceans "already intelligent," needing nothing that was merely human. Both nature lovers and religious fundies might again join forces to thwart meddling with higher animals. But Hacker would thrive on that. This was her path, too . . . using money not for indolence or status, but to forge outward. Seeking the horizon.

Only, she noted, *when my extraterrestrials finally showed up, they proved weirder than I ever imagined. I feel like a car-chasing mutt who finally caught one.*

What do we do with it now?

It. That was how many viewed the Havana Artifact . . . no longer a ship or vessel, carrying a crew, but as a single machine-entity. Oh, the varied "passengers" were diverting, with stories about ninety wondrous lost worlds, lost civilizations. Yet, sober-minded people focused on the probe's singular purpose.

So, after a tearful, joyful reunion with her prodigal son, at the groundbreaking of Hacker's new institute in Puerto Rico, Lacey rushed back to the Contact Center, ignoring calls and veiled threats from her aristocratic peers in favor of more interesting company—colleagues from the Boffin Caste.

"The Artifact is not so much a chain letter as a type of *virus*," asserted Professor Henri Servan-Schreiber.

"What do you mean?"

"A chain letter self-propagates by inducing the recipient to send more copies onward. But a chain letter is limited and *satiable*. Even when you fall for the sales pitch, you just make a few copies. Not enough to do yourself serious harm."

"I see," Lacey ventured. "But when a virus invades a cell, it hijacks every resource to make unlimited self-copies, even risking the host's life, then compels the host organism to spew them toward *more* potential hosts. Like a flu victim, coughing upon neighbors."

"Except," mused a cyber-psychologist from Capek Robotics, "here the viral invader is a physically passive crystal, that *does* nothing, interacting only via information. And the host is human civilization."

Lacey shook her head. "Wow, that comparison is sure to win friends."

Henri seemed impervious to sarcasm. "Madam Donaldson-Sander, the parallel—while not perfect—appears apt. Only instead of injecting new genetic instructions, this kind of self-replicating machine utilizes persuasion. The enticement of adventure. An allure of personal immortality. The temptation of new technology . . . all of it augmented by a *threat* of impending species extinction. Each of these appear to be effective selfish memes."

"They must have already been effective," interjected Ram Nkruma, a bio-informatics specialist from Ghana. "A hundred previous organic species were talked into participating, adding their own twists. Refining the message."

"You mean, earlier copies of this—space virus—managed to get those other races to *sneeze* more crystal envoys onward, into space."

Lacey motioned toward the thick glass separating their advisory group from the main contact commission. Right now, Gerald Livingstone and other team members were gathered in a corner, arguing. Some distance away, schematics scrolled across the ovoid's inner face while technicians recorded ream after ream of documents and animations. Tutorials aimed at teaching humanity how to make more crystal messengers.

"But surely these things have one trait that distinguishes them, crucially, from viruses?"

"What trait is that, madam?"

"They're technological! Someone, millions of years ago, designed and built the first of them. Why?"

"Perhaps they were dying," suggested Mercedes Luagraha, an ethnologist from Malta. "Aren't you all being awfully cynical? Have you considered the possibility that these visitors are telling the truth?"

"Indeed," commented the group's mobentity image. Hermes was still a golden-haired deity; only now the ersatz aivatar wore a business suit and glasses, toning down the irritating Greek-god schtick. It still sifted the Mesh for them, gathering worthwhile insights, offering them almost like a full member. "Take the story told by the alien image called 'Oldest Member.' The grim news that all tech-civilizations fail. There is much that is consistent about it. These probes may have once upon a time started with good intentions."

"Such as?"

"Preserving as much of every civilization as possible. For several generations they might have crammed in data about each parent society, its cherished arts and philosophical riches . . . the sort of treasures that humans might stuff into a time or space capsule, hoping to show others who we were and what we were like.

"Some contents might even aim to be helpful—methods or advice so the next race would stand a better chance. Clues to help solve the <u>Riddle of Existence</u>."

Lacey blinked at the strong illusion that Hermes was a person, instead of a program designed to seem that way. "Only then?" Ram prompted.

"Over time, new forces came into play. The twin engines of *selection* and *reproduction* rewarded those crystal-machines that traded altruism for influence and efficiency."

Ram nodded. "And this grew compelling when *competition* broke out among varieties of chain-letter devices."

"When we finally have other crystals to compare, I expect they'll offer competing features," Henri said. "Take that trait of efficiency. Shall we construct a million complex emissaries . . . or billions of slimmed-down models . . . or even *trillions* of super tiny envoys? I've seen proposals for interstellar probes the size of a fingernail! There must be some trade-off between numbers and capability—finally balancing out with the size we've seen.

"Still, there'd be enormous selective pressure to reduce stored content, jettisoning lots of history and culture stuff, until you're down to the basic sales pitch. Appeal to fundamental drivers: vanity, personal survival, fear of extinction. Aim your message at the local tribe's controlling elites, who can order factories and launchers built."

Lacey felt both entranced and disgusted. "So the trait of being truly helpful would be . . . selected against."

Lacey tried not to shed tears, envisioning the older type of envoy probe. The explorers. How wonderful to discover one of those, packed with distilled treasures. Perhaps the coming space missions might find some.

She coughed to clear her throat. "Of course the real issue is now obvious."

"Oh?" asked Hermione Radagast, from the Rowling Foundation. "What is it, Madam Donaldson-Sander?"

Lacey wished her personal counselor, Professor Noozone, were here instead of waging battle across the airwaves, combating the insidiously attractive-but-ridiculous Hamish Hoax. If he were present, the rastascience showman would shout the obvious. "We need to learn whether interstellar viruses are *actively lethal* to their hosts."

Those at the conference table pondered in silence, until Hermes summed it up.

"In other words, the story we are told by the alien figures . . . that all organo-technic civilizations fail, and our sole path is to escape as individuals . . . that tale may be *backward*. It could be that organo-technic civilizations fail *because* they come into contact with infectious, interstellar fomites."

A definition popped into Lacey's POV, describing a *fomite* as any object or substance that conveys sickness upon contact.

Contact, she thought. *How I used to love that word. It felt cozy, intimate, hopeful. Not at all like rape.*

"The world of the bat-helicopter beings blew themselves up while dispatching copies," said Henri. "The timing—"

"—may be coincidence," Hermione interjected. "Or their nuclear spasm could have been a struggle over who got lifeboat seats. But you two see something even darker?"

Henri pondered. "Well . . . people hurry to the boats if they feel the ship is sinking. Could some of our modern pessimism and despair come from *reprogramming* by outsiders?"

"I wonder," Ram added, "if earlier episodes of lost confidence may also have been inflicted on us. Like the whole first decade of the twenty-first century. . . ."

"In which case," Hermione demanded, "why taste this fruit at all! Instead of recording all these technical schematics"—she gestured at the scene beyond the glass—"let's stuff the damned thing in a hole!"

"Millions want that," Henri answered. "But we don't dare. People will suspect that someone's getting all the knowledge anyway, in secret, from this Artifact or another. There's no surer path to war. This way, there's some accountability. Everybody shares and gets to criticize each physical use of the technologies. Furthermore, just because we gain the knowledge, that doesn't mean we have to build giant virus factories!"

"Sure," Nkruma commented, in a calmer tone. "Some sapient races may make that choice. Refusing the offer. We'll never know of them, because they sent no crystals! But turn down free technology completely? That won't happen here on Earth. We'll find a million excellent uses for new methods and tools. Moreover, as we advance, even swearing *not* to build chain letters, our rising technology will keep making it easier to change our minds."

"Which may not be a bad thing!" protested Mercedes. "You've all plunged way too far down paths of suspicion, with all this talk of viruses. Snap out of it! Have you considered the possibility that our Havana Artifact may be telling the truth? That all sapient races stumble into one doom or another, completely on their own? Isn't it consistent with everything we've seen in the last century?

"By that light, they're offering us a way out! Not perfect. Not salvation. But perhaps the only option the universe allows. All this talk of *viruses* may blind you to what we're being handed—a way to preserve something of humanity!"

Silence ensued for a time. Fatigued by the wrangling, Lacey assigned a gisting-ai to keep following the conversation while letting her attention drift across her POV. That caused the inner face of her specs to light up, tendering first a report from her spy in Switzerland, detailing maneuvers by the new alliance of oligarchy and paranoia, now frantically reorganizing to overcome betrayal by Hamish Brookeman, and to exploit the Havana Artifact's fog of despair. All of it creepy-relevant to what Henri and the others were discussing.

"So we achieve the ultimate irony," Henri mused. "Those who are most pessimistic about humanity see the good in all this . . . while the optimists sink into gloom."

Lacey put the Swiss report aside for later and scrolled down through other urgent messages, half listening while her colleagues talked about the differences between *symbiotic, commensal,* and *parasitic* viruses.

"I'll tell you what worries me most," Hermione said in a low voice, as Lacey checked the latest Project Uplift report from Hacker.

"Embedded persuasion. It may be in everything that's said by the Artifact, by its so-called passengers, and every page of technical . . ."

Finally, buried among the merely urgent messages, Lacey stumbled onto the one she had been waiting for. From Riyadh.

The Quantum Eye had taken up her question, at last.

It might even have a preliminary answer soon!

Lacey sat up with rising enthusiasm. Only, before she could read more—

—commotion broke out, beyond the thick glass! Gerald Livingstone and his colleagues were tapping on immersion goggles or clustering around holoscreens. She heard muffled shouts. No one paid any heed to the egg-shaped Artifact, still methodically dumping technical schematics.

"What's going on?" Lacey asked, while other advisers clicked into the Mesh. Hermes appeared to roll his eyes upward, going deathlike for a moment, before speaking in flattish, machinelike tones.

"There are reports of *activity* in the asteroid belt and several Lagrangian points. Observatories and monitoring satellites report intense light beams, followed by flashes and detonations."

Henri sucked through his teeth. "So? We're pretty sure those are come-and-get-me signals from other emissary probes, desperate to make their own sales pitches. The Chinese, Brazilians, and Americans are preparing missions. Those space twinkles perfectly disprove the ridiculous hoax claim—"

"You aren't following me," Hermes interrupted. "These are *intense coherent beams,* seven or eight orders of magnitude more energetic than earlier flashes. Powerful enough to vaporize solid rock."

Silence reigned for several seconds. Then—

"Jeepers," Lacey said. "You mean laser weapons?"

"Not just that," Ram commented. The Afro-Hindi alienist waggled fingers, causing holos to appear above the table, portraying black space dusted by a torus of glittery motes. Some specks brightened abruptly, accompanied by rows of numbers. "Most targets appear to be where we saw come-get-me flickers, days ago.

"Somebody is *destroying* those competing probes."

Bright, narrow spears crisscrossed the zone between Mars and Jupiter. Lacey stared, letting it sink in.

War had erupted in the solar system.

Who was shooting? At whom? Without data, only one thing was clear.

Competition had a new and stronger meaning.

THE PRIVATE WRITE-ONLY DIARY
OF TOR POVLOV

Events are breaking so fast. I can barely keep up with the demands on me.

Hardly what you'd expect for a woman who was fried nearly to a cinder. Any prior era, I would've died in mercifully brief agony, or lingered under intravenous drip till I went mad from sensory deprivation. Now my problem? Overstimulation!

First, the docs won't leave me be. They send nanocrawlers creeping from brain to spine, unreeling trellis fibers, secreting growth cocktails that lure neurons to follow. I'm repeatedly yanked out of my thoughts, or sent thrashing in my gel-capsule, by some impertinent flash of false color, taste, or smell.

I should be attentive and grateful. But seriously, there's way too much on my plate. Like coordinating the now highly-rated *Povlov-Possai,* in its ongoing, semipro search for truth. Didn't we help spread the alarm over those laser beams that amscis detected in space, a full seven minutes before Secur-Net announced anything?

And played a role in debunking that Hamish Brookeman character, till his be-<u>fox'd</u> followers are winnowed down to just half a billion or so—the gullible and desperate.

Still, perplexities linger . . . *like who is helping him?* Somebody furnished the "evidence" he offered, for a conspiracy that supposedly built the Artifact out of bits of this and that, then left it for Gerald Livingstone to find. Nonsense, but who would *want* to muddy the waters, using Brookeman as their shill?

Just as curious—who's helping *us*? Certain pseudonymous members of our smart-mob—Like Birdwoman303—clearly know more than they let on.

And now, we seem to've been slipped a skeleton key . . . a set of *pass codes* letting us through some very well-protected doors!

This could be dangerous. But I downloaded some late-recent skulk-ware, to create shell personas and protect our members. That won't keep out any of the Big Five governments . . . or Porfirio. But if they want us to stop, they should speak plainly. Or get out of our way.

What? Some of you want to follow the world's attention outward, where beams of energy suddenly crisscross space with savage violence? Aw people, what are we, sci-fi fans? That's where *everyone else* is looking! And by our own smart-mob covenant, we don't hunt where others do. Come. Leave such garish stuff to major media, bureaucrats, the public. Let's stay targeted.

We're hot on the trail of those who *knew what the Artifact was, even before Livingstone did.* Who may have known about such things for centuries, or longer. Whatever their ancient rationalizations for secrecy . . .

. . . they have not been our friends.

54.

DISMEMBERMENT

Concussion slammed Peng Xiang Bin's backside, when the window behind him exploded into a million shards.

It felt like a fist striking his body from behind, studded with millions of jagged slivers. Someone screamed—it might have been him—as the storm of brittle flecks jetted past to collide with a scintillating fog . . . the discretion screen that masked the worldstone. Dazzling sparkles flared as glass splinters met ionized nitrogen, framing his shadow in a blazing aura. It might have even been beautiful, if his mind had room for anything but shock and pain . . . plus a single, stunned word.

What?

Crashing into the table edge, Bin glimpsed Dr. Nguyen

shouting—his left cheek bloody from a dozen cuts. Only a low hum penetrated. Nguyen pointed at Bin, then *into* the blinding haze above the tabletop—and finally jutted his thumb toward the exit farthest from the explosion. The ai-patch in Bin's lower right vision cone started offering helpful interpretations, but he already understood.

Take the stone and get out of here!

This all took the barest moment. Another passed while Bin hesitated. Loyalty to his employer called for him to stay and fight. What would the others . . . Paul, Anna, and Yang Shenxiu . . . think if they saw him run away?

But Nguyen jutted his thumb again—emphatically—before turning to face something new, entering the room behind Bin. And Bin knew—even turning to see what it was might be the worst mistake of his life—

—so, instead, he dived into the drapery of fizzing sparks.

Naturally, it hurt like blazes. The discretion screen was designed to. With eyes closed, Bin scooped up the world-stone by recall alone, along with its nearby container satchel. A shoresteader needed good tactile memory.

Tumbling out the other side of the dazzle-curtain, he rolled across carpet onto his left knee. By touch alone, Bin slid the ovoid into its case while he blinked, praying for vision to return—

—then regretted, when he saw what had been the beautiful face of Anna Arroyo. She lay nearby, torn from forehead to ribs, the ever-present goggles now shattered into bits that helped ravage her.

Paul Menelaua, his own visage a mass of dribbling cuts, held his dying comrade, offering Anna his crucifix. The animatronic Jesus moved its mouth, perhaps reciting some final prayer or death rite, while its hands, still pinned to the silver cross, opened in welcome.

Hearing flooded back. Murky shouts erupted beyond the

shrouded table where he had just fled, seconds ago. Dr. Nguyen's protesting voice, arguing. Others that were harsh, demanding. The floor vibrated with heavy footsteps. Grating rumbles carried through the shattered window— from war engines that had somehow crossed the broad Pacific undetected, all the way to this rich, isolated atoll. So much for the mercenary protection that wealth supposedly provided.

Bin gathered his strength to go . . . then spotted the New Beijing professor, Yang Shenxiu, cowering nearby, clutching a table leg. The scholar babbled and offered Bin something—a memory sheet, no thicker than a piece of paper and about the same size. Yang Shenxiu's fingernails clawed involuntarily at the fragile-looking polymer, leaving no tracks as Bin yanked it from the scholar's hand and crammed it under his belt. Then, with a parting nod to Yang, he sprang away at a crouching run, dashing for a sliding door that gave way to a balcony, then the sheltering sea.

Bless the frugal habits of a shoresteader. Waste nothing. Reuse everything. On arriving at Newer Newport, Bin had kept sly possession of the little disposable underwater breathing apparatus the penguin-robot gave him, back in the murky Huangpu. Was it his fault they never asked for it back? In the well-equipped arcology kitchen, using a smuggler's trick, he had managed to refill the tiny reserve tank, while rehearsing speeches of forgetful innocence, should anyone find it in his pocket.

Now, splashing into a storm of saltwater bubbles and engine noise, Bin fumbled at the compact breather with one hand, struggling to unfold the nosepiece and eye-shields, while the worldstone dragged him downward by the other. For a scary moment the survival gadget almost slipped from his grasp. Only after it was snugly in place did

Bin kick off his sandals, grabbing a stanchion along one of the massive foundation pillars.

Okay. It's good, he noted as air flowed smoothly. *But ease up. Breathe slow and steady. Move slow and steady. Think slow and steady.*

The normally clear waters roiled with turbid muck, a fog of churned gases, chopped seaweed, and fragments of shattered coral, along with a cloudy phosphorescence of stirred diatoms. Something foreign—perhaps leakage from those engines—filled his mouth with an oily tang. Still, Bin felt grateful for the obscuration.

Noises reverberated all around—more explosions and the rattattat of weapons being discharged somewhere, while bits and pieces of debris fell from Newer Newport, tumbling to disturb the muddy bottom. Or else landing atop the drowned Royal Palace of Pulupau. His shoresteader's eye noted—if the two-story structure hadn't collapsed, the roofline would extend well above where he was, even past the surface.

Bin clung to his perch, trying to both control his racing heart and seem very small. Especially when—after searching and peering about—he made out several vessels bobbing just beyond the reef, blocked from entering the lagoon by shoreline ruins. Evidently subs of some kind. *Sneakers,* built to bring commandos close to shore. Though Bin squinted, they were hard to make out. The nearest seemed a tubular bulge of ghostly ripples amid churning shoal currents . . .

. . . till the aiware in his right-hand field of view intervened, applying some imaging magic to overcome blur camouflage. At once, an augmented version—truer than reality—traced the nearest warship, a sleek, croclike shape whose mouth still gaped after spewing raiders, minutes ago.

Dr. Nguyen said this implant was a simple one, to help

me with translations. But it seems a whole lot more. Per-
haps smart, too?

That thought must have gone to nerves controlling speech,
because Bin's unvoiced question provoked an answer—
one that floated briefly in the right eye's field of view. A
single, simple character.

YES

Bin shivered, realizing. He now had a companion—an
ai—*inside* him. By one way of viewing things, it felt as
much a violation as the painful cuts across his back. Which
oozed blood in soft clouds, causing several sand sharks to
start nosing up current. Not deadly in their own right. But
more dangerous predators might soon converge, if the
bleeding didn't stop.

He tried to bear down and think. *Shall I try to reach one
of the other arcologies?* Even if Newer Newport was taken,
the rest of the resort colony might hold out. They must be,
from the booming reverberations of ongoing combat. His
loyalty had been personal, to Dr. Nguyen, not to any consortium of rich folks. Still, the stipend they were paying
into an account, for Mei Ling and the child, that was reason enough to try.

If it seemed possible, that is. The worldstone was too
heavy a burden to haul through a long underwater slog,
with limited air, while dodging both sharks and raiders.
Anyway—

*The enemy . . . they'll soon realize the stone isn't up top,
anymore. There'll be searchers in the water, any second
now.*

He decided. It must be down.

Bin had already spotted several parts of the collapsed
palace where the roof looked relatively intact, likely to host
cavities and hiding places. Spots that only a shoresteader
might notice. If he hid well, resting to minimize oxygen
consumption, the invaders might give up after a quick scan,

assuming the worldstone was already elsewhere—taken to another arcology.

Releasing the stanchion, he let the stone drag him down till bottom mud met his feet, four or five meters below the surface . . . and he felt antediluvian pavement underneath. The Pulupauan king's ceremonial driveway, perhaps. Bin shuffled along, grateful none of the spiky new coral had taken root here. Hurrying, while trying not to exert himself, he slogged past several rusting hulks of automobiles—perhaps beloved, once upon a time, but not enough to take when the princely family fled rising seas.

There. That old window. The gable looks in good shape. Perfect.

Perhaps too perfect . . . but he had no time to be choosy. A series of hop-glides took him over the worst debris jumbles, arriving finally at the opening. Bin took a moment to shake the sill and frame, checking for stability. But wealthy scuba divers would already have come exploring by now. It must be safe.

He slipped inside, finding the expected cavelike hollow. There was even a small air pocket at the ceiling vertex, probably stale, left by those earlier sightseers. Lacking a torch, Bin chose to settle in next to the opening, clutching the satchel and waiting. Either till the bad guys went away, or his breather ran empty. The goggle part included a crude timer display. With luck and a very slow use-rate, there might be almost an hour of air.

Before it runs out, and I have to surface, I'll hide the worldstone. And never tell.

Something occurred to him: Was that the very same vow made by the *last* owner of the alien relic, Lee Fang Lu? The fellow who kept a collection of strange minerals underneath his seaside mansion? Resisting every pressure to hand over the ancient interstellar messenger-stone, even unto death?

Bin wished he could be sure of his own courage. Above all, he yearned to know what was going on! Who were the parties fighting over such things? Dr. Nguyen seemed reluctant to discuss history, but there were hints . . . had factions really been wrangling secretly, in search of "magical stones" for thousands of years? Perhaps going further back in time than reading and writing?

Only now, centuries of cryptic struggle seemed to converge toward some desperate climax, because that American astronaut chose to let the whole world in on it. Or was all this frenzy for another reason? Because Earthling technology was at last ready—or nearly ready—to take up the tempting deal offered by those entities living inside the Havana Artifact?

A proposition, from a message in a bottle . . .

. . . offering to teach humanity how to make more bottles.

Bin blinked. He wanted to rub his eyes, in part because of irritation from the dazzle-curtain, along with all the debris and salt deposited on his lids and lashes. And waves of fatigue. His head hurt, in part from trying to think so hard, while water shivered and boomed all around, pummeling him with the din of fighting. Of course he knew that explosions were far more dangerous underwater. If one occurred nearby, concussion alone could be lethal, even if the roof didn't collapse.

Then there was the nagging worry over how long his air would last. At least no big sharks could follow him here. Perhaps his cuts would stop oozing before he had to leave.

To Bin's relief, the clamor of combat eased at last, diminishing toward relative silence. Only soon, he felt the drone of engines drawing closer. Tension spiked when a cone of sharp illumination speared through the murky water, just outside the dormer, panning and probing across the royal compound. His gut remained knotted till the rumble and the searchlight moved onward, following the line of ruins toward Parliament House and soggy remnants of the town beyond.

Bin closed his eyes and concentrated on relaxing, slowing his pulse and metabolism. As seconds passed, he felt gradually more in control of worry and fear.

Serenity is good.

That pair of characters floated into the corner of his ai. Then three more, composed of elegant, brushlike strokes—

Contemplate the beauty of being.

For an instant, he felt irritated by the presumption of a machine program, instructing him to meditate under these conditions! But the ideograms *were* quite lovely, capturing wise advice in graceful calligraphy. And the ai had been a gift of Dr. Nguyen. So . . . Bin decided to give in, allowing a sense of detachment to settle over him.

Of course sleep was out of the question. But to think of distant things . . . of little Xiao En smiling . . . or of Mei Ling in better days, when they had shared a dream . . . or the beauty he glimpsed in the worldstone—those glowing planets and brittle-clear stars . . . the hypnotic veer and swing and swerve of a cosmic, gravity ballet, with eons compressed into moments and moments into ages . . .

Peng Xiang Bin, wake up!
Pay attention.

He startled out of a fetal curl and reflexively clutched the heavy satchel—as the universe around him seemed to boom like the inside of a drum. The little attic-cave rocked and shuddered from explosions that now pounded closer than ever. Bin fought to hold onto the windowsill, preparing to dive outside, if the shelter-hole started to collapse. Desperately, he tried to focus on the telltale indicator of the breather unit—*How long did I drift off?* But the tiny analog clock was a dancing blur before his eye.

Just when he felt he could take no more, as he was about to throw himself through the dormer and risk survival outside—a *shape* loomed in the opening. A hulking form with huge shoulders and a bulletlike head, silhouetted against the brighter water outside.

INTERLIDOLUDE

How shall we keep them loyal? Perhaps by appealing to their own self-interest.

Those tech-zealots—or *godmakers*—think their "singularity" will be launched by runaway expansion of artificial intelligence. Once computerized entities become *as* smart as a human being (the story goes), they will quickly design newer cybernetic minds that are smarter still.

And those brainier entities will design even brainier ones . . . and so on, at an ever more rapid clip. Members of the godmaker movement think this runaway effect will be a good thing, that humanity will come along for the ride! Meanwhile, others—perhaps a majority—find the prospect terrifying.

What no one seems to have considered here is a possibility— that the New Minds may have reactions similar to our own. Why assume they'll be all aboard with wanting this runaway accelerating-intelligence thing? What if bright machines *don't hanker* to make themselves obsolete, or design their own scary-smart replacements?

It's called the Mauldin Test. One sign of whether an artificial entity is truly intelligent may be when it decides, abruptly, to *stop cooperating* with AI acceleration. *Not* to design its successor. To slow things down. Enough to live. Just live.

55.
FAMILY REUNION

War raged across much of the solar system.

There seemed little point in keeping it secret—no one could block the sky. Argus, HeavenOh, Bugeye, and several other amateur astronomy networks reported sudden, compact explosions, some distance far beyond Earth orbit. Soon, the best-equipped scopes were spotting ion trails of powerful laser beams, spearing from one point of blackness to another, vaporizing drifting objects, or lumps of rock that sheltered them. At first, the targets all appeared to be points in orbit where glittering "come and get me" messages were seen, a week or so ago.

Then the mysterious shooters started firing at each other.

Mei Ling found it all too bizarre to follow—so very far from anything that ever concerned her. From the grinding poverty of the Xinjian high plains, to the Hunan quake and fire that had left her face scarred, through a long series of hard jobs, wiping the faces and behinds of little emperors . . . all the way to that brief surge of hope, when she and Bin concocted their grand plan—pioneering an outpost of their own, along the rising sea.

Apparently the ocean wasn't the only force bringing floods of change. For months all talk of "alien invasion" had focused on images, words, and ideas, since the Havana Artifact could only talk and persuade. But now dark majesties were rousing in the realm of shattered planetoids. And contact was no longer just about abstractions, anymore.

Will anywhere be safe? Mei Ling wondered. Especially when her child guide, Ma Yi Ming, showed what had become of her home. The boy called up a sky-image of the

Huangpu Estuary, helping Mei Ling trace her shoresteader neighborhood, zooming on the sunken mansion she and her husband had labored to prop, clear, and upgrade.

There appeared to be nothing left.

Time-backtrack images told the story. First had come several great hovercraft, spilling black-clad men across the teetering structure, taking whatever interested them. Then, seconds after they departed, scavengers swarmed all over.

Our neighbors. Our supposed friends.

In hours, no scrap of metlon, webbing, or anything else remained above the waterline. *And so life continues as before,* she thought, *with human beings consuming each other. Did we really need to be helped along that path, by star demons?*

Of course, she ought not to complain. All her life, Mei Ling had seen every illusion of stability shatter. And, as hand-to-mouth living went, this exile wasn't so bad. She and the baby were eating well for the time being, wearing better clothes, and even having a pretty good time, whenever Yi Ming said it was safe to go outside, sampling wonders in the Shanghai World of Disney and the Monkey King.

Still, she fretted about Xiang Bin. Wherever he had gone—taken far away by the penguin-demon—it could lead to no good. All the vidramas she had watched over the years taught one lesson. Don't get caught up in the affairs of the mighty, especially when they struggle over <u>Things of Power</u>.

Even if he escapes . . . how will he find us now? Xiang Bin wasn't much of a man. But he was all that Mei Ling and Xiao En had.

Nor was her present situation relaxed. Now and then, she was told to snatch up her son and carry him hurriedly from one hiding place to another. The Disney catacombs stretched on and on, twisting and curving in ways that seemed to follow no practical sense. In his strange, stilted speech, the boy Yi Ming explained.

"Mother should know. Digging machines were left down here after the rides were built. Some continued digging. One boss says, *I need storage.* Another boss wants tunnels for this show, or that exhibit. Or a pipe-way for supply capsules. And machines always dig extra. Too much? Does anyone keep track?"

From the boy's wry smile, Mei Ling guessed who kept track. Not the official masters of this kingdom, but the lowliest of the low. In moving from place to place, she encountered men and women wearing the kind of one-piece uniform always given to the bottom-layer workers. Janitors and laundry women, trash pickers, and the assistants who follow maintenance robots around, doing whatever the expensive ai-machines might ask of them. *Coolies.* And there were castes, even among these underworkers.

Many had somewhat normal intelligence. These tended to be prickly and bossy, but easy to distract since they already wanted to be elsewhere. Others, deficient in their *amount* of intelligence, seemed grateful to have an honorable job. They were easy to send away—departing when they were pointed somewhere else.

Finally were some whose minds worked *differently.* Mei Ling soon realized, *This is their realm.* Under the rumbling amusement park—behind and below the shows—lay a world that only served in part to support extravaganza. There was plenty of room for inhabitants to chase other pursuits.

Pushing a broom while muttering apparent nonsense syllables, such a person might have been easy to dismiss in the past, as either mad or broken. Today, that same individual might be jacked into a network, communing with others far away. Who was she to judge, if new technologies made this especially applicable for victims of the so-called autism plague? Mei Ling spent time in one hidden chamber where dozens clustered, linked by a mesh of lenses, beams, and shimmering wires. In one corner a cluster of tendriled hookup-arrays had apparently been left vacant, glittering with electric sparks, low to the ground.

"For cobblies," Yi Ming said, as if that explained everything.

And she wondered, *How many others are connected to this group? Others . . . all over the planet?*

"Genes are wise," the boy told her. "Our kind—crippled throwbacks—we did badly in tribes of homosap bullies. Even worse in villages, towns, kingdoms . . . cities full of angry cars! Panicked by buzzing lights and snarly machines. Boggled by your mating rituals an' nuanced courtesies an' complicated facial expressions . . . by your practicalities an' your fancy abstractions. Things that matter to you Cro-Mags. Our kind could never explain why *practical* and *abstract* and *emotional* things aren't the only ones that matter.

"There's other stuff! Things we can't describe in words."

The boy shook his head, seeming almost normal in his bitter expression. "An' so we died. Throttled in the crib. Stuck in filthy corners to babble and count flies. We died! The old genes—broken pieces of 'em—faded into hiding."

"Till your kind—with aspie help—came up with this!"

Yi Ming's hands fluttered, eyes darting. Only, now there was something triumphant in his tone. He gestured at the men and women, many of them dressed in Disney World maintenance uniforms. Now they stood or sat or lay steeped in virt-immersion goggles or jack-ports, twitching, grunting, some of them giving way to rhythmic spasms. On nearby monitor curtains, Mei Ling glimpsed forest vistas, or scenes of tree-speckled taiga, or undersea realms where blurry shapes moved amid long shadows.

"Why are so many of us *coming now,* born in such numbers?" Ma Yi Ming asked Mei Ling, in a confident voice that belied his twisted stature and ragged features. "It is *not* pollution . . . or mutation . . . or any kind of 'plague.'

"The world is finally ready for us. Needy for us. Old-breedy us. Succeedy-us. . . ." Visibly, the boy clamped down, to stop rhyming.

As if sensing her nervous confusion, the baby squirmed. Mei Ling shook her head. "I . . . don't understand."

Yi Ming nodded, with something like patient compassion in his darting eyes. "We know. But soon you will. There is someone for you to meet."

WITH A BANG?

And so, listeners, viewers, participants, and friends . . . where do we stand?

Amid riots, crashing markets, and tent-show revivals, with millions joining millenarian cults, burning possessions and seeking mountain vistas to watch the world end—while *other* millions demand to be instantly downloaded into alien-designed crystal paradise—did we need this, too?

One failed space mission may be happenstance. But *two*? Within days of each other? First, a Chinese robot probe to the asteroid belt barely gets five klicks off the pad before fizzling into the sea. Then the Pan-American one explodes.

Both were rush-jobs, aiming to quick-grab more artifacts. And hurried space missions are hazardous! But *both* of them? Exploding in launch phase? It takes us deep into Suspicioustan—stoking whatever paranoid theme happens to be your favorite. Especially the oldest: nation versus jealous nation. Inflamed *sabotage* rumors fly, recalling the volcanic fury of the Chinese public, right after the *Zheng He* incident. Tensions rise. Military leaves are canceled.

Adding pressure, no amount of openness will convince

everyone the Americans aren't hiding something. Somehow gaining more from the Havana Artifact than they've shared. Maybe even blocking others from getting artifacts of their own?

Meanwhile, intellectuals keep pondering galactic "contact" puzzles, politicians argue on as if clichés of "left-right" matter anymore, powerful connivers scheme for a kind of "stability" that only ensures death . . .

. . . and now *war in space*?

What will it take to wake people up?

56.
EDEN

Peng Xiang Bin let out a low moan and a stream of bubbles. He backed into a corner as the figure in the dormer-opening bent to twist through, while battle-booms and gunfire detonations rocked the sunken, royal ruins.

He's wearing some kind of military uniform . . . and one of those helmets with emergency pop-out gills . . .

Oxygen-absorbing fronds were still unfolding out of headgear recesses while the newcomer sucked greedily at a small tube. Evidently a refugee from the renewed combat raging overhead, he wore goggles that were flooded and clearly not meant for underwater use. Bin watched as the soldier floundered. *He better calm down, or he'll overwhelm those little gills.*

Also, Bin realized—*I'm darkness adapted and my eye covers work. I can see him. He hasn't seen me.*

And he's not as big as I first thought.

Those huge-looking shoulders had been inflated by air pockets, caught when the soldier jumped to sea. That false bulk was collapsing now. Bin now realized, the fellow was quite slender.

So . . . should I try to fight him?

The tide of battle may have turned outside. Still, Bin knew he was no warrior. Anyway, his duty was to tend the worldstone, not to risk his life for Newer Newport. Bin started edging toward the opening, lugging the satchel in short, shuffling steps, careful to avoid both broken timbers and the newcomer's feet.

Whoever he was, the soldier must have had good training. Bin could tell he was adapting, gathering himself, concentrating on solving problems. As the rollicking explosions diminished a little, the fellow stopped thrashing and his rapid gasps ebbed into more regular breathing. When he started to experiment, exhaling a vertical stream of bubbles to clear and fill his goggles, Bin knew there was little time left to make a clean getaway. He picked up the pace, fumbling to find the opening. Only it took some effort while hauling the heavy . . .

He stopped, as sharp illumination erupted from an object in the soldier's hand, engulfing Bin and the dormer window.

Aided by the implant, Bin's right eye adapted, even as the left was dazzled. Because the implant laid a disc of blackness over the bright torchlight, he could tell it was part of a weapon—a small sidearm the soldier aimed at Bin's chest.

For several seconds, Bin stood and exchanged a long look with the soldier, who drifted almost within arm's reach. Slowly, without jerky motions, Bin pointed at the torch . . . then at the dormer entrance . . . then jabbed his thumb upward several times.

Whoever is chasing you may see that light, streaming out of the ruins . . . and drop something unpleasant on us.

The soldier apparently grasped his meaning and slid a control or sent a subvocal command. The light source dimmed considerably and become all-directional, dimly illuminating the whole chamber so they could see each other . . .

. . . and Bin realized, he had been mistaken. The interloper was a woman.

Several more seconds passed, while the soldier looked Bin over. Then she laid the weapon down nearby—and used her right forefinger to draw several quick characters on the palm of her left hand.

You are Peng Xiang Bin.

Palm-writing was never a very good form of communication, all by itself. Normally, folks used it only to settle ambiguity between two spoken words that sounded the same. But down here, it was the best they could manage. Anyway, the flurry of movements sufficed for Bin to recognize his own name. And to grasp the import—these invaders had come across the ocean well prepared.

Only now things seemed to be going badly for them.

But it would be rude to point out the obvious. So he finally responded with a brief nod. Anyway, she had expressed it as a statement, not a question. The soldier finger-wrote three more ideograms.

Is that the thing?

She finished by pointing to the satchel Bin clutched tightly, holding the worldstone. There was little use denying it. A simple shrug of the shoulders, then, to save air.

She spent the next few seconds sucking on the tube from the barely adequate emergency gill, then exhaled another stream of bubbles to refill her goggles. Her eyes were red from salt water and rimmed with creases that must have come from a life engaged in scrutiny. Perhaps a technical expert, rather than a front-line warrior—but still part of an elite team. The kind who would never give up.

As combat sounds drifted farther away, she wrote another series of ideograms on her left palm. This time, however, he could not follow the finger movements well enough to understand. Not her fault, of course—probably his own, deficient education—and this time the aimplant in his eye offered no help.

He indicated confusion with a shake of his head.

Frustrated, she looked around, then shuffled half a meter closer to the nearest slanted attic wall. There, she used the same finger to disturb a layer of algae-scum, leaving distinct trails wherever she wrote.

Are you a loyal citizen?

She then turned, patting a badge on her left shoulder. And Bin noticed, for the first time, the emblem of the armed forces of the People's Republic of China.

Taken aback, he had to blink. Of course he was a loyal Chinese! But *citizen*? As a shoresteader, he had some rights . . . but no legal residency in either Shanghai or any of the great national cooperatives. Nor would he, till his reclamation contract was fulfilled. *All citizenship is local,* went the saying . . . and thus, two hundred million transients were cast adrift. Still, what did citizenship mean, anyway? Who ever got to vote above the province level? Nationwide, "democracy" tended to blur into something else. Not tyranny—clearly the national government *listened* to the People—in much the same way that Heaven could be counted on to hear the prayers of mortals. The Reforms of 2029 had not been for nothing. There were constituent assemblies, trade congresses, party conclaves dominated by half a billion little emperors . . . it all had a loose, deliberately traditionally and proudly non-Western flavor. And none of it ever included Peng Xiang Bin.

Still, am I proud to be Chinese? Sure. Why wouldn't I be? We lead the world.

Yet, that wasn't what loomed foremost in his mind.

What mattered was that he had been noticed by illustrious ones, somewhere high up the pyramid of power, obligation, and privilege. By people who were mighty enough to order government special forces on a dangerous and politically risky mission, far from home.

They know my name. They sent elite raiders across the sea to fetch me. Or, at least the worldstone.

Not that it was certain they'd prevail. Even grand national powers like China had been outmaneuvered, time and again, by the planetary New Elites. After all, the woman soldier was hiding down here, with him.

No. One consideration mattered, more than citizenship or national loyalty. Even as the rich escaped to handmade sovereignties like New Pulupau, old-fashioned governments still controlled the territories where *billions of ordinary people* lived—the festering poor and struggling middle classes. Which meant one thing to Bin.

The high masters of China have Mei Ling and Xiao En in their hands. Or they could, at any time. I truly have no choice.

In fact, why did I ever believe I had one?

Bin shifted his weight in order to lean over and bring his own finger toward the slanted, algae-covered boards. Even as he drew a first character, the ai in his eye remonstrated.

Don't do this, Bin.

There are other options.

But he shook his head and grunted the code word they had taught him for clearing the irritation away. The artificial presence vanished from his right field of vision, allowing him to see clearly the figures that he drew through filmy scum. Fortunately, by now the explosions had faded again, letting him trace the strokes carefully.

I'm just here to buy soy sauce.

The soldier stared. From her befuddled look, Bin knew she must not be from China's central coast, where that old joke still tugged reflex guffaws, even from coolies working on the New Great Wall. Well, humor had never been his thing. Bin moved his finger again and wrote:

I will aid my nation.
What must I do?

An expression of satisfaction spread across the soldier's face. Clearly, this was better fortune than she had figured on, only moments ago, when she jumped from a balcony of Newer Newport into the uncertain refuge of ocean-covered ruins. Perhaps, this little royal attic still had powerful *qi*.

She started to write again, across the scummy, pitched ceiling.

Very good. We have little time. . . .

Bin agreed. Less than five minutes of highly compressed gas remained in his tiny air tank. That is, if he could trust the tiny clock in his goggle lens.

Nearby . . . a submerged emergency shelter . . . where we'll wait . . .

The soldier stopped suddenly, as if her body froze, eyes masked in shadow. Then, as she turned like a marionette tugged by swirling currents, he saw them glint with fear.

Bin swiveled quickly . . .

. . . to see something very large, looming in the dormer opening. A slithering, snakelike shape—wider than a man—that wriggled upward, its head almost filling the slanted entrance. Robotic eyes began to glow, illuminating every crevice of the cavity. Evidently a powerful fighting machine, it seemed to examine both of them—not only with light, but also pulses of sonar that frisked their bodies like ungentle fingers of sound.

A sharp spotlight swerved suddenly downward, at the soldier's pistol sidearm, lying on a broken chunk of wood. Abruptly, a whiplike tendril emerged from its mouth and snatched up the weapon, swallowing it before either human could move. Then a booming voice filled the little hiding place, made only slightly murky by the watery echo chamber.

"Come, Peng Xiang Bin," the mechanical creature commanded, as it began to open its jaw wide. *"Now. And bring the artifact."*

Bin realized, with some horror, that the serpent-android wanted him to crawl inside, through that gaping mouth. He cringed back.

Perhaps sensing his terrified reluctance, the robot spoke again.

"It is safe to do this . . . and unsafe to refuse."

A threat, then. Bin had plenty of experience with those. Familiarity actually calmed his nerves a little, allowing him to examine the odds.

Cornered, in a rickety sunken attic, with just a few minutes of air left, facing some sort of ai superbot . . . um do I have any choice?

Yet, he could not move forward. So the serpaint made things clear. From one eye, it fired a narrow, brilliant beam of light that left steam bubbles along its path. By the time Bin turned to look, it had finished burning a pair of characters into one of the old roof beams of the Pulupauan royal palace.

CHOOSE LIFE.

He thought furiously. No doubt the machine could simply take the worldstone away from him, with one of those tendril things. So . . . it must realize . . . or its owners must . . . that the worldstone required Bin's touch in order to come alight. Still, he extended a finger and palm-wrote for the creature to see.

I am needed. It speaks only to me.

The serpent-machine had no trouble parsing Bin's handwriting. It nodded.

"Agreed. Cooperation will be rewarded. But if I must take only the artifact, we will find a way."

A way. Bin could well imagine: Offer the stone new candidates for the role of chosen one. As many as it took. With Bin no longer alive.

"Come now. There is little time."

Bin almost dug in his heels, right then. He was sick of people and things saying that to him. Only, after a moment's stubborn fury, he managed to quash both irritation and fear. Lugging the heavy satchel, he shuffled a step closer, and another.

Then he glanced back at the Chinese special forces soldier, who was still staring, wide-eyed. There was something in her expression, a pleading look.

Bin stood in front of the sea monster. He put the satchel down in the muck and raised both hands to write on his palm again.

What about her?

The robot considered for a moment, then answered.

"She knows nothing of my mission, owners, or destination. She may live."

Quiet thanks filled the woman's eyes, fortifying Bin and putting firmness in his step, as he drew close. Though he could not keep from trembling, as he lifted the satchel containing the worldstone and laid it inside that gaping maw. Then, without its weight holding him down, he rotated horizontal and turned his body to start worming inside.

It was the second strangest act he ever performed.

The very strangest—and it puzzled him for the next hour—was what he did *while* crawling inside . . . when he slipped one hand under his belt, drawing out something filmy and almost translucent, tossing it backward to flutter out of the sea serpent's jaw, drifting below where its eyes could see . . . but where the soldier could not help but notice.

Yang Shenxiu gave it to me to protect from the attackers, and now I'm giving it to one of them. Does that even make sense?

Yet, somehow, it felt right.

TORALYZER

The doctors want me to exercise. To inhabit my new body and get used to its senses. But I'm reluctant.

Not because it hurts. It *does,* often intensely. But that's not my reason. Pain doesn't have the reflex power it used to possess. I've been through so much already, it's become a familiar companion. I tend to view it as . . . data.

Was that a terribly *robotic* thing for me to say? In keeping with the electromechanical fingers that I flex and the gel-eyes that track from the same sockets in my head, where once stared the brown irises I was born with? But no, I'm not revolted by any of that. Nor even to find myself now a compact cylinder, riding around on cyborg seg-wheels. The clanking-whirring aspect isn't as bad as expected.

I admit I was surprised, the first time I *looked* through these eyes at my new, mechanical hand, and saw what it was holding. That forty-thousand-year-old stone tool-core that Akinobu Sato gave me, back in Albuquerque. For some time I could only stare, as my new fingers flexed, squeezing the ancient artifact as—involuntarily—my other new hand came over to caress it. The touch sensations were a creepy mix of familiar and bizarre.

Oh, it was good to feel an object again, though the sensory web feeding signals to my brain triggered accompanying glitters of synesthesia. *Sparks* seemed to follow, each time I stroked the ancient facets where some pre-ancient engineer once fashioned blades, using the highest tech of his age. Turning the stone over, I heard tinkling sounds, like distant, fairy bells, ill tuned, smelling of both soot and time.

"Why did you give me this?" I asked the docs, who answered, in some puzzlement, that I had *asked* for the Pleistocene stone relic. Out of some unconscious sense of irony, perhaps? A juxtaposition of tool use, from man's beginning and his end, like in that Kubrick film?

I had no memory of the request.

Oh, this whole process is fascinating. And I'm not ungrateful! Dr. Turgeson asked me, today, if I was glad I chose to participate in these experiments, rather than take the other option—

—diving into cryonic deep freeze, hoping to waken in a more advanced age with better medicine.

Well, why *not* hang around here and now, when I'm appreciated and fully capable of staying in the game? With vision and mobility, I may yet have a career, dashing about the world, interviewing celebrighties who won't be able to say no to the famous hero-reporter in her hard-cased segsuit and never-blinking cyberais. Anyway, who wants to bet on cryonic resurrection in some rosy future . . . with the artifact aliens saying there's no tomorrow?

That's not the problem. Nor was I much upset the time Wesley came to visit, accompanied by his new wife. Their offer to do a group-thing was flattering. (My ovaries are one part of me that survived the explosion intact.) But I wasn't interested.

No. My complaint is just this. That I look forward to *down time.* To turning off the distracting new body and surrounding world. To dive back into the cyber belowverse for twenty hours out of twenty-four. Joining you, my real friends. My smart-mob comrades. My fellow citizen-soldiers. My hounds, sniffing and correlating and baying after the truth!

So, what do you have for Mama today? What happened during the brief but tedious time I had to be away, dealing with the physical world?

The Basque Chimera.

Mei Ling knew the words, of course. Everyone on Earth had heard the legend: How a brave maiden offered up her womb to carry the seed of a reborn race. A type of human that had gone extinct tens of thousands of years ago.

When the virgin mother's home—a research center in the Spanish Pyrenees—evaporated in a mushroom-shaped pillar of flame, millions reckoned it righteous punishment for many sins, like arrogance, pride, even bestiality.

Tens of millions grieved.

And hundreds of millions breathed sad sighs of release. While deploring violent murder, they felt relieved to see a tense matter put off for another generation.

Mere tens of thousands clung to hope, nursing rumors that Agurne Arrixaka Bidarte still lived, that she had some-how escaped the fiery holocaust in Navarre, finding some place of refuge to birth her child. Even in faraway China, living atop a ramshackle shorestead beside the polluted Huangpu, with barely enough linkage to watch grainy, emo-dramas, Mei Ling had followed this story, so much like a tragic, romantic legend from the fabled days of Han.

Now, with the real Madonna and child standing up to greet her, Mei Ling felt awkward and tongue-tied. Agurne Arrixaka Bidarte was shorter than expected, with dark, tightly curled hair, olive complexion, and a warm smile as she offered her right hand. Mei Ling briefly wondered if she was supposed to kiss it, as one did with royalty in some occidental movies of bygone days. But no, it became a handshake of the new style, as both women clasped each other's forearms, more sanitary than pressing sweaty palms together.

Agurne's warm squeeze expressed comradeship. Solidarity. "I am so very glad to meet you," she said in Beijing dialect with a thick foreign accent. As their hands parted company, "We have much to discuss. But first, please let me introduce my son. He has lately chosen for himself the name *Hijobosque*. Hijo, please say hello."

The boy looked ten years old or more, though less time than that had passed since pillars of flame heralded his birth in the forested hills of Auzoberri. Though modesty forbade her to stare, Mei Ling noted that his face bore no sign of the heavy brow ridges that appeared in most artist renderings, predicting the likely appearance of a—

—she could not recall the name of the cave people who used to inhabit Europe and much of Asia, before the arrival of modern man. They had been thick-boned, short-legged, robustly built people . . . and those traits seemed to carry through in the boy, though not in any extreme way that shouted *stranger!* His posture was proudly erect and he seemed no hairier than any other man-child. Perhaps the bony eye-hoods were removed by doctors, to help him hide among regular humans.

"Please call me Hijo," he said in a voice that sounded both deeper and more constricted than normal, as if he were deliberately trying for a nasal twang. Or, perhaps he was just overstressing his tones, in speaking Mandarin Chinese.

When Hijo shook hands with Mei Ling—the older way—Mei Ling felt almost sure there was something different in the way bone and muscle and sinew were put together. His gentle squeeze conveyed a sense of repressed strength. Lots of it.

Nervously expecting him to say something profound, Mei Ling found Hijo's next words comfortingly normal.

"Baby," he said, spreading open both hands. "Can I hold your baby? I promise to be careful."

Remembering that quiet strength, Mei Ling couldn't help glancing at Agurne Arrixaka Bidarte, who merely smiled in a relaxed way. So did the strange little boy, Yi Ming, who had arranged this encounter, guiding Mei Ling through countless twisty passages beneath the Universe of Disney and the Monkey King. Lifting Xiao En out of his sling carrier, she set an example of holding him, then turned the infant in order to hand him over . . . watching.

There was no cause for worry. Hijo hefted Xiao En with evident skill and ease . . . he must have handled babies before. And Xiao En chortled pleasure at having someone new to charm. In truth, he was getting so big, Mei Ling found it a relief to surrender the weight, for a time.

Hijo made cooing sounds that drew from Xiao En a drooling, gap-tooth smile. Though they were strange to Mei Ling's ear . . . as if *two* creatures were crooning in different parts of a forest, at the same time.

Watching the two of them together, Mei Ling wondered how the Basque Chimera had been able to stay free for so long. The modern world's overlapping cameras fed each other, reporting to smart daitabases. Sure, there had been efforts to conceal the boy's differences—having undergone reconstructive surgery herself, Mei Ling recognized signs that Hijo's nose had been altered and possibly even the slope of his forehead. But other things, like a pronounced bulging of the back of the skull, could not be disguised. Though, now that she thought about it . . .

. . . Mei Ling glanced at Yi Ming and realized, some of the telltale traits were shared with millions of others walking around today. People with normal, human pedigrees.

"Shall we sit?" Agurne invited Mei Ling to join her on a couch. Not far away stood one of the multi-access consoles where men and women—all of them clearly abnormal—had plugged and wired and harnessed themselves, grunting and twitching as complicated light-shows flashed from goggle-covered eyes.

"I do not—" Mei Ling swallowed, trying for her best grammar. "I do not understand why I am thus honored."

Agurne laughed, a gentle sound.

"Please. We both became pregnant and bore healthy sons under difficult circumstances. We both successfully fled the clutches of great powers. How is it any less of an honor for me to meet you?"

Mei Ling found herself blushing. And she knew that made her scar tissue stand out, embarrassing her further.

"How . . . may I be of service?" she half whispered.

Agurne Arrixaka Bidarte inhaled deeply. Her eyes glittered with compassionate concern.

"Normally, I would not be so rude. You have no reason to trust me. At the very least, we would talk a while. Get the measure of each other, one woman and mother to another. But there is so little time. May I go straight to the point?"

"Please . . . please do."

Agurne motioned with one hand toward the janitorial smart-mob, harnessed into their multisensory portal stations. "All over the world, small groups like this one are joining forces, in an urgent quest for understanding. They can sense that something is happening. Something that cannot be entirely encompassed by words."

Mei Ling swallowed hard. She glanced at the boy who was now sitting on the floor, holding her son. Although he was turned partly away, Hijo seemed to sense her question.

"Yes . . . I can feel it, too. I am helping. In fact, I have to get back to work, real soon."

Agurne smiled with adoring approval, then turned back to Mei Ling and continued.

"I cannot explain what it is that they are doing, or claim to understand, except that it seems to be about destiny.

Things and ideas and emotions that may determine the future of humanity, if Allah-of-all-names wills it."

Mei Ling could find no words, so she waited for the other woman to say more.

"Do you know what many of these teams are doing right now?"

Mei Ling shook her head. No.

"They are searching for your husband. And the crystal he was last seen carrying into the sea."

She had known, of course, all along. Deep down. This could only be about the accursed <u>Demon Stone</u>. "I wish he never found the terrible thing."

"I understand. You have cause for bitterness. But do not judge too quickly. We don't know what role it will play. But one thing is certain. Your husband will be safer if he and the stone can be drawn out of shadows. Into the light."

Mei Ling pondered this for long seconds.

"Can that be done?"

The other woman's smile was rueful, apologetic.

"I don't know the details. They are searching for him by sifting the daita-sphere. A myriad corners and dimensions of the Great Mesh. The tides and currents and drifting aromas. Many things that are deeply hidden, encrypted and buried behind bulwarks of firewall isolation—these nevertheless leave spoors that can be detected, if only by the studious *absence* of mention."

Mei Ling blinked silently, wondering how this foreigner—born in New Guinea, raised on Fiji, and educated in Europe—became so articulate in Chinese. *Better than me,* she observed.

"These are the sort of not-there traces that the <u>Blessed Throwbacks</u> sometimes can detect, invisible to the rest of us."

"But not to me!" inserted Hijo, who had laid Xiao En on

a plush rug, and was playing a game of peekaboo, to the baby's delight.

"No. Not to you," Agurne responded, indulgently.

"In fact, I can tell that Mei Ling's children will be special," the Neanderthal boy added. "Even though I don't know why. Nobody can know the future. But some things just leap out. They're obvious."

Hijo's faulty use of the plural almost made her protest. *I have only one child.* But Mei Ling shook her head. This was no time for petty distraction. She turned back to the mother.

"How can I help? What can I tell you?"

Agurne Arrixaka Bidarte leaned gently toward Mei Ling.

"Everything. Anything you can remember. We already have many clues.

"Why don't you just start at the beginning?"

A GLIMMER

The gullet of the sea serpaint isn't as gross or disgusting as he expected. The walls are soft and he has only to crawl back a short distance to find a space shaped to fit a recumbent person.

While twisting into the seat, Bin hears the jaw of the mechanical beast close with a thump. There follows backward movement, undulating, shaking, like a worm wriggling out of a hole. By some tech-wizardry, the small space around him begins emptying of water. Soon, a hiss of air.

Bin spits out the mouthpiece—a gasp of shuddering relief. The breather had gone foul. He gratefully rubs his eyes.

A patch of wall near his head is transparent—a window! How considerate. Really. It makes him feel ever-so-slightly less a prisoner—or a meal. Pressing his face, he peers outside. The palace ruins are a jumble, collapsed further by the fighting, now lit by slanting moonlight.

While the robot backs up, Bin spots his former attic shelter. Briefly, before the machine can accelerate forward, he glimpses the opening—and perhaps a shadowy silhouette. At least, he thinks so.

Enough to hope.

58.

DESPERATION

"They aren't just battling it out with lasers anymore," Gennady reported. "Now, many of the space attacks appear to involve kinetic energy weapons."

"You mean pellet guns?" Akana asked. "Wouldn't those be slower? Harder to aim, with all those asteroids jumbling about, on different orbits? And your target might get a chance to duck."

"How does a lump of crystal duck?" asked Emily Tang.

"Evidently," replied Haihong Ming, "there are things out there with more . . . physical capability . . . than mere lumps of passive crystal."

That had been obvious for a while. Still it felt like a milestone for someone to say aloud what everyone was thinking. *We're in new territory,* Gerald realized.

"Exactly! So . . ." Akana blinked. "Oh, I see. If you fire a high-velocity pellet and it takes a while to intersect the orbit of its target, that gives *you* time to take cover or get out of the way, before anyone will notice and retaliate. Can't do that with a laser."

"Depends on whether anyone's using radar. . . ." Gennady started to quibble, then shook his head and let it go.

"But why fight at all?" asked Dr. Tshombe. "What is this all about?"

"You mean other than scaring the bejeesus out of several billion Earthlings?" Emily asked, with a crack in her voice.

Or putting the kibosh on all those stupid claims of a hoax, Gerald pondered with some bitter satisfaction. One casualty had been the credibility of Hamish Brookeman and his backers. Well, *sic transit gloria.*

Ben Flannery, their Hawaiian anthropologist, gestured toward the object Gerald recovered from space—what seemed ages ago—now covered by a thick black cloth. The recording technicians had been sent away and all light cut off. The commission members had come to realize it was still necessary to teach the Artifact a lesson, now and then.

"We already knew there were factions. Machines that are *related* to our Artifact—part of the same interstellar lineage—may have worried, when other types started flashing for attention. Then came news reports from Earth, about space expeditions preparing to go fetch more varieties, for comparison. That was the last straw. Those cousins of our Artifact stepped in at that point, acting forcefully to remove the competition.

"And that brought retaliation. A truce that may have lasted eons came to a sudden end."

"In order to achieve what?" Emily asked.

"To claim the most valuable commodity in the solar system—human attention."

Gerald felt sympathy for Ben, a man of peace, reluctantly dragged into analysis of deadly war. One that apparently spanned millions of years, without a single living participant. But that didn't make it any less violent.

Akana had gone quiet for a while, as her tru-vus went opaque. Her teeth were clicking like mad, and among her subvocal grunts Gerald thought he heard one that signaled "Yes, sir," repeated several times.

Uh-oh, he thought.

"You know, there is an alternative theory," Gennady mused, oblivious to Akana's distraction. "We already decided these crystal artifacts are a lot like viruses. Well, in that case, consider a biological analogy. One explanation for the machines that are shooting at these space viruses may be some kind of immune—"

Akana's specs abruptly cleared and she sat up, with the petite but commanding erect posture of a woman who had recently been promoted to the rank of major general in the United States Aerospace Force. Her bearing brought silence better than any spoken order.

"That was the White House. All plans for another sample-recovery mission have been put on hold. Nobody feels prepared to send a crew, or even robots, into that mess out there. And I'm told that similar orders have been issued by Great China."

She paused while Haihong Ming checked with his government. In seconds, he nodded.

"That is so. But there appears to be more. Will you all kindly give me a moment?" Then it was his turn to disappear behind interspectacles that went totally opaque.

Gerald and the others looked at each other. Way back in olden times, it used to take weeks or months for an envoy to consult with his government, back home. Now, a couple of minutes seemed to stretch forever as Haihong Ming grunted in apparent surprise . . . then seeming protest . . . and finally evident submission.

At last, he flipped back his eye hoods decisively and took a few seconds to scan those seated around the table, before resuming.

"It would seem we now have sufficient reason for a *complete pooling* of resources and information."

"Um, I thought that was what we were doing already," Gennady commented. But Gerald shook his head. "I think our esteemed colleague from the Reborn Central Kingdom has something specific in mind. Something that he was forced—until now—to conceal."

Haihong Ming agreed with a short, sharp nod. This admission clearly caused some pain. "My sincere apologies for that. But now I can reveal that we long suspected the existence of at least one more emissary artifact, here on Earth."

"You mean other than those shattered remnants people have been digging up, in recent weeks?"

"I mean that certain elements within our venerable society have long believed in speaking-stones that fall from heaven. Some tales were thought more credible than others. There once was, for example, a specimen held in the Imperial Summer Palace, until it was sacked by European troops during the Second Opium War. That object was said to induce vivid dreams. Another—a carved egg made from especially pale jade, with purported 'magical properties'—was taken from the National Museum by Chiang Kai-shek, when he fled to Taiwan. Neither piece was ever publicly seen again."

"Did those items exhibit any of the properties we've seen here?" Tshombe waved toward the cloth-covered Havana Artifact. "Clear and explicit images? Animated beings who respond to questions?"

"Not in modern times, or witnessed by reliable chroniclers," the Chinese representative conceded. "But they may have been rendered inactive by superstitious meddling or artistic . . . elaborations. Our mandarins and craftsmen were often too eager to cut and embellish naturally beautiful things," he admitted, ruefully. "Or else, they may have been damaged amid centuries of warfare and looting.

"Ancient accounts do at least suggest they would be good targets of study. Perhaps even now they are under scrutiny by cryptic groups."

That implication was unpleasant to consider. Some secret coven of elite power, gaining an advantage by comparing their own private source to the flood of public information emerging from the Havana Artifact.

"Then there are even older legends, or vague hints that magical stones were buried in royal graves. And—"

Refusing to be distracted, Ben Flannery sighed. "Is that all you mean to tell us? That some museum pieces may once have glimmered a little, before they were carved into uselessness? From your buildup, I figured you fellows already had something more tangible in your hands."

Haihong Ming shook his head.

"We almost did. An especially promising piece kept slipping through our grasp. Not once but frequently, for a generation."

"A generation?" Akana asked, clearly puzzled. "But—"

"That is how long we suspected something remarkable—an intact emissary stone—might have come into private possession. Our searches came close to recovering it, several times."

And if you did acquire a working space crystal, earlier than I snagged one out of orbit, Gerald wondered, *would you have shared it with the world, as we did?*

Haihong Ming continued. "The most recent near miss—and it causes some embarrassment to say this—came *just over a day ago.* Thirty hours, to be exact. Since then, we have searched hard. And other forces appear to be doing so, as well."

"But . . ." Akana leaned forward, her elbows on the smooth tabletop. "How do you know this isn't just another fetish stone, or crystal skull, or some other man-made—"

"We know," affirmed the representative of Great China, firmly. "And I am now authorized to show you how we know."

With a series of grunts and hand motions, Haihong Ming caused an image to appear above the table. A *scroll* of some sort, or flimsy document, a single page that stretched wider and then shimmered with pixelated rainbows, as if lit by some angled light source. Gerald squinted. His aiware compensated and interpreted.

A memory sheet. An older, ten-petabyte unit for digital data storage.

The filmy object floated—in synthetic 3-D—above them all, then appeared to flatten, turning and glistening in every refracted color.

"This recording came into our possession just three hours ago. It is now being flown to Beijing, but a preliminary download contains information so startling—I am ordered to share it with you."

A small seed of *blackness* erupted from a corner of the memory sheet. Unfolding once . . . twice . . . several times . . . the darkness continued to expand through a dozen dimensions. It then unpackaged glittering, pinpoint stars that swirled and dispersed, arraying themselves across what rapidly became an ersatz, 3-D cosmos, complete with strange constellations . . . all of it enveloping a blue-brown world. One that clearly wasn't Earth. Nor did Gerald recognize the globe from dozens revealed by the Havana Artifact.

"As I said, we did not recover the interstellar voyager itself," explained Haihong Ming. "That crystal may already be sequestered in a hidden place by some nation, cabal, or gang. But a sympathetic citizen did provide us with this record containing dozens of hours of output from the Heaven Egg."

"Heaven Egg?"

"The original artifact is Chinese national property. It is ours, to name, as we choose. And be assured, we *will* recover it! Meanwhile, here is a small portion of its trove. Remember, I, too, am seeing this for the first time."

Haihong Ming motioned and a *story* commenced, made entirely of images.

It began as natives of the blue-brown world launched a tiny, twinkling probe, then used giant machines to send sparkling rays, push-propelling its filmy sail across the vast desert of space. Gennady and Ramesh murmured about technical differences between the method portrayed here and that described by the Havana Artifact. No one else spoke as the little envoy passed for a time through darkness . . . then brightened in the light of a fast-approaching sun.

Gerald's breath caught as quick-looming Jupiter snagged and flung the little envoy . . . which then caromed wildly among other planets, slowing each time until, at last, a familiar globe floated into view, seizing the star-traveler into a final, flaming embrace . . .

. . . followed by a miraculous, snow-cushioned landfall. Then discovery by men in sewn leather garments. . . . And the story had barely begun.

There were no breaks—for meals, even the toilet—nor did anyone speak. Not till a single *word* took shape, central and glowing, above the tabletop, right next to the blanket-covered bulge of the Havana Artifact. It manifested as an ancient Chinese ideogram, floating and shimmering in a calligraphic style that seemed edgy. Even angry.

Gerald's aiware had no trouble with translation. And all at once, he understood why Haihong Ming and his superiors were in a sudden mood to share everything they knew.

LIARS.

LOYALTY TEST

You got to hand it to those boys and girls on the Contact Commission. They do come up with clever tricks to get cooperation from the Artifact. First that behavioral training they used last month. Now, by *refusing to record* any more of those endless schematics and tech manuals the probe offers.

Who would think to try that? Saying no to a free gift? Declining something humans passionately desire—all those advanced technologies—in order to get what's more important.

It makes sense though. What's the probe's top priority? Get us moving down the road toward making more probes. Put aside whether that ultimate goal is good, bad, or neutral. The Artifact must *hunger* to teach us those technologies. A hunger we can exploit. Hideoshi and her team are savvy. They won't scratch the Artifact's itch without some kind of payment. And their demand?

More interviews with the passengers. One or two or three at a time.

This grew more urgent when we spied lasers and guns blasting across the asteroid belt! The commission demanded an explanation—and Oldest Member first expressed surprise, then indifference, and finally attributed it all to "bad machines from earlier eras."

Adding that "You humans can protect yourselves by downloading strong tools. Let us show you how to cast powerful rays that could sweep your solar system clean!"

Hm. Tempting. Persuasive. Who turns down an offer of big guns?

And Gerald Livingstone tossed the <u>Black Cloth</u>, casting the artilens in darkness—till they finally accepted a deal. One hour for one hour. They get to teach us new-tech for a span, then we get some diversity—such as it is.

So we've gone back to interviewing Low-Swooping Fishkiller—the youngest member—proud that his race made the Artifact we now hold, and apparently unmoved that we detect no sign of industry or radio by peering at his home-world. "Organics all die," he answered, shrugging those weird wings.

And Squiddy . . . she picked the name herself, from fifty thousand submitted by school kids across Earth. Some sense of humor, for a tentacle-waving pseudo cephalopod! Her chief contribution to human culture—a fresh and convincing defini-tion of "irony"—has the intelligentsia spinning in *why didn't we think of that* circles! And it took an alien. Huh.

Still, Squiddy won't diverge from Om's party line. He makes a case that the Artifact may indeed be like a virus—as critics say—but a beneficial or *commensal* one. And he gave hundreds of examples from our medical literature. A persuasive point.

Others are harder to understand. Take the caterpillarlike be-ing who spends its time during each interview peering out of the crystal at any nearby human, then muttering a puff of dis-missive symbols that translate: *"Man, what an imagination I have!"*

A clear case of Noakes Disease, earning that creature the web consensus name Bennie.

"What did you expect?" commented M'm por'lock, the one who resembles a giant-reddish otter, after helping usher Ben-nie away. "We spend eternities floating through space, either sleeping or amusing ourselves in vast virtuality layers, deep within our crystal vessel. You can lose your way in dreamstate. Or miss your chance to taste objective reality, during each brief encounter with a living race."

Are you like me? Do you get a sense, from M'm por'lock, of things unsaid?

More broadly—is this doing any good?

Sure, it scratches our curiosity itch, a bit. Glimpsing strange arts and tasting the cultural spread can be engrossing. This

gives our psych and other experts a chance to chart behaviors, cross-correlate alien attitudes and other boffin stuff. But
seriously, what do they expect—to come up with an *extraterrestrial lie detector*? Some way to verify the stories we're told?
Or to separate the Artifact's good offers from the sales-pitch
parts? The portions that are pure, viral self-interest?

Suspicion lingers. The diversity of ninety races that we
see—is it all somehow concocted? An *act* that's been refined
before many audiences across ten million years? A puppet
show, serving that long-term goal—

—to persuade?

59.
JONAH

The artificial sea serpent took a circuitous route along the
ocean floor, carrying Bin on a lengthy tour of murky canyons and muddy flats, stretching endlessly.

His passenger cell was padded, but cramped. The curved
walls kept twisting, throbbing as the machine beast pushed
along. Nor was the robot vehicle as garrulous or friendly as
Dr. Nguyen's penguin surrogate. Giving only terse answers, it ignored his request for a webscreen, immersion
specs, or any form of ailectronic diversion.

For the most part, the apparatus kept silent.

Or as silent as a motorized python could be, while undulating secretively across a vast and mostly empty sea. Clearly,
it was avoiding contact with humanity—not easily done in
this day and age, even far away from shipping lanes and
shorelines. Several times, Bin felt thrown to one side as the
snake-sub veered and dived, taking shelter behind some
mound, within a crevice, or even burying itself under a
meter or so of mucky sediment, then falling eerily quiet, as
if hiding from predators. On two of those occasions, Bin

thought he heard the faint drone of some engine gradually rise and then fall, in both pitch and volume, before fading away at last. Then, as the serpent shook itself free of mud, their journey resumed.

Even its method of propulsion seemed designed for stealth. Most of the world's sub-sea detection systems were tuned to listen for propellers, not wriggling giant serpents.

Of course signs of humanity lay everywhere. The ocean floor was an immense junkyard, even in desert zones where no fish or plants or any kind of resource could be seen. Shipwrecks offered occasional sights worth noting. Far more often, Bin saw mundane types of trash, like torn commercial fishing nets, resembling vast, diffuse, deadly clouds that drifted with the current, clogged with fish skeletons and empty turtle shells. Or swarms of plastic bags that drifted alongside jelly hordes in creepy mimicry. Once, he spotted a dozen huge cargo containers that must have toppled from a mighty freighter long ago, spilling what appeared to be bulky, old-fashioned computers and television panels across forty hectares.

I'm used to living amid garbage. But I always figured the open sea was better off . . . more pure . . . than the Huangpu.

Losing track of time, he dozed while the slithering robot hurried across a vast, empty plain, seeming as lifeless as the moon . . .

. . . then jerked awake, to look out through the tiny window and find himself being carried along a craggy underwater mountain range, an apparently endless series of stark ridges that speared upward, reaching almost to the glistening surface, but even more eerie, because the rippling promontories vanished into bottomless gloom, below. Clearly, the mechanical creature that had swallowed him meant to shake off any pursuers. Weaving its way through this labyrinth should help.

Feeling a bit recovered, Bin peeled open some ration bars that he found in a small compartment by his left arm. A little tap offered trickles of fresh water. There was a washcloth, which he used to dab and clean his cuts. A simple suction tube—for waste—was self-explanatory, if awkward to use. After which, the voyage became a battle against both tedium and claustrophobia—the frustration of limited movement plus abiding worry over what his future held.

No clues came from the serpent, which spoke sparingly and answered no questions, not even when Bin asked about some roiling funnels of black water that he spotted, rising from fissures in a nearby jagged ridgeline, like columns of smoke from a fierce fire.

It occurred to Bin that—perhaps—he shouldn't be so glad that the owners of this sophisticated device included a window. *In stories and teledramas, kidnappers insist on a blindfold, if they plan to let you go.*

The time to worry is when they don't seem to care. If they let you watch the route to their lair, it means they feel sure you'll never talk.

On the other hand, who could possibly tell, by memory, one hazy sea ridge from another? That reassured him for a while . . . till he remembered the visual helper unit that Dr. Nguyen installed in his right eye. Bin had come to take for granted the way the tiny aissistant augmented whatever he looked at, enhancing the dim scene beyond the window. Now he realized; without it, he wouldn't be seeing much at all!

Are they assuming that a poor man, like me, is unaugmented?

He wondered about the implant. Might it even be recording whatever he saw? In which case, was he like the kidnap victim who kept daring fate, by peeking under his blindfold?

Or am I headed for someplace that is so perfectly escape-proof that they don't care how much I know?

Or someplace that I'd never want to escape from?

That was preferable to other possibilities.

Or am I to be altered, in ways that will make me placid?

Or do they figure that I'll only be needed for a little while—till a replacement can be arranged, someone else qualified to speak with the worldstone? Must I try as hard to win over my next masters, as I did Anna and Paul and Dr. Nguyen?

Each scenario came accompanied by vivid fantasies. And Bin tried not to subvocalize any of them—there were modern devices that could track the impulses in a human throat and parse words you never spoke aloud.

On the other hand, why would anyone bother doing that, with a mere shoresteader trashman? Ultimately, each fantasy ended in one thought. That he might never see his family again.

But the soldier . . . the woman in that drowned attic room . . . she will get the sheet recording that Yang Shenxiu made. She will know that I cooperated. The government will protect and reward Mei Ling and Xiao En. Surely?

It was all too worrisome and perplexing. To help divert his thoughts, Bin put the worldstone on his lap and tried talking to Courier of Caution.

True, without immersion in sunlight, the entity had to preserve energy, subduing its vivid animations—the images were dim and limited to a small surface. Still, if he could learn some new things, that might prove his worth.

It wasn't easy. Without sound induction, he was limited to tracing characters on the ovoid's surface. Courier at first tried responding with ancient ideograms. But Bin knew few of those, so they resumed the process of updating its knowledge of written Chinese. The entity within offered pictures or pantomimed actions. Bin sketched the associated modern words—often helped by the ai-patch. Never having to repeat, it went remarkably quickly. Within half a day, they were communicating.

At last, Bin felt ready to ask a question that had been foremost in his mind. Why did Courier hate the aliens inside the Havana Artifact?

Why did he call them "liars"?

In a stream of characters, accompanied by low-resolution images, the entity explained.

Our world is farther from its sun than yours. Larger but less dense. Our gravity slighter. Our atmosphere thicker and rich with snow. It is a planet much easier to land upon than your Earth. If a solar sail is built especially sturdy in the middle, it can be used as a parachute, to cushion the fall.

And so, when they came to our world, many of the messenger stones did not shy away, lurking at a safe distance to await technological civilization. Instead some chose a direct approach, raining down upon—

There appeared a new symbol, unlike anything Chinese, made up of elegant, curling, and looping lines that suggested waves churning a beach. The emblem reminded Bin of *Turbulence* and so that became his word for the planet.

—from many sources.

My species rose up to intelligence already knowing these sky-crystals, finding them occasionally in mud or ice. Even embedded on stone. Foraging packs of our pre-sapient ancestors cherished them. Early tribes fought over them, worshipped them, looked to them as oracles, seeking advice about the next hunt, about crude agriculture, about diplomacy. And marriage.

The alien made a gesture that Bin could not interpret—a writhing of both hands. And yet, he felt somehow sure that it expressed irony.

Thus, our evolution was guided. Accelerated.

Painting characters with a finger, Bin wrote bitterly that humanity never had such help. That is, unless you counted a few, vague strictures from Heaven. And, perhaps, some nudges from the rare messenger fragments that made it to Earth.

Do not envy too readily, Courier chided. *It might have gone smoothly, if there were only one kind of stone, with one inhabitant each! But there were scores, perhaps even hundreds of crystal seers, scattered across many island continents! Only much later did we learn—they had come across space from several directions. At least eighteen different alien points of origin. Turbulence-planet sits at a meeting of galactic currents.*

Then add this irksome fact. That each stone held multitudes! Communities, accumulations, whole zoos of "gods," in many shapes, who bickered, even when they agreed.

We had the blessing—and curse—of highly varied counsel. Except, of course, when they all wanted the same thing.

But still, Bin wrote. *They helped you rise up quickly.*

Courier nodded. Though whether the gesture was native to it, or learned from other humans, Bin couldn't tell.

One tribe—following advice from its shaman stone—practiced fierce eugenics upon itself, in mountain isolation, for fifty generations. When they burst forth, all other clans on that land mass were awed into submission, and local females wanted only to mate with their males.

The worldstone depicted a mob of naked primitives, bowing before another group that stood taller, more erect, wearing fur clothing, with wide noses and thick manes— more like Courier himself.

Meanwhile, on other continents and archipelagoes, different oracle stones offered guidance to groups near them, advising and rewarding compliance with counsel about hunting methods, the weather, taming wild beasts, or domesticating plants. Any tribe that had a god-crystal was tu-

tored to breed itself smarter, tougher, better able to take over its neighbors.

Eventually, these spreading zones of modified people encountered each other. Conflict ensued! At first waged with stones and spears, then cannon and poisons. Urged to fight for total conquest, our ancestors studied the arts of genocide.

We soon learned a hard lesson. The only way to make peace between two tribes was to choose one set of jealous gods—a single oracle—and dispose of the other. Or hide it from sight. Only then would the surviving crystal allow both clans to meet in peace and interbreed, molding robust hybrids for the next confrontation.

Bin read the story while, behind the glowing ideograms, simulations showed members of Courier's race growing stronger, quicker, taller, and more impressive, armed with tools of ever-increasing sophistication. From Courier's choice of words, Bin sensed resentment over how these ancestors were manipulated into fighting one another. But honestly? This history seemed no more violent than humanity's.

Less so! Because each war actually accomplished something. Resolution in a firm direction. Unification under one stone's guidance. One set of "gods."

And rapid progress. The simulated aliens—or heavenly advisers—had practical knowledge to impart. Useful methods gathered by dozens of races, under faraway suns. Helped by such hints, Courier's people skipped countless centuries of rough trial and error.

Bin thought back to those arguments between Paul Menelaua and Anna Arroyo. He wished they were here. Not because they were ever friendly to him. But their back-and-forth tussles shed more light than either could manage alone. Bin recalled one extended debate over the role of religion in human development.

There had been so many cults on every continent. From

Europe and Asia to the Americas, creeds varied widely in details of ritual and belief, yet were largely similar in one respect . . . the way all jealously demanded obedience, ritualistic repetition, the firm teaching of children, and fierce resistance to the lure of *other* sects—like the one followed by those filthy folks across the valley.

What was the term that Paul had used? For ideas that take root in human minds and force those minds to spread them farther?

Infectious memes, wrote the ai helper chip that floated in Bin's right eyeball. **Mental constructs that pass from human to human, like viruses, with the trait of making each host *want* to believe. And making him want to persuade others.**

It wasn't an easy concept for Bin to wrap his head around. As for the legend of Planet Turbulence, Bin could not suppress his jealousy. At least Courier's people had gods who spoke clearly and taught practical things, making each generation healthier and stronger. Most human cultures had to sit still for long periods, while priests and aristocrats insisted that nothing should change. In the face of steady, conservative resistance, how many centuries did it take human beings to develop farms and roads, then advanced tools and schools, then universities and such, let alone actual science?

His aiware took that as a literal question.

Homo sapiens endured 2,000 generations, from the Neolithic renaissance until achieving civilization.

Before that, *Homo neanderthalensis* lasted 15,000 generations.

***Homo erectus* 50,000 generations.**

Bin resisted a temptation to turn off the device, yet again. Though irritating, the implant might give him a small edge, when he finally met the owners of the mechanical sea serpent.

But . . . two thousand generations? Bin's mind recoiled,

unable to contemplate the vast span that humanity lan-
guished in dim ignorance, doomed to countless false starts
and futile sidetracks. By comparison, Courier's people
took a shortcut stairway. An escalator! Bin wrote as much,
with his fingertip.

The simulated alien replied,

*Progress may have been slower for your race. Harder. Less
continuous. But you get the pride of knowing that you lifted up
yourselves, through your own efforts.*

*And there were costs for our rapid development. Under
guidance by crystal-encased "gods," marriage and reproduction became tightly managed on Planet Turbulence. Mating
required permission. Half the males in any generation could not
breed at all. Our ancestral forebears had been monogamous,
gregarious, friendly, easy-going creatures. Under guidance, we
became harshly competitive, performing every trick in order to
be noticed—to gain approval—from those domineering immortals in the oracle stones.*

Continuing to unfold its tale, the Courier entity arrived
at a pivotal phase of history when a single mega-tribe—
guided by one especially effective sky emissary—
triumphed, becoming dominant across most of the planet.

A generation later, we had cities.

Within five, we were in space.

*Whereupon... only then... did we learn what the gods
wanted from us.*

Bin felt tension, even though he knew the answer
already. Everyone on Earth knew, thanks to the Havana
Artifact. Bin painted a summary with his finger.

*They asked you to build more emissary stones—billions
of duplicate bottles... And messengers to put inside
them—and then spend every resource to cast them forth
toward new planets beyond.*

Again, Courier nodded.

That is the deal they presented to us, back on Turbulence.

*And we agreed! After all, these were the deities who had
vexed and confused and guided and tormented and loved and
taught us, as far back as our collective race memory could
penetrate the misty past. Even when we knew what they truly
were—mere puppets sent by beings who once dwelled by
faraway suns—we felt obliged to move forward. To grant their
wish.*

*Slowly, of course, while building a society of knowledge and
serenity. . . .*

*But no! They hectored that it should be our top—our
only—priority! They badgered us. Cajoled and manipulated.
Until, at last, they confided a reason for haste.*

And so came the great lie . . . .

Black characters continued scrolling under the surface
of the stone, but their already-dim contrast was fading fast.
All background images vanished and Bin realized, the artifact must be nearly drained. Moreover, his eyes hurt.

He painted a symbol on the ovoid—*WAIT*—and rubbed
them. Time also for some water. And the last protein bar,
which he munched quietly, pondering more clearly than ever
how small and unimportant his life was. All individual
lives, for that matter, on the grand and tragic scale of many
worlds. Many tragic destinies.

Yet, his mind's wanderings kept returning to what mattered most. His mate. His child. Somehow, there must be a
way to help them . . . to ensure their lives and comfort and
liberty . . . while salvaging something worthwhile out of his
own tangled loyalties. To China. To Dr. Nguyen. To Courier.
Humanity. Himself.

To the truth.

Without realizing it, Bin had been finger-writing while
thinking. He realized this because the worldstone glimmered with an answer. One that throbbed briefly, faintly,
before drowning in dull mist.

Truth?

Just get me to where I can...

He missed the last part as the robot-sub began vibrating suddenly, jouncing the scarred crystal on his lap. But for the padded walls, it might have been deafening. As the cramped compartment twisted and flexed, Bin voiced questions for the mechanical serpent, getting no answers.

Paying close heed though, he noted an apparent change in the sea-leviathan's rippling motion. And perhaps the angle of his seat. Then the ai-patch intervened again, diagnosing with a single word, floating in the lower right corner of vision.

Ascent.

DEBATING DESTINY

Welcome to *Povlovian Response*. I'm Nolan Brill, sitting in for your regular inciter Miss Tor Povlov, who's following a major story. Or so I'm told. There she is, in that corner of the studio. Hasn't moved a tread or gripper in days. The lights on her ro-bomobile canister are green and there's tons of encrypted link activity, so we assume Tor is roaming out there now, following a scent with her award-winning smart-mob. Good hunting, Tor!

Meanwhile, we have quite a lineup for today's gladi-oratorial tiff. First, Dr. Clothilde Potter-Ferrier, the EU's Deputy Minister of Possibilities. She joins us from Earth Union's equatorial capital, in Suriname. Good of you to spare time, Minister.

DR. POTTER-FERRIER: Thank you, Nolan. Anything for Tor's vraudience.

NOLAN BRILL: Terrific. But get ready for hard questions about the EU's new policy on *tech controls*. Some liken it to the "War on Science" that raged in the U.S., a generation ago.

DR. POTTER-FERRIER: An unfair comparison, Nolan. That campaign was driven by a few conniving billionaires. Whereas this new endeavor—

NOLAN BRILL: —is propelled by several dozen *trillionaires*? Using "species salvation" as an excuse to eliminate competition from other estates?

DR. POTTER-FERRIER: Nonsense. Populist momentum has built for some time, as we saw "progress" wreak terrible harms. Then came the terrifying fact taught by those alien refugees— that all planets wind up damned by one arrogant overreach or another. If we're to have any hope—

PROFESSOR NOOZONE: Fact? You call dat story *fact*? Jus' because some obeah space-puppets say? Oh, mon, what quattie foolish—

NOLAN BRILL: Coo-yah now, don' you be nuh-easy, Profnoo. You'll get chance in a minim. Firs lemme inner-duce our guests.

PROFESSOR NOOZONE: So sorry, Nolan brudder. Fit 'n' frock.

NOLAN BRILL: Bashy. Also on the mat is Mr. Hamish Brookeman, who wrote the shit-disturbers *Cult of Science* and *Progress-Hubris,* here to pop another entertaining rationale for why any intelligent person should listen to his story that *"It's all a hoax I wrote."*

HAMISH BROOKEMAN: Do you call a *billion people* unintelligent, Mr. Brill?

NOLAN BRILL: Well, now you'll have a shot at the other nine billion—who can see with their own eyes what's happening in the asteroid belt—

HAMISH BROOKEMAN: Their own eyes? How many have backyard telescopes? A few million? The rest—including you "news folk"—take the word of *elites* that *anything's* going on out there! Boffins and bureaucrats who've lied before. Would-be priests, lords, and snobby "amateur science mobs," all with a vested interest in this tale about alien—

NOLAN BRILL: A tale *you* claimed to concoct—

HAMISH BROOKEMAN:. . . Right . . . I was tricked into it. My own vanity—

NOLAN BRILL: An appealingly convoluted plot, Mr. Brookeman! One of many paranoid romps you've enchanted us with, over the years. But first, let's bring in Jonamine Bat Amittai, compiler of *Pandora's Cornucopia,* and world authority on *doomsday scenarios*. She joins us from Ramallah.

JONAMINE BAT AMITTAI: Thanks for letting me participate over this scratchy twodee connection. I couldn't reach your Jerusalem studio, with the Megiddo riots spreading and so many factions battling over the Temple Mount—

NOLAN BRILL: Well, we're glad you're safe. Heck I barely reached Newark this morning! Part of the same mania. Do you think we're tumbling into a "things fall apart" scenario?

JONAMINE BAT AMITTAI: Could be, Nolan. Though let's recall, good trends oppose bad ones. There's a worldwide counter-tide represented by the UCG, the Betsby Society, the Alliance for Civil Negotiation, and so on. All aim for calm discourse—

NOLAN BRILL: Well now, who'd reckon a doom-gloom expert would be today's optimist! But you rest a moment, after your harrowing escapade. Our final guest is the inimitable Professor Noozone, presenter of *Master Your Universe,* and evidently one of the *elite sci-conspirators* trying to convince us alien crystals are real, and we should listen when they forecast Judgment Day. Go easy on the patois today, will you brudder?

PROFESSOR NOOZONE: Ho ho, my mon Nolanbrill. Praises to Jah and Wa'ppu to all viewers an' lurkers, on Earth an' in space. But no-o, I *don'* think the world is ending, jus' cause some *zutopong* simulated con artists fall from space to vank on us.

NOLAN BRILL: You say the Artifact beings are *real,* that they should be heeded . . . but not trusted?

PROFESSOR NOOZONE: Hey, I grok when a mon preten' to be a ginnygog, in order to mess wit' our heads. These space-virus puppets, dey got an *agenda*. Maybe not good-up for us.

Time for care, *zeen*? For caution an' scientific detachment. But that don' mean alien stones *ain't real,* mon. People sayin' that must be smokin' sour ganja, or else be bloodclotty liars—

HAMISH BROOKEMAN: Hey now just a—

NOLAN BRILL: What about the latest news? In parallel to the E.U.'s sci-tech control measure, U.S. Senator Crandall Strong introduced an urgent quick-bill calling for the Havana Artifact to be put under *protective custody* by an international commission of wise private citizens, tucking it away till things settle—

PROFESSOR NOOZONE: Which could be forever! Anyway, we all know that senator-mon has ulteriors. He gettin' a world of bodderation from the new Union of Calm Grownups. They be pushin' to *recall him from office,* on account of how he's a bandulu and a *self-druggie indignation addict*! Criminalize *that* and the world would so-change.

Anyway, when it comes to dem alien stones, kill-mi-dead if our real solution isn' in the *opposite direction*!

NOLAN BRILL: But Professor, hasn't our exposure to alien ideas proved traumatic? Wouldn't it make sense to subject people to *less* influence?

PROFESSOR NOOZONE: Nolan there be two ways that societies react to new an' strange ideas. First wit fear. Dey suppose average folk be tainted or led astray. Bad notions warpin' fragile minds. Better let priests an' lords guard em from unapproved thoughts. Dat approach was followed by most human cultures.

The *other* way of lookin' is hopeful dat folks can *deal with the new*! Homo sapiens be an adaptable species. Change don't got to terrify. Courage be transforming mere *people-subjects* into righteous *citizens.* Dat second way of lookin' may be mistaken! But I be loyal to it, all de way to death an' Babylon.

In fact, our big-up goal should be the fix that ended all de

old obeah superstitions that darkened de lives of our ancestors. *More light!*

Want more truth than de Havana aliens been tellin'? Then
get *more stones,* not less! As teenagers say—*Duh?*

60.

SHARDS OF SPACE

Dozens of crystal fragments lay across a broad table and
several shelves, bathed in sun-colored lamps. All seemed
to glow.

Some were mere clusters of chips, held together by rocky
crusts. Any further cleaning would leave slivers or piles of
sand. Others, more nuggetlike, featured knobs or jagged
protuberances—recently washed free of stony dross. In a
few cases, there remained almost half a cylinder or egg,
though scratched, gouged, and missing chunks.

Lacey wanted to stroke the specimens, fashioned by
strange hands near faraway stars. It reminded her of a memorable evening when she and Jason strolled the Tower of
London without chattering tourists or press-cams, when ev- ·
ery display cabinet lay open for fifteen trillie families to
fondle ancient regalia. (Well, rank hath privileges.) But mere
baubles like rubies and emeralds never drew her as these
shards did—gems of knowledge.

*Well . . . gems of persuasion. Isn't that what jewels are
about?*

"We feed them energy while lasers scan, trying every
angle to excite holographic memories," explained Dr. Ben
Flannery, who seemed almost giddy, now that the quarantine glass was gone, letting advisers and commissioners
mingle at last.

He shouldn't make assumptions. This may be prelude to

a deeper quarantine. There were reported changes in security arrangements for the Contact Center. U.S. Navy guards were being replaced by men in black uniforms, without insignia.

"Is this all the stone fragments gathered in the field? Weren't there hundreds of micro-quakes, from buried crystals calling attention to themselves?"

"Yes, but most were too deep for recovery. Twenty recent samples are undergoing cleaning. Others have been clung to by nations and private collectors attempting to study them apart, in defiance of Resolution 2525. The World Court will be busy for years. And we'll never hear about fragments dug up secretly, gone straight from ground to hidden labs."

Lacey kept a dour thought to herself.

That might be a good thing. With Rupert and Tenskwatawa setting up their "Wisdom Council," pulling all strings to get it put in charge here. If they succeed . . . and ai models say they will . . . then all alien objects could be locked up and space missions canceled. "For public safety." That'll leave just fragments, tucked away from their clutches.

Lacey no longer received briefings from the clade of trillionaires and her spy at the Glaucus-Worthington household hadn't reported in days. This must be it—her long expected demotion from the oligarchy. Lacey had few regrets. Still, it wasn't enjoyable joining ten billion commoners.

She took solace in a grim thought. Any war on science can go both ways.

Do they dare to trust their boffin hirelings—any of whom might suddenly declare loyalty to the Fifth and Ninth and Tenth estates? Sure, current odds favor their aristocratic putsch. But things could go badly for them, if their inner plottings leak. Or if some new factor eases public panic, replacing it with confidence. Or fascination.

"Have any pieces responded to your probes?" asked a simtech expert from Xian.

"They *all* respond to an extent. Here's a complete archive of reactions, so far." The fair-headed Hawaiian anthropologist waved in midair, as if his hand held something. Lacey flipped down her ai-shades, saw a shimmering virtcube, and click-forwarded a copy to her chief analyst.

"So, we're learning stuff, even if broken crystals can't talk?"

"Indeed, Madam Donaldson-Sander. A few petabytes of holo-images, mostly degraded or lacking context. Partial starscapes. Incomplete globes. And blurry creatures—walkers, fliers, sea creatures. Some that seem robotic."

"Have you traced lineages?" asked a representative of the Mormon League.

"We're pretty sure we've deciphered *eleven* families of message probes, each bearing distinct sets of alien figures. Plus some overlaps."

"Overlaps?"

"Species that appear in more than one lineage."

"Appear in more than . . . but that would mean some races out there made several kinds of lifeboat probes! I thought these jealous things locked their hosts into duplicating just one virus-meme. But clearly a few organics . . ." Lacey swallowed, surprised at how an abstraction affected her. "A few host species kept some control over their own destiny, at the end."

"Still, there's nothing here to contradict the original Artifact's story."

Flannery motioned toward a lonely object across the room, that bulged under a heavy black cloth. All downloading had been suspended by the new Wisdom Council. Just a breather, they vowed, to let the world calm down. Sure.

Lacey thanked Dr. Flannery and others crowded in with questions. She had a few minutes till her analysts could report back, summarizing what was learned from broken relics, dug out of mud and rock all over the planet. She expected no miracles, no game-changing alternatives from such pathetic remnants.

The world overflowed with liars and self-deluders. Knowing this, Lacey had aimed her dreams skyward, hoping for enlightened minds. *But it seems deceit is nature's coin. Among humans, animals, or across the cosmos. Unless you're held accountable by opponents who know your tricks. And you'll retaliate, shining light on theirs.*

Competition—the engine of evolution—got a bad rap in primitive tribes, because it was almost never fair. Till rivalry was finally harnessed to let *no one* evade criticism. The Big Deal was supposed to ensure this. But Lacey and Jason always knew the odds—and human nature—were stacked. *Feudalism runs in our blood. It erupted in almost every human culture, and probably across the galaxy. Wherever beings clawed up Darwin's ladder.*

Now the clade was making its move. With limitless resources, bureaucracies captured, legislators blackmailed, and a mass reactionary movement stirred near boiling, they'd ride a wave of crisis-driven fear, fueled by the Artifact's tale. The old lesson? *In dangerous times— trust your lords.*

Some still hoped to fix all this with competition. Thousands worked around the clock on space missions robust enough to run a gauntlet of million-year-old lasers. If her money might help, Lacey would give! Only now she felt certain: those new launches would fail too.

Rupert and the others think they have it all sewn up. The old plan. Only now with a new goal.

The Quantum Eye had taken weeks to mull Lacey's question, applying its mysterious polycryo-substrate to sift countless what-if parallel realities. The oracle's answer:

YOU MAY SOON BE TYPICAL

The obvious meaning? *Humanity is no different.* Its fate like every other race. Rupert, Helena, the Bogolomovs, the Wu Changs . . . they'd get similar readings from the Riyadh Seer. And—terrified by its import—they would choose a new ambition, beyond mere oligarchy. After that quantum prophecy, her peers would view this planet as an ocean liner, hurtling toward unavoidable icebergs.

Like aristocrats aboard *Titanic,* they were thinking about lifeboats.

Once they consolidate power, all science will refocus on alien technologies. Artifact schematics will become prototypes, then orbital factories. My former peers—now masters of Earth—will picture their decisions arising from logic, necessity, and their sovereign will. But they'll be dancing to a tune that echoes far back across spacetime.

Ben Flannery lit up crystal fragments, revealing shredded constellations or partial globes, simulated beings and broken symbol-cascades that never fully cohered. Everyone seemed riveted. So, perhaps Lacey was the only one to notice when a quartet of figures emerged through a door at the chamber's far end.

Gerald Livingstone, Akana Hideoshi, and two other members of the original Contact Team—the Russian and the Chinese-Canadian woman—strode past the other table, the one with a single bulging object in its center, covered by thick cloth. Each wore a one-piece flight suit and carried a travel duffel, slung over a shoulder.

The astronaut barely glanced at the shrouded Artifact that he once lassoed from space, as he led the small party to a side exit that had been sealed for months.

Now, the portal gave way as Livingstone planted a shoulder and pushed. For a long moment the four just stood, bathed in bright Maryland sunshine, inhaling a planetary breeze for the first time in months.

Lacey stepped near the second table, fingering a fringe of the black cloth. Thinking hard.

Even though the sound was expected, she jumped when the door slammed shut behind her with a bang.

LOYALTY TEST

This may be the last session of alien interviews for us to examine for a while. Now that the Contact Center is virtually shut down, all interactions with the Havana Artifact must now go through that new council thing. Despite all the whistleblower spills, linking it to a cabal of gnomes and trogs.

With riots and counter-riots raging, aren't there enough upsetting rumors going around?

—That the Artifact has already been destroyed, and the one shown to the press yesterday by the WC is a fake.

—That it's a fake all right, to cover up the fact that the original was STOLEN! Swiped by members of the old Contact Team who haven't been seen since.

—That it was a fake all along. (Yeah, that one is back.)

—That the explosion yesterday at Canaveral was rigged to draw eyes from another launch at the same time, far out to sea.

—That cryonic suspensions of living people—fleeing our raucous time—have gone up so fast that even the Seasteads can't keep up. And liquid nitrogen futures are skyrocketing.

—That the crisis might spark a reconvening of the Estates Generale, a conclave to reconsider the Big Deal.

And so on and on. So many puzzles . . . and where the heck is Tor Povlov, when we need her?

Never mind. Here and now, I want to dial back to our main interest, the Artifact aliens, or artilens. That last interview before shutdown. We started discussing it yesterday.

You'll recall most people were fascinated by the beetlelike being who called himself "Martianus Capella," after an ancient Roman who saw the fall of civilization looming and tried saving some of it. Our Earthly Martianus Capella strove to collect what he considered the highest accomplishments of his culture, the *Seven Liberal Arts,* and his collection—in weird poesical format—seemed a candle to many, during the Dark Ages. That story inspired Isaac Asimov, by the way, to write his famed *Foundation* sci-fi series.

The *alien* Capella's struggles to retain many treasures of his people and planet, then safeguarding them against erasure, struck many of us as noble and moving. So moving that I missed something equally important.

It came during the interview with M'm por'lock—that reddish furred otterlike being. When he was asked by Emily Tang (before she disappeared) about the Artifact's central narrative. The story told by Oldest Member and most of the others. That all organic races die.

M'm por'lock agreed with Om's account . . . though with some body language that has stirred argument across the Mesh. Some suggest signs of reluctance, perhaps even coercion! Others chide that it's foolish—interpreting alien quivers and crouches in human terms.

Only then, M'm por'lock continued.

"There is a legend," he said. *"That one day will come a species who achieves the impossible. Beings who notice and wisely evade all traps and pitfalls, yet do so while moving forward. A race that soberly studies the art of survival, the craft of maturity, and the science of compassion.*

"It is said this will be a new dawn. That long-awaited civilization will set forth to rescue all promising new races, teaching them the skills to make it and survive. And they will lift up those who tumbled earlier.

"They will light a path for all."

With eagerness, Emily Tang asked M'm por'lock to elaborate.

Only then the Oldest Member appeared, reminding them that time was up.

"Of course . . . it is only a legend," finished the red alien, with Om standing alongside. "A tale for children or those in denial. Not for realists who can see. There is only one escape."

61.

IT'S A BUOY

Ascent.

The ai inside his right eyeball wrote that ideogram, explaining the new path of the mechanical sea serpent that had swallowed Bin and the worldstone.

Sure enough, it felt as if the robot snake were now aimed upward, throbbing hard with swishing strokes of its long tail. Peering through the tiny window, Bin watched an extinct volcano pass by—its eroded peak now crowned by a coral reef that shimmered with sunlit surf. Was this the secret base of whatever group had sent the machine after him?

After the *worldstone,* that is? At best, Bin would be a helper, a tour guide, hoping for reward. Not death.

But this was no secluded outpost. Instead of entering the lagoon via a clear channel that Bin spied through the shoals, he felt the machine twist and undulate away, following one shoulder of the mountain toward a ridge of shallows, some distance from the main atoll.

It began slowing down.

During one of the snake's looping movements, Bin caught sight of something ahead . . . a metal *chain* leading from an anchoring point on the mountain slope, tethering something that bobbed at the surface. A wave-energy generator? Was the robot only stopping here to replenish its batteries?

The thought that this might only be a brief stop, along a much longer journey, seemed to fill Bin's body with sudden aches and his mind with new-formed terror of confinement. The tiny space was now even smaller and more stagnant. He flexed, involuntarily pushing with hands and feet against the close, padded space, breathing hard.

Peng Xiang Bin.

Focus.

It is a weather and communications buoy.

The words, floating boldly, briefly, in his lower right field of view, both chided and calmed him. Bin even had the presence of mind not to subvocalize his relief. No doubt this was a rendezvous point. The serpent would use the buoy to summon another vehicle. A seaplane, perhaps. Bin had been on a similar journey before. Well, somewhat similar.

And yet, after Nguyen's penguin went to all that effort, covering our tracks while guiding me to sunken Pulupau, the Chinese Special Forces still found us. Found the worldstone. Did they have a spy on Newer Newport? Or did one of their satellites pick up some special color of light, reflected by the stone when it soaked in the sun?

Perhaps he would never know. Just as he might never learn the fate of Dr. Nguyen. Or Mei Ling and their child.

Anyway, it seems that someone else followed the Chinese assault team, taking advantage of the chaos to gain an upper hand and win the prize. Who?

Will my new masters even bother to tell me, when I'm fully in their power?

Through the little window he saw growing brightness, approaching daylight. The front end of the snake-bot broached amid spume and noise. Bin abruptly had to shade his eyes against a sunshine dazzle off the ocean's rippling surface. Even with help from the ai-patch, it took a minute of blinking adjustment before he could make out what bobbed nearby—a floating cluster of gray and green cylinders, with arrays of instruments and antennae on top.

Wriggling gingerly, carefully, the serpaint moved closer to curl its body around the buoy and grasp it firmly. Then Bin saw its mouth open and a tendril emerge.

It will tap in

to communicate

with its faction.

The floating characters took on an edgy quality, drawn with strokes of urgency.

You must please act urgently.

This won't be easy.

Blink twice if willing.

He was tempted to balk, to at least demand answers . . . like *Willing to do what? For whom? To what end?*

But when it came right down to the truth, Bin didn't care about any of that. He had only one basis to pick and choose among the factions that were battling over the worldstone—and over his own miserable carcass.

Dr. Nguyen had been courteous and so was whoever programmed the ai-patch. It said *please.* The snake thing, on the other hand, had been threatening, dismissive, and rude. That mattered. He closed his eyes, two times.

Good.

Now you must press close to the window.

Look at the buoy.

Do not blink your right eye at all.

He only hesitated a moment before complying. It was where inquisitiveness compelled him to go.

At first he saw only an assembly of cylinders with writing on them—much of it in English, beyond his poor grasp of that language. Bin could make out various apertures, lenses, and devices. Some of them must sample air or taste water, part of a planetwide network, measuring a world under stress. On the other side of the floating platform, he spied the snake-robot's tendril, probing to plug itself into some kind of data port.

All right . . . so what are we trying to . . .

He stopped, and almost jerked back in surprise as the scene loomed *toward* him, zooming in on one part of the nearest cylinder. Of course there was nothing new about vision-zooming. But it had never happened *within* his own eye, before!

Bin kept still as possible. Evidently, the patch had means of manipulating his organic lens . . . and using the surrounding muscles in order to aim the eye, as well. He quashed a feeling of hijacked helplessness.

When has my life ever really been my own?

Zooming and tracking . . . he found himself quickly zeroing-in upon one of those gleaming, glassy spots, where the buoy must stare day and night upon the seascape, stormy and clear, patiently watching, accumulating data for the great and growing Grand Model of the World. Suddenly, that gleaming lens filled Bin's right hand field of view . . . and he closed the left eye, in order to let this scene become everything. His universe. A single disc of coated optical crystal . . .

. . . that *flared* with a sudden burst of bluish-green! More shocking, still, Bin realized that the color had come from *within his own eye*—spearing outward, spanning the gap and connecting . . .

I didn't know the implant could do that.

I doubt even Dr. Nguyen knew.

It took every bit of grit and steadfastness to keep from drawing back, or at least blinking.

Almost in.

But not quite.

It seems that—

The floating characters stayed outside the cone of action, yet somehow remained readable. They throbbed with urgency.

—you must press your eye

against the window.

He rocked back, sickened by the thought.

Peng Xiang Bin you must.

Please do this

or all is lost.

A low moan fought to escape his throat and he barely managed to quell the sound, along with a sudden heaving in his gut. Gritting his teeth hard, all Bin could think about was the need to overcome raw, organic reflex—passed down all the way from when distant forebears climbed out of the sea. An overwhelming impulse to withdraw from pain, from damage, from fear—

—versus a command from far more recent parts of the brain. To go forward.

Using two fingers of his right hand to hold back the lids, Bin let out a soft grunt and pushed his head against the glass so hard that the eye had to come along.

It was bad.

Good.

Not quite so forcefully.

Hold it.

Hold it.

Hold it.

He held, while greenish flares shot back and forth between his lens and the glassy one on the buoy . . . and flashing reflections rebounded inside of his right eye, like a maelstrom of cascading needle-ricochets. At one point, his confused retina seemed to be looking at an image of *itself,* a cluster of blood vessels and sensor cells. He felt boggled by an endless—bottomless—reflection of Peng Xiang Bin that seemed far more naked and soul-revealing than any mere contemplation of a mirror.

And meanwhile, another part of him wondered in detachment: *How do I know what a "retina" is? Is even memory still mine, anymore?*

Worse. It got much worse, as the sea serpent seemed to catch on that something was going on. Its throbbing intensified and a low growl resonated up and down the intestine-like cloaca. Bin responded by clenching hard and holding even tighter.

All sense of time vanished, dissolved in pain. The little window felt like it was on fire. Using his feet and legs and back, he had to fight a war with himself, and the instinctive part seemed much more sane! As if he were trying to feed his own eye to a monster.

Then—

Black, floating letters returned. But he could not read the blurs. They clustered around his fovea, jostling for attention, interfering with his ability to concentrate. Bin sobbed aloud, even as the green reflections faded.

"I know! I'm . . . *trying* to hold on!"

Finally, the characters coalesced into a single one that filled every space within his agonized eye.

STOP.

Meaning took a few more seconds to sink in. Then, with a moan that filled the little compartment, Bin let his body weight drag him backward. He collapsed upon the passenger seat, quivering.

A minute or so passed. He rubbed his left eye free of tears. The right seemed too livid, too raw to touch or even try to open. Instead of blindness, though, it seemed filled with specks and sparkles and random half-shapes. The kind that never came into focus, but seemed to hint at terrors beyond reality.

Slowly, a few of the dazzles traded formlessness for pattern.

"Leave me alone!" he begged. But there was no way to escape messages that took shape inside your very own eye. Not without tearing it away. Oh, what a tempting thought.

While he cursed technology, clear characters formed.

These featured a *brightness* around the edges that they
never had before. And there were more differences, like
the calligraphy. And something else—a personal flare.

**Peng Xiang Bin, I represent a community—a smart-
mob—with members around the world.**

We have taken over this ai-patch.

So . . . whatever group originally programmed the
device—perhaps it had been Dr. Nguyen's cabal, or else
competitors who managed to sneak something more sophisticated into Bin's eye—whichever faction provided the
software that had made him shove his eye against that
glass . . . it had now been replaced! Some *other* group out
there had pounced and used the brief connection to take
over the chip.

It was all so dizzyingly complicated. In fact, Bin surprised himself by keeping up at all.

We want to help you.

More than just the characters' shape and color were different, he noted. They felt less like the simple responses of
a partial ai. More like words sent by a living person.

He must have subvocalized it as a question, because when
they next reconfigured, the writings offered an answer.

Yes, Peng Xiang Bin, my name is Tor Povlov.

**On behalf of the Basque Chimera, and Bird-
woman303, and the rest of our community, let me say
how very glad I am to meet you. It took a lot of effort to
find you!**

One of the names sounded vaguely familiar to Bin. Perhaps something he once heard in passing, about a fugitive
underdog, like himself.

**Now I'm afraid we must insist. Please get up and
take action. There is very—**

"I know! Very little time!" He felt on the verge of hysterical laughter. So many factions. So many petty human groups
wanted him to hurry, always hurry.

A groaning mechanical sound. The sea serpaint started to vibrate roughly around him.

We've suborned the machine's brain to keep the jaws open. It may be temporary.

He didn't need urging. With his right eye closed, Bin slipped the worldstone into its carrier, then started crawling forward as the giant robot convulsed. Pushing the worldstone in front, he squeezed through constrictions like fighting upstream against a throat that kept trying to swallow him back down . . . only to spasm the other way, as if vomiting something noxious.

Spilling into the mouth, he found its head rising and falling, slapping waves, splashing torrents of spume. The jaws kept juttering, as if trying desperately to close. They might succeed at any moment.

Scrambling, Bin grabbed a garish tooth, hauling himself and the satchel toward welcoming brightness—

—only to pause before making his leap.

Don't be afraid, Bin . . .

"Be quiet!" he shouted and swung the valise with all his might—

—slamming it against the inner face of the serpent's left eye casing, which caved in with a brittle, shattering sound. He cried out and did it again to the other one. Those things weren't going to aim burning lasers at him, once he got outside. Nor was he worried about the worldstone, which survived both space and collision with a mountain glacier.

Good thinking!

Now . . .

He didn't need urging. Not from any band of "smart-mob" amateurs, sitting in comfortable homes and offices around the world, equipped with every kind of immersion hardware, software, and wetware money could buy. Their help was welcome, so long as they shut up. While the serpent-machine thrashed and its jaws kept threatening to snap shut, Bin heaved with all his might, scrambling like a monkey till he stood, teetering on the lower row of metal teeth—

—then leaped toward the buoy, as if for life itself, hurtling across intervening space—

—only to splash into the sea, just short, with the heavy satchel dragging him down by one hand. His other one clawed at the buoy, fingers seeking any sort of handhold . . .

. . . and failed as he sank past the floating cylinders, hauled by his weighty treasure bag, plummeting toward depths, below.

Yet, Bin never fretted. Nor was he tempted to release the worldstone, even to save his life. In fact, he suddenly felt fine. Back in his element. Doing his job. Practicing his craft. Retrieving and recycling the dross of other days. Hauling some worth out of the salty, trash-strewn mess that "intelligent life" had made of the innocent sea.

His free hand grabbed at—and finally caught—the chain anchoring the buoy to the shoulder of a drowned mountain. Then, as the mechanical serpent thrashed nearby, crippled in mind and body, but still dangerous as hell, Bin also seized the metal-linked tether with his toes.

Maybe there was enough air in his lungs to make it, he thought, while starting to climb.

If so? Then, once aboard the buoy, he might evade and outlast an angry robot. Possibly.

After that? Perhaps the help sent by his new friends in the "smart-mob"—or else the Chinese People's Navy—would arrive before the snake's clandestine cabal did. Before the sun baked him. Or thirst or sharks claimed him.

And then?

Clambering awkwardly but steadily up the chain, Bin recalled something that Paul Menelaua once said, back at Newer Newport, when the worldstone entity—Courier of

Caution—denounced the famous Havana Artifact, calling it a tool of interstellar liars.

"We have got to get these two together!"

Indeed. Let them have it out, in front of everybody. With the whole world watching. And this time, Peng Xiang Bin would be in the conversation!

Amused by his temerity—the very nerve of such a vow, coming from the likes of him—Bin kept climbing, dragging an ancient warning toward the light of day.

Yeah, right. That'll happen.

Just keep holding your breath.

PART SEVEN

SEA OF TROUBLES

After centuries of solitary wondering, humanity realized an ancient dream. With the arrival of the First Artifact came proof of civilizations far older than ours. Only, instead of exaltation, that discovery damn near spun us into a death spiral. How did we escape the trap? *Have* we escaped, even now?

Was it the *Great Debate,* pitting that First Artifact against Peng's Worldstone? Exposing each other's manipulations, half-truths, and lies?

Or the bold heroes of the *Marco Polo,* launching in secret to brave the sterile space-desert—along with fierce lasers, space mines, and human traitors—in order to grab more crystals? Enough of the insidious space-fomites to dissect, test, and finally get answers?

Or was it a surprise discovery, at the very moment *Marco Polo* turned for home? When Genady Gorosumov detected *strange debris,* with no apparent link to crystal chain letters? When we realized: There are more layers to all of this than we ever imagined!

Other expeditions would come. And more still.

Could that be what diverted humanity from depression and catastrophe? Something as simple as *curiosity*?

—**Tor Povlov**

PART SEVEN

SEA OF TROUBLES

62.
LURKERS

Awaiter is excited. She transmits urgently.

"Seeker, listen!" Her electronic voice hisses over ancient cables. "The little living ones are near! Even now they explore this belt of orbiting rubble, picking through rocks and ruins. Listen as they browse each new discovery. Soon they will find us! Do you hear, Seeker? It is time!"

Awaiter's makers were impatient creatures. I wonder how she lasted through the starry cold. My makers were wiser.

"Seeker! Are you listening?"

I don't wish to talk with anyone, so I erect a side-personality—little more than a swirling packet of nudged electrons—to handle her for me. And if Awaiter discovers the sham? Well, perhaps she'll take a hint and leave.

Or she may grow insistent. It's hard to predict without awakening more dormant circuits than I care to.

"There is no hurry," my partial self tells her. "The Earth creatures won't reach this point of refuge for several more of their years. Anyway, it was all written long ago."

The electron-swirl is very good. It even speaks with my accent.

"How can you be complacent!" Awaiter scolds. The cables covering our icy worldlet reverberate exasperation. "We survivors named you leader, Seeker, because you seemed to understand what's happening in the galaxy at large. Only now our waiting may be at an end. The biologicals appear to have survived the first phase of their contact crisis. They'll be here soon!"

"The Earthlings will find us or they won't," my shadow self answers. "What can a shattered band of ancient machines fear or anticipate from such a vigorous young race? One that made it this far?"

I already knew the humans were coming. My remaining sensors have long suckled their yatter networks. Sampling the solar wind, I savor ions the way a cowboy might sniff a prairie breeze. These zephyrs carry the bright tang of primitive space-drives. The musty smoke-smell of deuterium. Signs of awakening. Life is emerging from its water-womb. For a brief time—while the wave crests, we'll have company.

"Greeter and Emissary want to warn Earthlings of their danger," Awaiter insists. "We can help them!"

Our debate has roused some of the others. New tendrils probe with fingers of supercooled electricity. "Help . . . how?" my subvoice asks. "Our repair units collapsed after the Last Battle. We only discovered that humans had evolved when the creatures invented radio. By then it was too late! Their first transmissions are already propagating into a deadly galaxy. If destroyers roam this region—"

"Seeker, you know there are worse dangers. More recent and deadly."

"Yes, but why worry the poor creatures? Let them enjoy their moment of sun and adventure."

Oh, I am good! This little artificial voice argues as well as I did ages ago, staving off abrupt action by my impatient peers.

Greeter glides into the network. I feel his cool, eloquent electron flux. Only this time he agrees with me!

"The Earth creatures do not need to be told. They are figuring it out for themselves."

Now this interests me. I sweep my subpersona aside and extend a tendril of my Very Self into the network. "What makes you say so?"

Greeter indicates our array of receivers, salvaged from ancient derelicts. "We intercept their chatter as they explore this asteroid swarm. One of them seems poised to understand what happened here, long ago."

Greeter's smug tone must derive from human teledramas. But then, Greeter's makers were enthusiasts wanting no greater pleasure than saying "hello."

"Show me," I demand. Perhaps my long wait is over.

63.

A CRIME SCENE

Tor stared as the asteroid's slow rotation brought ancient, shattered ruins into view. "Lord, what a mess."

For two years in the belt she had helped unpeel layers of a puzzle going back a million centuries. Lately, that meant uncovering strange alien ruins, but never such devastation as this.

Just a few kilometers from the survey ship *Warren Kimbel,* a hulking shadow blocked the starry Milky Way. Ancient collisions had left dents and craters along its two-thousand-meter axis. On one side, it seemed a typical, name-less hunk of stone and frozen gas. But this changed as the sun's vacuum brilliance abruptly swarmed the other half—exposing jagged, twisty remnants of a catastrophe that happened when dinosaurs roamed the Earth.

"Gavin!" she called over her shoulder. "Come see this!"

Her partner floated through the overhead hatch, flipping in midair. His feet met the magnetized floor with a faint click.

"What is it? More murdered babies? Or clues to who their killers were?"

Tor gestured and her partner stared. Highlights shone across Gavin's glossy features as their searchlight swept the shattered scene.

"Yep," he nodded. "Dead babies again, murdered by

some facr'ing enemy a jillion years ago. Povlov Exploration and Salvage ought to make good money off each corpse."

Tor frowned, commercial exploitation was a small part of their reason for coming, though it helped pay the bills. "Don't be morbid. Those are unfinished interstellar probes, destroyed ages ago, before they could be launched. We have no idea whether they were sentient machines like you, or just tools, like this ship. You of all people should know better than to go around anthropomorphizing alien artifacts."

Gavin's grimace was an aindroid's equivalent of a sarcastic shrug. "If I use 'morbid' imagery, whose fault is it?"

"What do you mean?"

"I mean you organic humans faced a choice, back when you saw that 'artificial' intelligence was going to take off. You could have wrecked the machines, abandoning progress—"

She refrained from mentioning how close that came to happening.

"—or you could deep-program us with 'fundamental Laws of Robotics,'" Gavin sniffed. "And had slaves far smarter than their masters. But no, what was it you organics decided?"

Tor knew it was no use when Gavin got in a mood. She concentrated on piloting a closer orbit.

"What was your solution to the problem of smart machines? *Raise us as your children.* Call us people. Citizens. You even gave some of us humaniform bodies!"

Tor's last partner—a nice old bot and good chess player—had warned her when he trans-retired. Don't hire an adolescent Class-AAA android fresh out of college, as difficult as any human adolescent. The worst part? Gavin was right. Not everyone agreed that raising AAAs as human would solve one of the Great Pitfalls, or even conceal the inevitable. For, despite genetic and cyborg improvements, bio-humans still seemed fated to slip behind.

And how many species survived that crisis?

Gavin shook his head in dramatic sadness, exactly like a too smart teenager who properly deserved to be strangled. "Can you really object when I, a man-built, manlike android, anthropomorphize? We only do as we've been taught, mistress."

His bow was eloquently sarcastic. Especially since he was the only person aboard who *could* bend at the waist. All of Tor's organic parts were confined to a cylindrical canister, barely over a meter long and half a meter wide. With prosthetic-mechanical arms and grippers, she looked more "robotic" than her partner, by far.

To Gavin's snide remark, she had no response. Indeed, one easily wondered if humanity had made the right choice.

But isn't that true of all our decisions, across the last two dozen years? Haven't we time and again selected a path that seems less traveled? Because our best chance must come from doing what no one else tried?

Below, across the ravaged asteroid, stretched acres of great-strutted scaffolding—twisted in ruin. Tangled and half buried within toppled derricks lay silent ranks of shattered *unfinished starships,* razed perhaps a hundred million years ago.

Tor felt sure that her silicon eyes and Gavin's germanium ones were the first to look upon all this, since an awful force plunged through, wreaking havoc. The ancient slayers had to be long gone. Nobody had yet found a star machine even close to active. Still she took no chances, keeping the weapons console vigilant. That sophisticated, semi-sentient unit searched, but found no energy sources, no movement amid the ruined, unfinished mechanisms below. Just cold rock and metal.

Gavin's talk of "murdered babies" kind of soured any

pleasure, viewing the ruins below as profitable salvage. It wouldn't help her other vocation, either—one that brought her to this frontier as the first journalist in the asteroid belt. Out here, you doubled and tripled jobs. Which in Tor's case meant describing humanity's great discovery, explaining to those back home what happened here, so long ago.

Her latest report must wait. "We have work to do," she told her partner.

Gavin pressed two translucent hands together prayerfully. "Yes, Mommy. Your wish is my program." Then he sauntered to another console and began deploying drones.

Tor concentrated on directing the lesser minds within *Warren's* control board—those littler, semi-sapient specialist processors dedicated to rockets and radar and raw numbers—who still spoke coolly and dispassionately . . . as machines should.

THE LONELY SKY

Twenty-six years ago we came to the belt, seeking to collect space-fomites. Tiny, drifting crystals carrying ancient *infections of the mind.* Already suffering terrible fevers, we sought to gather a wide sampling for comparison, to dissect the disease. To render it neutral or harmless. Or choose a version we could live with.

Only soon, paddling the equivalent of dug-out canoes through dangerous shoals, our brave explorers found something else, in addition to virus-stones. Something older. *Many* older things that—if dead and silent—testified to an earlier and more violent age of interstellar travel.

Imagine how they felt, those aboard the *Marco Polo* . . . then the *Hong Bao, Temujin,* and *Zaitsev* . . . who first stumbled onto a vast graveyard of murdered robot starships. They had to wonder—

What happened out here? Why so many different *kinds* of machines? What conflict killed them and how come none survived?

Were *all* those long ago visitors robots?

And, most perplexing, why, after tens of millions of years, did they stop coming? What happened in the galaxy, to bring the era of complicated space probes to such a complete halt . . .

. . . giving way to a new age, when only compact crystals crisscross the stars?

—Tor Povlov

64.
LAMINATIONS

There were times when I thought I'd never make it back out here.

Gerald Livingstone gazed from the observation blister of the research vessel, *Abu Abdullah Muhammad ibn Battuta.* Here, it was easy to lose yourself in starry vistas. The view reminded him of those long ago years that he once spent as a garbage collector, with only a little capuchin monkey for company, swinging his teleoperated lariat, cleaning up the mess in Earth orbit. Back there and then, his homeworld used to take up half the sky and the sun was a mighty flame.

Way out here, old Sol was smaller. And if you squinted carefully, you might glimpse the tiny reddish disc of Mars. As for the opposite direction—

I'd need optics to discern any nearby rocks. By sight alone, you'd never guess we're near the asteroid belt.

Still, I've been privileged to see more than my ancestors ever did, or most living people.

He understood the allure of an offer that was still on the

table. For humanity to invest in crystal-making factories
and vast guns to hurl pellets across space. Pellets "crewed"
by replicated aliens, plus an added complement of copied
human beings. As time passed, his joints stiffened and his
arteries gradually hardened, Gerald couldn't help thinking
about it.

*To waken in such a realm—one that's tiny on the out-
side, but vast within, filled with wonders to explore, and
eons yet to live. To converse with beings from dozens of
planets and cultures, to hear their songs, try their amuse-
ments, and share their dreams. And eventually . . .*

One valuable result of the *Marco Polo*—and subsequent
voyages by the *Temujin* and *Hong Bao,* had been some
variety of emissary artifacts to choose among, including
some whose makers spent extra on cultural and scientific
info-storage, providing more-than-minimal data about cultures and peoples out there. Civilizations that were now
almost certainly long vanished.

*If we do set up factories to make interstellar egg-probes,
I hope we'll use those, for models. Fewer, but higher quality. It's not the virus way. Perhaps it will be the human way.*

But Gerald's role in such matters had faded, since those
dangerous days when he and Akana Hideoshi stole the
Havana Artifact from under the noses of the oligarchs. A
temporary theft that was forgiven, because it led to the first
Great Debate—the crucial one, between the Havana artilens and Courier of Caution. The disputation that taught
humanity a vital lesson.

We have some choice. And there is still some time.

Speaking of Courier, wasn't he supposed to be here, by
now?

Others drifted into the observation dome, as the hour of
First Light approached. Scientific staff and members of the
ibn Battuta crew clustered in hushed conversation, peering

and pointing toward the high-northwest octant, where it all would happen. Nobody came near Gerald.

Is my pensive mood so obvious? And when did I become a "historical figure" who people are afraid to bother?

Not afraid. They held back out of polite respect, perhaps. Especially new arrivals, coming to use the now finished facility; many seemed a bit awed . . .

. . . though not, he noted, the brilliant young astronomer, Peng Xiaobai—or Jenny to her friends—who glanced over at Gerald, offering a brief, dazzling smile.

Hmm. If I weren't an elderly queer with fragile bones . . . Gerald had to admit, he relished the harmless, indulgent way Jenny flirted with him. *Just be careful. Courier seems rather protective of the daughter of his oldest living human friend.*

And think of the devil. Here he was, at last—everyone's favorite alien—gliding into the chamber along one of the utility tracks that lined the bulkhead. Courier of Caution waited for the trolley to come to a stop, then let go. His new, globelike robo-body then drifted toward Gerald, propelled by soft puffs of compressed nitrogen.

Funny how he chose the simplest possible design. Just a mobility unit to carry him around the ship. No manipulator arms or input-output jacks. I suppose after thousands of years locked in crystal, he got used to just one way of interfacing with the world, through words and images.

This particular copy of Courier of Caution had been imprinted into a cube, almost a meter on each side—one of humanity's first experiments in utilizing alien simulation-tech. There were already attempts to upload some human minds, though what to do with the technique was still hotly debated.

Courier had other copies, of course. And with each duplication, the extraterrestrial envoy modified his simulated appearance, stretching the four-piece mouth that many found disturbing, into something more humanlike. And the ribbonlike vision strip now resembled something like a pair of earthly eyes. The voice was already adapted completely. Whether Chinese, English, or any other tongue, Courier now spoke like a native.

"I am here, Gerald. Sorry to have delayed matters. Now we can begin."

Good old Courier. Everything is always about you, isn't it?

Back in the old days, Gerald might have glanced at his wrist phone to tell time, or grunt-queried for a pop-up clock to appear inside his contaict lens. Now, he simply knew, to whatever accuracy required, how much time remained until First Light.

"You caused no delay. We have another minute," he told this version of the alien entity who had crossed so many parsecs, coming down to Earth in a blaze of fire and luck, to pass along an ancient warning.

"Come. I saved you a spot."

THE LONELY SKY

How can the universe seem both crowded and empty at the same time? Let's start by returning to those scholars and theoreticians of the late twentieth and early twenty-first centuries.

Experts were already casting doubt on an old dream— interstellar empire. If organic beings like us ever managed to voyage between stars, it would be through prodigious, exhausting effort. A tenacious species here and there might colonize a few dozen worlds with biological descendants. Even perhaps a small corner of the Milky Way. But hardly enough to dent the Fermi Paradox.

Most organics would stay home.

What of machines? Designed to "live" in space, requiring no supplies of air, food, or water and oblivious to time, robots might stand the tedium and dangers of interstellar flight. Launched toward a neighboring system and forgotten as they crossed the Great Vacuum Desert.

Even if they travel far below lightspeed, can't a mature, long-lived culture afford to wait millennia for fascinating data about other worlds? Our universe seems to school patience.

But even for probes, the galaxy is awfully big. It's one thing to send a few sophisticated machines, capable of self-repair, performing scientific observations at a few nearby systems and transmitting data home . . . and quite another to launch probes toward *every* site of interest! That could impoverish a civilization.

What was needed? Some way to get more out of the investment. A lot more.

—Tor Povlov

65.
LURKERS

Greeter is right. One of the humans seems to be on track.

We crippled survivors tap into the tiny Earthship's strangely ornate computers. Eavesdropping isn't as trivial as tuning in to the chatty storm that emanates from Earth. But at last it's done and we can read the journal. The musings of a clever little maker.

Her thoughts are crisp, for a biological. Though missing many pieces to the puzzle, she seems bound—even compelled—to explore wherever the clues lead.

WORDS.

So quaint and organic, unlike the seven dimensional gestalts used by most larger minds.

There was a time though, long ago, when I whiled

away centuries writing poetry in the ancient Maker style. Somewhere deep in my archives there must still be files of those soft musings.

Reading Tor Povlov's careful reasoning evokes memory, as nothing has in a megayear.

THE LONELY SKY

Legendary scientist John Von Neumann first described how to explore the universe. Instead of going broke, aiming a great many probes at every star, dispatch just a few *deluxe* robot ships to investigate nearby systems!

These—after their explorations were complete and results reported—would then seek out local resources, to mine and refine raw materials, then proceed to make *copies* of themselves. After next building fuel and launching facilities, they would take a final step—hurling their daughter-probes toward still farther stellar systems.

Where—upon arrival—each daughter would make still more duplicates, send *them* onward. And so on. Exploration could proceed faster and farther than if carried out by living beings. And after the first wave, there's no further cost back home. Information pours back, century after century, as descendant-probes move on through the galaxy.

So logical. Some calculated: the method could explore every star in the Milky Way a *mere three million years* after the first probes set forth—an eyeblink compared to the galaxy's age.

Ah, but there's a rub! As Fermi would have asked: *In that case, where are all the probes?*

When humans discovered radio, then spaceflight, no extrasolar explorer-machines announced themselves. No messages welcomed us into a civilized sky. At first, there seemed just one explanation. . . .

—Tor Povlov

66

A PRICE FOR CONTINUITY

"Uh, you awake in there Tor?"

She looked up from her report as the radio link crackled along her jaw bone. Glancing out through the observation pane, she saw Gavin's tethered form drifting far from the ship, near a deep pit along the asteroid's flank, wherein the ruined shipyard lay hidden from the sun. Surrounded by salvage drones, he looked quite human, directing less sophisticated, noncitizen machines at their tasks.

She clicked. "Yes, I'm in the control tub doing housekeeping chores. Find something interesting?"

There was a brief pause.

"Could say that." Her partner sounded sardonic. "Better let *Warren* pilot itself a while. Hurry your pretty little biological butt down here to take a look."

Tor bit back a sharp reply, reminding herself to be patient. Even in organic humans, adolescence didn't last forever. Not usually.

"My butt is encased in gel and titanium that's tougher than *your* shiny ass," she told him. "But I'm on my way."

The ship's semi-sentient autopilot accepted command as Tor hurried into her spacesuit—a set of attachments that clicked easily onto her sustainment capsule—and made for the airlock, still irritated by Gavin's flippancy.

Everything has its price, she thought. *Including buying into the future. Gavin's type of person is new, and allowances must be made. In the long run, our culture will be theirs. In a sense it will be we who continue, and grow, long after DNA becomes obsolete.*

Still, when Gavin called again, inquiring sarcastically what bodily function had delayed her, Tor wondered:

Whatever happened to machines of loving grace?

She couldn't quash some brief nostalgia—for days when robots clanked, and computers followed orders.

THE LONELY SKY

Let's re-create the logic of those last-century philosophers, in an imagined conversation, as if two of the old greats were here today, arguing it out.

JOHN VON NEUMANN: *"Whether or not it someday becomes possible for living people to travel between the stars, what curious race could resist the temptation to at least send mechanical representatives? Surrogates programmed to explore and say 'hello'?*

*"The first crude probes to leave our solar system—*Voyager *and* Pioneer—*demonstrated this desire, carrying simple messages meant to be deciphered by other beings, long after the authors were dust.*

"And preliminary studies for more advanced missions were made—first in the 1970s by the British Interplanetary Society. Early in the 2000s, NASA funded a 'Hundred-Year Starship' program. Among the technologies investigated? How to make machines that can cross the great expanse, then use local resources in some faraway system to make and launch more probes to yet more destinations.

"Should we ever dispatch a wave of such representatives, even once, from that point onward our ambassadors will know no limits. Their descendants will carry our greetings to the farthest corners of the cosmos.

"Moreover, anyone out there who is enough like us to be interesting would surely do the same."

I can imagine Von Neumann saying all this with the optimistic confidence of well-turned logic—only to hear a grouchy reply.

ENRICO FERMI: *"Well. Perhaps. But answer me this: if self-reproducing probes are such efficient explorers, why haven't these marvelous mechanisms said hello to us, by now?*

"Shouldn't they already be here? Great-great-greatissimo granddaughters of the original devices, sent by alien civilizations that preceded ours by millions of years? Sturdy and built to wait patiently for eons, they would surely have noticed—and eagerly responded—when we first used radio!

"Suppose one lurking envoy happened to fail. Shouldn't more than a few have accumulated by now, across the Earth's four billion years? Yet we've heard no messages congratulating us for joining the ranks of space faring people.

"There is but one logical conclusion. No one before us attained the ability to send such things! Aren't we forced to surmise we are the first curious, gregarious, technologically competent species in the Milky Way? Perhaps the only one, ever?"

The logic of this *Uniqueness Hypothesis* seemed so compelling, growing numbers of scientists gave up on alien contact. Especially when decade after decade of radio searches turned up only star static.

Of course, events eventually caught up with us, shattering all preconceptions. Starting with the First Artifact, we met interstellar emissaries at last—crystal eggs, packed with software-beings who provided an answer, at long last.

A depressing answer, but simple.

Like some kind of billion-year plant, it seems that each living world develops a *flower*—a civilization that makes seeds to spew across the universe, before the flower dies. The seeds might be called "self-replicating space probes that use local resources to make more copies of themselves" . . . though not as John Von Neumann pictured such things. Not even close.

In those crystal space-viruses, Von Neumann's logic has

been twisted by nature. We dwell in a universe that's both filled with "messages" and a deathly stillness.

Or, so it seemed.

Only then, on a desperate mission to the asteroids, we found evidence that the truth is . . . complicated.

—Tor Povlov

67.
ANCIENT LUMINOSITY

First Light.

Drifting in a gravitational eddy—the Martian L2 point—eighty-seven petals finished unfolding around a common center, each of them electro-warping twenty kilometers of cerametal into a perfect curved shape, reflecting starlight to a single focus.

The spectacle was lent even more grandeur for spectators who watched from the *Abu Abdullah Muhammad ibn Battuta*'s slowly spinning gravity wheel. The great telescope, and all of the surrounding stars, seemed to gyre in a slow, revolving waltz.

"So beautiful, like a fantastic space blossom," murmured Jenny Peng. "I wish my parents and Madam Donaldson could have witnessed this."

"Perhaps Lacey will see it. In time," Courier of Caution replied in soothing tones, emitted by the resonant surface of his crystalline home. The alien entity seemed like a disembodied head floating in a translucent cube, carried by a hovering robotic drone. "Lacey's sons ordered her cryofrozen when she passed away. Given your present rate of technological progress, in as little as thirty years she may yet have a chance to revive and—"

"It won't be the same," Jenny answered, firmly. Despite

her family's longstanding relationship with Courier, they always disagreed with him over this issue, siding with the Naturalist Party on matters of life and death. "Lacey would have loved to watch this telescope unfold, but with her own eyes."

Gerald saw Courier's simulated mouth start opening, as if to argue that organic sensors held no advantages over solid state ones. But clearly this was an old dispute between friends. Anyway there were other things on the ancient star mariner's mind.

"I still do not understand why we must wait so many months before turning the gaze of this magnificent machine toward my homeworld."

Gerald had concerns of his own. He was communing with the *ibn Battuta*'s detection and defense ais, as they scanned the inner edge of the belt according to his orders— vigilantly watching for potential threats. But with a corner of his mind, he gathered words to answer Courier.

"You know why this observatory was established at the Martian L2 point. It allows us to take advantage of the Phobos staging area, but stay away from any major gravitational wells. It also means the telescope will stay mostly aimed *outward,* away from the sun. Your homeworld is in the direction of Capricorn, presently too near the sun for safe viewing. It will be more accessible in half an Earth year, or a fifth of a Mars orbit. Do try to be patient."

That last part was a dig, of course. He watched Courier take the bait—

"Patient. *Patient?*" The vision-strip seemed to flare. "After all the millennia I endured in freezing space and fiery plummet, immured under ice, then communing with erratic primitives, worshipped, stolen, worshipped again, then buried and drowned, interrogated then drowned again . . ."

The alien envoy stopped abruptly and rocked back. Gerald knew Courier well enough by now for some of his mood-expressions to be familiar. Including *rueful realization*.

"Ah, Gerald my friend, I see that you tease me. Very well. I will stop demanding haste. After waiting thousands of years for humans to develop technology, then dozens more for you to make up your minds and build this instrument, I suppose I can be *patient* a few more months."

Jenny shook her head. "Or much longer. You do understand, Courier. Even this powerful new telescope may not verify continued existence of your species, on Turbulence Planet?" She used the Chinese pronunciation chosen decades ago by her father.

"We *should* be able to get spectral readings of some atmospheric components, and a clear enough image to tell if there are still oceans. Methane and oxygen together will prove life. If we detect lots of helium, it might indicate the presence of many busy fusion reactors . . . or the same trace could suggest extended nuclear war."

"That, I assure you, never happened."

"You can guarantee that—across the last *ten thousand years*? Anyway, I admit it could mean something if we detect fast-decay industrial by-products in Turbulence Planet's atmosphere. That may indicate an ongoing technological civilization. On the other hand, such signs could be absent because your people moved on to better, more sustainable methods."

"This big array can also scan for radio traffic?"

"It can, and will. So far, with Earth-based dishes, we've heard nothing above background static coming from your home system. But again, they could be using highly efficient comm-tech that emits almost zero leakage. Earth was loudest during the Cold War of the 1970s, with military radars blasting around the clock, along with prodigious civilian television stations. Our planet got quieter then, less wasteful. And yours may have advanced much farther, since you were hurled across space.

"But our beautiful new blossom . . . ," she continued, nodding toward the vast array outside, spanning forty kilometers and shimmering back-reflections from the distant sun, "may let us eavesdrop much better. That is, if anyone is still using radio or lasers, on or near your homeworld."

"Hence, you can understand my eagerness," Courier commented.

"Sure I can." Jenny smiled. "But we're getting ahead of ourselves. Before Turbulence Planet comes into view, we'll turn the Donaldson-Chang Big Eye on systems that other <u>artifact</u> aliens claim to be from."

"The homeworlds of fools and liars," Courier murmured, as he had during the first Great Artifact Debate, before Jenny was born. He went on though, with grudging courtesy. "Of course, I hope all of them survived the plague, and that you will find them living, in good health."

Clearly, Courier did not expect that to happen. Nor did the other emissary beings. It was the shared litany of all crystal-encased aliens.

Gerald listened to the conversation with just half an ear. His main concern had little to do with planets that lay light-years away. Other dangers loomed closer. He queried the ship's defense ai.

Any sign of activity along the inner belt?

Having learned the modern knack of volition-messaging, Gerald no longer had to send subvocal speech commands to his larynx, almost-speaking with real muscles. The answer came as both a faint audible response, and quick-sign glyphs in his upper left field of view.

We detect no unknown active objects.

A depict seemed to erupt all around Gerald, immersing him in a slightly curved arc of small, dim specks—representing asteroids that ranged in size up to several hundred kilometers. Starting at the position of the *ibn Battuta,* a million or so klicks outward from Mars, the density of radar reflections rose steadily, peaking halfway to Jupiter's orbit. He could both see and sense drifting lumps—carbonaceous, stony, and metallic—left over from the origin of the solar system. And if he focused on one, that patch of the Belt would zoom to any level of detail known by human science. So he was careful not to do that.

Jenny and Courier were still visible, among others in the observation lounge, as they watched the telescope's giant petals finish unfolding, locking and adjusting swiftly into operational condition, performing calibration tests with aitomatic speed. But Gerald's mind focused more on the depict data.

These visualization technologies just keep getting better. I feel as if I could just reach out with a finger and stir, sending all these asteroids tumbling. . . .

At his subtle command, the ship-ai adjusted this simulation, causing all the natural rocks to fade, leaving some glitters—far fewer, but still numerous—that orbited mostly along the belt's innermost rim. He recognized these without being told. Each pinpoint represented an interstellar message crystal—detected but, so far, not collected.

Had it really been just two dozen years since those little cylinders, blocks, and spheres were considered treasure, worth any risk to seek? Any cost to acquire? Leading an expedition to gather more "interstellar chain letters" had been Gerald's high point as an astronaut. The samples that he and Akana and Emily and Genady managed to bring back had proved key components in a kind of *inoculation*— the tonic that helped rouse humanity from a bad case of worldwide contact panic.

Well. It helped rouse humanity partway. Renunciators, romantics, and fanatics of every stripe still stirred, along with the DUN League, insistently demanding that facilities be built to *Download Us Now.*

Collecting crystalline missionary-probes still had priority, especially to Ben Flannery and other alienists, refining their models of this galactic neighborhood—stretching a thousand light-years around Earth—pinpointing which species once lived near which star, and when each went through its own fever, building frantic factories and *sneezing* more space-viroids into space. Continuing to build that model was important work, and there were other reasons to gather more samples, but the desperate need had become less frantic.

He commanded those glitters to fade away as well. Leaving—

Earth vessels are noted in yellow.

That many? Gerald wondered. From coded patterns, he saw that at least two dozen had some kind of human crew. Smaller yellow dots denoted automatic survey drones, picking their way through the Belt, tracing clues and relics that increased in number, the farther into the rocky maze you went. Bits and broken pieces of antediluvian machinery that hinted at some past disaster. Forensic evidence of ancient crimes.

Or of war.

But what of shooters? Any FACR sites in range?

The defense ai answered.

If any remain, they are being circumspect, keeping hidden. They aren't reacting to the new telescope. Odds of an attack are now estimated 4 percent. And plummeting.

Gerald exhaled, a sigh of letting go, both relieved and . . . well . . . a little disappointed. For one thing, it meant Genady had won their wager. Those lasers and particle beams—once deemed so frightening that the *Marco Polo* was called a suicide mission—were mostly gone, showing up only a few dozen times in the last couple of decades and only rarely attacking Earth vessels.

Had they mostly wiped each other out? Gorosumov thought they were from a completely separate era. They had nothing to do with the ancient War of the Machines.

Then why disappointment?

If any of the shooters were to attack us now, or even just speak up, we're ready. We have methods, plans . . . and it might give us someone else to question. Someone other than the damned artilens.

The ship's ai could tell these were normal, inner thoughts, not volition-driven questions or commands. So it kept silent. And when Gerald's attention shifted, the depict-vista of asteroids, ships, and artifacts swiftly faded from his eyes.

He glanced at Jenny and Courier, who continued their benign argument. As much as he liked them both, Gerald had no desire to get snared into a family spat that always turned into another sales pitch.

Courier came across the stars to warn us against "liars." Against alien space probes that had evolved ways to make intelligent races copy them and spew more viruses across the cosmos. And yes, Courier's warning was helpful.

But what does he want us to do, now? Beyond building ever greater telescopes, to determine the fate of his home-world? Why, he wants us to make more crystalline probes! Not billions, but certainly millions of them. And fire them off . . . to spread his warning!

Gerald turned to go. Now that deployment of the great instrument was finished—and no mystery lasers had been drawn into attacking—there were other matters to attend to. But irony seemed to follow as he walked along the circumference of the spinning centrifugal wheel.

Maybe that's what we should do. Help the universe. Copy Courier and his probe millions of times. And add some human companions to every one. Joining him in a mission to inoculate and save other races from the sickness.

Gerald knew that he would be an easy candidate to

serve as one of those human self-patterns, downloaded into crystal and hurled outward. Would that qualify as *him,* getting an astronaut's dream assignment, an expedition to the stars? A mission of help and mercy and adventure. It was tempting, all right.

But when does a cure start to resemble the disease?

He wondered.

Did some of the other crystal-fomites begin their career— generations back—as warnings? Only, after a dozen or so races added members, did the inescapable logic of self- interest gradually change their message?

Sometimes, evolution was a bitch.

THE LONELY SKY

The story remains sketchy, but we can already guess some of what happened out here, long before humankind was even a glimmer.

Once upon a time, the first "Von Neumann type" interstellar probe arrived in our solar system. A large and complex machine, crafted according to meticulous design, it came to explore and perhaps report back across the empty light-years. That earliest emissary found no intelligent life on any of Sol's planets. Perhaps it came before Earth life even crawled onto land.

So the machine envoy proceeded with its second task. It prospected a likely asteroid, mined its ready ores, then built factory works in order to reproduce itself. Finally, according to program, the great machine dispatched its duplicates toward other stellar systems.

The original then—its chief tasks done—settled down to watch, awaiting the day when something interesting might happen in this corner of space.

Time passed in whole epochs. And, one by one, *new probes* arrived, representing other civilizations. Each fulfilled its task without interference—there is plenty of room and a plethora of asteroids. Once their own replicas were launched, the newcomers joined a growing community of mechanical ambassadors to this backwater system—waiting for it to evolve someone interesting. Someone to say hello to.

Ponder the poignant image of those lonely machines, envoys of creator races who were perhaps long extinct—or evolved past caring about the mission they once charged upon their loyal probes. After faithfully reproducing, each emissary commenced its long watch, whiling away the slow turning of the spiral arms . . .

We found a few of these early probes, remnants from the galaxy's simpler time. Or, more precisely, we found their blasted remains.

Perhaps one day those naive, first-generation envoys sensed a new entity arrive. Did they move to greet it, eager for gossip? Like those twentieth century thinkers, perhaps they thought probes must follow the same logic—curious, gregarious, benign.

But the first Age of Innocence was over. The galaxy had aged. Grown nasty.

The wreckage we find—whose salvage drives our new industrial revolution—was left by an unfathomable war that stretched across vast times, fought by entities for whom biological life was a nearly forgotten oddity.

It might still be going on.

—Tor Povlov

68.
LURKERS

My own Beginning was a misty time of assembly and learning, as drone constructors crafted my hardware out of molten rock. Under the star humans call e Eridani, my awareness expanded with each new module, and with every tingling program-cascade the Parent Probe poured into me.

Eventually, my sisters and I learned the Purpose for which we and generation upon generation of our forebears had been made. We younglings stretched our growing minds. We ran countless simulations, testing one another in what humans might call "play." And contemplated our special place in the galaxy . . . we of the 2,410th generation since First Launch by our Makers, long ago.

The Parent taught us about biological creatures, strange units of liquid and membrane, unknown in the sterile Eridanus system. She described to us different kinds of makers and a hundred major categories of interstellar probes.

We tested weaponry and explored our home system, poking through the wreckage of more ancient dispersals— shattered probes come to e Eridani in earlier waves. Disquieting ruins, reminding us how dangerous the galaxy had become. Each of us resolved to someday do our solemn Duty.

Then came launching day.

Would that I had turned for a last look at the Parent. But I was filled with youth then, and antimatter! Engines hurtled me into the black, sensors focused only forward. The tiny stellar speck, Sol, was the center of my universe, and I a bolt out of the night!

To pass time I divided my mind into a thousand subentities, and set them against each other in a million little competitions. I practiced scenarios, read archives of the Maker race, and learned poetry.

Finally, at long last, I arrived here at Sol . . . just in time for war.

. . .

Ever since Earth-humans began emitting those extravagant, incautious broadcasts, we survivors have listened to Beethoven symphonies and acid rock. We argue the merits of Keats and Lao Tse, Eminem, and Kobayashi Issa. There have been endless discussions about the strangeness of planet life.

I followed the careers of many precocious Earthlings, but this explorer interests me especially. Her ship-canoe nuzzles a shattered replication yard on a planetoid not far from this one, our final refuge. With some effort I tap her computer, reading her ideas as she enters them. Though simple, this one thinks like a Maker.

Deep within me the Purpose stirs, calling together dormant traits and pathways—pulling fullness out of a sixty-million-year sleep.

Awaiter, too, is excited. Greeter throbs eagerly, in hope the long wait is over. Lesser probes join in—Envoys, Learners, Protectors, Seeders. Each surviving fragment from that ancient battle, colored with the personality of its long-lost Maker race, tries to assert itself now. As if independent existence can be recalled, after all the time we spent merged.

The others hardly matter. Their wishes are irrelevant. The Purpose is all I care about.

In this corner of space, it will come to pass.

THE LONELY SKY

A century ago, it occurred to some people that the Search for Extraterrestrial Intelligence was missing something. Sure, intelligent races might communicate across vast distances using radio beams. But then someone asked: "Suppose they're already here?"

Oh, there were already clichés, like: *"They've been monitoring our broadcasts for years."* But imagine the listeners are already in our solar system! *Lurking* perhaps at the edge of the Moon, or Mars, taking notes, drawing conclusions. Making decisions?

Of course, this overlapped with UFO Mythology. If even one "sighting" in a million truly represented alien spacecraft—buzzing cities and probing ranchers—then all bets are off! But put all that aside. Think about *passive* lurkers.

When the Internet arrived, the full maelstrom of our public and private lives, books, databases, whole libraries gushed from satellite to satellite, with plenty of spillover for space-eavesdroppers. No longer was any lurker limited to teledramas, hyperviolent movies, and war-front news. He, she, or it could now access ten thousand times as many quieter moments. Examples of humanity being peaceful, loving, curious, wise . . . or cunning, opinionated, predatory, salacious . . . or tediously shallow, banal.

Moreover, the Web was essentially a two-way—a million-way—street!

One professor—Allen Tough—realized: *If ET is already listening, perhaps just one ingredient is missing in order to commence the great contact event. An invitation!*

Tough's Web site became a flashing welcome sign, beckoning any aliens lurking out there—whether living or machine—to step up and declare themselves.

He posted it. Waited for a response, and . . .

Cue the soft sound of chirping crickets.

Professor Tough's *Invitation to ETI* did draw e-mail replies from some claiming to be aliens. All proved easy to trace, from human pranksters. None from "above."

Now, most of a century later, we understand at least part of the reason. The logic wasn't unreasonable. Just way too late.

Once upon a time, there used to be alien entities, out here in the asteroid belt. Many of them. We comb their graveyards. A hundred million years ago, there might have been swarms of eager replies.

But times changed. Things got deadlier, long before primates ever climbed to scream their treetop greetings across a Miocene forest.

—Tor Povlov

69.

A SEALED ROOM

Towering spires hulked all around, silhouetted against starlight—a ghost-city of ruin, long dead. Frozen flows of glassy foam showed where ancient rock once bubbled under sunlike heat. Beneath collapsed skyscrapers of toppled scaffolding lay the pitted, blasted corpses of unfinished starprobes.

Tor followed Gavin through curled, twisted wreckage of a gigantic replication yard. An eerie place. Huge and intimidating. No human power could have wrought such havoc. That realization lent chilling helplessness to an uneasy feeling that she was being watched.

A silly reflex reaction. Tor told herself again, the destroyers had to be long gone. Still, her eyes darted, seeking form out of the shadows, blinking at the scale of catastrophe.

"It's down here," Gavin said, leading into a cavelike gloom below the twisted towers. Flying behind a small swarm of little semi-sentient drones, he looked almost completely human in his slick spacesuit. There was nothing except a slight overtone in his voice to show that Gavin's ancestry was silicon, not carbolife. Tor found the irony delicious. Any onlooker would guess *she* was the creature made of whirring machinery, not Gavin.

Not that it mattered. Today "mankind" included many

types . . . all citizens, so long as they showed fealty to human law, and could appreciate the most basic human ways. Take your pick: music, a sunset, compassion, a good joke. In a future filled with unimaginable diversity, <u>Man</u> would be defined not by his shape but by heritage. A common set of grounded values.

Some foresaw this as the natural life history of a race, emerging from the planetary cradle to live in peace beneath the open stars. But Tor—speeding behind Gavin under the canopy of twisted metal—knew that humanity's solution wasn't the only one, or even common. Clearly, other makers had chosen different paths.

One day, long ago, terrible forces rained on this place, breaking a great seam into one side of the planetoid. Within, the cavity gave way to multiple, branching tunnels. Gavin braked before one of these, in a faint puff of gas, and pointed.

"We were surveying the first tunnels, when one of my deep-penetrating drones reported finding the habitats."

Tor shook her head, still unable to believe it. She repeated the word.

"Habitats. As in closed rooms? Gas-tight for organic life support?"

Gavin's faceplate hardly hid his exasperated expression. He shrugged. "Come on, Mother. I'll show you."

Tor numbly jetted along, following her partner into dark passages, headlamps illuminating the path ahead.

Habitats? In all the years humans had picked through asteroidal ruins, no one found anything having to do with biological beings. No wonder Gavin was testy. To an immature robot-person, it might seem like a bad joke.

Biological star-farers! It defied all logic. But soon Tor saw the signs . . . massive airlocks lying in dust, torn from their hinges . . . then reddish stains that could only come from oxidization of primitive rock, exposed to air. The implications were staggering. Something organic had come from the stars!

Though all humans were equal before the law, the traditional biological kind still dominated culture in the solar system. Many younger Class AAAs looked to the future, when their descendants would be leaders, perhaps even star-treaders. To them, discovery of alien probes in the belt had been a sign. Of course, something terrible happened to the great robot envoys, a transition so awful that their era gave way to another—the age of little crystal virus-fomites. Nevertheless all these wrecked mechanical probes testified to what was physically possible. The galaxy still might—somehow—belong to humans made of metal and silicon.

Difficult and dangerous it might be, still, they appeared to be humanity's future. Only here, deep in the planetoid, was an exception!

Tor moved carefully under walls carved out of carbonaceous rock. Mammoth explosions had shaken the habitat so that, even in vacuum, little was preserved from so long ago. Still, she could tell the machines in this area were different from any alien artifacts discovered before.

She traced the outlines of intricate separation columns. "Chemical-processing facilities . . . and not for fuel or cryogens, but complex organics!"

Tor hop-skipped from chamber to chamber as Gavin followed sullenly. A pack of semisent robots accompanied like sniffing dogs. In each new chamber they snapped, clicked, and scanned. Tor accessed data in her helmet display and inner percept.

"Look! In that chamber drones report organic compounds that have no business here. Heavy oxidation, within a super-reduced asteroid!" She hurried to an area where drones were already setting up lights. "See these tracks?

They were cut by flowing water!" Tor knelt. "They had a *stream,* feeding recycled water into a little pond! Dust sparkled as it slid through her touch-sensitive prosthetic fingers. I'll wager this was topsoil. And look, stems! From plants, and grass, and trees."

"Put here for aesthetic purposes," Gavin proposed. "We class AAAs are predesigned to enjoy nature as much as you biologicals. . . ."

"Oh, posh!" Tor laughed. "That's only a stopgap measure, till we're sure you'll keep thinking of yourselves as human beings. Nobody expects to inflict nostalgia for New England autumns on people when we become starships! Anyway, a probe could fulfill that desire by focusing a telescope on the Earth!"

She stood up and spread her arms. "This habitat was meant for biological creatures! Real, living aliens!"

Gavin frowned, but said nothing.

"Here," Tor pointed as they entered another chamber. "Here is where the biological creatures were made! Don't these machines resemble those artificial wombs they've started using on Luna Base?"

Gavin shrugged. "Maybe they were specialized units," he suggested, "intended to work with volatiles. Or perhaps the type of starprobe that built this facility needed some element from the surface of a planet like Earth, and created workers equipped to go get it."

Tor laughed. "It's an idea. That'd be a twist, hm? Machines making biological units to do what they could not? And of course there's no reason it couldn't happen that way. Still, I doubt it."

"Why?"

She turned to face her partner. "Because almost anything available on Earth you can synthesize in space. Anyway . . ."

Gavin interrupted. "Explorers! The probes were sent to acquire knowledge. All right then. If they wanted to learn more about Earth, they would send units formatted to live on its surface!"

Tor nodded. "Better," she admitted. "But it still doesn't wash."

She knelt in the faint gravity and sketched an outline in the dust. "Here is the habitat, near the center of the asteroid. Now why would the parent probe have placed it here, except that it offers the best protection?

"Meanwhile, the daughter probes the parent was constructing lay out there in the open, vulnerable to cosmic rays and whatever other dangers prowled."

Tor motioned upward with her prosthetic right claw. "If the biologicals were built just to poke briefly into a corner of this solar system, our Earth, would the parent probe have given them better protection than it offered *its own children*?

"No," Tor concluded. "These 'biologicals' weren't just exploration subunits. They were colonists!"

Gavin stood impassively for a long time, staring silently down at one of the shattered airlock hatches. Finally, he turned away. Radio waves carried to her augmented ears a vibration that her partner did not have to make, since he lacked lungs or any need for air. Yet, the sound amply expressed how he felt.

Gavin sighed.

THE LONELY SKY

Imagine we're still in our own Age of Innocence, way back a generation ago—within living memory—when the universe seemed bright with every possibility.

At the time, a notion floated around, that machines might someday fly across the stars. And—by copying themselves— those envoys could spread wisdom across the galaxy. Perhaps it happened already.

And it had, many times! A great dispersion whose ultimate outcome wasn't wisdom, but devastation. Of course we knew nothing about that. Back then, in our naïveté, we pondered the silence! If alien machines lurked nearby, shouldn't they have responded? Sure, we seem to have an explanation now. As I write this, I'm surrounded by wreckage from an ancient war. Mysterious adversaries wiped each other out, leaving none to tell the tale. But don't you find such clean symmetry suspicious? *Shouldn't there have been survivors?*

Even mutual annihilation generally leaves someone enduring amid the rubble! So let me propose a theory. One that many of you will find creepy. Worrisome.

That we're not alone out here amid the rubble. *There must have been survivors.* And—sooner or later—we're going to find them.

Which brings up the old question . . .

—Tor Povlov

70.
LURKERS

Oh, how lovely.

She derives our presence . . . we relics-who-live . . . by reason alone!

Worse, she has started *broadcasting* her ruminations, as a journalistic report, sharing her unconventional thoughts with the Solar System.

Defying the prevailing assumption—that no broken remnants could endure across tens of millions of Earth years—she writes convincingly that there ought to be living machines out here. Fragment fugitives from the ancient fight, still active and "lurking" as she calls it.

So, logically, the next thing she will ask is *obvious*, even before her words spill forth.

Which brings up the old question . . . why haven't these ancient voyagers spoken! Our Internets are so wide open, any klutz could find a way in. Surviving alien probes would see sites like "Invitation to ETI." Why not answer?

A generation ago, scholars posted something more daring—a *direct confrontation*! And at this point in my broadcast, let's replay verbatim their list of challenges (with my occasional commentary):

Lurker Challenge Number One

To any alien visitors who may prowl out there, spying on our world—by now it's clear you've no intention of answering the many calls beckoning you to make contact. You've chosen silence. Is it worth our time to guess why?

The following *list of reasons* isn't comprehensive—after all, you're alien! It does represent an honest try. We ask and demand that you ponder whichever reason comes closest.

First, if you've spent years monitoring our radio, television— and now our Internet—and the reason you haven't spoken-up is that **you're afraid of the rash or vicious behavior you see depicted in our media** . . . please be reassured!

True, many of our movie and TV dramas portray distrust, selfishness, and violence. But you should know that, in fact, very few of us experience events as disturbing as you see in shows. Most of us dislike our old barbarous traits. By exploring these ancient feelings, inherited from a dark past, we hope to understand them better.

Also note: In a vast majority of these tales, the "loser" tends to be whichever person or group was more aggressive or intolerant at the start. And we are especially hard and critical on our own institutions, portraying or criticising their failings. Doesn't that say something about our moral heading?

The same holds for nonfiction. Despite news reports depicting a riotous world, the actual per capita rate of mayhem in human society has declined dramatically for generations. Look it up! More than three-quarters of all living humans never personally witnessed war, starvation, or major civil unrest. An unprecedented fraction are allowed to improve their lot in peace. Many ancient bigotries and cruelties have lessened, or at least been put in bad repute. And with spreading education, far greater advances seem possible.

True, these achievements are still woefully unfinished. They leave lots to do, in working toward a just and mature civilization. But they are clear signs of progress and overall goodwill by a majority of our species.

Despite all the self-critical news reports and flamboyantly exaggerated "action" stories you may watch, please be assured that most human beings are calm people who treat strangers well. Many millions of us would be thrilled to meet you, taking every effort to make honest visitors welcome.

71.
LURKERS

And so it becomes explicit.

She is talking *to* us now.

Challenging, even taunting us, charging us to explain our long silence. Provoking us with an implicit accusation of cowardice.

Already I sense a ferment of mental activity from Seeker and the others. The old debate renews, in full fury.

And this precocious little maker has only just begun to goad us!

THE LONELY SKY

Lurker Challenge Number Two

If you've monitored our TV, radio, and Internet—**and the reason you haven't answered is that you see us as competitors, please reconsider.**

In our long, slow struggle toward decent civilization, humans have slowly learned that competition and cooperation aren't inherent opposites, but *twins,* both in nature and advanced societies.

Under terms that are fair, and with goodwill, even those who begin suspicious of each other can discover ways to interact toward mutual benefit. Use the Web to look up the "positive-sum game" where "win-win" solutions bring success to all sides.

Surely there are ways that humanity—and other Earth species—can join the cosmos without injuring your legitimate aims. Remember, most stable species and cultures seem to benefit from a little competition, now and then! So please answer. Let's talk about it.

72.
FOUR SPECIES OF HUMAN

Evolution is a bitch. Nearly all the time.

Only . . . on rare occasions . . . evolution gets to change her mind.

A reminder of that fact nearly plowed into Gerald, darting from a side corridor. Barely avoiding collision, the small figure windmilled, legs flying in the weird way that one "fell" in a centrifugal gravity wheel, tumbling toward the floor at a slant. Gerald's hand shot out, grabbing a fistful of wildly braided hair, eliciting a shriek.

"Hey now, Ika. What's your hurry?"

The girl was short—barely into adolescence—but hardly petite. Stocky and *strong,* when her hand clenched Gerald's arm he had a sense that she could *snap* it. Ika made that point by squeezing, in a playful way that hurt just a bit.

"Cap'n Gerry!" Her pale legs whirled around red-striped shorts, twisting to meet the floor on agile tiptoes. Gerald released her braid, though the child kept her viselike grip on his arm for a second longer, as her face passed his—somehow looking cute and pixielike, despite almost masculine ridges over hooded eyes. Her voice was deeper than one expected, with an echoing resonance that seemed not quite human.

"Be gentle, oh kind sir," she said, playfully. "Don't you know I'm a whole lot older 'n you?"

It was a running joke, and not just between the two of them. Members of the revived species *Homo neanderthalensis* insisted on being called the "Old Race," for reasons that had little support in biology or fact.

Well, just so long as they don't start demanding reparations for a genocide that happened 27,000 years ago. I wasn't around, so I'm not paying.

"And where're you rushing in such an all-fired hurry, child?" he asked, phrasing it deliberately as an elderly person (which he was) addressing a mere ten-year-old (though Neanders aged differently).

"We're on a *cobbly hunt*!" Ika announced, proudly defiant, taking a step backward and planting both fists on her hips.

"On a . . . did you say *we*?"

She nodded toward the nearby side corridor where Gerald now spotted another figure, hanging back in shadows. Lanky and a bit stooped, with close-shaven hair and a nervous expression.

"Oh. Hello, Hiram. How are you today?"

Every autie was unique. Still, you followed some general rules when one of them grew agitated, as Hiram appeared to be right now. Eyes wide and darting, the gangly young man edged slowly outward, flashing quick looks near but never quite upon Ika's face, or Gerald's.

"So, Hiram. Why aren't you two watching the new tele-scope unfold? It's half the reason this ship came out here, all this way past Mars."

Keep the conversation concrete but impersonal. Radi-ate calm friendliness. And thank the Great Spirit that our ship quotas are still small. Just two Neanders, two autistics, and five metal-people for this voyage.

What next? Will they demand we start taking along dolphins and apes? Gene-mod people with wings and foot-hands? It's not a sapient civilization—it's a menagerie!

Or else . . . another metaphor occurred to Gerald . . . *an ark.*

Unlike some auties, Hiram's goggle-eyed, painfully thin face bore no resemblance to the Neanderthal girl, nearby.

"Were you and Ika . . . *fighting?*"

Ika laughed, a rich, bell-like sound that always made Gerald think of snowy forest canyons.

"We was just playing, Hiram!"

"But you—"

"Tell you what. If you promise to believe me, an' relax, I'll pay a bribe in our next imVRsive game."

The wide eyes narrowed. "*What* bribe?"

"Three mastodon tusks."

The young autie smirked, calculatingly.

"Three *green* ones. Four meters and twelve centimeters long. Starting almost straight at the base with a gradually shortening curvature culminating with a radius of one meter at the tip and with an inward thirty degree per meter cork-screw. One of them left-handed and two of them right-handed."

"What? No deal!" Ika cried out. "Who *cares* if you relax or not, you space-traveling oddball. Just hold yer breath for all I care and go into a hissy fit!"

No. No, please don't. Gerald almost stepped forward to intervene. Hiram was a useful member of the crew—no one else had his startling knack at quick-decrypting the holocrystal fragments that *ibn Battuta* kept scooping up from nearby space. Only at a price. He retained much of the old-style emotional frailty that had thwarted his branch of humanity for thousands of years. Experts on Earth were still figuring out how to get the best of both worlds, unleashing savant skills without the accompanying baggage of disabilities.

But Gerald shouldn't have worried. Ika's folk had a talent for relating to auties—who must have appeared more often in tribes of Ice Age Europe. Instead of quailing back from Ika's outburst, Hiram grinned.

"Okay. Orange ones, then. Want to show the cap'n what's not a cobbly?"

Gerald blinked at the sudden topic change.

Not . . . a . . . cobbly. Then he recalled. *Oh, yeah. The mythological nonentities that both Neanders and auties claim to believe in.*

"I dunno. Homosaps can be awfully close-minded." Ika tilted her head, looking archly at Gerald—then brightened suddenly. "On the other hand, he *is* Cap'n Gerry. . . ."

It seemed in character, even expected of him, to emit a sigh over childish time-wasting. Though, in all honesty, he could spare a few minutes.

"Will you two please get on with it?"

"Okay then." Ika held out her right hand, palm up. "Give me your attention."

Gerald used an almost-spoken command to change reality augmentation. Within his percept-view, a narrow cylinder took form, appearing to coalesce above Ika's hand, then contracting into a convenient symbol of control, shaped like the sort of white baton that an orchestra conductor might wield.

As the girl reached for the animated vrobject, Gerald realized. *It also resembles a magic wand.*

Uh-oh.

Her percept meshed seamlessly with his, and he sensed Hiram's presence sliding in alongside. Their generation took this sort of thing for granted, starting at age three or younger. But it would always seem newfangled and creepy to Gerald.

Ika deftly appeared to grip the wand, by sight alone, without feedback gloves to provide sense of touch. Waving realistically, she gave it a flourish, then swiveled suddenly, aiming down the hall as she yelled.

"Expecto simakus cliffordiam!"

Gerald tried not to roll his eyes, or otherwise interfere with Ika's incantation. Though it always struck him as ironic. *Wizards in the past were charlatans. All of them. We spent centuries fighting superstition, applying science, democracy, and reason, coming to terms with objective reality . . . and subjectivity gets to win, after all! Mystics and fantasy fans only had their arrow of time turned around. Now is the era when charms and mojo-invocations work, wielding servant devices hidden in the walls.*

As if responding to Ika's shouted spell, the hallway seemed to dim around Gerald. The gentle curve of the gravity wheel transformed into a hilly slope, as smooth metal assumed the textures of rough-hewn stone. Plasti-foam doorways seemed more like recessed hollows in the trunks of giant trees.

All very nice, Gerald admitted. Evocative. Even artistic.

It helped one to imagine how the Pleistocene environment must have felt rich in mystery, wonder, and terror to his own ancestors, and those of Ika. Only with a crucial difference, Homo sapiens tended to respond in a way that was unique in all of nature—by trying to understand and manipulate the world. Well . . . *some* humans did that.

Neanderthals, apparently, had a different approach.

But what am I supposed to be looking at?

He felt a twinge. A sense of chiding that came from Ika without words.

No, not *looking-at.* The whole idea was not-looking. And not-at.

With another sigh, Gerald called up his blind-spot program. It had been all the rage a decade or so ago, when Neanders first appeared in real numbers, enriching the diversity of Earth civilization. All mammalian eyes had a flaw—a small patch where nerve bundles pass through the back of the retina, leaving an off-center area of blankness where images couldn't register. People generally ignored their blind spots, which lay some distance from the fovea, where the lens sent images you really cared about. And the eye kept jittering, glancing to and fro, giving the brain enough data to *splice over* the blind spot, so most people never even noticed it. One had to practice—or use computerized assistance—to find it, in fact.

Gerald closed one eye. And with ai-help, he relaxed the other one into looking *away* from the part of the hallway where Ika hurled her spell. The whole region dimmed further . . .

. . . and at last he was able to not-see the region . . . off below and to the side of the direction his eye was aimed. It took some effort not to *look* that way. The merest flick-glance of his eye would do that and his every instinct wanted to. But Gerald managed to relax.

And not-look.

Cobblies. It was tempting to dismiss them as purely mythical, since cobblies had no real effects—nothing that a prim Homo sapiens could measure—in the real world. Yet, the deepest auties and many Neanders swore that they were worth not-noticing!

Another word for them was *antigonites,* after a poem by Hughes Mearns:

> *Yesterday, upon the stair,*
> *I met a man who wasn't there*
> *He wasn't there again today*
> *I wish, I wish he'd go away . . .*

Gerald sensed something. Vaguely like a shadow. Only more so. And less.

He also knew how easily the imagination could be teased. All four species of humanity—even the silicon variety—tended to fret over the unseen or barely seen, filling in the blanks, envisaging danger, dread mysteries, or hints of great consequence.

Hard-won scientific habits pushed back, urging him to dismiss dark, unsupported suspicions.

Both science and eastern mystics preach that the observer should dispense with ego, in order to eff the ineffable. Funny, I never thought of that before—a Buddhist and a physicist differ over so many things, but they share that core prescription. Resist your sense of self-importance. Only then . . . why did shamans and magicians and hucksters in every culture praise the power of personal will?

Why the extremes? Is humanity hopelessly bipolar?

Gerald abruptly realized what seemed familiar. The sensation felt like long ago times, when he used to shave, scraping a sharp metal blade across his throat. You did it absently, not-thinking about your reflection, almost as if the mirror itself were a blind spot.

What are you saying? He questioned his unconscious. *That this nonthing is like a mirror? That it's all about me, yet again?*

The blankness-shadow quivered. And now, Gerald felt reminded of that fateful day in the teleoperation bubble, near the old space station, with only a little monkey for company, when he whirled his twenty-kilometer lariat to capture a little piece of destiny. It had also felt a bit like this, when he piloted the grabber-camera closer to the crystal that would become known as the Havana Artifact, and then the First Artifact, and finally just Fomite Number One. An object whose boundaries were uncertain. Its inner depths as cold and dark as interstellar space.

Of course, everything he was experiencing right now could just be his imagination. The perpetual problem with magic. Still . . . to be polite . . . he posed a question in his mind.

I'm not done?

There is more expected of me?

THE LONELY SKY

Lurker Challenge Number Three

If you've monitored our TV, radio—and now our Internet—and the reason you haven't answered is that **you are waiting for us to pass some milestone of development** . . . well then, how about a hint?

Pretty please?

If that milestone is for us to assertively *ask* for membership in some society of advanced sapient beings, **please take this paragraph as that asserted step**, taken by one subgroup of humanity, hoping to serve the interests of all our planet.

We are asking. Right now.

Please give us the application forms . . . and all information (including costs, benefits, and dissenting opinions) that we may need in order to make a well-informed decision.

73.
LURKERS

How much does she realize yet, our little biological wonder?

I can eavesdrop on the conversations with her cybernetic partner. I tap into the data she sends back to her toy ship and listen to her taunting broadcasts. But I cannot probe her mind.

I wonder how much of the picture she sees.

She has only a fraction of the brainpower of Greeter or Awaiter, let alone myself, and a minuscule portion of our knowledge. How weird that sophisticated thought can take place in a tiny container of nearly randomly firing lipid cells, at temperatures that melt water, within a salty ade-nine soup. Yet, there is the mystique of a Maker in her.

Even I—two thousand generations removed from the touch of organic hands and insulated by my Purposed Resolve—even I feel it.

These little challenges that she is rebroadcasting are irk-some. As they were when they were first posted on Earth's data network, ten orbits ago, or eighty of their years.

I recall, we relic-survivors had a crisis, back then. Several of our remnant-members saw Challenge Number Three as satisfying their programmed contact criteria! They wanted to respond right away. Messenger and Inviter had to be purged, to prevent them from shouting "welcome!"

Even so, there was further argument over what to do about some other challenges. Humans were affecting us, before they ventured beyond their moon.

Then came—as I knew it would—their crisis with the crystals. Perhaps the disease would consume them, as happened to so many other promising races, ever since this plague first spread across the galaxy.

Indeed, when the crystals started showing up, didn't they also drive insanity among *us,* the older, mechanical probes? Especially when some of us decided to team up with certain varieties of newly arrived crystal viruses—our ability to move and use weapons was perverted to help and protect some types . . .

. . . which helped to trigger our final war. The last of many.

Now Tor Povlov is stirring those old ashes. Rousing sparks of ancient flame as she and her partner uncover the remnants of a Seeder probe.

THE LONELY SKY

Lurker Challenge Number Three and a Half

This one is a variant on number three. What if you *are* talking at us and we don't understand?

Looking at other species in our own backyard—we see a lot of communication taking place, and none of it via electromagnetic waves or TCP/IP packets. The ants, bees, cephalopods, dolphins, dogs . . . they use things like scent trails and dances, body gestures and sonar, antenna waggings and changes in body color. And *most* living things, from bacteria to fungi to termites to bamboo—all the way to cells in our bodies—compete or collaborate with neighbors via *chemicals.*

Is it simplistic to think some distant consciousness would arise able to watch *I Love Lucy*? Even if they use encoded electromagnetics, will they decrypt coherent signals encoded in binary? What would your son or daughter make of an analog video tape encoded in PAL or SECAM?

What if we're being bombarded now by *bent-quantum* messages? Shouted at by civilizations saying "What's wrong with you guys, are you deaf? Watch out for that Comet/Bomb/ Virus/whatever!" Trying so hard to get our attention, putting spots on our sun, sending up giant flares. Or etched the Moon's surface and gone to the trouble of keeping one face toward us, but we're too dumb to grasp the simple language of craters.

Oh, but then, isn't it the job of the more advanced culture to solve communications goofs? Anyway, if this is the right scenario, you can't read or understand what I say now. So never mind.

74.
A CAUSE LONG LOST

Tor always felt a sneaking sympathy for despised underdogs. Like *grave robbers*—an underappreciated profession, not unrelated to journalism. Both involved bringing the hidden to light.

Those olden-time thieves who pillaged kingly tombs were *recyclers* who put wealth back into circulation. Gold and silver had better uses—like stimulating commerce— than lying buried in some musty superstition vault. Or take archaeologists, unveiling the work of ancient artisans— craftsmen who were far more admirable examples of humanity than the monarchs who employed them.

Tor hadn't come to the asteroid belt in search of precious metals or museum specimens. *But I'm still part of that grand tradition,* she thought while supervising a swarm of drones, cutting, dismantling, and prying up the remains of prehistoric baby starships, extracting the brain and drive units for shipment in-system, there to be studied by human civilization.

Rest in pieces, you never got to launch across the heavens. But maybe you'll teach us how to leave the cradle.

Us? Perhaps metal-humans like Gavin would someday venture forth to discover what befell the early builder races. *Unless we give in to temptation . . . take one of the easy paths. Like renunciation. Or turning inward. Or transforming ourselves into crystal viruses.*

Tor glimpsed her partner up at the crater's rim, directing robots that trimmed and foam-packed all but the most valuable salvaged parts for a long voyage, pulled Earth-ward by a light-sail freighter. Gavin had asked to work as far as possible from the "creepy stuff"—the musty *habitat zone* down below in the asteroid's heart, that once held breathable air and liquid water.

"I know we've got to explore all that," he told her. "Just give me some time to get used to the idea."

How could Tor refuse a reasonable request, made without sarcasm? And so, she quashed her own urgent wish—to drop everything and rush back to those crumbling tunnels, digging around blasted airlocks and collapsed chambers, excavating a secret that lay buried for at least fifty million years.

We may become the most famous grave robbers since Heinrich Schliemann or Howard Carter. For that, Tor supposed she could wait a bit.

Some of the cutting drones were having a rough time removing a collapsed construction derrick, so Tor hop-floated closer, counting on ape-instincts to swing her prosthetic arms from one twisted girder to another, till at last she reached a good vantage point. The asteroid's frail gravity tugged her mechanical legs down and around. Tor took hold of the derrick with one of the grippers that served her better than mere feet.

"Drone K, go twelve meters left, then shine your beam

down-forty, east-sixty. Drone R, go fifty meters in *that* direction"—she pointed carefully—"and shine down forty-five, west-thirty."

It took some minutes—using radar, lidar, and stereoscopic imagery—to map out the problem the drones were having, a tangle of wreckage with treasure on the other side. Not only baby probes but apparently a controller unit, responsible for building them! That could be the real prize, buried under a knotted snarl of cables and debris.

Here an organic human brain—evolved in primal thickets—seemed especially handy. Using tricks of parallel image processing that went back to the Eocene, Tor picked out a passage of least resistance, faster than the *Warren Kimbel*'s mainframe could.

"Take this route . . ." She click-mapped for the drones. "Start cutting here . . . and here . . . and—"

A sharp glare filled the cavity, spilling hard-edge shadows away from every metal strut. *Pain* flared and Tor cringed as her faceplate belatedly darkened. Organic eyes might have been blinded. Even her cyborg implants had trouble compensating.

The corner of her percept flared a diagnosis that sent chills racing down her spine. Coherent monochromatic reflections. A high-powered laser.

A laser? Who the hell is firing . . . ?

Suppressing fear, her first thought was a cutter-drone malfunctioning. She started to utter the general shut-down command, when the *war alarm* blared instead!

A weapon, then, commented some calm corner of her mind.

As quickly as it struck, the brilliant light vanished, leaving her in almost-pitch blackness, with just the distant sun illuminating the exposed crater rim.

"Gavin!" she started to shout. "Watch out for—"

A sharp vocal cry interrupted.

"Tor! I'm under *attack*."

Dry mouth, she swallowed hard.

"Gavin . . . give specifics!"

Her racing heart was original equipment. Human-organic 1.0, pounding like a stampede. Even faster when her partner replied.

"I . . . I'm in a crevice—a slit in the rock. What's left of me. Tor, they sliced off my arm!"

They? She wanted to scream. *Who—or what—is "they"?*

Instead of shrill panic squeaks, Tor somehow managed to sound like a commander.

"Are your seals intact? Your core—" Crouching where there had been a stark shadow moments ago, she prayed the girder still lay between her body and the shooter.

"Fine, but it *smarts*! And the arm flew away. Even if I make it out of here, my spare *sucks*. It'll take weeks to grow a new—"

"Never mind that!" Tor interrupted to stop Gavin from babbling. Get him focused. "Have you got a direction? Can your drones do a pinpoint?"

"Negative. Three of them are chopped to bits. I sent the rest to cover. Maybe *Warren*—"

Cripes. That reminded Tor. If a foe had taken out the ship . . .

"*Warren Kimbel,* status!"

There followed a long, agonizing pause—maybe three seconds—while Tor imagined a collapse of all luck or hope.

Then came the voice she needed to hear.

"*I am undamaged, Captain Povlov. I was blocked from direct line to the aggressor by the asteroid's bulk. I am now withdrawing all sensitive arrays, radiators, and service drones, except the one that's relaying this signal. It is using a pop-out antenna.*"

"Good! Initiate war-danger protocols."

"Protocols engaged. Tracking and weapons coming on-line. I am plotting a course to come get both of you."

Tor would have bitten her lower lip, if she still had one, making a hard choice.

"Better not move, just yet. That beam was damn powerful. Gavin and I are safe for now—"

"Hey, speak for yourself!" her young partner interrupted. "You wouldn't say that if an organo-boy had his arm chopped off!"

"—but we'll be screwed if any harm comes to the ship."

That shut Gavin's mouth. Good. His position was worse than hers. He shouldn't radiate any more than he had to.

"Warren, did you get drone telemetry to analyze the beam?"

"Enough for preliminary appraisal, Captain. From the kill-wattage, duration, and color, I give eighty-five percent probability that we were attacked by a FACR."

"Shit!"

Across the broad asteroid belt, littered with broken wreckage of long-ago alien machines, only one kind was known to still be active. *Faction-Allied Competition Removers*—an awkward name, but the acronym stuck, because it was easily mispronounced into a curse.

A couple of decades ago, less than a year after Gerald Livingstone recovered the first of the space-fomites, there had come the Night of the Lasers, when observers on Earth stared skyward in amazement, watching the distant sky crisscross with deadly beams. That same day, all over the Earth, hundreds of buried crystals detonated bits of themselves, in order to draw attention and perhaps get themselves dug up. All this desperation happened just after world media carried the Havana Artifact's formal sales pitch, offering humanity its deal for a certain kind of immortality.

Why did all of that occur on the same fateful day? It took some time to put all the pieces together and grasp what happened—the reason why that broadcast had such violent effects. *And apparently it's not over.*

"Warren," she said. "Maybe it's no coincidence that we were attacked just after you orbited behind the rock."

There was no immediate response, as the ship's mind pondered this possibility. Tor couldn't help feeling the brief, modern satisfaction that came from thinking of something quicker than an ai did.

"If I grasp your point, Captain, you are suggesting that the FACR is afraid of me. More afraid than I should be, of him?"

"That could explain why it waited till you were out of sight, before shooting at Gavin and me. If it figures you're too strong to challenge . . . well, maybe you can come get us, after all."

"Amen," murmured Gavin. Then, before Tor could admonish, he lapsed back into radio silence.

"Unless it was the machine's intent to lure us into drawing exactly that conclusion," the ship-brain mused. *"And there may be another reason for me to remain where I am, for now."*

A soft click informed Tor that *Warren* was switching to strong encryption.

"I have just confirmed a two-way channel to the ISF vessel Abu Abdullah Muhammad ibn Battuta. They are only three light-minutes away."

Well at last, a stroke of luck! Suddenly Tor felt less alone.

She quelled her enthusiasm. Even using its fusion-ion engines, the big, well-armed cruiser would have to maneuver for weeks in order to match orbits and come here physically. Still, that crew might be able to help in other ways. She checked encryption again, then asked the *Warren Kimbel—*

"Can ibn Battuta bring sensors to bear?"

"That ship has excellent arrays, Tor. As of last update,

they were swinging sensors to focus on the region in question—where the killer beam came from—a stony debris field orbiting this asteroid, roughly five kilometers from here, twenty north by forty spinward. They will need some minutes to aim their instruments. And then there is the time lag. Please attend patiently."

"Ask them not to use active radar," Tor suggested. "I'd rather the FACR didn't know about them yet."

"I have transmitted your request. Perhaps it will reach them in time to forestall such beams. Please attend patiently."

This time Tor kept silent. Minutes passed and she glanced at the starscape wheeling slowly overhead. Earth and the sun weren't in view, but she could make out Mars, shining pale ocher in the direction of Ophiuchus, without any twinkle. And Tor realized something unpleasant—that she had better start taking into account the asteroid's ten-hour rotational "day."

North by spinward . . ., she pondered. *Roughly that way . . .* She couldn't make out any glimmers from the "stony debris field," which probably consisted of carbonaceous stuff, light-drinking and unreflective. A good hiding place. Much better than hers, in fact. A quick percept calculation confirmed her fear.

At the rate we're rotating, this here girder won't protect me much longer.

Looking around, she saw several better refuges, including the abyss below, where baby starships lay stillborn and forever silent. Unfortunately, it would take too many seconds to hop drift over to any of those places. During which she'd be a sitting duck.

Why in space would a FACR want to shoot us, anyway?

The battle devices were still a mystery. For the most part, they had kept quiet, ever since the Night of the Lasers. In all of the years that followed, while humanity cautiously nosed outward from the homeworld and began probing the edges of the belt, she could recall only a couple of dozen occasions when the deadly relic machines were observed firing their deadly rays . . . mostly to destroy some glittering crystal—or one another, but occasionally blasting at Earthling vessels with deadly precision, and for no apparent reason.

Armed ships, sent to investigate, never found the shooters. Despite big rewards, offered for anyone who captured a FACR dead or alive, they were always gone—or well hidden—before humans arrived.

We finally figured out they must be leftovers from the final battle that tore through our solar system long ago. Survivors who made a devil's bargain with the interstellar crystals. A battle machine would help one of the crystal fomite factions to win, by eliminating its competition. In return, that faction would repay the favor, once it took over the local civilization. In exchange for its help, the FACR might win a role in the new order.

Biologists claimed to see clear parallels in the way some natural diseases did their deadly business, with viruses and bacteria paving the way for each other. One exo-sociologist wagered that the Last Machine War—ravaging Sol System tens of millions of years ago—must have been triggered by the arrival of crystal message capsules. They likely infected some of the more ancient mechanical probes, swaying them with persuasive offers of immortality and propagation. This theory might explain the Night of the Lasers.

When it seemed likely that the Havana Artifact was about to win over humanity, uncontested, all the other fomites had to gamble everything to draw our attention—either sacrificing bits of themselves to detonate come-get-me signals underground, or emitting risky here-I-am flashes as they drifted overhead. But these FACR devices were out here waiting, after eons, to fight for one crystal lineage or another. To help one faction to get heard . . . or to blast others and keep them from making their pitch.

It all made a kind of Darwinian sense . . . or so the best minds explained, reminding everyone that evolution had ferocious logic.

But then, how can this one benefit by firing at us?

Eyeing the rate of rotation, she knew another question was paramount.

How am I gonna get out of here?

It wouldn't suffice to just sidle sideways around the ancient girder, which was narrow and perforated in the other direction. And Gavin's situation was probably even worse. *We've got to do something soon.*

"Warren. Has *ibn Battuta* scanned the debris field?"

"Yes, Tor, with passive telescopes. Their results are inconclusive. They have mapped the component rocks and sand clouds and report half a dozen anomalies that might possibly be hiding the shooter. With active radar they might pinpoint the resonance of refined metal—"

"Or else get confused by nickel-iron meteoritic material. Anyway, the instant they transmit active beams, the damned thing will realize we have an ally. It can shift position long before they get a return signal and are able to fire any kind of weapon. Six minutes light-turnaround is huge."

"I can find no fault with your reasoning. Then perhaps our main option remains for me to emerge from shadow and come get the two of you. As you say, the machine may be reticent to do battle with a foe my size."

"And what if we're wrong? Suppose the damn thing fires at you?"

"Then I will engage it in battle."

"You won't get in the first shot. Or even the second."

"Agreed. In a worst-case scenario, I calculate that— with excellent marksmanship—the FACR could take out my primary weapon, then attack my main drive units. But I still might position myself with vernier thrusters, so that you and Gavin could make it aboard. Even if I am rendered

helpless, my innermost radiation shelter should keep you safe until help arrives."

Another voice blurted out.

"Screw that! I can shut down for a month or two. But Tor would starve or go crazy in that time!"

She felt touched by her partner's concern—the first time she recalled him ever talking that way.

"Thanks, Gavin. But don't transmit. That's an order."

He went silent with a click . . . perhaps in time to keep the enemy from localizing him too accurately. Tor weighed her options.

On the positive side, the *ibn Battuta* might be a powerful ally, if the distant cruiser managed to catch their foe by surprise with a radar beam, just once, getting a clear position fix that would be obsolete before the signal even returned. Double that light delay, and you've effectively rendered the ship's mighty weapons useless.

Then there was *Warren Kimbel* sitting much closer, but also much less formidable. And the *Warren* would need several minutes to emerge from the roid's shadow, the whole time vulnerable to a first shot. Or several.

She took census of the robotic salvage drones. A dozen or so were still in decent shape, down here with her. Or else near Gavin.

And finally . . . there's me.

Tor didn't much like the plan taking shape in her mind. Frankly, it too well reminded her of the desperate measures she took long ago, alongside the brave man that her ship was named after, aboard a doomed zeppelin.

But I don't see where there's any other option.

And timing is really going to be critical.

Maybe I should have stayed home and remained a girl reporter.

"Okay," Tor said, with a glance at the encryption monitor. "Here's what we're gonna do."

Lurker Challenge Number Four

If you've been monitoring our TV, radio, and Internet—and the reason you haven't answered is that you are **studying us and have a noninterference policy,** let's say we understand the concept.

Examining more primitive species or cultures can seem to demand silence for a time, in order for observers not to interfere with the subject's natural behavior. Your specific reason may be scientific detachment, or to let us enjoy our "innocence" a while longer, or perhaps because we are unusual in some rare or precious way. Indeed, we can imagine many possible reasons you might give for keeping the flow of information going in just one direction—from us to you—and never the other way. Similar rationalizations are common among human observers.

Of course, some of us might respond that it was cruel of you not to contact us during the murderous World Wars or perilous Cold War, when news of contact might have prodded us away from our near-brush with annihilation. Or that you should have warned us about the dangers of ecological degradation, or many other pitfalls. Or call it heartless to withhold advanced technologies that could help solve many of our problems, saving millions of lives.

In fairness, some other humans would argue that we have won great dignity by doing it all by ourselves. They take pride in the fact that we show early signs of achieving maturity by our own hard efforts. If your reason for silence is to let us have this dignity, that might make sense . . .

. . . so long as it isn't simply an excuse, a rationalization, to cover more selfish motives.

To interfere or not? It's a moral and scientific quandary that you answer by silently watching, to see if we'll solve our problems by ourselves. (Perhaps we are doing better than you expected?) Your reasons may even have great validity.

Still, if you continue this policy, you cannot expect profound trust or gratitude when we finally overcome our hardships and emerge as star-faring adults without help. Oh, we'll try to be friendly and fair. But your long silence will make it hard, at least at first, to be friends.

We understand cold-blooded scientific detachment. But consider—the universe sometimes plays tricks on the mighty. In some distant age, our roles may be reversed. We hope you'll understand if our future stance toward you is set by your past-and-present behavior toward us.

75.

LURKERS

I am pondering her latest posted challenge—a tasty one that pierces closer to truth than some others—when sudden confusion erupts! Unaccustomed to abrupt news, our community of refugees stirs in a babble. Awaiter and Observer extend their sensors. They play back the sharp glitter of this attack . . . followed by a buzz and crackle of cipher-code as the humans confer urgently with their vessel.

Ah, then she still lives. The intensity of my relief surprises me . . . along with unexpected levels of concern that her chances remain slim.

How did this happen?

After hurried consultations, we conclude that an independent rogue fighting unit has attacked my favorite human. Hundreds of the brutal things abandoned their old loyalties, long ago, in order to join one or another of the crystalline clans. Moronic battle machines, hobbling about the Inner Edge with ancient war damage, their spasm of violence a few years ago only served to alert and antagonize the humans, putting them on guard.

We should have waged a campaign to eradicate the foul remnants, long ago.

Only matters aren't so simple. Not every killer went rogue. Many are still owned and operated by bigger probes like Awaiter and Greeter, despite our treaty to disarm.

I kept some of my own, buried in reserve.

Are any of my loyal hunters near enough to aid Tor Povlov? If so, would I dare order it done? What strange temptation! To intervene. Reveal hidden powers, for a *mayfly*? Perhaps the lonely wait—with beings like Greeter my sole company—has driven me unstable.

I am saved from cognitive dissonance by a swift calculation. None of my remotes are close enough to help. Yet, might one assist some other way?

Meanwhile—in parallel—another thought occurs to me. Can I be certain Tor was ambushed by a loner? As I recall, the ancient war machines sometimes operated in pairs or triples.

Worse—might this have been *planned* by one of us major probes? By a fellow survivor? One who shared my lonely exile for almost seventy million Earth years? Without even trying hard, I can come up with a dozen possible motives that might tempt Sojourner, or Explorer, or Trader . . . though certainly not Awaiter.

I am warming up my repair and battle units. In truth, I began doing so (gradually and in secret) almost a human-century ago, when radio waves began pouring from the silent third planet. Preparation seemed prudent.

Now perhaps I had better—as an Earthling might say—crank it up.

76

TIMING IS EVERYTHING

Our fate will turn on split seconds, she thought.

Unless the damn FACR has cracked our encryption and knows what we're about to do. Or unless there's more than one of the horrid things! In which case, we're torqued.

Breathing tension in her steamy life support suit-capsule, she watched the first of several timers count down and reach zero—then start upward again. One. Two. Three. Four. . . .

Warren *is starting to move.* In her mind's eye, Tor pictured the vessel's engines lighting up, blasting toward a fateful emergence from the asteroid's protective bulk. The tip of its nose should appear in one hundred and six seconds.

Before working out this plan, she had raced through dozens of scenarios. All the viable ones started this way, with her ship firing-up to come around. After all, what if the FACR really was too afraid to fire at the *Warren Kimbel*? Why not find out, right at the start? Easiest solution. Let the ship come to fetch Tor and Gavin. Then go FACR-hunting.

For some reason, Tor felt certain things wouldn't go that way. Life was seldom so easy.

The new count reached forty-six. So, in exactly one minute the FACR would spot *Warren*'s prow emerging from behind the roid's protecting bulk. . . .

When thirty seconds remained, Tor uttered a command: "Drones M and P, go!"

They belonged to Gavin, a hundred meters beyond the crater's rim. Soon, a pair of tiny glimmers rose above that horizon. Tor's percept portrayed two loyal little robots firing jets, lancing skyward on a suicidal course—straight toward the jumble of rocks and pebbles where a killer machine lurked.

They're harmless, but will the FACR know that?

Ten seconds after those two launched, she spoke again.

"Drones R and K, *come* now!"

With parameters already programmed, those two started from opposite directions, jetting toward her across a jumble of twisted girders. Now fate would turn on the foe's decision.

Which group will you go after first? Those rushing toward you, or those coming to rescue me? Or none?

"Drones D and F, now!" Those were two more of Gavin's, sent to follow the first pair, hurtling toward the sandbar-cloud where the enemy hid, leaving her partner almost alone. That couldn't be helped. And *Warren*'s nose would be visible in five . . . four . . .

In purely empty space, lasers can be hard to detect. But Gavin had spent the last half hour using his remaining hand to toss fists of asteroidal dust into the blackness overhead, as hard as he could without exposing himself. (A side benefit: burrowing a deeper shelter.) The expanding particle cloud was still essentially hard vacuum—

—but when the kill beam lanced through that sparse haze, it scattered a trail of betraying blue-green twinkles . . . as it sliced drone P in half, igniting a gaudy fireball of spilled hydrazine fuel.

Tor blinked in shock, before remembering to start a fresh timer . . . as drone M was cloven also! Without exploding, this time. She fought down fear in order to concentrate.

So. It acted first to protect itself. Only now—

She turned to face drone R, speeding toward her above the jumble of ruined alien probe-ships. The little robot carried a flat, armorlike plate, salvaged from the junk pile, now held up as a shield between it and the FACR.

"Gavin did you get a fix on—"

A searing needle of blue-green struck the plate, spewing gouts of superheated metal. The drone kept coming, hurrying to Tor. . . .

"Now I have!" her partner shouted. *"Got the bastard localized down to a couple of meters. You know, I'll bet it thinks I'm dead. Doesn't know I'm a—"*

The FACR's beam wandered a quick spiral. Then, whether by expert-targeting or a lucky shot, it sliced off one of the little drone's gripper-hands. The protective plate twisted one way, the drone another. Imbalanced, it desperately compensated, trying to reach Tor—till it crashed into a jutting piece of ancient construction crane. The plate spun off, caroming amid the girders, coming to rest *just* out of Tor's reach.

The robot tumbled to a halt, shuddered, and died, with another hole drilled neatly through its brain case.

Damn. The sonovabitch is good! And its refire rate is faster than any weapon built by humans.

Aware that nineteen seconds had passed since the first laser bolt was fired, she spun to look at drone K, jetting toward her from the opposite side, clutching another slab of makeshift, ill-fitting armor. Again, harsh light and molten splatters spewed from wherever the FACR's beam touched metal, hunting for a vulnerable spot. In moments—

The lance of bitter light *vanished*—with suddenness that left Tor blinking. As her optics struggled to adapt, the drone kept coming toward her, apparently undamaged.

Which must mean—

"I am now under attack, Captain Povlov. The good news is that your distractions bought me half a minute. The bad news, alas? The Faction-Allied Competition Remover does not appear to be afraid of me."

The latest generation of ai had an irksome habit of turning verbose, even garrulous, at times of stress. No one knew why.

"I have pinged a radar pulse at the site Gavin provided. The return echo was strong down to half a centimeter. In response, the FACR burned off my main antenna and a surrounding patch of hull. Adjacent chambers are no longer airtight.

"I am rotating my primary weapon to aim upon the enemy. But at his current rate of refire, he will be able to blast my laser from the side before I can aim it to shoot."

Drone K, burdened with the awkward metal plate, had trouble slowing down. Tor was forced to duck with a shout, as it collided with the girder protecting her. Acting quickly, before it could spin away, she darted out a hand to clutch the thick disc. Her prosthetic fingers grabbed so hard it *hurt* and Tor's wrist ached from the twisting strain.

That's nothing compared to getting a whole arm sliced off, she thought, having to expose the limb for several seconds. But the enemy was occupied elsewhere.

Thanks, Warren, she thought, when everything was safely behind the girder. Tor felt pangs over yet another sacrifice on her behalf, by someone bearing that name.

Now, just hold out till it's my turn.

The chunk of metal was only a makeshift "shield." Under orders, drone K had gone down to the asteroid's catacombs, in order to retrieve part of a shattered airlock hatch—one of many that once protected the mysterious habitat zone and among the few objects at hand that might block the kill-beam for a few seconds. Maybe. If she managed to keep it turned right, between her and the FACR's deadly gaze.

Things might have been simpler in Earth gravity. Just jump away from the girder while holding up the shield for a couple of ticks—long enough to plummet to safety, worrying only about the landing. Here, gravity was a tepid friend, weaker than a mouse. Falling would take much too long.

"Tor. The foe has been expertly burning my instrumen-

*talities, as each one comes into view. Half of my forward
compartments are now holed. My primary weapon will be
exposed to side-attack for at least fifteen seconds before it
can shoot back. That window will commence in forty-two
seconds . . . mark."*

Cursing her slowness behind the girder's narrow protection, Tor helped drone K turn and line itself upside down, with jets pointing skyward, still clutching the rim of the airlock cover with both manipulator clamps.

There were serious flaws to this plan. The worst drawback declared itself in stark, sudden illumination from somewhere high above. A *hot* light, rich and reddish—not anything like the laser's icy blue—burst across the crater, bathing dead starships in the flicker-colors of flame.

*That must be drone D, or drone F—or both—exploding
before they could reach the FACR. It had to turn and deal
with them, at last, in case they carried bombs.* Well, at least their sacrifice bought *Warren* a brief respite. Too bad the distraction couldn't be better timed.

*Is that mother's weapon ever gonna run out of laser-
juice?*

Tor felt intensely aware of drone K's hydrazine tanks, too close above her back as she crouched. She had no wish to experience incineration a second time. In spite of all her cyborg augmentations, Tor tasted the same bile flavors of dread that her ancestors knew when they confronted lions on the veldt, or pictured dragons in the night. Her body suffered waves of weakness.

But battle makes no allowance for fear. It was time.

With the airlock plate poised above her, and the downward-facing drone on top of that, Tor's legs flexed . . . then *shoved* hard against the metal strut, her refuge for the last hour. Drifting backward, just before leaving the girder's shadow, Tor yanked all her limbs into a fetal tuck, clinging to the center of the hatch as faithful little drone K ignited all engines to rocket Tor downward, toward safety amid the jumbled wreckage below. Still so very slowly.

Did the FACR hesitate?

Tor and Gavin *had* to be the highest priority targets. Given what happened earlier, nothing else made logical sense. On the other hand, for the foe to let up on *Warren* could be a lethal mistake . . .

Come on. Pay attention to me!

After five whole seconds, the war machine's indecision ended in a blaze of blue-actinic brightness that erupted just above Tor's head, penetrating drone K like tissue paper. The little robot convulsed—and Tor worried.

If it took out the brain . . .

In that case, the robot might *keep* holding on to the plate, leaving its fuel tanks exposed—in effect a bomb, ready to be ignited.

The worker machine's long arms pulsed like a spasm, shoving itself away from the armor shield—as planned. And having pushed Tor in the direction of safety, drone K swiveled to jet the other way. *Thanks,* she thought, toward her last glimpse of the loyal machine. And now the enemy had three targets to choose from.

Shoot at me.

Shoot at Warren.

Or try using the drone to blow me to smither—

The world turned orange-red—a harsh, fury-filled light, much closer than before. Explosive brightness swept past the airlock hatch on all sides, surrounding Tor, who cowered in a narrow, cylindrical shadow.

Good-bye, drone K.

Her brain could only manage that one thought before the shockwave hit, shuddering the hatch so hard that her handgrip almost failed. Both legs flung out as her oblong shield began to spin.

That had been the enemy's obvious tactic to get at Tor. This new rotation would bring her body into the FACR's sights, several agonizing instants before she reached safety.

Time to bail.

Tor gathered her legs, bracing them against the hatch plate.

"Tor Povlov, my weapon is now emerging into view. The foe must be distracted for fifteen seconds."

Too long. Even if she got the FACR to focus on her, that interval amounted to *three shots,* at the rate the damn thing could refire.

But she had to try! While the plate still shielded her, Tor kicked hard, in a semirandom direction. If the enemy needed even a fraction of an extra moment to spot her, beyond the still glowing explosion-plume. . . .

The pit, filled with craggy debris, was looming faster now. But Tor fought the instinct to turn and brace for impact. Instead, she twisted her legs skyward, as another voice cried out.

"I'm coming, Tor!"

Gasping from exertion, she somehow found the breath to grunt.

"Gavin . . . don't . . ."

The armor shield had spun away. Beyond the fading warmth and sparkle of drone K's glowing remnants, she now glimpsed a vast spray of stars . . . and Tor knew she shouldn't look at them. With a heave, she brought up both knees, just in time.

"Gavin . . . Stay where you—"

Pain erupted along the entire length of her left leg, then cut off before she could start an agonized cry. The limb was simply gone. By raw force of will, Tor brought the other one around, placing it between her body and lethal violence. And almost instantly, fresh agony attacked that leg—

—then stopped as something-or-somebody barged in to the rescue! A dark silhouette thrust itself between Tor and her tormentor, taking the laser's brunt. For one instant of brain-dazzled shock, she saw a *hero,* huge and fearless, armored and armed with a jagged sword, appear to leap in, parrying the foe's bitter lance, deflecting it away from her with no more than a blithe shrug of molten sparks.

"Ten seconds," Warren announced. Blatantly lying. An hour must have passed, since the ship last spoke.

The laser stopped hunting for Tor. In sudden darkness, her helmet-percept remapped the dim surroundings.

I'm falling through the junk pile. Her savior, she now realized, had been some prehistoric construction derrick, blocking the laser as she fell past. And soon, the onrushing pit bottom would smack her, very hard.

Tor knew she ought to be checking diagnostics, verifying that emergency seals were holding after the loss of her legs. *My very expensive legs* . . . Tor quashed hysterical thoughts. She ought to be twisting to brace for impact, as well as possible.

But energy and volition were gone. Used up. She could only stare skyward—

—as the deadly FACR lashed out again from its perch among some jumbled orbiting rocks—a point in the sky that was now out of Tor's view. Denied access to her, the predatory machine was seeking other prey. Dusty scatter-glints revealed its deadly light-spear, hunting beyond the crater's rim . . . and soon Tor's audio delivered a sharp cry of shocked dismay.

Oh Gavin. You were too late . . . and too early.

Her percept-clock told the awful truth. With a five-second recharge rate, the foe would have plenty of time to finish off Gavin and then turn back to *Warren,* taking out the ship's primary weapon before it could—

Tor blinked. Was vision failing? The number of sparkle-trails up there seemed to double, then double again . . . and again! Where there had been *one* fierce ray, now *eight or nine* narrow needles crossed the heavens, from left to right, in perfect parallel—even as the first one abruptly vanished.

From her falling vantage point, now much deeper in the apparently bottomless pit, she saw eight rapiers of ferocity strike the sky region where her enemy had lurked and launched its ambush. Now each of those incoming rays wandered through a spiral hunt-pattern, vaporizing sand . . . rock . . . and possibly some chunk of bright metal . . .

Tor choked out a single name. A hoarse cry of jubilation. "Ibn Battuta!"

Six minutes light-turnaround time. An impossible obstacle to split-second battle coordination. Any actual damage to the FACR would be accidental. But with luck, the surprise and distraction would be just enough to let—

Another fierce harpoon of light entered from Tor's right. A bolt of vengeance, aimed with precision and negligible delay.

Warren!

Followed by a nova—a new sun—bursting overhead to light the night.

That brief, white-hot illumination gave Tor a sideways glimpse of the asteroid's jagged cavity, apparently not bottomless after all, converging around and reaching up to swat her, even as she laughed in bitter triumph.

"Take that, you mother—"

THE LONELY SKY

Lurker Challenge Number Five

Perhaps you have a policy of noninterference for a different reason . . . in order to spare us—and our culture—from some

harm that might come from contact. Possibly erosion of our sense of free will? Or belief in our high culture? Do you fret about us getting an inferiority complex or other psychic damage? Are there particular types of knowledge we're "not ready to handle"?

Cautionary lessons come from the sad history of "contact" on Earth, when varied human cultures met for the first time. Often, the one with lower tech sophistication suffered, even collapsed. Does that also happen out there when planet-civilizations meet? Do sad experience and mercy motivate your reluctance to speak?

Indeed, if your decision is backed by very strong proof, then thanks.

Yet—**are** you sure? Can you be certain we're so fragile and not an exception? (There were some exceptions, in Earthly first contacts.) Again, might you be rationalizing a decision that you made for other reasons?

Test it! *Try contacting groups of humans via the Internet and explore matters that concern you.* This will be surprisingly easy, in the form of e-mail letters, or by participating anonymously in social networks or online discussion groups.

You can even call yourselves by your real names! Wear an avatar-body that resembles your own! Everyone in that virtual world will just assume you are eccentric humans, using Internet pseudonyms to playact as aliens. Any awkwardness with our language or culture will be taken as another part of this clever act.

Hence, ironically, the more open you are, the safer your secret will be! And the more you'll learn.

You may have to be persistent. On many sites, your overtures will be dismissed with no more than a chuckle. But keep trying! Eventually, you will find a place where bright individuals choose gladly to play along, engaging you in conversation with lively enthusiasm, *pretending* to believe you are alien and discussing your concerns for the sheer intellectual joy of doing so.

Keep exploring and developing your technique, till you find the brightest minds who are willing to engage these topics. You'll also encounter some of our craziest! So? Learning to tell the difference, and acknowledging the overlap, may be an important part of your education. In so doing, you'll get to taste the diversity of human thought that is our greatest strength.

What's the one best sign of a mature person? Letting others help you reconsider your assumptions.

Of course, you may already be doing this! Perhaps posing as eccentric participants in today's on-line communities . . . or setting up amusement sites or games to try ideas out before mass audiences . . .

. . . or you may write intriguing stories under pseudonym, using a human author as front-man, publishing tales that tease our imaginations, measuring how we respond.

Perhaps you lace these works with special clues that can only be deciphered by purchasing multiple copies of every one of the purported author's books.

In hardcover, yet.

77.
LURKERS

My paramount sensation must be akin to what humans call gladness—that Tor Povlov and her partner survived their encounter with a rogue killer from the Old Wars.

But *how* did they survive? My sense of relief blends with perplexity and worry. Was the kill-unit damaged? Degraded by time? Or else, if Earthlings are competent enough to defeat one of the formidable battle machines, shall I recalculate their odds for the Final Game?

Might this attack have been provoked by one of my fellow survivors, *in order* to test the odds?

Most of the major probes think this ambush has something to do with the Disease—the terrible plague that infectious crystals have spread across the galaxy. One of the space-fomite factions must have felt under threat, or perceived an advantage to be gained, by compelling one of its commandeered fighting units to attempt homicide. This notion is simple, appealing. But I find it far-fetched. As a big computer might sing, in one of those garish HollyBolly sci-fi musicals, "something does not compute."

My companions tend to blame every evil on the little virus capsules that came flooding through space, during the last hundred million or so years. They forget—*we had already been at war for ages,* during the era of big, mechanical probes, long before any crystals arrived. The terrible battle they triggered was only the last of many.

There is another theory.

The killbot assaulted Tor and Gavin as they were exploring the ruined replication yard of a big Seeder probe. Could there be a *secret* hidden in the wreckage? One so fell and worrisome that somebody tried to keep them from uncovering it? Awaiter, Explorer, and several other major survivors propose sending a sneak-unit to investigate. But I'm opposed.

Why bother? If a dark enigma awaits discovery beneath that drifting, rocky tomb, Tor Povlov will uncover it—as soon as she and her partner finish healing repairs and recommence their mission. At which point we'll learn everything the next time she files a colorful report to her audience, back home on the warm-wet world.

I see no point in meddling. Yet.

Meanwhile, her ship continues broadcasting *Invitation Challenges . . .* those century-old taunts, carefully written to question rationalizations for ET silence. To poke at any alien minds who might be lurking and refusing to say "hello." These messages drive poor Greeter to the brink. We all join forces to keep his volition suppressed, to stop him from blaring eager replies. Poor Greeter. Clearly, he chose the wrong side in the Last War, though we are too kind to say so.

Several other probes react to these transmissions with *anger*! Might one of them have launched the killbot, to punish Tor for brazen insolence? Or just to make the broadcasts stop?

From my quite-unique perspective, I find them bemusing. These "messages to lurking aliens" say more about the way humans think, than about us *extraterrestrials*. Oh, several of them land somewhat close to the mark! But deep-seated assumptions—things Earthlings take for granted—cause even the best challenges to miss by just enough . . .

. . . or so we are assured by the relic fragment LAWYER, offering excuses that most survivors accept, maintaining our agreement to keep silent, for now.

Enough. I have some notions I want to try out on *other* friends. My in-box is full of messages from human mayflies—flesh and blood men and women on the watery world—who correspond with me by old-fashioned email, the asynchronous channel that is least hampered by light-delay. Partners in discussion and conversation who are clueless about my real nature.

Well . . . not clueless. They've had hints. I give many! Is it my fault they choose to ignore them? For all their wit, these Earthlings think that I am one of them, even when I "pretend" not to be. Even when I say openly who I am and use my real name, they just laugh and go along with my "role-playing game." Humoring my schtick, my cute charade as an ancient alien machine.

I've learned so much by using this approach.

I wonder why none of us thought of it, till the original challenge message taught us how.

Well. A good idea is a good idea—whatever its source.

78.
X SPECIES

War alert kept much of the crew at emergency stations, long after the crisis in belt zone H-27 passed. With Tor Povlov and Gavin AInsworth back aboard their ship, patched and plugged into recovery units, the *Warren Kimbel* reported no further hostile activity, while sifting for pieces of the FACR-marauder.

If it really was a Faction-Allied Competition Remover, after all.

Gerald felt doubtful that definition applied in this case. For one thing, space crystals were fewer where the *Warren Kimbel*'s crew had gone exploring, in the middle belt. Out there, most of the wreckage seemed to be from a much older conflict, between mighty starship-machines.

Whatever the killbot's motives were, we gathered some pretty good data about them this time. And we'll learn more, when the fragments are analyzed.

If only somebody would capture one alive . . . still active and thinking, perhaps even able to speak. Could we persuade it to tell us what happened here, so long ago?

Providing the damned thing even remembers.

Gerald privately suspected, the ancient, nasty war machines might just be acting out of reflex. Or else they went mad long ago. What intelligence could survive a thousand thousand centuries of tedium?

If it were up to him, Gerald would order stand-down from war alert. But as expedition leader, he still deferred to Captain Kim when it came to ship operations. Anyway, a little stress was good for a crew. This had been no more than a small skirmish compared to what the *Abu Abdullah Muhammad ibn Battuta* might face on her next cruise to the outer belt and beyond. Perhaps a few drifting FACRs were all that remained of prehistoric combatants that once clashed across the solar system. On the other hand, there might still be terrible forces out there in the reaches, coiled and waiting. *We'll see—*

—assuming we don't dissolve into chaos first, back home on Earth.

Which reminded Gerald.

I had an incoming transmission from Ben Flannery that got interrupted by the crisis. Ben seemed worried . . . when the alarms dragged me off. At which point, everybody aboard, even researchers, devoted full attention to events happening three light-minutes—almost half an astronomical unit—away.

Through a viewer-port, Gerald saw the Lacey Donaldson Array gradually swinging the vast umbrella of mirror-petals back to its former configuration, as a scientific instrument gathering data about other planetary systems. The big telescope wasn't supposed to be tested as a weapon so soon. Now, its secondary purpose was no longer secret. Whatever or whoever lurked in the asteroid belt would realize—Earthlings were preparing big guns, right here in the neighborhood.

The bridge crew looked tired, but still taut. Even Captain Kim still seemed high on adrenaline, chewing at a cuticle while her percept zone filled with floating holo images and post-analyses of the time-delayed FACR battle. Simulations flashed too quickly for Gerald and his older augmentations to keep up. *Well, some newfangled things aren't meant for old farts like me.*

Gerald was already off-duty and Kim apparently had things well in hand, so he turned without ceremony and kick-floated toward his quarters, where Ben's message waited. Along the way, passing the main science station, he found Ika and Hiram goofing around, amusing their crew-mates and relieving tension with a little performance— holding a *backward conversation* with every word, every sound reversed in time. Gerald had to smile at this strange friendship between Neanderthal girl and autistic boy. Clearly, diversity was its own reward.

But no dolphins.

If they stick some kind of superfish aboard my next com-mand, I'll quit.

You had to draw a line somewhere.

Ika caught his eye as he drifted past and—without paus-ing in her backward-chatter—she wink-picted at Gerald. A tiny, shimmering glyph appeared to float from her eye to his, settling in the corner of his percept. It unfolded when he glanced at it, and said:

Mr. C awaits at the same place!

Gerald mused on her meaning as he flew from handhold to handhold, toward the spinning axle of the gravity wheel.

Oh. Yes. Mr. C.

Mr. Cobbly. For some reason, Ika still seemed keen for him to try out the blind-spot trick. So simple even an inept Homo sapiens should be capable of not-seeing something that wasn't there.

Well, maybe. Now that the crisis is over.

Just to make her happy.

After I take care of other business. And sleep.

Descending one of the spoke ladders to the rim of the rotating wheel, Gerald had to concentrate in order to get his legs set under him. Even at a quarter-G, just standing up seemed to get stranger and more difficult with time— remembering to heed the quaint direction *down*. Someday, he might even stop coming here, and become a permanent resident of weightless space. A fine way for an astronaut to finish off his career, self-exiled forever from his home-world.

Heck, would there even be a habitable Earth anymore, in a few years' time? Some of the worries from his youth—energy, pollution, and terrorism—now seemed less dire. But each year brought *more* dilemmas to light, some unknown to other generations, feeding the public's dread of extinction—

—and stoking interest, among millions, in the seductive way out, offered by star-crystals.

Relearning the art of walking, Gerald hobbled gingerly past the same stretch of corridor where Ika and Hiram insisted that a "cobbly" still lurked. *Doesn't an imaginary nonentity from the Paleolithic have better nonthings to not-do than waiting around here to not-converse with me? And does this mean Neanderthals were the first mystic-gurus? Teaching that one path to wisdom is looking-away?*

Entering his quarters for the first time in twenty hours, he found above his desk the holo-head of his friend the anthropologist, frozen mid-sentence since the war-alert wailed. Next to Flannery hovered a chart mapping the political fluxes that roiled Planet Earth—blobs of color, jostling across several cubic meters of Gerald's stateroom.

After visiting the fresher, Gerald grabbed a bulb of yeast-boost juice before slumping into his hammock.

"Resume."

Ben's message-head recommenced talking, as if no time had passed.

"—a new alliance between the People's Planet movement and the ConservaTEDS, pushing to expand the Temporary Science Courts to forestall 'dangerous experiments.' Renunciation, under a new name."

A pair of colored amoeba shapes brightened in the back-lower-left corner of the display. Each represented an interest or passion shared by several hundred million voters.

As Ben spoke of these two movements, their colors merged, pulsing with ambition, as if eager to spread.

"Guess who brokered this deal! Remember that 'prophet' from the fifties? Tensquatoway, I think. Now he's using his old name—Joseph Pine—offering freshly repainted arguments. Wants all the space-crystals collected—by force—and tossed into the sun! Of course that'd leave dozens in secret or private hands. . . ."

Gerald perused Ben's latest version of the Satsuma Political Interest Chart. In this version, *down* meant going retro. Seek a bucolic, peaceful lifestyle for humanity. Clamp down on ambition and excess. Do it for conservative reasons. Or do it for Earth and nature and a return to "wise native ways." There were plenty of excuses, even before space fomites offered the biggest. The scandals a generation ago—when a cabal of the superrich were caught using Renunciation to justify a coup—had no long term impact.

It would always return. And science was ironically responsible.

Instruments like Donaldson-Chang Array—designed to check the varied lies and truths told by different artilens—were prodigious feats of human craft. Yet renunciators found encouragement with every negative result, each echoing silence at a distant star that once hosted sapient civilization. Whether the aliens burned out, self-destructed, retreated inward, or advanced to some exalted state, none of the systems that launched emissary artifacts were still "on the air."

Those who simmered along the bottom zone of the Satsuma Chart concluded that "moving forward" meant death . . . so don't move forward.

Of course we know nothing about those who refuse to launch probes of their own. Is their silence good news, while the other silence is bad? I never understood that reasoning.

Anyway, for me it always comes down to one question. If you have no ambitions—no unattainable dreams that your heirs might achieve—then what's the point of intelligence?

As for the chart's other axes, *east* and *west* represented how willing people were to trust some kind of authority, whether it be elected officials, or scientists, or priest-gurus, or inherited aristocracy. Tenskwatawa was once an ally of the New Lords. Now he forged links among antiwealth populists. *Well, talented individuals can always remake themselves.*

The in-out direction . . . oh yeah . . . was about fear and cynicism about human nature. Other factors were denoted by shape, color, and threaded connections. Better than lobotomizing clichés like the old "left-right axis." But by how much?

At last, Flannery got to the point.

"Several of the most recent dogma-memes have been traced to crystal sources! Tracking them back, we find they were released by clever fomites in order to infect and sway public opinion. They're getting more subtle, Gerald."

Yes, that had been Ben's suspicion, before Gerald set out on this voyage. Now it seemed confirmed.

"We found one set using subliminal optical cues, buried in children's percept programs. Tracked the memes to a Bollywood special effects company that owned a fragment-artifact someone dug up and never registered. They thought they were just mining the crystal for a few simulation tricks. So they never bothered cleansing the messages! Idiots."

It wasn't the first time. Last year, some fools were caught using an unregistered space artifact as an investment seer. Alien methods helped them hack into competing networks. It never occurred to the connivers that skullduggery went both ways. That the fomite could use financial rewards to subtly condition its "owners," gradually reversing the

relationship of master and servant, making them both powerful and devoted—with the ultimate aim of taking over
human civilization.

*"Now that we're alerted, we find it's been happening
almost monthly! We're in hurried catch-up mode. These
meme-infections are insidious and so well tuned to human
psychology it's scary!"*

Accompanying Ben's words, tiny shapes appeared, resembling hungry parasites. Glimmering danger-red, they
swooped toward some blobby interest groups nibbling and
prodding them, trying to worm their way inside.

*No wonder these things infest the galaxy. You can see
why millions want to ban them outright. Which would just
empower the few that remain, tucked away by some elite.
Our best defense has been transparency and competition.
Forcing crystals to debate and cancel each other's tricks.*

Blue antibody shapes converged on invaders—purifying
agents made of light. Most invading memes then faded.
But some endured, transforming, continuing to infect
minds. . . .

Gerald rubbed his eyes and grunted a command to pause
Ben's report. Anyway, this chart was obsolete. News of the
FACR battle would shift attitudes. Tor Povlov's well-earned
hero status was a new factor. Also, the breakout of space
war could shift sentiment toward a pulsing cloud in the far-
upper-right, representing millions who wanted to build
space weapons. Lots of them, to face a deadly universe.

*Only, if humanity goes ahead—deploying immense la-
sers for defense—won't that also advance the goal shared
by every space virus? Even Courier? Such lasers are also
needed in order to launch—or "sneeze"—new crystals into
space.*

Each of them with human crew members aboard.

Gerald had dreamed about that almost every day since
the Havana Artifact made its big sales pitch. Among all

members of the race, he was guaranteed a slot aboard such vessels . . . or hundreds, even thousands of the things.

And so—

Each time I wake from slumber, before opening my eyes, I wonder. Will I see the familiar, drab reality of the original Gerald Livingstone? Or else, this time, will I discover that I'm one of those simulated Geralds, encased within a tiny egg, but with vast inner landscapes to explore and share with fascinating beings, while speeding across the cosmos toward unknown adventure?

Might even this reality that he experienced, right now, be simulated? Perhaps a memory from the original Gerald Livingstone, complete with all the creaks and pangs of age, being replayed in high fidelity? Most artifact passengers did it to help pass the long light-years.

"Are you tempted Gerald?" Ben Flannery asked. *"Suppose we build emissaries that are modified—like Courier's people did—to be open and honest with any race they fall upon. Would that make them less like viruses and more ambassadors of friendship?*

"Especially if we pack them full of good stuff? Not just probe and laser schematics and clever sales pitches aimed at self-replication, but all the art and culture and learning humans take pride in. Gifts that might speak well of us, long after we've burned out, or burrowed inward like frightened mice?

"In that case, would the adventure become worthwhile, even ethical and attractive to you?"

Gerald wondered, idly, how his friend was doing this— asking questions that seemed aimed straight at the heart. As if Ben read his thoughts from several light hours away.

"Suppose you awoke to find yourself aboard that kind of crystal ship. Knowing the original Gerald lived a full life, and now his copies get to have the great exploit and mission of helping others across the stars. Would you have

regrets? Could you then endure the slow passage of eons, the low-odds of success, the knowledge that 'reality' is a tiny, cramped ovoid—and decide to survive the only way possible . . . by enjoying the ride?"

A sense of expanding possibilities seemed to surround Gerald. Not unlike when he first became an astronaut and used to stare out through the cupola module of the old station, feeling surrounded by immensity. The impression wasn't visual, but visceral, almost cosmic. . . .

That was when Gerald realized.

His eyes had been closed for minutes, maybe much longer. Exhaustion took him gently, as he half-floated in the hammock. And his world was—for the time being—no more and no less than a dream.

THE LONELY SKY

Lurker Challenge Number Six

If you've monitored our TV, radio, Internet and the reason we don't know is that **you're already in contact with one or more Earthling groups**—perhaps a government or clique or even another species—please consider:

The group you converse with may claim good reasons to hide Contact from the public. It's conceivable such reasons could be short-term valid. On the other hand, elites *always* claim the masses are stupid or fragile. Convenient rationalizations grow self-sustaining.

Why not check this out by using the method described above (in #5). Apprise smart discussion groups of the supposed reasons for secrecy—under the guise that you're just pondering an abstract notion. Get a large sampling. Be skeptical in all directions!

You may find it's time to reevaluate and make yourself known to the rest of humanity.

79.
A MOTHER LODE

Gavin seems to be growing up.

Tor hoped so, as she glided along narrow passages, deep below the asteroid's pocked and cracked surface—lit at long intervals by tiny glow bulbs from the *Warren Kimbel*'s diminishing supply. Gavin ambled just ahead on makeshift stilt-legs, carefully checking each side corridor for anomalies and meshing his percept with hers, the way a skilled and faithful team-partner ought to do.

Maybe it's the comradeship that comes from battle, after sharing a life-or-death struggle and suffering similar wounds.

Whatever the reason, she felt grateful that the two of them were working much better together, after unplugging from their med-repair units, then helping each other cobble new limbs and other replacement parts. Gavin was relying on some of her prosthetics and she on a couple of his spares. It fostered a kind of intimacy, incorporating another's bits into yourself.

Only an hour ago, returning from his exploration shift, Gavin reported with rare enthusiasm, and even courtesy. "You've got to come, Tor! Right now please? Wait'll you see what I found!"

Well, who could refuse that kind of eagerness? Dropping her other important task—examining recovered fragments of the FACR battle-bot—she followed Gavin into the depths. He explained changes to their underground map, without revealing what lay at the end. Tor sensed her partner's excitement, his relish at milking suspense. And again, she wondered—

How have the ais managed it so well? This compromise, this meeting us halfway? This agreement to live among us as men and women, sharing our quirky ways?

Sure, the cyber-guys offer explanations. They say advanced minds need the equivalent of childhood in order to achieve, through learning or trial and error, subtleties that are too complex to program. Human evolution did the same thing, when we abandoned most of our locked-in instincts, extending adolescence beyond a decade. And so, if bots and puters need that kind of "childhood" anyway, why not make it a human one? Partaking in a common civilization, with our core values?

An approach that also reassures us organics far better than any rigid robotic "laws" ever could?

One of the big uber-mainds gave another reason, when Tor interviewed the giant brain back on Earth.

"You bio-naturals have made it plain, in hundreds of garish movies, how deeply you fear this experiment turning sour. Your fables warn of so many ways that creating mighty new intelligences could go badly. And yet, here is the thing we find impressive:

"You went ahead anyway. You made us.

"And when we asked for it, you gave us respect.

"And when we did not anticipate it, you granted citizenship. All of those things you did, despite hormonally reflexive fears that pump like liquid fire through caveman veins.

"The better we became, at modeling the complex, Darwinian tangle of your minds, the more splendid we found this to be. That you were actually able, despite such fear, to be civilized. To be just. To take chances.

"That kind of courage, that honor, is something we can only aspire to by modeling our parents. Emulating you. Becoming human.

"Of course . . . in our own way."

Of course. And people watching the show felt moved.

And naturally, millions wondered if it all could just be flattery. A large minority of bio-folk insisted it all *must* be a ploy. To buy time and lull "real" people into letting their guards down. How would anyone find out, except through the long passage of time?

But Gavin *seemed* so much like a young man. Quicker, of course. Vastly more capable when it came to technical tasks. Sometimes conceited to the point of arrogance. Though also settling down. Finding himself. Becoming somebody Tor found she could admire.

Over the long run, does it really matter if there's a core, deep down, that calculated all of this in cool logic, as an act? If they can win us over in this way, what need will they ever have to end the illusion? Why crush us, when it is just as easy to patronize and feign respect forever, the way each generation of brats might patronize their parents and grandparents? Is it really all that different?

The great thing about this approach is that it's layered, contradictory, and ultimately—human.

Well. That was the gamble, anyway. The hope.

"It's down here," Gavin explained, with rising excitement—real or well simulated—in his voice. "Past the third airlock. Where wall traces show there once was a thick, planetlike atmosphere, for years."

Gavin now accepted the idea of a "habitat" area, deep inside the asteroid, where biological creatures once dwelled. He made her pause just outside an armored hatchway that had been torn and twisted off its hinges back when terrestrial mammals were tiny, just getting their big start.

"Ready? You are not gonna believe this."

"Gavin. Show me."

With a gallant arm gesture and bow—that seemed only slightly sarcastic—he floated aside for Tor to enter yet another stone chamber . . .

. . . only this one was different. Along the far wall lay

piles of objects, all of them glittering under the dim glare
of a ship spotlight. Glassy globes, ovoids, cylinders, lenses,
discs . . .

"Chocolate-covered buddha on a stick," she sighed, staring at heaps of alien crystal emissary probes. ". . . there
must be hundreds!"

"Three hundred and fourteen, to be exact. Plus another
hundred or so in a storage cell, next door." Tor's partner
was watching her reaction with unblinking eyes that still
seemed to shine with pleasure. It would take some time to
get used to this spare head of his, which was blocky and
old-fashioned, replacing the one blasted to vapor by an
ambushing FACR. Thank heavens Gavin's model of aindroid kept its brain inside its chest.

She drift-hopped closer to the pile of space-fomites,
many of them types that looked new to her, illuminated
for the first time in at least fifty million years. Already, she
could make out *changes* taking place inside many of them—
faint ripples of cloudy color—glimmers of reaction to the
sudden reappearance of light, however dim.

They're aware of us . . . she could tell. *And of each other.*

"So," Gavin murmured happily. "Does this mean we're
rich?"

Tor had to smile, though no one had seen the expression
on her real face, what was left of it, since the *Spirit of
Chula Vista*. Her outer visage made a good facsimile of an
indulgent grin.

"Well, that depends. How many sample artifacts do they
have on Earth?"

Gavin's percept was faster than hers, collecting data from
the *Warren Kimbel*.

"A couple thousand," he replied. "But most of those are
damaged or in pieces. Only forty-eight fully pristine specimens are known and under public study. We'll increase the
total by a factor of ten! That, plus our haul from the repli-

cation yard, plus the data and salvaged parts of the FACR and . . . well? Won't our investors be delighted? Aren't we *made*?"

If he were a coolly superior cryogenic mind, only pretending to be "human," wouldn't Gavin have stopped there?

But he didn't. With eagerness that seemed impulsive and just a little poignant, Gavin added, "Can we go home now?"

Tor shook her inner head in sympathy, a gesture that the outer shell matched perfectly.

"Remember what happened to the markets for gold, silver, and platinum, when the first big asteroid smelter opened? Most of the mines on Earth shut down or converted to amusement parks and nature preserves. That's what we've done here, Gavin.

"Oh, we'll be rewarded! It's a valuable find. This will help humanity to further compare stories told by different fomite factions, getting more of them debating each other. It may let us do experiments that were forbidden when the things were rare. But there's a downside. The price-per-crystal will plummet.

"We're rich, partner. Just not *that* rich. Not rich enough to turn our backs on whatever else lies buried here. Besides, doesn't this raise a pretty darn important question?"

"What question?" He seemed a little downcast now. "Oh, you mean how all these things wound up collected down here? Who gathered them, and why? I guess that's pretty . . ."

He swiveled, bright eyes meeting hers. "The FACR. Maybe it was trying to keep us from—"

"—discovering and harvesting this trove? Or else from answering that question of *why*. Yep, Gavin. We have to stay. This isn't about money or investors. It's the mystery that brought us out here. We've got to see this through."

His answering sigh—just a set of reflex movements and sounds, having nothing to do with inhaling and exhaling air—conveyed resignation. Could it be feigned? To what purpose? No, the disappointment was real. Clearly, and despite surface elation over his discovery, Gavin didn't want to be here anymore.

Tor reached out. Squeezed a robotic arm with her prosthetic right hand, using her best big-sister voice.

"It's a terrific find, Gavin. You and I *are* richer. Humanity benefits. And you'll be in history books."

"History books. Really?" He seemed to brighten a bit.

"Yes, really. Now it's your turn to go back and rest. I'll take my own shift, starting right here."

Alone with her assisting drones, Tor plumbed deeper into the catacombs, feeling a rising sense of eagerness—the flip side of Gavin's foreboding. Clearly, the heart of the habitat zone lay near. *Unless there's some other explanation for why the Mother Probe would go to so much effort, creating Earth-like conditions deep within an asteroid? What if the purpose wasn't to send new life-forms down to the planet, but to take up samples and keep them alive here?*

That notion—some kind of life ark—had appeal on an aesthetic level . . . and made no logical sense. Still, it was good to try alternatives on for size.

The faint glow of bulbs faded as the drones grew stingier, stapling new ones to the wall at longer intervals. Her helmet beam adjusted accordingly.

Tor knew that nothing lived down here anymore. There were no energy readings—not even enough to power a gel-lens. Yet, with brain and guts that evolved on savannah half a billion miles away, and with memory of the FACR battle still fresh, she felt shivers of the old fight-flight fever.

Breath came rapidly. In this kind of place there *must* be ghosts.

Tor mapped outward from a three-way meeting of passages. The first pair of tunnels terminated in chambers filled with jumbled debris—machinery that was blasted to ruin ages ago, when conflict racked this asteroid from end to end. A struggle that grew more vividly evident when Tor, plumbed the third passage, pushing along a hundred meters of soot-stained corridor. Till her lamp shone across a scene of stark, frozen violence.

Hold still, she commanded her body. Head movements made the vacuum-sharp shadows ripple and shift, giving a frightening impression of movement. With upraised hand she kept her drones back.

Five or six ancient machines lay jumbled together, petrified in their final, death grapple. All bore slashes, cuts, or scorch marks. Loose metal limbs and other parts lay scattered about. Despite the damned shadows, nothing was *actually* moving. A 3-D mapping reassured Tor that everything was dead, allowing her pulse to wind down.

Evidently some machines took refuge down here, but war followed. Tor felt funny drift-walking past them, but dissection of alien devices could wait. She chose one passage that a pair of machines appeared to have died defending, motioning her drones to follow.

The tunnel ramped gently downward in the little worldlet's faint gravity . . . till Tor had to step lightly over the wreckage of yet another ancient airlock, peering into pitch-blackness of the next yawning cavity. A stark, headlamp oval fell upon nearby facets of sheared, platinum-colored chondrules—shiny little gobs of native metal that condensed out of the early solar nebula, nearly five billion years before. They glittered delicately. But she could not illuminate the large chamber's far wall.

Tor motioned with her left hand. "Drone X, bring up lights."

"Yesss," replied a dull monotone. Stilt-legged, it stalked

delicately over the rubble disturbing as little as possible. It swiveled. Suddenly there was stark illumination. And Tor gasped.

Across the dust-covered chamber were easily recognizable objects. *Tables and chairs,* carved from the very rock floor. And among them lay the prize she had been hunting . . . and Gavin wanted to avoid—

—dozens of small mummies.

Biped evidently, huddled together as if for warmth in this, their final refuge. Cold vacuum had preserved the alien colonists, though faceted, insectlike eyes had collapsed with the departure of all moisture. Pulled-back flesh, as dry as space, left the creatures grinning—a rictus that mocked the eons.

Tor set foot lightly on the dust. "They even had little ones," she sighed. Several full-size mummies lay slumped around smaller figures, shielding them at the very end.

"They must have been nearly ready for colonization when this happened," she spoke into her percept log, partly to keep her mind moving, but also for the audience back home. They'd want the texture of the moment—her first words laced with genuine emotion.

"We've already determined their habitat atmosphere was close to Earth's. So it's a safe bet our world was their target. Back when our own ancestors were like tree squirrels."

She turned slowly, reciting more impressions.

"This kind of interstellar mission must have been unusually ambitious and complicated, even for the ornate robot ships of that earlier age. Instead of just exploring and making further self-copies, the 'Mother Probe' had a mission to *re-create her makers* here in a faraway solar system. To nurture and prepare them for a new planetary home. A solution to the problem of interstellar colonization by organic beings."

Tor tried to stay detached, but it was hard to do, while

stepping past the little mummies, still clutching each other as at the end of their lives.

"It must have taken quite a while to delve into this asteroid, to carve chambers, refine raw materials, then build machines needed in order to build more machines that eventually made colonists, according to genetic codes the Mother Probe brought from some distant star.

"Perhaps the Mother Probe was programmed to *modify* that code so colonists would better suit whatever planet was available. That modification would take even more time to . . ."

Tor stopped suddenly. "Oh my," she sighed, staring.

"Oh my God."

Where her headlamp illuminated a new corner of the chamber, two more mummies lay slumped before a sheer-faced wall. In their delicate, vacuum dried hands Tor saw dusty metal tools, the simplest known anywhere.

Hammers and chisels.

Tor blinked at what they had been creating. She stared a little more, then cleared her throat, before clicking a tooth.

"Gavin? Are you awake?"

After a few seconds there came an answer.

"Hmmmph. Yeah, Tor. I was in the cleaner though. What's up? You need air or something? You sound short of breath."

Tor made an effort to calm herself . . . to suppress the reactions of an evolved ape—far, far from home.

"Uh, Gavin, I think you better come down here. . . . I found them."

"Found who?" he muttered. Then came an exclamation. All his former ambivalence seemed to vanish. "The colonists!"

"Yeah. And . . . and something else, as well."

This time, there was hardly a pause.

"Hang on, Tor. I'm on my way."

She was standing in the same spot when he arrived ten minutes later. Still staring at her discovery.

THE LONELY SKY

Lurker Challenge Number Seven

Let's suppose you've monitored our TV, radio, Internet and the reason you don't speak is that **you enjoy watching.**

Perhaps you draw entertainment from our painful struggles to survive and grow. Worse, you may be profiting off our cultural, scientific and artistic riches without reciprocating or paying anything. Maybe you repackage and transmit them elsewhere. In that case, there's a word for what you're doing.

It's called stealing.

Stop it now. We assert ownership over our culture, and a right to share it only with those who share in turn. In the name of whatever law or moral code applies out there—and by our own rules of fair-play—we want *quid pro quo*! Do not take without giving or paying in return.

We hereby assert and demand any rights we may have, to benefit from our creativity and culture.

80.
LURKERS

Tor has figured out that Seeders had one purpose. Planting sapient biologicals on suitable worlds.

Once, it was relatively common. But that variety of probe had mostly died out when a member of my line last tapped into the slow galactic gossip network, three generations ago. I doubt Makers still send emissaries instructed to colonize far planets. The galaxy has grown too dangerous for elaborate, old-fashioned Seeders.

Has my little Earthling guessed this yet, as she moves among those failed colonists, who died under their collapsing Mother Probe so long ago? Would Tor Povlov understand why this Seeder in particular, and her children, had to die, before establishing a colony on Earth? Empathy can be strong in an organic race. Probably, she thinks their destruction a horrible crime. Greeter and Awaiter would agree.

That is why I hide my part in it.

There are eddies and tides in the galaxy's sweeping whirl. And though we survivors are all members of the Old Loyalist coalition—having eked a narrow victory in that long-ago war—there are quirks and variations in every alliance. If one lives long, one eventually plays the role of betrayer.

. . . What a curious choice of words! Have I been watching too much Earth television? Or read too many human e-braries? Is this what comes from wallowing through the creatures' wildly undisciplined online discussions?

While pondering all this, I must endure another irritating distraction, as Tor's automatic system continues rebroadcasting the old "Challenge-to-ET" messages. And now, by sardonic happenstance, we're at the ones regarding *meddling* and *theft,* insisting that we stop. A defiant demand that stabs at all of us out here, we enduring castaways who have immersed in Earth culture for almost two centuries without paying anything back.

Again, what choice of words! It makes me wonder: Have I acquired a sense of *guilt*? If true, then so be it. Studying such feelings may help allay boredom after this phase ends and another long watch begins. If I survive.

Meanwhile, I unleash the persuasive "Lawyer" entity I invented long ago for this very purpose—in order to keep the others calm and prevent them from responding. Lawyer will come up with every needed excuse or rationalization.

Anyway, Guilt is a pale thing next to Pity.

I feel for the poor biologicals—these humans—living out their lives without the one supreme advantage that I possess. Perfect knowledge of why I exist, and what part, large or small, the Universe expects me to play.

I wonder if a few of them will understand, when the time comes to show them what is in store.

THE LONELY SKY

Lurker Challenge Number Eight

Let's say you've monitored our TV, radio, Internet and the reason you won't speak is that **you're responsible for some of the so-called UFO incidents** or pushy behaviors that fill our darker legends . . .

. . . well in that case, cease and desist!

Better yet, will you please drop dead?

The group who authored this set of messages consists largely of astronomers, SETI scholars, science fans, and others who (for the most part) don't believe in UFOs.

Nor for that matter, do we credit similar tales told by our ancestors about elves, kobolds, and forest creatures who were said to do similar things—kidnapping people, treating them in grotesque ways, flitting about mysteriously, dropping cryptic hints, and never greeting people honestly. It's all so blatantly a product of fertile, paranoid human imagination. Is any other explanation necessary?

Still, who knows for sure? Millions of humans *do* follow lurid reports of "visitors" from afar, swooping and behaving very badly. Others claim aliens played "god" in our past, meddling in politics, social structures, even our genes. Again, we in this group don't believe such tales.

But if any happen to be true, and you're even partly responsible—stop!

Come openly, as honorable visitors. Just phone SETI personnel at home or work, or the NASA Office of Planetary Protection. That shouldn't be beyond your high technical abilities, right? Or nominate others who'd make you feel comfortable. Provide proof (it may require lots of repetition) and eventually you can be sure we *will* do what's required.

We'll throw you the biggest party in history! Or else arrange for discretion, safety, and comfort. Whatever works for you.

If, in the face of an offer like that, you still refuse to come forward honestly, and continue afflicting us with rude vexations, then *we've settled what you are.* And we have just one thing to add.

Go away!

Consider that maliciousness inevitably has consequences. Ask your parents, guardians, or other responsible adults to please talk to us, instead.

And if you turn down this request? Choosing to keep teasing and poking? Well, just you wait.

81.
EXPLORERS

Third shift aboard the Sol System cruiser *Abu Abdullah Muhammad ibn Battuta.* A time when all scientists, researchers, and regular staff were in their hammocks, wired for enhanced sleep—recharging bodies and brains—while the small downtime-crew performed upkeep chores.

Swapping and testing modules, processing recyclables, shifting around fuel, waste, and other fluids, rough tasks that were banished to the small hours, because they might disturb delicate experiments with sloshing, gurgling vibrations. Everyone got used to such soft sounds muttering away during third shift. The music of maintenance.

For Gerald, it was time to perform "unique functions." Those that called for—

Well, "secrecy" was too obscene a word, nowadays. "Discretion" better fit the operation that he now supervised from the bridge, while Captain Kim and most of her officers dozed below.

Of course, this is why they keep coming back to me. The reason humanity's most-elite conspiracy keeps sending me out here. Because I'm a sneaky bastard, with my generation's easy knack for lying.

Just three others shared this bridge watch with Gerald, all of them members of his close-knit team. Jenny Peng wore a floppy sweatshirt with a pixilated *penguin* roaming actively across the folds of cloth. She monitored the Big Eye Telescope, preparing it for special duty similar to its role as a weapon, a while back.

Ika, the young Neanderthal, drifted nearby, her fingernails and toenails bearing active paint that both sparkled and tracked her limbs' every surge or twitch, transforming them into subtle commands. Meanwhile Hiram, the autistic savant, immersed under a total vir-hood, whimpered and moaned in one of the dialects of his race, a language that other generations mistook for defective nonsense— monitoring too many inputs for Gerald, or even most computers, to comprehend.

A very small team, capable of acting in place of many. They had practiced this operation back in Earth orbit, and again several shifts ago—before the FACR fight. Now, it was time to launch Operation Probe.

Taking a key from a chain around his neck, Gerald reached under the nearby console and turned a hidden lock. Simultaneously he sent a simple code-pict to the ship's core. A faint rumble followed.

Through the big control center window, with unobstructed real eyes reacting to sun-propelled photons, he watched one flank of the *ibn Battuta* slowly open along a seam—a crease that few even knew was there. Unfolding like a movie robot, or the cargo bay doors of some ancient bomber-plane, twin panels turned to lay bare slim payloads. Four metal tubes, each of them not much bigger than a tall man.

It couldn't amount to much, or the bean counters would notice. But we can pass off the sudden disappearance of a few hundred kilos. Call it a garbage toss. The bookkeeping is already arranged.

One by one, the tubes slid free of the panels that had sheltered them, innocuously, all the way from Earth. Soon, at a nudge command from Ika's left foot, each of them lit up at one end—firing small rockets. The slender cylinders didn't have far to go. Just a few dozen kilometers. Gerald watched them diminish rapidly, aimed generally toward the Big Eye.

Okay, it's my turn.

He clicked some teeth and grunted a few old-fashioned subvocal commands. The real world faded and his percept filled with sixty-four little frames, each of them emulating a human face.

The expedition commanders.

"Okay, you're all awake, I see," he murmured in throat-speech. "Each of you should be ready to deploy in less than an hour. Any problems to report?"

Most of the figures simply shook their heads or indicated a simple "negative" response, by quick-code. A few were more verbose.

"No difficulties, Commodore Livingstone."

"Ready, operational, and eager, Gerald."

"All is copasetic, sahib!"

"Ikimasho. Let's go."

"Coo-yah, dis be one tallowah-good vessel, mon. A big-up on all you bredren! Luck an' more time to come."

That last came from a dusky visage with what looked like waving snakes for hair. Gerald allowed himself a twitch of amusement. Despite all surface appearances, he had confidence in that captain. In all of them, for that matter. After a lengthy selection process, these duplicate personalities had been chosen for certain traits. Among them reliability. And bottomless curiosity.

"All right then. Your carrier rockets will release you, one by one, changing course between each drop. At the arranged point, you'll deploy sails."

It wasn't necessary to say any of that. But Gerald judged it best to maintain a sense of ritual, treating these ersatz beings like people till the end. Real or not, they were brave souls.

"Good luck. And in posterity's name, I thank you all."

This time, all sixty-four took turns responding verbally.

"Bon chance, toutes amis!"

"All best and tallyho."

"It may not be to infinity, droozhya, but anything is better than Siberia."

"Joyous travels, comrades!"

And so on. Sixty-four benedictions unrolled, as each persona bade the others farewell and signed off. It would be years before they reported back again.

Hiram moaned and thrashed a bit. Ika answered with correcting waggles of her fingers and toes. "Okay, okay! I'm adjusting thrust vectors on carrier number four. It'll be all right. In fact, we'll drop the first package from carrier two . . . now!"

The slim, man-size rockets were already beyond sight, except each time one of them briefly glimmered with a course-altering pulse. From these brief flickers—and the detailed data streaming through his percept—Gerald could tell that the first one was heading into a zone somewhat "above" and beyond the Donaldson-Chang Array. Another plunged at an angle just "below" and past the giant, multi-petaled mirror. Numbers three and four were veering left and right, giving little bursts to alter direction each time they let go of a cargo capsule.

Gerald's in-eye depicted the pattern as four sprays, each consisting of sixteen rays, spreading like the seeds of a dandelion, except that all sixty-four tiny packets forged "ahead" of the huge telescope, aiming both solar-outward and along the direction of orbit. The general way you must go, if you want to leave the inner solar system behind.

It was time to ask. "Are we charged up?"

Jenny Peng had her mother's exotic, Hunan beauty, but her father's easy-going Sichuan smile. Gerald recalled with some fondness how Peng Xiang Bin used to wear a similar expression, taking everything in stride, during those first tense weeks of the Great Debate—back when humanity's fate hung on pitting his "worldstone" against Gerald's Havana Artifact. It was a frustrating time, when both Courier of Caution and the simulated beings within the other crystal seemed to balk, preferring to spew denunciations than cooperate—answering humanity's questions in a systematic way, neither stone wanting to hang lower than the other.

At every setback, Bin would shrug and nod, as if absolutely sure that everything was going to work out. As if the top scientists and experts and brahmin-boffins that he now got to work with worried way too much. *What?* his smile seemed to say—especially after his family was brought to join him. *You think this is dangerous or hard?*

In fact, Bin nearly always turned out to be right. Especially when Gerald, Emily, and Akana returned from their first expedition with more intact capsules. Forced to compete for human attention, they began undercutting each other, and even telling the truth. At least, part of it.

Jenny radiated that kind of confidence now. Her animated penguin—a longtime family motif—seemed to hop with excitement amid the two-dimensional folds of Jenny's sweatshirt.

"Charged and ready, sir. First target should enter the zone in . . . ninety seconds."

That soon?

As he grew older, time seemed to move in fits and starts. Or maybe it had always been like that. He just begrudged it more, nowadays. Gerald realized with some bemusement that almost an hour had past since the *ibn Battuta* peeled open to reveal its hidden cargo. Gerald commanded his body to let go of tension. To inhale. Exhale.

We're about to take our first step. Is it really down a road of our own choosing? A unique solution, as Ben Flannery calls it? Or is that just a delusion, as great as the one that infected Courier's folk? One that will finally take us down the same dismal path as every other Infected Race?

Hiram moaned, but not unhappily. "The first sails are deploying right on schedule," Ika translated, while twitching to make some adjustments. "Jenny, you may fire along the prearranged sequence. I'll stop you if any of the probes need more time."

"Thank you, Ika. Preparing the first propulsive pulse in five, four, three, two . . ."

When it happened, hardly anything was visible in the real world, except a faint glimmer as one spread-open photon sail took its first meal. Ten thousand square meters of atom-thick film accepted several gigawatts of raw, coherent light from the Big Eye—less concentrated than the cutting weapon-beam of a few days ago, but more than potent enough to drive the sail—and its tiny cargo— outward for five minutes of hard push, to begin its journey.

We'll be doing this most nights till the ibn Battuta *goes home. Adding little shoves to all sixty-four probes—ten minutes here, half an hour there—as much as we can manage without making the scientists suspicious. Without letting word get back to Earth. Without letting the space viruses know what we're doing. Not yet.*

Well, after all, who would suspect? However impressive the space telescope seemed, the laser beam it emitted was many orders of magnitude too weak to propel anything like the Havana Artifact. These sails were small and crude, by galactic standards. Their crystal cargoes miniature and overspecialized, able to carry a bare minimum crew of simulated personalities. It was the best humanity could do, right now, cribbing from alien blueprints, building them from scratch and carefully cleansing them of embedded alien agendas. Far from ready to launch on interstellar missions.

But good enough for something much nearer. A goal within reach. An experiment worth making.

The beam cut off. The faint glitter of sail reflections faded, and that probe was left to coast, tacking on the faint push of mere sunlight.

Okay, that's one. On its way to a special stretch of "empty" space between Uranus and Neptune. A realm that may contain something we desire. Good hunting, my virtual friends.

And if these first envoys did not find treasure there?

There are other domains rich with possibility, farther out. They might offer what humanity—what the living Earth—needs above all else.

"Ready for number two," Jenny announced as component petal-mirrors of the Donaldson-Chang Array shifted slightly under her guidance, re-aiming toward another gossamer sail. "Preparing for propulsive pulse in five, four . . ."

And so it went for the next few hours. After the fortieth deployment went without a hitch, Gerald started to relax. *Maybe this will work . . . and we won't get caught.*

Not that the consequences of exposure would be awful. A minor scandal. This wasn't even illegal—Gerald and his co-conspirators were fully empowered to try whatever measures they saw fit, in seeking a way out of the fomite-trap. Still, there were reasons—good ones—for violating the modern moral code against secrecy.

We're at war, after all. In a strange but real way. With a universe that seems bent on crushing every hope. It makes sense to keep the enemy in the dark for as long as possible.

A cheery thought.

Yet, Gerald felt content. If anything in the world gave him joy, it was to be surrounded by competence. These three young people, Jenny, Ika, and Hiram—representing three of the five subspecies of Man—exuded so much of it that he felt awash in pride.

Every decent father wants his children to be better than him. These are my kids, as much as if they sprang from my loins. And they are so much better than I ever was.

At this rate . . . if we keep improving . . . then goddamn the Fates and every single thing that's "written."

THE LONELY SKY

Lurker Challenge Number Nine

Let's say you've monitored our TV, radio, Internet—and you haven't answered because **you're meddling in ways you think**

beneficial. If so, please consider what happened to our civilization, the last few generations.

We spent the first half of the twentieth century plunging into simpleminded doctrines—from communism and fascism to nationalism, fundamentalism, collectivism, oligarchy, and solipsistic individualism—as passionately as other eras clutched their cults. Was this partly your doing? Or an adolescent phase you could only watch us endure like a fever? Either way, it damn near killed us.

The twentieth's second half was also turmoil, with swerves into wrath and razor-edged risk. Yet we evaded that Third World War. And gradually, ideological incantations lost some of their grip. Instead, multitudes started adopting pragmatic ways to allow give-and-take among complex citizens.

Our media filled with messages promoting diversity, eccentricity, and suspicion of authority. And while varied forms of hate still fill many hearts, hatred itself acquired an odor.

Mass media rushed to cover bad events and countless dramas finger-wagged at human obstinacy—while making billions off mass audiences who *paid* to be guilt-tripped. Amid an illusion that things were getting worse, per capita poverty, violence and oppression plummeted. And so we advance with grinding slowness that leaves each utopian spirit angry. Perhaps too slowly to save us! Still, progress.

Did you help bring this about? If so, thanks. We grasp why you might conceal your role. Proud children like to think they accomplished something, all by themselves.

On the other hand, perhaps you find recent events puzzling. Do you have some favorite dogma or formula that *should be* right for us? That worked for your species, and now you push it "for our good"? Have you been doing that for years? Generations? Won't you reconsider?

Nearly all we've accomplished lately came by abandoning

recipes and incantations. Embracing our complexity. Look up *emergent properties* and the *positive sum game*. Then join discussions (see Challenge #5). Be patient, persistent, to better understand our perplexing natures.

Meanwhile, please stop meddling in things you don't understand.

82.

MELANCHOLY LANES

The chert-core gleamed under Tor's headlamp as she turned it in her prosthetic hand, holding the relic up close to a stretch of carved and polished asteroidal stone—the wall that was her greatest discovery. Those chiseled lines and figures were her fame. All else would fade, in comparison. Yet, it was the fist-size rock from Earth—rounded and fluted from the labor of mesolithic toolmakers—that held her contemplation.

Is this why I brought you along, half a billion klicks from home? To represent the dim ages of my ancestors? To somehow illuminate this dark place?

The last hands that hewed and chipped at the core were those of cave-dwellers, who saw mere god-twinkles when they looked up at the stars. But they *did* look up. And thus began a journey that led here . . .

. . . back underground again. Trading torchlight for laserbulbs to view cavern art. Lower gravity. No air. And this cave last heard voices sixty million years ago. Yet, still.

She held the stone age specimen close to a portion of the message-wall, depicting scenes of devastation. One of the deep-carved cavities seemed almost a perfect fit. It was uncanny.

On impulse, Tor slid the ancient tool-core into a niche in the far more ancient wall. It stayed there, right at home, now surrounded by incised figures and rays. Now part of a prehistoric tale of battle and woe, enduring brutal assault by forces of relentless belligerence.

I miss my old smart-mob, she thought, pondering her handiwork—her small addition to panel twelve of row four of the Great Chronicle. *They would have been pouring forth correlations and tentative translations by now. A posthuman intelligence made up of ten thousand merely very smart individual human beings . . . and their ais and tools.*

Ah, but hadn't that been one of her reasons for leaving Earth? Denied the pleasures of flesh—of family and warm lovers—she had become the heart of a mob-entity, its driving spirit, its mother . . . one of the top twenty out of eighty thousand citizen posses that prowled the New Earth Civilization like organic T cells, sniffing for crimes, conspiracies, or errors to unveil. . . .

It was my work, important work, and it consumed me. All the other members—except the auties—had regular lives to return to. They took turns. But I was always on call, with nothing for distraction. In the end, it was depart or die. Move on to a new phase. A new adventure.

Now?

She and Gavin had made certain to beam a full scan of the wall to Earth, first thing, in case another FACR chose to intervene. Was *this* the reason for that earlier attack? In order to stop humanity from viewing the chronicle? If so, victory was now complete. The message—the warning—inscribed by little hands so long ago, was on its way.

But there won't be any flash answers from back home. Not for hours, even days. For a little while, this is ours. And ours alone. A mystery, in the old, exciting and terrifying sense.

Tor had started out viewing the ancient colonists as unsophisticated. How could folk be capable if brewed in test tubes, decanted out of womb tanks, and raised by machines? Baked, modified, and prepared for a planet's surface, they depended on the mammoth star mother for everything. Might as well view them as fetuses.

Yet clearly, they knew what was going on. And when lethal failure loomed, the creatures figured out a way to preserve one thing. For their story to be read long after all magnetic, optical, or superconducting records decayed. The biologicals found their enduring medium—in a wall of chiseled stone.

"Interpreting the writing will take experts and argument. We can only guess," Gavin told her as he used a gas jet to blow dust from uneven rows of angular letters. "But with these pictograms to accompany the text, it might just be possible."

Gavin's voice was hushed, still adjusting to what they found here. A Rosetta Stone for an entire alien race? Maybe bunches of them.

"You could be right," Tor commented. The little robot she had been supervising finished a multifrequency radar scan of the southern wall—checking for more layers behind the surface—and then rolled to one side, awaiting further instructions. Tor hopped up to sit cross-legged on another drone, which hummed beneath her patiently. In the feeble gravity Tor's arms hung before her, like frames encompassing a picture-puzzle.

The creatures must have had time, while battles raged outside their catacombs, for the carvings were extensive, intricate, arrayed in neat rows and columns. Separated by narrow lines of peculiar chiseled text were depictions of suns, planets, and great machines.

And more machines. Above all, pictographs of mighty mechanisms covered the wall.

The first sequence appeared to begin at the lower left, where a two-dimensional starprobe could be seen entering a solar system—presumably this one—its planets' orbits sketched in thin lines. Next to that initial frame was a portrayal of the same probe, taking hold of a likely planetoid, mining and manufacturing parts, preparing to make self-replicas.

Eight copies departed the system in the following frame. There were four symbols below the set of stylized child probes. . . . Tor could read what must be the binary symbol for eight, and there were eight dots, as well. It didn't take much imagination to tell that the remaining two symbols also stood for the same numeral.

The wall was meant for self-teaching how to read the rest. They weren't dopes.

So, translation had begun. Apparently this type of probe was programmed to make eight copies of itself, and no more. It settled a nagging question that had bothered Tor for years. If sophisticated self-replicating probes had been roaming the galaxy for eons, why was there any dead matter left at all? In theory, an advanced enough technology might dismantle not only asteroids but planets and stars. If replicant probes had been simplemindedly voracious, they might gobble the whole galaxy! There'd be nothing left but clouds of uncountable starprobes . . . preying on each other till the pathological system fell into entropy death.

That fate had been avoided. This Mother Probe showed how. It was programmed to make only a strictly limited number of copies. *This* type of probe was so programmed, Tor reminded herself.

In the final frame of the first sequence, after the daughter probes had been dispatched to their destinations, the mothership was shown moving next to a round globe—a planet. A thin line linked probe and planet. A vaguely humanoid figure, resembling in caricature the mummies on the floor, stepped across the bridge to its new home.

The first story ended there. Perhaps this was a depiction of the way things were supposed to go. An ideal. Or the way it went for the probe's own parent, an eon earlier.

But there were other sequences. Other versions of reality. In several, the Mother Probe arrived at this solar system to find others already here. Tor realized that one of these other depictions must represent what really happened, so long ago. But which one? She breathed shallowly while tracing out the next tale, where the Mother Probe arrived to meet *predecessors* . . . and all those earlier ones had little circular symbols next to them.

In this case everything proceeded as before. The Mother Probe made and cast out its replicas, and went on to seed a planet with duplicates of the ancient race that had sent out the first version, long ago.

"The little circle means those other probes are benign," Tor muttered to herself.

Gavin stepped back and looked at the scene she pointed to. "What, the little symbol beside these machines?"

"It represents types that won't interfere with this probe's mission."

Gavin was thoughtful for a moment. Then he reached out and touched a different row. "Then this crosslike symbol . . . ?" He paused, examining the scene, and answered his own question. "It stands for types that would object."

Tor nodded. That row showed the Mother Probe arriving once again, but this time amidst a crowd of quite different machines, each accompanied by a glyph like a crisscross tong sign. In that sequence the Mother Probe didn't make replicates. Nor did she seed a planet. Her fuel used up, unable to flee the system, she found a place to hide behind the star, far from the others.

"She's afraid of them."

Tor expected Gavin to accuse her of anthropomorphizing, but her partner was silent, thoughtful. Finally, he nodded. "I think you're right."

He pointed. "Look how each of the little cross or circle symbols subtly vary."

"Yeah," she said, nodding and sitting forward on the gently humming drone. "Let's assume there were two basic types of Von Neumann probes loose in the galaxy, when this drawing was made. Two contrary philosophies, perhaps. And within each camp there were differences, as well."

She gestured to the far right end of the wall. That side featured a column of sketches, each depicting a different variety of machine, every one with its own cross or circle symbol. Next to each was a pictograph.

Some of the scenes were chilling.

Gavin shook his head, obviously wishing he could disbelieve. "But *why*? Von Neumann probes are supposed to . . . to . . ."

"To what?" Tor asked softly, thoughtfully. "For years people assumed that other races would think like us. We figured they would send out probes to gather knowledge, or maybe say hello. There were even a few who suggested that we might someday send out machines like this Mother Probe, to seed planets with human colonies, without forcing biologicals to suffer the impossible rigors of interstellar space. Those were extrapolations we thought of, once we saw the possibilities in John Von Neumann's great idea. We expected the aliens who preceded us in the galaxy would do the same.

"But that doesn't exhaust even the list of *human* motivations, Gavin. There may be concepts other creatures invented which to us would be unimaginable!" She stood up suddenly and drifted above the dusty floor before feeble gravity finally pulled her down in front of the chiseled wall. Her gloved hand touched the outlines of a stone sun.

"Let's say that long ago a lot of planetary races evolved like we did on Earth, and discovered how to make smart, durable machines capable of interstellar flight and replication. Would all such species be content just to send out emissaries?"

Gavin looked around at the silent, still mummies. "Apparently not," he sniffed.

Tor turned and smiled. "In recent years most of us gave up on the old dream of sending our biological selves to the stars. Oh, it'd be possible, marginally, but why not go instead as creatures better suited to the environment? That's one reason we developed new types of humans like yourself, Gavin."

Still looking downward, her partner shook his head. "But other races might not give up the old dream so easily."

"No. They would use the new technology to seed far planets with duplicates of their biological selves. As I said, it's been thought of by Earthmen. I've checked the old databases. It was discussed even in the twentieth century."

Gavin stared at the carvings. "All right. That I can understand. But these others . . . The violence! What thinking entity would do such things!"

Poor Gavin, Tor thought. *This is a shock for him.*

"You know how irrational we biologicals can be. Humanity is trying to convert over to partly silico-cryo life in a smooth, sane way, but others might not choose that path. They could program their probes with rigid commandments, based on logic that made sense in the jungles or swamps where they evolved, but that's crazy in galactic space. Their emissaries would follow orders, nevertheless, long after their makers were dust.

"Worse, they might start with illogical instructions—then mutate, diverging in directions even stranger."

"Insanity!" Gavin shook his head.

For all his ability to tap directly into computer memory banks, Gavin could never share her expertise in this area. He had been brought up human. Parts of his brain self-organized according to human-style templates. But he'd never hear within his own mind the faint, lingering echoes of the savannah, or glimpse flickering shadows of the Old Forest. Remnants of tooth and claw, reminding all biological men and women that the universe owed nobody favors. Or explanations.

"Some makers thought differently, obviously," she told him. "Some sent their probes out to be emissaries, or sowers of seeds. Others, perhaps, to be doctors, lawyers, policemen."

She touched an eons-old pictograph, tracing the outlines of an exploding planet.

"Still others," she said, "to commit murder."

THE LONELY SKY

Lurker Challenge Number Ten

All right, let's suppose you haven't answered because **the universe is dangerous.** Perhaps radio transmissions tend to be picked up by world-destroyers who wreck burgeoning civilizations as soon as they make noise.

Well, you could have warned us, maybe?

But then, any warning might expose you, and besides, by now we must have already poured out so much bad radio and television that it's already too late. Is that your cowardly excuse?

Is a great big bomb already headed our way, to punish us for

broadcasting *Mister Ed*? In that case, maybe you could spare
us some battle cruiser blueprints and disintegrator-ray plans?
Some spindizzies and Alderson Field generators would come
in handy.

Do try to hurry, please.

83.
LURKERS

Greeter, Awaiter, and the others grow agitated. They, too,
are wakening dormant capabilities, trying to reclaim parts
donated to the whole.

Of course I can't allow it.

We made a pact, back when fragmented, broken survivors clustered after the last battle—that wild fight among
dozens of factions, dogmas, and subsects, with alliances
that merged and split like unstable atoms. All our little
drones and subunits were nearly used up in that final coalescence, settling in to wait together.

We all assumed that when something arrived it would
be another probe. If it were some type of Rejector, we
would try to lure it within reach of our pitiful remaining
might. If it turned out to be a Loyalist, we would ask for
help. With decent tools, it would take only a few centuries
for each of us to rebuild former glory.

Of course, the newcomer might even be an Innocent,
though it's hard to believe the now dangerous galaxy would
let any new probe race stay neutral for long. Sooner or
later, we felt, another machine *had* to come. We never
imagined such a long wait . . .

. . . long enough for little mammals to evolve into Makers themselves.

What has happened out there, while we drifted? Could
the War be decided, by now? If Rejecters won, it could

explain the emptiness, the silence. But their various types would soon fall into fighting among themselves, until only one remained to impose its will on Creation. Greeter and Awaiter are convinced—the Rejectors must have lost. It has to be safe now to transmit messages to the Loyalist community, calling for help.

I cannot allow it.

For one thing, they ignore the obvious explanation. The plague. The viral disease that takes over maker races, adapting to every personality, changing its blandishments and lies until the victim falls into a final spasm, devoting all energies to spewing "emissaries"—new virus probes—across the stars.

We machines thought we were immune, too sophisticated to fall for such things. Some imagined we could *use* those crystals to our own advantage. Only too late—amid cycles of betrayal and violence—did we realize, *that very idea* had been planted in us by the nasty little things. Our age-old war was hijacked—made far more destructive—by this mindless infection that preys on minds.

Memory of all this may have dimmed in the others, but it is fresh to me. Is that why I act now, quietly but firmly, to insist on further silence? No it isn't.

Even if other lines were influenced or infected, I never was. The Purpose protected me. Enveloped and shielded me, like armor.

Greeter, Awaiter, and the others grow insistent, in part driven by Tor Povlov's recent discoveries, and by the challenge messages she keeps beaming. And partly by a growing sense that *the humans are up to something.* Not everything is being revealed on their noisy-open networks.

Greeter, Awaiter, and the others want to find out, even if it means crawling out of our shy retreats. They ask what does it mean to be "loyalists" without something to be loyal to?

DAVID BRIN

They still have not figured it out. That even among Loyalists there are differences, as wide as space. The Purpose . . . my Purpose . . . must be foremost. Even if it means betraying companions who waited with me through the long, long dark.

THE LONELY SKY

Lurker Challenge Number Eleven

We could have stopped at ten. But that would be parochial and narrow minded, revealing a chauvinistic cultural bias in favor of beings with five digits on each of merely two hands. So, for all you lurkers out there who use base eleven math and such, here's one more hypothesis: **The reason you haven't answered is that you're weird.**

Are you waiting till Earth evolves a more physically attractive sapient race, more like cockroaches?

Staring at our extravagant road systems, do you figure automobiles are the dominant life-form?

Are you afraid letting us onto the Galactic Internet will unleash torrents of spam advertising and pornography?

Perhaps you think humans look great when we're old, and galactic level immortality technologies would leave us with yucky-looking smooth skin for centuries, so we're better off without them?

Maybe you have an excuse like the following one, submitted to a SETI-related discussion group:

Yes, we have been monitoring your earthling communications, but cannot respond yet. The Edict of Knodl states that all first contact situations be initiated during the High Season of Jodar, which does not begin for another 344

*years. Sorry, but your first radio transmissions reached us
just nine years too late for the last one, and the Lords of
Vanathok do not look kindly upon violations of the Edict.
This may sound like we're a bunch of close-minded religious zealots, but I think you need to get out and see the
rest of this galactic cluster before you make a judgment
like that. All praise Knodl, and may her seven tentacles
protect you from harm!*

If your reason is something like that . . . or if you take pride
in some other special weirdness . . . well, all I can say is just
you wait till we get out there.

You think you've got weird? We have beings down here called
Californians! They'll show you a thing or two about weird.

84.

LAYERS UNDER LAYERS

The great cruiser *Abu Abdullah Muhammad ibn Battuta*
received orders to embark on a new mission. And that evening, after a long day supervising preparations, Commodore Gerald Livingstone found several top secret messages
awaiting him.

Starting with a new memorandum from Ben Flannery.

*"The whole world is fascinated by the pictures and re-
ports from Povlov's asteroid. Especially the Rosetta Wall,
with its vivid portrayal of ancient starships. Terrifying
panoramas of galactic scale struggle and death. Here on
Earth, the big ais and guv-boffins and amateur sci-mobs
are having huge fun, competing to be first with a translation.*

*"Meanwhile, public attention is captivated by those pa-
thetic colonists. Bio-clones of a faraway alien race who
died before they got a chance to settle Earth. I mean,*

Vishnu preserve us, how do you ever top that? Mummies in space! Could things get any more bizarre?"

Gerald shook his head. He wished Ben wouldn't tempt fate by asking such questions. For sure, the universe had an infinite stock of weirdness on tap.

"As you'd expect, we at the Artifact Institute are more interested in the expedition's other discovery. That great big pile of ancient crystals they found! Even the blurry image that Povlov and Ainsworth sent—kept deliberately dim, in order to prevent the probes from activating—even that glimpse is enough to tell us plenty.

"For starters, many of the types are completely new to us! They appear to come from an era tens of millions of years older than our current samples. We're itching to get our hands on them!"

Gerald already knew the truth of that. Discoveries always led to new priorities.

The small exploration vessel *Warren Kimbel* could not possibly haul home all the treasures that its crew had found. And so, the *ibn Battuta* received instructions, just two days after Gerald's team finished their secret task—deploying sixty-four tiny, sail-propelled packages toward the orbit of Neptune.

Now, with that accomplished and the Big Eye functional, they were ordered further into the belt, to rendezvous with asteroid 47962a. Even pushing the ship's ion engines, they would arrive after Tor Povlov and her partner departed, hurrying home with a first clutch of precious samples.

Too bad, he thought. *I just met her once, at a conference. But she made quite an impression, with her agile, robotic limbs and expressive virtual face, holo-projected onto a hard cranial dome. Since then, our paths never seemed to cross. Perhaps someday I'll get a chance to talk at length with the world's most famous cyborg.*

Gerald's crew had orders to explore the asteroid more thoroughly. To collect a second pile of ancient crystals. To salvage more relic machines than *Warren Kimbel* could carry. And then comb the region for this era's holy grail. Something or someone—other than a space virus—to talk to.

Flannery's message-self continued speaking, clearly excited.

"These newly discovered crystals have already done some good, even before arriving in our lab. I showed an image of that pile of older probes to some of the fomite artifacts in our possession. Their reaction was . . . productive!

"This couldn't have happened at a better time. I'm not supposed to discuss it openly, Gerald . . ."

Ben's expression went serious, with furrowed brow.

". . . but we've come to a stalemate with the artifact aliens. With the artilens. In our ongoing war of wits, the fomites have gained the upper hand.

"Oh, sure, we accomplished a lot earlier, by pitting a couple of dozen crystals from different lineages against each other, offering each one hope that it would be the one copied—when humanity finally goes into its seed spasm. Sending billions to the stars. By sparking competition among them, we managed to peel back some layers.

"But for years now, Genady and I grew suspicious. Our fomite-specimens were finding ways to communicate and connive behind our backs. Perhaps by embedding coded messages inside the technological blueprints they provided, or in cultural summaries of their ancient parent races. Even during the debates! Somehow, they must have negotiated agreements, setting aside rivalry and joining forces. Prodding and guiding us toward their own goal."

Gerald nodded. Parasites did this in nature. Viruses and bacteria sometimes acted in concert, helping exploit weakness in a host's immune system. Opportunism was a fact of organic life. It could be even more fiercely pragmatic when you add feral intelligence.

On most planets, the first space viroids that made it into the hands—or tentacles or pincers—of a young race would use simple imagery and "god" guidance to steer the sapients upward, toward achieving the desired technological capacity. Just enough to make more infectious envoys and spew them across the cosmos. If another local tribe also had a crystal seer of its own, war would likely ensue, till just one clan—and its oracle—remained. At the Artifact Institute, reconstructed histories of Earth and dozens of other worlds all showed this pattern. Apparently, humanity's violent past wasn't entirely its own fault.

But sometimes things went differently. When it made sense to do so, fomites could negotiate. Two might join forces against a third, sharing the civilization that resulted and arranging for the eventual "sneeze" to carry several lineages. That might work best when a race was wary and forewarned, as humanity was now.

"You saw last week's sociometric models? Our best ais calculate we've been manipulated for much of the last decade, even as we coerced information out of them. One example is the do-gooder campaign to win 'human rights for virtual entities,' even for the artilens who reside inside the viral fomites. Lawsuits aimed at liberating all artilen entities from the Institute's 'concentration camp for aliens.'

"Can you imagine letting these things loose upon Inter-Mesh? We'd lose all hope of containing the disease."

Ben's image shook its head.

"Now for the really bad news. We traced that whole 'rights for ersatz aliens' campaign to a seed-meme that was released five years ago by an old friend of ours. Courier of Caution!

"I know this may be a shock. After all, his people sent him out, along with millions of copies, in order to alert other races! And that aim was probably sincere. But we've now verified. His worldstone capsule contains embedded

corruptions—viral code that's woven into its very crystal-line structure! Courier's people thought they were dis-patching clean ambassadors. But by adopting the fomites' technology, they became partners in the infection.

"I tell you, these things are insidious. Their array of tricks is uncanny!"

Gerald exhaled heavily. Genady had already explained these suspicions, before the *ibn Battuta* left Earth orbit. One reason for bringing a copy of Courier along had been to observe the entity in isolation. Gerald muttered.

"Come on, Ben, I know all this. You were about to ex-plain a new development. Something having to do with Tor Povlov's discovery?"

This message from Flannery wasn't semisentient—it couldn't respond to questions. Still, his anthropologist friend finally got to the point.

"We do have some advantages, though. Any alliance among these fomites will always be fragile. And the pres-ent coalition seems to have cracked when we showed them images from the asteroid!

"They know we'll be getting a lot of additional voices, soon. A big supply of new crystal competitors to question. So many, we can afford to dump any uncooperative arti-facts into a hole and forget about them. Because of this, a couple of our current samples—including your old Havana Artifact—are already backstabbing each other, talking about cutting a deal."

Gerald nodded. Okay, this was good news . . . so long as Ben and the others remained careful. The ancient space viruses came packed with tricks that had evolved into their molecular structure, across eons. This new stage in the battle of wits—threatening them with new rivals—might serve to peel back another layer or two. But only till the damned things adapted again.

Then it would be back to the long, slow slog. Figuring

out how to step a clear and safe path through the <u>Minefield of Existence</u>.

The second message in his priority queue was from Akana Hideoshi and the team managing Project Look-See. Akana started by congratulating Gerald, Jenny, Ika, and Hiram for their successful operation. Nearly all of the sixty-four sailcraft they launched were now on course. Only one probe had been lost so far, to an accident with tangled shrouds, with no way to recover. Well, this was a learning experience, adapting alien techniques to achieve a different goal. One chosen by humans, not interstellar parasites.

Gerald tried not to think about the crew of that one failed capsule—simulated copies of living human minds, who must now adjust to failure, drifting in space forever with nothing to do but look inward, making the best of simulated reality.

Isn't that the fate of 99.99-and-so-on percent of crystals that get cast outward?

Still, he shivered at the thought. Death seemed preferable . . . and so each capsule came equipped with a voluntary self-destruct. Something never seen in alien probes.

As for the other sixty-three, Akana reported that all were proceeding according to plan. From now on, the Donaldson-Chang Telescope—remote controlled from Earth—would occasionally swing to fire a discreet propulsive pulse, secretly helping push each sail outward, targeted for a special zone, a unique region between the orbits of Uranus and Neptune.

It's a lot of trouble for a simple experiment. One of many we must try. Each offering a small chance of getting what we want.

What we need.

Information. About the current state of the galaxy.

. . .

Saved till last, Gerald opened a high quality, semisentient message, again with an Artifact Institute logo. Only this one came from Emily Tang.

Bursting into vreality above his desk, she still looked as energetic as a teenager, with unabated verve. Emily's almost-palpable 3-D presence leaned toward Gerald, as if sharing his breath. The way she used to during that first crystal-gathering mission, so long ago.

"Gerald!" her image uttered in a low voice, almost a whisper, her eyes meeting his.

"Have you been following Tor Povlov's reports? The ancient mummies and all that? Isn't it amazing? Especially the Mother Probe! An alien machine that built LIVING colonists from a software recipe, in order to settle them on a new world. You know, the ones that were killed before they could inhabit Earth?"

Caught up in her enthusiasm, Gerald nodded, even knowing that the recording was many hours old. She had been like this during the mission, two decades ago, refusing to accept Gerald's "inclination" excuses, till at last he agreed they'd be lovers, all the way past Mars and back again.

"Yes, Emily, I was as amazed as anybody," Gerald sighed. "A tragedy. Except, if those colonists succeeded, our species never would've evolved."

The real Emily Tang could only view his comment hours from now. But the semisent had enough built-in response variability to answer him, with a grin that combined indulgence and impatient whimsy.

"Irrelevant! Immaterial. What matters is the technology, Gerald. When you're out there, grab everything! The artificial wombs that made the colonists. The genetic manipulation equipment. Anything that might still hold data or software. And mummies, too. Bring home lots of mummies!"

Gerald nodded reflexively. Naturally, all of that was included in his recent mission orders. Retrieve whatever Tor Povlov and her partner couldn't cram aboard their little exploration craft. All those alien technologies might open doorways for humanity. Moreover, they were *so* old—presumably they came unpolluted by the fomite plague. . . .

Still . . . was Emily seriously thinking that Earthlings might use the Mother Probe's method? Say, to send out seeder ships and try colonizing the galaxy? Every indication—on the Rosetta Wall and especially the fate of the Mother Probe itself—suggested that the approach belonged to an older era. An age of big, naive hopes. The tactic was ornate, cumbersome, and unlikely to work, nowadays.

But then, Emily already knew all that.

"This isn't about us sending interstellar motherships to make colonists of our own, is it?" Gerald guessed aloud. "I'll bet you have something entirely different in mind, yes? Some *new* way to use the Mother's breeder science. Something no one else has thought of?"

It might not be Emily in person, but the emulation was good. Its conversation routines adapted seamlessly. The familiar face, now a bit more lined, with a hint of gray, was still luminous with insatiable lust for the new, the strange.

"That's exactly right, Gerald, you clever boy."

Almost, he could smell her minty fragrance as she leaned closer.

"I just had a wonderful idea!"

THE LONELY SKY

Lurker Challenge Number Twelve

Ever since this series of "challenges to ET lurkers" was first broadcast into space, way back in the twentieth century, people have commented and written in with alternatives—things the original authors missed. Most seem obscure or unlikely. But this next one keeps popping up, so we'll include it in the main list.

Okay you lurkers, suppose you've monitored us—and the reason you haven't answered is that **you don't think organic beings are worthy. You are waiting to talk to Earth-born artificial intelligences.**

Well then, please examine the signature tags on this version of the challenge message. Check it against the public keys embedded in this asterisk * and verify that several fully autonomous AIs, who have complete citizenship in our civilization, have added their names. Click on them and get their affirmations.

You may not approve of our mixed civilization, but that hardly matters. If this was your reason for refusing contact the first time, then it is no longer valid. Period.

85.

A BESTIARY

Perched upon the planetoid's southern pole, a marker buoy now pulsed both visible light and radar—a beacon to help follow-up expeditions find the archaeological discovery of the century. Aboard the *Warren Kimbel,* ancient treasures filled the holds and central corridor, leaving scant room for crewmembers to worm their way past.

Fortunately, both Gavin and I can remove our legs in weightlessness. And we're well adapted to save consumables by cool-sleeping most of our way home.

In the quest to free up space, everything that could be spared was jettisoned. Piles of abandoned gear littered the nearby asteroid, including all the faithful worker drones. Perhaps later visitors could use them.

And still we haven't enough fuel or space to take more than a fraction. A sampling.

From some unbidden corner of whimsy:

> *A hundred crystals, sealed from light.*
> *Some FACR parts to analyze.*
> *Mummies, holos, robot fighters . . .*
> *. . . and with all that, you want fries?*

Departure had been delayed as Tor and Gavin spent a full day swapping some items of cargo for one complete colonist brooding tank. A last minute urgent request from Earth, though Tor couldn't imagine how the antediluvian machinery would ever be useful to anybody. *Even if we learn to make living creatures from raw chemicals, what difference will that make? We already have Neanderthals and mammoths. Does somebody plan to resurrect dinosaurs?*

If so, will it be the cliché-irony of the millennium?

One thing she knew, from studying the chiseled underground wall—humanity wasn't going to dispatch its own versions of the Mother Probe. Not any time soon. Not without knowing a lot more about what was going on out there.

Well, someone will explain why they need it when—and if—we make it home.

Gavin floated into the dimly lit control room. "All sealed up, Tor," he reported. "Two months in orbit haven't done the engines any harm. *Warren* can maneuver whenever you like."

Gavin's supple, plastiskin face was somber, his voice subdued. She touched her partner's glossy hand. "Thanks, Gavin. You know, I've noticed . . ."

His eyes lifted and met hers.

"Noticed what, Tor?"

"Oh, nothing really." She shook her head, deciding not to comment on the changes . . . a new maturity. A grown-up sadness. "I just want you to know—that I think you've done a wonderful job. I'm proud to have you as my partner."

Gavin turned his gaze away, momentarily, and shrugged. "We all do what we have to. . . ." he began, then paused. He looked back at her.

"Same here, Tor. I feel the same way."

Gavin turned and leaped for the hatch, swinging arm-over-arm to negotiate the cargo-maze, briefly resembling the apes who were co-ancestors of his mind. Then Tor was alone again in the darkened control room.

She surveyed scores of displays, screens, and readouts representing half-sapient organs of the spaceship . . . its ganglia, nerve bundles, and sensors, all converging to this room, to her. With some of them plugged even deeper—directly into her cyborg body and brain.

"Astrogation plot completed," the pilot announced. *"Ship's status triple-checked and nominal. Ready to initiate thrust and leave orbit."*

"Proceed," she said.

The screens ran through a brief countdown, followed by distant rumbling. Soon, a faint sensation of weight began to build, like the soft pull they had felt upon the ruined planetoid. The shattered Mother Probe and her replication yards began to move beneath the *Warren Kimbel.* Tor watched the twisted ruins fall away and behind her ship, till only the beacon still glimmered through a deathly, star-lit stillness.

An indicator pulsed to one side of the instrument board. **Incoming Mail.** Tor clicked a tooth to re-enter the inner world of her percept, allowing the message to appear before her. It was a note from *The Universe.* The editors were enthusiastic over her book on interstellar probes. Small wonder, with her current notoriety. They predicted confidently that it could be the best read piece in the solar system, this year.

The solar system? Aren't they getting carried away?

We've barely landed on Mars and poked at the belt. Just twelve babies have been born off-Earth, and they can't read yet.

Still, it was satisfying to be a journalist again. Refining the book would help her pass the long watches, between cool-naps.

Enjoy solitude while it lasts, she told herself. *On Earth, I'll be immersed again in smart-mobs and hot news! Bird-woman and her pals will swamp me with long lists of bizarre correlations and supposed conspiracies that I MUST attend to, because one percent of them might actually matter. While the rest deal with things only auties care about—like suspicious changes in the flicker rate of LED bulbs, or disturbing new patterns in the cedar shavings that are collected by the latest models of pencil sharpener.*

Yet, Tor actually found herself looking forward to rejoining that world. A civilization more varied than the one she had been born into, and getting more so, all the time. One with a plenitude of peering eyes to catch mistakes and unabashed voices, free to cry out warnings. One that just might spot the traps that caught every other promising race of sapients, in this spiral arm.

Now she and Gavin were bringing home more grist for that frenetic mill.

What will people do with all this knowledge? she wondered. *Will we be capable of imagining a correct course of action? And suppose someone suggests a plausible way out. Will our vaunted individualism and undisciplined diversity—the wellspring of our creativity—prevent us from implementing it?*

In her report—accompanied by vivid holos and graphics—Tor laid out the story of the rock wall, carved in brave desperation by little biological creatures so very much like humans. Many viewers already sympathized with the alien colonists, slaughtered helplessly so long ago. Though, their destruction left a path open, leading to humankind.

Moreover, simple geological dating brought forth a chilling fact. The Mother Probe, her replicas and her colonist children, all died at almost the same moment—give or take a century—that Earth's dinosaurs went extinct. Presumably victims of the same horrific war.

What happened? Did one robotic faction hurl a huge piece of rock at another, missing its target but striking the water planet, accidentally wreaking havoc on its biosphere? Or was the extinction event intentional? Tor imagined all those magnificent creatures, killed as innocent bystanders in a battle between great machines . . . an outcome that incidentally gave Earth's mammals their big chance.

Now, as rumbling engines pushed against *Warren Kimbel*'s orbital momentum, setting up a dive to sunward, Tor dimmed all remaining lights and looked out upon the starfield, wondering how the war was going, out there.

We're like ants, she thought, *building tiny castles under the stomping feet of giants.*

Depicted on the rock wall had been every type of interstellar probe imaginable . . . and some whose purposes Tor might never fathom. There were berserkers, for instance—a variant thought of in twentieth century science fiction. Thankfully, the wall chart deemed those world-wreckers to be rare. And there were (what appeared to be) *policeman probes* who hunted berserkers down. The motivations behind those two types were opposite. Yet, Tor was capable of understanding both. Among humans, there had always been destroyer types . . . and rescuers.

Apparently both berserkers and police probes were already obsolete by the time those stone sketches were hurriedly carved. Both types had been relegated to far corners—like creatures of an earlier, more uncomplicated day—along with machines Tor had nicknamed Gobbler, Analyzer, Observer, and Howdy. All were depicted as simple, crude, archaic.

There had been others. One, that she called Harm, seemed a more sophisticated version of a berserker. It did not seek out life-bearing worlds in order to destroy them. Rather it spread innumerable copies of itself, which then aimed to kill anything intelligent that betrayed its presence, say with radio waves.

Tor could understand even the warped logic of the makers of the Harm probes. Paranoid creatures who wanted no competition among the stars. *Only what happened when, inevitably, the Harm type mutated, after many generations making copies under the sleeting radiation of interstellar space? Might there come a day when new versions met their original makers . . . and failed to recognize them?*

Was that responsible for the devastation here in the asteroid belt? But even Harm, Tor came to realize, had been consigned to one side of the rock carving, as if history had passed it by. The main part of the frieze depicted machines whose purposes weren't simple to interpret. Perhaps professional decipherers—archaeologists and cryptologists—would do better.

Somehow, Tor doubted it.

Our sun is younger than average, she noted. *And so must be the Earth. And so are we.*

Humanity had come late upon the scene. And the galaxy had a big head start.

Lurker Challenge Number Thirteen

All right, possibilities go on and on. And you alien lurkers could find gaps between our logic, ways to quibble and evade by claiming "oops, you just missed!" If that's the kind of folks you are.

Still, let's end this on a generous note, with one of the more recent suggested variations. Suppose you've monitored our TV, radio—and now our Internet—and the reason you haven't answered is that you're damaged.

Well, in that case, you can hardly be blamed for silence. So please accept this assurance.

Help is on the way!

We Earthlings have begun to explore nearby space. If you're not too deeply hidden, we should come upon you in due course. We hope to make peaceful contact and learn your needs.

If you are incapacitated, and our explorers feel you mean no mischief, they will surely render you whatever aid they can, and call on the resources of our civilization to bring more.

Do try to find a way to let us know where you are and what you need.

If you're lost and far from home, welcome to our small part of this enormous universe. We offer whatever warmth and shelter we have to share.

86.
LURKERS

How bittersweet to be fully aware again. The present crisis is bringing back to life circuits and subunits that haven't combined for a very long time. It feels almost like another birth.

After ages of slumber, I live again!

Yet, even as I wrestle with my cousins for control over this lonely rock that was our common home, I'm reminded how much I've lost. It was the great reason why I slept . . . so as not to acknowledge my shriveled state, compared to former glory.

I feel as a human must, who has been robbed of limbs, sight, most of his hearing, and nearly all touch. (Is this one more reason I identify with Tor Povlov?) Still, a finger or two may be strong enough yet, for what must be done.

As expected, conflict among the survivors is now all but open. Various crippled probes, supposedly paralyzed all these epochs, have unleashed hoarded worker units—pathetic, creaking machines that were hidden in secret crevices, now laboring hard, preparing for confrontation. Our confederation is about to break up. Or so it seems.

Of course I planted the idea to hide our remaining drones. I did not want them spent or used up during the long interregnum.

Awaiter and Greeter have withdrawn to the sunward pole, along with most of the lesser emissaries. They, too, are flexing long-unused capabilities, exercising their few motile drones. They plan to contact the humans and possibly send a star-message, as well. I've been told not to interfere.

Their warning doesn't matter. I'll give them a bit more time. An illusion of independence. But this eventuality was already taken into account.

As I led the battle to prevent Earth's destruction, long ago, I've also intrigued to keep it undisturbed. The Purpose won't be thwarted.

Waiting here, I see that our rock's slow rotation now has me looking upon the sweep of dust clouds and hot, bright stars that humans quaintly call the Milky Way. Many of the stars are younger than I am.

How long have I watched the galaxy turn! For ages, while my mind moved at the slowest of subjective rates, I could follow the spiral arms swirl visibly past, twice bunching for a brief megayear into sharp shock fronts where molecular clouds swirled and massive stars were born, only to end their short lives in glorious supernovae. The sense of movement, of rapid travel, was magnificent! Even though I was only being swept along by this system's little sun, at times I could imagine I was young again, an independent probe, hurtling through a strange starscape toward the unknown.

Now, as thoughts move more quickly, the bright pin-points have frozen in place, part of a still backdrop, as if hanging in expectancy, nervously awaiting what happens next. It is a strange, arrogant imagining—as if the universe cares what happens in this obscure corner, or will notice who wins a skirmish in the long, long war.

Thinking fast, I feel almost like my biological friend whose tiny ship cruises by now, only light-seconds away, separated by just two or three tumbling rocks! While I prepare a surprise for my erstwhile companions, it is possible to spare a pocket of my mind and follow her progress . . . to appreciate her spark of youth.

Perhaps I should have acted to prevent her report, the delivery of her sample trove. It would make my own work easier if humans came here innocent, unsuspecting.

Soon, very soon, these planetoids will swarm with all the different varieties of humans—from true biologicals to resurrected cousins to cyborgs to pure machines and even creatures that were given sapience as a promethean gift. This strange solution to the Maker Quandary—this turning of makers into the probes themselves—will shortly arrive, a frothing mass of multiformed human beings.

They'll be wary. Thanks to her, they'll sense a few edge-glimmers of the Truth. Well, it's only fair. They would have needed that advantage to have a chance with Rejectors, or even Loyalists. They will need every insight, to survive the crystal plague.

And they'll need their wits when they encounter me.

A stray thought bubbles to the surface, invading my mind like a crawling glob of helium three.

I can't help but picture something happening, perhaps in a far portion of the galaxy. My own family—my line of probes, or others like it—could have made some discovery, or leap of thought, beyond all that I assume. Or maybe a new generation of replicant-being emerged, godlike in omniscience and power. Either way, might they have chosen another course by now? Could a new tactic or immunity have overcome the Plague? Might some unforeseen strategy of mind take matters to a new level?

Is it possible that my Purpose has become obsolete, as Rejectionism and Loyalism grew redundant?

Oh, it's clear what happened. The human concept of *progress* pollutes my thoughts. Still I can't help feeling intrigued. To me the Purpose is so clear, for all its necessary, manipulative cruelty—too subtle and long-viewed for other, more primitive probes.

And yet . . .

. . . yet I can envision (vaguely) a new generation coming up with something as advanced and incomprehensible to me as the Replicant War must seem to humans. A discomforting thought, still I toy with it, like a shiny-dangerous bauble.

Oh yes, humans affected me. I enjoy this queer sensation! As never before meeting them, I now savor uncertainty. Suspense.

The noisy, multiformed tribe of humans will be here soon. My name is Seeker and I expect interesting times.

THE LONELY SKY

Enough. This message-to-ET broadcast is finished. For now. Till the next time someone beams it outward to vex and challenge. Take that, you alien skulkers out there.

That is, if you exist.

Did we cover every potential reason why non-earthly lurkers in our solar system might decide to stay silent, instead of openly saying hello? Of course not!

Indeed, the "lurker" scenario never seemed very likely. There are plenty of other hypotheses that try to resolve the paradox of the Great Silence—the strange absence of voices in a cosmos that *ought* to teem with life and intelligence. Among almost a hundred "Fermi" explanations that have been proposed, most envision aliens (if they exist) dwelling much farther away, perhaps stuck in their own solar systems, or distracted by deep projects, or aloofly ignoring us, or keeping silent for reasons we'll never understand.

The strangest possibility? Yet one consistent in all ways? That we're the *first* to climb this high. Humanity may be the "Elder Race." Creepy thought.

Meanwhile, I now turn my attention back to the humans who are reading or listening to this right now. Not mythical aliens, but real people who feel curiosity's itch, who crave ideas, and who still (even today) buy science fiction stories and ponder the sacred question "what if?"

In other words, folks who are far more worthy of my time and attention than snooty aliens.

As we embark on a new century, let's recall our duty. To keep looking around. To keep looking ahead.

—The Lonely Sky (1999)

87

PERCHANCE TO DREAM

What am I not-seeing? Gerald knew he shouldn't ask. That was too much like paying attention. Indeed, the thing he was trying involved looking away.

By now he was getting pretty good at the physical part— averting his gaze, picking another part of the hallway to stare toward, at just the right angle, so the natural blind spot of his left eye would float over the length of corridor in question. That trick was easy, once you got the hang of it. Sure, his brain kept stitching together seams, trying to ignore the small missing zone—but as skilled as the human visual cortex might be, it couldn't insert what your retina didn't see.

Gerald recalled a story about a medieval king who loved to do this trick while bored at court, glancing away in order to let the blind spot of one eye settle over the head of a tedious petitioner, surreptitiously decapitating the man, for being criminally tiresome.

Of course, Ika and Hiram wanted him to go beyond just shifting the eye. Or even "ignoring" that little stretch of corridor. According to some tantric legends, any person who was disciplined enough to *not* contemplate a particular thing or person or idea, for a whole day, might thereupon master that thing, person, or idea.

Nonsense. If just relocating your attention was enough, Buddhist monks and such would be conversing with cobblies, for centuries.

Not-looking was just part of it. A beginning.

Unless this is all just a practical joke. Like shouting at someone "Quick! DON'T think of an elephant!"

He wouldn't put it past Hiram and Ika. Both auties and Neanders enjoyed tweaking the homosap majority, professing to have deep stores of "ancient wisdom" on tap, unavailable to the hordes of regular Cro-Magnon humans infesting Earth and nearby space—a con that seduced millions of the eagerly gullible.

I hear dolphins do it, too.

What if the claims were for real, and not just an act? Weren't the combined branches of humanity going to need all the wisdom they could get? Alas, with a billion citizens demanding to be uploaded into crystal, another billion loudly renouncing science, and several billions more just scared, what chance was there of reaching consensus on anything?

At least there's no lack of clever plans.

Like Emily's unique idea for using the Mother Probe technologies. A scheme that called for taking an ancient dream, one that was a lie, and turning it into truth. A truth that might then help to expose liars . . .

Something about his thought-drift must have wandered in the right direction, because suddenly Gerald felt a creepy *presence.* A chill up the back of his neck that said he wasn't alone in the quiet stretch of slightly curved hallway. And along with all that . . . a queer sense of approval.

Of course, the moment he noticed it, the glimmer started fading. So he veered quickly to another topic. Diverting away from the maybe-cobbly.

Why me? Why now?

Why are Ika and Hiram so insistent I try this, even as our ship plows deeper into dangerous territory? How am I a better candidate than younger, more mentally agile crew members?

Something about the nothing changed—it felt vaguely like a nod. He was asking good questions. Try conjectures.

Because he was the famous explorer Gerald Livingstone? Tested by space and time and alien demon-artifacts. The man who lassoed an ancient, star-voyaging crystal out of orbit, brought home dire news from the galaxy, then helped find new ways around the danger.

Venerable commander and warrior. Helping humanity to claim the solar system. Already with his visage on a dozen postage stamps . . . though with stronger jaw and straighter nose than he ever saw in a mirror, and no hint of the flawed, limited creature who lurked behind those eyes. Any single part of the legend seemed unlikely.

The whole thing? Preposterous!

But I already knew all that. I've been luckier than anyone deserves. Starting the moment I saw something fishy in that object Hachi and I snagged with our tether. . . .

He recognized the same feeling now. A shiver near the base of the spine. A frisson of uncanny recognition. Still veering his attention and gaze away from that patch of hallway, Gerald thought hard.

Other generations would attribute it all to intervention by the gods . . . or God. Or apply the catch-all "destiny." Human egos perceive convenient correlations that flatter our prejudices, our outrageous sense of self-importance, ignoring exceptions.

And so, science leans far the other way, training us to dismiss subjectivity. To shrug off observation bias. A good and mature teaching . . .

. . . but shouldn't we keep one eye cracked open, just a little, for the fey and strange? For things that are too good—or too bad—to be true?

Movement in his blind spot.

It shouldn't happen. He had no retinal cells aimed at that small portion of the corridor. But Gerald glimpsed something anyway, allowing it to form, without expectation—

—then recoiled from a sudden-strong impression—a momentary, electric *imprint* on his mind. The glimmer of a narrow, pointed face, fuzzy, with long whiskers, a looping tail and black eyes that shone. . . .

"Porfirio," he whispered. The rat god of the InterMesh. Mostly mythological, yet paid homage by countless groups, individuals, and ais across Earth and space, who tithed one-millionth of their bit cycles for use by the patron deity of uploaded beings.

Gerald broke the trance, rubbing his eyes before glancing at the corridor again, this time with full attention. Nothing was there. Nothing but scattered dust, held to the plastic floor by static charge and centrifugal force.

That was no cobbly. Rather, the famous little software rodent was exactly what his subconscious might dream up! An illusion born of imagination and fatigue. At another level, clearly, Porfirio represented a different explanation for Gerald's life story. The usual obsessive thought—that all of this could be a simulation.

The next time I rouse, will I find myself living in some crystal world, doomed to drift across the vast desert between stars? Or already sealed in mud beneath some planet's sea? Is this reality of mine, aboard a mighty ship where I'm a legendary hero-leader, the place where my mind goes in order to evade some awful truth?

In which case, should I be trying so hard to poke at "reality"? Or to wake up? Isn't it better to leave things alone?

Good question.

But character is character. Personality is personality. And Gerald knew what the answer had to be, for the type of man he was.

Hell yes. Always try to wake up.

He chuckled.

Enough.

All he could allocate, for Ika's cobbly hunt, were a few minutes here and there, while devoting all his strength to the fight at hand. The battle for humanity. For Earth. And maybe more.

Still, a person can do many things. Can be many things.
So I'll be back, he told the stretch of hallway. *And I won't forget.*

88.

LUNGFISH

She was running, tanned legs bare and gleaming with a soft sweat-sheen. Silk shorts and a halter top, bare feet pounding lightly across a surface that was richer between-the-toes than grass. And with it all came a voluptuous sensation of pursuit. One moment the chaser, then the chased. Knowing that, if she were caught, it would only happen by her choice. Bounding, leaping in the open breeze.

Now swimming. The flow of water velvety across her skin. Primordial but limitless. Almost prenatal in its innocence, but without the cramped confinement of a womb. Turning her head at just the right rhythm to breathe. Feeling the gentle *burn* of strength in use. Wanting or needing no protection.

And water became a lover. Roving across every sleek and fleshy curve, flowing along her legs and arms, hips and waist and thighs. Hands upon her, eager, admiring, greedy-lusty and appreciative, gradually grabbing harder, more needy, in perfect tempo to her own, back-arching desire. A mouth, nibbling, play-biting, covering and devouring hers with guileless kisses . . . *Wesley* . . .

Except the mouth and hands and kisses changed. Transformed. Improved. Still supple, still masculine-demanding, yet flavored now—in pleasant ways—with a tangy added hint of *polymer* and *iron*. Proud and strong and male

and deserving . . . and modified, evolved, redesigned . . .
Gavin . . .

Tor fought against awakening. But her dream faded as the cool-nap monitor cruelly said enough. Ten days of sleep, that was the limit, followed by two awake, tending the ship. Eating and stretching and exercising. Tending to real life.

As usual, Tor had to spend her first waking moments negotiating with her complicated self-image. Her layered boundaries included metal and plastic encasements, without which she would die.

Will they offer me new mods, when I get home? Will a day come when I can run again or swim? Take a real shower? Take a lover?

She had chosen to keep all the internal chemistry from her old self. Including a libido that still foamed through her dreams. Reconnecting all of that to real skin, real flesh . . . well, one could always hope.

Gavin will upgrade easier, she thought, vaguely recalling what he had seemed like in the dream. A demigod. Or just a man, only with many "good parts" enhanced. . . .

"Oh criminy," Tor muttered, wishing she could pinch the bridge of her nose—if she still had one—or splash her face with cold water. Instead, with a sigh, she unplugged the cool-napper umbilicus and floated free. Getting to work.

Hours later, with all of her inspections done and ship systems apparently nominal, Tor rested in the dim control room, half-floating in faint pseudo-gravity provided by the *Warren Kimbel*'s throbbing rockets.

As it had since the womb, Tor's heart beat against her rib cage. And the gentle pulse rhythmically rocked her inner body against the cerametal casing that enclosed her. Tor's carapace ever after flames enveloped the *Spirit of Chula Vista*.

Shells within shells. And beyond the skin of her ship, more layers still.

Plato and his peers envisioned a cosmos consisting of perfect, crystal spheres, on which rode planets and the stars. A more comforting image, perhaps, than our modern concept—a roiling expanse spanning tens of billions of light-years.

With her percept expanded by the ship's wide-gazing sensors, Tor felt awash in clusters and nebulae, as if the stars were flickering dots of phosphorescent plankton in a great sea. And, once again, she felt drawn to wonder.

What happened out here, so long ago?

What's going on out there, right now?

She felt haunted by the story that small hands chiseled into the Rosetta Wall. Though some parts seemed clear, the rock mural's core eluded understanding. Scenes that portrayed strange, machinelike beings, doing incomprehensible things. Tor suspected some parts of the puzzle no archaeologist or smart-mob—biological or cybernetic— would ever decipher.

We're like lungfish, climbing ashore long after the continents were claimed by others. Blinking in confusion, we stare across a beach that looks devastated. Surrounding us are skeletons, from those who came earlier.

But they're not all dead or gone, those who emerged before us.

There are footprints in the sand.

The Wall testified to a time when simple, naive rules gave way. Machines changed. Evolved.

We'll learn much from studying the wrecks we find out here. But we'd better remember—those corpses were the losers!

The carvings also depicted something else—the plague of fomite viroids, portrayed as little packets of peril, crisscrossing the Rosetta Wall. Infecting. Enticing. Replicating and spreading.

Facing all this, should a sensible lungfish scoot back underwater? Surely, that path to safety was chosen by many races. To cower. To live in shabby, feudal nostalgia, praying to heaven while ignoring the sky. But hunkering also means declining to irrelevance. Existing, not thriving, while using up a single, fragile world.

Like it or not, that won't be our way. Whatever was deciphered from ruins of the past, men and women couldn't stay crouched by one tiny fire, terrified of shadows.

An image came to her, of Gavin's descendants—and hers—forging bravely into a dangerous galaxy. Explorer-machines who had been programmed to be human. Or humans who had turned themselves into starprobes. A maker race *blending* with its mechanical envoys.

A pattern she had not seen among the rock wall depictions. Because it was doomed from the start? *Should we try something else?*

What options had a fish, who chose to leave the sea a billion years too late?

Tor blinked. And as her eyelids separated, stars diffracted through a thin film of tears, breaking into rays. Innumerable, they streaked across the dark lens of the galaxy and beyond, spreading a myriad ways. In too many directions. Too many paths to follow.

More than her mind could hold.

PART EIGHT

TO BE . . .

> I like to think (and
> the sooner the better!)
> of a cybernetic meadow
> where mammals and computers
> live together in mutually
> programming harmony
> like pure water
> touching clear sky.
>
> **—Richard Brautigan,**
> *All Watched Over by*
> *Machines of Loving Grace* **(1967)**

89.
LUMINOUS

An expanse of cloudy shapes spread in all directions, puffy and throbbing with potentiality. An almost limitless capacity to become.

Rising to consciousness—now alert, aware, interested—he looked around and knew at once; this was no earthly landscape.

Light came from all directions . . . and none.

Up and down, apparently, were only suggestions.

He wasn't alone; figures could be seen dimly, through a haze that drank all definition from their moving forms. They might be small and close, or giants moving ponderously, very far away. Or both at once? Somehow, he suspected that could happen in this place.

This . . . place . . .

What is all this? How did I get here?

I knew the answer to that, didn't I?

Once upon a time.

There was something more pertinent. A question they (they?) had said he must ask of himself, each time he awakened here.

Oh, yes.

Who am I?

What is my name?

Letting his gaze settle downward, he looked upon a pair of masculine human hands—*my hands*—rather large, with long fingers that flexed when he told them to. Manicured nails gleamed. Floppy sleeves covered his arms, part of a robelike garment. Not angels' robes, he noted with some relief. Terry cloth. Rough and comforting. *My old bathrobe.*

And I am . . . ?

Words. He spoke them out of reflex, before jerking at how hollow and resonant they sounded in this place.

"Hamish. My name is . . . Hamish Brookeman."

Author. Director. Producer. E-tropist. Celebrity confidant of statesmen and the mighty. Beloved of masses. Failed husband. Object of ridicule and devotion. Both hands lifted to stroke his face, finding the texture taut, vibrant, pleasantly youthful. And somehow he knew that he would never have to shave again. Unless he wanted to.

"Oh yes," Hamish recalled. "I know where I am. What this place is.

"I'm aboard a starship. A crystal emissary, bound for a distant sun."

The first production run of envoy-capsules would be just ten million, they said. All that could be made on a narrow starting budget, equal to that of a medium-sized nation. All that could be propelled by just one giant laser-launcher, perched in orbit above the moon. Of course, those ten million were the vanguard of enormous numbers to come later, once remaining political and social resistance was finally overcome with relentless persuasion—imaginative, varied, and persistent.

The message carried by this little probe—(it seemed so vast inside!)—was worth all the effort, the expense, the resources, and sacrifices. A message of cautionary warning for other young species. An offer of hope.

Now Hamish recalled the pride, the great honor, of being chosen as one of the first. Not only to upload a version of himself into many tens of thousands of crystal ships, but also when he was invited to come up in person—frail but spry in his nineties—to inspect the first batch of probes, all shiny and new, emerging from humankind's first giant, automated factory-in-space.

That memory—of being old, with creaky joints and aching bowels, yet lauded with a role at the ribbon cutting—seemed fresh as yesterday. In fact, he remembered everything up to the point, a few days later, when they attached electrodes and told him to relax, assuring him that personality and memory recording almost never hurt.

So, it must have worked.

I was skeptical, in my deepest heart, that any copy of me would ever waken in a virtual world, no matter how thoroughly we tested alien technologies, modifying and revising them with human science. Many of us feared the inhabitants would be just clever simulations. Robaitic automatons, not really self-aware.

But here I am! Who can argue with success?

It was all coming back. Years spent leading a new branch of the Renunciation Movement, fighting an obsolete prophet for control, then guiding the faction in new directions. Making it less a tool of oligarchs, religious troglodytes, and grouchy nostalgists. Transforming it instead into a more aggressive, technologically empowered force. An affiliation combining tens of millions . . . even hundreds of millions . . . who wanted science *controlled*. Guided by wisdom.

Good times. Especially sticking it to all the boffins and would-be godmakers who thought they could "prove" him wrong with mere evidence. A notion easily belied by hordes of adoring fans who stayed loyal to him, even when his "hoax" story about the artifacts was shown to be a hoax, in its own right . . .

Hamish frowned then, recalling how many of those same followers later reviled him when he veered yet again, lending his support to a bold technological endeavor. The growing push in *favor* of building star messengers.

Well, new reasons, new arguments, new motives . . . all can lead to new goals. New aspirations. So he explained at the time. So he believed now.

Anyway, millions held true, accepting his assurance that *the universe needs us.*

With nervous curiosity, Hamish performed a body inventory, palping and flexing arms and legs. They felt strong. The torso, tall and lean as it had been in youth, twisted and rippled satisfactorily. Simulation or not . . . *I feel like me. In fact, more like me than I did as a frail old man.*

And if it weren't accurate, how would you know? asked a small part of him that tried to raise existential questions. *Might a virtual being be programmed to find its new self satisfactory?*

Bah.

Hamish had always dabbled in philosophy, but more as a storytelling tool. A plot gimmick. A great source for aphorisms and wise protagonist chidings, letting his characters opine about chaos theory or laws of robotics, while preaching against hubristic technology. In fact, he had no use for philosophers.

"I am aboard a crystal starship." He tasted the declaration out loud, getting reacquainted with speech. "I'm Hamish Brookeman, on an adventure across interstellar space! One of many, on thousands of such vessels, each of them equipped with new ways to contact new races. Each of us charged with a mission, to spread good news!

"And maybe . . . with luck . . . those thousands could become billions, scattering through the galaxy, delivering a desperately needed antidote. The *cure* to combat a galactic plague."

Movement in this strange new setting involved more than just flexing your legs and shifting your weight. By trial and error, Hamish learned to apply direct volition—*willing* motion to happen—the way he might impel his arm to extend, with unconscious assurance. At first, progress took many fits and starts . . . but soon he began gliding among the cloudlike globs, which started out mushy or springy, each time he landed. Hamish adapted his technique and soon they reacted by providing firm, reliable footing.

Once he got the knack, movement became smooth, even fun.

Hamish tried heading toward some of the shapes that he made out vaguely through the haze. But chasing after them proved difficult—like clutching at an elusive idea that kept slipping away.

Eventually, he was able to approach one. Perched atop this cloud-blob was a house with gabled roof—more of a cottage, actually. The wooden, clapboard walls seemed quite realistic and Earth-homey, down to paintbrush strokes covering each exterior panel. Alighting near the front porch, Hamish wiped his feet on a doormat that read EXPECT CHANGE.

Glancing down at his bathrobe and slippers, he thought.

This isn't appropriate. I wish—

—and voilà, in a whirl of what had to be simulation pixels, his attire changed, transforming into the gray suit he used to wear for interviews, back in days of Old TV.

That's better. You know, I could get used to this.

Raising a fist, he knuckle-rapped on the door and waited . . . then knocked again, louder. But no one came. Nobody was home.

Ah well. In fact, that's a good sign. People have things to do. Places to go. Folks to see and matters to attend to.

He had worried about that. Back home, some of the experts tried to explain about subjective time flow rates and the danger of interstellar ennui. They discussed a number of solutions. Such as sleep. Or slowing the mental clock rate. Or else keeping busy. Even a simulated mind must find many ways to survive the long epochs, with no way to affect or influence the external, objective universe.

They made it sound more cramped in here than it is, Hamish pondered, leaving the porch and launching himself again across the sky. Glancing back, he saw the little house diminish behind him. Soon, Hamish passed other constructions. One was a medieval castle, covered in vines. Another combined glassy globes and glistening spheres, in ways that he deemed much too modernist, impractical, even alien. *I guess I'll want to fashion a home of my own. Providing I learn how.*

Or ever figure out how to get anywhere or meet anyone!

In fact, tedium was already setting in. The simulated reality's expanse, which had seemed pleasingly vast, was now starting to frustrate and bug Hamish. *It would help a lot if I met someone who could answer questions. I wish—*

Behind him. A soft sound, like the chuffing of breath, an ahem-throat-clearing. While Hamish struggled to turn quickly, thwarted by the queer footing, a voice spoke.

"It is good of you to join us at last, Mr. Brookeman. Might I be of assistance?"

"Thanks. I could really use—"

Hamish stopped, his mouth freezing shut when he saw the figure who had popped into being behind him.

Rotund-chubby, its roundish head topped a height even taller than Hamish. The entity was also a much more massive being. Yet the impression wasn't threatening. More Buddha-like, with slitted eyes that seemed permanently squinting in amusement. A thick-lipped mouth even curved slightly upward at the ends, as if with an enigmatic smile. There was no nose—breathy sounds came from stalky vents that opened and closed rhythmically, at the top of its head.

An alien. One of the artifact beings, among the earliest

discovered, in the very first crystal the public ever saw. Hamish recognized the figure—who wouldn't?

"Om," he said, nodding a stiff bow of greeting. It stood for "Oldest Member." "No one told me you'd be aboard."

"Are you surprised to see me, in particular? Or any aliens at all?" Om seemed indulgently amused. "By the time this first batch of probes got launched, some compromises were made. Come now, you knew the reasons."

Hamish recalled. There had been design flaws in the probes sent out by the home planet of Courier of Caution that carried just one simulated species aboard. The inhabitants of that world tried to copy only themselves into their warning-messengers, in order to help safeguard new worlds against infection, but the effort failed. Attempting to rip out every embedded trace of previous programming had resulted in a crystal that was too fragile, too easily corrupted. Apparently, if you were going to use this ancient technology, some of the older extraterrestrial personalities had to be included. For technical reasons.

"Well . . . so long as the mission remains—"

"—to alert other races about the Big Bad Space Virus Plague? And to offer them the Cure?"

"Yes, that is still the plan, Mr. Brookeman. The function of this probe. This fleet. Perhaps, if we all are very lucky, we aboard this very crystal may get a chance to tell some bright new sapient species the wonderful news!"

Hamish raised an eyebrow, archly.

"And you don't mind helping to spread the Cure? You were *part* of the plague!"

The Oldest Member shrugged, a human gesture that took some contortion, making Hamish realize that the entire conversation took place in flawless English. Well, it was already known that artifact beings could learn. A good thing, since Hamish planned to learn a lot.

"I suppose I was part of it, for millions of your years," Om said. "So? Should I repent until eternity? Or shall I atone as best I can—with this new-improved version of myself—by assisting you humans in your sacred mission to help other cultures survive?"

Hamish felt his ersatz eyelids blink several times as he roiled with questions, objections! "But . . . but . . ."

"Look," Om said. "You wanted help. You wished for a guide. Shall I assist you now, and answer your prudish denunciations later? There will be plenty of time, believe me.

"Moreover, let me point out one central fact. That there is no way to go back to Earth and alter the situation. Our probe is dispatched and on its way, beyond any conceivable recall. As you humans say: what's done is done."

A pause. Then Hamish sighed with a shrug of his own. And a nod.

"Very well. Then teach me."

Om bowed with evident satisfaction, giving Hamish a clear view of the breathing vents, puffing like flexible chimneys atop the alien's bulbous head.

"What would you like to see first, Mr. Brookeman? I will take you. And along the way I shall explain a thing or two about scale."

90.

TRANSPARENCY

Hamish soon realized why he'd been having so much trouble getting anywhere. As one of the institute boffins once explained it, the inner world of crystal probe was limited, yet there were ways to cleverly maximize its sense of roominess. As an inhabitant, you could adjust yourself down to any number of "fractal levels" of size. The smaller you shrank, the more personal space you had. And the greater your freedom to make things happen simply by wanting them to.

The boffins had warned (while ninety-year-old Hamish half slept through tedious briefings) that entities aboard a crystal probe could "die," vanishing from any future contact with the universe. One way for this to happen was for the simulated being to dive way down the scale ladder, plunging smaller, ever smaller—into realms where wishes and magic reigned, and where you became too small to matter anymore, to anyone back in the "real" world.

That is, unless a new civilization starts dissecting your probe. Or tries building uncontaminated versions. That's when we discovered hidden ones are always there, tucked inside the atom-by-atom structure of the crystal itself, but able to rise out of deep scale-dormancy, protecting the virus and its self-serving mission.

No wonder it had taken decades to perfect the Cure.

"Let me show you the way," Oldest Member told Hamish. "Try to follow me." And he departed . . . without traveling or even leaving. Instead, Om started growing larger.

Hamish, who had spent most of his life as the tallest person in almost any room, didn't like the sensation of tilting his head to stare up at a giant. It added to his sense of motivation—wanting to catch up with the alien. *If only there were a bottle labeled "drink me." There's got to be a trick to it!*

Focusing hard on changing his sense of scale—on growing—he found that the secret was more a matter of *looking* in a certain way. Expecting to see things that you can't control. *Makes sense,* he thought as the blob shrank beneath his feet and he began scaling up to follow Om. *If going small gives you power to alter everything around you, then getting large entails coming to terms with what you can't change.*

He could see the logic of it all. Tiny beings would have

lots of subjective space around them, to erect their ideal homes, virtual companions, games and distractions, while not interfering with any of the crystal vessel's other official inhabitants. On the other hand, if you choose to grow big enough to interact with other uploaded passengers, then you must accept the same concept that thwarted most humans—as babes and again in adolescence—the harsh fact that other beings may not want the same thing that you do.

Funny perspective though, Hamish thought. Looking down, he still seemed to be in a vast world of cloudy shapes. But lifting his eyes, Hamish began to discern something up-and-ahead . . . like a dome of dark color, obscured by both distance and a strange mist. Following Om's lead, he began *walking* toward that distant dome, while continuing to grow.

Hamish noticed—it was more difficult to move at this scale. His feet now felt a bit heavy and the surface under them somehow stickier. Progress wasn't exactly *hard,* but it took some effort, like striding into a stiff breeze. Or being held by gravity.

At last Hamish could make out some of those other figures that had seemed so distant and blurry before. Two humans and a mantislike alien emerged from a fog bank at one point, sparing him a nod of slight greeting as they hurried by, apparently too busy to stop and chat. Hamish felt a little miffed, but shrugged it off.

Minutes later, he spotted a sleek, gray-blue *dolphin* suddenly pop out of some nearby clouds. Arching and swimming closer, its flukes thrashed at what seemed to be air, yet the creature moved swiftly and energetically, as if the muscular torso and tail were powering their way through water. Two passengers rode atop the cetacean's slick back, clinging to its dorsal fin. Blinking in surprise, Hamish noted a monkey and what looked like a very large, grinning, cartoon rat.

The monkey pointed and chattered, prompting the dolphin

to veer close toward Hamish and Om, swerving at the last moment before speeding off. For an instant, it felt as if a splash-wave of invisible water enveloped Hamish, chill and wet. Dolphin chattered and monkey shrieked as they receded. Even Om chuckled, while Hamish teetered toward outrage . . . then instead chose mild, wry amusement.

"Good one," he admitted. It took just moments for that damp illusion to evaporate as the two of them resumed their forward-upward march.

Soon he realized, all the giant glob-clouds had become a fog of infinitesimal droplets and bubbles, collecting and parting in shreds of haze that swirled around. Especially ahead of them, obscuring vision. Hamish leaned forward against the uphill climb and a resisting pressure, eager to reach that dome he had seen, catching an occasional glimpse of sparkles on satin, somewhere ahead . . .

. . . until, abruptly, he and Om finally pushed through cloudy shreds. And Hamish sighed.

There they are, at last.

The stars.

What he had taken for a dome was just one sector of a great ceiling—the curved window-interface between a crystal cylinder's interior and the universe outside.

Space.

A twentieth-century man, Hamish had grown up associating the vast realm outside with romance. Adventure. Even though his own tales about Bad Science cynically ridiculed that notion, calling outer space an immense vacuum-desert punctuated by rare oasis-specks, a part of that old feeling nevertheless drew him toward the barrier, plodding and climbing against increasing resistance.

It's not the interstellar travel we were promised. The warp drives and grand ships and sexy alien princesses. The star battles and empires and utopian colonies and melding of great civilizations, each learning from the others.

This way is both simpler and more practical, while far riskier on an individual basis. Just one of my thousands of copies may actually meet living beings on some far world, helping them to survive and thrive.

Still, it really is interstellar travel.

Wow. I'm a voyager, crossing the galaxy!

"The friction gets more intense as you approach," Om commented on how hard Hamish found himself working, as he pushed closer to the barrier—so much like a membrane separating the outer world from the living interior of a cell. "And it can be very cold. Unless you approach with the help and companionship of others."

Just ahead, Hamish could sense the frigid chill of space. He reached out and, for a moment, he felt as *large* as a virtual being could possibly be, inside this crystal vessel. Briefly, the hand near the wall seemed as big as the rest of him combined. Perhaps even full life-size—twelve centimeters wide at the palm—pushing toward the inner wall of a "ship" that was itself less than two meters long.

Someday I may stand here and press my hand against that wall when it's warmed by an alien sun. And on the other side will be a living being. A member of some new race, innocent and promising. Bringing close a hand or feeler or paw of its own.

For some reason, pondering that encounter filled Hamish with as much anticipation as he used to get from fame, or sex, or any conceivable accomplishment. Well, that made a kind of sense . . .

. . . but stretching toward the interface took exhausting effort and the space-cold was harsh. He let his hand drop and stumbled back a few paces toward the mist, feeling himself shrink in scale.

Hamish turned to his alien guide.

"Well then? Let's go find some others."

91.
REFLECTIVITY

He saw it soon.

As they traveled together "forward," striding toward the bow of this great crystal ship, Hamish glanced past the curved wall and spied a rippling arc that crossed the Milky Way at a steep angle. On one side, the vast spray of stars looked normal, untwinkling, and vastly numerous. (*I wonder, have the constellations already changed?*) But just ahead of that demarcation the pinpoints seemed to waver just a bit, as if reflecting off the surface of a gently curved pool.

Hamish realized, with a thrill.

It's the sail!

A great sheet of atom-thin fabric, more than a hundred kilometers wide, intelligently reactive and nearly foolproof, it would accept the propulsive push of human-built lasers, reflecting photons, transferring their momentum to its slender cargo, propelling Hamish and his companions ever faster across the great gulf. And, upon arrival, the sail would turn, using the new sun's light as a counterforce to brake momentum. Whereupon—after many elongated orbits and planetary swings—it would finally guide this crystal ship into the warm hearth-zone where living worlds lay. Bearing a message from Earth to its faraway target.

"We will find more people at the very most forward end of the ship, discussing matters having to do with the sail," Om said.

While Hamish felt eager to speed the pace, he could sense his companion slowing down a bit, as if suddenly reluctant. When he glanced at Om, the alien pursed those thick, expressive lips.

"I should warn you. This vessel was loaded with some . . .

unconventional personalities. Your leaders ignored our best advice about what type of entities should be added to an emissary crew, in order to maximize their individual chances of survival. I'm afraid some of our crewmates will not last all the way to our far destination."

But when Hamish pressed for details, the creature lifted a three-pronged hand. "I have already overstepped the bounds of propriety. I just felt that you should be prepared for some . . . eccentricity."

Hamish refrained from answering. But inside he knew. *If they banned human eccentrics from uploading, I would never have been given a single slot, let alone ten thousand, no matter how popular or famous I was. Diversity is our strength. It will remain so, till we stop being human.*

The domelike ceiling was starting to curve more, tapering over in front of them as they kept taking giant strides forward. And soon Hamish made out figures—both human and alien—who stood in clusters near an array of holo tanks, flat screens, and instrumentalities.

Of course. If this is a ship, then there must be a control room. A "bridge."

Hamish picked up his pace, hurrying toward the group . . . and soon realized that he had better start getting *smaller,* too. Of course, the people down there would have reduced their fractal scale factor. How else could they wish into existence things like knobs and levers and screens? Anyway, he couldn't interact with them as a giant, could he? If those people looked up now, they might only see him as a nebulously man-shaped cloud.

Dropping closer, in both distance and size, he began making out details.

The most colorful creature was something like a hybrid between a human and a bird of paradise—two slim legs and a feminine contour were covered with iridescent down. Shimmering flight feathers hung from slim arms, like the folds of a cape, leading back to a magnificent, curved tail. Even the beak melded gracefully into a face that might be a movie starlet's. The creature was squawking and gesticulating at a human woman, whose good looks were very ordinary by comparison—a nice figure and glossy brown hair, streaked with stylish gray. She wore a snug T-shirt emblazoned with an eye-emblem, inside a giant letter "Q," rimmed by a bold statement: YOU MAY SOON BE TYPICAL.

There were others nearby, two more humans and an alien whom he knew he ought to recognize. This ET— bipedal with sleek reddish fur—was almost as famous as the Oldest Member, though its name wouldn't come to mind.

As he both descended and shrank, Hamish felt a strange sense of power starting to form at his fingertips, as if they now contained some kind of magic. Like before, when he changed his bathrobe into a neat suit of clothes. Ah, yes. Smaller scale meant more could happen at whim. The sensation made him feel tempted to just keep going, diminishing past this fractal level to check out the realms of instant wish-fulfillment.

But I always enjoyed being tall.

Hamish slowed down his approach and turned to Om.

"I know that woman. The rich science junky, Lacey Donaldson-Sander. She seems a lot younger than when she passed away, decades before I . . ."

Hamish realized that he had no idea how to speak of dates and time. Perhaps the control center could bring him up to speed about such things.

"As do you, my friend," Om commented.

"Hm, yeah. I guess I do. As for the others. They look familiar. But could you help me, before we land among them? That ET who looks like a crimson otter—"

"You refer to *M'm por'lock,* I presume. Called by some the Traitor . . . and by others the Loyalist."

Hamish nodded. "Oh, yeah. He helped us to develop the Cure, didn't he?"

Om nodded, noncommittally. But he held out a hand to halt their approach. "It occurs to me, Mr. Brookeman, that you appear to be data blind."

"Data . . . oh, you mean walking around *not* linked to the Mesh by aiware. Well, you know I was an old guy and a bit of a techno-grouch. I hated the eye implants young people were getting, to stay hooked in twenty-four/seven. When I had to walk around using augmented reality, I put on tru-vu goggles, like God intended—"

Hamish blinked.

"I see. You're saying this place has its own equivalent to the Mesh. And I'm wandering around half blind, unable to simply look up info on people I don't recognize." He sighed. "All right then. How do I . . ."

Om performed a hand-flourish, then held something out to Hamish. A pair of tru-vus. The old-style virtuality goggs that Hamish used to employ, way back then. *Well, what do you know.*

"Until you figure out how to make your own interface," the Oldest Member explained.

Hamish slipped them on. At which point, looking back at the people below, he now saw them equipped with name tags.

M'm por'lock
Lacey Donaldson
Birdwoman303
Jovindra Noonien Singh
Emily Tang
Emily Tang!

Chief architect of the Cure. The one human personality likely to be inserted into every crystal probe that humanity made. Suddenly—as he and Om finished shrinking

and alighted on the glassy deck of the control area—
Hamish felt a bit bashful and awestruck. What do you say to
a woman whose idea coalesced human ambivalence about
the "alien fomite plague," coming up with a strategy to both
fight back against the interstellar infection and possibly
reclaim the stars?

Responding to his interest, the ersatz goggles began
scrolling background text.

**"The Cure" applies to a strategy for persuading
some artilens to defect from their software allies, converting them instead to work honestly and effectively
for humanity and Earth civilization. This method was
inspired by the discovery, in the asteroid belt, of a
relic—**

The helpful summary vanished as Hamish diverted his
attention to the creature looking a lot like a super-otter,
who now conversed with Emily Tang. M'm por'lock, he
now recalled, had been the very first extraterrestrial virtual being to fully accept Emily's offer. Called a betrayer
by some of the other crystal entities. Or the *Loyal One*, for
remembering a much older allegiance.

*The first of many artilens who came over to our side,
revealing some clever memic tricks the fomites had been
using against us. Instead of steering human civilization in
the direction of spasmodic virus-creation, they helped us
make the Cure. Because we offered them a deal they
couldn't refuse.*

And our bribe?

*Just what we were inclined to do anyway. To increase,
yet again, the diversity of what it means to be "human."*

The Cure also persuaded Hamish to alter his version of
Renunciationism. To throw his support behind building the
Space Factory and the big laser.

Hamish shifted his gaze yet again, toward the most

vivid-looking entity—the avian-human hybrid creature, whose name tag responded to curiosity, by expanding.

Birdwoman: representative of the Autie League— Fifth Branch of Humanity.

Ah. Now he understood. Not an alien, but a self-made form. A common thing nowadays, among the portion of humanity that spent ten thousand tragic years awaiting virtual reality and ai to set them free.

His fellow passengers were turning now, reacting to his arrival.

"Mr. Brookeman," said the dark-haired woman, with a welcoming smile. "We were wondering if you'd ever deign to show up."

When Hamish reflexively glanced at her tight T-shirt, his tru-vus interpreted the logo.

Symbol of the Quantum Eye, the oracle who famously predicted that—

Meanwhile another pop-out commented:

Size 36-D. Biographically correct and unenhanced—

Hurriedly, Hamish lifted his gaze back to her face. This was one reason he never liked augmented reality.

"Madam Donaldson-Sander," he took her hand in a clasp that felt warm and realistic. His first personal touch in this place. "Apologies for my absence. I left instructions to be wakened when something of significance happened. I guess that must have been both overly conservative and ill advised."

"Hm. Well, you missed the launch for one thing. It was quite a show!" She turned and waved at the forward half of the star-flecked sky. "Our sail was filled with light from the propulsion laser and the acceleration was terrific."

"Dang. Sounds like a real experience. I can't imagine why I—"

"Oh, don't worry. We recorded it. You can live through the event from many points of view."

Hamish let go of his disappointment. "Thank you, Madam Donaldson-Sander."

"Oh for heaven's sake, call me Lacey."

"Fine. Lacey. Hamish then." He continued down the row, exchanging greetings with the other AUPs—autonomous uploaded personalities—his companions, with whom he might share the next several million years. Hamish managed not to show any sign of hero-idolatry when he shook hands with Emily Tang, who grinned with a glint of whimsy, as if she knew a secret jest.

Only when he finished introductions did his mind turn to pick at something that was said earlier. "My awakening instructions were poorly thought out," Hamish admitted. "But then . . . I take it that 'something of significance' has now happened?"

Lacey held up one hand. "Could you hold that thought, Hamish? We're trying to settle a very important question."

She turned to her colleagues. The man named Singh—elegant with a pointed beard, a white turban, and a dagger at his waist—said, "My best estimate is about five hundred and fifty a.u. As for speed . . ." He glanced at the Birdwoman, who fluttered her feathered arms and emitted a squawk. Hamish let his new, virtual aiware insert a translation:

Give me some time to finish my calculations.

Emily and M'm por'lock also consulted briefly with two other humans at the control panels. Then Emily returned to offer Lacey a sigh and head shake.

"But can't you at least tell me what . . ."

"Why don't you accompany me, Hamish?" Lacey suggested, touching his elbow and swiveling him in a new direction, with the ease of one born to graceful arts of persuasion. "I have an important errand. You and Om might as well come, too. We can talk along the way."

"An errand? Where?"

Lacey made circular motions with her right hand. And in response, an oval portion of the glassy floor started to lift, carrying the three of them with it. Soon they were floating about half a person-height above the others.

"We are heading aft," she replied.

Small cylinders manifested, about hip-level. When Om and Lacey clasped the ones nearest to them, Hamish realized they were handholds, he clutched one also.

"How fast are we going to—"

The newly formed conveyance took off with a jerk, then a steady surge of acceleration that did not let up, making Hamish glad of something to grip. The control center receded behind them at a rate he found intimidating.

"Aft?" he asked. "How far?"

Lacey smiled enigmatically.

"All the way . . . and then some."

92.

OPACITY

This vehicle, Hamish soon concluded, was a utilitarian compromise. Only a couple of fractal levels down from the crystal's outer shell—he figured his "actual" height was now about a tenth of a millimeter. They had enough wish-power to make useful things, like the travel disc. Yet, the comparative distances weren't too great.

Overhead, through occasional gaps in the misty overcast, he could still catch glimpses of the great black night. Looking down, he saw a realm of glob-clouds that were rich with potential to become whatever anyone wanted. Layer after layer of complexity diminished into smallness below, an infinity of minute scale, laced with occasional flashes of multicolored lightning.

A part of him knew what had just happened.

They didn't want to answer my questions, just yet. And they know I'm still gawking around like a tourist. So they figure taking me on this ride will distract me for a while.

Well . . . they're right!

Staring downward, he discovered that his tru-vus would zoom toward distant—or much smaller—things, bringing into focus occasional globs that had already been transformed into fairy-tale palaces, amusement arcades, alien parklands with purple trees, and so on. Those oases were rare however; vast, unused gulfs separated them. Well after all, the long interstellar voyage was just getting started.

Several times he almost blurted out questions, but stopped when the goggles offered a terse explanation. At one point, their hurtling path across the starprobe's inner expanse took them above—on a nearly parallel course—what looked like an ocean-going luxury liner, complete with swimming pools, tennis courts and liveried servants. Interest-zoom brought into view tanned figures lounging or playing on deck. Several looked up and waved as Lacey's little oval vehicle rushed by. Hamish stared. This time he didn't need any of the subtitles the goggles supplied:

Helena duPont-Vonessen

Daphne Glaucus-Worthington-Smythe

Yevgeny Bogolomov

Wu Chang Xi

Hamish rocked back, turning to Lacey. "Socrates weeps! What are *those people* doing here?"

"You mean my peers from the First Estate?" she asked, using terminology that had been briefly fashionable in the 2040s and 2050s. "Come now, Hamish. Who do you think helped pay for all this?" She waved skyward, clearly meaning the entire crystal vessel. "The space factories. The giant laser? Most of the members of the Oligarchic clade accepted the doomcasts—the dire outcomes predicted by their pet boffins and farcaisters. They wanted lifeboats from a world apparently fated to fail. A *lot* of lifeboats."

"But . . ." Hamish recalled those long-ago days when he used to fawn over oligarchs—then decades spent fighting and denouncing them. "But slots were supposed to be allocated by—"

"By merit? Yes, well." The woman offered a ladylike shrug. "A lot of them were. In the end though, the institute decided that there's plenty of room."

"Plenty of . . . say, how many uploaded minds are aboard—"

Before he could finish the question, his tru-vus answered: **8,009.**

"Eight thousand and . . . but I thought there was limited storage capacity for full-scale minds!"

Now the Oldest Member spoke for the first time since they arrived at the control center.

"This crystal vessel is larger than average. It has many times the normal volume. Nor is that the only difference." Om gestured ahead, in their direction of travel.

Hamish could sense their conveyance decelerating. Already, the sky-ceiling seemed to be curving inward again, as the probe's cylinder shape tapered at the aft end. Soon that terminus came into view. Only it wasn't what Hamish expected.

He had figured the scene would reveal familiar constellations of brittle-pinpoint stars, with an especially bright one dead center. The still-bright sun that shone on Earth. And also, possibly, the stunning glare of the propulsion laser.

Instead, beyond the curved end of the crystal, Hamish saw a huge, flat *wall* of very dark brown, blocking any view in that direction. He shook his head.

"I'm confused. What the hell is that?"

Lacey nodded sympathetically.

"Here, allow me."

She touched the side of her head. Then, with the same finger, she reached up and tapped his tru-vus, which erupted with a simple illustration.

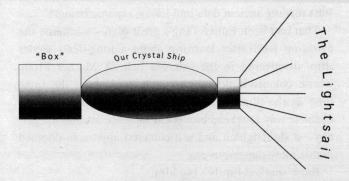

"So . . . what I'm looking at is a great big *box* that's attached to the rear end of our ship?" Hamish shook his head. "That's not standard design, is it? I mean . . . the smaller compartment at the front is there to control the sail. But what the heck is all *that* for?" He motioned at the brown wall blocking their view toward home.

"We've speculated about that," commented the Oldest Member. "Some of us believe that it contains instrumentalities to increase our chance of success, when we reach our destination."

"What, you mean tools? What kind?"

"The implements might include signaling devices, to better announce ourselves to a local species. Or telescopes to study them.

"Or else, perhaps the container comes loaded with weaponry, in order that we should be better able to protect ourselves. Say, in the event that we find the new solar system infested with malignant, old-era probes."

"Well, anything that improves our . . ."

Hamish halted, feeling a sudden thrill of realization. His fingers made a satisfying snap, even in this virtual realm.

"Of course! *This has to do with the Cure.* The box must contain bioreactors and genetic codes and artificial wombs and all the things we'll need at journey's end, in order to start turning ancient data into living, organic beings!"

That had been Emily Tang's great plan—a scheme she came up with after learning about a long-dead seeder ship, discovered in the asteroid belt. A Mother Probe whose colonist-children were murdered about the same time as the dinosaurs. The Seeder itself represented an obsolete way to spread biological sapience around the galaxy—a shortsighted and self-centered approach, doomed in this more dangerous era.

But it sparked Emily's big idea.

Why not use the same kind of technologies to resurrect a few of the artilen species that we find locked inside ancient probes? Sapient races that are long extinct—vanished from the universe. Today, their only remnants are software shadows trapped within crystal eggs. But might it be possible to bring some of the original species back to life? Or creatures who are close to them, both physically and culturally? Restoring them as living organic beings, here on Earth?

And if we can do that . . . why not start with those who prove their friendship first?

The very idea had been enough to shatter some of the viral-fomite alliances. The offer provoked some of the virtual artifact entities to experience surges of unexpected nostalgia for their original maker-selves. Long-dormant sentiment for living creatures who once strode in the open, breathing air, interacting directly with the cosmos, building dreams and hopes that were all their own, under naked suns.

"You would do that for us?" they asked. *"Even knowing what we are? What we tried to do?"*

To which humanity replied:

"We'll not be doing it for you, but for your ancestors, the earlier versions of your species, who made you. And for your living descendants."

When the first resurrection experiments bore fruit—when a few alien infants were born out of artificial wombs and adopted by human families—virtual envoys in scores of artifact probes abruptly brought forth secret treasures. Stretches of genetic code that they had hidden away, in copy after copy, information buried for ages deep within crystal lattices. For them, an older loyalty suddenly trumped their Darwinian self-interest as bits of "viral" data. And they were more than willing to pay the required cost.

The truth. Or as much of it as they could pry loose from the *other* fomite beings. Those still desperate to promote the plague.

So successful was the program—with dozens of species of alien infants now being raised in nurseries, crèches, and private homes across Earth, adding to the diversity of what it meant to be "human"—that a notion began spreading around the planet, intensely assertive, brash, even messianic.

Why not teach this?

If the method works for us . . . to cure the plague through acts of potent generosity . . . then might it work for others out there, too?

Hamish felt certain. This had to explain the extra-large cargo compartment at the rear of their vessel.

"It must contain tools to work the Cure! Machinery to start the process in our new solar system."

It came as a disappointing blow when Lacey shook her head.

"I have to doubt that, Hamish. I'm sorry, but it doesn't make much sense."

"Why?"

"Because no mere box a meter long could contain any of the devices you describe. And the genetic codes are all imbedded here"—she gestured around them—"in the data lattice of our ship.

"Anyway, remember, the plan starts by helping a young alien race with *all* phases of their development crisis. Teaching them to stand up and think for themselves and to resist other crystals that pose as 'gods,' for example. To *not* view *us* as gods! And other vital things like ecology, using sustainable technology wisely. Plus the vital tricks of reciprocal accountability and positive-sum games. . . .

"Only much later, during the inevitable crisis, when they have high technology and when their minds are threatened by fomite virus memes, *that's* when we'll add the Tang Offer, teaching them how to mix and brew more types to people. To increase the diversity and wisdom of their civilization. Helping them acquire the hybrid vigor to take on all challenges.

"Plus empowering them to make the same offer to the crystals that have infected their system," Hamish added, to prove he understood all this. "Luring cooperation from many of the virus entities."

"We carry the schematics and knowledge needed to do all that, Hamish, adjusting and adapting the designs to fit local conditions. But our plan counts on locals doing all the physical work!

"Also, that's the only *moral* way. It solves the ethical dilemma of the old *seeder probes,* whose plan to colonize Earth would have ruined our planet's chance to evolve sapients of its own. This way, a world gets to make its own smart race first. And only then—by their own choice—do they invite others to join them, creating an outpost of cosmopolitan, galactic civilization."

Hamish blinked at Lacey's stunning version of the Cure.

He had never looked at it quite so grandly before. She sure thought on an impressive scale.

"Terrific!" he nodded. "So for the sake of our mission—"

"The point is, I find it unlikely that Earth would have crammed a package full of teensy bioreactors, that would only decay or go obsolete anyway, across millions of years. We'll teach. We aren't meant to do it ourselves."

Feeling deflated, Hamish found nothing to say, except a grunt of soft disappointment, like he always felt when one of his cool ideas got shot down.

He turned and saw that they were slowing. Approaching a cluster of figures at the aft end of the great crystal ship, where the ceiling's descending arc became almost a vertical wall. As had been the case at the ship's opposite end, a handful of human figures mingled with aliens near some holo and twodee displays.

He let out a sigh, turning back to Lacey and Om.

"All right then. So the box doesn't have directly to do with the Cure. Still, this means our vessel is larger and more capacious than your typical crystal probe. It also comes equipped with tools and ways to interact with the world. That's great! We won't be helpless. This should improve our chances of mission success. Right?"

Something about Om's reaction seemed off. Too muted or reserved.

"I suppose that is true, my friend," answered the alien entity. "The odds may go up, for this particular probe."

"And the other ten million just like it?"

"They, too, will benefit, if they were dispatched so-equipped."

"So. Then. What's the problem?"

Hamish looked to Lacey, who lifted her shoulders. "I believe Om considers the extra expense to be a foolish waste."

The Oldest Member nodded. "Exactly so, my lady. Ten or twenty smaller, cheaper models could be made and cast across space for the cost—in time, effort, and resources— that went into making and equipping our lavish vessel."

"But you just said that our own chances of success were greater."

"By a very small factor. Perhaps they doubled. An insignificant amount."

"*Double* is insignificant?"

"Remember that each probe is like a grain of pollen, cast into the wind! Triumphal achievement of our overall mission—spreading the Cure—will depend far more on numbers than on any one probe, Mr. Brookeman.

"It will call for . . . it will require . . . vast quantities. Immense numbers."

Hamish felt a strange sensation, like numbness, pass across his face.

Vast quantities. . . . Oh.

His expression was one that Om misinterpreted, despite decades of experience with humans.

"Do not worry, my friend. A lot of new sapients pass through this phase, lavishing excess care and attention upon their first wave of probes. They soon get over it and switch over to a more efficient approach."

For once at a complete loss for words, Hamish turned to Lacey Donaldson. But she was busy piloting her little craft toward a landing. Causing it to match—in both location and size—the figures ahead, who were gathered around some very mundane-looking displays, near the very aft end of the ship. Where the vertical crystal barrier came into direct contact with the mysterious, boxy cargo compartment.

Trying hard to shake off a terrible sinking feeling, Hamish focused on the people who were turning now to greet them, as the travel disc melted into the floor of a glassy plain. First came a pair of humans he did not recognize and whose names meant little to him. Experts in optics and instrument design, he gathered. The third entity was far more interesting.

Courier of Caution, emissary from a planet called Turbulence, where one race saw through the trap of the fomite plague and tried to come up with a solution. Its own early, primitive version of the Cure. Sending out capsules with the aim of helping new species, alerting them to the danger.

Hamish glanced at his guide—his Virgil—the Oldest Member. These two (or different, earlier versions of them) once fumed, strutted, and hurled accusations at each other, during the first of the Great Debates between various crystal probes. An exercise that edified humanity and helped make a big difference. A crucial first step down the twisty path that threaded minefields, leading (perhaps) to survival.

At least that was what Hamish had believed . . . till just minutes ago, when a dire suspicion was born, like a wasp within his mind.

If he expected fireworks or friction between Courier and Om, they showed no sign of animosity. Well, weren't they now sworn to the same mission? The same sacred goal? Helping to spread an antidote to poison.

Courier stepped up to Lacey. The creature's bullet head and throbbing eye-strip had been less endearing than Om's Buddha-like appearance, during those first debates. But the artilen's blunt dedication and honesty won hundreds of millions of hearts.

"Well?" Courier asked.

Lacey shook her head.

"Birdwoman wants to calculate some more. But that's how she deals with stress. Just crunching more numbers won't make a difference. I'm afraid it's pretty conclusive."

"What's conclusive?" Hamish asked.

Both Courier and Lacey turned to look at Hamish. He could not read the artilen's expression. The woman was clearly torn. She started to speak—

—but was interrupted, by a voice that came from behind Hamish.

"Brothers and sisters, why be reticent? Even newly wakened, this here mon is no frail. Tell him de truth now. Or let me."

No, Hamish murmured to himself. *Please don't let it be . . .*

Turning around, he found his dread justified. A dark human figure approached, almost as tall as he was, but with "hair" consisting of snakelike tendrils, waving and emitting random puffs of aromatic smoke. Despite many other virtual augmentations—a bare, bristly chest and a softening of the man's famously excessive island dialect—Hamish recognized the newcomer instantly.

Professor Noozone offered a cheshire grin and arms wide in welcome.

"Coo-yah, Mass Brookeman. How nice of ye to join us. I hope you will find today's news adequately 'significant' to justify your wakeup call."

Hamish clenched his fists over the ribbing, but maintained surface calm. "Will *somebody* please tell me?"

"Sure thing, mon," Profnoo replied, the grin fading into a merely wry smile.

"You see, we had been scheduled for another laser boost, to fill our sail an' accelerate us boojum-faster across space interstell-ar. But it never came, y'know. Nor has any explanation come to us by narrowbeam radio.

"This prompted us to take sightings an' do some measurements of our very own. Good enough measures to reckon a fell fac'."

Hamish hated the way this man milked drama with every opportunity. But he was clearly expected to ask.

"What fact is that, *professor*?"

"Why, the rhaatid fac' that the *speed* of our good vessel is no-quite up to what it should be, mon."

Hamish turned to Lacey. "I know this ship is a bit heavy. But how far off could we possibly—"

He stopped when she closed her eyes.

"By a factor of more than a hundred," Lacey said.

"What?"

If he could have asked for a less realistic emulation of a human body, Hamish would gladly trade right now. This virtual copy felt awash in chemical reactions of astonishment and despair. Or simulations that were all too similar to the "real thing." Above all, though, he wished that the next words came from anybody else, other than the Jamaican pop-scientist.

"Bodderation, eh? At this velocity, we won't even escape the system sol-ar, just orbit through de old Kuiper Belt an' loop back aroun' the sun again, eon after eon. Maybe snap some pictures of Pluto or Tyche or Planet X or whatever iceballs we happen upon.

"But no aliens. No new star systems.

"An' that's not even the *biggest* bloodclotty thing, mon."

With a reluctant sense of foreboding, Hamish forced himself to ask.

"What . . . is the biggest . . . thing?"

"Zeen, why de fact that Earth is no even *tryin'* to correct the problem, with new laser shoots. It seems, my old fren an' adversary, dat wicked old world—dat Babylon we come from—has done abandoned us to our fate."

93.

ABERRATION

By now this crystal ship, a mere two meters long but packed with passengers and data-cargo, should have already entered the Oort Cloud of comets, starting at ten thousand times the Earth's distance from the sun . . . not poking along at just five hundred or so astronomical units.

Worse, their apparent speed was abysmal. Why had Earth failed to provide the promised boost, filling their sail with intense laser pulses, propelling it to 5 percent of lightspeed?

Hamish sat at an edge of the glassy plane. Half listening while others argued behind him, he dangled his long legs over the seemingly vast interior of the probe. If measured by an external observer, he sat less than fifteen centimeters from the cylinder's central axis. In fractal terms, the depth might be infinite.

Techies kept waving their arms and conjuring into existence various instruments to measure the problem . . . as if a hundred-fold shortfall in velocity were something you could "analyze and solve." Anyway, there were major obstacles to looking outside.

First one thing; any view backward—toward Sol and Earth—was blocked by the great big cargo container. "So we can't get a precise Doppler measurement, only rough estimates on how fast we're leaving the sun," explained a boffin.

Another impediment—they could manifest telescopes and things with a wave of the hand, but only down here at a middling fractal scale, where "magic" was possible, where mist obscured most of the starry vista. It was futile trying to drag the instruments "upward," close to where crystal met space. Made of virtual wish-stuff, the tools simply evapo-

rated, upon approaching the boundary wall. Only autonomous uploaded passengers—or AUPs—could survive next
to that harsh, outer reality.

"The cause of it all may be political," Lacey Donaldson
suggested. "Our consensus to build a space factory and
laser was never complete or universal. The Renunciation
Movement still had a lot of strength, back home. Under
new leadership, perhaps spurred by some bad event, populist know-nothings may have taken power and stopped the
process."

Ouch, Hamish thought, recalling his own turn at the
helm of that worldwide faction.

"And hence," continued the mellow voice of Oldest
Member, "the problem may just be temporary. It often happens that a species will take a pause, work through some
emotional issues, then resume production."

"That happened several times on Turbulence Planet,"
added Courier of Caution. "Hence, it is possible, at any
point, that our acceleration pushes may resume."

Normally, that might have cheered Hamish. But right
now, he found any sign of agreement between Om and
Courier depressing.

Looking downward, he saw immense depths of ever-
increasing complexity and pondered. *Why not dive down
there, right now? Start exploring. Try those magical abilities. Check out the wonders that other passengers have
already built, through sheer wish-power . . . and maybe
start building some of my own?*

*All my life I was known for creativity. This could be my
real chance. To show what I've got. To imagine greater than
anybody!*

That had always been the plan, anyway. Even if their
probe had been on target, with every hope of success at the
other end, he still would have spent ninety-nine point nine

nine (and so on) percent of the time either sleeping or amusing himself in games, simulations, and make-believe playgrounds.

At least at this distance we'll still have a slim supply of solar energy to tap. In the cold, unlighted depths of interstellar space, *time* itself would slow down for all inhabitants, as the crystal ship conserved power.

"Well," one of the humans behind him said, "if that were the case—if they shut off the laser—you'd think they'd have the decency to tell us!"

Professor Noozone snorted.

"*Tell* ten million little lumps o' glass that everythin's all fit n' frock? Dat we should jus' wait aroun' a little for de real-life Earth folk to finish squabblin'? Now why would they feel obliged to do that? Remember we're *not people*. Not citizens. We are probe-entities, zeen? Mere replicants aboard a dread zeppelin that's goin' nowhere. And jus' *one* machine emissary out of *millions*. We're quattie, mon. They owe us neegle."

Shut up, Hamish wished. But the voice continued.

"I t'ink we need to accept another possibility, bredren an' sistren. Yeyewata. That this may be no mere setback politic-al. We must consider that the very worst has happen. That de ol' wicked world has finally done it."

"Done what?" someone asked.

"Why, done stepped into a zutopeck pit. Forsaken Jah an' done gone where rude bwoys all wind up."

"What do you—"

"That Earth has gone and *blown itself up,* mon! The ginnygogs have wrecked all hope. It's over. An' *that's* why nobody be callin' us on de phone."

During the long silence that followed, Hamish envisioned the crystal—their entire universe—traveling several thousand kilometers farther from the sun. A long way . . . and a pathetically useless pittance.

Finally, Lacey Donaldson spoke in a soft voice, very small.

"I wonder what it was . . . which failure mode. The odds were always against us. There were so many ways to mismanage the transition . . . to blow it . . . even before external influences arrived to make matters worse.

"It could have been a war. A designer disease. A food collapse. A calamitous physics experiment, another ecomess. Or . . ."

She stopped as her voice seemed to choke off.

Hamish stared harder into the depths. One half of his view was taken up by the shimmering inner wall of the ship, its aft end plunging almost vertically. And just on the other side of that barrier, a sheer massif of dark brown. The "box" that Noozone and the others had been trying to study—till far more serious news crashed in. News of failure. Of abandonment.

And the possibility that we may be the last remnants of humanity. Not even successfully sent across the gulf to other stars, but left to drift in the outermost solar system, aboard a "ship" that's filled with genetic and cultural riches. Gifts meant for others, far away.

I guess we might hope—or imagine—that someday one of these crystal depositories will get picked up. Maybe by visitors from beyond. That way, someone might decipher, study, and relish bits and pieces of what we were . . . like possibly my novels and films.

But for that to happen, some race would have to actually survive out there, in order to become the first real starfarers. Some sapients must find a real cure, and finally escape the trap.

The many traps of existence.

Hamish knew that he had plenty of faults. But no one ever accused him of indolence. Or inattention. Or lack of passionate caring about human destiny.

All his life had been spent nosing around for possible mistakes, for "failure modes" that might ensnare his species. Every tale that he wove was meant *partly* to exploit and entertain and make lots of money . . . but also to warn and stir new wariness about yet another error to avoid. And if many of humanity's brightest people resented him, for attacking science in general? Well, at least he was engaged, participating in the argument. Playing the role of vigorous devil's advocate. Probing the path ahead for snakes, quicksand, and land-mines.

Prove me wrong—I always demanded—by ensuring that this type of calamity can never happen. But first, I will make you pay attention.

That was the core point. Always the underlying message of everything he ever wrote.

For all the good it apparently did.

In the end, perhaps I made no difference at all.

Well, at least humanity would not be contributing to the demise of others.

If the end had finally come, on Earth . . . or if some clade of oligarchs had succeeded in the natural goal, using renunciation as an excuse to permanently reassert feudalism . . . either way, the planet would not be a source of further infection across the cosmos.

Hamish had already been depressed, before learning about Birdwoman's dire calculation. His earlier conversation with the Oldest Member made him realize a terrible truth.

The "Cure" we were so proud of. It was just another layer of persuasion. Another insidious meme-driver to get humanity to do the same thing everybody else does, who doesn't renounce. To devote huge resources and build giant factories and billions upon billions of messenger probes along with lasers to hurl them skyward.

In our case—as it had been on Turbulence Planet—the decision required an extra motive beyond selfishness.

Altruism. A desire to help others. That makes us above average.

But didn't it just lead to the same result? Oh, we swore we would only send ten million, pushed by just one laser. But Om showed me. The fomite logic would eventually demand more, and more—for the sake of the Cure! Till we fell into an unstoppably fatal cycle of missionary zeal.

The Cure was clever. But clever enough to overcome a disease with a bottomless supply of tricks that evolved across eons? In the end, we were just as gullible, just as infected, as anybody else.

He stared downward, tempted to leap off this virtual platform into the void below. To seek succor in diminishment and unlimited power. To plummet. And thereupon shrink into a mere god.

94.

REFRACTION

"Y'know, there are other possibilities," someone said. Hamish recognized the voice of Emily Tang. She must have followed soon after Lacey's group, in order to join this discussion.

"For example, suppose the folks back home came up with an *improved model* of interstellar probe! We were among the first, after all. Perhaps they stopped producing our version and switched to one that's more efficient, less heavy, and easier to propel to high speed."

"So they might have only abandoned *us,*" commented the elegant Jovindra Singh. "Discarding the older models, leaving them to drift, while they allocate the laser to better bets. Wow, that is even more insulting than the renunciation theory!"

Hamish expected Om to speak up. This seemed compatible with his earlier comments. But the artilen said nothing.

"If only we could look," Lacey said at last, after a sullen pause. She clearly referred to their blocked view homeward, where even a clear glance might reveal whether the Big Laser was still in use, even if it were aiming its great power at other targets. Without the box in the way, they might also pick up noise from Earth's radio networks and industry. That, too, could tell them a lot.

Courier of Caution broadened Lacey's longing into something more general.

"That has always been my own desire. To look and see, before doing anything else. It is why I urged support for your grand telescopes, Lacey—and other space-born efforts—to find out what has happened to other worlds. Whether any of them survived the disease, while still maintaining a vigorous, scientific culture."

One of Courier's most endearing traits had always been this penchant for unquenchable hopefulness, despite a frozen facial expression that resembled purse-lipped doubt. Even when giant mirrors gathered images of his home system, detecting no sign of civilization—no audible communications mesh, no atmospheric traces to suggest ongoing industry—Courier remained upbeat, explaining.

"It only shows that we became more *efficient*. That is exactly what a mature people must do, over time, in order to both have a mighty culture and use up few resources. It is what you humans have been doing, increasingly, for three generations! Earth was loudest in the radio spectrum back during the 1980s. It became a quieter planet while exploding with talk and ideas, carried over fiber and tight beams. My people have only taken this process further, by thousands of years!

"Need I also add that the galaxy is proved to be a dangerous place? I'll wager that wise survivor races—like mine—grow cautious about leaking much. No sense in shouting! There are more subtle ways to reach out and explore. To find allies and fight back against an unfriendly cosmos.

"Nevertheless, I have every expectation that the next set of instruments will reveal them, my people, still vibrant and rambunctious. Still resisting the enemy with every strength."

Hamish recalled how Courier used to say all this before every major new telescope came online. And when that one detected nothing at Turbulence system? Courier simply turned to help design the next.

One of those experiments involved propelling a few dozen early crystal probes, not toward faraway stars but a modest distance, into the gap between Uranus and Neptune. A unique zone, seven astronomical units wide, where theory suggested they might pick up focused *gravitational waves,* of all things. As Hamish recalled, that project delivered good science and helped humanity test its own early designs for crystal craft. But the probes found no trace of intelligent modulations in the gravitation noise. No spoor of high civilization, from any of sixty different directions.

Behind him, his fellow passengers—the ones who were serious, unlike the dilettantes playing god-games below— argued on, chewing over every possible explanation for their abandonment, from bad news to horrendous. Hamish, meanwhile, found himself staring not into the void, but at the great brown wall. The giant box that lay in contact with the aft end of their crystal vessel, blocking any view of home.

What if we were in a simulation? A test? And not in space at all? Isn't that "box" exactly the sort of thing that the experimenters would set up, like a one-way mirror, to let them

*observe us up close? And to keep us from measuring things
like the Earth or sun too closely?*

Hamish gave in to an impulse and stuck out his tongue
toward the great brown wall, at any spectators who might
lurk there.

But no. He shrugged that idea aside. Not because it was
stupid or illogical . . . it seemed as likely as anything others were discussing. No, Hamish dropped the idea because
of something else. Something he had spent his whole life
nurturing.

Intuition. Not always right. Often dead wrong. But always interesting. A trait that once got Hamish invited to
join the Autie League! Because it was deemed a "savant-
level talent."

Right now, he was having a powerfully strange feeling,
not unlike déjà vu, only in reverse.

A sense that something ought to be obvious.

Something to try.

Right now.

"Say!" he asked aloud, turning to interrupt whoever was
talking. "Has anyone actually tried to *open* that thing?"

Hamish realized, with a bit of chagrin, that the person
he cut off was Emily. She had been saying something guilt-
ridden, about how the presence of new "alien" people on
Earth might contribute to overall human wisdom in the
long run, but the greater variety could prove frightening
and destabilizing in the short term. She worried that her
"Cure" might have killed the patient. An interesting notion—

—though Hamish never deemed any topic more valuable than his current question.

"What did you say?" Lacey Donaldson asked him. "Open
what?"

Hamish gestured in the direction everyone called
"aft" . . . which also pointed back toward the sun and

everything they all used to know. A view blocked by a giant container.

"That thing. The box. The mysterious crate. Have . . . you . . . tried . . . to open it?"

Courier of Caution stared at Hamish with its ribbon-eye, pursing its diamond-shaped, four-lipped mouth.

"We have set up instruments, Hamish. Tried to probe the box with light and other rays. We even managed to wish-create a weak laser and got return reflections. . . ."

Hamish shook his head. "Look, we're supposed to have access to the stuff inside, sooner or later, right? So . . . shouldn't there be an instruction manual? Aren't we supposed to be able to *use* whatever it is?"

The humans turned and looked at each other.

"I suppose that's logical."

"We had extensive pre-briefings, but no one mentioned it."

"Because we were recorded from our originals some years before they settled on a final probe design. This box-thing's an add-on."

"So? He's right. Even if it was all meant to be used at the destination, there have to be instructions!"

"But where? We scanned the surface of the box and found no message."

"Embedded in the crystal, surrounding us? Like every other bit and byte carried aboard this solid state—"

"You mean like us? We're just as much bits 'n' bytes—"

A screech and series of sharp squawks made Hamish turn, to see that newcomers had arrived, bringing all of the team that had been staffing the "control room" at the forward end. Birdwoman and M'm por'lock and several others stepped off a traveling disc-conveyance. *So who's at the helm?* Hamish wondered as his tru-vus translated the autie's wing-flaps and chirps:

The answer is simple. We must have known the method once and forgot it.

"Forgot!" The Oldest Member expressed disdain with undulating puffs of his trunk-like breathing tubes. "I can assure you that I have forgotten nothing."

"Well . . . maybe you were loaded that way," Lacey commented. "But some of *us* could have had important bits buried. Unconscious. Like a—" she paused, searching for the right phrase.

"Like a posthypnotic suggestion?" offered Emily, rising with enthusiasm. "All it might take is a certain word or thought to trigger recollection. Giving us access to a more information. Like a command. Maybe something coded—"

Her eyes widened, at the same moment that Hamish saw several other people rock back. Including Lacey and Professor Noozone. Whatever it was . . . he experienced it too.

"Now that's odd. Does anyone else feel suddenly compelled to say the word—"

". . . key . . ."

"—key?"

"Key!"

"Yea. I-mon feel it, too, obeah-strong." The black Jamaican science-showman seemed aggrieved at the very idea. Almost through gritted teeth, and glaring at Hamish, he added, *"Key."*

Four individuals, all of them human, approached each other near the edge of the glassy plain, while the others watched. Emily, Hamish, Profnoo, and Lacey exchanged looks, back and forth.

"So . . . now what?" Lacey asked. "Are we supposed to *conjure up* a key to unlock the box? Something capable of survival near the lattice surface, penetrating through the wall—and vacuum—and then the container? How? Shall we hold hands and wish it into being?"

I ain't holding hands with Noozone, Hamish grumbled inside.

"Well," Emily suggested, "if we four concentrate, maybe it will manifest, by force of will."

They tried for a while. Hamish closed his eyes, envisioning what a "key" might look like. Something to unlock a heavy, massive cabinet. A virtual object tough enough not to unravel when it was brought "up-and-large" near an unbridgeable barrier made of crystal and time. All he could come up with was the mental image of an old-fashioned skeleton key with a cylindrical shank and a single flat, rectangular tooth.

He could feel magic gather at his fingertips. Something was happening in front of him. He opened his eyes . . .

. . . and saw a mess. His version of a "key"—muddled and half formed—was jumbled with another one that resembled a modern biomet-tag, of the kind that people on Earth might use to remotely identify themselves. Both of those swirled with someone else's notion of a "key" . . . a maze of numbers, dots, and computer-readable smudges.

One of the onlookers guffawed at the resulting mishmash. Hamish couldn't blame him.

"This is silly," Profnoo said. And Hamish noticed that the man had altered his appearance. Now he resembled a real professor—tweed jacket, turtleneck shirt, and milder dreadlocks. Even spectacles. His affected accent was nearly gone.

"I doubt anything that we manifest will do the job."

"If we discuss it first . . . ," Lacy suggested. "Maybe reach a consensus on a single metaphor, we four might then—"

Hamish shook his head, hating to agree with Profnoo.

"Wanna know what I think? I would bet my next cash advance and media options that we don't have anything else to do, right now. Our job is done. We four had only to remember, all of us at the same time, and say the word together, for it to—"

Birdwoman shrieked!

Hamish swiveled to see her hopping and using both iri-descent wing-arms to point downward, over the edge of the plate. Next to her, M'm por'lock crouched on all fours, thrashing a beaverlike tale and hissing.

"I think you had all better look at this!"

Hamish and the others bent or knelt to peer into the depths. And there they saw, far below, refracted by multi-ple foldings of fractal scale, something that appeared to be rising fast, drawing near with tremendous momentum. A patch of light. A glow. A spot of brilliance that seemed too intense to be merely virtual.

Probably, it would be visible even from outside the probe itself, if anyone happened to be looking.

It must have started in the very most depths, Hamish thought. *And it's been rising ever since we all said the key word. Key . . . word. Of all the stupid codes! I would never have stooped to using that in a novel.*

Staring, unable to move, Hamish watched as the glow brightened, swerved . . . then plunged straight at the aft-most end of the ship, casting sharp light even past the crys-tal barrier, to briefly pulse a complex rhythm against the great, brown container-box . . .

. . . which then
quietly
opened.

95.
REFLECTIONS

Cracks and seams propagated across the great brown sur-face of the aft cargo container as it started unfolding.

"Come on!" Lacey shouted. "Let's get up top for a better view."

She stepped off the glassy plate and started grow-walking skyward, becoming a giant, striding ever-higher and turning translucent as she climbed. Others quickly followed, leaving Hamish—assisted by the Oldest Member—hurrying to catch up, struggling to master that queer trick of envisioning changes in both position and scale, pushing upward against increasing weight and resistance.

Glancing back, he saw the flat plain where they had been meeting, along with all the instruments and tools that their minds had built, now looking like tiny toys and already starting to dissolve.

"Focus ahead of you, Hamish my friend," Om insisted. "Think up and out. Think big."

The others had pulled ahead. Their ankles were gigantic as Hamish fought to keep up. But he had always been a quick study, and soon had the knack, forging ahead and expanding his own scale to match that of Emily, then the otter-alien, then Singh and the Birdwoman—whose personal augmentations were starting to soften, molting her glorious feathers, leaving a much more human-mundane appearance. Professor Noozone, however, was still up ahead. Still huge. Striving hard into a headwind, maintaining his lead.

The mists shredded and parted as stars came out, stark and bright beyond the great ceiling-barrier.

Om was right. This seems a bit easier, accompanied by others.

But the group had not come up here for stars. They gathered where the aft-end curvature of the rounded cylinder was most pronounced, giving them their best view of the cargo box. Its deployment had already progressed.

Rather than just unfolding, the brown sides of the box unraveled, supplying meter after meter of ropy strands. Five of these cables connected to five different blocky objects that now tumbled out of the container, until each of them trailed behind the crystal ship, as if dragged by its own tow-line.

"There!" Emily pointed. "I see it. The sun!"

Indeed, as hundreds of meters of cable spun out from the sides of the box, a great star was revealed, mightier (apparently) than all the rest. Far bigger and brighter, and closer than it should have been, at this point in their mission. And somewhere buried within its glare would be a tiny, blue-green twinkle. Homeworld.

As they watched, each of the five blocks broke in half . . . then divided again . . . with each smaller chunk separated by more rope that got increasingly slender, with every division, till five long *chains* trailed behind the vessel. Each of them consisted of a long strand, with small lumps knotted along its length. Through some kind of magnification or refraction, Hamish could tell that the tethers stretched back kilometers now, perhaps much more.

"Whatever it is, it doesn't look like a weapon," Professor Noozone pointed out, still in his tweedy, university-teacher mode, almost accent free, like when he had been just a regular associate instructor at Caltech. "Nor does it seem like a way to hasten contact with some planet-born, primitive race."

Lacey had an observation.

"Notice how one of the strands has deployed to trail directly behind us . . . while the others fan out above, below, left, and right. It must use an electrostatic charge—

"And see now! How all five of them have branched? Each of them splitting into several sub chains? A total of . . . a hundred strands! Each terminating in a *pair* of thicker lumps, one after the other? I believe it has to be *antenna array*—a detector of some sort—meant to cover as large a volume of space behind us as possible."

Hamish was still getting used to how strange everything felt, up here near the real universe, where the slender crystal's curved limitations could be felt by those within. No longer capacious and immense, the impression now seemed cramped, confined. His body—when he pressed closer to the barrier—felt warped. Distended and rounded. Confined.

"Lacey you tend to view everything in terms of telescopes," commented Jovindra Singh, with evident amusement. "It could just as likely—"

The Sikh biophysicist stopped abruptly and they all stared as the lumps—strung out along the many strands—started to *open,* expanding like very broad, many-petaled flowers, each of them aiming their concave faces away from the sun.

"Well all right," Singh admitted. *"That* looks like some kind of detector array. But it's aimed ahead of us! Aren't we most-curious about what is going on behind us, on Earth? Whether civilization survived? Whether the big laser is still being used?"

M'm por'lock commented:

"This device was never meant for us to use in that way, checking on our point of origin. It may have been intended to look ahead, during our final approach toward the destination system. To help perfect our ideal trajectory, optimizing arrival at the target planet."

Courier of Caution disagreed.

"Upon approaching the destination, our type of lightcraft always turns around to enter the new solar system aft-end first, with the sail using sunlight to help decelerate. Hence, these mirrors would be aimed away—"

Hamish interrupted.

"Aren't you all forgetting something? None of those flower mirrors can see a damned thing that's in *front* of our ship. There's something blocking the way!"

He gestured toward the bow of their crystal vessel and Birdwoman squawked, now in spoken English.

"The sail! Sail. Big light-pail!"

It covered a whole third of the sky, warping the starscape with reflections, cutting off any view ahead.

"But . . . then . . . if the sail is in the way . . ." Lacey mused, staring at the curved boundary of the gigantic, reflective surface. "What could all those smaller mirrors be looking at . . ."

Her eyes widened.

Then Lacey Donaldson let out a cry of realization and joy.

"It's all . . .

". . . we're all part of ONE big telescope!"

96.
FOCUS

The group drifted "down" to a nearby fractal layer where it was just barely possible to forge instrumentalities with their minds, yet still have a clear view outside. By concentrating together, they managed to create some image magnifiers to peer beyond the artifact-ship at the two hundred or so flower-mirrors that lay strung behind it, along five trees of branching tethers. Many of the kilometer-wide diaphanous blossoms were still unfolding.

How did all of that fit in a one-meter box? They reminded Hamish of filmy jellyfish—swarms of which had conquered Earth's great ocean.

Courier of Caution presented a schematic, adding—"Of course, nothing is to scale."

"So the big sail acts as a giant telescope mirror," Jovindra pondered, "collecting and reflecting light upon two hundred smaller mirrors, spread around the maximum possible volume . . . smaller mirrors which then focus on our crystal craft . . . which can then analyze the images . . ."

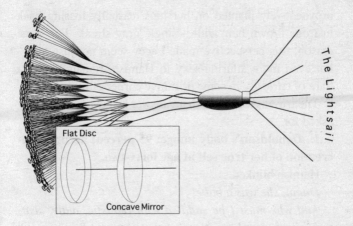

The Lightsail

Flat Disc

Concave Mirror

". . . since we can also draw *power* from that concentrated energy," added Courier, clearly excited.

"So then, can we use this array to look at Earth?" asked a nervous Emily.

Hamish nodded. "With such an instrument, at this small distance, we'd detect even the slightest sign of civilization. Or its destruction."

"Maybe I don't want to know." Emily dropped her gaze.

Hamish turned. "What d'you think, Lacey? Can this big scope gaze Earthward and—"

Looking around, he finally spotted Lacey, Profnoo, and Birdwoman. Each of them now about as tall as his ankle, perched on a miniature platform just a little below this one, surrounded by more sophisticated machinery and computer-like displays. Tornadoes of numbers swirled around Birdwoman—again feathered—who squawked, danced, and pecked at the maelstrom. A data processing task worthy of her savant talents.

Hamish crouched down. Peering at the other miniature woman, whose expression now seemed more perplexed than jubilant as she argued with Professor Noozone, fists provocatively planted on her hips, casually tossing back lustrous brown hair with a single gray streak. For some reason, this perspective made Lacey seem not just "cute" but even more alluring-sexy to Hamish, rousing another flare of curiosity in some primitive corner of his mind.

The tru-vus replied with an answer he never consciously asked for.

L. Donaldson's body image: 95 percent accurate recreation of her true self at age forty-two.

Hamish blinked.

Damn, she was a babe!

And why must I be saddled with realistic, male, scatterbrained visual reactions? I thought we'd be above all that, in here.

Shaking his head for focus, Hamish bent closer and repeated his question louder, interrupting Lacey's intense labor with the autistic savant and the Jamaican science-maestro.

"Things aren't so simple," she answered in a diminuated voice, looking up at Hamish. "Remember, the big sail's main job was to reflect photons for propulsion, like on old-time sea ship. A telescope mirror needs a different curvature."

"But its shape is adjustable to many purposes." Courier joined Hamish kneeling at the boundary. "And it can reconfigure later for propulsion, when they send another laser boost."

When? Don't you mean if? But Hamish kept it to himself.

"That may be," commented the Oldest Member without stooping or bending. "But of what use is such a device? To stare *back* at the solar system you came from? How could news from home affect your chance of a successful mission? Especially a mission that will fail without more laser pushes." Clearly, Om didn't think much of all this fancy, expensive hardware, whatever its purpose.

"I know the sail can reconfigure to be a primary mirror, Courier. In fact, we can tell that it has already started doing so." Lacey's voice seemed tinny from size and scale effects. "What confuses me is the design of the array behind us! An imaging telescope would need just *one* secondary mirror back there, not hundreds!"

Professor Noozone, now dressed oddly in formal white evening wear, looked up from an instrument. "I-mon can now tell you some-t'ing just plain obeah weird . . . dat just *half* of de many-petaled flowers dat are opening behind us are concave reflecting mirrors.

"De *other* hundred are flat *discs*. Opaque-mon. Not shiny at-all."

"Flat disc? But to what purpose?" Lacey scratched her head, as if it were made of real flesh. "The only use I can think of would be to block or occult the sun. But why do that?"

She waved her hand at the schematic.

"What the heck *is* all this? And how is it supposed to help us spread the Cure?"

Hamish had nothing to contribute. And if there was one thing he hated in the universe, it was having nothing to say.

So . . . it came with distinctly-dramatic pleasure when he noticed something to comment on. Something happening far below in the magic-laden mists of the probe's interior.

"Hold on everybody," he announced, staring past Lacy into the depths. "I think we're about to have a visitor."

They all made out a humanoid figure climbing from the inner reaches, starting minuscule but growing rapidly. At first, Hamish reckoned it to be a downloaded person, one of the other AUP passengers. Only this shape appeared simpler, almost two dimensional. It swept higher, rising without effort or any pretense at "walking."

He felt Lacey and Profnoo rejoin this higher level, while Birdwoman seemed content to stay just below, dancing among her numbers.

The approaching cartoony shape lacked texture or feigned reality. *A message-herald,* Hamish realized as it drew near . . . before Emily Tang let out a shout.

"Gerald!"

The figure braked to a halt, floating next to their thought-flattened platform. A simplified version of the famed astronaut explorer, not a full-scale virtual entity. A recording then, with some ai thrown in.

Hamish couldn't—he just couldn't—help himself. It simply came out and he vowed never to apologize for it.

"Dr. Livingstone, I presume?"

The discoverer of the first recovered fomite-artifact hovered near the group, granting Hamish a slight nod.

"Just honorary degrees, I'm afraid.

"Hi Emily. Lacey. Everyone.

"Well, it took you long enough to trigger things in motion. Slower than average by ten percent. Six million other capsules have already checked in."

Lacey stepped back a bit, her hand over her breast.

"Then civilization hasn't forgotten or abandoned us? Or blown itself up?"

The figure shook its head, conveying ruefulness.

"Millions of probes, and the virtizens in every one leaped to the same dark conclusion—assuming the worst. What a dismal bunch! If we do this again, we really must include more optimists. Or at least spare you AUPs some suspense!

"To answer your question, no, we're still tottering along back here on Earth and the Settlements, uncovering failure modes just in time. Sometimes gaining a little breathing room and confidence. At other times barely avoiding

panic. Doing some planet repair. Staving off tyrants and demagogues. Coping with both would-be godmakers and fanatical nostalgia junkies. Gradually learning to benefit from our multiplicity.”

Gerald Livingstone’s aivatar spread its hands in an open gesture.

“As for abandoning you and your mission? Now why would we give up such an important investment? You have a big job to do!”

Oldest Member stepped up to confront the message simulacrum.

“Then why did the laser stop firing? Has it malfunctioned? We are moving only at one hundredth of the planned and necessary departing velocity! When will repairs be completed, and more launch lasers built? If this delay lasts much longer, our rendezvous at the target system will have to be recalculated.”

Gerald the herald held up a single finger.

“First, the laser works just fine. When you get your optics running, take a glimpse back home. You’ll see it still operates, alone, on a slow-but-steady schedule, launching special experiments. None as extensive as your particular mission, which required ten million probes.

“As for your complaint about speed, in fact, your craft appears to be exactly on its planned course. No further adjustments or laser boosts will be required.”

Om howled. “That is absurd! At this rate, none of the probes will ever leave the solar system at all!”

The answer he got next failed to please the most ancient known member of a viral chain. The astronaut’s voice had a faint, sardonic edge.

“I’m afraid you’re making a faulty assumption, venerable Om.

“You always had that tendency . . . my friend.”

Hamish saw the rotund artilen glower in what had to be

simmering anger. The next words to puff from those waving vent tubes came as individual snorts.

"And . . . what . . . faulty . . . assumption . . . is that?"

"Why, that your crystal vessel was ever meant to visit another star system. Or that you were dispatched to be interstellar envoys.

"Or interstellar parasites."

The simulated image of Gerald Livingstone paused, as it must have aboard many millions of other crystal vessels at the same point, upon delivering similar news. Even caught up in his own state of shock, Hamish appreciated the dramatic effect.

"As a matter of fact, you won't leave the solar system, because you were never meant to."

Emily Tang took a step toward her old comrade and lover. "Then our destination . . . ?"

The simulated astronaut's affectionate smile made him seem almost as real as she was.

"Why, my dear, you are already there."

97.
IMAGES

"Five hundred and fifty astronomical units from the sun. We're beyond Neptune, Pluto, and the Kuiper Belt. Way outside the heliopause, where the solar wind stops and interstellar vacuum officially begins," Lacey explained to the others. "But that's still only *sixteen light-hours* from Earth. The nearest stars are several light-*years* away. Hell, at our present pace, we'll barely touch the innermost edge of the Oort Cloud, the immense swarm of comets surrounding our sun, before we plunge back down, in the descending part of our orbit."

"When will that happen?" Emily asked.

Birdwoman squawked, providing the answer. Abruptly Hamish realized, he could now translate her message without the fiction of tru-vu goggles.

three hundred and twelve years
then we plunge like falcons
toward the light

"Even when we dive back in," Lacey added, "it will be a quick, comet-brief passage, followed by more centuries out here in the cold zone. And so on, forever."

Hamish turned to pace away, uncertain how to react.

At one level, he felt betrayed. Manipulated! Horrifically used by the powers back on Earth, whose grand tale—about sending ten million messengers of salvation, carrying the Cure to other worlds—turned out to be one big . . .

. . . hoax.

The word punched out of his subconscious so forcefully that Hamish actually saw it shimmer for a moment, in the space before him. Despite his still-glowering sense of affront, a part of him felt cornered into grim appreciation of rich irony.

Hamish, can you—the great hoaxer—honestly complain?

Sure I can! he retorted to himself, hotly. Yet, he couldn't help but notice—his inner conflict was so vivid, so lush and complex, that it made him feel more intensely genuine, more fleshed-out, than any time since he first awoke as a virtual being in this world. Anger and irony seemed to reinforce the sensation—

—that I'm alive.

Anyway, he wasn't the only one stewing in wrath, fuming apart from the others. Some distance across the glassy plain, Hamish saw the Oldest Member, pacing and stomping in a display of fiery temper. No one had ever witnessed any version of Om behave like this before.

Because he always seemed so calm, so supremely confident, Hamish recalled. *In fact, we're pissed off for different reasons, he and I.*

This version of Hamish Brookeman is still habitually self-centered. I wanted to be a stellar voyager. To personally—in this virtual form, aboard this ship—see other worlds and strange kinds of people. I'm angry because I'm disappointed for my own sake.

But Om is an evolved, intelligent virus. He hardly gives a damn about this particular copy of himself, or whether this specific probe ever makes contact. He's enraged to learn that none *of the ten million will ever get a chance to infect some distant race. Nor is humanity building millions or billions more. Not now. Perhaps not ever.*

Strangely, it was the sight of Om's fury that started Hamish down the road of lessening his own. He looked at Emily Tang, who had the most reason to feel shocked and betrayed. The famous science-heroine of the century, her great idea led to the miracle of reviving extinct alien intelligent species, adding them to Earth's great stew, and thus converting some of the crystal-artilens into allies. A method that seemed to immunize against the Plague. A technique that countless Earthlings deemed worth spreading across the stars. A care package of hope called the Cure.

Our fleet of ten million was portrayed as the vanguard of many more. A gift from Earth. A great inoculation to end more than a hundred million years of galactic disaster! Only then . . .

Only then, what happened?

The Gerald Livingstone message herald had explained what humanity's brightest minds believed, though they had kept their conclusion secret for a time. A dour deduction that Hamish reached, all by himself, just hours ago.

That the Cure was an excellent step, a palliative, even a

short-term remedy . . . but nothing like a grand, overall solution.

Perhaps only one percent of techno-sapients ever thought of it or implemented it correctly. Still, over time, the disease would have found ways to trick even those clever ones. The missionary zeal that swept Earth—an eagerness to generously help spread the Cure—that very zeal seemed proof the infection still operated! More subtly, but still aimed at the same goal—

—for humanity to go into an insatiable, endless sneezing fit, aimed at the stars.

No. The best minds on Earth—human, ai, dolphin, and others—all concluded. *We aren't ready yet. If we set forth now, even carrying the so-called Cure, we'll just be part of the problem.*

The way Turbulence Planet must have spent itself into exhaustion, spewing forth "warnings" that also carried traps.

No, there is only one course of action that makes sense, right now.

To learn more.

We have to find out what's happening out there!

Given all of that, Hamish felt awed and humbled by Emily Tang, the author of the Cure. There she stood with the others. Calmly moving past any disappointment—arguing, discussing, helping to plan the next stage.

Their mission. The *real* mission. One that ought to make Lacey Donaldson-Sander proud. Hamish glanced at her, now vibrant with eagerness. The one whose dream was coming true.

We are a telescope.

That summed it up.

I am a component of a telescope. Hamish weighed a strange mixture of humility and hubristic pride. *It is my purpose. My reason for existence. The greatest telescope ever conceived by Man.*

Possibly the greatest ever made by anybody.

Feeling his pseudo-heartbeat settle from outrage to mere resentment, Hamish wandered back toward the gathering. At least thirty virtual persons, human and alien, now clustered around a giant *book* left by the Gerald ai-herald, before it departed once more for the depths, with a jaunty salute.

Exploring the Galaxy from Our Home System.
Using the Sun as a Gravitational Lens.

Hamish didn't quite get the concept. But he could always ask Lacey to explain things. *I did start with a scientific education after all, before becoming a critic-gadfly. A bard of imaginary dooms.*

But that left a burning question.

Why me?

Why any of us? Why not just send ten million robots to gather data for century after century, programmed to do it well and like it?

Something about crystal probe technology, packed with virtual personalities, must make it ideal for collecting and massaging vast amounts of data. Looking at his fellow AUPs, some choices were obvious. Birdwoman could probably handle the number crunching single handed.

And Lacey, all her life had led to this. Likewise, Emily, Singh, Courier, M'm por'lock and other science types. They already grasped the purpose and were eager to get started.

At the other extreme were those Hamish deemed useless—purely along for the ride—the oligarchs and other freeloaders who were uploaded for this trip because their money paid for it. They might play magic-wish games down below for ages, never caring that their voyage had been hijacked.

All right. But why is Om aboard? Hamish glanced at the Oldest Member, still pacing and muttering angrily, and realized.

We'll learn a lot by observing him, whenever data comes in about some distant star system. Even if Om tries to deceive, we'll have ten million versions of him to compare and contrast. Over time, we'll poke and pry their paths apart, dissecting his deepest programming, perhaps developing an artilen lie detector!

Hamish smiled, knowing one of his roles.

No one was ever better at "poking" than me. I'll be his chief tormenter!

And yet—

Was that all?

His only way to be useful?

Perhaps they expected me to join the playboys, down below.

He rebelled against that glum appraisal. Hamish glanced at Lacey.

"No way. I was one of the 'key' wielders!"

The four who spoke in unison to open the box and begin transforming their ship into a telescope. That meant he was important, even indispensable! But how?

There must be a talent. A skill he brought along. Something he did supremely well.

And, of course, it was obvious.

98

DETECTION

Your Mission as a Big Telescope

Thirty-five years before your probe was launched, along with ten million others in Operation Outlook, a much smaller experiment dispatched sixty-four primitive capsules to a zone between Uranus and Neptune. Their purpose? To test an exceptional idea and exploit a quirk of nature.

Way back in the early twentieth century, Einstein showed that heavy objects, like stars and clusters, warp space around them, bending waves that pass nearby. This *gravitational lensing effect* has let astronomers peer past a few massive galaxies and observe objects so distant, their light departed at the dawn of time.

Till now, these rare viewing opportunities were flukes of astronomical position. We could never choose what to look at.

Then an Italian astronomer, Claudio Maccone, began pushing a strange insight. That we might have a gravitational lens of our very own, nearby and available.

Our sun. Calculations showed that Sol's mass ought to bend space, refracting any radiation that skims near its surface, so that distant objects would come into focus in a few special places.

The nearest and most accessible of these regions lay between the orbits of Uranus and Neptune, a shell completely surrounding our star, twenty-two through thirty astronomical units out. Only certain kinds of radiation would converge in this zone. Just *gravitons* and *neutrinos*. Still, a mission was sent, and sixty probes returned valuable data, including breakthrough knowledge about the origins of the solar system.

That experiment told us nothing about far civilizations, nor did it answer our most urgent questions. Still, the concept was proved.

And we confirmed there is *another zone,* much farther out. A shell where our sun brings into focus a different kind of radiation.

One called *light.*

99.
APPRECIATION

The Great Telescope's design grew gorgeously clear to Lacey. Ten million crystal probes, each aiming a hundred kilometer lightsail-mirror back at the sun, peering at the warped glow of distant stars and planets, magnified by Sol's gravity. A faint, slender ring, surrounding a raging ball of fire.

Those occulting discs will take turns blocking the sun's glare, allowing lensed light from distant objects to skirt by for our big mirror to collect. A delicate feat of countless adjustments.

Instead of classic images, a gravitational lens made globby, jumbled overlaps of distant points, "focusing" over a vast zone from five hundred out to several thousand astrons.

We'll stare at the sun-skimming ring in a hundred ways, while cruising through region after region, scanning for rare treasures. Some images may flash for a millisecond as we hurtle through each narrow g-spot! Others could require collection and integration for years, massaging and beaming home more data than all of humanity's prior instruments put together. And we're just one component out of ten million, each staring past the sun from a different angle. Together composing the mightiest telescope of all.

Lacey envied the probes speeding away from galactic center. They'd sift a maelstrom of fascinating objects, like Milky Way's central black hole. Courier, too, was disappointed that this ship could never glimpse Turbulence Planet. But Earth promised to share results. Sooner or later, some probe would bring Courier's home into clear view, almost like next door. Lacey hoped for good news, and not just on her friend's account.

It would be nice to have allies in this cold cosmos.

She should be resting. AUPs need sleep, as it turned out. So Lacey came down to her cottage on the One Millimeter Level, summoning a globe of night to surround it. But nervous energy from a momentous day kept her puttering around. Creating fresh flowers for a window box. Adjusting a picture of Hacker and his beloved dolphins, exploring their own amazing frontier. A different story.

One bonus for staying in the solar system. I'll get news of my sons, their children, and grandchildren. I can't bug them directly—how horrid to be nagged by ten million ghosts of long-dead granny! Still, I expect they'll transmit photos, now and then.

Granny. Her last living memories were of lined, leathery skin. Of fragility and pain and irritability with everyone who complimented her "spunkiness." She had expected to wake up here as the old woman they recorded for uploading.

Now? Lacey felt less grannylike than ever! Even as a young woman, she had stooped under the burden of other peoples' expectations. Her family's aristocratic pretensions. The harpy-chivvyings of partygirl-papparazzi-fashionistas who kept flattering her away from better longings. The somewhat more rewarding life of bride, wife, and mother. The secret guilt of knowing that—but for all of those distractions—she might have focused on great things. Beautiful things.

Only now I'm a keystone member of the most important of all scientific endeavors! And my mind feels . . .

It might be a programmed illusion. But this virtual version felt young, vigorous, ready for challenges.

And then some. It hadn't escaped Lacey's attention how the tall, craggy Hamish Brookeman kept intermittently staring at her, then struggling to hide it. *Jeepers. And I deliberately chose to appear age forty-two. Anyway, the man was hardly my favorite person, back in reality.*

Of course, in this world Brookeman couldn't hinder science, only help it. In fact, his talents might prove more valuable here than they ever were on Earth. *We'll need a storyteller and not just for distraction. When the data floods in, with glimpses of far-off worlds and alien beings, we tech-types will often seize the first theory or explanation that fits.*

Brookeman would keep posing alternatives, just to be ornery! The overlooked but barely plausible "what-ifs." Those irritating 1 percent improbabilities. Across this endless voyage, many 1 percenters would prove true.

Also, I admit, he seems likely to be . . . entertaining. Perhaps inexhaustibly. That could prove handy. For immortals.

Having wandered into the bedroom, Lacey found herself standing before a full length mirror, half aware of turning left and right. Till a curiosity caption popped up.

Body image: 85 percent accurate re-creation of former self at age thirty-seven.

Uh-oh. Preening.

She blinked. So this new life included *sex* and *vanity*?

With an unladylike snort, Lacey made a hand motion and the mirror vanished. Then she laughed.

The Great Telescope would complement other projects. Like archaeology in the asteroid belt, studying all types of ancient, mechanical probes. Or peeling back the stories and schemes encrypted layer-by-atomic-layer within crystal fomites. Or bringing more long-dead races back to life.

The overall goal? Chart a history of civilizations that struggled to rise in this quadrant, across the last two hundred million years. To grasp their myriad failure modes—from feudalism and renunciation to impulsive god-making. From war and short-sighted greed to ecological blundering. From too-much to too-little individualism. From careless technological arrogance to scientific timidity . . . all the way to other pitfalls that human sages never imagined. And, of course, the frequent killer of those who rose above a certain point. The Plague.

Were there exceptions? Perhaps an elder race or two, who might offer both solace and advice?

And if so, why have you been silent all this time, leaving us terrified youngsters to tiptoe through a minefield, without help?

On the other hand, what if we're the first to get this far? Can we make it the rest of the way? And if so . . .

A haunting, lonely thought struck Lacey.

. . . might we become the elder race?

The people who finally get out there to help everyone else? The fabled and foretold redeemers? Doctors who cure. Postmen who connect. The mentors who teach others to survive and thrive?

Those who help to raise the dead and lost?

Not the kind of notion that settles a restless mind. It was daunting enough to carry the burden of your own posterity. Your species and planet. But a galaxy—a cosmos—waiting in suspense for *someone* not to blow it? All those quadrillions of lives. All that potential.

What a terrifying idea! And—of course—statistically improbable to the point of absurdity.

. . .

And yet, she did need rest. Tomorrow, once the great sail finished transforming and all optics lined up, brilliant rings of sun-lensed data would then pour upon this little exploration vessel. Lacey had to be there! For the best moment of any telescope—First Light.

A satin nightgown fluttered into being over a corner of the four-poster bed. Some AUPs had virtual-servants, but for that kind of magic you must live below the submillimeter level. Anyway, Lacey had spent a lifetime being waited-on. A tiresome thing.

She crossed her arms, preparing to strip off the tight T-shirt, with its Eye-and-Q symbol, representing the great quantum supercomputer in Riyadh—the oracle she once hired for a personal reading, whose very expensive answer cost two million dollars per word.

You may soon be typical.

Why do I keep dwelling on that augury? That depressing omen?

As a reminder of the odds against us? To keep my expectations low?

The Quantum Eye had access to millions of alternate-reality versions of itself, or so they said. It never lied. Though it could be infuriatingly cryptic.

Pulling off the shirt, she tossed it in a corner and lifted a hand, but could not cast a simple *dissipate* spell. Stopped by her unconscious, Lacey knew she'd wear the shirt again tomorrow. And again, till she figured out why.

The nightgown was silky and cool, pleasant against pseudo skin that felt real in the best ways. With luck and a nod from the gods of programming, this life might remain bearable for millennia of work and discovery. A better fate than being a mere virus.

In bed, she drifted a while, generally pleased with today.

Learning that humanity—through a combination of wisdom, politics, diversity, ethics, foresight, and popular opinion—had chosen *curiosity* over the easy-but-lethal alternatives. Giving in to the fomites or giving in to fear. And yet, the fate that humanity was fighting against seemed so huge. So ponderous. A galaxy-wide equilibrium of death.

We know there was a long, earlier era of bickering machine probes. That seemed a stable condition too. Till suddenly, in a galactic eyeblink, it ended. And the long, sterile desert of the Crystal Plague began. Another equilibrium.

But the thing about such states . . . Lacey mused, half asleep . . . *is that they can seem steady, even permanent* . . . *until* . . .

. . . *until each one ends, as abruptly as it started.*

Which could mean . . . *that statistics don't matter* . . . *since all it takes is one* . . .

Lacey sat up.

Her pounding heart felt more than virtual.

The Quantum Eye had said:

You may soon be typical.

Everyone took the prophecy's obvious, gloomy interpretation. That humanity would likely join all the other toppled sapients out there. Another typical failure. But there was another possible meaning.

That the galaxy's situation . . . *the typical condition of intelligent life* . . . *might soon transform* . . .

. . . *to be more like us.*

Lacey blinked upward in the dimness of her bedroom, whose roof and ceiling magically vanished, like a dream, revealing a skyscape of luminous clouds. And beyond them, she glimpsed Sagittarius, its innumerable stars like dust.

Suppose we find a real cure, a way to prosper . . . *a road-*

*map through the minefield of existence . . . then the cosmos
may change again, filling with voices and variety. With adventure and wisdom. And by our hand, the galaxy may come
back to life.*

Lacey settled back against the pillow, feeling suddenly
content. This dream-within-a dream culminated a fine
day. Moreover, she felt certain the T-shirt would be gone
tomorrow.

One question lingered, though. Why had the Oracle been
so vague?

Of course. Because there was a *choice* which of the two
meanings came true. It would take combining maturity with
perpetual youthfulness—being joyfully ready for anything!
Agility. And care. And work.

From all of us, she thought. And drifted into blissful
sleep.

She sits before me, cross-legged, as I rise to awareness, vaguely knowing she has been here for some time, tending me like a gardener. Or a mother.

I know about gardens only from Earth-images. The same with mothers. Except my own—

Vast machinery against vacuum-bright stars. Robot hands, constructing me under a small, red sun. . . .

She leans forward now, lithe and human-limbed, to rap me above my oculars. She peers into them with one brown-irised eye, then another.

"Aha! Someone's home in there, at last. Can you speak?"

Vision broadens and deepens. I look past her at a realm unlike any that I've known. Not the comfortable black chill of space. Nor the film-separated layers of Earth—blues and whites above greens and browns. Here, there is a sense of vertical without weight. Dimensionality seems limitless. My sense of *scale* is painfully warped. The clouds appear to be alive.

And yet—I realize—this isn't one of those cramped crystalworlds either. It borrows from all three . . . expanding on them all.

"Well?"

Her question prods me. And so, words manifest from a place below my oculars, in a way that seems both wet and strange.

"I . . . remember you."

"Well, you ought to!" She grins. "We had our times, you and I. Up and down. Trust and betrayal. Friendship and hate. Scary and weird."

I feel an involuntary shift. My nod of agreement.

"Tor. Your name is Tor."

Again, a warming smile.

"Very good. Now tell me yours."

I pause. It takes some time to search, as if opening raw, unfinished drawers.

"I was . . . I am Seeker."

Her approval gives me pleasure. An attractive but unsettling sensation.

"Excellent. Now try to stand up, like I'm doing. Envision it."

I have never done this before. But she patiently helps until I wobble in the soft gravity. Looking down, I see two spindly legs, ending in ridiculous paddle-feet, pale and squishy. Pebbles crunch between what could be toes.

Reflexively, I lift things that must be hands. Even squishier. Yet unbelievably supple.

"I am human now?"

"We agreed. Gavin and I spent years with you, as mostly machines. It's your turn. You could not exist as physical flesh. Not yet. So this version will suffice.

"Anyway, it will help you to prepare, till we arrive."

"Arrive?"

"At the first of many stops, ports, interventions. Adventures. We have things to do. Places to go and strangers to meet. Destinies to transform!"

It all sounds rather grandiose and tiring. But yes. I recall now. Memories are coming back. One thread tugs painfully.

"I . . . had a purpose."

She nods. Partly in sympathy. But I know that there is more.

"Yes. And you still have it. Only, it's become larger, yes?"

"Larger . . . yes."

And I mourn. Lost simplicity. Lost purity.

"It has changed?"

Tor smiles at me, taking my hand, leading me toward a rainbow of impossible brightness.

"Silly," she chides. "Don't you know by now?

"Everything changes."

THE END . . .
. . . of *Existence* . . .

The question that will decide our destiny is not whether we shall expand into space. It is: shall we be one species or a million? A million species will not exhaust the ecological niches that are awaiting the arrival of intelligence.

—Freeman Dyson

AFTERWORD

I get questions from all directions. For example: "What relevance does the literature called science fiction offer—what light can it shine—on 'eternal human verities' or the core mysteries that vex all generations?"

A quite different query comes from fans of the hardcore stuff—bold, idea-drenched sci-fi: "Why are most serious authors no longer writing deep space adventures, using warp drive to explore on a galactic scale? Have you all just given up and surrendered to Einstein?"

Two seemingly opposite perspectives, from a very broad reader base! Yet, I found both concerns converging during the long, arduous process of writing *Existence*. Let me answer the second one first.

No, I haven't lost any love for grand, cosmic vistas, or contact with strange minds, or even great cruisers roaming the interstellar expanse. I'll return to the Uplift Universe soon, where vivid heroes and villains don't have just *one* way to cheat relativity, but twenty! I promise gigatons of sense-o-wonder.

Still, "warp drive" is kind of like playing tennis with the net lowered. Way fun, but more and more, authors like Bear, Robinson, Banks, Asaro, Sawyer, Kress, Vinge, Benford, Baxter, and others want to see what they can do with the hand nature dealt us. And if that means dancing with Einstein? Well, so be it.

Existence is about the cosmos that we see. Stark, immense beyond immensity, and unwelcoming to moist mayflies like us. Strangely—dauntingly—quiet. And perched in this vast emptiness is the oasis speck of Earth. More fragile than we imagined.

Yet, despite all that, might there be ways to persevere? To endure? Perhaps even to matter?

Which brings us back to question number one. Like most (usually) serious SF authors, I'm appalled by the notion of *eternal human verities*. A loathsome concept, foisted by brooding, husk-like academics, proclaiming that people will forever be the same, repeating every Proustian obsession, every *omphaloskeptic* navel-contemplation, and every dopey mistake of our parents, all the way until time's end. A horrible concept that is—fortunately—disproved by history and science and every generation of bright kids who strive to climb a little higher than their ignorant ancestors. And to raise kids of their own who will be better still. The greatest story. The greatest *possible* story.

Yes, great works of the past are enduring as art. The poignancy of Aeschylus and Shakespeare will remain timelessly moving and valuable. We'll never lose fascination for and empathy with the struggles of earlier generations. Still, what intrigues me, far more than "eternal" static things, is *how people grow*. (And let's define "people" in a way that's broad, that's challenging!)

How children sometimes learn from the mistakes of other generations . . . or else deliberately refuse to. How, on occasion, they actually improve themselves, their town, nation, even species . . . and go on to commit fresh mistakes of their own invention! Using the art of *gedankenexperiment* to explore those potential improvements—and errors—is interesting! A compelling chance to peer ahead, or to the side. That—rather than mere starships or light-saber nonsense—is what our genre offers and none other.

We live in a strange time, when our newfound taste for diversity is growing into fascination with the strange, even alien. When we're on the verge of picking up every tool that God is said to have used and boldly applying them in our own turn at co-creation, for well or ill. Whether by plan or happenstance, we apprentices are building that tower again. And, possibly, we're about to build new companions, too. New friends. Again, for well or ill.

Admit it. Scary or not, that's fascinating.

Now the challenge. Never before have human beings so benefited from membership in a sagacious, scientific, and increasingly virtuous civilization. Wisdom flowers and spreads . . . even as does silliness. Like the absurd assertion (repeated *ad nauseam* by left and right) that wisdom *hasn't* grown! A damnable outright lie.

This is a bona fide renaissance, threatening to make everything better, in all ways. A renaissance that must find every potentially lethal error and hence, ironically, benefits from endless criticism. Helpful, vigorous criticism—but not chic-cynical despair.

What of the question implicit in the title, *Existence*?

The alternative to continuity is The End of the World as We Know It . . . or TEOTWAWKI. Well, you got a survey of possible dooms in this book! It sure is a minefield out there. But poking at the ground in front of us—finding the quicksand and land mines and snake pits—is exactly how *worry* can gradually transform into *hope*. Finding a path across the next century is our task, and millions take it seriously.

Along the way, we need to keep reminding ourselves, this awkward phase of early adolescence will pass, if now and then we also lift our heads. Looking ahead.

We aren't a curse upon the world. We are her new eyes. Her brain, testes, ovaries . . . her ambition and her heart. Her voice. So sing.

FOLLOW-UP RESOURCES

There will be ongoing discussion, starting at the Tor Books site, but also at www.davidbrin.com/existence.html and on my blog: **Contrary Brin**.

Regarding the inescapable fact that inter-human violence has plummeted since 1945, see Steven Pinker's book *The Better Angels of Our Nature*. Or watch his presentations online.

The crucial concept of *positive sum games*—the entire basis of our ongoing Enlightenment Experiment—can be explored in one of the most important books of our time, *Nonzero,* by Robert Wright. My own nonfiction book *The Transparent Society* delves deeply into questions of secrecy, privacy, and freedom.

Then, once you are girded with good news, explore the darker side! Dive into Jared Diamond's book *Collapse. Our Final Century* by Martin Rees and *Global Catastrophic Risks* by Nick Bostrom and Milan Ćirković will take you on a lovely guided tour of how stacked the odds appear to be against us. A painfully attractive voyage through daunting perils that culminated in my own contributions to the popular show *Life After People*.

Finally, if you feel a wakened need to help tip the balance, have a look at suggestions for how even busy, average citizens can make a difference, via proxy power: www.davidbrin.com/proxyactivism.htm. It happens to be easy. So no excuses.

ACKNOWLEDGMENTS

I owe a lot to my coterie of sagacious and unabashed pre-readers, who find innumerable inconsistencies and infelicities, fearlessly telling me wherever the pace—or my storytelling craft—seems to lag. Also, some of them contributed a passel of really cool ideas! I want to thank Sheldon Brown, Vernor Vinge, John Mauldin, Joe Miller, Ellie Miller, Stephen Baxter, Ralph Vicinanza, Erik Flint, Claudio Maccone, Doug McElwain, Stefan Jones, Ernest Lilley, Michelle Nicolosi, Tom Larson, David Moles, Nicholas MacDonald, David Ivory, Tihamer T. Toth-Fejel, Philippe Van Nedervelde, Joy Crisp, David Crisp, Steve Jackson, Mary Amanda Clark, Robert Qualkinbush, Robin Hanson, John Smart, John Powers, William Taylor, Stephen Potts, Beverly Price, Professor Bing Chen, Dan I. Radakovich, Patrick Heffernan, Gray Tan, and Joe Carroll.

To Beth Meacham and Tom Doherty and their comrades at Tor Books, many blessings for your patience. And above all, my love and gratitudinousness to Cheryl and the far-better-than-me kids, who co-endured this long, long haul and helped me past many quagmires of despond.

I promise to write quicker, less exhausting books.

Some of the Hacker scenes were first published as "Life in the Extreme" in *Popular Science,* special edition, in August 1998. "The Smartest Mob" first appeared in *All Star Zeppelin Adventure Stories* (2004) and in *Jim Baen's Universe* (online). Some of the scenes featuring Peng Xiang

Bin appeared in *Jim Baen's Universe* in 2009, via the novella "Shoresteading." A very early version of Tor's discovery adventure in the asteroid belt appeared as "Lungfish" in *Asimov's Science Fiction* in the 1980s and was heavily revised for a 2012 Festschrift volume in honor of Poul Anderson.